## *Bestseller*

Olivia Goldsmith is the author of the international bestsellers *The First Wives Club*, now a major Hollywood film, *Flavour of the Month* and *Fashionably Late*. Also, with Amy Fine Collins, *Simple Isn't Easy*, a practical guide to stylish dressing. A native New Yorker, she now lives mostly in Florida.

Acclaim for *Bestseller*:

'A highly entertaining tale.' *Publishers Weekly*

'Olivia Goldsmith's forte has always been the writing of revenge novels with great, good humour . . . There's lots of romance and revenge here . . . Plenty of awful people get their comeuppance and there's more satisfactory coupling at the end than in a Shakespeare comedy.'
*Washington Post*

'The achievement of *Bestseller* is that Olivia Goldsmith takes the sometimes arcane publishing industry and makes it interesting as well as completely credible. Her descriptions of the pressures on authors, the often arbitrary editorial process and even the bottom-line problems of small booksellers are dead right.'
*New York Times Book Review*

'Goldsmith hands out her characters' rewards and comeuppances like Jane Austen dealing blackjack . . . You keep licking your fingers and reaching for the next page as if it were another potato chip.' *Newsweek*

BY THE SAME AUTHOR

Fiction

*The First Wives Club*
*Flavour of the Month*
*Fashionably Late*

Non-Fiction

*Simple Isn't Easy*

Olivia Goldsmith

# Bestseller

HarperCollinsPublishers

HarperCollins*Publishers*
77–85 Fulham Palace Road,
Hammersmith, London W6 8JB

This paperback edition 1997
1 3 5 7 9 8 6 4 2

First published in Great Britain by
HarperCollins*Publishers* 1996

First published in the USA by
HarperCollins*Publishers* 1996



ISBN 0 00 649673 3

Set in Meridien by
Rowland Phototypesetting Ltd,
Bury St Edmunds, Suffolk

Printed and bound in Great Britain by
Caledonian International
Book Manufacturing Ltd, Glasgow

To Larry Ashmead
Editor of Genius
Cultivator of Tomatoes

Whose stories of writers, agents, editors, and publishers
inspired, awed, and amused me.
This is your book as much as it is mine. Let them sue *you*.

# ACKNOWLEDGMENTS

So many people contributed to this book that I am going to leave them all out, and instead write a special sucking-up acknowledgements the way a lot of bestselling authors do. Special thanks however, are due to those who were so supportive on a day-to-day, listen-to-my-whining basis. Thanks to: Paul (No Coast) Mahon, for his manic good humor, his wit, and his eternal, unjustified optimism and spirit of fun. Keep taking the medication, Paul! To Nan Robinson, a total piece of work, and I mean that in the nicest possible way. To Walter Mathews for his patience, humor and decorating advice; To Charlotte Abbott as well as her dog; To Jason Kaufman, with thanks for his unfailing good humor and patience, though I do miss the ponytail; To the brilliant Patricia Faulkner, guide at the V & A who helped so much with Canaletto, art history, and the insider's view of the guide's world; To Amy Fine Collins, a constant friend and inspiration; To Philip Gwyn Jones for his insights on British class distinctions and background on the vagaries of the U.K. school system; To Rachel Hore, even though she *didn't* name the baby after me; To Peter Straus; To Faith Sale, whose brilliant explanation of the role of an editor inspired and awed me; To Barbara Turner, whom I love dearly and who knows everything worth knowing. Hang in there, Binny; To Carmen Callil, for her brilliant critiques of my work; To Hugh Wilson, a writer, a director and a total charm boy; To Gail Parent, because you're right—it is all high school; To Anthony Cheetham; To Louis Baum, because I truly adore you *and* I like going to the Groucho; To Anthony Blond; to George Craig, for his belief in authors, particularly this one; To Lenny Gartner, whose creativity dwarfs my own; To Gail Rebuck; To Jane Austen, because everybody's been writing about her lately; To Sir James Goldsmith—you know why, "Uncle Jimmy". To Frances Coady; To the mysterious but always witty Horace Bent; To Val Hudson, with thanks for the book party and apologies to the rug; To Christopher MacLehose; To Melody Smith, for her endless galley slaving; To Ian La Frenais for the inspiration I received from his masterpiece "Scotland: The Vital Market". To Martyn Goff; To the Number 14 and 22 London double-decker buses—I wrote most of the first half of this novel in the front left upstairs seat; To Jonathan Lloyd; To Dick Snyder for publishing me in the first place; To Sherry Lansing for her continuing friendship and for buying the film rights to this book; To Matthew Evans; To Liz Calder, most delightful and eminent of English editors; To Alexandra Elovitz, with thanks for your company, Big Girl in London and Bath; To Robert McCrum; To Rachel "Where's the Cream" Dower for the fun we had on King's Road; To Ben Dower, as long as he stays close to the candles; To Paul "Badah" Smith, with love always; To Nicholas Clee of *The Bookseller*; To Gerry Petievich, my brother, sage and West Coast Muscle; To Christopher Gasson; To Scott Rudin, my all time idol; To Michael Elovitz, the best cook at Bonchino's; To Georgina Capel; To the London Library, for letting me be a member and with thanks for the use of the hall; To Caroline Michel; To John Bloom, for keeping me in the picture; To Maureen Egen, because we love the same movie; To Dori Berinstein, with love to Mitchell, Sammi, and Pooh; To John Baker for his delightful wit and support of "New Voices"; To Liz Knights, whose contribution to the book world will be remembered; To Carole Little for extending her amazing hospitality to me and letting me enjoy her exquisite taste; To Roberta Rubin of the original Book Stall; To Tom Maschler for my own reasons; To Philippa Harrison for being my gal-in-publishing idol; To Nick Webb because you're so damn adorable; To Rosie Cheetham, for entertaining me more than anyone—and I haven't even met you! To Eddie Bell, because of all that you have taught me; To Helen Fraser of Penguin, with my deep appreciation and regrets; To Imogen Taylor of Little, Brown, even though you left me flat; To Karen Duffy for everything; To Corinne Gotch; To June Formby of Pan Bookstores, because she always provides a good read; To WH Smith for making me a hero (or heroine) for a month and to Graham Edmonds; To David Singer for putting my name on the wall of the London tube; To David Schad of Selfridges, because he's so much fun to flirt with; To Roger Katz of Hatchards for "loaning" me his Academy pass; To Caroline Milliken of Harrods, for all those book signings. To Fred Newman of *Publishing News*, even though you won't name a Nibbie for me; To Robin Baird-Smith because he, too, loves Georgian houses; To Brian Stone for being so tall and forgiving me for foot-in-mouth disease; To Tom Rosenthal; To Richard Charkin, for not suing me; To Paul Hamlyn, though you ignore me at drink parties; To Bob Gavron; To Tim Hely Hutchinson—I'll never forget that night, Tim. To Simon Master, for just being you; To David Whitaker, for your particular charm and wit; To Peter Mayer, because you're my physical type; To Barry Winkleman, with the hope *you* send *me* a gift; To Deborah Rogers, for her deep understanding; To Gill Coleridge, because I care; To Carole Blake, one of the few great agents; To Michael Sissons; To *all* the Chapmans: Ian, Ian S. and Nick; To Chris Weller; To Manfred Herriger, because you're the only Manfred I know and that should count for something; To Dan Franklin, for being so unpretentious; To Jonathan Burnham, a book lover extraordinaire; To Steve Rubin and his adorable, charming wife Cynthia; To Mark Barty-King; To Patrick Janson-Smith, because I think we might be distantly related; To Paul Scherer; To Geraldine Cook, because she knows what English girlfriends can be like; To Mike Petty; To Celia Brayfield, for her description of the butterflies; To all my friends at the Basil Street Hotel.

Also, and with deep apologies, thanks to the unsung heroes of the book world; the sales reps who schlep to the independent bookstores and know not only what their publishers are selling but also what their bookstore clients need. Their love of books and their unfailing humor never fails to impress. I had a whole subplot around a book rep in this novel, but it wound up on the cutting room floor. My apologies to all book reps everywhere but especially to: Edward Tobin, Moira Reilly, Ian Bell and Barbara Flood of the Ireland Sales Division; John Grahamslaw, Steve "The Man" Newell, Val Clark, Mick "Lashes" Fawcett, Ronnie Allan, Peter Hawtin, Jim McMullan, Mike "Macho-bay" McQueen, Harry Ward, Stephen Ward, and Chris Moody of the North Sales Division; David Crombie, John Faiers, Jane "Let's Go Shopping" Harris, Roseanne Bantick, Robin Birch, Elizabeth Dawson, Daren "Have I Got A Book for You" Hall, Keith Jenkin, Richard "Big Mac" MacDonald, Kevin Paul, Bob Payne, James "Cute Thing" Prichard, Ellen Tucker and Ian Wood of the South Sales Division.

Most of all, thanks to everyone else in the book world, particularly my readers. My experiences, bad and good, have been thrilling because they are all a part of the process of creating the things that have always been most exciting and precious to me: books. So, to all of you, recognized and unrecognized, thanks for letting me be a tiny part of the long history of publishing.

Lastly, for those few I have felt it best to omit, I remind you of Alexander Pope's lines:

> Satire's my weapon, but I'm too discreet
> To run amuck, and tilt at all I meet.

The year I returned to active publishing there were five varied manuscripts submitted to Davis & Dash; five manuscripts, each by a different author, each with different aspirations. All five made the enormous jump from unpublished manuscript to published book, but only one among them was destined to make the next leap to become the bestseller.

—Gerald Ochs Davis, Sr.

## PART ONE

# *A Novel Idea*

One day God decided he would visit the earth. Strolling down the road, God encountered a sobbing man. "Why are you crying, my son?"

The man said, "God, I am blind." So God touched him and the man could see and he was happy.

As God walked farther he met another crying man and asked, "Why are you crying, my son?"

The man said, "God, I am crippled." So God touched him and the man could walk and he was happy.

Farther down the road God met yet a third man crying and asked, "Why are you crying, my son?"

The man said, "God, I'm a writer." And God sat down and cried with him.

—Gerald Ochs Davis, Sr.
*Fifty Years in Publishing*

# 1

> Nobody ever committed suicide while reading a good book, but many have tried while trying to write one.
>
> —*Robert Byrne*

Terry was looking down at the pilled cuff of her sweater when she saw Roberta approaching. Roberta had an even sadder look than usual on her plain face. Terry was not surprised. Business at The Bookstall had dropped off a lot over the summer, when any West Sider with disposable income uses it to get out of Manhattan on the weekends. But now, with Christmas coming, business had not picked up, probably because of the superstore that had planted itself on twenty thousand square feet just two downtown blocks away.

Roberta was a little woman, small-boned and birdlike. Terry liked the way the older woman looked. Her skin had those tiny, even fine lines that fair-skinned brunettes are often saddled with, though Roberta's hair had gone from brown to gray long ago. Now Roberta laid her hand on Terry's ratty sleeve. Reluctant, Terry looked into Roberta's sad brown eyes.

"I have some bad news," Roberta said, but Terry didn't need to be told. She'd seen it coming. Still, Roberta was from the old school, the one where people took responsibility for their actions and felt they owed explanations. She lived up to her name: Roberta Fine. "I don't think I have to tell you that it's not your performance, and that it's certainly not personal," Roberta began. "You know how much I've enjoyed working with you the last year and a half." Terry, a writer, heard the nuance. She didn't need Roberta to continue, though she did. "But even on a part-time basis, I simply can't afford . . ." Roberta paused, shook her head, and briskly licked her lips for a moment, as if moistening them would make the words come out more easily. "The only other option . . ." Roberta began, then stopped.

Terry merely nodded her head. They both looked over at Margaret Bartholemew. Poor Margaret. Older even than Roberta, lumpy Margaret was hunched in the corner, awkwardly packing a box of returns. She lost her grip and half a dozen books fell to the floor, one of them tearing. No credit for the return. Roberta closed her eyes briefly and sighed. She lowered her already quiet voice.

"I can't let Margaret go," Roberta almost whispered. "She only has this and Social Security. Without a place to come to each day, people to talk to, well . . . I've been over it a hundred times, Terry, but I just can't—"

Terry smiled and shook her head. "No problem," she said. She tried to muster some humor. "I mean it. It's not like you were paying me what I was worth."

"A price beyond rubies," Roberta nodded, her face still serious. She patted Terry's pilled cuff. Then she sighed again. "The truth is, I don't know how long I'll be able to keep the store going. But that's not *your* concern." Roberta shook her head. "After twenty-seven years, you'd think that people would have some loyalty, that they would . . ." She paused. In all the time Terry had known Roberta, first as a customer at The Bookstall and later as an employee, she'd never heard Roberta bitter. Well, she didn't hear any bitterness now, exactly. Just disappointment and, perhaps, a little hurt surprise. Terry knew all about both of these feelings.

Roberta just shrugged her birdlike shoulders as if to end the conversation and reached up to pat Terry's arm. "You're young and talented. You'll move on to other things soon. But I'm so sorry, dear." And it was that, the word *dear*, that made the tear slip out.

*

The tear had been Terry's only surprise. She had seen the end coming—and not just the end of her little part-time job at The Bookstall. As she swung north up Columbus Avenue, Terry was numb. She carried her pilled sweater, a hairbrush, and a few other personal belongings in a biodegradable Bookstall bag—along with the copy of Alice Thomas Ellis's new short-story collection that Roberta had inscribed and insisted Terry take as a gift. Terry felt no anger, no pain. After all, the job hadn't given her enough to live on, not even in the limited way she lived, including the tiny income from the manuscript typing she did on the side.

Terry thought of Roberta and how the older woman had called her young and talented. So why did Terry feel so old and used up? After she had finished her Columbia dissertation, and after she'd spent the tail end of her loans and grants, she had managed to support herself for the last eight years on marginal jobs at copy centers, word-processing services, and then at The Bookstall, while she wrote, edited, rewrote, submitted, and resubmitted her manuscript, her magnum opus, the book that explained the world as she saw it. And she'd failed.

While friends around her took real jobs, got promoted, married, and moved on, she'd only written. And not just written—she'd also tried to sell her work. She wasn't one of those slackers who was so terrified of rejection that they never attempted to be published at all. Terry *had* tried. She'd kept careful lists. She knew how to research. She'd figured out the best, most literary editors and submitted the book to them at the ever-dwindling number of publishing houses in New York, holding her breath while an editor considered her work, living through the rejection and watching her target shrink as one firm was subsumed by another. Well, the corporate-acquisition ballet hadn't mattered in the end because they'd *all* rejected her. Some had shown initial interest but in the end considered her novel "too literary." Others felt that it lacked focus and pacing.

Or that it was too long. Or that the humor was too coarse, too farcical. It was too political, too serious, too depressing. Some simply rejected it out of hand and advised her to get a day job. But most sent the standard rejection letter, the one that meant that nobody had even bothered to look at an eleven-hundred-page unsolicited manuscript that hadn't been touted by an agent or bid on by Hollywood.

Terry actually smiled at that. Imagine Hollywood trying to film *The Duplicity of Men*! Hollywood was all *about* the duplicity of men, and they weren't ready to give away any of their secrets.

She shook her head, switched her bag to her other hand, and waited at a red light to cross Broadway. At this point she was down to only one hope. The manuscript, edited yet again, had been out for close to five months at Verona Press, and a subeditor, Simon Small, had actually written her *two* letters, each with a few intelligent questions. This was the longest time anyone had considered *Duplicity*. But it had been weeks since her last inquiry, and he wasn't responding to her calls or her letters. She sighed. It was a bad sign. She had almost nothing in the bank, and now she was unemployed again. Her hopes hung on a very small Simon because she would not, she could not, ask her mother for yet another loan.

Opal was still back in Bloomington, Indiana, still working at the college library and still foolishly believing that her daughter was a genius. Poor Opal, Terry thought. She'd already had so many disappointments. Terrance O'Neal had courted Opal but quickly revealed himself after marriage as nothing more than an Irish drunk. He then abandoned her and their infant daughter. Opal got the job as librarian but then was passed over time and again for promotion.

But Opal was a stoic from an Indiana farm family. Alone, she'd gotten herself through the classics, not to mention the library-science program at the state university. When her father wouldn't "waste money on school for a girl," she'd done it all herself. Opal had worked and raised Terry alone and helped her get scholarships to both Yale and Columbia. Opal had molded her daughter into the writer who would tell the world what men were and why they were the way they were. Opal had taught Terry that life consisted of pain, false hopes, hard work, and the exaltation of great talent. They had read Tolstoy together, and Trollope, Dickens, and Austen. Terry had been the only girl in the seventh grade to know that George Eliot was a woman. And that George Sand was, too. If it made her a bit of a freak, she didn't mind. Terry loved books as passionately as her mother did and was grateful that Opal had shown her the door through which she could escape their limited world. Greedily, guiltily, Terry had stepped through it, leaving Opal behind.

But now, eight years later and with several initials at the end of her name, Terry not only found life as painful and tragic as Opal had predicted but had to bear the burden, the horrible realization, that perhaps the pain was not going to be ameliorated by the benison of talent. Books, her mainstay and her escape, had turned on her. Every published book taunted her. Words, which had been her comfort, her tool with which to weave a story, were now a chain that was dragging her down.

Terry had never meant to write a commercial book, a million-copy bestseller. Certainly not. If there was a God and that God looked into the deepest, darkest place in her heart, there wouldn't be the smallest bit of envy for John Grisham or Danielle Steel. Terry didn't want a six-figure publishing contract or her name on the bestseller list at the 20 percent-off rack at Barnes & Noble. She wasn't that modest. She wanted immortality. She'd suffered loneliness and poverty to string her words together, one by one, for more than a thousand pages. And all to find her true friends, a small, serious readership. Now, after enough submissions to make her dizzy, Simon Small, a man she'd never even met, was the only one left who could grant her a chance at that.

She passed Ninetieth Street and the only neighborhood tavern that was still cheap enough for her to nurse a beer at. But Terry didn't have the heart or the money for that. Soon it would be the unemployment line and a begging letter to Opal. No. She shook her head. None of that, none of that ever again. Opal had deceived her, and she in turn had deceived Opal. They had created a world of false hope. She had, like the girl in the fairy tale, tried to sit in a roomful of straw and spin it into gold. But she had failed.

Terry shrugged and turned left, walking along her block toward Amsterdam Avenue. This was one of the dicey streets where the West Side renaissance had not yet taken hold. A few brownstones, their façades raped in the fifties by white brick fronts, stood among nondescript apartment buildings too shabby to go co-op. Her own, the shabbiest of all, had been converted into tiny studios. She walked down the two steps that led to the entrance and through the narrow hall to her apartment in the back. Chinese take-out menus littered the floor, but today she had no energy to pick them up. Nor would Mr. Aiello, the super, who lived in the front. Terry stopped at the tarnished brass mailbox and took out her key. Maybe there would be a letter from Opal, filled with the small goings-on of the library and of her garden and her reading. Yeah, and maybe there'd be an overdue notice from ConEd, and another from the phone company. But once Terry inserted her key, her heart dropped. It was much worse than that. She saw the package that all writers hate and fear. It was a big envelope, and for all intents and purposes, it could just as well have been a bomb. Because it stopped Terry O'Neal's life as completely as a terrorist.

She wrestled the package out of the narrow box, forgetting to relock the brass door. There it was, return address Verona Publications, 60 Hudson Street, S. Small. Terry had been submitting her work long enough by now to know what a returned manuscript looked like. Especially this one, her only one, which ran to 1,114 typed pages. And had been returned twenty-six times. No, she corrected herself. This would make it twenty-seven.

Terry hefted the package under her arm, walked down the dark hall, and fumbled with the keys to the apartment. She had rented the place eight years ago after finishing her dissertation and leaving Columbia. It was just a single room, but there were ornate moldings on the wall from when the broken-up space had been something more. There was a crystal chandelier, which miraculously no previous tenant had ruined or stolen, and a marble fireplace, which, though smoky, actually worked. The apartment was dark at noon, it had virtually no closet space, and the hot water was never more than tepid, but it had charmed her. Back then, it had echoed *la vie bohème*. In a hopeful, flamboyant mood she had painted it peacock blue with white trim.

Now the blue was faded and the white had grayed. The room looked not like a writer's lair, an artist's garret, but like a cheap, dark, and nasty place to have to begin or end a life in. Terry sat down on the Salvation Army sofa and tore open the envelope. The letter clipped in front of the manuscript was no surprise. There were never any surprises.

Dear Ms. O'Neal,

It is with real regret that I am forced to return your manuscript *The Duplicity of Men*. Despite some beautifully written passages and an interesting theme, the editorial board, upon consideration, has decided it is inappropriate for our list at this time.

I am therefore returning it to you with sincere regret. I would be most willing to look at any other novels you may be working on in the future.

Simon Small

Any *other* novels? In the future? For a moment, Terry almost laughed. She sat there, drained and empty. She was a big girl, and her heavy thighs sank into the sofa, her arms hanging between them. She didn't move for a long time. Until she knew.

Enough is enough, she thought. Soundlessly, she pushed herself up and went to the battered file drawer where she kept the other letters, the rejections she had collected from Putnam and Simon & Schuster, from Little, Brown and Houghton Mifflin, from Viking, Davis & Dash, Random House, and Knopf. From *all* of them. There were dozens. Could she say that fairly? She was always exact with her words. To be sure, she counted them one last time. There were twenty-six, with Simon Small's making the twenty-seventh. So, in fact, she could say there were dozens. And she'd done no better with the university presses than with the commercial houses. Well, what had she truly expected? She knew nobody and nobody cared to know her. She had poured all of her reading, all of her love of language, all of her experience of life into these carefully constructed, crystalline pages of prose and had been foolish enough to think that somebody would care enough to read them. Well, she was wrong. The whole folly was over.

Carefully, meticulously, she went to the fireplace and crumpled up some old newspapers and torn cardboard. She started a blaze. Then, slowly, a few pages at a time, she fed the manuscript to the flames. It felt surprisingly cleansing. It didn't take long: less than a half hour perhaps. Certainly not long considering the thirty-three years it had taken her to learn to read, to learn to write, to imbibe the great works, to develop her own style, to have a story to tell, and to tell it. It had been a hard life, often full of pain and frustration. Now she had to add defeat. But, Terry knew, if she couldn't live a writer's life, she didn't want to live at all.

Once her manuscript was burned she looked around, as if waking from a trance. She didn't stay still long. It had felt too good to stop. Before the fire died, she fed an earlier draft into the flames, then her latest marked copy. Next she began to scour the apartment in earnest. She found every note, every draft, every partial photocopy, and fed all of it into the bonfire. After all, there was no point to saving it anymore. She had run out of publishers, time, money, and belief. And the anticipation—the waiting for the rejections—had been more painful than the rejections themselves because somehow she had always known that her vision was too dark, her world too sad, to be lauded by publishers or her professors. Terry had been the type of student who never found a mentor, who never shone in seminars, who never got to be the pet at workshops. She was too rawboned, too raw altogether, too unfeminine and clear-eyed. She was not likable, and her professors saved their compassion—if they had any—for others. She had lived in obscurity, and that's just where she would die.

The fire was nearly burned out. Terry looked around the apartment. With all the papers burned there was very little else: a few nondescript skirts, a gray tweed dress, some reams of printer paper, her battered laptop, her good leather purse, a canvas book bag. Things that didn't matter. She took the three back-up computer disks and placed them, last of all, into the dying embers. They stank as they melted and bubbled. The bitter smell in the air mingled with the fear at the back of her throat.

She thought about writing a note to Opal. But what was there to say? I was wrong? You were wrong? She'd written thousands of paragraphs, millions of words. It was enough for one lifetime. Yet she didn't want her mother to feel her blame. So, when at the last, the very last, Terry picked up the carefully labeled file of rejection letters, she paused before consigning them to the guttering flames. She needed no other explanation, no other note. Almost gaily, she found some transparent tape and walked around the room, decorating the walls with the only visible reward of her eight years of endless, single-minded toil. The letters papered the room nicely. They proved she'd left no stone unturned. With all that done, she went to the window outside the kitchenette and cut down the clothes-line that, long ago, she had strung across to the fire escape of the next building. Terry dragged the kitchen chair to the center of the room and sat with the coil of rope upon her lap. Before she did anything else, she thought she'd simply sit back, staring at all the nos, all the negative votes, hanging on the wall and—in her own mordant way—enjoy the view.

# 2

> I think of a writer as a river: you reflect what passes before you.
>
> —*Natalia Ginsburg*

Camilla Clapfish pushed the lock of brown hair behind her ear with her habitual little twist, wrote the last line, and then slowly looked up from the manuscript she had just completed. Outside, beyond the open window, the dull gray cobbled streets of San Gimignano were offset by the vibrant blue of the Italian sky. Camilla sighed and put down her pen. She had given herself a week here, undisturbed, to finish the book, a book she had been working on for almost a year, and she'd achieved her goal a day early. She smiled to herself. It felt like "the hols"—what upper-class British schoolchildren used to call vacation. She looked across the rooftops to the crazy stone towers of the ancient hill town. She'd go out and celebrate. She could spend the little she had left of her money on a good bottle of wine and a slap-up meal. She wouldn't eat at the hotel tonight; she'd find a really good restaurant. But first she would walk in the tiny park, climb the steps of one of the towers, and look out over the Tuscan plain.

Oddly, Camilla felt as much sadness as triumph over finishing the book. Writing had come late to her—well, if at twenty-nine anything could be considered late. She'd found how she loved to record what her eyes took in, to create with words instead of paints. She was a failed artist, an unsuccessful art historian, and a quiet person—not a talker. But words on paper had become her companions this last year, and the characters she had drawn had become her friends. She'd written about a group of middle-aged ladies on a bus tour. She felt she'd come to know and like them all, even the troublesome Mrs. Florence Mallabar. She would miss them.

Camilla added the last page to the neat stack of manuscript, rose from the table, and went to the wardrobe, where her plain brown linen jacket hung. She was tall, and her light brown hair and her dark brown eyes set the tone for her wrennish dress. Camilla was not one for bright carmine or aquamarine. She wore no lipstick. Too much early exposure to nuns, she supposed. You wound up dressing like either a tart or a novice. She was certainly of the novitiate school. And although her English skin and regular features were enough to draw some attention from Italian men, she didn't—as her mother had frequently reminded her—"make very much of herself."

Now she carefully locked the door to the sparely furnished hotel room and walked down the stone stairs to the lobby. The clerk at the desk greeted her in Italian and asked if she was having a good day.

*"Sì. Buono. Grazie."* Yes, it was a *very* good day. The day I finished my first novel, Camilla thought, but she merely nodded. Her Italian was passable enough to discuss the practicalities of life but not good enough to describe this quiet joy. The clerk, an older man with a grizzled mustache, smiled. To him she was only another tourist. San Gimignano was a famous tourist town, a perfectly intact fourteenth-century wonder. There were those who called it "The Medieval Manhattan of Tuscany" because of the beautiful and bizarre stone towers that graced it. Once there had been sixty or seventy of them, but now only fourteen remained, making a strange and beautiful silhouette against the green Tuscan landscape. She would go out and enjoy looking about.

She walked out the stone portal of the hotel onto Via S'Porto, the secondary street that led to the main piazza. She paused, took a deep breath, and rubbed her eyelids with the very tips of her fingers. She was tired but elated, and more than a little surprised. *I didn't think I could do it, but I did,* she thought. *I've finished it. I've finished my first book.* She smiled and—for the first time in months—felt a pang of loneliness. Camilla was quite used to being alone. But now, without the comfort of her book to work on and keep her company, she wished there was someone she could tell her news to.

I suppose I never thought I'd complete it, she realized. After all, she had never been taught what was now called "creative writing." Camilla had attended the Convent of the Sacred Heart in Birmingham, a dark, failed industrial city in the English Midlands, and her salvation had been that she was taken under the wing of Sister Agnus Dei, stern Sister Agnus, her sixth-form teacher, who had recognized her intelligence and championed her cause. It was Sister Agnus who had insisted that Camilla sit for A levels—the all-important testing that got British schoolchildren accepted to university.

No one in Camilla's family had been to university. Well, in point of fact, all of them had left school at the earliest legal opportunity. Camilla's father had been a lorry driver until an accident resulted in a bad back that ended his days behind the wheel. Her mother, not to put too fine a point on it, had been what once was referred to as a "char."

Perhaps that was unfair. Camilla, walking over the cobblestones, reconsidered her words and edited her thoughts. Well, if Mum was not as little as a cleaning lady, she certainly was not as much as a housekeeper. She had been the "daily" whom the Beveridge family had called in as needed, and she had spent a good part of her life cleaning up the messes of those she still referred to as "her betters." In fact, it seemed to Camilla that her mother had always been more interested and more willing to clean and cook and listen to the children of the Beveridge family than to her own. The Clapfish flat was messy, ill-managed, overcrowded, and damp. Mrs. Clapfish rarely bothered with housework at home—"Don't get paid to do it, now, do I?" she'd ask. Thinking of their home even now, under the warm Italian autumn sun, made Camilla shiver. Her three younger brothers had been in a constant clamor, their noses always wet, as were their socks and vests. When they weren't shouting at one another they were being shouted at by their mother, who was just as often being shouted at by their father. Camilla sighed, her loneliness deepening. No point in writing to them, telling them she had finished a novel, Camilla thought. Her mother would only ask, "Whatever for?"

As she continued walking toward the center of San Gimignano, she decided that she certainly wouldn't tell Lady Ann Beveridge about her novel. But maybe she would write to Sister Agnus Dei tomorrow and give her the news. Sister Agnus, despite her name, wasn't the least bit lamblike. She'd be fiercely glad. In the meantime, Camilla would enjoy this day, the Italian sun, and the beauty of the stonework, being responsible for no one but herself.

She did not have to guide anyone through either of the two main churches, or point out the Roman ruins, or wait while calculatedly naïf souvenirs were purchased. Camilla had spent the last year and a half in Firenze, first studying and then supporting herself there as a tour guide. All of her higher education in art history in New York—which her parents had neither understood nor approved of—had, in the end, come down to this: She was a tour guide. Because, only after Camilla had struggled through college and graduated, only after she'd finished her dissertation, did she realize that—without connections in either the art world or academia and without any particular personal charm—she would never get one of the few and highly coveted museum or teaching jobs. So, adrift, she had left New York and wound up in Florence, giving guided tours and, in her loneliness, writing fiction in her spare time.

She liked giving tours, but only to Americans. They were used to standing in groups and were eager to improve themselves. It seemed almost a religion with them. British tourists never would stand together—they were always wandering off or directing their gaze somewhere else, while the French were absolutely impossible—rude and arrogant, the lot of them. Camilla had never finished a tour without one of them walking out on her while she spoke. Yes, Americans were nicest, most grateful. And although she became frozen with a paralyzing shyness if they asked her to coffee or lunch after a tour, Camilla spoke with authority during her stint as docent. She could guide people more easily than be with them.

Camilla lived frugally, watching every penny, but she'd already had a lifetime of experience with that. She also had to put up with the occasional condescension of wealthy visitors who wanted their art predigested and their history reduced to four-hundred-year-old scandal. But she persevered. She was actually rather well-suited to the job. She had a surprisingly strong voice, physical stamina, and a good memory for details. If at first speaking to groups was difficult, she found, in time and with good notes, that it was easier than talking to people one-to-one. Although hers was by no means a glamorous or lucrative life, she had at least managed to live among the splendors of Italy and have her evenings free. Free for Gianfranco and, on nights he couldn't see her, for her novel.

Along with the writing, the fresh flowers she always kept in her room kept her loneliness at bay. A solitary life did not mean a lonely one, and it comforted her to recognize flowers in the Firenze markets, just the same as the ones she bought at The Angel tube stand and at the Korean greengrocers in New York—the delphiniums, tuberoses, and gladioli, all as familiar as old friends.

Now she walked into the flower-bedecked square that opened before her. The sun was just beginning its slanting descent. One side of the square was already in shadows, while the other was illuminated by a golden light. The old stone buildings, gilt by the sun, glowed as if lit from within.

The air was so clear that each lintel, each doorstep, each window mullion showed a line as clean as a pen stroke. Geraniums, nasturtiums, and ivy exploded from window boxes, breaking the austerity of the stone with their riot of color. For once she wouldn't have to stand against a building, her calves aching, the expense of a café out of reach. No. Tonight she'd splurge and enjoy the view in comfort. Boldly, Camilla walked toward a café table beside the well in the center of the square, ready to take a seat. She would have an aperitif here and, in doing so, pay for the rental of a comfortable chair. It would allow her to watch while the sun set and the square emptied, as it did each evening at this time.

Camilla had made her life—such as it was—on such small pleasures. Snatched hours with Gianfranco, walks among the splendid architecture, hours spent in museums. It had always been so. While her classmates back at the Sacred Heart looked forward to country-house weekends, Christmas gifts from Harrods, and, later, cordon bleu classes in Paris or a stint at what passed as the season in London, Camilla had comforted herself with small, sometimes even tiny, pleasures but ones that deeply satisfied: a good library book and a bag of boiled sweets; hot toast spread with Marmite eaten alone in her room; a long afternoon visit to the Birmingham Museum, or a special program on the telly that she could watch undisturbed while the boys were out playing football. Even a hot bath with a rare dollop of scented bath oil was a treat to be looked forward to.

Then later, when she was older, there was the wider world of art—the hours she could spend at the Tate staring at—no, *devouring*—the Turners—her favorite artist save for Canaletto. The Van Huysum at the National Gallery. Taking the Wallace Collection one lush room at a time. Whole days whiled away at the V & A. Then there was New York, mooning around the Frick, sitting in a quiet spot at the Cloisters. The Metropolitan Museum of Art gave particularly good value—for the investment of looking there was so very much to see. And now there was today, when she would enjoy her comfortable seat and the beauty and activity all around her in the square.

But as she approached the table, the chair at the other side was appropriated by a pale, ginger-haired man who helped an older woman into the seat. Camilla's hand was already on the corner of her own chair, and as the stout woman slid her bottom onto the metal seat, Camilla's hand brushed the man's. She pulled back as if burned. He must have seen that it was her seat, her withdrawal, because he immediately began to apologize.

"I'm so sorry. Are you sitting here? I didn't mean to . . ." He paused, and in the silence Camilla tried to bite back her disappointment and come up with a plan B. All of the other tables were taken, so she would have to sit inside the café, away from the quiet beauty of the piazza. She shook her head and was about to leave, but he continued. "Mother, we've taken this young lady's table."

The older woman looked up. "What?" she asked. "I don't think so. I think this table was free." The older woman glanced at Camilla. "Sit down, Frederick," she told him. She was flushed, with a round, heavy face in late middle age. But despite her weight she had a good haircut and discreet but excellent makeup. "*Were* you sitting here?" she demanded.

Camilla shook her head wordlessly. "No, Mother, but she was *about* to," the man explained. Then he smiled at Camilla. They were Americans. The ginger-haired man had a nice, crooked smile, and his irregular nose and tiny freckles gave his face a pleasant aspect. "We'll take another place," he said.

"Well, why don't we just share the table?" the older woman asked, irritated. Clearly, she was not planning to move. Camilla stood motionless for a moment and looked again at the young man.

"Yes. Would you let us sit at your table?" he said, and his absolute good nature was easy to give in to. Yet, after months of taking tourists through the major sites of the quattrocento, Camilla didn't relish another tourist conversation. She paused. She had so longed for this seat and this view and the beautiful light, fading even as she stood there. She took her seat.

A waiter—handsome, negligent, and self-absorbed—casually asked for their order. "A Martini," Camilla said. The older woman's eyebrows seemed to rise as her eyes narrowed.

"Shall we share a bottle of Montepulciano?" the man asked his mother.

"Yes, that would be fine."

The waiter nodded briskly and left them to their silence. Camilla was relieved by it and stared across the slightly hilly cobblestone path to the archway that led to the road out of San Gimignano. Camilla knew it was likely that at any moment her thoughts would be broken into by the nervous, idle chatter of these two tourists: Where are you from? Oh, we've been there. How long are you staying? Where do you go next? She had better savour this silence for as long as it lasted.

But she was wrong. The older woman opened her purse and seemed to be ransacking it, while her son simply sat, one long freckled hand on the table, looking across the courtyard and occasionally up at the birds that were settling into the hundreds of niches in the walls. Surprisingly, the silence was not awkward, and after a few moments Camilla found herself relaxing, slowly but inexorably becoming a part of the scene. This was what she liked. The sensation—unusual for her—that she was a part of the pageant, rather than a mere observer. For just as surely as she was sitting there beside the freckled man and his mother, there were tourists across the way snapping pictures. Pictures that they would bring home to Cincinnati and Lyons and Munich, pictures in which she would appear, a stranger in the square beside two other strangers, her hands lying idly on the empty white table.

Camilla's heart suddenly lifted in her chest. She didn't have only the beauty of the scene in front of her, she was also a part of the scene, now and forever in those snapshots and her own memory, the woman dressed in brown at the table beside the well. She couldn't repress a small sigh.

"It is lovely, isn't it?" the man asked. She had to nod. "I tell myself that I won't forget it and I tell myself that I know how beautiful it is. But each time I come back I am taken by surprise all over again." She nodded again. She felt that way about so many of the beauties of Italy—about the Botticelli room in the Uffizi, the Medici Chapel, the Giotto frescoes in Assisi. About all of Venice, and, of course, about Canaletto.

The older woman looked up for the first time. "I think I've lost my sunglasses," she said.

"Oh, Mother. You do this twice a day. They're probably back at the hotel."

"Well, they won't do me any good there."

"Shall I get them for you?" her son asked, rising from his seat.

"Don't be silly," she told him. "I'll go." She got up and without another word left the table. How unpleasant. Camilla watched her bustle across the square and wished the woman's hotel was in Umbria. But she disappeared into a doorway right on the square. One of the better hotels in the town, Camilla noticed. And the one with an excellent restaurant.

"She's tired," the man explained to Camilla, although she hadn't inquired. "She spent the day sitting in churches, and she finds it tedious after the first hour."

"And you don't?"

"Oh, not at all. But then, I'm an architect."

There was a silence. To be polite, Camilla smiled and asked, "Then it's not your first visit to San Gimignano?"

"Oh, no," he said. "I try to come back every year, although I haven't been able to make it for the last two. We spent the day at Saint Peter's, and then we climbed all three towers." He paused. "How did you spend the day?" Somehow, it was irresistible not to tell him.

"I finished writing my novel," Camilla said.

"Good for you! Do you write novels often?" he asked, and she saw the mischief in his grin.

"This is my first," she admitted.

"Well, I am most impressed. How are you going to celebrate?"

Just then the waiter appeared with her drink and the bottle of wine. "This is my celebration," Camilla told him.

His face crumpled in dismay. "But we spoiled it for you! Oh, I'm so sorry. Mother isn't usually like that, but she was tired. She's been under some pressure." He stood up. "Excuse me," he said again.

"No." Camilla put her hand out. "Please don't go." Her voice had more feeling in it than she had intended, but it was too late now. Suddenly it seemed as if being alone would become unbearable. The man hesitated for a moment, his reddish-brown eyes not quite focusing on hers. He wasn't at all handsome, not in any way, Camilla thought. But there was an attractiveness about him, a pleasantness that, though it could not make up for his total lack of beauty, still had a certain charm.

Hesitantly, he sat down again. "Well, what's the name of the novel?"

"I'm not certain," she told him.

"Then what is the name of the novelist?" he asked, and she had to smile again.

She extended her hand. He reached out but fumbled for a moment in the air before he took hers in his own cool, long, freckled one. "Camilla," she said self-consciously. "Camilla Clapfish."

"Well, Miss Clapfish, permit me, Frederick Sayles Ashton, to be the first to congratulate you on the completion of your as-yet untitled debut novel." His formality was very un-American but quite endearing.

"Thank you," she told him and took back her hand

reluctantly. She picked up her drink, but he quickly stopped her by lifting his own glass. Some of the wine slopped over one side, but he didn't seem to notice.

"Before you sip, permit me." He tilted his head and looked over the rim of his wineglass at her. "I think my mother thought you had ordered a mixed drink," he confided. "It may have induced her departure. She doesn't approve of cocktails." He put his glass down, dipping his elbow in the puddle of wine on the tabletop. He didn't seem to realize it.

Camilla looked at her own innocent aperitif. "Oh. She must have thought I was asking for a gin martini. No. Here it's a brand name for vermouth."

"Yes. Well, *I* know that, but I don't think Mother does. Father was a drunk, you see." Camilla nodded, silent. Having lived in New York, she was familiar with Americans and their candor, but it did often leave her speechless. Luckily, Frederick Sayles Ashton was not. "To the alliterative Camilla Clapfish and the future publication of her first book."

And then, for the first time, dismay hit her. My God, she thought, the book had been hard enough to write. It had started so tentatively as an exercise, then became absorbing, a labor of creation and love and also a torture that had filled her empty evenings. But now that it was finished, she'd have to try and get it published. How in the world, Camilla thought, would she ever manage that?

# 3

> I am not a snob, but rich people are often a lot of fun to write about.
>
> —*Noël Coward*

Susann Baker Edmonds lay on the *chaise-longue* staring out toward the Mediterranean as if somewhere out there she would find chapter twenty-eight. There shouldn't even be a chapter twenty-eight. The book was too damned long. The distant sea glinted, but Susann hadn't a reflecting glint of an idea. She stood up and paced the north side of the marble-edged pool. She heard Edith, her secretary, recross her heavy legs and sigh.

"Could you be still for just a moment?" Susann snapped.

"I'm sorry," Edith said, but she didn't sound sorry. She sounded bored and impatient and eager to get away. As if something in Edith Fischer's boring, middle-aged life was more important than a new novel by Susann Baker Edmonds. Susann knew she had to calm down. God, she hated to feel this way, so edgy, so nasty. She was *not* a nasty person. She put her hands up to either side of her lovely, lifted face and looked over at the dreary Edith. Physically Edith was everything Susann despised—dowdy, overweight, and drab. She was spunkless, and yet Edith was exactly the audience that devoured Susann's books. That's why bland Edith, sitting there knitting in the sun, was not simply an annoyance that could be terminated by the termination of her employment.

Because to Susann, Edith was a secret touchstone. When they were working together and she saw Edith's eyes glowing, her mouth slightly open, and her breathing quickened with interest and excitement, Susann knew she had a story that worked. But how long had it been since Edith had been responsive like that? Certainly not while they worked on *A Mother and a Daughter*. And not while she struggled through *The Lady of the House*. Perhaps Edith was merely jaded. Both books had come out on Mother's Day of the previous two years, and each had climbed to the top of the bestseller list, as all Susann Baker Edmonds's books did. But even Susann had to admit that the past two had climbed a little more slowly and held the vaulted top slot for a far briefer period.

Susann knew she was at a nerve-racking place: Realistically, she knew that being at the top so long simply meant it was sooner that she'd fall. But Susann *liked* the top. She wanted to stay there. She prided herself on being a number-one bestselling author. From out of nowhere to number one: She'd been one of the very few to make the leap.

And Edith had watched her climb. Back when both of them worked together as legal secretaries, Susann had brought in her stories, page by page, and Edith had devoured them, always asking the question sublime to any writer—"What happens next?" It was because of that enthusiasm that Susann—just plain Sue Ann then—had kept writing. If not for Edith, Susann would surely have quit. Because it had been hard, so hard, to work all day and spin stories at night.

It was still hard. Now a bestseller, a number one, was *expected* of her. Now, at last, she was paid an enormous advance for her stories.

Susann paced the length of the pool again and turned to look out at the horizon. "Any mail?" she asked.

Edith shook her head without even looking up from her knitting. "Nothing important." Edith handled all the bills, forwarding them to Susann's accountant to be paid, and all of the fan mail, sending customized responses. Actually, the only thing Edith didn't handle for Susann was Kim and her begging letters. But Susann hadn't heard from

Kim lately. She would like to think that perhaps her adult daughter had finally begun to behave like an adult, but from long experience she doubted it.

Susann rubbed her hands as she paced. The sun on them felt good but freckled her skin. She looked around. It was still so hard. Her work had bought her this villa, the beautiful furniture in it, the Rolls parked in the garage, the services of Edith and the French couple who cooked and cleaned and drove for her. But it hadn't bought her daughter's love or happiness. And wasn't Susann slipping? She pulled her arthritic fingers through her artfully streaked blond hair and walked back to the *chaise*. She crossed her legs and her arms and told Edith crossly that she was through for the day.

Edith gave her a look and shrugged her rounded shoulders. The woman would have a dowager's hump in no time, Susann thought distastefully. "All right," Edith said, but Susann knew it wasn't all right. She had a deadline, Edith knew she had the deadline, and Susann always delivered on time. Her books came out each Mother's Day, as regular as jonquils in March. But this one would be different. It would be on the fall list. Her publisher demanded it. And she would not disappoint them.

Almost two decades ago she and Alf had been among the first to spot the hole in the marketplace between the heavily promoted spring list and the most important fall offerings. When her first successful book came out fourteen years ago, Alf had taken advantage of the women's market just waiting there at Mother's Day, and it had made her name.

It had also made her a rich woman. Well, not the first book. Of course she'd gotten screwed out of *that* deal. Each year since she had followed up the success of *The Lady of the House* with another Mother's Day novel, and with Alf's help, each one had sold hundreds of thousands of copies in hardcover and millions in paperback. She'd become a tradition among some women—daughters giving mothers a Susann Baker Edmonds, and now their own daughters gave *them* copies. Three generations reading her uplifting stories. Yes, she felt proud of what she'd accomplished. She'd become famous and wealthy, and Alf had become her full-time agent and taken over her affairs and fired the incompetent lawyer who'd given her first book away. They'd retained a PR firm. Her name popped up regularly in the columns. Four of her books had been made into television miniseries, and another three were optioned. She was the most profitable woman novelist at her publishing house, and they treated her appropriately.

But there was the rub. Susann put her hands over her eyes to shield her face from the sun. She was the most profitable *women's* writer, but there were all those men out there, turning out their techno-thrillers, their legal-suspense stories, and those other testosterone-driven books, all of which were being made into feature films by those bastards in Hollywood who ignored middle-aged women. It was so unfair. Susann had never had a movie made of any of her books. Women would go to see Crichton movies and Grisham movies and Clancy movies, but men wouldn't take their wives out to see a woman's saga. Women's books were only good enough for the pink ghetto of television. And without the extra heat that films generated, it was getting harder and harder nowadays to keep a bestseller up at the top of the list. So this new one would come out in the autumn. Would it help? There were one hundred and fifty romance titles released each month. As if that wasn't enough, most tried to interest book buyers, stores, and readers with all kinds of giveaways and undignified trash. Joan Schulhafer of Avon Books had put it succinctly when she said, "We have a higher nicknack-per-author ratio than any other genre."

Edith was gathering up her steno pad, her bag of pencils and yellow Post-it notes and paper clips. She was taking off her reading glasses, putting them in her skirt pocket and putting her sunglasses on her sun-burned pink nose.

In the last two decades, while she worked with Edith, Susann had married, divorced, become slimmer, younger-looking, better dressed, and blond. While Edith . . . Edith hadn't changed at all, except to age. She looked like a drone. It actually frightened Susann, partly because—even though she looked at least a decade younger—Susann knew she was actually four years *older* than Edith. And Edith knew it, too, being one of the few insiders who knew Susann's real age.

Hell, Edith didn't just know her real *age* (fifty-eight), she knew her real name (Sue Ann Kowlofsky), the real number of marriages Susann had been through (three), the real number of face-lifts Susann had had (two), and even where she kept most of her money (the island of Jersey). Edith knew all the sordid details about Susann's daughter, Kim—the drug rehabs, the DWIs, the bad men. Perhaps that was why Edith so exasperated her. Edith had neither improved herself, nor did she seem impressed with Susann's improvements. There was no softening mystique between them. And Susann didn't like living without mystique. She had become dependent on her publicist-generated bio, Alf's respect, the publisher's kid-glove handling, and the aura that fame and wealth had given her.

"Alf ought to be back soon," Susann remarked. "I have to get dressed. We have a dinner party tonight." Edith didn't much like Alf, and the feeling was mutual.

"The chapter's more important than the party," Edith said. "It needs work."

Susann felt her temper rising, but she bit back the words she wanted to spit and, instead, gave Edith one of her best smiles. "Why don't *you* see what you can do with it?" she asked.

Edith stood, finally, and shuffled off the terrace into the house. Susann got up and crossed to the balustrade, leaning against it and looking out toward the water. The autumn sun slipped behind a cloud, and Susann, clad only in a bathing suit and chiffon cover-up, shivered. The problem was that as tacky and annoying as she was, Edith was right. The new book was not only coming slowly, it was coming badly. And there was no room for shoddiness. At this point in her life Susann could not afford to slip out of the golden circle of bestsellers and back into obscurity, back to Cincinnati. The very thought made her shiver again.

The women's fiction market was changing. Alf said it was moving forward and might leave her behind. But without her books, without her fame, without the money that she brought in, where would she be? *Who* would she be? What would Alf do if her business fell off? Managing her had made him, but as he'd taken on other clients, hadn't his interest in her waned a bit? Would even Edith stick with her if all of this ended?

Susann closed her eyes, shutting them tight despite the crow's feet. Plastic surgery still couldn't do anything about crow's feet, though it had erased the bags and tightened the sags under and over her eyes. Still, good as she looked, young as she looked, slim as she looked, Susann clutched the railing with her arthritic hands and knew she was just a fifty-eight-year-old woman, frightened and alone.

# 4

> What no wife of a writer can ever understand is that a writer is working when he's staring out of the window.
>
> —*Burton Rascoe*

Judith stared out the window, looking up from the typewriter on the card table she was using as a desk. She was alone, except for Flaubert, who snorted and whimpered in his sleep. Judith wondered if the dog was dreaming. She stretched in her chair. From her seat she could see King Street and a tiny corner of the state university campus. A girl was leaning up against the brick wall of the student center, and, as Judith watched, the dark, lanky young man who was standing beside her leaned in, encompassing her with his hands. Then he quickly kissed her on the mouth. The girl laughed and tossed her head. Even through the dirt of the windowpane Judith could see the white flash of her teeth.

It seemed so long to Judith since she'd been a student, even though it was only two semesters ago. And it seemed even longer since Daniel had kissed her that way. Perhaps he had *never* kissed her that way. Daniel was not what anyone would call the spontaneous type. Brilliant, yes. Ambitious, definitely. But spontaneous . . . No, Judith could never remember Daniel kissing her like that.

Of course, he hadn't been free to kiss her on the campus, she told herself, trying to be fair. Judith always tried to be fair. She remembered reading somewhere that her name came from the Old Testament, that Judith might have been one of the judges, or perhaps she was just in the Book of Judges. Something like that. Daniel would know. He knew everything. So why was she being so critical? Judith felt confused. When she sat up here, working on the book, she sometimes let her mind wander, and she didn't always like where it led her.

Below her, in the sunlight, the young man bent and picked up a backpack, swinging it easily onto his shoulder. He said something, and Judith could see another flash of teeth from the smiling girl. When was the last time I smiled, Judith wondered. Well, she reminded herself, I've always been a serious girl.

And theirs had been a very serious affair. After all, Judith had been a student and Daniel was her teacher. Not only that, he was married. Of course, his marriage had already been troubled for some time. Daniel was an honorable person, so he told her right from the beginning, and he had told her that he was deeply attracted to her. He thought she had talent—real talent—and that someday she could be a successful writer.

No grown man had ever paid that kind of attention to her. She had blushed with pleasure and confusion. And she had accepted his praise and his offer to go out for a cup of coffee. "You'll be a successful writer," he'd repeated, and there, under the table in the coffee shop, he'd taken her hand and squeezed it. Writing was her dream, her secret ambition. She'd never told anyone, much less a college professor, that she wanted to be a writer. They would laugh at her. But Daniel hadn't laughed. He knew her secret, and he encouraged her.

She'd believed him, and here she was, actually married to him and working away, 279 pages into the manuscript. It wasn't exactly the book she had planned to write. Not art. Not even close. It was a book they were sort of doing together. Not exactly for the art of it, and not exactly together, but . . . well, they needed the money now.

Her parents had been furious about Daniel, about his religious background, his marital status. They had threatened to sue the school and had cut her off without a penny.

Not that Judith really cared. They'd always been well-off, and her father had always used money to control them all. That was probably why she'd gone to a state college in the first place. He'd been livid that she hadn't applied to one of the Seven Sisters schools. But Judith, in her serious way, had told him she was sick of exclusivity and didn't care about money.

Daniel didn't care about money either. It was one of the reasons she loved him. At first she'd even been afraid to tell him that she was one of the Elmira Hunts. Daniel hated capitalism and inherited wealth. He told her that straight out. Like her, he believed in a meritocracy.

But now they were short of money. Really short. Daniel had to pay alimony and child support. So they were writing this book for their future, a book that could be commercial, that could make them some money and free Daniel from teaching so he could get to do some serious writing. Then *she'd* have time to get back to her first novel, the one that Daniel had praised so highly.

Judith heard the apartment door slam. Flaubert jumped up.

"I don't hear you!" Daniel's accusatory voice floated up the stairs from the kitchen. He often came home between classes for a sandwich and a quickie. Judith sighed. It just all seemed different now, when sex wasn't forbidden but expected. Somehow the romance was—well, not gone exactly, but lessened.

"I don't hear you," Daniel called again. He loved to hear the sound of her old typewriter. He thought it was quaint that she refused to use a word processor. He called her his little Luddite. Judith wasn't sure what that meant, but she'd never asked.

Now she gave Flaubert a settling pat and shouted out to her husband, "I'm thinking. Sometimes I'm allowed to think." She immediately regretted the snappish tone in her voice.

Daniel hopped the three steps up to the little room in

the turret that Judith used as an office. He wasn't exactly handsome. He was a little too small, a little too tight-featured. But with his steel-rimmed glasses, his curling black hair, and his grin, he had an insouciance that always affected her. He was so different from her cold, controlling father. Even now, she couldn't believe that she had attracted him. He'd graduated from Yale! And he'd been on scholarship. He'd spent a year at the Sorbonne. Daniel Gross was *really* educated, and Judith knew that her mediocre grades at the Elmira Academy did not measure up to Daniel's prep-school education. He'd already read *everything,* and he'd even met some of the writers who wrote the great books he taught. His two courses on contemporary American literature were always overregistered. In her first semester Judith had actually been shut out of it. She almost smiled. Imagine that! And now she didn't just get to admire his pepper-and-salt tweed jackets and his hand-knitted sweaters and his perfectly rumpled corduroys, she got to live with him and make love to him. I *am* happy, she told herself, looking up at him. I am very lucky and very happy.

Daniel approached her and put a hand on either shoulder. Flaubert growled, as he always did when Daniel touched Judith, but she told him to hush. Daniel's hands were small, but his fingers were powerful, and he gently gripped the tense muscles in her neck and shoulders. "So, how's it coming? Daydreaming, or have you got a junior case of writer's block?"

She smiled at the little pun. Judith hadn't graduated. She left last year, her junior year. Somehow, after Daniel, the degree didn't seem important anymore. And as Daniel pointed out, what the hell use was a B.A. in English from a SUNY school? It was, he joked "as good as a one-way ticket to Palookaville." Judith knew there were few teaching jobs anyway, and she had no interest in reading *Silas Marner* with a class of hormonally challenged seventh-graders. No; she wanted to write, and she wanted to be taken seriously, and Daniel was helping her to do both.

"Have you made the changes to chapter eleven?" Daniel asked. Although the plot was basically her idea, Daniel had worked it into an outline, and it was that outline she was working from. He'd given her a schedule and insisted she produce six pages a day. Each evening he read and reread the pages she worked on and corrected them, edited them, and made suggestions. She spent the following day making his changes and getting on with the new stuff.

"No, but I finished chapter twenty-four. Only two to go!" She looked up at him, hoping for a smile of surprise at her industriousness. But he only reached for the pages and started to read. Silently, his eyes devoured the first page, then the next one and the one after that. She tried not to squirm while she waited for his reaction.

"Okay," he said. She colored. From Daniel, that was praise. "This looks okay. I'll take it with me, back to class." He stopped and looked at his watch. "In fact, I better go. I need some prep time."

Judith stood up, trying not to let her disappointment show. A quickie was better than nothing at all. "Are you sure?" she asked. And tentatively she snaked her hand around his back, letting it rest on the tweed of his jacket just above his buttocks. She moved her hand lower. Through the scratchy fabric she could feel his round little behind. But Daniel kept his eyes on the chapter, then folded it in half, and—giving her a quick peck on her cheek—turned to go. No quickie today.

He ran down the three little steps and into the kitchen. She followed him, as lonely as a kid in a grammar school hallway, watching as he grabbed his beat-up leather briefcase and stuffed the new chapter into it. Flaubert stood beside her, his tail wagging as Daniel rebuckled the case, put it under his arm, and then—just as Judith felt completely let down—reached over and hugged her. "You did good," he said and gave her a big kiss on her forehead, just as if she were a little girl. She smiled with pleasure.

"See if you can get to those chapter eleven corrections this afternoon," he told her, and Judith silently nodded her head.

# 5

> Someday I hope to write a book where the royalties will pay for the copies I give away.
>
> —*Clarence Darrow*

Gerald Ochs Davis tapped the mouse twice and sent the new chapter off to the print queue. He had—finally—succumbed to the lure of technology and had allowed installation of a sophisticated PC, which was housed in a mahogany neoclassic cabinet. But he had drawn the line at having a clattering printer in his office. He leaned back in the tall, leather-upholstered chair and shot his cuffs so that they protruded out just the appropriate inch and a quarter beyond his perfectly tailored blazer sleeve. He wore a Patek Phillipe wristwatch—he called thin as a small novella. In discreet white thread his initials were embroidered on the *inside* of his white cuffs. He looked down at the monogram—GOD. He allowed himself a very small smile.

His friends would consider the inside, white-on-white monogram just another one of his small idiosyncrasies. All endearing—at least to his friends. His enemies, and they were legion, would simply chalk it up as another one of his nasty affectations. But Gerald knew his enemies, and following the Arabic advice, he kept them close to him. He also knew why they hated him: simple jealousy. Gerald had had the good fortune to be born into a wealthy, prestigious family, he had had the fun of being thrown out of the very finest prep schools, he had bedded, married, and divorced (not always in that order) four of the world's most beautiful women. As if that wasn't enough, he now not only ran one of the oldest and certainly the largest publishing company in New York City, but he also wrote some of its most touted books. Not to mention having the coveted corner table reserved for him in the Grill Room of the Four Seasons every day of the week he was in the city. Gerald's life was full and rich, and he understood that those with a more paltry portion were, naturally, envious. It came with the territory.

And quite a large territory it was. Gerald looked around his office, an enormous room almost fifty feet long, which contained not only his magnificent English Regency partner's desk but two separate seating arrangements, a floor-to-ceiling library of first editions, a massive window with a view across to the Chrysler Building and the East River, as well as an original Chippendale conference table that seated eighteen—in original Chippendale chairs. Aside from the large and luxurious bathroom (complete with sauna), his suite also consisted of a small private dining room, another conference room for larger groups, an impressive reception area, and two secretarial offices. In fact, his offices took up so much space in the building and were so luxuriously appointed that many of his employees referred to Gerald's floor as "God's Little Acre". It was virtually an acre of space—Gerald had once had it measured—and at eighty-two dollars a square foot, it was probably the most expensive executive suite in all of the city. That made Gerald smile, too. In an industry noted for its lack of frills and style, Gerald had more than his share of both.

But there were complications and tragedies in a life of such privilege. Gerald got up from his desk and checked himself in the Duncan Phyfe mirror that hung between two windows of the south wall. He adjusted one eyebrow. His hair, all of it, was false, glued on every morning. Gerald suffered from alopecia areata, a disease that had rendered him totally hairless from the age of three. Some doctors thought it hereditary, others felt it was psychologically based, the product of an unloving home. Gerald didn't know the reason. All he knew was that each morning he put on his wig, his eyebrows, and even his upper eyelashes.

There was a knock at the brass-inlaid door. Gerald ran his hand across his eyebrow, smoothing it, and called out. Mrs. Perkins appeared, the printout in her hand. "Do you want this now?" she asked.

Gerald's good mood evaporated as he eyed the manuscript pages in his secretary's age-spotted hand. The woman should do something about those. "Yes," he said curtly. "And I'd like some coffee. Jamaican Blue Mountain."

Part of Mrs. Perkins's job was to grind and brew Gerald's dozen or so daily cups of coffee. And he was very particular about his coffee. He had given up red meat, dairy products, other fats, cigarettes, and even—with great reluctance—red wine. But he'd be damned if he was giving up his caffeine. He planned to live forever, but he wanted to be alert while he was doing so. And if he was going to drink coffee, he was only going to drink the *best* coffee. Only Gerald and the Queen of England bought Jamaican Blue Mountain in bulk. At sixty dollars a pound, it was expensive, but there was a line on Davis & Dash's annual budget that read "executive office canteen supplies," and Gerald's exorbitant coffee bill was buried in there. To Gerald there was nothing that heightened the pleasure of a luxury more than not having to pay for it himself.

Because, despite his six-figure salary and his seven-figure bonus, Gerald was always short of cash. This came of living well in New York City and of having three expensive wives, two of them exes, along with four children in college, as well as a demanding mistress to support. Even Gerald, long used to profligate spending, could be shocked by his current monthly expenses.

Part of the problem was that Gerald had been raised among the very, very rich and moved among the very, very rich but was, actually, himself, only moderately well-off. His family had created no trust funds. Gerald's only sinecure had been the publishing firm, his stock, and his job at Davis & Dash. But his father had sold the firm when Gerald was a young man, and although some of the family still retained shares, Gerald's portion of the sale money had been spent long ago.

Since then, unforeseen by Gerald's now aged father, the company had been sold again, and yet again. This last time it had been acquired by a major communications conglomerate. Davis & Dash was the corporate jewel in their crown. Through all of the acquisitions, while other heads rolled, Gerald had managed to keep his above water. After all, he was a member of publishing royalty, he was *the* Davis of Davis & Dash. He knew everyone in the business, and he brought in the top money-making books, not to mention the most prestigious (though not always profitable) authors. No one would dare to fire Gerald Ochs Davis. He was a resource of the firm as important as the backlist. He knew it, and so did the corporate moguls, Philistines though they were. Gerald was, after all, the most well-known publisher in New York.

And Gerald was an author himself. In the early years of his career, he had become vaguely unhappy, working as an editor, then editor in chief, and, finally, publisher. It seemed to him that all of it lacked a certain *je ne sais quoi.* Being the midwife at the birth of an important book was exciting, but after a dozen years of it Gerald had realized that the spotlight was never on the midwife but always on the mother and child—and some of them were real mothers. Gerald had realized, rather late in life, that he wanted to write.

Well, that wasn't exactly true. Gerald did not want to *write,* he wanted to have *written.* He wanted to see *his* name in the *New York Times Book Review,* on the spines of books, and on the cover of volumes displayed in bookstore windows. He wanted to be mentioned in "Hot Type" in *Vanity Fair.* He wanted a black-and-white photo of himself, taken by Jill Krementz, on a dust jacket. Gerald wanted the thing that writers got, which eluded all editors: He wanted credit.

He also wanted money. After all, there he was making million-dollar contracts with barely literate horror-genre writers, people who thought that brand names were adjectives, for God's sake, while he himself was perennially short of spondulicks. Something was wrong with the picture.

But Gerald had not been sure he could write. He had a deep fear of making a fool of himself—after all, he was already Gerald Ochs Davis and didn't need to make his name. He also didn't need to destroy the name he had by doing something louche or stupid. So he had begun cleverly, dipping his toe in the water of words, so to speak, by writing a nonfiction book called *Getting It All*. He had used every contact he had to launch and promote the book. He had also mounted a campaign to have each secretary at Davis & Dash call bookstores across the country and buy multiple copies. It had all managed to get the slim self-help volume onto the bestseller list. He had been clever and picked the right subject at the right time. Twenty years ago his book gave people permission to be selfish. The altruism of the sixties had faded, but the outright greed of the eighties had not fully kicked in when his book, a sort of updated Machiavelli, had pointed the way.

He had his first success, but Gerald didn't want to write nonfiction. There was no status in that, unless you did exquisitely researched biographies of important artists or political figures. Definitely *not* his style. Nor was there any real money in it. So, with a certain amount of fear but propelled by the success of *Getting It All* and his need for more cash, he wrote his first novel, a roman à clef. It was a scabrous tell-all about two sisters, one who marries the president and the other who manages to sleep with her sister's husband along with almost everybody else. He'd gotten lots of dish from Truman Capote, Louis Auchincloss, and Gore Vidal, and the book had sold like hotcakes. The only downside was that Jackie never spoke to him again. But that was not such a bad thing—after all, there was a certain éclat in feuding with the Queen of New York, and anyway, she worked for a rival publisher. The book had certainly raised society eyebrows. But it had raised his income as well, and for the second time, Gerald Ochs Davis had a bestseller. If critics tore it apart and those in society pretended shock at his disclosures, Gerald knew their invidious cavils were based on envy.

But the truth was, it had been more onerous since then. The novelty of a well-known publisher-turned-writer and the rehash of a well-known scandal wore off quickly. Sadly, there weren't that many unknown skeletons for Gerald to rattle as a basis for his plots. His second novel, *Polly*, was the story of a prostitute who worked her way up to become the madam of the most exclusive whorehouse in New York and, eventually, the wife of a corporate chairman. Once again, Gerald based the story on reality—he used Davis & Dash staff to help with research—and those in the know were aware that he was writing about Molly Buchanan Dash, now a widowed doyenne in her eighties. It may have been ungallant, but *Polly* was a modest success and paid tuition bills and alimony for two years—though it didn't quite make the lists.

But with the precedent set, Gerald felt free to write himself a three-book, million-dollar contract, and that was back in the days when a million dollars was real money. Then, dutifully, he had written a book each year since, mainly because he needed the money. Each book sold a little less well than the one before, but if the royalty payments were smaller, the advances got bigger. Yet they were spent so fast.

Now, working on his latest novel, Gerald needed the money more than ever. But he also needed *this* book to succeed. If he had been hurried and lazy on the last two—and he had—it must have shown, because he had been punished.

Publishing was unlike any other business. When books were ordered and shipped, it did not mean that they were bought. Booksellers had the right, unique among industries, to return books that didn't sell. As Alfred Knopf had wittily put it, "Gone today, here tomorrow." (It was considered very bad form to wish authors on their birthdays "many happy returns.") With his last book, he had picked a subject that never seemed to pall: Lila Kyle, the murdered starlet. He didn't call her Lila Kyle, of course. Still, the story of a Hollywood brat raised by her wacky movie star mother to become the flavor of the month, only to be assassinated by a crazed fan, was in a way the story of the American dream turned nightmare. Despite Gerald's exhortations to the sales force and his insistence on a first printing of 150,000 hardcover copies, the book had shipped only 100,000 copies. Of course, it hadn't helped that Laura Richie, the celebrity gossip, had written a book on the same subject. Hers sold, making all the lists. His did not. On top of that, an unbelievably humiliating *80,000* had been returned. Even now they were stored in a Midwest warehouse because Gerald was too proud to remainder them and see them on book tables all around the country at a dollar a copy. He thought of Jonathan Cape, the prestigious London publisher, who was once asked by an Englishwoman if he kept a copy of every book he printed. "Madam," he replied, "I keep thousands."

Gerald's returns had been a major débâcle, and he was still licking his wounds and fudging numbers to cover the failure. Because now, when he needed the money more than ever, Davis & Dash was publicly held, and accounting was trickier and more difficult. If Gerald did continue to use Davis & Dash as a private fiefdom, at least he was smart enough to cover his tracks. Even in a huge, publicly held company there were ways to manipulate numbers, to move inventory credits from one author and have them assigned to another. You had to be smart and careful. Gerald was both—and his returned books had been moved to the columns of other, more successful writers like Peet Trawley, who would never notice the difference. After all, what were they going to do? Stand in the warehouse and count all the printed and shipped volumes?

But Gerald's contract would run out with this latest book, and to justify another huge advance he would have to see some sales. So he was doing his best. It was actually the story of his aunt and uncle, both prominent New York socialites in the Roaring Twenties, who were famous for their style, their parties, and the dissolute ending of their lives. Gerald's uncle had shot his aunt dead after finding her in bed with another woman—one *he* had been sleeping with. And Gerald, desperate for a plot, had used this family scandal as the basis for his glitzy potboiler. If he had nothing new to disclose—after all, he'd only met his uncle once or twice—the book revived a forgotten juicy scandal.

The problem was, what if his best wasn't enough?

Now he looked up at his secretary, patiently waiting for him. "Did you review them?" Gerald asked Mrs. Perkins. Gerald enjoyed being recondite—he always tried to use words people would not know. But despite his multi-prep-school education—or because of it—Gerald's spelling and punctuation still weren't what they should be, and his senior secretary was allowed to review his draft simply to make it understandable.

"Yes," Mrs. Perkins said. "But I think the lesbian love scene is too graphic."

"Mrs. Perkins, editor of genius," Gerald snapped. What he did not need now was negative feedback. What he had to do was push forward, finish the goddamned book, and see what happened then. If worse came to worst, he could always bring Pam in to edit it. Pam Mantiss was his editor in chief, a woman he had slept with, promoted, and piled work onto for more than a decade. She was smart and hard and hardworking. In fact, she did most of *his* work because he didn't have the time for it anymore. Now he looked up from his desk, "When I want an editorial opinion, I'll ask Pam," Gerald told Mrs. Perkins. "What I'd like from *you* is some coffee."

Mrs. Perkins merely nodded and put the pages down on the right-hand corner of his desk. "Ellen Levine called about that contract," she told him.

"Ellen Levine *always* calls about *all* contracts," he snapped. "She reinvents the wheel with every one. Tell Pam to handle it."

Mrs. Perkins left the office, and Gerald turned back to the screen of the word processor, staring at its gray and empty face. How would he fill another three hundred manuscript pages? He hadn't a clue. But he knew he had to do it before the end of next month if he wanted to collect his acceptance money. He rubbed his glabrous hands together nervously. He turned to face the huge windows of his office. Somewhere out there he had to find half a million people who would spend twenty-three dollars each to buy his book. Because Gerald *had* to be a success this time to keep his show rolling.

# 6

> Manuscript: something submitted in haste and returned at leisure.
>
> —*Oliver Herford*

Opal O'Neal trudged around the corner, stopping to check the numbered sign to make sure she was on the right street. She'd always disliked the idea of numbered streets—it seemed so impersonal, so anonymous. But, she supposed, that was what New York City was all about.

She slowly walked along the block of run-down brownstones and tenements. She tried to recall by sight which one had been her daughter's, but all the buildings looked alike. She'd visited Terry twice but not in the last three years. There hadn't been extra money for that. Opal's eyes filmed over with tears, and though she didn't allow them to fall—not in public—she had to pause a moment until her vision cleared. Then she spotted the black-painted "266" over a building entrance and knew this was the place, the address to which she had mailed so many long and loving letters. The place where her daughter had died.

Opal had gotten the news over the telephone, from a woman police detective. She barely believed it then, and these few days hadn't brought much more acceptance. She could have believed that Terry had been mugged or even murdered, but not that she had killed herself. Still, even over the phone, the woman had been quite convincing. There had been no break-in, she said, there were no signs of a struggle, and there were the carefully taped rejection notices, signposts to suicide. Last, there had been the "choice of modes," as the woman put it. Apparently, women under forty chose hanging more frequently than any other suicide method. Opal wondered, for a moment, what the preferred method for women over forty was. But she shook that thought from her head. It was cynical and mean-spirited, and Opal tried to be neither. She simply wanted to be a good and loving person, a good and loving mother, but it seemed *that* was out of the question now.

Opal squared her shoulders and walked down the three steps leading to the just-below-street-level entrance to the building. In New York real estate it was called a "semibasement"—Terry had once written that to Opal—but it seemed basement enough to drop the *semi* altogether, Opal thought. She went through her handbag and took out the case she had carefully secreted in the side pocket. The police had sent Opal her daughter's keys and requested that she collect not only Terry's body, which had been held at the Center Street morgue, but also her personal effects.

Opal had trouble with the key to the building's front door. The lock seemed loose, as if a million keys had jiggled it, but she finally got the key to fit properly and the door gave under the weight of her shoulder. Dank air met her—there was no lobby or foyer, just the dark hallway that led past one door, on to the metal-tipped stairs upward, and then finally to the door of Terry's apartment in the back. Opal had just managed to get the second key into the second lock and was pulling the door open when a man's voice stopped her.

"Hey! What the hell are you doing? And who the hell are you?"

Opal straightened herself to her full height of almost five feet. In the dimness she could just make out his stooped shape. "I am Opal O'Neal, and I am here to get my daughter's things."

The man paused for a moment, as if he was thinking about whether or not to be embarrassed, then deciding not to be. "Well, all right," he said grudgingly. As if he had anything to say about it at all. Opal merely nodded her head curtly, stepped into the last home her daughter had ever known, and closed the door behind her.

It was a sad room. Swiftly, Opal took in the battered table, the daybed, the single squat, overstuffed chair. Somehow, when she had visited Terry, it hadn't seemed so grim. Why hadn't she noticed? Had the bright presence of her daughter obscured the lurking darkness? Although it was a sunny, cold day outside, the room was murky as a cave. The dark blue was a bad color. Opal fumbled for the lightswitch, and the harsh overhead chandelier flicked on. She couldn't keep her eyes from flicking upward to the place where Terry had chosen to tie the noose. Quickly she looked away. By now the undertaker had picked up Terry's body from the morgue. Tomorrow Terry would be cremated, and the following day Opal would bring her ashes back home to Bloomington. Their home. A town where streets had names, not numbers. The town she never should have let Terry leave.

Opal opened her large purse and took out the canvas zipper bag she had folded within it. She went to the dresser and pulled open the top drawer. Inside were half a dozen pairs of white underpants, a single pair of unopened panty hose, a few nightgowns, and two brassieres. There was also a diaphragm in its plastic case. Opal blushed when she thought of the police searching through her daughter's private things. But Opal wasn't a prude. She knew that Terry had had a lover—at least one—and she had not disapproved. She may be a fifty-four-year-old librarian from Indiana, but Opal thought of herself as a modern woman. In fact, she was only against *marriage*, not lovers. In her experience, men seemed to turn bad only after another man performed the ring ritual over them. She shook her head, scooped up the drawer contents, and opened the next drawer down.

Opal knew that her daughter had spent the last decade working on her novel. She had encouraged and supported Terry while she worked. And Terry had even shared bits of it with her. Not much, and always diffidently. But it had shown her that Terry knew men, and the writing had been good, very good. Opal was *not* an indulgent reader. Years at the library, and at home in the evenings reading Flaubert, Turgenev, Austen, Forster, and the other greats had given Opal an informed and exquisite taste. She knew that Terry shared that taste and, moreover, had the creative wellspring to do more with it than Opal ever had. Terry had been her own harshest critic and most merciless editor. But on those few occasions when she had shared sections of the book with Opal, Opal had seen how brilliant it was.

Yet the police told her that there were no manuscripts, no papers of any kind found. Only the burnt offerings in the fireplace. Opal simply couldn't believe that. A mother might kill herself, but she would never kill her child. Or Terry wouldn't have. Opal *knew* the manuscript was here. They'd simply overlooked it.

But at first all she saw in the drawer were neatly folded clothes—a few sweaters, two old shirts. Then, underneath them, she glimpsed a cigar box. Not big enough for a manuscript, but perhaps . . . Opal's heart began to beat faster. Terry had been scribbling since she was a toddler. She wrote about *everything*. Terry's whole life had been dedicated to writing, and Opal's to preparing her and helping her to write. Surely Terry wouldn't go without leaving some explanation, some clue, to help Opal through this. The box looked just like the one Terry had kept letters in back in high school. Opal knew that the box was waiting for her.

She carefully lifted out the brightly colored box and wedged her thumbnail under the lid, flicking it open. Inside there was nothing but a collection of pencil stubs, markers, and the kind of click-top ballpoint pens that had the name of various businesses on their sides. Opal bit her thin lower lip and threw the box in the trash. She put the sweaters and blouses into in her canvas bag. Terry was—had been—a big girl; Opal couldn't wear these things, but somebody could. Neither of them had approved of waste.

One drawer left. Something had to be there. Slowly, Opal opened it. But all it held was a few pair of neatly folded corduroy slacks and a Columbia sweatshirt. Opal remembered Terry wearing it on her last visit to Bloomington, and her eyes filmed over again. Fighting back the tears, she emptied the contents of the drawer into her bag.

Next she went into the tiny bathroom. Terry had never been one to fix herself up much—she took after Opal in that respect—but even Opal was surprised by how little there was. A toothbrush and a plastic cup, toothpaste, a stack of neatly folded washcloths, a bar of soap, and a hairbrush were all the objects laid on the sink and shelf. Opal cast all but the hairbrush into the trash and looked carefully at the brush before she put it in her canvas bag. Terry's hairs were wrapped around the bristles. Was that all of herself that Terry was leaving behind? Opal opened the medicine cabinet, but it was stocked as sparely and impersonally as a hotel's. A can of Band-Aids, a deodorant bar, cheap hand cream, tampons, aspirin, and a plastic tube of petroleum jelly sat primly on the little glass shelves. Opal shook her head and didn't have the heart to clean any further. She'd leave that for the next tenant.

She walked out of the bathroom, past the fireplace and over to the single closet. Even with the light on it was difficult to see into it, but Opal didn't need to see much to know how little there was inside. A worn London Fog raincoat (which Opal had given Terry for Christmas six or seven years before), a brown cloth coat that Opal did not remember, and a few skirts hung there beside a broom and a small upright vacuum cleaner. On the shelf above, two blankets and a pillow were arranged neatly. There was Terry's computer, which the police told her had been emptied of all files. On the floor was a pair of rubber boots, two pairs of sturdy shoes, and a dustpan, along with a box of unused garbage bags. There was also a cardboard carton.

Opal squatted down, her heart racing as she reached for

the box. Is this where Terry had stored early drafts of the book? But as Opal pulled the box toward her, its weight and its clanking gave her the bad news. She opened it to find nothing more than empty cans and bottles, ready for recycling, that was all.

Opal looked again at the room. She felt so very tired, it was as if she could not stand up for another minute. For her whole life, it seemed, Opal had stood for something. She had stood for education, she had stood for the idea that one could better oneself, she had stood for single women getting a place in the world and for individuality in a place that preferred conformity. She had stood up for her daughter's dream, her talent and creativity, and believed that Terry could become a writer. Now Opal could stand no longer. She sank onto the daybed as if she, like Terry, would never rise again. She looked at the fireplace and the ashes in it. That was what her life was reduced to—ashes. There was no point in going back to Bloomington, to go on cataloging books, to go on reading. Terry was dead, and she had left nothing behind her.

Opal knew she was neither pretty, nor well dressed, nor well educated, but she was not so naive that she couldn't see the message in the lack of a message. Terry was—had been—furious, not just at those publishers who had rejected her work, but also at Opal herself, who had encouraged her in the first place. Otherwise she would have left a word of comfort.

From all she had read, Opal knew that the writer's life was a lonely one. But surely Terry had the muscle to live with that. As Opal had told Terry over and over during her childhood, you can never be lonely if you have a good book. And in this dingy apartment, on the bookshelves flanking the fireplace, there were plenty of those. But Terry *must* have been lonely, and desperate enough not to care. Lonely and desperate and angry.

At last, Opal began to weep. There was nothing that Terry had left behind—no message, no manuscript, no nothing. Just these rejection letters the policewoman had given Opal. They'd come from the ignorant, stupid, shallow publishers who had helped to kill Terry. Those were the key to this death scene. That is all that Terry meant for me to receive, Opal thought. That and my guilt. The hardness of it was shocking.

Opal cried as she hadn't cried for thirty years. And while she wept, she cursed herself for encouraging Terry in a life so difficult. She carried my hopes with her, and the burden was too heavy. It's my fault, Opal told herself. But what else could I have done? Terry was talented. Terry was an artist. It wasn't just that she was my daughter. She *was* brilliant. Did she blame me because nobody else agreed? Did she lose faith in herself because mine was the only voice that supported her? Did she come to hate me? Opal looked around the grim room that accused her. She must have. She did. Opal moaned and nearly choked. She felt as if she'd go on crying forever.

The knock on the door startled her. She wiped her eyes with her hand and looked for a tissue. Before she could fumble for her purse, the rapping at the door began again. "I'm coming," Opal said, and managed to get to the door. But she didn't open it. She wasn't stupid, after all, and she read the newspapers. In fact, she read the *NewYork Times* every day at the library. She knew what trouble could lurk outside a New York City door. "Who is it?" she asked, her voice wet and deep from her tears.

"It's me."

Well, that was the least helpful response she'd ever heard. "Who are you?" she asked.

"Me, Aiello, the super."

Opal rolled her eyes and then wiped them again. Just what she needed! Some stranger's condolences and morbid curiosity. If she wanted that, she'd have brought Terry's body back to Bloomington, where all the townspeople could gape. She opened the door. "Yes?" she asked.

"I'll need the keys back," the man said. No "excuse me"

or "I'm terribly sorry" or "Can I help you in your moment of need," but a baldfaced demand for the keys! Opal was outraged. This city was heartless. No wonder Terry hadn't been able to face it.

"I believe the rent is paid till the end of the month," Opal informed him, "so I believe that gives me a legal right to the keys until then."

The grizzled man's face reflected his surprise. Then he shrugged. "Yeah. If ya want to stay in there." He shook his head. "If I was you, I'd just want to clear out." Opal *did* want to clear out—more than anything—but there was the cremation and the memorial service tomorrow.

"If you were me, which is unimaginable, you would be polite and helpful."

Aiello stood there and blinked. Opal watched while his Neanderthal mind processed what she had just said. Light dawned on Marblehead.

"Oh, well, if you need anything . . . you know, boxes or something . . ." His voice trailed off.

It seemed the man did know shame. Good. Opal nodded to him. "I'll be just fine," she lied and firmly shut the door.

# 7

> You have to sink way down to a level of hopelessness and desperation to find the book that you can write.
>
> —*Susan Sontag*

Camilla spent her single day of holiday doing what she liked to do best—simply looking. But first she slept in, and after a breakfast of delicious hot chocolate and biscotti, she further indulged herself by sitting in the sunny hotel courtyard and reading a few chapters of Forster's *A Room with a View*. It was fun to read another British writer's send-up of tourists in Italy. Camilla, of course, didn't put herself in Forster's league. But she had just finished writing her own novel about the subject.

The pots of evergreens and homely violas, the beautiful stonework all around her, the blue of the sky, all were improved by the piquancy of anticipation. It was delightful to have the evening dinner with her new acquaintances to look forward to. It made this time alone seem splendid, and the coming company a nice contrast.

But from time to time, as she read about Lucy Honeychurch and her meddling, silly aunt, Camilla had to stop. Her attention would wander until she found herself reading a whole page without taking in a word. Instead she felt a vague shadow, as if the brilliant sky had clouded over. It was because of what Frederick Ashton had brought up. *How shall I ever get my book published*, she thought, and a chill ran through her. Who did I think I was, to write it? Who will ever look at a book about a coachload of middle-aged ladies in Italy and want to give me money for it?

Funny, really, how she had words to write for her characters and words for artists dead for hundreds of years but no words for herself. She blushed at how tongue-tied she'd been with Frederick Ashton. Her shyness—self-consciousness really—embarrassed her.

Camilla believed that for some reason her fate was to always be an outsider. She had felt different—had *been* different—from the rest of her family. Then, as a scholarship student from a working-class background, she'd been singular, distinct from the other girls at the convent school. Afterward, at college in America, she had felt unlike the Americans—who seemed somehow younger and more carefree than she. Now, living in Italy, although she'd made a few Italian friends and had certainly been passionate about her Italian lover, Gianfranco, she knew that, once again, she was different, an outsider. They all had the strong ties of family, of homes they had lived in for generations, of allegiances to the city in which they were born. Being an outsider had made her self-conscious and had helped her to write. In a way, it cleared her vision. But it certainly didn't make for a warm and pleasant personal life.

Despite living alone she could never be totally lonely if she had a good book. Books spoke to her, more directly, more deeply, than most people did. Her greatest pleasure had been reading, and now she found that she could write as well. Not well, not really well, not as well as Beryl Bainbridge or Kay Gibbons or Anita Brookner, but well enough to entertain herself—and maybe others.

The secret she had discovered, known to all other writers, was that when she wrote she wasn't lonely. It did more than just fill her mind and empty pages. It also seemed to be a communion, a communion between her feeling self and her observing self, a communion with her future reader—if there ever would be one.

Now, thinking of the publishing business, she realized that once again she was an outsider. How in the world would she manage to break into *that* elite group? Who in London did she know? Camilla was good at slogging and perseverance, but she was simply useless at putting herself forward, at pushing herself on anyone. What would she do now that she had finished her little book? In some secret part of her heart, she had written it hoping that it was a way out. Because she knew she had hit a dead end, here in sunny Italy. But what if the book was simply another dead end?

At noon she put the Forster away along with her dark thoughts and energetically walked out of the town and down to the plain below. She'd wanted both to escape her anxiety and to admire San Gimignano's unique skyline—its crazy towers, so odd against the Tuscany backdrop. She ate a sandwich she'd brought with her, but it was unseasonably hot and she was thirsty. After picking a handful of irresistibly red poppies, she walked back up to the hill town and found a *taverna* in which to sit and drink white wine. She had to keep away that question, that feeling of fear that accompanied the thought "Now what?"

She didn't want to eat much because of the dinner that evening, but she also didn't want to get tipsy. After a second glass of wine, Camilla made her way back to the hotel, where she bathed and then, in the luxurious thoughtlessness of the wine's embrace, slept through the rest of the afternoon. She awoke at a little after six and stretched, idly watching the light reflected on the ceiling. Then her mind turned to the immediate problem of what to wear.

Last night when Frederick Ashton had suggested dinner he said that they could "dress up a bit" to celebrate. But in fact, she *had* been wearing her best clothes yesterday evening.

She dressed in the other skirt she had with her and looked at herself in the glass. She smiled ruefully. You could take the girl out of the convent, but you couldn't take the convent out of the girl. Mrs. Clapfish had sent

Camilla to Sacred Heart rather than the local school simply because Lady Ann Beveridge had kindly arranged it. Once or twice, when Mrs. Clapfish had been called to the Beveridge home in an emergency, she had been forced to bring little Camilla, who was told "to sit very still and not touch nothing." This Camilla did. She had been awed and enchanted by the proportions of those fine Georgian rooms. She loved the light that poured in and the sheen of the furniture. And Lady Ann noticed.

"She seems a bright child, if a bit quiet," Lady Ann had said. "It would be a pity to have her bullied by the children from the council houses at school." The fact that Camilla was bullied by those same children at home—after all, they lived in council housing—seemed not to have occurred to Lady Ann. But she *had* sent a note to Sister Agnus, which was enough for Camilla to have been brought for an interview to the convent. From her first walk down the long stone entrance hallway, the convent had changed her life, and Camilla would always be grateful. Even at six years of age she had responded to the hush, to the light, and to the compelling beauty of the stone. The convent school, in all its peace, austerity, and magnificent organization, had given her something important.

But it had also separated her forever from the rest of her family. Because, although she was only a day girl and went home to *chez* Clapfish every night, once she had seen another way of being, she took to it. The uniform allowed her to gratefully lose herself among the other, wealthier, more confident students. And, if she applied herself, the nuns gave constant, if cool, approval, a commodity as lacking at home as order.

Of course she had been a bit of a joke, a curiosity. To start with, there was the name. Working-class girls in Birmingham were named Tracey or Sharon, not Hermione or Jemima or Camilla. Truth was, her mother had named her Camilla after one of Lady Ann's dogs. The name was so clearly upper-class that its appearance in her humble family made it laughable. How many times had she seen a new sister eyeing the class register and raising her eyebrows as she came to what Sister Agnus had dryly called "the girl with the highly unlikely name of Camilla Clapfish." Because of her background and patronage, she was expected to do well but not *too* well. On Visitors' Day, when Camilla had won a prize, Lady Ann—an old girl—had raised her brows and told her she'd done very well "for a Clapfish out of water." Everyone who heard her had laughed. Camilla had just shrugged and supposed she had.

Now, gazing at her reflection in the mirror, she realized she looked the perfect postulant. Well, it would have to do. She left the hotel at exactly half-past seven, her hair still slightly damp. It took her only a few moments to get to the square, but once there, she was dismayed not to see Frederick anywhere about. She would have to sit down, and that would wrinkle her skirt. Of course, she would have to do that at the restaurant, but by then he would have already seen her at her best, such as it was.

Dismayed, she lingered beside the well for a few self-conscious moments. How long could a girl stand beside a stone well and look interested? A thought chilled her. What if Frederick didn't come? What if his mother had refused? A proper Gorgon, she was. What, Camilla asked herself, if she had wasted the whole day in silly anticipation of an evening that wasn't even going to happen? And she didn't have the dosh for a restaurant dinner. A blush heated her face. It was at that exact moment that Frederick tapped her on the shoulder.

"Do you need some money?"

She looked at him, startled. She knew Americans were much franker than the British, but it took her a moment to realize that he wasn't reading her mind, nor was he quite as daft as to be inquiring into her bleak financial situation. He was only asking if she needed a coin to throw into the well! Wordlessly, she shook her head. Still, he handed her a coin.

"Well. Squander your lira," he suggested. "Make a wish."

Camilla looked into the well. I *want my book published,* she thought and dropped the coin. *And maybe, someday, to own a great painting.*

"Well done," he said. "Are you hungry?"

She nodded and realized she hadn't yet spoken a word. She was a wordless writer. "Yes," she said. "Yes. I'm famished."

"Great. I'm just the guy who knows just the place where they'll serve just the meal you need." And with that, he gently took her arm and led her across the square.

Perhaps his mother *wasn't* going to join them. Camilla was glad, but while she would enjoy dinner more if she were alone with Frederick, she would also have to be more on her guard. After all, he was a stranger, and an American, and he *had* said that his mother would join them. He might just be on the make.

But as they stepped inside the main room of the restaurant Camilla saw Mrs. Ashton, already ensconced at the best table, at the end of the room in the corner. It had a window view in two directions, facing out across the darkening plain below. Mrs. Ashton seemed to be deeply engrossed. Seeing her, Camilla didn't know whether she was relieved, disappointed, or both, but before she could make up her mind Frederick had escorted her across the room. He seated her beside his mother so that she, too, had the benefit of the exquisite view. Frederick seated himself opposite. "I almost hate to do it," he said. "To sit here, I mean. I hate to block the scenery."

"Why don't you sit here?" Camilla offered. "It is quite the best spot." For a moment, Camilla thought again of Forster's tourists and the fuss over the room with a view.

"I disagree. I'm the one with the view of two beautiful women." It was corny, but Camilla felt herself color again.

Mrs. Ashton snorted. "I think your arithmetic is faulty.

Or else it's your grammar. No need for plurals. There is only one beauty at this table."

Camilla, embarrassed, knew she should thank both of them for the compliment, but it was hard to look directly at Frederick, while Mrs. Ashton had been so very cool in her correction that she almost made the compliment seem a by-product. Or an insult. Certainly it wasn't true. Camilla knew she was not unpleasant-looking. Her skin was clear, her features regular, and her hair—a light brown with a coppery undertone—was nice enough. But nice was not beautiful. Camilla decided to sidestep the comment altogether. "Have you eaten here before?" she asked.

"Every time we come to San Gimignano," Mrs. Ashton told her. "Frederick is fond of the gnocchi." She sighed and shifted her weight. "He can eat whatever he wants without gaining an ounce. It's really aggravating."

A waiter approached just then and asked what they wanted to drink. Camilla asked for a Martini, while the Ashtons ordered a large mineral water, *con gas*. When the drinks were brought, moments later, Mrs. Ashton looked over at Camilla's innocent glass of red liquid.

"But that *isn't* a martini," she said.

Frederick smiled. "It isn't gin, Mother. *Martini* is the brand name for sweet vermouth."

Mrs. Ashton regarded Camilla's glass. "Ah, vermouth," she said in a voice full of approval.

Frederick beamed at the two of them. "I *told* you she thought it was an American martini you ordered yesterday," he explained. "My father was a gin drinker. They make mean drunks."

Camilla blinked. Would she ever get accustomed to American candor? Shyly, she tried to suss out Mrs. Ashton. But the woman seemed unflustered by the remark. She did, however, notice Camilla's eye upon her.

"I'm used to Frederick," she explained to Camilla and calmly picked up her menu.

With Frederick's help, Camilla ordered what turned out

to be a splendid meal. She ate the roasted peppers, the gnocchi, and the wonderful snapper with pleasure. They talked about San Gimignano, the odd architectural war between the Guelphs and the Ghibellines, and church frescoes. Mrs. Ashton commented occasionally, but the conversation was mostly between Camilla and Frederick.

"So, where are you from?" Frederick asked.

"Hard to say," Camilla said, smiling. "I grew up in Birmingham. In England. Not very romantic, I'm afraid. And then I went to school in the States and studied art history, and now I'm here being a tour guide. Where are you from?"

"Well, I usually say New York, but that's a lie. Actually, I grew up in Westchester County. Mother still has a house in Larchmont. Very suburban."

"There's nothing shameful about being from Larchmont," Mrs. Ashton said.

"No. As long as you don't stay there after you grow up. My sister and I both moved to the city," he explained, "though I've been living back in Larchmont the last few months."

He sounded apologetic. Camilla knew that a lot of young people had moved home. What had they called that in the States? "Returning to the nest" or something? For Camilla, it was an impossibility. *Anything* would be better than the council house in Birmingham.

She tried not to judge Frederick harshly. Still, she had to wonder at a man in his thirties who lived at home and traveled with his mother. She wondered if he was a homosexual. But if so, why would he feign an interest in her? Perhaps it was simply to divert his mother. Camilla looked down at her plate and decided it was best to keep her attention on her dinner.

"Who is your favorite Italian painter?" Mrs. Ashton ventured.

"Canaletto," Camilla told her without hesitation. This was comfortable ground.

"Canaletto?" Frederick asked. "God. I never would have thought it. He's so fixed. So mathematical."

"That's part of what I like," Camilla replied. "He combines the fairy tale of Venice with the control of an architect."

"It's very British of you," Mrs. Ashton said approvingly. "Didn't Joseph Smith send Canalettos by the boatload to London?"

Camilla nodded, impressed with the old woman's knowledge. But Frederick was clearly not in agreement with her choice. "When it comes to Venice," he said, "I prefer Guardi. He does backwaters and different lights. It's not always midday on the Grand Canal."

"I suppose I like midday on the Grand Canal," Camilla said primly. She felt like adding that she'd spent enough of her time in backwaters, but she restrained herself.

"So, tell us about your book," Frederick proposed. Camilla's mouth was full of the potato pasta, and she nearly choked as she swallowed.

"What is it about?" Frederick prompted. Camilla thought for a moment but didn't come up with an answer.

"It's hard to say, really." She paused. The pause grew too long. "I mean, it's a group of American women on tour in Italy, but that's not what it's *about*, if you know what I mean." God, she sounded awkward and daft.

"Is there a plot?" Mrs. Ashton asked.

"Not much," Camilla admitted. "They come to Firenze and they tour by coach and then they go home."

"Send it to Emma," Mrs. Ashton sniffed. "She always thinks highly of books without plots. Now, I prefer a story. Daphne du Maurier. But you ought to send it to Emma."

Camilla looked from Mrs. Ashton to Frederick. What had she missed? "My sister," he explained. "She works in New York for a publisher. Are you determined to publish first in London? Have you already promised it to someone?"

Camilla very nearly laughed. As if the whole publishing world were waiting breathlessly for her manuscript! "No," she said demurely, "I haven't promised it to anyone at all."

"Well," Frederick said, "we'll have to talk about this." Camilla took another sip of wine. Was this happening? Or was this just the empty talk of strangers? She could hardly believe her luck. She told herself not to get too hopeful. She'd just wait and see. Yet her head felt light, as if she'd already had too much wine.

Somehow, hazy as it all felt, they began to talk about their favorite cathedrals, and Frederick listened as Camilla chin-wagged about Assisi and Giotto's frescoes. At last, realizing what she was doing, she stopped. She must be drunk, she realized. She'd dominated the conversation. The three of them sat for a moment in the silence.

"I'm so sorry," she said. "I seem to have run on and on." She looked down at her empty plate, abashed.

Frederick ignored her apology. "You have a lovely voice," he said. "Would you show me the church at Assisi sometime? I've been, but I always focused on the structure more than the decor." He paused. "Would you come with me to Assisi?"

"At the risk of interrupting where I'm not wanted, Frederick, I must ask if you think that's wise?" his mother said.

Camilla blushed again and looked from Frederick's enthusiastic face to his mother's cool one. She shrugged. "I have to go back to Firenze tomorrow anyway," she said. "I have a tour group to meet."

"Just as well," Mrs. Ashton said calmly.

"Well, when would you be free?" he asked, ignoring his mother.

"Frederick, leave the girl alone," Mrs. Ashton said. "She doesn't want to go to Assisi with you."

"Oh, no!" Camilla blurted out, surprising herself. "That's not true. I mean, yes, I would like to go." She surprised herself even more because she meant it. "But I simply can't. I mean, not now. Not this week, anyway." She thought of Gianfranco, back in Firenze. He was what the French called a *cinq-à-sept*, a five-to-seven kind of lover because, she had only recently realized, he regarded her as a mistress, not a potential wife.

"Some other week?" Frederick asked. "Next week?"

"Well, I will be flying home at the end of next week," Mrs. Ashton said. "It appears that *I* can't go to Assisi."

Frederick looked across the table at Camilla and smiled. "But that doesn't mean that we can't, does it?" he asked.

# 8

> I write for women who read me in the goddam subways on the way home from work. I know who they are, because that's who I used to be. They want to press their noses against the windows of other people's houses and get a look at the parties they'll never be invited to, the dresses they'll never get to wear, the lives they'll never live, the guys they'll never fuck.
>
> —*Jackie Susann*

A technician was winding a cable across the beige rug of the living room. "Susann Baker Edmonds Interview," read the clapper board, waiting among the other flotsam and jetsam of television recording for the camera to begin taping. Susann herself, beautifully dressed in a Carolina Herrera suit, stood quietly as the makeup artist dusted her with one more layer of glare-reducing powder. After more than a dozen years of these interviews, she still got nervous, but she had taught herself to breathe deeply and calmly and to empty her mind of everything. Susann and Alf had worked hard at creating a seamless image of herself—an image of a woman that every one of her readers might want to be. She knew that they didn't only love her books—they loved her story. Her own story. Because if *she* could rise from the misery of her legal-secretary job in Cincinnati to the dizzying heights of international living at its best, so could they.

Of course, they didn't know how frightening it was to look at the monthly bills when you were living at this level. Susann lived very well—Alf insisted that she deserved it. And he clearly enjoyed it, too. He enjoyed this house in

France more than she did. Hell, she didn't even speak French. The view was lovely, but the expenses increased the pressure on her, demanding that she produce a book every year. Still, she was lucky and she knew it. This was not the time to think about the pressure, only about happiness and complete satisfaction. It took energy to project that, and Susann used these last moments to gather hers.

Then, "What the hell do you think you're doing! Do you know how much that rug cost?" All heads but Susann's snapped around to face Alfred Byron, Susann's lover and literary agent. He was a short, burly, white-haired man with a face too easily red. It was scarlet right now. Susann didn't have to turn to know that. She froze, closing her eyes.

"Six thousands francs a square meter! Do you know how much that is in dollars? Do you know how much that is in *yards*? I had this rug hand-stitched in Portugal for Susann! And now you're snaking some greasy cable over it!"

A production assistant began apologizing while two techies quickly moved to lift the offending electrical cord. Smoothly Susann moved to Alf's side and patted his hand. "It won't do any harm, Alf," she said quietly. "It isn't covered with grease. They don't use grease for TV." She turned to the assistant producer, a kid who couldn't be thirty. "I'm sure it's fine as it is," she told him, giving him her best smile. He looked doubtfully from her to Alf's red face. Why was it that everyone took Alfred as the authority? Was it simply because he was louder? Because he was older? Or was it because he was a man?

Susann kept herself from audibly sighing. She knew that all Alf wanted was to protect her, to be helpful, and to be sure that everything went right. He was as involved and concerned about her career as she was. Sometimes she was afraid he was *more* involved. She should be grateful, she told herself, and she *was*, but sometimes Alf could be so . . . so . . .

"Well, they shouldn't be taping it down. Should they? Should they be taping it? Won't that stuff leave marks on the carpet, the tape?" They all looked down at the gray gaffer's tape that held the cable in place.

"We don't have to tape it, Mr. Byron. We'll take that tape right up."

Susann doubted the tape would have done any damage, but she smiled her best smile, patted Alf's arm again, and then went back to the mirror. She didn't like what she saw. She should have had her eyes done again when she had the second face-lift, she thought as she looked at the puckerings of skin that held the powder in little crepe lines under her eyes. She hadn't been sleeping well, and it showed. Brewster Moore, her surgeon, hadn't wanted to do the eyes now—he had felt she should wait. But what in the world for? Wait until she looked *older*? Until she looked even *worse*? It wasn't *his* damn eye pouches that were going to appear on television or on the back of a new book. He was good but too conservative. She wanted to stamp her foot and push the damn mirror away.

"Is everything all right, Mrs. Edmonds?" the makeup woman asked. What was the woman's name? Louise? No, Lorraine. Susann made it a point to remember the names of all the gofers, drivers, assistants, and secretaries who crossed her path. It was the least she could do. So she looked back helplessly at her reflection and the pouches under her eyes, then smiled her best smile at the girl.

"Yes, Lorraine, it's terrific. I wish you could do my makeup every day."

The girl smiled and, mercifully, took away the damn mirror. Susann stared blindly out the window, across the pool, and began her breathing. Now was not the time to think about Alf and his disloyalty, her daughter's wasted life, or the deadline she felt strangled by. Now only remember that half of all mass market paperbacks sold were romances—almost a billion dollars in annual sales. She was ready to clear her mind and assume the state that allowed her to project an air of happiness and complete satisfaction. That is what her readers wanted to see. That is what her readers wanted to *have*. It was what all of her heroines wound up with at the close of all of her books. Happiness and complete satisfaction. She took another deep breath.

"Who the hell is smoking?" Alf yelled. "Who the hell is smoking in here?" He stopped yelling momentarily as he apparently found his culprit, then resumed. "Don't you know Susann has asthma?"

Susann didn't have asthma, as it happened. Alf did. She turned and saw Alf's big back hunched over. Oh, my God! He was yelling at Tammi Young, the newscaster who was about to conduct the interview. Alf must not have recognized her. The girl *had* seemed a brainless little twit, but she worked for the network and Susann did *not* need a hostile interview right now. Not when her last two books had barely held the number-one spot for more than a week!

But at that moment, before she had a chance to straighten things out, a sound technician—Kevin? or was it Brian?—approached her and asked, very quietly, if she could snake the thin black microphone wire up under her jacket for him. She nodded; it seemed Alf and Tammi were working things out on the other side of the vast living room. She'd be grateful for that. She'd be even more grateful if he'd just butt out. She looked up and saw Edith grinning. Edith loved it when Alf made an ass of himself.

There *was* a time when Susann had been grateful for Alf's constant involvement and his enthusiasm and strength. She had been writing for five or six years, her third marriage had failed, and so had her books. No one believed in her except Edith, and that wasn't enough. It was only when she met Alf and he began not only to fight and negotiate for her, but also to *believe* in her work, that things had started to fall into place. He'd gone out and gained her exposure; finding all kinds of publicity angles, and that, plus his relentless nagging of the publisher to advertise and promote her book, had finally propelled her out of the paperback ghetto into hardbacks and up the list. Alf couldn't have been more proud if he wrote the books himself, and sometimes Susann thought he believed he *had* written them. He always talked about what was owed to "our work," and how many copies of "our latest book" had sold. For years he had negotiated every contract, taken care of all of the business, managed and invested her money, and supervised all publicity and book tours. He also had started sleeping with her.

Their affair was on-again, off-again. She knew Alf would never marry her—he wouldn't offend his two sons. Because Alf, despite the poetic last name, was a Boronkin, not a Byron. The joke was he'd dropped his old friends along with the "kin." He'd adopted the name when he left Cincinnati and set up shop in New York. But he kept close to his sons and was a Jew who refused to marry a shiksa. No matter how successful either of them became.

Susann looked at him now, earnestly talking to the director. Somehow Alf had not adjusted to success. He had fought his way to the top with her, but once there, he continued to fight. What was that called? A bunker mentality? Sometimes Susann thought that if Alf didn't encounter difficulties, he considered it his job to create them. Just so he had an obstacle he had to overcome that day. But Susann was tired of obstacles. Though she appeared ten years younger than her fifty-eight years, she *felt* ten years older. She looked down at her hands, swollen from arthritis. She'd do everything she could to keep them off camera. Her hands did not look happy or satisfied. She supposed she wasn't either.

She had met Alf when she was forty-three. She had felt young then—although she probably hadn't looked as good. Still, she'd had lots of energy and enthusiasm, despite the lousy job and the failed marriages. Life seemed an adventure. Alf had been older and, it seemed, wiser. He'd had his own insurance agency and had invested a little in Cincinnati real estate. His first wife had died, and his two sons were grown. He had half-romanced, half-adopted Susann.

It had been a lovely time. Alf had thought of her writing as magical, not a business. He'd read every word breathlessly. And just as her writing had rescued her from a mundane life, it had given him a new and exciting second career. Alf was more entranced with the glamour of the entertainment world than Susann had ever been. It was he who kept the scrapbooks, dusted the shelf of her books, and had the first of each of "our new editions" bound in blue calfskin and stamped with gold.

Now, somehow, Alf felt like a burden, along with all the other burdens Susann felt she was carrying. He had insisted on this last contract—for two new books—in addition to the other new one they already had to deliver on. And he'd pocket almost a quarter of a million dollars in fees, while she was saddled with delivery. Finally, she and Edith had finished the first draft of the new book, but Susann knew it was flat. It was a funny thing: Back when she was penniless and living from paycheck to paycheck, when she didn't have time to be a good mother to Kim, she had written about success and wealth, family love, and the glamorous life with a lot more passion and clarity than she did now, now that she was living it. There was an irony there, but Susann was not the type to ferret it out. And she was too tired.

Alf had proudly and overaggressively negotiated the blockbuster twenty-million-dollar contract, but the pressure that had put on her seemed to Susann almost unbearable. After all, money wasn't everything. He'd made her leave the publisher she had been with from the beginning. He made her leave her editor, Imogen.

In the old days, she had gotten relatively small advances and her enormous sales had meant big royalty checks. The publisher had treated her like a fine piece of jewelry.

Imogen never forgot a birthday. But Alf had insisted that it was bad business to let the publisher sit on the money until—twice a year, and then reluctantly—it paid out the royalties she was owed. "Why should we let them be our bankers?" Alf asked. "They don't pay interest." He had gotten bigger and bigger payments up front, but when her publisher balked, he had shopped her around to a new house—Davis & Dash—where she had been given a huge advance. Susann was afraid that neither this new book or the next one would earn out the advance money. She couldn't bear having Gerald Ochs Davis, her new publisher, looking at her like she was a bad investment instead of a jewel in the crown. She had been a winner, and every bit of success had been a thrill and a surprise. Now, behind the eight ball of the two contracts, she was expected to perform at the very highest commercial level; anything less would be considered failure. And one thing Alf Byron would not tolerate was failure.

"We're ready for you now, Mrs. Edmonds," the unbelievably young assistant director told her. Susann came out of her reverie, depressed and dissatisfied. But that's not what she was allowed to be right now. What she had to be was happy, with an air of complete satisfaction. And that is what she *would* be.

"I'm ready," Susann said, and gave the boy her best smile.

# 9

> I'm not a big believer in disciplined writers. What does discipline mean? The writer who forces himself to sit down and write for seven hours every day might be wasting those seven hours if he's not in the mood and doesn't feel the juice. I don't think discipline equals creativity.
>
> —*Bret Easton Ellis*

Daniel Gross sat in his small office, his back to the door, his shoulders hunched over the notebook he was writing in. The typewritten copy of Judith's latest chapter—well, *his* chapter, really—was secreted under the flap of the back cover. As he copied the chapter carefully into his notebook, he made a few revisions and cross outs. But Judith had done a good job typing up his ideas, and there was really very little—surprisingly little—he had to change. Too bad her typing was so lousy. He looked at the name on the title page. "Jude Daniel." Perhaps he should have picked a different nom de plume: something more commercial like Paige Turner of Bess Cellar or E. Z. Reid. He corrected another one of Judith's mistakes.

Judith could sit down every day and pound it out. That's how he knew she wasn't truly sensitive, not really an artist. For him it was necessary to feel the creative urge. The muses did not dance to your command, he thought. Who had written that? Perhaps he had. He jotted it down in the margin of his notebook.

Each time Daniel finished copying a page, he tore Judith's typewritten version into many strips and, instead of throwing them in his wastepaper basket, put them into his pocket. It was better to be safe than sorry, as his grandma used to tell him. Safe from what, or sorry about what, he wasn't exactly sure.

And the fact is, he didn't feel safe and he might indeed be sorry. He hadn't received tenure last year, but then how could he reasonably expect to after being caught in adultery, breaking up his marriage, and marrying a student? Eleanor, his first wife, had been well liked in the department. Although it wasn't illegal, leaving your no-longer-so-young-looking wife for a much younger student certainly was *not* approved of. A definite frost had descended upon the women professors in his department, and Daniel wondered if now, despite his good work, he might never achieve tenure. No, he certainly wasn't safe.

But sorry? Was he sorry he'd married Judith? Well, he surely was sorry that her father had taken it so badly, the anti-Semite. The old bastard was loaded, and if Daniel hadn't exactly counted on living off some of the Hunt glassworks fortune, he had at least looked forward to the possibility. He had already played the we're-young-and-in-love-and-poor-as-college-students game once with Eleanor, and he no longer found it amusing. But Judith might, in the end, be his ticket out of here. Daniel looked around the cramped cubicle that was his office. It was painted a shiny khaki color, God knows how long ago. Sometime after the Korean War? Or World War II, or maybe even World War I? The paint was flaking in more than half a dozen places. If he ever wanted to commit suicide, Daniel reflected, he probably had enough lead in the available paint flakes for effective poisoning.

Daniel looked out the drafty window. The room was so badly heated that he kept his coat on all the time. Except, of course, in the summer, when the room was so hot that he sweated. Now it was hard to believe that he had once spread Judith on this very desk and had the energy, in the heat, to make love to her. Daniel shook his head.

He was about to finish copying out the last page when

there was a knock at the door. Guiltily, he folded up the final page and thrust it deep into the unused pages of his notebook. He left the notebook lying open on the half-finished page. "Come in," he called.

The shining blond head of Cheryl Jenkins hesitantly peeked around the door. "Is it all right?" she asked.

"Fine," Daniel said, "just fine." The girl entered the room, and it seemed as if the sun entered with her. It must be her hair, Daniel thought. It was so very blond. It must be natural, because dyeing it would never leave it so glossy, so very shiny.

"I'm sorry to bother you," Cheryl said, "I mean, I know you have lots to do—"

"No, don't worry about it. I'm just doing a little editing on my novel."

"Your novel?" Cheryl breathed. "Oh, I *really* shouldn't be bothering you." She turned as if to go, and Daniel lurched across the small room and took her hand.

"It's all right, Cheryl. I'd be happy to help you. What is it?"

The girl colored and took her hand away but looked up at him. She was very short, and suddenly two thoughts occurred almost simultaneously to Daniel. The first was how ungainly Judith was compared to this tiny sprite. And the second was whether Cheryl's pubic hair was as blond as the shiny cap of hair on her head.

Cheryl was rummaging through her purse. She took out two crumpled sheets of paper. "I've never read anything aloud at the writers' circle," she said, "but I thought this wasn't too awful. I mean, not *really* bad, and so I thought, maybe . . . well . . ."

Daniel took the two sheets from her trembling hand and read them quickly. The writing was clear and a lot more forceful than Cheryl was herself. In fact, it was better writing than the stuff Chuck Tasity, another student, turned out by the truckload and read promiscuously. "This is really good, Cheryl. You should read it."

Her smile of pleasure was a delightful reward for his praise. "Really?" she asked. He nodded.

"Really," he told her.

"Oh, I'm so glad you think so. I've gotten so much out of your class and the writers' circle. It's really improved my work." She paused and blushed again. Daniel wondered if her nipples were truly pink—the girl was a china doll. "You've done so much for me, I wish I could do something for you," Cheryl said.

Daniel smiled, resisting his impulse. Jesus Christ, it was hard to be married. "Maybe you could buy me a cup of coffee sometime," he said.

She hung her head, then looked up from under her lashes at him. "I could type for you," she suggested. "I noticed that all of your drafts are handwritten. And the typed versions are—well, I could type for you," she repeated in a very small voice.

Daniel smiled. Not only was Judith a lousy typist, but she insisted on using her stupid high school portable typewriter. "Maybe we could talk about that. Have you got a word processor?"

"Oh, yes. I've got a laptop. And a laser printer," she told him.

Daniel wondered where she got the money for that kind of equipment. He looked down again at the sheets of paper in his hand. "You have real talent, Cheryl."

"Do you really think so?" The girl blushed again. She was adorable.

"Yes, I do. Someday, with the right guidance, you could be a successful writer."

The girl said nothing, but she was clearly transported. Those were the magic words, the words that all neophytes longed to hear. Cheryl looked up at him, full in the face for the first time. "I feel like you've given me so much already," she breathed.

Do you know I'm deeply attracted to you? He had almost said it. The words had formed in his brain and his lips were about to begin moving when there was another knock on the door. This caller didn't wait to be asked in. Don Kingsbury, the head of the department and just about the only member who still spoke to him, smiled in the doorway. Cheryl turned and, without another word, walked past him and out of the room.

Don, oblivious, raised his brows. "How's it going?" he asked. Daniel shrugged. Don was a big guy, well over six foot, and chunky. He sat himself on a corner of the desk and crossed his massive legs. Daniel stood up to be above his eye level. He wondered how much Don had overheard of his talk with Cheryl. Don merely glanced down at Daniel's notebook.

"Ah, the book. How's *that* going?" Don asked.

"Not too badly," Daniel admitted noncommittally. "You know, I'm not attempting art here. Just something that's workmanlike, something that can be published."

"Yeah. Something the movies will buy," Don said, laughing. "Will you read it at the writers' circle?" Twice each month Daniel led a writers' group meeting in which participants read their current work and got feedback and, sometimes, criticism. Especially from Daniel.

"I already have," Daniel said. "I might read some more tonight."

"Well, I'll walk you over there. I thought I might sit in. You know, I really do admire the way you've sustained that group. And you've done an excellent job on the seminars. Bringing up those first-time novelists for the panel discussion was a great idea."

"I did have to pull a few strings," Daniel said modestly. Actually, it hadn't been too difficult to get them. After all, who the hell wanted to hear the experiences of a literary first novelist?

"And I was amazed when you got Alfred Byron up here."

Daniel nodded. That *was* a coup. Alfred Byron was a prestigious agent, but when one of the young writer's books had taken off—a young writer Byron represented—he'd been appreciative that Daniel had invited him. In return he'd agreed to give a brief talk. He'd come back again to moderate a panel discussion. And Daniel secretly planned for Alfred Byron to do much, much more.

"I think you are really bringing a breath of reality to the department," Don said. "You know, we have so many students who want to write and don't have a clue about what the business of getting published is all about. And then we have our ivory-tower academics who believe that any writer still living can't be worthwhile. You've really added positive diversity to the department." Daniel felt his heart lift. Maybe he wasn't as unsafe or as sorry as he had thought.

"I'm certainly trying. I'm trying to make a difference." Did that sound too corny?

"Well, you're succeeding. I don't know how you manage to teach your classes, schedule these events, *and* write a novel on the side. I certainly couldn't do it." Don laughed heartily. Of course, he could afford to—*he* had tenure. He was the head of the whole fucking department.

Daniel paused for a moment. He ought to mention that he was working on the novel with Judith, that she was drafting much of the book, but somehow he felt constrained. Best not to bring up Judith and all of that again, not at this moment, when Don was being so positive. "Yes, it's hard," Daniel admitted, "but I'm interested in it all. That takes the edge off."

"So, do you mind if I sit in on the writers' circle? Would it be too intrusive?"

Daniel thought of how shy Cheryl Jenkins was, and of nervous Bob Hadley. Of course it would be an intrusion, to have the head of the department casually eavesdropping on their work in progress. But Daniel knew that Chuck Tasity would grandstand, and perhaps—just perhaps—he himself would read some from his notebook. That wouldn't hurt.

"It wouldn't be an intrusion at all," Daniel said and smiled at Don. "Why don't you join us?"

Judith typed the last words of the last sentence of the last chapter of the book and then sat for a moment, her hands still raised above the keyboard. She felt empty and almost frightened.

Slowly, she brought her hands down to her lap. Before her, carefully piled on the card table, were all of her completed chapters, each one neatly revised and retyped according to Daniel's critique. They made a large, squared white stack. A stack of her work—well, their work together. In the silence and space of the deepening darkness outside the small turret room, Judith felt the question hanging over her.

What next?

She thought she had read somewhere that writers often felt a sadness, and emptiness, when they finished a book. But sadness was not exactly what she felt. Bravely, she sat still and tried to feel what it was that felt so constricting. She was relieved the book was finished, because it had been such hard work. Each morning she had had to force herself to sit down at the card table. Each empty sheet of paper stared at her like a challenge; each crumpled sheet in the wastebasket was a silent rebuke. And it had been hard, too, being so often criticized by Daniel.

But, she realized, it had kept her occupied. The feeling she had now was close to fear. What else did she now have to do? Her labors were over, and from here on it would be Daniel who had to do the work. Daniel would have to begin using his connections to get the book published and bring in the money they so desperately needed. She should be elated, but she was frightened instead. Don't be silly, she told herself. You've done it. You've really finished it. You never thought you could.

Judith felt another little chill. What if, despite his boasts and the people he had "collected" at seminars and panels, what if Daniel was wrong and the book was no good? What if he couldn't sell it? Had she wasted so many hours, so much energy and pain? And whose failure would it be?

Because Judith had not written what she had wanted to write. That book, both she and Daniel agreed, would have been too uncommercial, too literary. How large a market was there for the story of an upper-middle-class girl whose father virtually ran the town they lived in? The girl would find herself pregnant by a boy from the wrong side of the tracks, if there were tracks in their town. It was, as Daniel told her, "too revelatory," "too small," and "too artsy." Just another sensitive coming-of-age book.

This book would be bigger than that one could ever be, if less felt and less real. Like the authors of many commercial books, she—well, they—had plucked the idea from the newspapers. Judith had been reading the horrific story of a woman who had reported her three children missing, only to later admit that she herself had murdered them. Judith had cried over the story, not only for the babies but for the woman's demented state. Somehow, Judith understood that kind of desperate forlornness. It was Daniel, listening to her talk about it, who had recognized the hook. And so they had come up with the plot for *In Full Knowledge*.

Now the finished work sat before her, and looking at it, Judith shivered. Although she had invented Elthea, the heroine, Judith felt as if her character was real and Judith knew her: her desperation as her husband cheated and her marriage crumbled; the claustrophobia of being left with the three little boys; the fear and drabness of living on a single mother's inadequate salary; her father's refusal to give her financial help; her grasping at the chance for a new beginning with another man, and her hysteria when she lost him, too. Was it coincidence that the real murderess had been abandoned by three males and that she subsequently murdered three? Judith knew that while her fictional Elthea was not a typical sympathetic character, Judith's own understanding and compassion for her had illuminated every page.

The truth was that Judith identified with Elthea. After all, hadn't Judith been a victim of her father and of her first boyfriend back in Elmira? The book revealed more of her than she had planned. And perhaps, she thought, I'm also frightened now because I'm afraid no one will understand Elthea. Maybe that's all it is. But a deeper voice told her that wasn't all: Somewhere lurked the fear that without this book to talk about, Daniel might not talk to her at all.

"Well, Flaubert, I did it. This occasion justifies a Milk-Bone for you." The dog gave her a bark.

Judith's back was stiff, and all at once she felt as if she had to move. Slowly, she pushed away from the card table, stood up, and stretched. What was wrong with her? The book was finished. Daniel would be pleased, and tonight they would celebrate. She walked down the three steps that led to the kitchen and the hall closet. Daniel kept his suit and sports jackets in their bedroom wardrobe, and Judith used the hall closet as her own. She took down the blue wool dress, the one she had bought with her mother the last time they shopped together in Poughkeepsie. She held it up against herself, looking in the hall mirror. It brought out the blonder tones in her light brown hair and the depth of color in her eyes, but she wondered if she could still get into it. "What do you think, Flaubert?" The dog cocked his head. Nothing but approval and a desire for Milk-Bones there. She looked back to the mirror critically. She'd gained weight sitting at the typewriter and moiling around the empty apartment, snacking nervously and out of boredom. She thought she could still manage the dress.

She decided to shower, dress, put up her hair, and apply all the makeup she didn't bother with most of the time. She'd look her best when Daniel came home tonight, and they'd go out to dinner and have a bottle of wine and celebrate. The book was done, and once they sold it, they could go on to live the life they had planned. Maybe she could even have the baby she wanted so desperately. Judith shook off her gray mood and tried to be cheerful. *In Full Knowledge* might not have been the book she wanted to write, but she had written it well, and she knew that Daniel was pleased, despite his criticisms. She had made Elthea live, and no one could read the book without understanding why she had done what she did. Perhaps readers might even feel that they, in the same situation, would have done the same thing.

Judith stepped into the shower and let the hot water run down her sore neck and tense back. She used the expensive almond shampoo she saved for special occasions and enjoyed its clean, evocative scent. It was only when she was rinsing off that Judith remembered that tonight was Daniel's writers' circle and that he wouldn't be home for dinner.

# 10

> When I am dead,
> I hope it may be said:
> "His sins were scarlet, but his books were read."
>
> —*Hilaire Belloc*

"What about the new Callard book?"

"Crap," Pam Mantiss told Gerald Ochs Davis. "Midlist crap."

"But we'll have the Peet Trawley," Gerald said to reassure himself. "That will fly. Especially with the movie coming up."

"I hope we'll have it. He's really sick."

"He's been sick for thirty years. He *likes* to be sick. Münchhausen syndrome. It matters not. Just slap an omega on the cover. It will still sell." Gerald thought of Dick Snyder's directions years ago to the Simon & Schuster editor who was trying to cope with an impossible Jackie Susann manuscript: "Just turn it into a book somehow; that's all I ask." Gerald looked over the list in front of him. "When does Edmonds deliver the new one?"

Pam shook her head. She read his thoughts. "Forget it. Apparently her old house is still getting returns from her *last* book. She isn't going to do it for us."

Gerald stopped going over the printout before him. Pam had already accused him of buying Edmonds when she was past her peak, paying top dollar. "We're *not* forgetting this one," he told Pam. "I paid twenty million dollars. Her books are going to sell no matter what we have to do to sell them."

Pam shrugged. She was smart, but sometimes he wanted to murder her. He thought she actually enjoyed writing off authors. Like Tom Callard, the hot first-time novelist whom Pam had snagged (and probably shagged) before an auction could take place. The book sold two hundred thousand copies. Now his second was suddenly chopped liver? They must have had a lover's quarrel.

"How about the Chad Weston book? I've heard it's raw."

"It's graphic, violent sex. I like it."

"I'm not surprised," Gerald said dryly. "But will anyone else?"

"Well, the pussies around here are scandalized, but they don't know the difference between fiction and politics," Pam said. "I love the book. It's a *satire*. He's satirizing our disposable culture. Smart people will get it." She paused and grinned. "It will raise a lot of eyebrows."

Involuntarily, Gerald put his hand up to one of his own glued-on brows. Sometimes he hated them. "Will it raise our profits?" he snapped.

"Absolutely. It's a book of our times, about how the nineties came out of the eighties. It's about how man, without civilization's restraint, fears and destroys that which created him. It's about tit-biting boys, Gerald. It will move."

Gerald winced at her crudity. Weston was another ninety-day wonder. His first book had hit—his second had not. "It better do more than move," Gerald said. "It's got to run. I want to see the manuscript. What's the title?"

"*SchizoBoy.*"

Gerald barked out a laugh. "Clearly autobiographical." Pam merely shrugged, her blond hair bouncing, as did her breasts. "There's my book, of course."

"Of course," Pam said noncommittally.

"Have you read it?"

"Not yet," she admitted.

"Any nonfiction?" he asked, trying to keep the annoyance out of his voice.

"Yeah. Oprah's back and we got her," Pam said caustically. When Oprah Winfrey had reneged on delivering her autobiography to Knopf, it had nearly ruined their bottom line. Pam and Gerald both knew the trouble with commercial nonfiction: Lots of people had one good story in them, but few had more. The nonfiction editors were like sharks; they had to keep moving or die. After all, how many autobiographies could Dolly Parton write?

"What else can we do?"

"I'll call around," Pam said. "I'll see what's being pushed. But it wouldn't hurt you to get the lead out and circulate. Put your ear to the ground."

"Is there a cliché you've left unspoken?" Gerald asked her as he rose. "I'm off to the Citron Press party. Maybe something will turn up."

Gerald looked around at the party crowd and had to restrain a visible shudder. In the old days, even ten years ago, book parties were low-budget, dreary affairs held in offices or building lobbies. Now, with publishing turning into what Gerald scathingly called the "literary industrial complex," parties were much fewer but often high-budget, flashy offerings. Gerald couldn't decide which was worse. This one was one of the old school, celebrating the opening of a new small publishing house, Citron Press. Craig Stevens was hosting it, and Gerald hoped Stevens had deep pockets. He was joining the trend that Permanent Press and Four Walls Eight Windows had begun—boutique publishers. Good luck to him.

Gerald smiled, nodding at HarperCollins's Larry Ashmead, king of salt-and-pepper-shaker collections, and moved on. Fredi Friedman, the only soignée woman present, was as usual talking to someone about her latest discovery, telling him how it was certain to climb the lists.

Gerald sighed. One couldn't start a literary house anymore. Things had changed. Look at Farrar, Straus. In the past, "quality literary fiction" was defined as Farrar, Straus & Giroux. Roger Straus and Robert Giroux had started right after the war with only twenty-five thousand dollars.

Straus had a vision that informed and shaped his list into something beautiful. Even Gerald had to admit that. They had made canny domestic purchases and bought translation rights to the best European literature as well.

Just as Farrar, Straus had been known for the best fiction, Harper & Row had been known as the quality nonfiction house. Cass Canfield had liked history and biographies and so had shaped a dignified, cohesive list. At Doubleday it had been commercial fiction and nonfiction. For three decades, Doubleday ruled the bestseller list. That was what it did best.

But those days were over, Gerald reflected. Publishing had changed so much. Now all everyone wanted were bestsellers. Roger Straus had sold his firm. Harper was bought by Rupert Murdoch, and HarperCollins had expanded in half a dozen directions. Doubleday was now a part of the Bertelsmann empire. The tax laws had made it necessary: Even his father had sold out. The days when a personal influence held sway on a house, on a list, were over. Everyone had to scramble for bestsellers now just to keep in the business. Look at what had happened at Knopf—another house known for its great literary fiction: When Sonny Mehta had taken over that venerable firm, he acquired Dean Koontz! Gerald had to laugh, thinking of how all the snotty literary people at Knopf, so proud of their designer fiction, must have felt swallowing that.

Gerald was proud now to be able to say, "There is no such thing as a Davis & Dash book." He wanted books that sold, that made a splash and that kept him afloat. Like the other sharks, Gerald had to keep moving forward, keep making visible progress, to satisfy CEO David Morton's corporate lust for ever-increasing profits, a return on investment almost impossible to make considering the outrageous advances paid to authors and the quaint tradition of stores returning books.

Gerald surveyed the room. His eyes were attracted to the red hair of Joanna Cotler, the head of the eponymously named Joanna Cotler Books, a bright face in the usual drab publishing party. Generally, Gerald avoided these affairs, but he knew Pam's recommendation to "get his ear to the ground" was a good one. Still, did the women dress so badly because they were paid so little? Surely it was easier for a camel to pass through the eye of a needle than it was to find a smartly dressed female editor.

Gerald could hold his own against any competitor, acquire almost any author he sought, and manage to fight off the corporate hordes, but he had done so more through guile and bitchiness than through direct confrontation. Gerald ruled as totally as Tsarina Catherine had ruled Russia, and probably with a similar style.

This party was a waste of time. What had he been thinking of? Book parties, especially literary ones, were not the place to troll for a hot book *or* a hot body.

Gerald had one dreadful weakness: He liked his women not only attractive but also intelligent. That was where all his difficulties came in. You couldn't please them. Right now Anne, his mistress, was dissatisfied because he wouldn't buy any of the books she was hawking and couldn't help her career as much as she wanted (he'd never sleep with an agent again). His wife, as always, was either depressed or angry. Neurotic, intelligent women were a pain in the ass. They were also his specialty.

Gerald looked around one last time to decide who, if anyone, he would grace with his presence. Robert Gottlieb of the William Morris Agency was there, surrounded by visiting British publishers. Gerald would not have said no to Gottlieb's top client Tom Clancy, but he certainly wasn't going to mix with the Brits. Patrick Janson-Smith, the old charmer, young Ian Chapman—time for a haircut?—Clare Alexander: half of London seemed to be here and all, no doubt, would like to add another giant name to their lists.

Sometimes, he reflected, not just an agent but a whole publishing house was held hostage to a single author. As publishing had followed Hollywood in its search for megahits, bestselling authors were coddled almost like movie stars. Where would Doubleday be without Grisham, Putnam without Clancy, Viking without King, Harper without John Gray, Knopf without Crichton? Even losing a literary bestselling writer could rock a house's stability, as when John Irving left Morrow. Without Sidney Sheldon, Morrow could fold. It gave a whole new meaning to the term "house arrest."

Karen Rinaldi, vibrant with her red hair and Comme des Garçons suit, was a far better option. She'd been at Turtle Bay, the imprint that Joni Evans had founded at Random House. They'd signed some big books—*Girl Interrupted* and a couple of others—before Alberto Vitale had pulled the plug. Turtle Bay interrupted. After its demise, the books it published had sold so well they vindicated Joni, who was a smart girl. Joni, interrupted, went on to become a top agent. She only looked bad when she came up against Joan Collins in court.

It seemed to Gerald that all of the women who had worked at Turtle Bay in its townhouse office near the Random House building, which he referred to as the Brownstone of Babes, were those constantly seductive smart girls who look *Vogue* and talk *The New Yorker*. They all were thin and had great hair. Did anyone have a smaller waist, or a nicer smile, than Susan Kamil? He was making his way toward Karen when someone bumped into him and staggered against the wall. It was Erroll McDonald, noted for being the senior black editor in the ever-so-lily-white publishing world. He was noted for a few other things as well, and Gerald gave him the cold shoulder.

He'd lost Rinaldi in the crowd. There must be an easier way to meet women. On the Internet or something? Hadn't Rush Limbaugh met and married a fan? Maybe Gerald was going about this all wrong. He'd focus on business. Who else was around that might send him a book? Robert Loomis, the Random House editor and one of the grand old school, nodded and said hello. Gerald smiled but kept his distance. Loomis probably spoke with Gerald's father on a regular basis. He didn't need to talk to the gentleman publishing contingent—Loomis, Cass Canfield, Jr., Larry Hughes, Simon Michael Bessie (and his beautiful blond wife, Cornelia), Buz Wyeth, Star Lawrence, or the rest. Not that there were many left. Like his father, they were a vanishing breed. There was so little room for class, to say nothing of old-fashioned values, in a publishing conglomerate.

What Gerald needed was a hot young agent, preferably female. He kept one eye out for Karen as he scanned the room. In one corner Michael Korda was holding court, surrounded by his Simon & Schuster minions—Chuck Adams and the rest—and a few hungry authors hoping for crumbs. Korda had written a viciously funny piece for *The New Yorker* about Jackie Susann in which he managed to deeply bite the hand that had once fed him well. Very distasteful. He noticed Ann Patty, editor in chief at Crown. Her hair wasn't as red as Rinaldi's, but she was as smart as they got and had a nose for picking successful first-time novelists. Well, he needed that skill now. He nodded and walked on.

The press of bodies became unbearable. Really, he wondered, were any of these people enjoying this? Who could be expected to like sipping room-temperature chardonnay and eating little bits of rubbery cheese impaled on toothpicks? The combination reminded Gerald of a handstamp set he'd had as a child—all the letters of the alphabet and most punctuation marks carved out of rubber and backed with wooden handles so that he could "print" his own "books." It had been a messy, onerous job, and Gerald remembered how frustrated he'd been to have only one *e* and one *s* when he had to use those stamps so often. But after he'd finished his first "book," he'd brought it in to his father and Father had praised him. Gerald still remembered how his father had been sitting with an older gentleman, Mr. Perkins. When Gerald presented them with the book,

Mr. Perkins had laughed and called Gerald "a chip off the old block." His father had been so pleased that he had reached out and ruffled Gerald's bare pate, a rare and never-to-be-forgotten occurrence. From the time Gerald, at three, had exuviated his hair, his father had seemed reluctant to touch him, as if his depilous condition were communicable.

Gerald reached up reflexively to smooth his wig and looked around the room. He shot his cuffs. James Linville, standing alone, seemed to be sipping a nonalcoholic drink. This was a man who had been called in print a stick-in-the-ass. Gerald walked past him. Susan Blum, the editor in chief at this new publishing house, was approaching him. She was a dishy, if abrasive, smart girl, and he liked her. He briefly considered sleeping with her but decided she'd be too much trouble. Anyway, she'd keep any good book that came her way for Citron Press. Jay McInerney walked by. "Don't you see him everywhere?" Susan asked. "*So* boring."

"Some people mistake publishing parties for life," Gerald murmured.

"And books about them for art," Susan added with a laugh. They watched the crowd together in silence for a while.

"Gerald," she said finally, "is it true what I hear about Chad Weston's new one?"

"Depends on what you hear."

"That the little lizard has really exposed himself."

Gerald looked at her blandly. "We think it's a fine book," he said. "A rich commentary on the times in which we live."

"Fuck that flap-copy shit," Susan said. "He slices and dices. Doesn't he fuck dead women's bodies?"

Gerald raised one of his glued-on eyebrows. "It's fiction, Susan."

"The limp dick would do it in real life if he could," Susan replied. "Come on, Gerald. You're not going to encourage that kind of crap? There are a lot of women in publishing who are not happy about this book."

"There are a lot of women in publishing who are not happy about anything," Gerald replied coolly. "It's one of the reasons they go into publishing." He looked Susan over. Maybe he *would* enjoy sleeping with her. She was feisty. "You must be working hard, launching this house," he said. "You look like you deserve a vacation in the sun."

Susan tossed her head and laughed. "Gerald, I don't *ever* want to see you in your Speedo." She turned and walked away, to begin talking with Peter Gethers—an author who wouldn't take Susan anywhere but traveled with his cat, and wrote about it. Gerald moved on. Sharon DeLano of Random House stood at the drinks bar talking with Gore Vidal, whom she edited, and Tim Waterstone, the British bookseller. Well, he'd avoid *them*. Sharon might be the worst-dressed woman in publishing, where the competition for that title was keen. Gerald and Gore had been feuding for almost twenty years—putting Gerald on a list that was long and distinguished, but Gerald thought he would still prefer to read a novel by Gore than a novel by Waterstone. The Englishman had become a millionaire from selling books (hadn't they even opened some stores in the US?) but Gerald was not inclined to help him make his next million in his new career as a writer. Altogether too close to home.

No rest for the weary, thought Gerald. Now *there* was someone helpful: Gordon Kato. The smartest in the crop of new, savvy agents, the young Hawaiian might actually have something for him. Without appearing to, Gerald moved toward him. Kato had an incredible memory and a chesslike overview of the publishing world: He knew where the players used to be, where they were now, and where they were going. He had his own small agency and would certainly thrive. More than anything Gerald envied the boy his crop of thick black hair.

Will Bracken, a literary writer whose books sold in the

hundreds of copies—when they sold at all—wandered by, ghostlike. "*He* writes good stuff," Gordon said, nodding toward Will.

"Yes. We once published him," Gerald admitted. "His hardcover sold two thousand copies, and a thousand of those were computer error."

"Still, he's smart and his work is beautiful."

"Um-humm. If he'd just make all of his characters black or Native American, he might have a bestseller on his hands. Like Louise Erdrich or Terry McMillan."

"I don't think Will knew a lot of blacks up at Yale."

"Yale!" Gerald snorted. "The school of prissy, male whiners."

"Speaking of male whiners, what's going on with that Weston book?"

Goddammit, the industry was just a little hotbed of gossip. He didn't mind being talked about; he just wished that he could be envied for *more* mistresses and *better* book sales. Why wasn't Gordon asking him about his own novel instead of Weston's? "The book has literary merit, Gordon. We're publishing it. God, if the world gets any more politically correct, it will be so boring I'll kill myself."

Gordon smiled. "That might make a few authors happy," he said blandly.

The boy was insufferable, but he did have some hot new writers, and that was the blood of the business. "So, Gordon, what have you got for me?"

"An auction on Friday of Tony Earley's book."

"I don't want an auction. If I wanted to bid against these cretins, I wouldn't have walked up to you in the first place."

"No inside deals, Gerald," Gordon Kato said. "If I'm not giving one to Craig, who's throwing this party, I'm surely not giving one to you." Gerald strode away without a good-bye.

The brilliant Susan Moldow walked by but didn't say hello. When she was editor in chief at HarperCollins, her husband, Bill Shinker, had been publisher. They were called "Ma and Pa" by their staff, and she referred to him as Fur Face. They had signed up John Gray, and his books had earned a good portion of Harper's profits last year. Now both had moved on in the ever-changing kaleidoscope of publishing-house musical chairs.

Gerald approached a cluster of people. Tiny Harry Evans was in the center of it with Colin Powell, whose autobiography he'd published with S. I. Newhouse's approval and money. Rupert Murdoch had published Newt Gingrich. Clash of the titans! Which publisher would get to sleep in the Lincoln bedroom, down the hall from his bestselling author? Gerald smiled grimly. When it came to serious nonfiction, include me out, he thought, quoting Sam Goldwyn. Gerald stuck to movie stars and gossip—it never went out of style or got you bomb threats in the mail. He was glad he hadn't published Salman Rushdie. This controversy over Chad Weston was more than enough for him.

Alice Mayhew, the self-appointed Washington expert at Simon & Schuster—a distinction she seemed to feel was enviable—had arrived and was talking to some young woman. What did she have to feel so proud of? In the seventies she had published all the Watergate principals; it was called "the felon list."

Charlotte Abbott, one of the new young hopes at Avon, smiled at him. The girl was tall, fair, and intense, the kind who wouldn't be intimidated by big words. "Hello, Charlotte," he said.

"Hello, Gerald. Is what I hear about the Chad Weston novel really true?"

This was becoming extremely irritating. "Yes, Charlotte, it is," he said in a bored voice. "Chad has decided to switch genres. He's moving from literary novels to thrillers." He feigned excitement. "Move over, Thomas Harris! There's a new Hannibal Lecter, and I've got him!"

Donna Tartt walked by. She had been touted as a literary

second coming when her first novel was published. Despite the hype, the profiles, and its substantial sales, it was what Gerald referred to as a media blow job. In his opinion her book had been a slightly-above-average, somewhat pretentious murder mystery. After all the furore had died down, nothing more had been heard from Ms. Tartt. But then, it had taken her something like eleven years to write the first book. "She hasn't written anything in years," he said to Charlotte. "I hear she just can't be alone with her work."

"She should be an editor then," Charlotte laughed.

"Yes. Or have my debts." Gerald smiled at Charlotte. "I need a drink," he said and wandered off toward the door. He certainly needed something. Liz Ziemska, the stunning and bright young agent with Nicholas Ellison, caught his eye. Ah, there were *two* opportunities there. But Gerald remembered Susan's put-down, and for a moment he held back. In that moment, Liz was captured by Lawrence LaRose, who moved her toward one of the windows. Gerald despised LaRose. He was too smart, too young, too good-looking. So much for that.

Gerald nodded at Alberto Vitale, head of Random House. Gerald despised him too, but they did share something: Both craved publicity. Gerald merely acknowledged him coolly and moved on, a shark making headway through turgid water.

There was no prey here. This high-end boutique publishing house didn't draw much glitter. He waved and turned his back on the crowd, which, he reflected, would give them such a nice opportunity to talk behind it. Gerald knew he wasn't noble, but he tried always to oblige.

# 11

> I don't believe in personal immortality; the only way I expect to have some version of such a thing is through my books.
>
> —*Isaac Asimov*

Opal sat alone in the smallest room at the funeral home, but even so the room seemed cavernous. There were, perhaps, ten rows of chairs, and aside from Opal and the young man in the back who had handled the cremation arrangements, there wasn't a single other guest. Opal had cried all of her tears the day before, back at Terry's grim apartment, so here she had merely sat, white and wordless, while an unknown minister mouthed a few trite, awkward generalities and Albinoni's Canon played over the PA system. Then Terry's ashes were given to Opal. It hadn't taken long—less than fifteen minutes—and that included the inexcusable mangling the minister had done of the Langston Hughes poem—one of Terry's favorites. All of it had flown by, and Opal had merely sat, exhausted. She hadn't slept very well in Terry's narrow bed. All night long she had thought of the lines from the Hughes poem:

> Sometimes a crumb falls
> From the tables of joy,
> Sometimes a bone
> Is flung.
> To some people
> Love is given.
> To others
> Only heaven.

Had anyone flung a bone from the tables of joy to Terry? Opal had given her daughter love, but is a mother's love ever enough? Certainly it wasn't for Terry. There had been no comfort for her. And now Opal was alone, left with only Terry's dust to comfort her. She sat with the small metal box on her lap, and somehow it seemed as if it weighed enough so that Opal would never again be able to move from under the burden.

Now, while the Albinoni droned on endlessly, Opal merely stared at the front of the little room.

She jumped when she felt the hand on her shoulder and turned to look into the face of a woman slightly older than she. "I'm sorry," the woman said. "Did I startle you?"

Opal nodded. The woman had a long, kind face, and Opal could see that tears had gathered on her reddened lower lids.

"I'm Roberta Fine. I worked with your daughter."

Opal tried to gather herself together. Of course. Terry had written to her about Roberta. What was the name of her shop? The Book Stop? No. The Bookstall? Opal tried to smile and was about to say something—one of those things that people say—about how nice it was for you to come or how thoughtful you were to remember, when the woman's face seemed to reconfigure itself, morphing into a rictus of sorrow. She burst into noisy, hysterical sobs.

"I'm so sorry. I'm so sorry," she cried. After that Opal couldn't understand much of what she said except for something about letting Terry go, and how it hadn't been Terry's fault, and how Roberta felt so responsible. "I just had no idea," Roberta gulped. "I didn't know the job meant so much to her. I can't tell you what this has done to me. But it must be so very much worse for you." Once again the woman's face collapsed, and she began searching in her neat black purse for a handkerchief.

Opal handed her one of her own. She also reached out and patted Roberta Fine's thin, black-clad shoulder. The woman did look ravaged. She had fired Terry, apparently. But for her to think that Terry had killed herself over that! Well, Opal had lived long enough to know that everyone thought that their own experience was the true reality, the center of the world. Now she took Roberta's long, thin, damp white hand in her own ruddier one. "It's not your fault," Opal said. "Please, please don't think that for a minute. Losing the job didn't do this to Terry. If it's anybody's fault, it's mine. I shouldn't have encouraged her. I shouldn't have pushed her—"

"But you inspired her! She loved you, she admired you. She talked about you all the time." The woman paused. "Oh my God, you don't think this is *your* fault, do you?" The two women looked into each other's eyes for an endless minute. "Perhaps I've been very foolish," Roberta said.

"Perhaps I have, too," Opal agreed. "And perhaps blaming ourselves is very self-indulgent. Disrespectful of Terry, too."

Roberta continued to look into Opal's eyes. "It is easier to feel guilt than pain, isn't it?"

Opal nodded. "Yes." She paused. "It's also easier to feel responsible than to feel powerless." Roberta looked away, then nodded.

After a moment Opal reached into her own battered purse and took out the letters, all of Terry's rejection letters. "If anyone is responsible, here are the culprits. But I think we have to give Terry the dignity of making a choice. She was tired of all this. They'd worn her down."

Roberta took the pile of letters and began to thumb through them. She pulled out her glasses, put them on, and read one letter after another, shaking her head and making small clicking noises with her tongue. "Oh, really!" she said to one letter and pushed it to the bottom of the stack. At another one she silently shook her head. After a few more, she looked back at Opal. "But I had no idea," she said. "I mean, I knew about Terry's work, but I had no idea . . . Do you know the trick Doris Lessing pulled?"

Opal shook her head. "Doris Lessing submitted a new manuscript of her own to four or five publishers. But she used a different name. And she was rejected by all of them." She paused. Then, gently, she asked, "Is the book any good?"

Now Opal felt tears rising in her own eyes. "I don't know," she admitted. "The parts I read were brilliant, but I never read the whole thing."

"Well, read it now," Roberta urged.

Then Opal's tears overflowed, and though she kept calm and could speak, she couldn't wipe her eyes quickly enough to hide them. She sniffed. "I can't read it now. Terry has destroyed it. There's nothing left but ashes in her fireplace." Opal looked down into her lap. "There's nothing left of her life except for ashes."

Roberta reached out and patted Opal's arm, briefly and with the lightest touch imaginable. Opal could tell that—like herself—Roberta was not a huggy person. "Tragic," was all that Roberta said for a few minutes. And then, "You must, you *must* bring those ashes of the manuscript back with you as well," Roberta said. "They are as much a part of Terry as whatever is left in that box."

Opal looked up, and—for the first time since she had gotten the call, the phone call from the lady detective with the terrible news—she smiled. "Yes. Of course. That's what I'll do." And somehow the thought of mingling her daughter's ashes with the manuscript ashes not only made perfect sense but also gave some small comfort to Opal O'Neal.

"Do you want any help?" Roberta asked. "Is there anything I can do?"

"You've already done a lot for me," Opal told her.

"And you for me," Roberta responded. Then she took out a card and handed it to Opal. "My shop is only a few blocks away," she said. "Come by, or call, or write. And let me know if you need any help or want a ride to the airport."

Opal thanked her, and then, somehow, she found the

strength to stand. Together the two women walked slowly out of the graceless parlor.

Opal had finished packing, and her suitcases stood by the door. She had given away all of those things of Terry's that could be of any use to the homeless, then carried out two large bags of garbage, which she left in the rubber containers at the side of the door. Last, she had swept up the ashes from the fireplace grate and carefully added them to the contents of the metal box. She had washed her face and hands, put on some lipstick, combed her gray, permed curls, and made two final telephone calls, to ConEd and Nynex to terminate service. Then she took one last look around the room and went to the door, ready to leave.

But it seemed that, despite the few belongings of Terry's that she'd saved, there was more luggage than Opal could handle. She tried to lift a suitcase and a bag in each hand, but that was too heavy and awkward. She couldn't get through the door. She would have to make two trips, and she was afraid to leave anything on the New York sidewalk—even for a moment—while she went back in to get the remaining baggage. She reached into her purse for the keys and pushed all the luggage into the hall. She thought for a moment of calling Roberta Fine for help, but that was silly. She would just have to inch it all out, rather like a sheepdog moving a flock. But as Opal got to the front of the hallway, one of the bags she was pushing fell against the super's door. And, surprisingly quickly, he flung it open.

"Oh. It's you." He looked down at the little herd of luggage and back at Opal. "You leaving?" he asked. He was a master at stating the obvious. Opal merely nodded. "You clean out the apartment?"

Really, he was beneath contempt. But Opal merely nodded again. What was his name? Some name unknown in Indiana. Aiello. That was it. But she didn't know if it was his first name or his last. Well, she didn't have to speak to the brute.

"I gotta get those keys back," Aiello told her. Wordlessly Opal reached into her bag and handed them to him.

"Ya might wanna take a cab, what with all that luggage and all."

He didn't even offer to help her, but Opal was not surprised. She just kept sliding the bags toward the front door.

"And you might wanna clean out the mailbox," he continued, in his very limited attempt to be helpful.

"Mailbox?" Opal asked. "Where *is* the mailbox?" She imagined a row of rural tin canisters on posts, each with its little flag raised or lowered, but surely they didn't have mailboxes like that here. Aiello shrugged and with a twitch of his shoulder indicated the tarnished brass fronts inserted into the wall behind him. The whole affair looked like the grates of a heat register to Opal.

"These are the mailboxes," he said. "Hers was number two."

"How do you open them?" Opal asked.

"With the key, the little key."

"Oh, yes, one of the ones you've just taken," Opal said coolly.

Aiello shrugged and handed the keys back to her. "There's a lot of stuff in there," he said, looking through the grate.

With a sigh, Opal took the key chain and turned to the boxes. She inserted the smaller key into the round keyhole at the bottom of the box but could not get it to turn.

"Sometimes they're a little tricky," Aiello said. "Ya gotta dick around with it." He stopped, embarrassed, "I mean ya have to screw around with it." He felt the inadequacy of his correction. "You *know*," he said, exasperated. "You know what I mean."

Opal pushed the key in a little deeper, but it still wouldn't turn, so she pulled it out a bit, jiggled it, and found the place where it began to rotate. What was it with

New York City locks? None of them seemed cooperative. Finally, the key turned 180 degrees. She felt the lock disengage, and by pulling on the key itself, she lifted the front of the box.

A couple of envelopes fell onto the dirty tiled floor. There was also some kind of newsprint circular and two magazines, *The Writer* and *Poets & Writers*, but both of them were badly bent and torn because the major space in the box was taken up by a large jiffy bag, a huge padded envelope sealed with packing tape. It was wedged into the box so tightly that Opal, her hands shaking, couldn't pull it free.

"Here. Let me." Aiello pulled out the heavy package, tearing the wrapper and then handing it to Opal. He turned back to extricate the other mail and pick up the pieces that had fallen. But Opal didn't care about any of that. Right there, right there in the dirty, dark hallway, she tore into the big envelope and pulled out the manuscript inside. It was like being a midwife at a birth. Opal let the caul drop to the floor, exposing the gift inside. She voraciously read the cover letter.

> Dear Ms. O'Neal,
>
> In going through our files, we have found this photocopy of your submission from last year and, although I see in my records that we returned the original to you, I thought you might want to have this copy.

Opal didn't bother to look at the signature. Instead she tore the letter off the pile and looked. Yes! There was the title page. *The Duplicity of Men* by Terry O'Neal. The manuscript! Terry may not have meant to leave it behind, but here it was. Opal clutched it to her chest, a prize far more exciting, far more precious, than buried treasure or a winning lottery ticket. She could resubmit it. She *would* resubmit it, and she would get these jaspers in New York to pay attention. She didn't care if they'd said no to Terry, or even to Doris Lessing. She would get them to read and publish her daughter's masterpiece. Terry would not have lived her life in vain after all. Opal hadn't misled her. And she would prove it. While the publishers may have ignored Terry in life, they would acknowledge her now. Though Terry may have lived in obscurity, in death she would be known.

"It's something good?" Aiello asked. And, to his astonishment, the middle-aged woman kissed him.

# 12

> Writing is a form of therapy; sometimes I wonder how all those who do not write, compose or paint can manage to escape the madness, melancholia, the panic fear which is inherent in a human situation.
>
> —*Graham Greene*

Camilla returned to Firenze with her finished manuscript and the promise from Frederick Ashton that he would look her up. She had a tour to meet, and good docent that she was, she arrived early and crossed the Piazza della Repubblica at a slower-than-usual pace. She never enjoyed the moments before she met a new group. Some groups were very pleasant, eager to learn what she knew and as delighted by the city as she was. But others never seemed to coalesce or were made up of difficult or apparently stupid individuals who were either too shy or too uninterested to respond to her. She hoped she didn't have one of those on her hands. It would be so dispiriting just now when Camilla was pleased with herself, with her book, and with her new friend.

And then, almost at the door to the Hotel Excelsior, she saw Gianfranco. He was walking along the far side of the square with an older woman—perhaps his mother or his aunt. He was walking in her direction, facing her, but then he turned. Camilla was almost certain that he had seen her and, though it was he who should be ashamed, she felt her own face redden.

Gianfranco's family were well-off but certainly not among the oldest of Florentine families. They owned several hotels. Not the enormous ones, or the very best, like the Excelsior, but they were large enough and good enough to keep the family comfortable. His father was a judge, and Gianfranco himself was an *avvocato*. He would probably, in the fullness of time, be a judge as well. In the meanwhile, he spent as little time in the office as he could get away with and quite a bit of time in the bars and cafés of Firenze.

He had the dark good looks of an Italian film star—his features a little less regular than an American hero's but still incredibly attractive. Camilla had been surprised when he approached her at one of the few Florentine parties she had been invited to. Gianfranco had seduced her with his charm, his attentiveness, and his good looks, but while she had taken all of that as a sign of romantic and perhaps marital interest, he had meant it as the almost formal announcement of his interest in her—as a mistress. And *only* as a mistress. I have been stupid, Camilla thought. It was only after she had been dazzled by him, after she had slept with him, that she had realized her mistake. She thought they were in love, but he had laughed when she had asked about meeting his family. "Whatever for?" he had said, and she had realized that the rules of the game were very different among his class. Here you romanced a mistress while you married into the best family you could possibly manage. Rather like England, but Englishmen often omitted the bother of a mistress altogether.

Realizing her mistake, Camilla had tried to break up with him, but he was always so sweet, so sexual, and so clearly astonished by her pain. He cried with her and called her "*tesauro*." His treasure. And she—who had never been *anybody's* treasure—was touched, and found it impossible to go back to the emptiness of her life before she slept in his arms.

But she never got to sleep in his arms for long. Gianfranco would meet her at an apartment he kept only for his assignations. He never stayed overnight, nor did she. They met there at five and left around seven, he to have dinner with his mother and father, to take his place as the only son, the beloved only child, while she went home to her single room and her cold plate. Camilla had begun writing because of the long nights she spent awake, longing for Gianfranco. Yet when she was with him, every kiss, every stroke of his hand on her hair, was enough to cause her pain, pain that came from the knowledge that he might love her but never marry her.

"But why should you care about this?" he asked her reasonably. "It is you I love now. My father had a mistress for twenty-two years. *Tesauro*, why should you not be happy?"

She was too proud and too shy to explain that she did not want to be *one* of his loves: that for her he was an *only* love, and she wanted him to feel that way as well. But he didn't.

And so her book got written in the nights she spent alone, first as a distraction and then as an end in itself. Slowly, Camilla had been drawn into the web of words she was creating, rather like a spider getting trapped in its own grid. The power that writing gave her, the power to create a character, an event, a whole world, seduced her more deeply than Gianfranco had. She found herself obsessed, challenged, and despairing—fascinated by both the problems and the triumphs that came as she doggedly moved forward.

And now her book was finished, and so was her affair with Gianfranco. She had told him so before she had left for San Gimignano. He had laughed at her, as he had when she'd told him that before. But for her, this time it was different. Now she had something to keep her from being alone in that room. She would not go back to Gianfranco.

Still, seeing him there was enough to both humiliate her and set off a longing for him that she knew was dangerous. Camilla straightened her shoulders and walked into the Hotel Excelsior. She would guide these people through the wonders of Firenze, and if, like Dante before her, she was also a guide leading them through her own personal hell, she would not show it.

The group was *not* a good one, and it made Camilla all the more ready to accept Frederick's invitation to dinner when it came. He took her to a pleasant restaurant not far from the Palazzo Vecchio, something Gianfranco would never do for fear of being seen. She enjoyed the way Frederick took her arm and seemed pleased to be seen with her. But then, he was very plain. There was none of the sleekness, the feral but flashingly attractive looks of Gianfranco. Frederick's physical awkwardness with her was complimentary, though anything but sexy. Camilla smiled when he fumbled at the table and pulled out her chair too far. She was the one who had the power in this relationship. If there *was* any relationship. The French, those masters of orchestrated love, had once defined each member of a couple as "the one who kissed or who was kissed." With Gianfranco, Camilla had been the one who did the kissing. Now, if there was any kissing to be done, it would be Frederick's job. She looked across the table at him calmly. This was not a man to raise your temperature. But he seemed a nice man. And no one else had shown any interest in her. His eyes, which seemed very vague and almost unfocused, were the color of sherry. Camilla liked his eyes.

They ordered dinner, and he asked her about the tour group. She inquired about his mother, who was, apparently, leaving Italy the following morning. "But don't you want to have dinner with her on her last night?" Camilla asked.

"No. I'll see her in New York soon enough."

"I thought she lived in Larchmont."

"She lives in two places, actually. Larchmont and East Eighty-sixth Street and the park," he told her. That must mean Central Park and that they were wealthy. Camilla knew the rents in New York. "It's actually my apartment,"

Frederick explained. "But Mother is staying there to oversee some work that's being done to it."

Camilla nodded. They were unusually close, this man and his mother.

"How did you wind up in school in New York?" Frederick asked.

"Divine intervention." Camilla laughed. But now, years later, even joking about it was still painful. She had never spoken about the misadventure. Yet, tonight, under the influence of a fine bottle of Montepulciano, she felt as if she might. Frederick was easy to talk to. He seemed to have no expectations of her. She need not entertain or work to charm, as she did with Gianfranco, but if she did, she felt as if Frederick would like it, rather than being put off (as some men were when a plain brown wren became a more outgoing bird).

"I was meant to go to Cambridge," Camilla began to explain, and the words, spoken aloud for the first time in her life, actually hurt her throat. She picked up her wineglass and took another sip. "I was a scholarship girl at the convent school. The nuns took an interest in me, and when I seemed about to do very well on my A levels we filed an application with their written reports. The mother superior helped me get an interview at Cambridge." She paused, remembering back to the preparations for that day.

She hadn't known what to wear, and that was one way Sister Agnus had failed her. After all, how could a nun be expected to keep up with university fashions? So Camilla had worn her bright blue crimpolene Sunday suit and gone up to Cambridge with her mother. But despite her convent studies in Latin and Greek, despite her mastery of European history and her strong background in English literature, Camilla had been woefully unprepared for Cambridge.

The colleges on the banks of the Cam were more beautiful than she had ever imagined, and more bewildering. She smiled at Frederick, but the smile cost her. "It's existed for more than five hundred years, and it's based on an assumption that those who were about to be initiated were those in the know, while those who are uninitiated should remain so. Do you understand?"

Frederick nodded. "Despite propaganda to the contrary, we do have a class structure in America," he said.

"Well," Camilla continued, "colleges each had their specialities, and their names, which are often pronounced totally differently from the way they're spelled. There's Magdalene, pronounced 'Maudlin' (and spelled without the final *e* at Oxford). There's Petersborough, which was a college, but the only one that was never *called* a college." She paused. "I humiliated myself by asking for it incorrectly. Anyroad, interview times and places were posted, but I had no idea where, and there seemed no central desk, no registrar's office to inquire of, so I completely missed my first appointment when I discovered the listings on a board in a sequestered quadrangle." Camilla winced, recalling how her mother, horrified, began to yell at her—which certainly hadn't helped Camilla's composure. She had only found the history don, a mild, pleasant man, as he was leaving. He took pity on her in her dishevelment and humiliation and graciously suggested they reschedule the appointment for later in the day. But his only available hour conflicted with her other interview. "I was just naive," she explained to Frederick. "I should have told him how much I wanted to see him, how I hoped to read history, but all I managed was, 'Well, you see, I am seeing the classics don then.' He looked at the crimpolene, and I babbled, 'I haven't decided whether to do history or classics. I suppose I'll do classics in the end.'"

"So what happened then?" Frederick asked, as if it mattered.

"He told me, 'Then it's all come out right,' and wandered off, a bit bemused, his black gown flapping in the spring breeze."

Camilla smiled at Frederick, but it cost her. She'd only

realized the ghastliness of her mistake after her interview with the two supercilious classics dons, who eyed her with an unconcealed coldness that was as good as a poster announcing they knew she was NOKD—Not Our Kind, Dear. Under their merciless interrogation Camilla had wilted quickly, knowing too late that as a female, a Catholic, and a tongue-tied, badly dressed upstart from the working class she had as much chance of winning their approval as she did winning the Olympic decathlon.

All of this she explained to Frederick, whose long face lengthened and whose deep red-brown eyes darkened in sympathy. "What happened then?" he asked.

She shrugged. "I wasn't offered a place at Cambridge."

"So, what did you do?"

"Well, I deeply disappointed Sister Agnus. And I proved my mother's thesis right when she said that Cambridge wasn't the place for the likes of us." Camilla took another sip of wine and then tried a bite of her meal. But she'd lost her appetite. She put her fork down. Even now, years later, the experience was raw.

Frederick reached his hand across the table and patted hers just for a moment, very gently. "I mean," he said, "what did you do about school?"

"Well, I did well in my A levels. Well enough for Sister Agnus to put me in for a full scholarship at Marymount. It's a Catholic girls' college in New York City, and she knew one of the deans. I did my undergraduate work there and then my graduate work at Columbia."

"So you lived in New York," Frederick said.

"Yes, for a long time."

"And those are fine schools."

"Yes. Marymount might have been stronger—there were a lot of spoiled rich girls there—but the faculty was kind to me. And Columbia was top-drawer."

"Still, it wasn't Cambridge."

"No, it wasn't." She looked over at him, into those red-brown eyes. Somehow they seemed to understand a great deal about pain. Had he experienced so much? It didn't seem possible. After all, he was a wealthy, young American man with a devoted mother and a good education. Once again, Camilla wondered if he was gay: If that was the burden he carried, it gave him an insight into the burdens of others.

"It wasn't Cambridge," she repeated. "Cambridge was my last chance to find a place where I fit in among my own kind. I might have found a niche among other bright scholarship students. You know, all the other smart ones who didn't fit in at home. And then I would have gone down to London and been a part of that world. But it didn't work out. So, instead, I was a poor Brit in New York, a scholarship student among debutantes. Then, in graduate school, I was a woman among men, and an expatriate to boot. I had no connections, no way to get any. I was passed over for all the good jobs."

"Then what?"

Camilla shrugged. "Here I'm just a foreigner. I can't go back to Birmingham, and I'm not sure where to go next."

Frederick waited, as if he understood her feelings. "So you wrote a book," he coaxed. She nodded. "And now what?" he asked.

Camilla thought of Gianfranco. She sighed. "I don't know," she told him truthfully and raised her glass of wine to her lips.

"Well, I think it's obvious. I think you have to send your book to my sister."

"I'm not sure about that," she said.

"Yes," he told her. "My sister in New York. Remember? She's an editor with Davis & Dash. And it sounds as if she would like your book. Of course, there are no guarantees. But what have you got to lose?"

What indeed, Camilla thought. Would he send the book as a quid pro quo, a payment for future services rendered? He certainly didn't seem that type. Camilla looked at him, this very plain American who had entered her life, made no demands, and seemed to offer so much. What did he expect of her? What could she deliver? "I couldn't," she said, "I really couldn't."

"Sure you could," he told her. "You'd be silly not to."

"But I always thought I'd publish it in England. After all, I'm English."

"Yeah, but it's a book about Americans, and you've lived in America. And I know an American editor. I promise you, if I had a sister who was editing in London, I would send it to her. But since I don't, you'll have to live with this."

Camilla laughed. "All right," she said. "I guess I will live with it."

# 13

> Each publishing season seems to bring us another photogenic female author trying to get funky with pulp fiction.
>
> —*James Wolcott*

Susann waited while the driver stepped out of the limo and opened the door for her. She had a lot to do today, and the phone call from Kim had been upsetting. Not that Kim had sounded high or even hostile. Actually, her daughter had sounded unusually calm. But was it the calm before the storm? Susann had agreed to meet Kim for tea at the New York Palace, and then she was off to Alf's office to wrap up some final details, now that her new book was handed in.

Susann stepped out of the limousine and gave her best smile to Ralph, her driver when she was in New York. She walked through the elaborate gate and the hotel courtyard where the eight poplar trees were perennially wrapped in tiny white Christmas lights. She entered the hotel and turned right, walking up one side of the elegant staircase, her gloved hand barely touching the ornate railing. Despite her age, Susann had kept her posture and height thanks to her Alexander technique sessions. It was only her hands . . . She walked to the entrance of the Villard Room knowing she looked far too young to be the mother of the woman who waited for her.

But Kim looked surprisingly well—at least for Kim. She had gained some weight, but she always did that when she wasn't on cocaine. Kim looked more like Susann's second husband than she did Susann. She was chunky and dark-haired. Now Kim must be about the same age that

Alan was when Susann had married him. What an ill-fated marriage it had been. Alan had abandoned them when Kim was seven, but not before beating both of them regularly. Perhaps that was another reason Susann didn't like to see Kim: She reminded Susann of those days and made her feel guilty because of them.

"Hello, Sue," Kim said. For some reason, Kim had never called her Mommy or Mother. Not even when she was little. Susann hated to be called Sue but said nothing. Didn't Kim's greeting have a slightly ironic cast to it? Susann ignored it and merely took a seat opposite Kim. They didn't kiss.

"How are you?" Susann asked.

"Do you mean am I straight? Yes, I've been clean and sober for eight months now."

"Good. That's very good." Susann could have bitten her tongue. She knew she sounded prissy, but what could one say? I hope that this time you won't go back to your five-hundred-dollar-a-day habit? And, if you do, know that this time I will absolutely not intervene. No. They had established that already.

Susann was relieved when the waiter came and asked for their tea order. "Darjeeling," she told him with her best smile. Kim asked for chamomile. In moments the waiter reappeared with a trolley of tiny sandwiches—cucumber, smoked salmon, tomato, and cheese. Kim, despite her weight, asked for two of each, but Susann only had one thin cucumber. The waiter placed their teapots before them and left them to face each other. Susann took a bite of her sandwich. "Well," she said, "you said you had some news."

"Yes," Kim said. "I wanted you to know. I've written a book."

Susann paused for a moment, almost choking on her food. "You've done what?" she asked.

"A book. I've written a book," Kim repeated. "You're not the only one who can do it, you know."

Susann was at a loss for words. Now what? Was she expected to find Kim an agent, to edit her work, to find a publisher? Would the demands on her never end? "I didn't know that you wrote. You never told me. I'm just surprised—"

"Don't you remember? I showed you a story I wrote years ago. You cut it to shreds." Susann tried to recall it. Kim had had so many interests, gone off in so many directions, but never pursued any of them seriously. There'd been figure skating, ballet, and horseback riding. Photography, too. She had decided to go to art school instead of college but then dropped out. Then she wanted a restaurant, which failed, and a weaving studio, but that had come to nothing. All of Kim's enthusiasms were expensive, short-lived, and ultimately doomed. But when had writing been sandwiched in among the other activities? Susann tried to remember. Was it before the restaurant or after?

"Yes, I remember. You wrote a little story. I edited it for you."

Kim set her jaw firmly. "It wasn't 'a little story,' Sue. I had worked on it for months. And when I asked you your opinion, you tore it apart."

"I edited it," Susann repeated. "If you were serious about it, you would have listened to my suggestions and improved it. That's what professionalism is all about."

Kim shook her head. "You decimated me. It's taken me ten years to get the nerve to try again. And I've done it on my own. I've finished my first book, and I've sold it."

"You've finished it? You've sold it?" Susann parroted. She could hardly believe what she was hearing. "To whom have you sold it?"

"To Citron Press," Kim said defiantly. "And they've paid me enough to live on my own for the next year while I work on the next one."

Susann stared at her daughter, thunderstruck. Why in the world had Kimberly chosen this, of all things? And what was she to say? "Well. Congratulations. I hope you allow me to read it."

Kim smiled. "You'll get the first reader's copy," she said. Reader's copies were the typeset, uncorrected paperbound editions of a book that went out to critics and reviewers before publication. "Maybe you'll give me a blurb," Kimberly said, smiling. "I think you'll like it. The main character is a famous woman author."

Susann felt her own smile disappearing. She thought of the way Cheever's children had written about him. And she was no Cheever. She had read the Danielle Steel unauthorized biography by Nicole Hoyt, and the similarities between her and Danielle were a bit frightening. They had both married and become mothers at a young age; they both had second husbands who were sex perverts, but, Susann thought to herself, at least Alf wasn't a drug addict the way Steel's third husband had been; and she hadn't remarried and had five more children as Steel had. She felt her face flush; unlike Danielle, she may have to worry that her unauthorized bio would be written by her daughter. "Well, I wish you had let me know earlier. Perhaps I could have helped you. Or maybe Alf could have."

"Fuck Alf," Kim told her. "I wouldn't accept anything from that dirty old bastard." Susann shook her head. She hoped Kimberly wasn't going to bring all of *that* up again. The legitimate tragedy in their lives had been that Robert Edmonds, Susann's third husband and Kimberly's stepfather, had molested Kim. But since then, Kim had seen advances in everyone from the gardener to her teachers at school. She'd even accused Alf of inappropriate behavior.

Susann tried not to roll her eyes, but failed. Kimberly leaned over and hissed at her. "Don't give me that look. Don't belittle me, and don't try to make me feel like I'm crazy. I've written this book and I've sold it, and I did both of those things myself. And I don't want anything from you or from Alf, or from my father or from my stepfather, either." She paused. "Nothing. Except my name."

"Your name?" Susann repeated.

"That's right. I'm using my stepfather's. He owes me that, at least. My name. Kimberly Baker Edmonds. That's the name I'm using. So it looks like you will have a little more competition, Sue."

# 14

> The writer is always tricking the reader into listening to their dream.
>
> —*Joan Didion*

Judith woke up with a smile on her face, which was unusual. Since she'd finished the book she'd felt rather bereft. Then she remembered: Daniel had woken her up when he came home from his writers' group last night. He'd been hungry for her, and she had fallen asleep feeling well and deeply loved.

She turned over in bed. She felt absolutely adorable cuddled up in the bedclothes. Daniel was already up and showered, dressed in his underpants, his back to her, rooting through his closet. She hoped he'd look over at her, come back to bed and kiss her or hold her. "Where's my blue sports coat?" he asked instead.

"Oh. I think it's in my closet," she admitted. Judith felt a stab of guilt. Daniel was so particular about his clothes. He had asked her over and over again to remember to take them out of the plastic film and hang them up in his closet when she brought them back from the cleaners. Too often she forgot. Like today. She had *meant* to take the hanger from her hall closet, but when she had struggled up the stairs with the groceries, the dog, and the dry cleaning, she had temporarily stuck it there and never gotten back to it. Somehow, though she was home all day, there was so much she didn't get to.

Judith didn't know why she felt so sad lately. Somehow, since she'd finished the book, she had spent most of her time in a daze, finding herself with a mug of coffee cooling in her hand, staring out the grimy windows. She didn't know what she'd been doing, what she was looking at or looking for. But she knew she didn't feel good.

Maybe it was because she had finished the book. She told herself that was it. That this was normal for a writer, if that was indeed what she was. Also, she was anxious about getting published because maybe, just maybe, they *shouldn't* be published.

Judith had done her best with the book, but she wasn't sure if it was true. Of course it was fiction, though it was based on an incident from real life. But the truth of research was not what Judith was thinking of. She—with Daniel's help—had created Elthea from her own imagination, and she wasn't sure that Elthea was true—not in the way that great characters had been true for Judith. Growing up, nothing had been more important to Judith than reading: She had widened her horizons, escaped her boredom, found her friends, and experienced life through books. Now she wondered if she had contributed, in a small way, to that long list of heroines that for her included Jane Eyre, Anna Karenina, Elizabeth Bennet, Dorothea Brooke, and a dozen contemporary ones whom she had loved. Judith knew she was no Flaubert, no George Eliot. But if she wasn't a genius, she didn't want to be a liar, and she was afraid that she might be. She had had to do things—write things—because Daniel demanded it. He said it made the book more commercial. But Judith was torn. Aside from Daniel, books were the only thing Judith truly loved. She would hate to betray either one of them.

Daniel was buttoning his shirt—one of the few French-cuffed shirts he had. He fumbled with the cuff link. She had bought those for him for his birthday, and she smiled to see him use them. He rarely wore a formal shirt, preferring his oxford cloth button-down or flannel ones. Judith sat up, about to get him his jacket, but he slipped into his good woolen trousers and was out of the room before she could manage to untangle herself from the duvet. She met him in the hallway, where he was angrily discarding the polyethylene and struggling into his jacket. He had a new, beautiful briefcase waiting at the door. When had he gotten that? she wondered. And how would they pay for it?

"Boy, you look good," she said. And it was true. Daniel rarely bothered to dress up, but he looked adorable in his good clothes. Now he didn't say anything—he just looked at her, and all of her sexy, adorable feelings vanished. Judith looked down at herself, in her creased, bedraggled nightgown and her tousled hair. Her cold bare feet—never pretty at the best of times—looked almost blue on the dark linoleum. She saw Daniel take her in, and she saw herself through his eyes. It was not a pretty picture.

"I've got to go," Daniel said. He picked up his new briefcase, pecked her on the cheek, and was gone.

Daniel took the train into New York. He wanted to use the time to review the manuscript and check, once more, Cheryl's typing job. But it was very competent, very professional. Cheryl was a much better typist than Judith would ever be. Daniel wondered what else she was better at. What was the Thomas Wolfe line? "I can always find plenty of women to sleep with but the kind of woman that is really hard for me to find is a typist who can read my writing." Daniel almost laughed. The train clacked along, the car occupied only by Daniel and a few lawyers on their way from Albany. Daniel wondered idly if he needed a lawyer. He would ask Alfred Byron today.

Alfred Byron was one of the movers and shakers among the heavy New York literary agents. Along with Mort Janklow, Lynn Nesbit, Owen Laster, Binky Urban, Esther Newberg, Andrew Wylie, and less than a handful of others, Byron was famous for making seven-figure deals. Daniel had had the audacity to invite Byron up to the school, first to speak on a panel and then, later, to chair another one. Daniel had been as surprised as anyone that Byron had accepted, but the old man seemed flattered and showed up. It still surprised Daniel that some people were so easily conned by a little attention from academia. Because, apparently, the invitations had been enough to ensure this meeting. And not many unpublished writers got in to see Alfred Byron. He represented Susann Baker Edmonds and a few other commercial megazoids. Not exactly "writers"—more like people who filled pages that other people bought by the millions of copies.

Daniel looked at the manuscript. Was this a megazoid in the making? "*In Full Knowledge* by Jude Daniel," had been typed in large, boldface letters by the obliging Cheryl. Daniel winced guiltily. He reminded himself that he hadn't done anything he wasn't supposed to. He may have *encouraged* Cheryl, but wasn't that a teacher's job? And he had not asked her to type this for him. She had offered. It wouldn't change her grade. She was going to get an A anyway. He hadn't done anything wrong.

Then why did he feel so guilty? I am allowed to have feelings, he reminded himself. As long as I don't act on them. And he hadn't. He hadn't acted on them. That was the important thing. He hadn't told Judith, either. Not about meeting Cheryl for coffee or getting Cheryl to retype the manuscript or . . .

Well, he hadn't told Judith about this meeting. Maybe he should have. But why get her hopes up for no reason? It wasn't as if he was lying to her. Not at all. He was doing this for her, for both of them, and if he failed, if he was shot down or rejected, there was no need to share that humiliation with Judith. It would only depress her, and God knows, she was depressed enough.

Daniel knew the manuscript was his ticket out of the endless, unrewarding life he'd somehow gotten stuck in. And he knew he had to get out.

"Daniel, Daniel, good to see you," Alfred Byron roared as he pumped Daniel's hand. Everything about the man was loud. "Please, Professor, come on into my office."

The office was wide, as Byron was, and somehow it

seemed almost too perfect—rather like the way a movie would depict an agent's office. There were floor-to-ceiling mahogany bookshelves with glass fronts on three walls, a dazzling antique Persian rug, a leather-covered worn chesterfield, and an enormous desk that was almost as ornate as Alfred Byron was himself.

Even the dust and piles of manuscript seemed placed for effect. Byron wore a strange suit—a kind of dark green color with odd reddish brown pinstripes that looked to Daniel like strings of dried blood. Well, didn't most writers think of agents as bloodsuckers? The suit was double-breasted with a pocket handkerchief in a paisley print protruding from its pocket. His gray-and-white striped shirt with a white collar was set off by a blue polka-dot tie. It was a very bad imitation of an English gentleman, and it certainly didn't fool Daniel Gross. The name didn't fool him either. Alfred Byron had been born Al Boronkin, but Daniel didn't mind any of the man's affectations, because Byron was a money player and Daniel wasn't in this for the art.

Byron sat behind his desk and placed his hands wide and flat upon the sea of mahogany that was his desktop. "So, Professor, what can I do for you? Another seminar, perhaps? I have an idea for one. I thought we could forget some of this sensitive, lyrical bullshit and talk about commercial writing. Let's tell your little kids what really works. I could put together a panel with some of my clients. Only first-rate. And I could get *Publishers Weekly* to—"

"It sounds really interesting, Alfred," Daniel interrupted, forcing himself to use the old charlatan's first name, "but I really didn't come here about a seminar. I mean, not this time. I thought that we could talk about this." He pulled the manuscript out of his new briefcase and set it down in the middle of Byron's huge desk. Daniel looked up at the agent's face quickly enough to see his smile fade. Daniel could almost hear the thoughts of dismay behind Alfred Byron's wide forehead. "Not another schmuck with a manuscript," he was thinking. But Byron quickly recovered, replacing his consternation with a cold professional smile.

"Well, well, what's this? You have been busy. A book, huh?"

"It's not what you think," Daniel began lamely.

"It's not a book?"

"What I mean is, it's not the kind of book you think." Daniel looked directly at Byron and tried to muster as much force and belief as he could. "It's a page-turner, Alfred. I swear to God it is."

The agent nodded his big head sagely. "I'm sure it is, Professor, I'm sure it is." Byron turned the book toward him but only glanced at the title page. Then he raised his white winged brows. "Jude Daniel?" he asked.

Daniel was about to explain that he had written the book with Judith, but the coolness in the room was so disconcerting that he couldn't muster up the strength to do it. What sounded lamer than a book written by an untenured college professor? A book written by his *wife*. "It's a pen name, Alfred," Daniel explained.

"Well, Professor, I don't really read unsolicited manuscripts. And we're not taking on new writers right now." Daniel knew that, as well as the rest of the circular ironies in the publishing world: that publishers were always looking for the next new success, while virtually none of them accepted or read new writers' work. Publishers depended on agents' submissions, but agents only received 10 or 15 percent of a writer's income, so they tried to limit their stables to writers who would earn huge advances. And most of the agents didn't take on new clients. So how was a new writer to get published, and how were publishers going to find the next new thing?

"I'd be happy to take a look at it," Byron said. Daniel realized it was unlikely. Most agents employed assistants who did the initial read. Byron stood up. He moved around his desk and put his hand on Daniel's shoulder. It was not so much a friendly gesture as the literary equivalent of a vaudevillian hook. Daniel stood up as he was expected to. "I'll be happy to take a look at it," Byron repeated as he walked Daniel to the door. "I'll get back to you as soon as I possibly can."

Daniel realized he had badly miscalculated. He was of interest to Byron only as an outlet for his clients, as an academic ego-booster. But Daniel decided to make one more attempt. "Please read it yourself, Alf," he said. "I promise you, you won't be disappointed." He paused. He couldn't help himself. He had to ask. "And if it is good, Alfred, how much could I get for it?"

Byron merely pursed his lips. "Well. One step at a time, Professor. One step at a time." Byron shook his hand, and Daniel felt more impotent than ever. How many other pathetic, unpublished writers had failed using lines as hackneyed as his? Daniel added the name Jude Daniel to the list.

# 15

> Could any modern publisher contemplate such an undertaking?
>
> —*Patrick O'Brian*

Gerald sprawled on the Chippendale sofa, Chad Weston's manuscript in a box on his lap. He had only read seventy-one pages, but he thought he'd read no more. Gerald looked down at the page before him.

> He took her severed arm and slowly, lovingly, sliced off each of her fingers. The blood had stopped flowing, but it was still a messy job. His Oyster Rolex was covered in blood—lucky it was waterproof.
>
> He took her arm, now reduced to a fingerless fist, and spread her legs wide, securing them to the sides of the radiator with more wire. He stepped over the pools of blood to keep his Cole Haan loafers clean. Then he took her arm and, using it as a dildo of her own dead flesh, he . . .

Gerald lay the manuscript down on the coffee table. He felt positively queasy—actually quite sick to his stomach. The book—*SchizoBoy*—wasn't just perverse. It was also bad *and* boring; not an easy trick. Weston had clearly lost his mind. No wonder there had been so much party buzz.

I should have read it earlier, Gerald thought. And why hadn't Pam told him how grotesque, how utterly vile . . . sometimes Gerald thought Pam might actually try to sabotage him. Other times he simply thought she was non compos mentis. She probably did like the book.

Gerald knew Chad Weston was a desperate man. He knew it because he himself felt the desperation of having each book he wrote diminish in importance and sales. It was a kind of dwindling, the sign of a writer's tapering potency. Gerald himself was using an old scandal to get back some of his verve. Chad had picked this one—this obscene, misogynistic hat trick. Its very perversity would get attention in the media. Gerald shook his head. My God, he had already defended this repulsive pile of excrement at publishing functions. If he hadn't been so busy on his own book, he'd have read this one. The publishing community would tear at him for this decision and despise him if he backed out.

What to do, what to do? His pride would not let him back down, but his taste was deeply offended. For a moment, he thought of the old joke that asked the different definitions between sexy and kinky. The answer was that sexy was when you made love using a feather; kinky was when you used the whole chicken. But this book of Weston's was way beyond kinky. Gerald added a definition to the joke: Perverse was when you did it to a *dead* chicken.

Disgusted, Gerald stood up and threw the pages onto the table. He walked over to the window and back, pacing off some of his nausea and anxiety. Time for some legal assistance.

Gerald went to the phone and dialed Jim Meyer's extension. He tapped his fingers impatiently as he waited for an answer, the words of a Warren Zevon song running through his mind: "Bring lawyers, guns, and money. The shit has hit the fan." Well, Gerald reflected, he had two out of three—if he could get his hands on Meyer.

At last the phone was answered. "Mr. Meyer's office."

"Is he in, Barbara?" Gerald snapped.

"Yes, but he's in a meeting and—"

"Get him *now,*" Gerald snapped. It didn't take more than a minute, and the second Jim got on the line, Gerald dispensed with the small talk. "Jim, we have trouble here.

The Weston manuscript is an obscenity. Where do we stand on it?"

"What do you mean?" Meyer asked in the calm, totally annoying way that lawyers did. "Do you mean, where do we stand in regard to the contractual obligation to the author, or in terms of our policy on pornography? Or do you feel the house will be jeopardized? My department vetted it, and I can assure you that—"

"Jim, spare me the blather. Do we have to publish this?"

There was a pause. "You mean you don't want to do the book at all?"

"That's right."

"Hold on. Let me take a look at his contract. Can I get right back to you?"

"*Right* back." Gerald strode up and down his enormous office. All writers—with the notable exception of Joan Collins—lived in fear of the acceptance clause. Payment wasn't made if the book was "unacceptable"; and it was up to the publisher to determine what that consisted of. It was a cudgel, a threat, a sword hanging. Gerald hoped he could use it now. When the phone rang he snatched it up before Mrs. Perkins could get to it. "Yes?" he snapped.

"We've accepted it, Gerald. There is an acceptance letter signed by Pam Mantiss and a memo indicating that the acceptance check was not only mailed but also received and cashed."

"So we have to publish it?"

"We don't have to. But we have already given him his acceptance check."

"Goddammit!" Pam had sought out Weston and had seduced him away from his first publisher with a lucrative three-book deal. Then she'd approved of the book. "Christ, how bad is the damage?"

"We're talking six hundred thousand dollars," Meyer told him.

Gerald winced. It was a big hit to take, and just at the end of the fiscal year. Gerald didn't want to do it. What would David Morton say if he knew? The board hated large advances and hated writing them off. What to do, what to do? How in the world had the book gone so far without him looking at it? Christ, he was overextended. There were publishers who had responsibilities as great as his, and there were authors who sold as well or better, but there were no publishers who were also authors, at least not in his league.

Yet he *had* to continue the writing. For both the money and the prestige. He simply had to. Not that David Morton liked that either. Nervously, with a little hunching motion of his narrow back, Gerald transferred the phone to the crook of his neck. God, he hated this Weston book. How could he, with any kind of conscience, allow the Davis & Dash imprimatur on a work as totally repellent and simultaneously as nugatory as this one? It was an abomination, and Gerald nearly blushed thinking of what his father would say when he saw the manuscript—as he inevitably would.

On the other hand, squandering the advance and acceptance money was unthinkable, and, to tell the truth, Gerald could not bear the thought of backing down and looking ridiculous in front of the tight little publishing community. He supposed it was better to look tasteless and mercenary than to look stupid.

Well, in one way this was a solution to his problems. The notoriety this book would receive would ensure sales, at least at first. And if those were enough to get it onto the bestseller list, the book would take on a life of its own. Readers today bought what they were told to; if it was on the list and discounted, they bought it.

The money the book would make would be his justification to David Morton, and to his father he'd merely say that he had to live up to his word, though his father would feel Gerald had turned Davis & Dash into a cloaca. Gerald still needed something to pick up the fall list. Maybe with this and the movie of Peet Trawley's first trilogy coming out he had the beginnings of a chance at squeaking by. Especially if he managed to stir up sales for his own book. He absolutely could not let David Morton and the stockholders know he had made such an egregious error on the Weston thing. He would publish the book and stand behind it.

"Gerald? Gerald, are you still there?" Jim Meyer asked.

"Certainly," Gerald answered.

# PART TWO

# *Lincoln's Doctor's Dog*

As difficult as it is for a writer to find a publisher—admittedly a daunting task—it is twice as difficult for a publisher to sort through the chaff, select the wheat, and profitably publish a worthy list.

—Gerald Ochs Davis, Sr.
*Fifty Years in Publishing*

# 16

The only good author is a dead author.
*—Patrick O'Connor*

"He's *dead*?" Pam Mantiss nearly yelled into the phone. "What do you mean, he's dead?"

"I think the traditional definition is meant here," Jim Meyer told her dryly. "Heart stoppage, lack of respiration, no measurable brain activity." Spoken as a true lawyer, Pam thought.

"How can he be dead? He owes us a manuscript in less than three months." Pam put her hand to her forehead. Peet Trawley dead. It was unimaginable. She'd been working with him for close to twenty years, and he'd been sick every day for all that time—or imagining he was. She'd just seen him. He'd looked awful, and said he couldn't get out of his chair, but he *always* looked awful, and Pam had long suspected that he used the wheelchair more as a prop than a necessity. It was protection for him, a kind of exoskeleton. And he needed the protection, what with a voracious ex-wife constantly after him for money, a voracious current wife always after him for money, and a less-than-winsome collection of children and stepchildren from both marriages, all voracious and always after him for money.

"Jesus Christ, Jim. He was the only sure thing I had for the fall list."

"Uh-huh. That and *Lincoln's Doctor's Dog*."

"Yeah, right." It was an old publishing joke: that books about Lincoln sold; that books about dogs sold; and that books about doctors sold. Therefore, a guaranteed bestseller would be *Lincoln's Doctor's Dog*. The joke, of course, was such a title that would clearly go nowhere. Well, there might be no sure things, Pam thought, but with Peet's track record and a movie coming out, his books were as close as it comes.

"How do you know he's dead?" she demanded. Publishing was rife with gossip. Maybe this was just bullshit. Jim Meyer was only corporate counsel, a lawyer, not a book person.

"His attorney, the one handling probate, called. Peet died on Wednesday."

"Probate already? My God, that was fast!" Well, knowing Edina, his wife, and the rest of Peet's family, they'd be squabbling over the will before Peet was cold.

"Too bad about your sure thing," Jim said, nastily.

Pam clutched at the receiver. God! Just because she didn't want to sleep with him again, he took it personally. As if Pam didn't know that there was no sure thing. And even though it sometimes drove her crazy, it gave her daily work the edginess she seemed to crave. Actually, when she thought about it, cravings were the major portion of her life: She'd craved booze in the seventies, then switched to sex and coke in the eighties, and had moved on to food in the nineties—until her weight gain and depression drove her to Prozac. No doubt about it, she thought ruefully, she was definitely a woman of her times.

She was also editor in chief at one of the most successful, yet still prestigious, publishing firms in New York—the world's capital for publishers. And being the *only* woman who had achieved that position at Davis & Dash, she, better than anyone, knew there were no sure things in publishing. Too bad she needed one so badly now.

She went to the small refrigerator concealed in a cabinet. In it were bottles and bottles of Snapple, carefully lined up in rows. Another obsession. No one was allowed to touch her precious Snapple, though occasionally she offered some to a visiting author. She counted the bottles now and took out a raspberry iced tea, popping the top and downing a swig, though it was early. Here's to you, Peet, she thought. And here's to me, too.

Pam had gotten where she was because of her enormous ability, her former willingness to work long hours, her scary, edgy talent at picking winners, and the ballsiness she had in backing up her selections. It also didn't hurt that she had what she thought of as a nice pair of tits, not to mention long legs. Those she had been willing to open for Gerald Ochs Davis when he had fallen between marriages—in the crack, as it were. Pam smiled at the vulgarity. She liked to be vulgar. And sexy. And edgy. But lately motherhood, Prozac, and Old Father Time were wearing off the edge. This news about Trawley might have, in the old days, given her a thrill of terror, an adrenaline high that would make the next steps fun. No more. She was tired. Holy shit, wasn't there one goddamn thing she could count on?

Well, she could count on the editorial meeting that she was already ten minutes late for to be both overlong and unproductive. She'd have to listen to all the little editor girls complain about the Chad Weston book and hear Lou Crinelli, one of her younger, more macho editors—and already bucking for her job—give a forty-minute summary of a manuscript that she could read in half the time. Pam sighed. By now all of the editors were sitting around the table waiting for her.

"Listen, I have to go over a contract," Jim said. "I just wanted you to know. Will you tell Gerald, or should I?"

Like he was the only one busy. Pam rolled her eyes. This was not good news to give GOD, especially along with the other news that his book's opening sucked. "I'll tell him," she said. Christ. She wasn't going to look forward to *that*.

Pam hung up her phone and moved to the window. Feets, get walking, she told herself, but she didn't move. She sipped the Snapple moodily. If they started the editorial meeting without her, they'd only have to begin again, because *she* made the decisions. It was raining: a gray, thin drizzle that made all of Manhattan look like a bad French film. Pam bit her lower lip. What would she do without the Trawley book? How could she replace it? What else could generate that wave of revenue?

She thought, bitter for a moment, about all the money she had made for Peet. Twenty-four books in sixteen languages that had sold over fifty million copies. There was still the backlist, but if she lost new revenues, she lost part of her power base. Pam felt the cold window with the tips of her fingers and shivered.

Good old Peet! Despite his hypochondria and constant complaining, he had pumped a book out every nine months, and he had a million fans who would buy it in hardcover and three times that number who would buy it in paperback. And Peet had been Pam's *own* discovery. In fact, it was because of Peet that Pam was where she was today.

Back in the Jurassic age, when Pam herself was a little editor girl, she used to take home manuscripts from the slush pile—publishing's name for the unsolicited books that came in over the transom. Nowadays, no one even bothered to read them. Even back then they were rarely worth the bother. But two decades ago Pam had believed—or at least hoped—that she could pluck the new Fitzgerald, or maybe the new Grace Paley, out of the endless pile of unknowns. After reading dozens, and then scores, and finally hundreds of pathetic, poorly plotted, badly typed, ineptly written submissions, Pam had realized it was an impossibility. It was like panning for gold in the sewer: all you wound up with was crap.

Until, just as she was about to give up, she hit upon Peet's Gothic tale. Set in a wind-battered New England coastal town, it was the story of a monstrous child, hidden from the town, growing up scorned and resented. It was unbelievably badly written—Peet believed strongly in the use of adverbs—but its energy was undeniable. Pam knew the book would need an incredible amount of work before it was close to publishable, but she was willing to do it. There was something primal about the book, and the resentments of the monster—which mirrored Peet's own—were deeply felt. After she'd cleaned the manuscript up and made it more presentable, she'd shown it to her boss and begged him to support her in the editorial conference. He'd refused, and—in desperation—she'd gone over his head. She'd lost, and it broke her heart when they rejected Peet.

Then she had the task of calling him, after she had prematurely written to him with good news. He had said it was the omega—the end of his attempts to be published. After all the rejections he'd received and the false hope that Pam had given him, he was giving up. It was only then that she found out that Peet was crippled. He'd been injured in a motorcycle accident and couldn't get out of his wheelchair. Today that kind of information would roll off Pam's battle-scarred back, but then it inspired her for one more effort. She succeeded, to a point. Hardcover wouldn't touch it, but she'd gotten the paperback division to put it out as a paperback original. Jubilant, Peet had insisted they put an omega on the cover art. It had become his symbol. Not an end, but a beginning.

But it was the end for Pam. When her boss found out, he fired her. However, a few months later the book went on to sell three and a half million copies in paper. There were a lot of teenagers out there who identified with the resentful, monstrous child. Peet became the nine-hundred-pound gorilla, and bless his heart, he wouldn't do another book without an omega somewhere on the cover, or without Pam as his editor.

Of course Pam was not only rehired, but treated with kid gloves. Peet's next book, once again totally rewritten by Pam, sold half a million hardcover copies and over four million in paper. Two more titles, plus a few other less enormous successes, and Pam got her own imprint, a big raise, and—eventually—her boss's job. She also attracted, for the first time, the attention of Gerald Ochs Davis.

Although public opinion sometimes held otherwise, Pam Mantiss knew that she didn't have her job because of her on-again, off-again sexual liaison with Gerald. She kept her job because she was tough and smart and because she delivered. She avoided the *Lincoln's Doctor's Dog* books and sought titles that moved off the shelf. She had a lot more hits than misses. After all, there were a lot of little editor girls who had slept with Gerald Ochs Davis. But there were very few little editor girls who wound up as editor in chief of a publishing house. Only Pam and a very few others had managed that.

But times were changing. The book business was tougher than ever. Pam remembered the good old days—only a decade ago—when sales of eighty thousand made a book a bestseller. Now it took three or four hundred thousand. The book market was bigger than ever, but the majority of book buyers were looking for only a few kinds of books. To make things worse, there were barbarians at the gate. The conglomerate that owned Davis & Dash looked at it as only another profit center. There had to be profits, and they had to get bigger every year. The pressure made her head hurt. Pam had a nine-year-old son to support. After she dumped Julio, her ex-husband, he'd headed down to Miami, or maybe the West Coast. Anyway, wherever he was playing bad saxophone and dealing good drugs, he wasn't paying any child support. She was always short of money.

Pam lived with an ongoing resentment that came from knowing that while she was smarter and more literate than most of her successful authors, they outearned her twenty or thirty to one. She negotiated the contracts, so she knew. Somehow it didn't seem fair. Peet Trawley was a prime example. He had been neither bright nor particularly talented. There had been a spark of something, and he had—with enormous help from her—prospered from it. While she, meanwhile, could barely pay Christophe's private-school bills and the ever-increasing co-op maintenance.

She gathered up her stuff for the editorial meeting: notes, pad, cigarettes. (She'd promised Christophe that she'd quit, but there was no way she could get through an editorial meeting without even looking at smokes.) As she was about to leave the office a thought occurred to her: Maybe Peet had recognized her in his will. He had often told her how grateful to her he was, when he wasn't busy cursing her for the revisions and endless rewrites she forced on him. Peet had never been one for gifts, but he had said things like, "I'll never forget you." And "You'll always be taken care of because of what you've done for me."

Didn't that mean that he was leaving her something? The realization burst upon Pam like a sunrise. What would a million dollars be to Peet Trawley, especially after he was dead? Never generous in life, he would make up for it now, as he'd always intimated he would. Perhaps that was why the estate lawyers had called Jim Meyer and why Jim had called her, but typically lawyerlike, he had been too discreet to say anything.

Pam's legs weakened, and she sank into her chair. Yes! Absolutely. Peet Trawley's death could very well make her a wealthy woman, or at least more comfortable. She could pay off her co-op mortgage. It would mean one less hefty payment a month. Christophe's overdue school bills. Summer camp. A fur coat. Maybe one important piece of jewelry—something to remember Peet by. Pam smiled. As her grandmother used to say, there was no cloud that didn't have a silver lining. Actually, she would just as soon have this lining platinum.

# 17

> One of the signs of Napoleon's greatness is the fact that he once had a publisher shot.
>
> —*Siegfried Unseld*

Opal sat neatly, her knees tightly together, her left ankle tucked under her right. She always had good posture and had frequently reminded Terry to stand up straight. Of course, Opal couldn't stand there in the ninth-floor reception area at Simon & Schuster. She had to sit on one of the curving banquettes that snaked along one wall. There was no back to them, only the back wall—which was also used to display the current successful books on the S&S list—so Opal had to sit completely unsupported, with her back erect and her hands neatly folded on top of Terry's massive manuscript. Opal had her brown leatherette shoulder bag tucked beside her, and she tried to make as neat a figure as possible.

She had dressed carefully—black polyester twill pants, a plain blue blouse, and her lavender raincoat. She had been especially careful not to carry anything except her purse and the manuscript, and that not even in a bag. It was difficult to manage, because the manuscript was such a bulky pile, and without a sack, Opal was afraid it might slip from her hands. She had it wrapped up in six large rubber bands—two stretched across the manuscript and four crisscrossed lengthwise. It was awkward and tiring to walk with the heavy burden, but when she stood on the subway or the bus, Opal held the manuscript to her like a baby. When she got a seat she put it carefully on her lap the way she did now.

The black woman at the reception desk seemed oblivious

to her. That, she supposed, was better than the day before—when Opal had been ejected from the lobby of Crown Publishers after trying for almost two hours to get upstairs. Opal had tried other means to get the manuscript read, but so had Terry, and they simply didn't work. Opal had decided that any means necessary was justified in getting Terry's manuscript published.

With the miraculous resurrection of Terry's manuscript, Opal had found a purpose. Although New York was an unknown maze to her, and publishing an even more frustrating, secretive world-within-worlds, Opal had not been a librarian for twenty-seven years without learning how to research. What she learned was not reassuring, nor did it give her any reason for hope, but hope had nothing to do with this mission. Opal would see this project through to the bitter end.

Luckily, alternative approaches were possible. Security guards were usually surprisingly lax at elevator banks when a little old lady, dressed neatly, smiled and told them she had an appointment with a name they knew upstairs. It was only once Opal got herself into the reception area that the trouble began. Since she didn't really have an appointment with Ann Patty of Crown, Arlene Friedman of Doubleday, Faith Sale at Putnam, or Sharon DeLano at Random House, when Opal got to the reception area she tried a few different techniques. Occasionally she insisted that a mistake had been made. Sometimes she admitted she had no appointment; she said that she was somebody's mother and she'd just wait. Because of her age and her innocent look the girls at the desk occasionally only raised their eyebrows or shrugged and let her sit there. But most had told her waiting was impossible—she couldn't see the editor without an appointment, and no, she couldn't even wait. So now Opal pretended she had an appointment and that she was deaf or stupid when they told her she didn't. It was humiliating, but time had given her this gift: Years ago she would have been far too shy and embarrassed to pull any of these routines.

Opal surprised herself with an amazing lack of concern about appearances anymore. Perhaps it was just age, or her pain. Maybe it was wisdom. She knew that being polite, that doing things the right way, following all the rules, hadn't helped Terry at all. And Opal no longer cared about herself. So, when one or another of the receptionists had called security and had her ejected, Opal hadn't been the slightest bit embarrassed. She had simply consulted her list and gone on to the next publishing house.

Many of the publishers were on multiple floors in one tower. The towers seemed to be clustered along Sixth Avenue, Broadway, and Third Avenue. Opal used the rejection letters as a start, though she didn't try any of the same names. Instead she went publisher by publisher, building by building, floor by floor. She made daily phone calls and went to the library to research every editorial name she could. Sometimes she would happen on a chatty receptionist who would tell her the names of the editors on that floor. Opal surreptitiously wrote them down for future reference and sat waiting for *any* of them to walk in or out. But the depressing fact was that once she had cornered one, she was almost invariably told that "we don't read unsolicited manuscripts" and was asked to leave. The chatty receptionist would look at her, stricken and betrayed. Each time that happened Opal had left, only because she didn't want to jeopardize the receptionist's job. But each time she vowed to herself that she would be back.

Today, on the ninth floor of Simon & Schuster, the receptionist had let her sit for a long time simply because she hadn't been able to get through to Michael Korda's extension. Opal had picked his name because he was editor in chief and most likely to have an engaged phone. That had worked, temporarily, at a couple of places. Now, it seemed, the woman had forgotten all about Opal. She was too busy on a long personal phone call with someone named Creon—or something like that—who didn't seem to want to meet her later that night. So when a tall, good-looking, middle-aged man walked through the double glass doors and interrupted the phone call to inquire if a package had been delivered, Opal heard the black woman tell him, "No, Mr. Adams, nothing's come for you." Opal jumped up and walked across the carpet to him.

"Mr. Adams?" she asked. "Could I speak to you a moment?"

The man looked at her, his face pleasant and open.

"You are Charles—Chuck—Adams, the senior editor, aren't you?" Opal asked. Her research had paid off. He nodded and smiled.

"Well, I have a book here—I mean, a manuscript—that I would like you to read." The smile faded from the tall man's face, but Opal continued. "Don't worry," she tried to reassure him. "It isn't mine." Opal had learned already that it was certain death to say you had a book of your own you wanted read. "I'm sort of the agent for it," she explained. Mr. Adams nodded. "My daughter wrote it." A mistake. The man's face stiffened. Darn it! She shouldn't have mentioned that Terry was a relative. Opal could see the indulgence on the man's face. He wasn't unkind; he seemed truly pained at their encounter.

"I'm sorry. We have a policy of not accepting unsolicited manuscripts."

"How can a person get a book published if nobody will read it?" Opal snapped. But the man had already turned his back and walked toward the doors leading to the inner sanctum where, she thought bitterly, he would be safe from little old ladies with manuscripts.

Well, Opal shrugged, he couldn't be expected to buck corporate policy. Or to believe that her attempted submission was different from the rest. At least he had not thrown her out or called security. It could have been worse. Opal took her seat again. But now the receptionist had—finally—noticed her and was getting off the phone.

"You don't have an appointment with Mr. Korda," she said, sounding indignant. "You don't have an appointment listed at all."

Opal opened her eyes as wide as she could but kept her seat on the banquette. "Well, I'm *certain* it was for today," she said. "Why don't you call back and see if they could fit me in for just five minutes? I did come all the way from Bloomington, Indiana."

The woman narrowed her eyes, trying to size Opal up. But Opal simply sat there, as calmly as she could, the heavy manuscript cutting off the circulation in her legs from her knees down. "I'll wait," she said brightly, and—after another minute of eye contact—the woman shrugged. "I'll just wait," Opal said again, more softly. And she would. She would wait for as long as it took.

# 18

> You ask for the distinction between the terms "Editor" and "Publisher": an editor selects manuscripts; a publisher selects editors.
>
> —*Max Schuster*

Emma Ashton sat behind her desk, which was completely stacked with manuscripts, galleys, memos, and the paper detritus that threatened to engulf her. She was as busy as a bad outfit, answering Pam's correspondence as well as her own. She picked up the letter on the top of the stack.

Dear Ms. Mantiss,
I am genuinely shocked that something as fickle as personal taste—which Duchamp about seventy-five years ago suggested the intelligent person put in a cupboard when viewing any work of art in case of infantile prejudice—can dictate something as important as publication. I am surprised and saddened that people in a position of relative power can have such limited perceptions. Can you suggest another publisher whose "personal taste" my *Cunning Beautiful Bitch* may suit? It's a novel that deserves an audience. Thank you.

Emma almost laughed. She'd have to answer this bitter, disappointed woman who had written to Pam. But what was the point? Emma sighed. The woman was a nut case, as well as a truly terrible writer. She believed that "personal taste" shouldn't affect an editor's choice of what to publish. What, then, should? It still amazed Emma that so many people attempted to write books with so little encouragement and so little talent. She used to agonize over these, but now she'd just send out another terse letter.

Emma had piles of other letters, papers, cover art, reader's copies, and actual books all over the edges of the carpet and on the shelves of three walls. Why had she ever thought that editorial work would be elegant and romantic? She had to smile.

Actually, Emma remembered why. When she was nine years old an important speaker had come to Larchmont Grammar. All of Emma's third-grade class had assembled in the library and been addressed by An Author. She was a large woman with a huge head of gray hair, and she talked about Her Life As a Writer; what it was like to put together the mystery novels she was famous for. But for some reason, the nine-year-old Emma had not been taken by the idea of writing books, even though she loved to read. She merely listened politely, interested but not inspired. It was only when one of her classmates raised her hand and asked what happened to a manuscript after the writer was finished with it that Emma perked up. "Well," the lady explained, "I send it in to my editor, a woman who sits in a big office in a tall skyscraper in New York City. She is paid a great deal of money to read my book, and then she tells me whatever way I have to fix it. I *do* fix it, and then the book gets printed and bound and sent out to bookstores."

Emma was suddenly transfixed with the image, not of the writer before her, but of the mysterious editor sitting "in a big office in a tall skyscraper in New York City." Emma had been to New York many times with her parents and her older brother, Frederick, and it seemed the center of all things. Imagine having a big office of your very own there and spending all day reading books. She was good at that. To Emma it sounded like the most divine thing in the world. To be *paid* to read books! To have an office in a *skyscraper*! From that moment, Emma knew exactly what she wanted to be.

And now that she was an editor there were three great ironies to swallow. The first was that she was paid very little, the second was that her office—virtually *all* offices in publishing—was laughably small, and the last was that she rarely had any time at work to read. Her days were taken up with list meetings, editorial meetings, rare lunches with authors, cover-art meetings, marketing meetings, and more phone calls than she liked to remember. The workload was crushing.

During her first year at Davis & Dash she had come in to the office to work on both Saturday and Sunday. In fact, that was when she got most of her editorial work done. During the week the noise, the phone calls, the meetings and distractions couldn't let you sink into the reading. Back then—just five years ago as an editorial assistant—she had only a desk in a cubicle along a row of other cubicles in a long hallway. But after a year or so, coming into the office every day of the week and working at the same windowless, exposed place had become too depressing. Now Emma differentiated her days not by taking the weekends off, but by spending them working at home.

At first that, too, had been hard. When she'd come to New York she'd shared a one-bedroom apartment with two other girls from college, and her space was only a corner of the living room. One of her roommates was fussy. The living room had to be kept straight. Laying out a manuscript and having to clean it up at the end of each work session was time-consuming, unproductive, and frustrating. As soon as she got a raise, Emma had moved out.

It was all for the best. She hadn't felt comfortable living with the two roommates anyway. It caused embarrassment. She buried herself in work and never had dates, and they seemed to want to know why. Living alone was easier. There were no questions, and she had all the space for her work that she needed. But sometimes she was lonely.

I should be grateful that I have my own place now, been promoted to editor, and have my own office here, Emma told herself. And usually she was. Her studio in the Village was large and sunny—even if it was still mostly unfurnished. But she had decided not to accept help from her mother, and she was making it on her own, with the little extra help from the trust fund her father had left her. She was managing, she reminded herself. A kid from the slacker generation making a pittance but making good.

At that moment the phone rang, and Emma couldn't help but wince. She paused and hoped that Heather, the assistant she shared with two other editors, would be at her desk and take the call. But it was unlikely. Emma listened to the second ring. She could simply not pick up, but then there would be another call for her to return when she laboriously copied down her voice mail. So, at the third ring, she picked up the phone.

"Emma Ashton? Is that you?" the querulous voice of Anna Morrison greeted Emma. Emma sighed but made sure that Anna wouldn't hear it. Not that Anna heard much: She was quite deaf, and Emma had to shout her end of their conversations.

"Emma Ashton? Is that you?" Mrs. Morrison asked again at the top of her voice. Emma assured Anna that indeed it was she. "So glad I got you. I'm quite excited, really. I was thinking about a new edition of *Green Days, Black Nights.*"

The woman was really quite dotty, but Emma knew that she wasn't so crazy as to think her old book would ever sell again. She just wanted to talk to someone.

Anna Morrison had once been a bestselling author. That wasn't in Emma's time, or in Pam Mantiss's time, or even in Gerald Ochs Davis's time. Anna Morrison was a kind of editorial mastodon, a throwback to the days of Frank Yerby and *Foxes of Harrow.* All of her books were out of print, available only in musty library stacks. And the last was probably borrowed back in 1954, no doubt. The trouble was that, unlike other relics, Anna Morrison didn't *know* she was dead. For years after she'd gone out of print she had hounded Mr. Davis, who eventually handed her off to Pam Mantiss, who, pitilessly, handed her off to Emma. Every house had these ghosts. Poor Emma wasn't heartless enough to ignore hers. She knew the old woman's problem: loneliness. And Emma wasn't mean enough to simply hang up on the old woman the way Pam used to. Instead, Emma settled more comfortably in her chair and gathered her energy so that she could shout responses to the poor old woman's questions.

They went on interminably, it seemed. At last she was done—at least finished talking about business. But Mrs. Morrison wanted contact—personal contact. "And you, Emma? How are you? Are you all work and no play? Is there a nice young man in your social life?"

Emma almost snorted at the question. She had no social life. Although last night, she had actually gone to The Gray Rabbit, and despite her habitual shyness and withdrawal she had actually met someone: Alex. She wouldn't want to shock old Anna Morrison by telling her that she had given Alex her phone number in a bar the night before. Well, she probably would never hear from Alex again.

"Nothing to report, Mrs. Morrison," she said as cheerfully as she could. She couldn't restrain a sigh. Why did people bother to take your number and then never call you? Emma shared a little spicy gossip about Chad Weston's new book and then managed to get rid of Anna Morrison at last. She looked at the work in front of her. Carefully, methodically, she began her sorting, watching as her "to do" list grew to three pages.

Without a knock, the door flew open and Pam Mantiss stuck her head in. "The motherfucker died on me," Pam said. "Now what the fuck am I going to do?"

"What?" Emma asked.

"Peet Trawley. The prick died. You know what his lawyer just told me? He said Peet has arranged his own tombstone. And you know what it's going to say?" Emma shook her head.

"'I told you I was sick.'" Pam laughed maniacally, took a swig from her Snapple bottle, and threw a stack of papers onto Emma's desk. "I'd like to chisel a fucking omega on it. The End. I don't know what the fuck I'm doing," Pam admitted, throwing herself into Emma's spare chair. "I just can't believe this has happened to me. Go through this shit and put together the sales report. I can't do it. Goddammit! I can't believe the motherfucker died on me." Pam finished the Snapple, threw the bottle at Emma's wastebasket, got up, and walked out of the room.

Emma looked at the shelf of Peet Trawley's oeuvre. All of them had the omega symbol, which she and the other editors cattily referred to as "the ancient Greek symbol for dreck." Peet was dead. Pam was shaken. Emma was merely thirsty. She wished she had some Snapple, but Pam never shared.

Now she'd have to review the sales report. It was hours of work. She picked up the rumpled sheaf of papers dumped in front of her and wondered how she'd find the time to add one more thing to her "to do" list.

# 19

> Often while reading a book one feels that the author would have preferred to paint rather than write; one can sense the pleasure he derives from describing a landscape or a person, as if he were painting what he is saying, because deep in his heart he would have preferred to use brushes and colors.
>
> —*Pablo Picasso*

Camilla and Frederick arrived in Assisi at twilight, and the driver expertly maneuvered the narrow street that led first up the hill to the apex and then down through a gate, passed the church of Saint Francis, and wound around to the venerable Hotel Subiaso. It was the only hotel perched beside the huge basilica. The suite had a terrace large enough to host a small drinks party on, and Camilla couldn't help but be drawn through the French doors. There was a spectacular view of the Umbrian plain seven hundred feet below. Despite her horrid nervousness, her concern about the sleeping arrangements and the lot, she couldn't help but be seduced by the scene, if not by Frederick himself.

"It's wonderful," she said reverently. He joined her and nodded. "It's like the landscape behind a Leonardo painting."

"You have a good eye."

"I would have been a painter if I had the talent," Camilla told him.

"And I'd have been a painter if *I* had the talent." She looked at him, surprised. Then she was lured back to the view. "Do you like it?" he asked.

"I like everything. Especially you." Then she was

embarrassed by her warmth. "With the exception of your sadly misguided preference for Guardi over Canaletto."

"Hah!" He put his hand up and examined her hair. "You're showing your bourgeois roots, my girl."

She jumped involuntarily, then stared back out at the view, not knowing what to feel. She felt exposed somehow. Her roots were not bourgeois at all—they were far lower than that. What did his little joke mean? Below them lights were beginning to twinkle. "It's wonderful," she said. "I've never stayed in Assisi overnight, and I'm sure you don't get this view from anywhere except the hotel."

"That's nothing," Frederick said. "Take a look at this." Gently he took her arm and turned her to the right. There, abutting the side of the hill, the church of Saint Francis extended itself to the very end of the peak, illuminated and as nobly beautiful as the prow of a ship. Camilla actually gasped. Although she had seen the basilica by night, lit at the entrance, the massive stone portals viewed from the piazza didn't reveal even a tenth of the structure.

"Amazing, isn't it?" Frederick said. "And they built it in three years."

The building was astonishing. It was, essentially, a full church built upon a full church. Although there was no dome, the double height of the two floors combined, built into and rising out of the hill of Assisi itself, made the whole deeply impressive. The rows of riblike flying buttresses were like the exposed bones of a fossil along the escarpment of the Assisi cliff. It was a breathtaking sight, and it brought Camilla great joy—the kind of joy that cannot be planned for or sought but that comes serendipitously. Suddenly she was flooded with it, nearly drunk with it, and it must have showed.

Camilla wished she could talk about it, could thank him and tell him how much the sight meant to her. But she wasn't good with words—not unless she wrote them down. She hadn't even been able to broach the subject of his intentions—whether Frederick expected her to sleep with him. She hated being so tongue-tied.

Maybe Frederick understood. "I'll leave you here," he said. "My room is next door." Before she could say anything, he withdrew. She felt a momentary stab of guilt: It had so far been so easy. No embarrassing fumblings, no need for gentle explanations or—far worse—awkward struggles and recriminations. She was, apparently, free. No strings attached. Free to take in this beauty without having to bonk him. She had misjudged Frederick.

Tonight she felt herself among the privileged. On other day visits she had looked up and seen people on the many terraces and balconies of the Subiaso. She had known that it was not, as her mother surely would have put it, "for the likes of us." But now it *was* for her. She smiled in the dark. Looking out at the view was like owning a wonderful painting. She tried to memorize the sight, so that she could recall it at will.

Just then a shutter door opened and, on a much smaller balcony, Frederick appeared. He waved. "Do you think you might consider relinquishing the view if I tempted you with dinner on the terrace below?" He gestured, and though she couldn't see his hand in the increasing darkness, his white shirt cuff gleamed. She looked down. Two or three stories below was a vast piazza. She hadn't noticed it because it was completely roofed with green leaves. Just below the verdant canopy she could glimpse the diners who were beginning to take their tables. "I have a reservation. I wanted to be sure we had a seat by the railing," he told her. His head was cocked in that funny way of his—birdlike and pushed almost down to one shoulder. "Do you think you could stop drinking all this in and start eating instead?" His white teeth flashed in the darkness. She nodded, then realized he wouldn't be able to see her gesture.

"Yes," she called to him. "I'm starving. But aren't you knackered?"

"What? Knackered? Sounds like something done to a horse." She heard him laugh, and she blushed.

She always said the wrong thing. She probably sounded like a yob. "Tired," she said, flustered. "I meant tired. Anyway, knock on my door when you're ready. I'll go down on you." She realized then what she'd said and blushed furiously. "Go down *with* you," she corrected.

"Well, I think I prefer the former, but I'll do the latter," Frederick laughed.

Perfect. He was genteel, and I throw in the smut! What a balls-up. Camilla wondered about Frederick again. He was certainly attentive, but so were so many homosexual men. And why else would he be traveling with his mother? But perhaps he was *not* gay. Nervously Camilla went back inside and only then realized the room was actually a small suite. The parlor was furnished in old but tasteless Italian furniture of the if-its-gilded-or-painted-it-must-be-*bellisimo* school. A small door led to the minuscule bedroom. There was only enough space there for a large bed painted with garlands of peonies and a huge matching wardrobe. But there were shutters that opened to a small balcony, similar to the one Frederick had stood on. Camilla looked from the balcony to the bed and realized that she could sleep tonight with the shutters open and wake up to a view unsurpassed in all of Umbria. She smiled, then forced herself to get down to business, washing up and dressing. She was just finishing up when she heard Frederick's tap at the door. Grabbing a jumper to throw over her shoulders, she joined him in the hallway.

Camilla was charmed by the dining room—if a veranda covered with vines could be classified as a room. Once again, as in San Gimignano, she and Frederick were led to the best table, in the corner where the two railings met. The leafy roof rustled, and Camilla put the jumper around her shoulders.

"Cold?" Frederick asked. "Shall I give you my jacket?"

"No," she told him, "it's perfect."

And it was. The meal was perfect, the view was perfect, and the wine was perfect. Despite her awkwardness, they talked about Saint Francis and Saint Claire and planned how they would spend the day tomorrow. The dining room buzzed pleasantly with the talk of couples and families enjoying themselves.

At last, when Frederick ordered an espresso, Camilla shook her head. It was too late in the evening for her to drink coffee, and she had never really grown to like it despite her years in America and Italy. She was a PG Tips girl, though in New York she'd gotten used to instant coffee. She'd never admit that was all she drank.

"I tell you what," he suggested. "Why don't we have dessert and my espresso on your veranda?" He turned to the waiter, who immediately nodded.

Oh no, Camilla thought. Now all of the messiness would begin. She should have known. She had no one to blame but herself. She got up, reluctantly, as Frederick held her chair. He took her arm just above the elbow, and they walked across the dining room. "They have a miraculous fruit sorbet that they serve in a hollowed-out frozen peach," Frederick murmured. "I've ordered you one."

Camilla nodded stiffly. Frederick walked very slowly, almost holding her back, his head cocked to the side in his habitual way. They entered the lift, and when they reached their floor, she led Frederick to her room. She fiddled with the big, ancient key but couldn't get the door to open. Her hands were shaking. Gently, Frederick took the key from her and deftly placed it in the keyhole, opening the door. This was it, then, she thought, her heart sinking. They walked through the salon and out onto the balcony. A waiter followed them, threw a white cloth over the table, and wiped down the two painted chairs. They both took seats while he served the espresso to Frederick and placed the peach before Camilla with a flourish. It looked like nothing so much as a Chinese baby's face, the top cut off and replaced as a little cap. Despite her anxiety, Camilla had to smile. And it was delicious. Somehow the frozen crystals tasted even more peachlike than the best peaches she had ever had. She took the long spoon and silently offered some to Frederick, but he didn't see her gesture or else ignored it. Perhaps he didn't care for sweets. Or he was waiting for dessert of another kind. He had finished his espresso and now leaned forward. "Camilla, I would like to ask you to do something with me. I know it's a lot to ask. It involves a lot of trust, but I think you can trust me."

Oh God, she thought. Here it comes. This was what happened when one wasn't good at talking. She decided it was best to take control herself. "You want to sleep with me," she said, her voice flat.

Frederick leaned back. He was silent for a long moment. "That's a very kind offer, and I'm sure it would be much more than pleasant, but I wasn't actually thinking about that." He paused, and Camilla tried to get over her monumental embarrassment. "I was talking about something more intimate." Frederick said. "I hoped you would read me your manuscript."

They had moved into the salon for the light. Frederick was lying on the uncomfortable-looking sofa, propped up by an even more uncomfortable-looking bolster. Camilla sat across from him on the small chair beside the lamp table. She had her manuscript on her lap—she carried it with her all the time since she'd finished it. Frederick had called for a bottle of Pellegrino, and Camilla stopped now, at the end of the chapter, and took a sip. She was afraid to look at him. She was still far too embarrassed. And she was also far too excited. She had never shown the manuscript to anybody, and she had certainly never read it out loud. Hearing it made a lot of difference. She saw awkward phrases and some redundancies. But on the whole she thought it came across, and she had been thrilled when he laughed at the funny bits. She'd even dared to glance across at him from under her lashes as she read the scene introducing Mrs. Florence Mallabar. She couldn't be sure, but his face looked pained.

She finished the fizzy water and put the glass down. They were both silent for a moment. "Are you tired?" he asked.

She shook her head, but she didn't want to bore him. "I'll stop," she assured him. "It isn't very good, is it?" The eleventh commandment in Britain was "Thou shalt not blow thine own trumpet." She still adhered to it.

Frederick threw his legs over the side of the sofa and sat up. "Camilla," he said, "it's wonderful. It's a really wonderful story. Your descriptions . . . well, they're brilliant. I see everything that you write about." He paused. "But that's not it. That's not even important. It's the characters. Those women are so alive. I know them. My mother is friends with them. They're funny. And brave." He paused. Camilla's heart beat so loudly she was sure he could hear it too. "You have so much insight, and so much compassion for them, Camilla. You're really, really good."

She sat still, utterly still, for a long moment and then put her face in her hands. She began to cry, silently at first, but she couldn't help making some sound. She wept because she believed him. This book that she had started, purely out of loneliness and desperation, that she had worked on with discipline, and then with all of her concentration and all of her love, really *was* worth something. It had taken on a life of its own. It wasn't just because Frederick said so. His words had unlocked the knowledge in her own heart. She looked across the room at him.

"Thank you," she said.

# 20

> That's very nice if they want to publish you, but don't pay too much attention to it. It will toss you away. Just continue to write.
>
> —*Natalie Goldberg*

Judith lay on their bed. Her feet were cold, but it seemed too much trouble to untangle the blanket and cover herself. She had no energy. With great effort, she turned her head to the right so that she could see the electric clock on the night table. It was eleven twenty-five already. Time in the dusty little apartment had a very strange way of going unbearably slowly and then telescoping, so that now, somehow, it was almost time for Daniel's return.

She had managed to lie here for almost five hours, disturbed only by her own thoughts. The phone hadn't rung. Since the break with her family, she never heard from them—except for the letter that her mother sent her every month. And she had no real college friends. When she married Daniel, she had had to drop her two college roommates—they'd seemed so young, and Daniel hadn't liked them. Since then Judith hadn't replaced Stephanie and Jessica with any of the cold faculty wives or professors. They certainly disapproved of her. Anyway, she had to spend hours alone on the book, so it seemed as if the writing life didn't make it easy to make friends or to keep them.

While she was writing, Judith had been holed up in her little office room all day without the time to think of herself as lonely. At night she'd been tired, and then she had Daniel's company. Only now that the writing was finished had she realized how alone she was without the book to keep her company. The days stretched endless and empty before her, a burden rather than a gift. She imagined this was a little bit like postpartum depression. But then didn't your obstetrician give you pills? Wasn't there some young mother who told you she'd had this too and what to do about it? Judith felt as if she had given birth to Elthea and the other characters of *In Full Knowledge,* but there had been no celebration afterward. There was no pink little baby to delight in. Instead, all the labor and pain had yielded nothing but a dead manuscript that Daniel had taken away and that no one seemed to be celebrating.

Judith sighed and turned over. She had meant to get up early this morning and begin to clean the apartment. She had planned to start in the bathroom, but when she had awakened at half past six it was still dark out. Once she did force herself up and had walked across the cold, splintery wooden floor and smelled the mildew in the bathroom, Judith had felt so overwhelmed with despair that she had simply crawled back into bed. There was so much that needed to be cleaned—the windows were coated with dirt, the floors had dustballs and dog hair on them, the windowsills were gritty. Even the sheet she was lying on needed to be changed. Judith rolled over and opened her eyes. The pillowcase under her cheek had old mascara marks and an irregular stain the shape of Australia where she had drooled during the night.

Somehow it seemed the more she rested, the more tired she was, but Judith couldn't manage to just tell herself to snap out of it. Anyway, what was the point? If she washed the windows, a cold and messy all-day job, they'd only be coated with grime in a day or two. And the bathroom! She could scrub the grout with a toothbrush, and the stains still would reappear. The worn linoleum of the floor didn't get really clean no matter how much scrubbing she did, and anyway, once Daniel peed and missed the bowl it would just need scrubbing again.

Still, despite her overwhelming fatigue, Judith hadn't

meant to be lying in bed in a dirty nightgown until lunchtime. How had the morning gone by? What was wrong with her? She was frightened, but she didn't know who to talk to. She felt too guilty to tell Daniel, and anyway he was so wrapped up with his classes and his workshop and his phone calls to agents that he seemed almost unaware of her. Perhaps if they marked the occasion or if he had seemed more excited about the completion of the book . . . perhaps if there had been some good news about it . . . But Daniel had told her it was far too early to hear anything. When she had handed *In Full Knowledge* over to him, Daniel had simply put it in his new briefcase and said that he would read it and think about "a submission plan." And that had been that.

Judith looked over at the clock: 11:31. Daniel would be home in ten or fifteen minutes. She couldn't let him see her like this. In a panic, she stood up, dizziness hitting her as she did so. She dragged herself into the bathroom, peed, and realized she didn't have the time or the energy to shower. She couldn't think about what to wear. She would pull on her jeans and her sweater from yesterday. She didn't have the wherewithal to plan another outfit. She went to the sink and washed her face quickly, not bothering to use the facecloth but merely splashing the water on with her hands. She brushed her brown hair back and put an elastic band around it. It was too greasy to let it hang down any other way.

She walked back to the bedroom. She didn't have time to make the bed now, not if she wanted to have some lunch waiting for Daniel. The apartment was very quiet. Where was Flaubert? Usually he slept with her at the foot of the bed. Now even her dog was avoiding her. Judith walked out of the bedroom and closed the door on the chaos. She would hope that Daniel didn't open it and her sins could go undiscovered. She promised herself that she'd clean it up this afternoon, before he came back. In the kitchen, and another wave of despair hit her. The bread was out, and the skillet still bore the remains of eggs from Daniel's breakfast. The sink was filled with the dishes and pots from the dinner of two nights ago, while the pizza box and the paper plates and forks from yesterday's take-out meal still littered the small table.

Judith looked at the kitchen clock. Ten minutes! Quickly, she gathered up the garbage, but as she tried to fold the pizza box and throw the rest of the trash into the can under the sink, she realized it was already full to overflowing. And then she found there were no more garbage bags. She'd forgotten to get more.

Judith went into her office and found an empty carton under the card table. She hadn't been in her office in over two weeks—not since she'd finished the book. She looked around for a moment. Though those days had been hard and isolated, they now seemed a golden time compared to this emptiness. She sighed and picked up the box. Then she noticed the dog. Flaubert was lying in the farthest corner, his soft brown eyes sadly watching her, his muzzle pressed into the floor beside his two front paws. "What are *you* doing here?" she asked. No wonder she had forgotten him. Did Flaubert hate her, too? He'd gone to the corner of the apartment farthest away from her and the bed.

My God, she thought, when was the last time he was walked? No wonder he hated her. Pity for the helpless dog overwhelmed Judith. Had Daniel walked him this morning? She didn't think so. "Come on, Flo," she coaxed. But the dog only looked away. What was wrong with him? Was he sick? She approached him and scratched behind his ears, right in the place he liked, but she didn't get the usual responsive thump of his tail. Well, she didn't have time to think about it now. She'd fill the carton with trash, put the dog on his leash, run him downstairs for a quick pit stop, and then rush back upstairs to make something for lunch. It would have to be grilled cheese on stale bread, but at least it was better than nothing. Daniel would know she'd tried.

She was dressed and the kitchen would be reasonably neat; these were improvements over Daniel's return yesterday. She wondered why she could only mobilize herself to do things for the dog or her husband, not herself. But she didn't have time to think about it now. She filled the carton with the kitchen garbage, called the reluctant Flaubert, and hooked the leash to his collar. Then, balancing the odorous carton in one hand and holding the leash in the other, she walked through the kitchen and into the dark hallway to the door. Her foot descended on something soft, and she nearly slipped. She had to put down the carton and fumble for the lightswitch. She looked down. "Oh, Flaubert!" The dog's ears went down, and he turned away in shame and trotted back through the kitchen to the cold little office. Daniel *hadn't* walked him. Judith looked down at her messed shoe. She had been lying in bed all morning while the dog had been suffering. Tears sprang to her eyes. From the day they had gotten him from the pound until this morning, Flaubert had never had an accident in the house. This wasn't the dog's fault; it was hers. He had obviously tried to get himself out. She could see that by the scratch marks on the door. The disgusting smell wafted up to her. Nauseated, she lifted her right foot and removed her sneaker, trying not to touch the dog shit.

It was then that Daniel opened the front door and stepped into the hallway.

# 21

Almost anyone can be an author; the business is to collect money and fame from this state of being.
—*A. A. Milne*

Well, he had finally finished. Gerald looked at the screen and the last words of the last chapter of his new book. He'd written it, and now he'd revised it, and he had only two wishes left: one, that it sold a million copies—hardcover—and two, that he never had to see the benighted, leprous, disgusting, and disappointing thing again. One fact that Gerald had learned in his writing career: It was just as hard to write a bad book as a good one. He had undoubtedly worked hard, but he was smart enough to know the book was bad.

The good news was that bad books sold just as well, *better*, than good ones. But was this one of the bad ones that would sell, or was it so bad that it would embarrass him?

Somehow, revealing the awful secrets of his aunt and uncle, adding imagined conversations, sexual liaisons, gossip, and scandal, didn't shame him in the least. After all, Joe McGinniss imagined and published what Rose Kennedy said when Ted told her of Robert's assassination. That took balls—fucking with history and national tragedy. Gerald was only retailing a small family scandal. Everyone did it. Why, Caroline and John Kennedy, Jr., had even auctioned off their mother's household trifles for a few dollars. It was the idea of the book lying on remainder tables that humiliated him. Gerald no longer hoped for a *succès d'estime*; a *succès d'argent* would be plenty good enough.

He rose from the davenport and walked to the tantalus, pouring himself another glass. The wine decanter was all that was left of the old decor of his study. Stephanie, his third wife, had recently redecorated the room for the second time. Gone were all the passé hunting prints, wood paneling, and old chintzes. Now the room looked like a Fifth Avenue version of an Oriental monastery. Actually, Gerald rather liked the austerity, and it set off the David Hockney painting to perfection.

Yet all of this cost a tremendous amount of money. Money to buy it, money to run it, and money to move Stephanie and himself among the wealthy who controlled the spigots from whence the money flowed. Only this morning Steph had presented him with another sheaf of unpaid bills—her Sonia Rykiel statement, the garage, the caterer's, and florists. Gerald had stuffed them into the Korean chest and closed the door on them for the time being. He had to focus on the manuscript, and he had. He'd completed it.

The phone rang, but he would let the housekeeper get it. She knew he was not to be disturbed. He had taken five days from the office grind to hole up and get this editing job finished. As soon as he handed it in, he could expect his acceptance check, and then the overdue maintenance, the assorted bills, the money he had borrowed on his margin account, the car-lease payments, and all the rest could be brought up to date.

Gerald looked out over the top of the Metropolitan Museum and beyond, into Central Park. For a man who had not inherited great wealth, he was doing very nicely, thank you. Remember that, he told himself sternly. He decided to celebrate and moved to the liquor cabinet. He took out the last bottle of 1912 port. There was enough for one drink. He would drink it, indulgently, leisurely, toasting himself. It was these small pleasures, these private ceremonies that gave life zest. He may have inherited his access to Davis & Dash, but he ascended based on his own merits, and he'd managed this lifestyle by spinning straw into gold.

There was a timid knock on the door—everyone but Stephanie was nervous about disturbing him—and Puri, the Philippine housekeeper, inserted her head. "It is your father," she said, before he could tell her not to disturb him.

Gerald put down the untouched port. He and his father adhered to certain rituals: lunch once a month at the Knickerbocker Club; a phone call at the office every other Monday; Christmas dinner, Easter lunch. It was neither a warm nor rancorous relationship, yet somehow, despite his fifty-eight years, Gerald still felt a thrill of anxiety, tinged with something less pure, when his father summoned him.

He walked back to the desk, regretting the port. It would be spoiled now. Gerald lifted the phone. "Hello, Father," he said, keeping his voice as neutral as he knew how.

"Gerald. Something has come to my attention. I must say, I am concerned."

Christ in a corset. Gerald knew business wasn't great right now. He didn't need Senior to second-guess him. "I know that sales aren't quite as strong as we predicted, but I don't think I'm going to have any problems with the board," Gerald began.

"I'm not talking about the financials, Gerald. I'm talking about this rumor—at least I am *assuming* it's a rumor—about your latest work."

Gerald felt his stomach quiver. Why did his father always make him feel the way he used to when he was called down to the headmaster's office at Deerfield? "What about it, Father?" He rubbed one hairless hand nervously over the other.

"It isn't possible that you're writing about your uncle, is it?"

Well, there it was. And on some level, hadn't Gerald been expecting this? Hadn't he been afraid of just this question? "Father, I am writing fiction. That's really all you need to know. It's fiction."

There was only the minutest of pauses. "I know the difference between fiction and a roman à clef. You are not hanging out our linen, are you?"

Gerald tried again. "Times have changed, Dad." He never called his father Dad. It was a mistake. It showed his discomfort, his concern. But it was too late now. "I've borrowed some bits from their story, but I've made it my own."

Gerald could hear his father's rasp of breath. "I simply can't believe it. You know how I felt when you did that last book, the one about the poor, dead hermaphrodite. It was sensationalism at its worst. But at least he—or she—or *whatever* the poor creature was, was not your family. Gerald, I insist that you send over the manuscript."

Gerald needed the acceptance check. He needed time. "Father, it's not even close to finished," he lied.

He could feel the ice forming at the other end of the line. "You forget, son, that I have read works in progress before," Senior said. "I'll read it this weekend." It wasn't a request, it was an order. The question: Was it an order that Gerald would obey?

Gerald put down the phone, picked up the port, swilled it down in a single gulp, and wondered what in the world he would do next.

# 22

> There are two kinds of editors, those who correct your copy and those who say it's wonderful.
>
> —*Theodore H. White*

Emma stood beside Mrs. Perkins's desk at the entrance to God's Little Acre. Gerald himself had called her in and asked if she would "take a look" at his book's opening. Emma didn't really have a choice. Gerald was not the kind of person who would willingly listen to criticism. The fact that he asked her opinion meant the book must be in a lot of trouble, which would make him more defensive than usual. Now she stood waiting for the opening chapter. Mrs. Perkins, however, was busy gossiping with Andrea, her assistant. Emma shared Heather with two other editors, but Gerald's *secretary* had an assistant of her own. "So now my husband wants a dog," Mrs. Perkins said.

Andrea shook her head. "One more thing you'll have to clean up after," Andrea said. "You need a dog like I need a bigger ass." Emma couldn't help but let her eyes flick over Andrea, including her wide butt. As she cleared her throat, Mrs. Perkins looked up at her.

"I'm having trouble with the printer," Mrs. Perkins smiled. Somehow, Emma doubted it. Mrs. Perkins simply liked to make editorial staff wait. The phone rang. Mrs. Perkins answered. "I'll tell him you said so," she said after a moment. "Another enraged call about *Schizo Boy*," she told Andrea.

"Did you see the old lady?" Andrea asked Mrs. Perkins.

"Is she in the reception area *again*?" Mrs. Perkins asked.

Andrea nodded. "Sandy should send for security, but

she doesn't have the heart. She says the old babe looks like her grandma."

"That's no excuse," Mrs. Perkins said. "If we let every homeless person into the lobby, the building would fall over."

What homeless person, Emma wondered?

"She isn't *homeless,*" Andrea said. "She's just—"

The intercom buzzed, and Gerald's voice snapped out an order. "Mrs. Perkins, I'm waiting." As Mrs. Perkins strode toward Gerald's door, she turned to Emma. "I'll have to get that to you later," she said. "We'll leave it at reception."

Emma walked back to her office. She looked at her watch: quarter to five. Usually she worked until six or seven, but she was tired. It had been a long week, and her work wasn't nearly finished. "Taking a look" at Gerald's opening was only the icing on a very large cake.

Well, she told herself in her mother's voice, no use putting off the inevitable. She eyed the piles of paper that not only covered her desk but were also neatly stacked all around the floor. Despite the tiny size of her office cubicle, she managed to stuff in an incredible number of manuscripts, galleys, and finished books. Emma sighed. For people in Pam's job publishing offered the rewards of serf and turf: Emma was enslaved while Pam ruled her fiefdom like a feudal lord. Emma sighed. She had better begin packing up her work to take home for the weekend.

Today she felt put upon. Pam had dumped the Susann Baker Edmonds manuscript on her, and Emma was looking forward to neither reading it nor editing it. It was a no-win. Edmonds was a high-ticket author and had to be handled with kid gloves. Emma didn't like women's commercial fiction to begin with, but even if she did, editing a bestselling author was most often a nightmare. If all authors believed that their words were holy, bestselling authors had their large advances and royalty checks to prove it. There was an insider's editing story about Dwight

D. Eisenhower: He'd written his memoirs, and they were significantly cut by his editor. When the book was ready to go to print, the editor met Eisenhower, who took out a small box and put it on the table between them. "What's that?" the editor asked. Ike opened the box to expose snippets of all the deleted words. They had been cut from his book with a razor blade. "I wrote them," Ike said. "Surely they shouldn't be wasted."

Susann Baker Edmonds wasn't a commander in chief or an ex-president, but she'd sold more copies of her books than Ike ever had. If Emma got Ms. Edmonds's nose out of joint, how hot would Susann make it for her?

Up until now, Pam had handled Susann. But with the problems Pam was having on the Trawley book and the heat she was taking for the Chad Weston thing, Emma had guessed she'd be stuck with Edmonds. It was a thankless task. If she suggested a lot of changes, Susann would be angry. If she didn't, Emma doubted the book would sell. So, in the end, it became not just the tricky task of untangling plot, character, style, and pacing, but also presenting the problems and possible solutions to Susann in a way that would make her see the need for the change *and* the way to make it. Emma was an excellent editor and could do the often brain-splitting work involved, but being diplomatic to stupid authors was something Emma knew she was *not* good at, probably because she didn't really care.

She knew there was a time, not too long ago, when she was thrilled with her work, when she felt that it was exactly the right job for her and that nobody could do it better. Now she wondered what in the world was *significant* about any of it.

There are two kinds of editors—the ones who like to sit over a manuscript and really edit, often brilliantly. Then there's the second kind, who are too busy. Emma knew she was the first kind and Pam was the second. She put the rubber-banded manuscript into her canvas backpack.

Then she added a short-story manuscript, and the final galley corrections of Annie Paradise's latest novel, which needed flap copy. How do you sum up a book in a hundred words in such a way as to make readers buy it? And do it without using grandiose superlatives or clichéd phrases like "this heartfelt novel explores the deepest reaches of the human heart" or "touchingly and sensitively told, you won't soon forget this coming-of-age saga." Emma was self-conscious about this. After all, could one sum up a whole book and seduce a prospective book buyer in a few paragraphs *without* distorting the truth, or promising more than the novel could deliver? *Should* one even try? With a grin, Emma remembered a description of *Warrior*, an obscure book by Donald E. McQuinn: "Brilliantly blending post-apocalyptic science fiction, historical frontier adventure, medieval-style warring between church and ruler, and even a futuristic Romeo and Juliet story, this riveting novel has something for every reader . . ." Now, without being ridiculous, she had to write something for Annie's book, hoping she could help sell it.

Emma struggled with it into the heavy backpack. Wearily, she picked up the memos and interoffice mail and stuffed them into her purse. Dispiritedly, she closed the door to her office and walked along the cluttered hallway, past the open-plan space where all of the junior people sat, to the reception area. A neatly dressed old lady sat on the couch. She must be the one Mrs. Perkins had been talking about. Emma looked away, feeling sorry for the woman. Sandy, the receptionist, stopped her. "Mr. Davis was looking for you," she said.

"I already spoke to him," Emma told her. Then she remembered she had yet to review his opening.

Sandy looked concerned. "Well, he said you shouldn't leave until I gave you something. He had an envelope for you." Sandy began looking through her desk, and Emma groaned inwardly. Sandy looked up at her. "I don't know *where* it is. It was right here. Let me call his office." Emma sighed and looked idly around the reception room. The small, older woman with curly gray hair didn't *look* like a nut job.

Emma felt the straps of her backpack slicing into her shoulders. She would have to straighten it. Sandy got off the phone. "It's not here. I'll just run down and get another printout for you." Emma nodded and went over to the seating area, using the back of it to readjust the pack.

"Can I help you?" the old lady asked. She carefully moved the wrapped stack of papers from her lap to the coffee table.

"Thanks," Emma smiled. "If you could just lift the straps and move them forward." The woman did, and Emma's backpack slipped more comfortably into position.

"That looks awfully heavy," the woman said. Emma nodded.

"It's filled with manuscripts," Emma explained.

"Oh. Are you an editor?"

"Yes." Emma was pleased. With her black leggings, running shoes, and leather jacket, she'd occasionally been mistaken for a messenger.

"Then I have a favor to ask of you," the old woman said.

Uh-oh. As a new resident in New York City Emma had quickly learned the rules of survival, which included never sitting in empty subway cars, never counting your cash in public, avoiding eye contact with everyone, and never talking to a crazy. But *was* this woman crazy? Emma watched as the woman lifted her carefully wrapped stack of papers. And then, too late, she realized what kind of crazy the woman was. To an editor, she was the most frightening kind of all: an unpublished writer with a book. "I'd like you to read this manuscript," the woman began, but Emma was already shaking her head.

"We don't accept unsolicited—"

The old woman was nodding her head. "I know that, dear. Believe me, I know. You can't get an agent unless you've already been published. You can't be published unless you've already been published. And you can't be considered for publication if you don't have an agent." There was no bitterness, only fatigue in the woman's voice. She looked at Emma. "Don't you think that if there was another way, I would do it?" For a moment her voice sounded exactly like Emma's mother's. Emma blinked.

But she couldn't—shouldn't—get involved. The world was a minefield of people with exploding manuscripts: Emma had only to mention she was an editor for taxi drivers, dentists, and even her doorman to pitch her a book idea. At first Emma had been encouraging, but too many DOA, incompetent, derivative, boring, mad manuscripts had detonated on her desk since then. She looked at Opal, about to blow her off.

"It's not mine," the woman said. "It's my daughter's. She's dead. It's good. Please." And to her horror, Emma saw tears rising in the old woman's eyes. You must just walk away, Emma told herself sternly. It's hopeless, and it's not your problem. "Help my daughter be heard. Stop the oppression of the women's voice in literature." It was then Emma knew she was doomed.

"All right," she sighed. "But I can't make any promises as to when I'll read it. I'm very busy right now."

God, that sounded awful! So pompous and unkind. The woman's pale face suffused with color. She bit her thin lower lip and nodded. She handed the gigantic manuscript to Emma. "My name is Opal O'Neal. I'm serving as my late daughter's agent." Emma wondered if there *was* a dead daughter or if this was simply another scam, designed by an old lady to get her manuscript read. Emma felt guilty for having the thought, so she just nodded her head. Well, she'd only read the first ten pages and then send it back. At least that was something. She scrabbled in her pocket for a card and, finding none, pulled out a pen and wrote down her name and extension number on a slip of paper, which she handed to Opal.

"Thank you," Opal O'Neal said, her voice small. Her gratitude was so disproportionate that Emma couldn't bear to look at her. Hefting the new burden, she turned and walked out the door, forgetting to wait for the opening chapter from Gerald Ochs Davis's book.

# 23

> The writer who can't do his job looks to his editor to do it for him, though he wouldn't dream of offering to share his royalties with that editor.
>
> —*Alfred Knopf*

Pam couldn't believe it: Peet Trawley, the cheap bastard, hadn't left her a penny. First the motherfucker dies on her, leaving her with a gaping hole in the fall list. Then he forgets her in his will. Unbelievable! Pam blamed the piranhas, the family he had spent nearly two decades complaining to Pam about. Well, so much for author care: She'd written his books, listened to his complaints, found him an endless stream of doctors, and once or twice even serviced him sexually. Her reward for all of that was absolutely nothing except a hole in the fall list. Somehow it seemed worse than unfair. Pam felt truly sick. She was afraid she was getting one of her dreaded migraine headaches.

Pam rubbed the place on her forehead where her migraines seemed to begin and looked down, one more time, at her printout. The numbers for the quarter were not as healthy as they should be, and she knew that this month they would not make their projected budget. It was dangerous not to hit budget—it was an invitation for the big boys at Communications General to stick their noses into the business. And Gerald hated that. More than anything else, Gerald hated to have his private fiefdom interfered with by outsiders, especially David Morton. The fact that the outsiders now owned the company made little difference to Gerald. Pam knew that screwing up the profit picture and bringing down the wrath of the suits was the only thing that could cost her her job.

And she *liked* her job. She'd paid her dues and, after almost twenty years in publishing, had finally worked herself into a position where the pay was good and the status was high. Just as she had once been Gerald's lackey, now she had a woman who was bright, hardworking, and willing to pay *her* dues. Pam had picked Emma Ashton out of the crowd of bright young things. The essential quality of any editor should be that anytime they pick up a manuscript they should be prepared to be surprised. Emma hoped for surprises. Pam knew she was long past them. Pam paid Emma a little bit more than the pathetic salary most little editor girls got, and for that tiny extra wage and for the equally tiny window Emma had in her minuscule office, Pam had bought not just intelligence, hard work, and stick-to-itiveness, she had also bought loyalty. Because Emma, unlike Pam herself, was not the type to fuck her boss—in either sense of the word.

Peet Trawley's lawyer and widow were coming by in an hour, but Pam didn't want to see either of them, unless they had a big check for her. Meanwhile, she had this fucking sales report to go over while Gerald was off finishing his book. She wasn't really a numbers person. For that, both she and Gerald counted on Chuck Rector, the vice president of finance and a lizard. What Pam was brilliant at was the instinct for what would sell and what wouldn't; that and how to present and package a book in a way that would make it happen. But looking over the printout, she didn't see *anything* from their last list that was going to happen.

Susann Baker Edmonds's first book for them didn't look good, and Pam looked down at the huge printing planned, most of which she was sure they would have to eat. She had told Gerald not to poach the stupid woman from Archibald Roget, but Gerald's ego had gotten in the way. Pam herself hated all those stupid women's books, those long tales of a woman's struggle, her romances, her marriage, and then the renewed struggle she had with her children. In the U.K. they called them "Aga sagas," named for the upmarket kitchen stoves that often were a centerpiece of the stories. Pam hated too the unrealistic glitz-and-glamour stories of women with improbable names and impossible beauty having imprudent affairs. Pam lumped the two kinds of women's books together and disdainfully called them "Pinks." And why were they so often written by women with three names? Barbara Taylor Bradford, Mary Higgins Clark, Susann Baker Edmonds, Susan Fromberg Schaeffer! Jesus, if Mary Baker Eddy came back from the dead, she'd be a natural!

Pam looked back at the printout. While Susann Baker Edmonds was about to disappoint, Gerald's last book had bombed so badly that they could both be fired for it! Why he insisted on writing books—which he did badly—instead of publishing them, which he could do well, was beyond her. If someone in corporate took a careful look at his numbers and his new contract, they'd *both* be history. Luckily the suits in Communications General weren't as good as Chuck Rector was at deciphering the numbers.

But Pam knew she was good at picking hits. She did it season after season. After all these years, Pam had come to believe there were only five kinds of books that had a chance at commercial success in the American mass market: Pinks, Spooks, Dicks, Uh-ohs, and Hots. "Pinks" were what she called the women's books (though a few—a very few—men read them). "Spooks" were all of those Stephen King/Peet Trawley/Dean Koontz scary weird monster books. The type where a neighborhood grandma becomes possessed by the Evil of All Creation and begins microwaving tots. "Dicks" usually had black-and-red dust jackets featuring swastikas, daggers, planes, and the occasional Medal of Honor. Clancy, Ludlum, Follett (before he converted to cathedrals) all did those to death, and men bought them by the millions. Though she wasn't political, Pam believed that publishing's greatest loss in the decade had been the end of the cold war, since Dicks were one of the guaranteed infusions of blood that circulated money through the industry. "Uh-ohs" were probably the biggest category, because, unlike Pinks or Dicks, both men and women bought them. They were the mystery and suspense books, where a character the reader liked was in some kind of jeopardy or a detective, amateur or otherwise, solved impossible murders despite their odd character quirks. Grisham, Elmore Leonard, Sue Grafton, and a host of others kept Uh-ohs going endlessly, though they bored the shit out of Pam.

Finally, there were the Hots—the true wild card, the hardest to predict. They were books that either were the first to exploit a new idea or were "written" by the celebrity-of-the-moment. Ivana Trump, Fabio, Naomi Campbell. The good news was that a Hot could be ridden to the top of the *New York Times* list, but you rarely, if ever, got a second successful book out of the author. Try to imagine a second O. J. Simpson Q and A book. Crichton was about the only fiction writer who specialized in Hots; his commercial sense constantly read America's pulse and pulled out dinosaurs, Japan-bashing, or sexual harassment at the very moment they were ripe. But aside from Crichton, Hots were usually fast rides that ended quickly. Pam made it a credo never to give a new Hots author a multibook contract.

She'd have to focus on what was coming up for the all-important fall list. There were a few Pinks, two Spooks that might do all right, a guaranteed Dick, but other than that, *nada*. The big goose egg. Pam shook her head. She saw Gerald's new one listed, and the dreary sales of his last book made her close her eyes. She could depend on Gerald for another book, but she could almost count on it not selling. Then she smiled. He might collect on his contract, but if she were Gerald, she wouldn't count on collecting his pension.

Anyway, what she needed were some new Hots—something quick and dirty that she could make a killing on. But Hots were so unpredictable; nothing was guaranteed. She thought *SchizoBoy* was one, but there were no sure things.

When the artsy writer A. M. Holmes had tried a slice and dice, she'd been excoriated by *The New Yorker*, which had called the book "This rotten novel." So Pam went back to combing the list for guaranteed successes. She thought of her pal Judith Regan's formula for picking winners: When she read the manuscript, her nipples got hard. Pam smiled, despite the furious pain in her head. Yeah, *Lincoln's Doctor's Dog*.

Mrs. Trawley and Burt Schuloff, her lawyer, sat in the conference room with Jim Meyer. Pam, as usual, was late, but she didn't give a shit. As far as she was concerned, Jim could handle this himself. Pam almost grinned when she looked at Edina Trawley: The stupid drama queen was not only swathed completely in black, but she was wearing a black patent-leather hat with a veil.

Who the fuck would have thought you could buy a patent-leather *hat*? Well, Pam admitted to herself, at least it was practical. Edina Trawley could wipe it off with a rag and use it again the next time a husband died. And somehow Pam didn't think it would be long before there was another husband—perhaps Burt Schuloff, by the look of it.

The fat lawyer stroked the widow's hand. Mrs. Trawley looked up at Pam. "Oh! Excuse me if I don't get up," she said.

"She's very weak," Schuloff told Pam.

Pam just took a seat, crossing her legs, hoping that Schuloff got a flash of beaver. Fuck him, the bloodsucker. Fuck both of them.

The widow was scrabbling in her black patent-leather purse. She took out a handkerchief—Pam couldn't believe that it, too, was black—and a tissue-wrapped lump. She handed it to Pam. "I know Peet would have wanted you to have this," she said.

Pam grabbed it. Jewelry? The antique obscene netsuke Pam had always admired? She tore off the paper. It was a disk—a three-and-a-half-inch Memorex disk. Pam looked at it blankly.

"His last disk," Schuloff explained.

"What a beautiful gesture," Pam said and threw the disk flatly onto the conference table where it skittered like a Frisbee to the corner, teetered, then fell to the carpet. "Oops," Pam said.

Jim retrieved the disk and served the widow coffee from a tray brought in by a secretary. He didn't offer Pam any, so she poured herself a cup. "Pam," Jim said, "we have something that Mrs. Trawley would like to discuss with you. Something they want from you."

Pam waited. Perhaps Edina wanted a receipt for the disk.

"No one knew Peet's work the way you did," the black widow said. "It was loved. *He* was loved. His work should continue."

Pam looked at her. She wasn't just greedy and stupid. She was crazy.

"What Mrs. Trawley means is that she'd like you to finish Peet's book," Schuloff said. "To, um . . . edit it to completion."

"Edit it to completion?" Pam asked. "Last I saw, there were only a few chapters—twenty pages or so."

"Well, you always said you wrote his books," Mrs. Trawley said. "So . . . write 'em."

Her lawyer jumped up. "No. No. That's not exactly what we had in mind," Schuloff said. "Not writing. Well, there's this one, with some of it outlined and some fleshed out. And then the two remaining books on the contract—"

"The contract is invalid," Jim Meyer was quick to point out. "The obligation is with Peet Trawley, who is deceased."

Mrs. Trawley began to cry. "But his books don't have to be."

Pam snorted. It had all become clear. Well, she'd always rewritten Peet. Now she'd just get paid for it. David Morton, Edina Trawley. All in all, a good day.

"A quarter of a million dollars," Pam said.

# 24

> I'm not a jealous woman, but I can't see what he sees in her, I can't see what he sees in her, I can't see what he sees in her!
>
> —*Sir Alan Patrick Herbert*

Susann stood by the window, looking out at New York's Central Park. Her Central Park West apartment was small—really just a pied-à-terre, but she'd been spending more and more time in New York. Maybe she needed a bigger place, Susann thought. She certainly needed *something*.

What, exactly, was wrong? What was missing? What she really needed was for her new book to be a smash. It was the success of her books that had changed her life, that had given her this apartment, the house in France, Alf, Edith's help, the wonderful clothes, the television appearances, even the looks she had bought through surgery.

But her success had also given her excitement. Nothing could match the feeling of opening the newspaper and seeing her book at the top of the list, or strolling into a bookstore in any airport, any mall in the country, and finding her books—sometimes a whole wall or a window full—proudly displayed. She never tired of the thrill of seeing her name on the side of a bus in New York or on a giant poster in the London underground. She loved going to book signings, being ushered by the store manager to the table laid specially for her. Most of all, she loved looking up at the long line of fans, each waiting for her signature, each waiting to tell her how important her books had been to them.

That's what was missing! Not the fans or the interviews or the ads but the feeling that she was important. At Davis & Dash they acted as if she were just anyone. How she wished she'd never left Peterson! *They* had treated her with dignity. They had also known how to sell her. And she'd *always* earned out. Only since she'd taken on this big contract had she felt not only such dreadful, almost unbearable, pressure but also the dislike or disappointment of her publisher and editor. The truth was, she didn't like them much, either, and sorely missed Imogen Clark, her editor at Peterson, who always knew how to tactfully coach her through the painful editing process. And Archibald Roget, the publisher, had always been so charming to her. At Davis & Dash she was afraid of Pam Mantiss and knew that to Gerald Ochs Davis she might only represent a bad investment.

Susann turned and looked at the ormolu-and-marble mantel clock. Alf was late. Though he had recently given her the clock, it seemed that she got less and less of his time. He always used to come see her in France or London. But in the last year or two he traveled to her less and less. Was it his age? Alf, after all, was no spring chicken. Whatever the reason, that was why she spent so much time in this pokey little apartment. To be with Alf. Who was late. Susann smoothed her finger nervously along the silk curtain. The place had been done by Duarto, the fabulously expensive society designer known as the "Sultan of Silk." The fabric was Scalamandre, $192 a yard. Susann had to smile. Why was she being so dark, so depressed? Things *had* changed, and they'd stay changed. This wasn't as pokey an apartment as the one she used to wait for Alf in, back in Cincinnati. No; this apartment was a palace compared to *that* hole. She looked around in satisfaction at the beautifully furnished, spotlessly clean living room. This apartment was four very luxe rooms overlooking the park. For a moment she felt calmer, but then the dissatisfaction rose again. The location and decor had changed, as had her bank account, but why was she still alone and waiting?

Of course, there was Edith, upstairs. The apartment had come with a tiny maid's room and hall toilet up in the attic of the building. Most other people used the rooms for storage, but Susann had the place painted, and Edith stayed there when they were in New York. If Edith minded, she didn't say anything. And it was a relief for Susann. Although she didn't like being alone, she hated being stuck with depressing Edith, who seemed only to get fatter and more boring with age. And her endless knitting! Sometimes Susann thought she'd go bonkers if she heard one more click of those needles.

Edith was the only one, though, that Susann had dared to tell about her daughter's latest caper. "Typical," was all Edith had said, and though it was, Susann resented her for saying it. This afternoon Edith had shown her a tiny item in *Publishers Weekly* that mentioned "a first novel by *Kim* Baker Edmonds" to be published by Citron Press. It was only a question of time before Alf and the Davis & Dash lawyers knew about it. What would happen then?

Well, Susann thought, things could be worse. There was Patti Davis, first betraying her family in her tell-all novels and then forgiving them in her "loving" memoir. And now she was writing yet another paen to her father—for Knopf, for goodness' sake. If the Reagans could survive, Susann supposed she could, too. But with her sales slipping, would yet *another* "Baker Edmonds" book steal part of her market share?

Susann had to tell Alf about the situation Kim had created. Imagine, her own daughter stealing Susann's name! She sighed. If she told Alf tonight, he'd begin yelling and calling lawyers—even though it was past ten o'clock. And Susann would—in the end—have to calm him down. She knew she had to tell him eventually, but now she needed some affection, some calm and loving care.

She heard Alf's key in the door. She moved quickly to

the sofa and snatched up a magazine. She didn't want him to think she had been despondent. Alf hated what he called her "moping." There was no point in spoiling the time they would have together.

"You still up?" Alf asked. He looked tired, and when he came close and brushed his lips against her cheeks, Susann could smell both brandy and cigars on his breath, two things he'd been told by his doctors to quit. His eyes looked a little bloodshot, too. As always, his suit was crumpled and his tie askew. Susann had to smile. Her Alf.

"Well, if you're tired, let's go to bed," she murmured, and ruffled his white hair.

"I wouldn't mind lying down," Alf agreed. Susann took a breath of happiness. "I have tons of reading," he added, and Susann's smile faded. She watched Alf pull his jacket off and throw it across the chair. Then he sat and tugged off his Belgian loafers. He had dropped his trench coat over one end of the sofa when he came in, and now he pulled over his briefcase, opened it, and began disgorging stacks of papers, contracts, and manuscripts. Susann was always amazed at how quickly Alf could mess things up, whether it was one of her rooms or one of his suits. But she smiled indulgently. It was nice to have him here with her, rather like having a child to clean up after. And better a messy room than the emptiness of its earlier neat perfection. Alf knew how to fill a room with life. He was like a child in that respect.

Susann definitely wouldn't bring up Kim tonight. It could wait until breakfast.

When Alf shuffled off to the bedroom clutching a manuscript, Susann followed. She was wearing a turquoise silk nightgown and a peignoir to match. The silk dragged a little along the carpet, and Susann tripped, falling against Alf. But he didn't seem to notice. He was already reading a memo at the top of his pile.

They got into bed. Susann pulled up the plump coverlet. One of her many splurges had been on linens—she could afford the very best, and Anichini was what she bought. Sinking into the white comfort was pure pleasure. It cost almost a hundred dollars a week just to have the sheets and pillowcases laundered and ironed at Madame Paulette's. Susann sighed with satisfaction.

Alf, sitting on the other side of the bed, had stripped down to his underwear. He pulled off his socks and rolled onto the sheets, oblivious to their quality. She felt his back against her side. This is what she waited for and wanted, Susann told herself. A little comfort, a little animal warmth. The white lilies in the gold-rimmed crystal vase scented the room. Everything was first-class. There was nothing to worry about, she told herself. Nothing was missing. She curved up against Alf's side. Absently, he patted her shoulder and turned his back as he reached for his pile of papers.

Was that it, then? A few quick pats and back to work? Was *that* what she had waited all night for? Angrily, pointedly, Susann reached across to the night table and shut off her light. "This won't take long," Alf mumbled. "I probably won't read more than a few pages." Susann said nothing, merely snatching the downy duvet up over her head.

But after a little while she got too hot under the covers. Anyway, she was ruining her hair. She poked her head out and looked over Alf's shoulder. It was a manuscript that he was looking at now, and she could just see the title: *In Full Knowledge*. It sounded like another one of those lawyer novels. He represented dozens of those, none of which had gone anywhere. She sighed.

In ten days he'd be off to the Frankfurt Book Fair to sell foreign rights to her books and try to palm off a few of his losers on the Dutch, the Danish, or the Italians. He'd leave her alone for almost two weeks, since he'd stop in London on the way over and rest up in her house in France before he came back. She wished he wouldn't go, but he loved the schmoozing—dinners with Adrian Bourne and Eddie

Bell, appointments with attractive editors like Helen Fraser of Heinemann or Imogen Taylor of Little, Brown.

Susann didn't know why he bothered. She was making plenty of money for both of them, and if he'd only focus a little more of his energy on *her*, she could perform even better. Why must he persist with this idea that he could find *other* bestsellers? He'd never had another writer whose book even made the lists, though, to be fair, he had managed a few big advances. Alf was always wheeling and dealing, but he put more time and effort into all his little deals than they were worth. She was the only real moneymaker in his stable. She knew it and so did he. Yet he refused to give up his other clients, just as he refused to marry her.

Susann thought of her daughter and shivered, despite the beautiful comforter. Should she interrupt Alf's reading with her bombshell? *That* would get his attention. She lay in bed, Alf's weight and bulk at her back, and waited for him to put down the manuscript. She heard the mantel clock in the living room chime eleven, and still she waited. Finally, when it seemed as if he had been at it for close to an hour, she turned to him. "Don't you think it's time to turn off the light?" she asked, using the sweetest voice she could.

Alf looked over at her. For a moment his bloodshot eyes behind his reading glasses were unfocused, as if he had been a million miles away. Then he came back to her. "This is good," he said, tapping the manuscript. "I mean, it's really good. This could be a blockbuster."

For some reason, his statement filled her with rage. But she wouldn't let him see that. Wordlessly, she snatched up the front pages of the manuscript. *In Full Knowledge*, by Jude Daniel. Who was Jude Daniel? she wondered. Was she attractive? Was Alf interested in her? The way he had been in her? His eyes, though red-rimmed, were alive with excitement.

"I'm telling you," he said, "you can't put this down. It's a real page-turner. Take a peek."

When was the last time she had seen that look? Certainly not when he read *her* last manuscript or even the one before. It was that look that in the early days had motivated her to keep on writing. She missed that look, more than the sex, more than the little gifts and small attentions Alf used to pay her.

"Who is she?" Susann asked.

"She?" Alf repeated. Then he looked at the title page. "Oh, you mean Jude Daniel? It's not a she. It's a he. That professor kid from the upstate school, the one I did the panel for. I tell you, I'm surprised. The little son of a bitch can write."

Susann knew she should have felt relief, but somehow she didn't. She looked at Alf's excited face. "I could make something happen with this," Alf was saying. "I could definitely make something happen." With a pang, Susann realized that what she felt for Jude Daniel—male or female—was pure jealousy.

# 25

> Beginning writers must appreciate the prerequisites if they hope to become writers. You pay your dues—which takes years.
>
> —*Alex Haley*

Camilla stood beside Frederick at the *tabacca*-store counter. Oddly enough, to mail a parcel tied with string required a visit to the state-run tobacco and salt shop—both, along with matches, an Italian-government monopoly. Camilla lifted the brown paper-wrapped parcel and opened the edge so that Frederick could insert his cover letter to his sister. She wondered, briefly, what he had written. Here's a manuscript that had been read to him by a woman he didn't really know but might (possibly) want to sleep with? Camilla suppressed a smile.

Their visit to Assisi had been wonderful. She'd shown him the frescoes in the basilica, and each evening she'd read to him. Then they'd sat at the small café by the central fountain and eaten in the mediocre restaurant above it. Frederick had told her that he loved her book. And she had believed him. Nothing else had happened, but to Camilla it seemed a lot.

She'd returned to a grueling five-day tour and hadn't seen Frederick—except he'd popped up twice: at the Bargello museum one afternoon and then at the Boboli Gardens. She'd been touched, though she hadn't had time to exchange more than a word or two. Today was her first half day off, her first chance to see him alone. And they didn't have much time before she took the group to see the view from the top of the Duomo this afternoon.

She smiled at Frederick as she wrapped up the

manuscript in brown paper again and handed it to the disheveled old man behind the counter. "This is very kind of you, Frederick, especially considering you're a man who prefers Guardi to Canaletto."

"And proud of it," Frederick said as he secured the ends of the string with sealing wax, supposedly ensuring that nobody would pry into the package. "Only a man of discernment would recognize the merits of this manuscript."

Together she and Frederick stepped out into the sunshine of the square, about to walk along the north arcade to the post office. But Frederick stumbled over the step down from the *tabacca* shop, and just in time Camilla caught his arm. He was both extremely generous and extremely physically graceless. He tripped, he knocked over glasses, he bumped into things all the time. For a moment Camilla couldn't help but remember Gianfranco's incredible physical grace. She sighed and took Frederick's arm. What would happen to her manuscript? Would mailing this change her life, or was it merely another dead end, as Firenze and Gianfranco had been? After all, who did she think she was? "Shall I just drop it in the post?" she asked Frederick.

"No. Let's do it together. Maybe it will bring us luck." Frederick smiled at her.

Camilla nodded. "Let's," she agreed, "although I think an Italian post office is the bleakest place in the world." They turned into the *stazione* post office. The noise was an assault, and the people in the crowd—who seemed not to be divided into any queues but milling randomly, more like an unruly mob—seemed about to assault one another. For a moment Camilla felt Frederick shrink back. Was he timid as well as being what some of her American tourists would call ""a klutz"? Camilla couldn't help feeling more than a little put off by a man who was less physically secure than she.

But after a moment he launched them into the crowd and finally managed—after ten minutes of pushing and gesturing and speaking his broken Italian—to get them up to an air-mail window. Another disheveled Italian, this one an unshaven young man in a wrinkled uniform, took her precious parcel, applied the appropriate colorful stamps, and then flung it over his left shoulder onto a pile of other parcels as if it were less than a pair of discarded shoes. Camilla winced, but Frederick laughed, turned to her, and put his long hand against her cheek. "It's okay," he told her in a voice that was surprisingly comforting. "It will get there safely." And then he bent down and kissed her softly and sweetly on her mouth.

"Ah, *bellisima*," said the man waiting behind them at the front of the mob. "*Bravo*," called out someone else. Camilla colored.

"Can I trust a man who prefers Guardi to Canaletto?"

He stopped her. "Listen, let me explain. I am an architect—"

"That's why you should recognize the merits of Canaletto. His combination of fantasy and precision."

"No, he does things by rote. He's lost the soul of Venice. Guardi paints with feeling."

"I believe he painted with a brush." Her face was flushed. She was annoyed.

The Italians, looking for divertissement and always interested in love, were watching their row. Camilla was far too shy to be put in this awkward position. Frederick was truly sweet, but . . . what could she say? Before she had to say anything he turned them around and, arm in arm, they walked out of the post office, leaving the bedlam behind them.

"Where are you taking your chickadees today?" Frederick asked her, joking about the tour group. They were Americans, a group of doctors and their wives from Philadelphia. They had been particularly nice but demanding. Today they'd leave for Rome. She'd be both a bit sorry and a bit relieved. It was also the day she was paid, and she was hoping for large tips.

"I'm taking them up to the top of the Duomo and then to the Campodeiglia," she told him. "Photo ops, you know." Was he planning to come? Since they'd come back from Assisi, each time she had looked up during her lectures and seen Frederick at the edge of the crowd she'd been flattered, but today she'd find it embarrassing to have him watch her palm gratuities, like a common waitress. Sister Agnus Dei would call it false pride. Anyway, she was too tongue-tied to tell him how she felt. "Should I expect you?" was all she asked.

He shook his head. "No," he said. "Regretfully not. But will you meet me for dinner?" Camilla nodded, very relieved and quite pleased.

"Come to my hotel," he suggested. "The dining room is terrific." Camilla had never been to the restaurant in the Helvetia & Bristol. It was expensive, and attracted the young, moneyed Florentine crowd. She wondered, briefly, if Gianfranco might be there. Well, what was that to her? She hadn't seen him in weeks.

"Yes," she said, "I would love to." And they parted at the corner with her manuscript in the mail and an agreement to meet at seven-thirty that evening.

The tour group had broken up after a stunning last view of Firenze. The city was as beautiful to look at from the hills around it as it was to examine from within. And the gratuities had been even more than Camilla had hoped for. Thank God Americans were so generous! She had been a bit in the hole after taking off those days for Assisi, though she had refused, of course, to accept anything from Frederick. Despite his insistence that she had been—as he put it—a miraculous tour guide, she didn't want to be his employee. He had been so complimentary—he'd said she'd given him new eyes. She'd been pleased by that, but she'd still only accepted the dinners, the hotel room, and the companionship; she wouldn't take money.

Now Camilla had a few lire to spare, as well as an hour or two to herself. But the long day had worn her out. She thought she would just lie down for a few minutes before she'd think about bathing and dressing for dinner.

When Camilla woke, it was already twilight. She sat up with a start, her heart pounding. She had overslept. Well, she hadn't meant to sleep at all. She looked at the little clock she kept on her bedside table. It was the only valuable thing in the room, a small enameled carriage clock that Gianfranco had given her. It was already seven o'clock! She almost ran to the little basin in the corner. She'd have no time for a proper bath or to wash and dry her hair. She would have to sponge herself and put her hair on top of her head.

Camilla hated to rush. She realized, as she washed and dressed, that she must have slept away her free time to avoid thinking. She had, after all, quite a lot to think about. Frederick clearly liked her, and she liked him, too. But in what way? She could still feel his kiss on her lips. But she didn't feel *that* way about him, did she? Was this just another useless adventure? She was twenty-nine, and she'd already had "adventures" in New York and here in Firenze. She had loved but not been loved in return. She was tired of being only a diversion. Was she merely a diversion as part of Frederick's holiday and nothing more?

The thought led her to the bigger question: What in the world was she doing? She seemed to be bouncing about the globe, as empty as a ping-pong ball. Where did she belong? She had had to leave Birmingham and her dreary, hopeless family to get her schooling, but she hadn't managed to find a place for herself in New York. Without money or friends she'd found it a hard city. So she'd come to Firenze, a soft and beautiful place, only to find there was no niche for her here, either. There were women—older, fatter, faded women—who got stuck here working as guides and living in lonely bed-sitters in *pensiones*. The idea of winding up with that life chilled Camilla.

And what about the manuscript? She tried to imagine where it was right now. Had it been loaded on a plane yet? What would happen when Frederick's sister received it? Would it be read? Would it be liked? Would it be published? She'd been quite chuffed by Frederick's praise, but now she'd lost her confidence. What if her manuscript was misplaced or, worse, rejected?

No wonder I fell asleep, Camilla thought. She had tried over and over to figure out the puzzle: how to fit in, how to forge strong connections with people, how to build a life. Somehow, though, she didn't have the knack. It seemed to her that love and work were the only two solutions to her loneliness. But working as a tour guide was not, in the end, either a deep connection to people or deeply engaging. She'd hoped her writing would matter. And it had. She'd felt intimate, connected, to the growing book. She'd come to love her characters. It seemed a natural thing for her to do, an outgrowth and explanation of who she was. But now it was finished. She had written it alone and she was still alone. Would it always be this way?

It was all so unsettling. She knew only one thing: She would like to write another book. She would like to tell more stories. It seemed to be the thread that ran through her life: She was a good tour guide not because she spoke well but because she wove an interesting narrative into her explanations. She retold the old myths and made the history of Firenze and its artists and rulers come alive. She thought she might also have made the characters in her novel do the same. She had watched her characters, her narrative, spin out before her, as amazing to her as if she'd been able to throw out silk and spin a web. But would it hold? Was it enough to build a new life on?

Camilla looked at herself in the little mirror over the basin as she pinned up her hair. She was almost afraid to admit how much she wanted this to happen. What if her book *was* bought? What if she did find a niche for herself? If she could write and make a living at it, she felt as if she had taken care of half of the formula.

That left only love to consider. Camilla put the last pin in her hair and walked out the door to dinner with Frederick, wondering what his sister in New York was like.

# 26

> Your manuscript is both good and original; but the part that is good is not original, and the part that is original is not good.
>
> —*Samuel Johnson*

Emma Ashton lay on the sofa, the Susann Baker Edmonds manuscript arrayed on the floor in stacks before her. She was truly and deeply miserable. It was in a mood like this that the sofa—an expensive down-filled splurge that she had spent some of her trust fund capital on—really paid dividends. Emma was embraced by the cushions. The deeper she sank into the mess of the Edmonds manuscript, the more deeply she was soothed by the comfort of the sofa. She thought, for a moment, of a line she'd heard credited to Jackie Kennedy Onassis. "If we all have to be miserable, it's better to be miserable in sable."

Emma put down her pencil. She pushed herself up from the sofa and looked at the mess that surrounded her. She'd been hoping for a call from Alex, but the call hadn't come. Emma sighed, wearily, and thought about going out this evening, just to clear her head. But she hated the bar scene and going to the movies alone, and Alex still might call. Anyway, she had so much work to do.

Emma stretched and walked across the big empty room to the single enormous window that looked over a group of gardens. Though her dubiously dubbed "studio loft"—basically one large room—was only on the fourth floor, it got a lot of sun, since it overlooked three-story brownstones to the south. But the day had been cloudy, and now dusk had already turned the tangle of unpruned trees and bushes below into darkness. Across the way, in the top-floor windows, lights had gone on and Emma could watch a mother feeding a toddler his dinner. She sighed. Twilight always made her melancholy.

She turned to face the mess of soiled pages on the floor. When she had gotten into the book business she had hoped for more than this. She had hoped to work on books that mattered, on stories that illuminated life, that gave solace or described life's great pains and great joys in a way that was beautiful.

But what was this manuscript? Mere distraction, and a bad job of it, too. The Edmonds book was stillborn, a pathetic effort to update what—to Emma—was already an insincere, empty style. Edmonds had written wish-fulfillment books up to now: long sagas of a woman's struggle, filled with descriptions of relationships, clothes worn, meals eaten, and the rest of the tedious details her fans once seemed to crave.

This new book had lost all of that, so the reader was left with nothing but character and plot, neither of which were Susann Baker Edmonds's strong points. The story was a middle-aged romance, something Emma thought of as "old adult." If "young adult" books were aimed at the netherworld of readers too old for children's books but too immature for regular fiction, "old adult" existed for those grown-ups too dumb or too lazy for real books. Like all of the new genre, this story set up a character disappointed by life, as "old adult" readers must be. But, unlike the reader, the main character got rewarded with everything she needed. Yet it was all so dead, so formulaic, that it was virtually unreadable. *"Paul looked at her and she turned away in shame. The varicose veins . . . the stretch marks. 'You're beautiful,' he breathed."* Ugh. Emma thought of what her mother's reaction would be and winced.

Well, she thought, it could be worse. She could have been assigned *SchizoBoy*, and then she would have had to resign. This manuscript was only silly, not evil. Reading the Chad Weston book had made her physically ill. She and the other women editors could hardly believe that Davis & Dash would publish it. She'd started a petition to ask them to refrain, but most people were afraid to sign it. Emma had been disappointed by that.

But what would she do about this? Tell Susann, tell Pam, that the book merely had to change plot, characterization, and style? Wouldn't they welcome *that* news. Emma shrugged. And who knew? In this business it was so hard to tell what would sell. *The Celestine Prophecy, Mutant Message Down Under, Border Music*! For all Emma knew, this empty, manipulative novel could be on the list the week it was published.

She sighed and went into her small kitchen to boil some water for pasta. She'd eat in, and maybe take a walk to the river later. She grated some cheese and emptied a plastic tub of pomodoro sauce into a pan. Across the room, near the archway to her sleeping alcove, her backpack lay on the floor, its drawstrings open, its contents scattered. She would clean that up just in case Alex *did* call. She strode across the wide, empty space and bent over the bag. It was surprisingly heavy, and when she looked into it she saw the wrapped manuscript that the old woman—what was her name?—had thrust at her. No doubt it was crap. She'd wait a week and then give it back. But as she turned to hang the backpack on its hook, her eyes crossed the Susann Baker Edmonds mess. Could anything but *Schizo-Boy* be worse? Emma thought again of Jewel, or Pearl, or whatever the old woman's name was. She remembered her look of pain. Was it really her dead daughter's manuscript? With one last sigh, Emma pulled it out of her backpack and took it into the kitchen.

The phone rang. Emma answered, hoping it would be Alex.

"Hello, Emma."

"Mother. Are you calling from Italy?" It was funny: Emma hadn't heard from her mother in almost a month, but now she instantly felt smothered.

"No, dear. Larchmont."

"Similar but not matching, and the board goes back," Emma said. But of course her mother never watched television and would not get the reference to the old game show. "When did you get home? I thought the two of you weren't back until *next* week?"

"Wrong on both counts. We were both scheduled back yesterday, but Frederick has stayed on."

"Alone?" Emma asked, surprised. "He's staying alone?"

"Let us hope so," her mother said. "They take good care of him at the Helvetia & Bristol, and he hired a driver. But I do worry."

"You worry too much," Emma said. "If he wanted to stay, I guess he can manage." But she wondered herself. Why had Frederick stayed? Perhaps he, too, was feeling suffocated by their formidable mother. Of course, both of them had long ago run away from Mrs. Ashton, but poor Frederick had had to return. Emma shook her head over the tragedy and couldn't help but think—not for the first time—that a tiny bit of their mother was glad that Frederick had to return to the nest. Emma shivered.

"Did you enjoy Florence?" Emma asked, because she didn't want to discuss anything else with her mother right now. Not her brother, not her job, not her sex life.

"It was lovely as always, but I thought if I had to see one more duomo, I would come down with a duomodenal ulcer. There are a lot of churches in Italy that only an architect could love."

"When is Frederick coming back?" Emma asked.

"That isn't clear. He's met someone."

Well, that was news. "Oh. Then he's touring with a friend?" *That* would make sense. Why hadn't she said so before?

"No. Not exactly. He appears to have made a kind of conquest. A girlfriend."

"No kidding! Great!" And unusual. Emma loved Frederick and wished him the best. "Does she know?"

"I'm not certain. And it wasn't my place to ask. I don't know if I should have left him, Emma." There was a pause. "I felt I had to do what he asked me to do, but I don't know if it was the right thing. I haven't called Dr. Frye yet, but I want you to promise me that if your brother calls you, you'll encourage him to come home."

"Mother, we've had this talk before. Frederick has to live the way he wants, just as I do. I'm sorry. Believe me, I'm sorry about everything that makes you unhappy about Frederick and me. But you have to accept us as we are, just as we have to accept ourselves." Emma rolled her eyes. Talking to her mother too often made her sound like a badly written self-help book. Was that the reason she avoided it? "Mother, I have to go." Never complain, never explain. That was the rule Emma tried to follow with her mother. Actually, it was a rule her mother had taught her. They said good night, and Emma hung up the phone.

The water was boiling, and she threw enough pasta for two into the pot. As if Alex just might drop by. And, if Alex didn't, Emma would eat all of it at the counter, reading just the first chapter of this mammoth piece of work. She looked at the title. *The Duplicity of Men*. Not bad, Emma thought. Just the first chapter, she told herself. That was all—well, that was more than—she owed the woman.

# 27

> A ratio of failures is built into the process of writing. The wastebasket has evolved for a reason.
>
> —*Margaret Atwood*

Pam threw down her pencil in disgust. She was surrounded by yellow sheets of legal paper, most of it crossed out and crumpled. And all of it added up to nothing. Absolutely nothing.

What the fuck was going on? She had spent three weekends and every evening writing "Peet's" book, but she hadn't come up with a usable chapter, page, or paragraph. After years of contempt for the writers she worked with, after years of envy at their royalties, she was having to examine one of her most basic beliefs: that she could write better.

Apparently, she couldn't.

Yet she *had* to have this book for the fall list. And she wanted the money. How could she possibly give up a quarter of a million dollars? She thought of Gordon Lish's writing commandment. "You have to make love to the page, to fuck it, to suck it off . . ." Well, she could do the sex, it was the writing that was hard.

If I could just go away, she thought, if I could take off a month or two and work quietly in a comfortable hotel in Saint Bart's or Cape Cod.

Pam looked around. Her apartment was a shithouse, and she looked worse. She hadn't washed her hair in three days. She'd eaten two pints of Ben & Jerry's Chunky Monkey, and she didn't even *like* bananas or nuts. The fact was, she was *going* nuts.

She had to write this book.

She couldn't write this book.

She had to pull herself together, dress, and go uptown. She had a lunch, and she had to go to the office. And next week she was off to Frankfurt for the book fair, where she would hunt desperately for the rights to anything that might be a hit. She'd have to leave Christophe at home with a sitter. God, it was all too much!

The lunch with Alf Byron was a waste of her precious time. Pam hated meeting with agents anyway. They were the blood ticks of the publishing world, as far as she was concerned. When they were engorged with the red blood of a successful author's 10 or 15 percent, they were insufferable. And when they were empty, hungry for new blood, they were desperate and useless. Yet they had come to virtually control the publishing marketplace. Very few authors negotiated their own contracts, and Pam supposed that publishers had brought this curse upon themselves when they had stopped reading manuscripts except for those submitted by agents.

Pam had been beating the bushes, covering the waterfront, and every other overused cliché she could think of, hoping to find a hot book or two to add to the Davis & Dash fall list. But despite meetings with a dozen agents, from Mort Janklow to Ellen Levine, she'd come up empty. There was a kind of law among agents: They serviced those who had paid them before. And Pam had always tried to buy cheaply. She wasn't popular with any of them. A few had tried to sell her swine, but why should they give her their pearls?

Today, because she had to, she was lunching with Alfred Byron, a real pain in the ass. Not that she expected anything there. She merely had to respond to his constant kvetching about Susann Baker Edmonds, his only major client. It wasn't that he didn't try for others. For years he had touted a stream of second-rate books by go-nowhere authors. He'd managed to burn Random House and Simon & Schuster a few times with manuscripts that he had created a buzz about but that had ultimately gone nowhere. And he represented Stewart Campbell, a loser suspense writer whom Pam published but paid dick for. Stewart was the kind of author whose books are worth more unsigned than signed. He had gone to a book signing in September and had found signed copies of his last book that still hadn't sold a year later. Alf had made a career out of a single author, but unlike a few other agents who had hitched their mediocre wagons to a star, Alfred Byron actually thought he was legitimate. That was what made him such a joke in the industry. Pam sighed. Lunch would be a crucifixion. Still, to keep Susann quiet and to be sure she got the massive changes Pam was going to need in the new manuscript, she had to do it.

Worse yet, they were going to Michael's. It was *the* publishing lunchroom, located behind a discreet glass front on West Fifty-fifth Street, and often called "The William Morris Agency Cafeteria" because the agents from around the corner ate there so often. Pam was sure she would see Owen Laster as well as at least half a dozen other people she knew. Working on the Trawley book she had done nothing but eat; she had gained more weight, she looked like shit, and she wasn't in the mood to smile and act as if *she* were the one with six books on the *New York Times* list. She'd prefer some Sixth Avenue dive where no one knew her. But she would have to go. Byron, wanting to be seen, had made the reservations, and she was stuck with it.

Pam showered, got dressed, blew out her blond hair, and looked in the mirror. Everyone else on Prozac lost weight. What was it with her? She favored clingy knit dresses, but the bronze Karan Kahn dress was just too tight, clinging not just to her large breasts but also to her ever-widening thighs. God, she *had* to lose weight. That had been one of the advantages of snorting coke—she'd been thin. Well, she'd given *that* shit up. Now she'd have to just not eat. That was all. She would just stop eating, starting today. She'd have nothing for lunch but a salad.

The resolve made her feel better. She ran a comb through her hair and put on bronze lipstick. That helped. So did the earrings. But her roots were showing. Then she noticed a spot on the dress, just above her left nipple. Oh, well. She took her raincoat off the hook and slipped into it, though there wasn't a cloud in the sky. She'd just keep her raincoat on. And she'd go back to exercise class with Bernie and Roy, the torture twins. She wouldn't drink, she'd only have a salad, she'd sit through Byron's boring bullshit, and then she'd insist on the editorial changes that Emma Ashton had suggested for Susann's book. Pam tied the trench coat tightly around her waist and scooped up her heavy shoulder bag. It was a hell of a way to make a living.

Michael's was crowded, as always. Peter Cocuzza, the manager, kissed Pam hello and, before she could stop him, took her coat. She'd forgotten about the spot on her dress and then had to make her entrance, had to walk down the two shallow steps and pass half a dozen tables in the front where the real heavy hitters were sitting. It was humiliating to have to pass Nan Talese, Howard Kaminsky, and Norman Perlstein, and smile, taking her seat with Byron in purgatory at the back of the bus.

Pam tried to steer the conversation with Byron to the Edmonds book, passing off Emma's initial comments as her own: how flat it was, how dull, and how to fix it. When Emma was finished writing the editorial letter, Pam would send it on to Byron with her signature. But Byron first had to shovel the shit: talk about Susann's latest foreign-rights deal, who he was seeing in Frankfurt, and his negotiations for a miniseries. Yeah, right. Now Byron was busy talking about some new first novel that he swore was going to go through the roof. How a dozen publishers were dying to see it. How Viking and Putnam were both hot for it. But how Byron, out of loyalty, would show it to

Pam first. *If* she gave him some concessions. *If* she promised more marketing support for Susann's book. Yeah, like I believe you, Pam thought. Like I give a shit.

". . . truly extraordinary," Byron was saying. "I had no intention of reading more than the first page or so, and then it kept me up all night. I mean, everyone *knows* about the case, but that's why this is both hot and unique. You remember what Laura Ziskin and Gus Van Sant did with *To Die For*. Well, he's brought a freshness to it, the insider point of view, and the compassion he creates for this mother who murdered her children is just . . . unsurpassed."

Pam yawned. She couldn't remember the last time she'd been this bored. The waiter brought their entrées and placed the pork chops, prune dressing, scalloped potatoes, and escarole in front of her. She'd already eaten her salad. She'd only ordered an entrée to be polite. She'd just have one bite. Pam picked up her knife and sliced off a piece of the meat. She was *starving*. "I'm not really interested in crime novels," she told Byron as she chewed. The pork was heavenly. "It's just not my thing." She added a mouthful of prunes.

"That's the beauty part, Pam. It's *not* a crime novel. Not that people into them won't buy it. They will. Big-time. But so will women readers. *All* women readers. It's got the romance thing, the bad-marriage thing, the revenge thing. It really transcends *any* genre."

Yeah, right. And Susann Baker Edmonds was the new female Shakespeare. "It's the guy's first book. And written from a female point of view?" she said doubtfully. "No one can do that."

"Wally Lamb did. Remember? *She's Come Undone*."

"Great book," Pam admitted.

"You know what they say: Everyone has one book in them."

"Yeah. And most of them should keep it there," Pam told him.

"Not this one. You gotta look at it."

She gave up. "Okay, Alf. Why don't you give me the first chapter, and I'll let you know. Meanwhile, we have to talk about Susann's new book." Pam stuffed some pork into her mouth and scooped up another forkful of the potatoes, washing it down with a gulp of Chablis. The escarole had been sautéed; she couldn't help but finish it. Well, it was only a green vegetable; how many calories could that be? Pam took the last bite of the second pork chop and couldn't resist picking up the bone and pulling the clinging, savory bits from it.

"No," Byron said. Pam looked up from her plate.

"No, what?" she asked.

"No. I'm not going to give you the first chapter to take with you. I'm not giving it to anyone. If you want to read it, read it here." He opened his briefcase and took out the manuscript.

"Are you kidding?" Pam asked. She put down the pork chop bone. Who the fuck did Byron think he was, Andrew Wylie? "Forget it."

"Fine." Alf shrugged and began to put the pages away. The waiter asked for their dessert order. Pam was already stuffed. Her hand lay on the bulge her belly made under the napkin. God, how had she done that? She'd eaten like a pig. "Nothing for me," she said automatically. Her eyes watched Alf Byron as he stuffed the manuscript back into his attaché. He wasn't even going to *show* it to her?

"Let me tempt you with the specials," the waiter intoned. "Crème brûlée, double chocolate cake, apricot tarte—"

"I'll have the crème brûlée," Byron said.

"Me, too," Pam said automatically. What the fuck. Then her sugar requirement would be taken care of. She narrowed her eyes at Byron. He was bullshitting her. No doubt about it. But what if the thing was good? What if Putnam really *was* interested? Phyllis Grann was smart. Really smart. Maybe, for once, Alf Byron *did* have something worthwhile. It could happen. It was a ridiculous demand—who reads manuscript in the middle of lunch?—but Pam held out her hand. "Let me see it," she said. "I'll read it right here."

Pam hadn't been this excited about a manuscript in a long while. It wasn't just that *In Full Knowledge* was a great read. She also liked the fact that it was written by a man. There was publicity value in that. She could imagine the flap copy: "A woman's book that reveals a woman's soul, written by the only man in America who understands." This wasn't Fitzgerald, it wasn't literature, but if she knew flapjacks from jack-offs, it would fly off the shelves. That, of course, was the question. Were her instincts still good? Pam shook her head. Christ, it was a bitch. The book business was nothing but a crapshoot. Pam could have just as easily been a commodities trader or a compulsive gambler. Like either of them, to keep in the game she had to follow her hunches and bet the farm.

God, she was tired. She wanted to sit back and rest on her laurels. But it was always, "Have you got a book on the list?" This year, more than anything, Pam wanted to win the Editor of the Year award. It was PR and bullshit and politics, but she felt it would finally show everyone that she wasn't a fluke. She needed the Trawley book to succeed. She needed *SchizoBoy* to hit. She needed the Susann Baker Edmonds to make the list. And now she needed *In Full Knowledge*.

Since her failure on the Trawley book she was doubting herself. Was it possible she *couldn't* write? Maybe she couldn't even pick winners anymore. Could she afford to spend a fortune on a first novel? Could she believe in it, in herself? Pam felt the food in her stomach churn.

But the beauty of this possible deal was that maybe she *didn't* have to bet the farm. Maybe Alf Byron would work something out with her. He had seemed to intimate that she could prevent an auction *if* she called him by Monday.

Was he bluffing? Probably not. Other editors would gobble this up. Pam hated the feeding frenzy that went on when two or three houses glommed onto a commercial first novel. Advances rocketed. The sky became the limit. *The Horse Whisperer, Thief of Light* kind of deals happened. It was ironic that a buzz—about an author without any track record—was more attractive than a known commodity. In fact, Pam knew a lot of authors who simply had to change names and come out with three or even four "first" novels, hoping one would hit. Dean Koontz had written under eight names. Since his first book, *Star Quest* in 1967, he'd churned out sixty novels—from science fiction to Gothic romances. He'd called himself Leigh Nichols and Deanna Dwyer. Now he had 150 million books in print, and his three contracts with publishers since '89 reportedly earned him $32 million. Hitting was almost a one-in-a-million chance, but every season or two somebody copped the jackpot. Pam felt that *In Full Knowledge*, Jude Daniel's book, just might be the Next Big Thing.

It was Sunday, and Christophe was at a friend's for the weekend. Half the time that left Pam feeling empty, abandoned, and anxious. The other half of the time she was relieved. Christophe was adorable but exhausting. He'd gone through eleven au pairs and baby-sitters in the last five years.

Pam got up from Christophe's bed, where she had curled up to reread the Jude Daniel manuscript, and wandered into the corner of her dining room that she used as her home office. She wondered what Jude Daniel was like. Was he good-looking? Was he hot? He had certainly written a few sticky-fingered sex scenes. Did he fuck like that? she wondered. She also wondered if she should call Byron now. She certainly didn't want to seem too eager. She never called *anyone* on the weekends, but he'd only given her until Monday morning. Pam tidied the manuscript and then pulled open the middle drawer of her desk. She'd promised Christophe that she'd stop smoking cigarettes, but she pulled out a secret stash of Marlboros and lit up. It was another luxury of having the weekend to herself.

She sat down at her desk, where she had left the Trawley mess. She just couldn't do it. Hired as a ghostwriter for a dead author, she herself needed a ghost. Maybe *that* was it. She could hire one of her hacks, one of her midlist authors desperate for money, and have him write the book. Then she'd edit it. Yes. Of course. That would work. No one would have to know.

The Jude Daniel manuscript would take a lot of marketing, a lot of PR and advertising, but it was part of the solution to the terrible problem of the fall list. Along with the Trawley book, *SchizoBoy*, and Susann's, she'd really have something going. But she wouldn't call Alf Byron until tomorrow.

Pam snuffed out the cigarette and took the butt into the bathroom. She had to flush it down the toilet, or Christophe would be sure to lecture her. She rolled herself a joint, took a hit, and pulled out her Filofax. Now all she needed was a ghost's ghost. She held the smoke deep down in her lungs. Okay. But first she would call Alf Byron and see if she could cut some kind of deal.

# 28

> In the publishing business you have to learn to greet failure with the same handshake as you greet success.
>
> —*Eddie Bell*

The Frankfurt Book Fair was the largest, most important international trade show in publishing. This was the eighteenth year that Gerald had attended, staying at the Hessischer Hof Hotel, where everybody who was anybody had reservations a year in advance. Gerald had a suite. He also had a sore throat. Was it strep, or was he merely still dehydrated from the flight? Not that it mattered. He, like everyone else, had half-hourly meetings scheduled with barely an interval between them to go to the bathroom. Gerald almost smiled; one of the questions he asked himself at Frankfurt each year was how the fat, German bathroom matrons managed to put up with the book crowd. Although Gerald tipped them the requisite five marks, tipping the toilet help was alien to most Americans, and the Brits were too cheap.

Gerald entered the enormous book-fair space. Same old thing. All that was different about this year was that for the first time David Morton was actually attending—not that he would acquire any books or sell foreign rights. Morton was there only to show up at the big social event. Raising his profile in the industry. Gerald was only worried about raising his white-cell count and how to get through the day avoiding the pitch-meisters while managing lunch. *That* was the true challenge of Frankfurt—all the restaurants were booked. Anybody who was anybody managed a quickie, but only that. With an hour off, everyone scurried. The losers were forced to gobble bratwurst in the *platz*.

When Gerald got to the Davis & Dash booth he found David Morton pacing back and forth alone in a space that was usually jammed. Gerald, surprised, awkwardly shot his cuffs and planted a smile on his face. "David," he said, as warmly as he could manage, "what a pleasant surprise."

"Are you crazy?" Morton asked him, his southern drawl stretching out each syllable.

"I think several of my analysts would vouch for my sanity," Gerald said coolly.

"Then what is your excuse for this?" David Morton asked, hefting the manuscript of *SchizoBoy*. Oh, Christ, Gerald thought. Someone has taught him to read. "It is, without a doubt, the most disgusting, perverted, sick piece of . . ." He paused, restraining himself. As a born-again Christian he rarely used profanity.

Gerald shrugged. "Just one man's view," he told David.

"It is not one man's view," David Morton said vehemently. "If it goes out with the Davis & Dash name on it, it indicates that we *share* that view. And I can tell you that I do not."

Gerald purposely sat down and forced himself to cross his leg in a casual, jaunty way. Body language meant so much, and he certainly wasn't going to bother to explain the First Amendment to Morton the Moron from a standing position. He would take his stand sitting down, thank you. "David," Gerald said with a smile, "I don't believe in channeling, but we sold a million and a half copies of that book by the fool who believes she's communicating with a Native American shaman—though why *he* would want to talk to that boring creature is beyond me. I'm not a vegetarian, but we publish vegetarian cookbooks."

"We're not talking about a damn cookbook, my friend," Morton said from his great height.

Gerald realized he'd made a tactical error. Sitting down

while Morton stood meant that he had to crane his neck to see him. It also meant that Morton was looking directly down on his wig, the worst angle to view it from. And rather than calming Morton, Gerald's position, both physical and corporate, seemed to further outrage him. "This boy is one sick cookie, this writer. Wanting to disembowel women and then—" Morton was making a sputtering noise. His face was very red.

"David, it's just a prolonged joke about shopping and the disposable culture. It works on two levels, and misogyny sells. Look at what Howard Stern's book did. Thirty-four thousand copies in its first day at Barnes & Noble."

"That was based on Stern's personality and cult. This is different. What if there's some nut who uses this as a how-to? People will hold us responsible."

The man was impossible. And Gerald was not going to allow Morton, an illiterate, to dictate editorial decisions. "It's *fiction,* David," he said in a tired voice. "That's what we put on the spine of the book. *SchizoBoy: A Novel.*"

The tall man flushed. "Don't condescend to me, you New York hustler. I will not be a party to this. Davis & Dash will not publish Chad Weston."

Gerald felt the fiat as a slap in his face. Perhaps he needed to regroup. After all, he himself had been offended by the thing, but he'd be damned if . . . Perhaps another approach would work. "We are under a contractual obligation to—" Gerald began.

"We have lawyers. Let him sue us."

"But we'll never get the advance money back—"

"To hell with the advance money." Morton had raised his voice. "You don't seem to be hearing me. This book is a hideous degradation of American women. I would not let this book be read by my wife, my mother, or my daughters. We are not, I repeat, *not* publishing this book."

Gerald stood up and tried to conceal the fact that his hands were shaking. He could feel the blood rush from his head, and knew he must have gone livid. "I . . ." He paused. What, exactly, was he going to say? "I resign"? "I won't do it"? "I think you're an ass"?

But it really didn't matter, because David Morton had already turned his back on Gerald and was moving out to the front of the booth. He stopped for a moment at the open doorway. Gerald wondered how many people had overheard this dressing-down and how long it would take for the news to ebb and flow throughout the book fair. Gerald had seen Judy Quinn from *PW* earlier; the last thing he needed was coverage of this fiasco in the "Hot Deals" column. Humble pie did not go down easily. In fact, he felt as if he might choke.

"Gerald, I am deeply disappointed in the lack of judgment you have displayed," David Morton said. "I will have to hope that it does not occur again."

With that implicit threat, he walked away. Gerald was left alone. He tried to swallow but found it difficult because of the pain in his throat and because of the size of his pride, a sharp-edged thing that he choked on.

"I've bought three books," Pam told Gerald gleefully. She was wearing an ugly dress, which in Gerald's opinion showed too much cleavage for a business party, but then Pam had never been known for quiet good taste. "I stole one from John Brockman, the nonfiction king. He wanted six figures, but I jewed him down."

Gerald winced at the slur. "It's not going to replace *SchizoBoy*, but then, what will?"

"Fuck that little bastard," Pam said. "The book wasn't going anywhere, anyway.We'll live without it."

"We have no choice."

"Morton was a prick to get involved in a publishing decision," Pam said.

Gerald doubted her sincerity. "So, what to do?"

She smiled. "I'm keeping busy. Elves aren't going to leave a manuscript on my pillow tonight."

"If they do, we'd have to call it a nocturnal submission," Gerald managed.

She leered. David Young, the handsome, charming managing director of HarperCollins U.K., was walking by. Pam raised her brows. "I'd like *that* on my pillow," she said, and took off after him. "Fun time."

Gerald was not having fun—not by any means. His sore throat had bloomed into what felt like an open wound, and the chewing out he'd received from David Morton was, by now, common knowledge. Still, Gerald was there at the Bertelsmann party with his head held high—though he was doing his best to avoid David Morton. Bob Gottlieb of *The New Yorker* drifted by and nodded. He was never to be confused with Robert Gottlieb, the William Morris superagent, though even reporters sometimes did. Gerald decided to avoid him and moved across the room. He spotted Jack McKeown, elegant as ever, in a heated discussion (was there any other kind?) with Judith Regan. Probably plotting another megahit. Screw them. He nodded to Phyllis Grann, the chairman of Putnam, despite his envy. Last year she'd made *Entertainment Weekly's* Power 101. Gerald had, for the first time, dropped off the magazine's list, while David Morton had moved up two notches. Phyllis had that pulled-together dress style that made her look like a woman newscaster. He passed Maureen Egen, the savvy and charming new publisher at Warner Books. Another woman a little too smart as far as he was concerned. If only he could do what she'd done with *Scarlett*. Ah, who should he talk to? Gerald didn't know how long he could continue this crucifixion. He headed to the bar to get a drink and passed the detestable David Rosenthal, with what looked like a smirk on his face. He was talking to Cindy Adams, the only newspaper columnist who bothered to mention authors when she talked about movies based on their books.

He considered going back to the hotel to avoid being sneered at. No. He wouldn't show the white feather. After all, he was not a little schoolboy sent to Coventry. He would speak to someone. He noticed the agent Helen Breitweiser standing quietly near the window, observing the glittering display with a look of amused detachment on her pale, delicate face. He inhaled deeply, shot his cuffs, and approached her. "What's the matter, Gerald? A little too much starch?" Helen asked quietly. He spun on his heel and walked away.

He needed someone unimportant. Ah . . . there was Paul Mahon, a literary lawyer-agent, talking to some dowdy brunette. Gerald forced himself to address the young man. "Hello, Paul," he smiled, though the grin hurt his face and the words hurt his throat.

"Hey, Gerald," Mahon said brightly. "Heard you got plowed on this Chad Weston thing. Are you going to have to eat all the advance money?"

Clearly, Gerald had picked a fool to speak to. He shrugged. "It's not much," he said, as cavalierly as he could.

Mahon raised his brows. "Six figures . . . not much? Let me introduce you to my client, Justine Rendal. She writes children's books, but I'm sure for six figures she'd be willing to write anything you want."

"Not anything," the brunette corrected. "I wouldn't write a Chad Weston slice-and-dice."

Gerald grimaced. "It's a slice-and-dice *commentary*. An *hommage*," he said with a tired sigh and a perfect Parisian accent.

"Too much *hommage* and not enough critique for my taste," she returned. As if her taste mattered. *You'll* never ever be published by Davis & Dash, Gerald thought, making a mental note of her name and crossing it off at the same time.

"So, it looks like Chad's agent is already talking to Archibald Roget of Peterson. You paid through the nose for stealing Susann Baker Edmonds from him, but it looks as if he's going to get Chad Weston cheap."

What fresh hell was this? Had that little worm already

cut a new deal? "Roget is publishing *SchizoBoy*?" Gerald asked, his voice reduced to a croak.

"That's the word, hummingbird," Mahon confirmed cheerfully. "Nothing's been signed yet, but boilerplate is being churned. Archie said it was a First Amendment thing—that he despised censorship in all its forms." Mahon giggled. "Guess that means you don't, hey, Gerald?"

Gerald very nearly groaned out loud. Oh, Christ! He could see it all now: his father's freezing blame, the attacks in the liberal press, and the stupid boy's book—which was barely literate—turning into a political *cause célèbre*. The publicity alone would sell a hundred thousand copies of the wretched thing. Archie Roget was getting his revenge. It was unbearable. Gerald began to walk toward the door. "Hey, where are you going?" Mahon asked, but Gerald found that his voice had completely disappeared.

"See ya. Wouldn't wanna be ya!" Paul Mahon sang out as Gerald left the party.

# 29

> Grief fills the room up of my absent child,
> Lies in his bed, walks up and down with me, . . .
> —*William Shakespeare*

Opal slowly got off her knees, dropping the wet rag into the bucket. In the wake of her daughter's suicide, it seemed that she could only do two things: scrub and read. This morning it was scrubbing.

It was odd to Opal that no matter how much cleaning she did, Terry's little apartment never took on the glow of cleanliness that made a home attractive and welcoming. The dirt must be embedded in the walls, the floors, the very fabric of the old building. Opal didn't know why she bothered, anyway. She wasn't all that fastidious in Bloomington. She let the newspapers mount up and waited till she had a full load to run the dishwasher or washing machine. But here she kept scrubbing. Perhaps, on some deeper level, she wanted to make this grim place a better last home for Terry. Of course, that was hopeless. Still, Opal washed down the walls, polished the windows with glass wax and newspaper, scoured the stove with steel wool, and mopped the floors with both detergent and bleach. It had become a kind of moving meditation for her. Then, when she got tired, she lay on the daybed and read the extra copy of her daughter's manuscript.

Opal was convinced that the book was brilliant, but reading it often caused an actual pain in her chest. She put her hand to her breast. When had she had her last X-ray? she wondered. She shook her head at her somaticizing. She was immensely sad and equally proud that Terry had achieved this vision, and she was absolutely committed to the book. It would be published. But she would have destroyed every word of the bulky, polished manuscript for just an hour, just ten minutes, with Terry.

Opal heard the mail arrive and put down the pages to get up and fetch it. She had to remember to bring both the mailbox and the apartment key with her so she wouldn't lock herself out. She'd made that mistake once, and it had cost her a favor from the super: a phone call, not to mention the hundred dollars cash she paid for a locksmith.

She could ill afford the unnecessary outlay. Money was certainly an issue. She had written to the library, taking a leave of absence after her vacation and sick pay had run out. The chief librarian, a young man whom Opal did not particularly like, had written a kind letter. But he could only keep the job open for one semester. She'd expected more, but she'd have to live with that.

Her final paycheck should have arrived by Monday, and it was already Thursday. Somehow Opal didn't trust the mailman, the flimsy boxes, or the whole New York postal system, though she knew it was as much a part of the federal post office as her suburban mail route. She opened the battered brass box, but all that was inside was a ConEd bill, a bank statement, and a letter from her real estate agent back in Bloomington. Opal had inquired about renting out her house. She hated to let it with her things in it, but in a college town that was the easiest way.

Opal walked back into the apartment, carefully locking the door behind her. She scanned the letter from the realtor; he assured her he could probably rent it to a couple of students for about six hundred a month. As if that was assuring at all! Opal shook her head. She hated to think of her china, her furniture—even her bed and sheets and linens—being abused by thoughtless kids. But she certainly could use the money.

Despite the very modest way she was living, she was about to have no income at all and she had to pay the rent and eat. She had already drawn up a careful, tight budget, and she'd stuck to it. She'd only spent money on buses, a few basic groceries, and laundry. She didn't eat out or go to the movies, but she did allow herself a weekly visit to the bookstore that Terry had worked in, though she'd only once bought a book, a guide to New York. Even with all her frugality, the totals at the bottom of her neat columns meant that each month she would be $744 poorer. After sixteen months, she would have no choice but to take early retirement or give up and go back. And have no job to go back to! Well, she didn't have to think about that right now, she told herself firmly. No use borrowing future trouble. She had plenty right here in the present.

Opal thought about the young editor at Davis & Dash. It was hard to believe that a woman so very young, and in an outfit like that, had power over books. Once again, Opal found herself worrying about it. Would she lose the manuscript? Perhaps she had been lying. Perhaps she was merely an assistant to an assistant—which was certainly what she looked like. Did a girl dressed like that *read*? Opal told herself not to get her hopes up. In five weeks of relentless assaults on more than two dozen publishers and agents, Opal had induced only this Emma Ashton to look at the manuscript. And she knew she couldn't expect an immediate hit. Well, it was a start. She'd just be prepared for a rejection and keep trying. If she could talk that child in a motorcycle jacket into it, she could talk other people into reading *The Duplicity of Men* as well.

Opal was about to pick up the manuscript again when the buzzer sounded. It startled her: Nobody ever rang except Aiello, the super, and that was only when she left several notes to him about the faulty washer in the bathroom sink, or the whining noise the refrigerator had been making. But she hadn't left Aiello a note this week. Opal went to the door but was citywise enough to first look out the peephole. It was Roberta, the woman from the bookstore. Opal had spoken briefly to her once at her shop. Surprised, Opal fumbled with the latch and pulled open the door. "Hello," Roberta said, smiling and holding out a bunch of cheerful yellow tulips. "I saw these and thought of you. Don't know why. Actually, you don't seem the yellow type. Did I do the wrong thing?"

Opal shook her head and took the flowers from Roberta. She didn't think she had a vase. "Come in. Sit down," she told Roberta, and took the flowers over to the sink. She had to settle for putting them in two mugs, one of which she put on the tiny dinette table and the other beside the daybed. "They're beautiful," Opal said. "Flowers always change a room, don't they?"

Roberta had perched herself on the daybed. Opal was disappointed to see she had not taken off her coat, but she had untied her beautiful scarf. She probably didn't mean to stay but a minute. Well, it was thoughtful nonetheless. "Yes, we're lucky in New York," said Roberta. "The Korean markets have made flowers so available, and so reasonably priced. I think the Chinese say that one way to judge the quality of a civilization is by the wide availability of affordable flowers."

Opal nodded. "I've always thought the Chinese have been better judges of civilization than the West has been." Then she remembered her manners. "Would you like a cup of coffee? I can only give you instant."

"Never drink the stuff," Roberta said. "Now, tea, on the other hand . . ."

Opal smiled. She filled the kettle and opened the cabinet over the sink. "I have Earl Grey or English Breakfast," she told Roberta.

"Earl Grey, please."

Opal took out two tea bags and put them into two cups. She'd used the mugs for the flowers, but she was embarrassed to see she had no matching saucers. She thought for a moment, with regret, of her Lennox china at home. Ah, well. It was odd to have anybody here with her. Her entertaining skills, never at the Pearl Mesta level to begin with, had atrophied. She brought over the tea and sat down in the straight-backed chair opposite Roberta. Roberta leaned forward. "May I ask you a question?" Roberta said, her voice low and confidential. Opal nodded, bracing herself.

"What are you doing here? I know it's not my place to say, but there doesn't seem to be anyone else to say it to you." Roberta's plain, serious face grew even more so. "I've seen you on Broadway, shopping at the market. And at the bookstore. But it worries me. There's nothing here for you, Opal."

"Yes, there is," Opal said. And in a rush she told Roberta about recovering the manuscript in the mail, about her campaign, her memorial to her daughter.

"You found the manuscript?" Roberta asked more than once, her eyes shining with enthusiasm or tears. "You found it?"

"Yes. And now I've even submitted it!" Opal told Roberta about every office she had tried, every call and visit she had made, culminating in her meeting with Emma Ashton. "Have you ever heard of her?" she asked.

Roberta shook her head regretfully. "But what a surprise! My goodness. When I saw you come into the bookstore I thought you were probably paralyzed. You know, just frozen here. And now I find you've accomplished all this . . ." She finished her tea, stood up, and walked to the long window that overlooked waste ground at the rear of the apartment. Her back turned, she said, "Why don't you come and work with me, Opal? I really can't pay much, but I honestly need the help. It would be good for you, and it would be good for me. After all, you can't spend twenty-four hours a day flogging the book."

Opal was glad Roberta's back was to her. It wasn't the money; it was the offer of friendship that touched her so deeply. "I'd like that very much," Opal told her, in what she recognized as one of the more profound understatements of her life.

Without turning, Roberta said, "Good. And I'd like very much to read the manuscript, if you'll allow me to. And to help in any way I can." She glanced back at Opal. "I know a few people in publishing, and a lot of booksellers, though I don't know how much it will help. Would you allow me to?"

"I'd be grateful."

Roberta stared out the window at the ugly bit of yard. "Do you garden?" she asked. "I have a garden on my terrace. You actually get some sun out there. I think that empty space could be made lovely." She looked at Opal, who had joined her at the window.

"Perhaps it could," Opal agreed.

# 30

You need a certain amount of nerve to be a writer.
—*Margaret Atwood*

Daniel stepped off the elevator and walked through the glass doors into the Davis & Dash reception area. Nervously, he ran his hand over his hair and then pulled at his tie. Perhaps he shouldn't have even *worn* the tie. After all, he wasn't a businessman or an academic. He was a novelist.

For a moment his conscience pinched him. He wasn't really the novelist either; Judith was. On this deal he was the businessman. But the important thing was getting the deal made. He shook his head, as if to loosen these distracting thoughts. No time to worry about credit right now. He hadn't told Judith about *any* of this. He didn't want to have to deal with her anxiety as well as his own.

He looked down at the receptionist, who had a tiny Davis & Dash name tag on her left shoulder. "Hi, Sandy," he said, "I'm Jude Daniel here to see Mr. Davis and Ms. Mantiss." He had never lied about his name before, never actually said this nom de plume out loud, and for a moment he expected the girl to narrow her eyes and contradict him. Instead, she merely lifted up the phone, punched in an extension, and murmured his name. Then she smiled at him.

"They'll be right out," she said. Almost immediately he was greeted by a portly, well-dressed woman who introduced herself as Mrs. Perkins. Daniel strolled with her down two long, messy corridors. Piles of manuscripts and papers were everywhere. Shelves were stuffed with books, posters, and reams of other, unidentified paper. Despite his pretended experience to Judith, he never actually had been inside a publishing house, and he tried, surreptitiously, to look into the small offices he passed. Everything seemed surprisingly disorderly, with chairs, tables, and desks stacked high with manuscripts and books. There were also cartons piled willy-nilly in the hallways. The walls had no art other than blowups of book jackets. Soon, he dared to think, his own might join them in the invigorating squalor.

At the end of the corridor he was ushered into a suite of rooms that was completely different. Here elegance and order reigned, and the furniture was not utilitarian Formica but antique wood. Daniel was brought through a private reception area, past an enormous conference room, and up to a mahogany door with gold lettering that read GERALD OCHS DAVIS. The great man himself. Even though Byron had told him that the fabled name wanted a look-see, it still felt unreal that he, Daniel Gross, was about to meet one of the most influential publishers in New York. Quickly, before he passed through the door, Daniel wiped his sweating palms against the side of his slacks. He didn't want to give a wet, wimpy, handshake to the guy who might make him wealthy.

"Well. The talk of the town," said the small, dapper man sitting behind the enormous partner's desk. He had the worst rug on his head that Daniel had ever seen. "I'm Gerald Davis." He put his hand out, and Daniel grasped it firmly—maybe too firmly, he realized as he saw Davis wince.

"I'm Jude Daniel," Daniel lied for the second time.

"And I'm Pam Mantiss, the editor in chief. I just loved your book." Daniel turned to a woman with wild blond hair, feverish eyes, and—he couldn't help but notice—enormous breasts. He held his hand out to her, and this time he was the one who nearly winced from the handshake. Pam sat down in one of a pair of low chairs in front of Davis's desk. Daniel took the other.

"Mrs. Perkins, I think we'll have some coffee," Gerald Davis said. He turned to Daniel, and his eyebrows raised. "So? Espresso, cappuccino?"

"Just coffee, thanks," Daniel said. Then he wondered if that was a mistake. Was coffee gauche? But Gerald Davis only nodded to Mrs. Perkins, and she left them.

Pam Mantiss was the first to make a move. The low chair had pushed her center of gravity to the very back of her seat. All that Daniel seemed to see when he looked at her were her eyes, her cleavage, and her legs, which were exposed to the top of her thighs. She was an attractive woman, in a frightening way. "I loved your book," she said again. Her voice was deep, almost mannish. "It's absolutely astonishing. I don't think any man has written in a contemporary woman's voice with such authority." Daniel smiled. Did this mean they definitely wanted the book? Was it a done deal? And how much would they pay? Before he could say anything, Gerald Davis chimed in.

"It's not only that," Gerald said. "It's that you turned a well-known tragic story into a really thrilling read. Of course, everyone has heard about the actual case. We know the outcome. But you make it new and hair-raising. The pacing is extraordinary. It's hard to believe it's your first novel."

"What's hard to believe is that a man wrote it," Pam Mantiss said, laughing. Daniel thought of Judith, and his face paled. He felt tiny beads of sweat break out along his hairline. Pam looked at him and half-closed her glittering, heavily lidded eyes. "When I read it, I came back to Gerald and said, 'I've got to meet this guy. Someone who *really* understands women.'" She smiled.

"Great," Daniel managed to croak. "Great," he said again, a little more enthusiastically. Now was the time. It wasn't too late; he could tell them about Judith. He could explain they were coauthors. But would he lose this offer if he did? Was there going to *be* an offer? And how much? As if reading his mind, Gerald gave him a toothy smile.

"You are going to be a very rich man," Gerald told him. Daniel let out a breath. Could he ask how rich? Or was that also gauche?

"Very rich?" he managed to echo.

"Oh, yes," Gerald told him with a laugh. "You'll be in the Bentley Turbo R class."

Daniel had no idea what Gerald was talking about. Was that a legal term? A financial term? Publishing? He tried to make a mental note of it to ask Alfred Byron about later. He wished that Byron had come to this meeting. But Byron said they wanted to meet him alone, "just a look-see," whatever that was. How should he play it?

Mrs. Perkins returned with a china tray carrying three cups. She placed it on Gerald's desk, nodded, and excused herself. Gerald and Pam began to reach for their incredibly tiny, fragile-looking demitasse cups. Daniel quickly rose from the difficult chair and passed Pam's cup to her. His own large coffee cup looked like a definite gaffe. He should have had espresso too, he thought. Though he liked cream and sugar, he was too nervous to try to pour them. He took the large cup and sat back in the uncomfortable chair, awkwardly balancing his burden on his knee.

"Well, where have you come from?" Gerald asked. "Before you take the book world by storm, we want to know who you are." Daniel managed to swallow the incredibly strong black coffee without choking.

"Originally from Westchester," he told them.

"And you teach now?" Pam asked, her eyes still half closed.

Daniel nodded. "Upstate. You know. The usual English survey courses, plus a little creative writing." He shrugged modestly. They asked about his classes, his status at the college, and when he'd begun the book. Pam asked if he was married and made a point of sighing when he said he was.

"And when did you finish the book?" Gerald asked.

"About two months ago," Daniel told them and—

briefly—thought of Judith's black mood since then. "It's been hard, you know. I've felt very empty since it's finished."

Pam nodded and leaned forward, putting her hand on his knee. Through the fabric of his trousers he could feel the heat from her palm. "Oh, you've gotta start on your next one, right away," she advised. "It's the only solution for that feeling." She smiled at him again, and he nodded.

They both seemed totally positive. It was going to happen. Would he get a million dollars for the book? He had read of huge advances for first-time novelists. He guessed that Byron would have to make the deal, but he wanted to get a feeling from them. It all seemed so complicated. What was the etiquette?

"Have you thought about your next book?" Gerald asked.

Perhaps that was it, Daniel thought. Well, he was prepared. "Oh, yes," he told them. "But I'm torn. I have three ideas, and I don't know which one to begin with." Briefly he outlined a few plots he had been thinking about, all dealing with women as both victims and perpetrators of crimes. As he talked, he saw Pam throw a look at Gerald. Did Gerald imperceptibly nod? Maybe the meeting was all to prove that he wasn't a one-book guy. Was that what a "look-see" was about? Would they want a two-book contract? Would that bring him more money up front?

"Well, what an embarrassment of riches," Gerald told him when he was through. "You have a real facility for taking an old story and casting it in an updated way. And your writing has so much belief and energy. I *saw* Elthea with those children at the lake. I felt the youngest son's arm when she pushed him. Quite astonishing."

Daniel blushed and nodded. He'd criticized that part to Judith. He'd said it was too brutal.

"And we *love* the title," Pam added. "*In Full Knowledge*. It's evocative, it pulls you in. It's really quite a gift, to title a book. A lot of times we have to change the title for the market. Authors find it painful." She again put her hand on his knee, this time giving a gentle squeeze to the flesh beneath his trousers. He must have been mistaken. He looked over at her, trying not to show any surprise, but her eyes, still wet and nervous, didn't reveal anything. "We really want this book," she said. "We might have to ask for a few editorial changes, but I'd really like to work personally with you."

Gerald nodded. "We think you have a brilliant future, and we want to be part of it." He rose. Quickly, Daniel placed his cup on the desk so that he, too, could stand. He nodded, and Gerald put out his hand. Without time to wipe his own, Daniel had to shake it. Was he dismissed? Pam stood and took his arm at the elbow, walking him across the huge office to the door. Was this it, then, Daniel wondered? He was ready to scream. How much money? How much? But surely he had impressed them. They wanted him. They said he would be rich. Surely that meant a million-dollar advance. He would be in the Bentley Turbo R class, whatever that was. He felt Pam lean against him; her large breasts pushed for a moment against his arm. She was totally terrifying. Daniel thought of a de Kooning painting—all teeth, wild energy, and frightening eyes. But he had to admit that Pam Mantiss was very arousing. He felt himself stir.

"I can't wait to work with you," she said, her voice deeper than ever. And both her eyes and her teeth glistened. "We'll be talking to Alf this week," she promised, then let him go, to be shown out by Mrs. Perkins.

# 31

> Serious books can find their audience in the United States.
>
> —*Herbert Mitgang*

On Monday morning, Emma put *The Duplicity of Men* manuscript into her backpack along with the Susann Baker Edmonds manuscript and notes. The Edmonds was going to need an entire rewrite! Despite the heavy load, Emma decided she would walk all the way from her Village apartment to Davis & Dash. She needed the time to concentrate. The day was gray and misty, but the air was soft against her cheek. It was early enough so that the traffic in the Village had not yet begun. She walked across Hudson Street; the wind from the river riffling her short hair. Emma smiled.

It had happened at last. She had found a masterpiece, the kind of book she had dreamed about publishing. She felt that this was a test. What had she gone to school for all those years, what had she been working toward, if not to get a wonderful, enlightened, and enlightening book like this one published? Surely Pam and the other members of the editorial board would see its luminous truths . . . if she could get them to read it. Emma crossed Fourteenth Street at Fifth Avenue and increased her pace.

Yes. *If* they read it. Pam and Gerald and the other editors would have to see the brilliance of Terry O'Neal's book. But what if they didn't? What if they only saw its length, its denseness, and, Emma admitted to herself, the unlikelihood of it racking up anything much in sales? It was a serious book, and Nan Talese had estimated that there were only four thousand serious readers in the country.

It would certainly be an expensive book to produce. But surely that was the reason why they—she herself—had done so many commercial books: to subsidize a brilliant, lyrical book like this one. That would justify publishing crap like Peet Trawley and Susann Baker Edmonds. In the pit of her stomach, Emma felt her excitement changing into anxiety. Everything was up to her. She *had* to present it properly. She had to get Pam behind her.

Though she was difficult, undependable, and often lazy, Pam Mantiss was not stupid. That was one of the reasons why Emma had been glad she'd been chosen to work for her. Though she often published crap, Pam never mistook it for gold. Surely she would recognize this gold that Emma had, amazingly, panned out of the river of slush that was unsolicited manuscripts.

It wasn't as if Pam hadn't published truly good books. She had. She'd discovered Mary Keene and Thomas Sutton. Both were literary, both respected. But that had been years ago. And both had left Davis & Dash. Word was that Pam tended to resent her authors once they achieved success. Anyway, for the last eight or ten years Pam had been more involved with commercial books. Emma could point that out—that Pam needed a new literary author. But perhaps that would be presumptuous.

Alternatively, Emma could present this as her own big find, since it was. But then would Pam be envious that it wasn't *her* discovery? Pam's territoriality and jealousy were frightening. That would be the other danger. Emma knew that for the sake of the book she would have to make sure that Pam not only loved *The Duplicity of Men*, but also never felt that Emma would take the credit for it. If it succeeded, it would become Pam's book.

When she became an editor, she was given the right to one editor's choice a year—publishing a book even if the rest of the editorial board didn't agree. But at her very first editorial-board meeting Pam had pushed for a new Dick book. "Is that your editor's choice?" she'd been asked.

"No, it's Emma's," she'd replied with a grin. Emma still hadn't confronted her over that. Emma sighed and adjusted the straps of her backpack. This morning it was a heavy load.

But she shouldn't feel burdened, she told herself. She should rejoice. She had been privileged to read this manuscript, and now she would simply have to accept—as her mother always told her—that along with privilege came responsibility. She would whip the Susann Baker Edmonds nonsense into shape—no matter what it took—and that would justify the publication of this book.

She did have one last strategy, though she hated to use it. If all else failed, she would just threaten to resign. And if that failed, she would actually do so. It was a gamble, but at this point Pam was lazy and dependent enough to fear losing her. Emma hated the risk, but she'd take it. Because if Davis & Dash didn't publish this book on her recommendation, Emma knew that there was no reason for her to remain there.

"I don't care *how* good it is," Pam said, her hand thumping the big pile that was *The Duplicity of Men*. I don't want to *know* how good it is! I need an eleven-hundred-page masterpiece like I need congestive heart failure."

"You have to read it," Emma repeated for the third time, as calmly yet strongly as she dared.

"What should I read it for? If I like it, it will just be more difficult to say no. And if I don't like it, then I've wasted a weekend." Pam Mantiss paused, crossed her arms, and settled them and her large *poitrine* on the desk before her. "What is it? A Pink? An Uh-oh?"

"It's nothing like that," Emma admitted.

"Look," Pam said, "you're no tyro. You know the economics of this. We're not an artsy-fartsy little literary house funded by some rich guy's ego and a grant from the National Endowment of the Arts. This isn't Citron Press. We're a business."

"Yes," Emma agreed, "but we're the *book* business." She paused. Over time Emma had found that her best argument with Pam was silence and repetition. "Pam, you *have* to read it."

She wasn't getting through to Pam, and she could feel the chance—the precious single chance *Duplicity* had—slipping away. She tried to keep down the panic she felt. Like some kind of primal jungle animal, Pam could smell fear and would just dismiss her and the book if she did so now. Emma took a deep breath. "Look," she said, "this is the kind of book that will get someone named Editor of the Year. When it's published by someone else, reviewed by Christopher Lehmann-Haupt, and then makes the front page of the *New York Times Book Review*, everyone will find out that you rejected it. How is *that* going to help Davis & Dash's credibility?"

Pam Mantiss narrowed her yellow eyes. "Who the hell is representing it?" she asked. "And why didn't they come to me directly?"

God! What could she say now? Emma swallowed. Pam was actually weakening, but here was another ego trap, one Emma hadn't foreseen. If she told the truth, about the old woman and her story of the dead daughter, Pam would laugh her out of the office. Sentimental she was not. If, on the other hand, Emma lied and pretended that Lynn Nesbit or some other important agent was representing the book, Pam would find out the lie or, worse, resent the agent for going to Emma. It was best to sidestep the issue. Pam could, sometimes, be distracted. "Look," Emma improvised, "I got it from a friend. No one knows I have it, and it hasn't been submitted anywhere yet. She'll lose her job if her boss finds out."

Pam grinned in the infuriating way she had whenever Emma mentioned a woman friend. But maybe she was smiling at the idea of a coup. Pam loved intrigue, subterfuge, and treachery—as long as she was on the winning end. Her paranoia was justified by her own shady methods.

The idea of snatching an illicit manuscript away from the jaws of the other hungry publishers out there would definitely have appeal.

"How long do we have before the submission?" Pam asked.

She was buying it? Emma took what felt like her first deep breath all morning. "Until next Monday," Emma said. She'd have to give Pam a weekend to look it over. "Will you promise to read it?" Emma asked.

"Well, I'll try to get to it."

"That's not good enough," Emma said.

*"What?"*

"You have to promise to read it or I have to give it right back," Emma told her, her heart thumping against her chest.

Pam squinted again. "I told you I'd try."

It was now or never, Emma thought. "I feel very strongly about this book, Pam. I feel that it's the best thing I've read since I've been here. And if that isn't enough of a recommendation to ensure that you'll read it, I don't see how I can continue working here." There. It was said. Emma watched Pam's mobile face freeze, while her eyes glittered even more electrically. They both stood silently for a moment. Emma had time to wonder if she'd be fired, have to quit, or win this round.

"All right," Pam said. "I'll read it."

Emma could hardly believe it. She tried to show no triumph, no excitement. This was Pam's victory. "Great," she said. "You'll like it. You really will."

"Maybe. But I *don't* like ultimatums. You used your chip. Okay. Just remember that you cashed it in. Better not use it again." Pam looked past Emma, out toward the hall. "How's the Edmonds manuscript?"

"It needs a lot of work," Emma told her.

"I *know* that."

"It can be fixed," Emma told her.

"Good. And now, if you'll excuse me, I have a meeting

about another first novel. Except it's a good one, a commercial one. One that will make us money, which is, after all, our job." Coldly, Pam walked past Emma, out of her own office, and down the hall toward God's Little Acre. Which gave Emma the space and the privacy to do a short, silent, victory dance all around the room.

# 32

Getting even is one reason for writing.
—*William Gass*

"We're suing. *Of course* we're suing. We're getting a goddamned injunction against her and her publishers and stopping the sons of bitches now," Alf nearly yelled.

Susann stiffened. She wondered how much privacy a privacy panel in the limo really guaranteed. She'd picked Alf up at the airport—he'd been in Frankfurt, checked up on the house in France, and had flown in from Nice. They were going straight to the Davis & Dash meeting. She'd *had* to tell Alf about Kim. A blurb about Kim's book deal with Citron Press had appeared in *Publishers Weekly* while he was in Frankfurt. He wasn't taking it well. "Do we have to tell them?" she asked, and she knew her voice sounded pathetically like a frightened child's. She'd done the best she could to prepare for this meeting: her hair was freshly done, her suit was immaculate, and her makeup perfect. But she was still very frightened.

"Of course we have to tell them," Alf snapped. "It will be a joint suit. Do you think Gerald Ochs Davis has paid for the Baker Edmonds name to see some *schprintz* buy it for a buck three-eighty? We know she's a thief. But Kim hasn't just ripped off your *name*; I'll bet they copy your cover style and your titles, too. This isn't a situation like Mary and Carol Higgins Clark. *They're* friends as well as mother and daughter. They agreed to share the name. But you're not friends with Kim." Alf was breathing hard. Susann wondered if he'd taken his pills. He was tired and cranky from the trip.

"She's done nothing but bleed you and exploit you for

years," he continued. "This is one exploitation she is not going to get away with. I can't stop you from giving her money, but I can stop her from stealing your name."

Susann winced. The fact was that in publishing, like all other American businesses, brand names sold. Bookstores prepared for a new shipment of Collinses or Clancys or Steels knowing that shoppers bought by the name. They flew out of stores. Only this year, Grisham's publisher shipped three million hardcover copies of his new novel, *The Rainmaker*, and had to guarantee that they'd arrive at all the nation's bookstores on the same day.

So Susann understood that her name had value—and that seeing it on another book, a book not by her, was a sort of infringement, legal or not. Fans might buy it—would buy it—by mistake. Bookstores would order it, counting on that mistake. And even the book clubs—who rarely took up a first novelist—might buy something with the "brand recognition" Kim's book would automatically have.

Susann felt sick to her stomach. It wasn't that what Alf was saying was untrue; the fact that it *was* true and the nastiness of his description was what she found so extremely unsettling. Kim had stolen before—money for drugs, and she'd shoplifted, too. But calling her a thief was so . . . hard. And now that burden was added to the already frightening prospect of the editorial meeting she was about to face. She smoothed the skirt of her suit.

Susann hated to be edited. It made her feel criticized and misunderstood and stupid. Imogen had always been very gentle with her. Pam certainly wouldn't. She knew that there were problems with her new book. When she'd asked Edith to grade it, as she always did when they completed a manuscript, Edith had looked at her coolly and said, "C minus." That alone was enough to make Susann feel faint, but though she resented Edith's judgment, she accepted it. Edith was not a liar, nor malicious. Before this Edith had never graded her lower than a B plus. Always, they had worked together to raise it to at least an A minus. But Susann didn't know how to fix this slight book. It wasn't her métier. This meeting, to go over editorial "suggestions," would be tense enough with Susann remembering Edith's grade as well as the disappointing performance of her last book. But now the additional problem of Kim's knockoff book seemed too much. It was *all* too much. For the dozenth time, Susann wished she'd never left her old publisher.

"Stop the car," Susann said. Her voice rose. "Stop the car, now." The limo slowed, and the moment it was stopped Susann threw open her door, not waiting for the driver's help. She stepped out onto the pavement, her feet encased in dainty Christian Louboutin heels. Bending from the waist so she would not muss her bouclé Sonia Rykiel suit, Susann vomited all across the back fender of the immaculate stretch limo.

"I don't understand," Gerald said stiffly. "When did you find this out?"

Susann sat quietly. She might not feel calm, but at least she would *look* calm. Susann knew what she had to do. She would give them her best smile. She looked up at all of them and tried to move the corners of her mouth—but found that, as if she'd had a stroke, her mouth could not obey. Alf had warned her not to mention the meeting with Kim. He spoke for them both: "We read it in *Publishers Weekly*, just the way you did. I should explain that Susann has been estranged from her daughter for some time. The kid's been in every rehab joint in the country. She's a drunk and a druggie, completely undependable."

Susann tried not to wince. She thought of the afternoon she had walked into her bedroom and found her husband fondling poor Kimmy. Robert Edmonds had only been Kim's stepfather, but he'd raised her far more than her real father had. Susann had never gotten over the shock and the disgust at seeing Robert's hairy adult hand covering Kim's crotch. Even now, in this immaculate office, she felt as if she might be sick again, right there on Gerald Ochs Davis's superb English antique table. Susann knew that Kim had been badly damaged, and she also knew that Kim had blamed her and manipulated her for years. Both realities were equally true. Susann had simply tried the best she could to cope. She had left Robert Edmonds, she had found a therapist for Kim, she'd gotten launched on her writing career, and she had tried to live with Kim's anger and instability. When she met Alf and the money started coming in, she'd used a lot of it to try and assuage Kim's pain.

But, as with Humpty Dumpty, all the king's horses and all the king's men didn't seem able to put Kim back together. Once broken, she remained broken, and both of them had to cope with the result as best as each could. Today the result had not taken Susann to court, to bail Kim out for passing bad checks or for shoplifting, nor had it brought her to yet another hospital or intervention. Instead it had brought her to the private conference room of Davis & Dash's publisher, where she sat before these two strangers, humbled and humiliated, and could explain almost nothing about the truth behind the visible situation.

"I'd like to call Jim Meyer in, if you don't mind," Gerald said. "You remember him. He's our corporate counsel." Had he sneered? Susann knew that Alf had negotiated for months with Meyer to get every penny, every concession he could. Exposing this mess to Meyer would be one further humiliation.

Susann sat as still as she could. Somehow all of this had taken on a life of its own. What if she simply stood up and screamed, "Leave Kim alone! Leave my daughter alone!" But she sat frozen, doing nothing.

Alf cleared his throat in the silence. "The thing you need to know is that legally she has no right to the Edmonds name. Kim is Susann's daughter by a previous marriage. She was raised, in part, by Robert Edmonds. But he never legally adopted her. She did use the name growing up, but there might be an angle there," Alf suggested.

Under the table Susann felt her hands clench, and her perfectly manicured nails dug into the flesh of her palms. Why had he told them that? He was such a bulldog. He was always so ready to fight. Why couldn't he just leave Kim alone? Or put this in Davis & Dash's hands and walk away? For a terrible moment Susann could not help but compare Alf's attitude toward her daughter with his attitude to his sons. He would never do anything, anything at all, that would hurt *them*. Not even marry the woman he loved. Or *said* he loved. For the first time since she had taken her seat in the exquisite conference room, Susann moved, but only to shake her head. Suddenly she felt exhausted—as if lifting even a pen would be far beyond her strength. I need a good, long rest, she thought.

"Well," Pam Mantiss said, "clearly this is going to take some time and legal action. In the meantime, why don't we focus on some of the editorial issues that have to be addressed?" The editor in chief looked across the table at Susann. "You see, Susann, the thing is, this book just won't cut it. You need a hit, and you need one badly. I'm afraid this book—as it stands—is not that hit. We're asking for significant changes. It's going to take a lot of work."

# 33

Some editors are failed writers, but so are most writers.

—*T. S. Eliot*

Pam Mantiss looked at the manuscript in front of her. *The Duplicity of Men*. It was badly typed, and to make that worse, it had been badly photocopied. The pages were blurry, and reading all 1,114 of them had been a bitch. It had taken all weekend. But Pam had to admit it was a brilliant book—perhaps the most brilliant book she'd ever read in manuscript. The question now wasn't whether the book was good, but whether it would be good for *her*.

There were certain things about *The Duplicity of Men* that Pam liked. She liked its intelligence, and she liked to be thought of as intelligent. Only an intelligent editor would handle this book. Was that enough reason to publish it? What would be the consequences? It would burnish her reputation, tarnished over *SchizoBoy*, but what would it do to her bottom line? Because being intelligent was certainly not enough. Pam Mantiss also had to be successful.

Pam luxuriated in success and all that it brought with it. Except, perhaps, the workload. For the last five years, Pam had been able to work at a manic pace for four days a week and have Friday, Saturday, and Sunday to herself. Many senior editors in publishing managed to do that. But the only way she could manage was because of Emma. Pam hadn't liked the threat Emma had made and the way she had made it, but she had to admit to herself that she didn't want to have to give Emma up. So the question on the table today, along with the mammoth manuscript, was how to keep her success, her reputation, her profits, *and*

Emma. The only answer seemed to be by publishing *The Duplicity of Men*.

Well, maybe that wasn't so bad. After all, she'd gotten the Jude Daniel book for a song. And she had a good feeling about that one—it had "bestseller" written all over it. Plus, the giveaways she'd had to promise to Byron was all stuff the Edmonds book needed anyway to keep the old bag on the list. And with what they'd paid for it, they'd have to spend to keep her on the list. After yesterday's meeting, Pam thought that Susann was pistol-whipped enough to make any changes necessary to resuscitate the pathetic manuscript. And Jim Meyer, the creep, would handle the daughter/author issue.

Pam looked up at the clock. It was almost two-thirty, and she had a meeting with Stewart Campbell at three. She struggled into a pair of black jeans but could barely get them half-zipped. Well, she'd throw a long sweater over them. Campbell was a nobody—she'd published two of his mysteries, and they'd gone nowhere fast. She was about to reject his latest, but then she realized he was the solution to her Peet Trawley problem. In the immortal words of Don Corleone, she was about to make him an offer he couldn't refuse.

So, she decided, she'd do this Terry O'Neal book. Anyway, she'd manage to buy *Duplicity* before any other house got to see it, thanks to Emma's anonymous "friend." The list was shaping up, if only she could bag a couple of other good things and get the new Trawley book finished.

Pam sat in the bright light behind the Formica table at Ollie's Noodle House. Stewart sat across from her, playing with the huge bowl of soup he had ordered. Pam should have stuck with the soup, too. Instead, she'd had fried dumplings, the irresistible scallion pancakes, and the chow fun for which Ollie's was famous. But tomorrow, she decided, she was going to go on a water fast. She'd stop on her way home this afternoon and buy two cases of

Evian and have them delivered. Now she looked across the table at Stewart. She'd better talk fast, because in just three-quarters of an hour the dinner crowd would begin to trickle in and the joint would be jammed, with the excess spilling out in lines along upper Broadway for the next five hours. Pam didn't need to have this conversation overheard.

Stewart looked at her. He had nice eyes, and the kind of dark, thick hair that stood up from his head in a healthy-looking thatch. He was a little younger than she was—maybe thirty-five or -six—and not bad-looking. But there was a softness about his face that in men always turned Pam off. She'd never slept with Stewart. Or maybe she had, once, after his first book party. It was hard to remember. She used to drink. Whatever, it had never happened again, and it never would.

Stewart's books sold, but not much. They certainly weren't art and not quite popular enough to be money-makers. That made him a hack. He'd put together a plot, he'd plod through it in a workmanly way, and he'd get his stuff in on time. He'd done two books, and she'd never paid him any more for the second than she had paid him for the first. He had a day job, substitute teaching in Brooklyn. She knew nothing else about him, except she thought he'd once been married.

"So, what do you think?" Stewart was asking. He mistakenly believed she'd called him about his work. As if she cared. He was talking about creating a new detective, as if Pam needed another goddamned Uh-oh. She shrugged, and before she had a chance to tell him no, she watched his shoulders droop and his lip extend. This was a man who expected defeat.

"Forget about it, Stewart. I have something more important to talk to you about. How would you like to make some real money?"

"Who do I have to kill?" Stewart asked. It wasn't such a funny joke: Pam remembered that last year Stewart had been stabbed, badly, by a junior high school student. It had taken him months to recover, and his case against the Board of Education was dragging on endlessly.

"No violence involved, except of the psychic kind," Pam assured him. She paused. "Aside from your recent near-death experience, did you ever think of ghosting?"

Stewart smiled, his grin lopsided. "I wasn't sure my writing was good enough for anyone to hire me to write *for* them," he snorted.

Time for some pop psychology, Pam decided. The guy had to be enthusiastic and motivated. At the same time, if the poor fuck wasn't desperate, he wouldn't take the gig. "Hey, don't be so down on yourself. Your work's not so bad. It's just not succeeding financially. If you had more time to hone it, to work on it . . . but that takes money. I have a way we both can make some money." She paused, certain she had his attention. He'd stopped picking at his rice noodles, and she nodded toward the bowl. "Are you done?" she asked. When he said he was, she pulled the dish in front of her and began to shovel the noodles into her mouth. Stewart just sat there. What a schlemiel. But one she could manipulate—one she owned. "Do you know that Peet Trawley died?" she asked. He shook his head. "Well, he did. And I have a manuscript of his—well, a kind of outline—that's got to be smoothed out. Well, actually, finished. Uh . . . written, really. It's got to be written."

Stewart was silent, but he wasn't stupid. "You mean you need a ghostwriter to finish *Peet Trawley's* book?"

She nodded, her mouth full of noodles.

Stewart watched her eat for a few moments. "Is it legal?"

"Sure," she said and wiped her hand with her mouth. "*He* gets the royalties," she reminded him, her resentments still fresh.

"But he's dead."

"Okay. So his family gets the royalties. You get the drift.

The point is, I need someone who'll take on the work for hire. Flat fee. No credit. Just the money."

"And you think I could do it?"

She'd have to play this part carefully. "I think with my help you can do it," she said. "But then Peet needed a lot of my help, too." Just then, as she had feared, a noisy group of Columbia students walked into the restaurant. Pam hoped they wouldn't sit anywhere near her. She also hoped they weren't from the law school. She'd have to make a side deal with Stewart on this. Jim Meyer and the others could never know. She'd tell Gerald but no one else. They'd crucify her. She crossed her arms and leaned forward. "I need this work done fast. I tell you the story, you write it, I edit it. You make any revisions needed. You're paid upon completion, not before. You agree not to reveal your involvement. Ever, for any reason. Not to your girlfriend, not to your mother. No one. And then you get a hundred thousand dollars."

His eyes opened wide. He'd never been paid more than twenty thousand for any of the books he'd done for her. Now for the clincher. "Plus I'll pay you twenty-five thousand for your new book idea," she said. "Just a one-book contract, but it's a new start." She could see he was reeling from his good fortune. "Still, the Trawley book has to come first," she continued. "Ya gotta work fast, Stewie, *and* this has to be absolutely confidential. Otherwise, you'll be in breach of contract. No one can know. Not even people at Davis & Dash."

"And you really think I can do it?" Stewart asked. Pam hid her smile. He was hooked.

"I *know* you can do it," Pam told him. She handed him a fortune cookie. "You don't need to open this," she said. "You've got a great future now."

# 34

> I'd like to have money. And I'd like to be a good writer. These two can come together, and I hope they will, but if that's too adorable, I'd rather have money.
>
> —*Dorothy Parker*

"A hundred and fifty thousand dollars?" Daniel repeated into the phone. "Is that *all*?" It was more money than Daniel had made in his entire teaching career, but he knew it was peanuts as an advance. He bit his lower lip with disappointment. What had all that talk in Gerald Ochs Davis's office been about? Hadn't Davis promised him he'd be rich? A hundred fifty thousand dollars was not rich.

Since the meeting Daniel had found out that a Bentley Turbo R was a quarter-of-a-million-dollar car. Hadn't Davis said he'd be in that class? Well, not with a hundred and fifty G's, parceled out in three payments—one when he signed the contract, one when he finished the final edit, and one when it was published. And from that he had to deduct taxes and the 20 percent that Alf Byron was demanding as his agent's fee. It must be a ridiculously low offer. And, to add insult to the injury, Alf was telling him to *take* it. Daniel could hardly believe his ears.

"I thought you said this was a million-dollar book!" he said.

"No. I said this was a *potential* million-dollar book," Byron reminded him. "But someone—some publisher—is going to have to spend a lot to make a lot. And Pam *loves* the book. She'll spend. They're ready to promote it, advertise it, tour you. There is chemistry between you.

That's what's important. It's worth more than up-front money."

Nothing was worth more than money, Daniel thought. And the "chemistry" between him and Pam made him shiver. "Can't you take it somewhere else?" Daniel asked, and he could hear the whine in his voice. "Couldn't you auction it or something?"

"This is where the expertise of a really good agent becomes so important," Byron said in a soothing voice. But Daniel wasn't soothed. "This was a careful match I made," Byron went on. "It's why I insist on twenty percent instead of ten or fifteen. Because I am going to be deeply involved. I guide careers. I build careers. I made Susann Baker Edmonds. You know, she's dedicated four of her books to me. I virtually wrote them with her. And I'll do that for you, Jude."

"Daniel. Not Jude: Daniel," he snapped. Jesus, he thought, he didn't need anyone else to write his books. He merely needed cash.

Alf continued. "I thought of a lot of other options, other houses. I promise you that. I know everyone in the business. But this felt right. Trust me on this. I think Pam really gets your book. You know, the union of a writer and an editor is like a marriage. The right vision, the right temperament—"

"We were talking about money, not marriage," Daniel snapped in disappointment. "I didn't write this book . . ." he paused for a moment, his own words guilty and loud in his ears. "I didn't write this particular book for love," he continued. "I wrote it to be commercial. I wrote it for the money. So that I could be free to write what I wanted—"

"Yes. Yes, I know that," Byron interrupted. "And the money and the freedom will come. That I promise you. But a writer's career is like a building. It has to have a solid foundation. And your first book is the key to that. If it succeeds, you make all the rules. But if it fails . . ." Byron paused, and in the silence Daniel felt the fear rush in. He swallowed, though his mouth had gone dry. Yes, there was that. What if the book failed?

"Is that the absolute most they'll offer?" Daniel asked.

"Remember it isn't just the money. You're going to be judged by the house you come from, and nothing is too good for you. You should go with the Cadillac, not the Buick of publishing. In the end, it'll make more money for you anyway. Well, she seemed firm. But I have my ways," Byron chuckled. "This is where you get the benefit of my leverage. Believe me, they don't want to piss off Susann Baker Edmonds—or her agent. I carry a lot of weight at that house. You couldn't be in better hands. I'll see what I can do. We give them the paperback rights, that's where the real money is anyway. Remember . . . there's also the possibility of a movie sale, serialization. I'll also be sure the contract includes bonuses for book-club sales. And extra money for making the bestseller list. Why, you'll get five thousand bucks for each week you're on the list. If you're only on for a month, that's twenty thousand right there. And if you're on it for a year—"

"I know how to multiply," Daniel said dryly, but he felt a little better. He'd had no idea how complex these deals were. "All right, Alf. I'll trust you. Let's take the deal."

"You won't be sorry," Alf told him. "You're going to be a giant. You're no hack. You can really write, son." Then, with a voice deep with portent, he said: "You're going to be the next Sidney Sheldon."

"Come on, Pam. You can have him signed, sealed, and delivered for another twenty-five thousand. What's twenty-five thousand to Davis & Dash?"

"It's twenty-five thousand, Alf," Pam said coldly. Pam Mantiss wasn't just a cold, smart bitch like everyone in the industry said. She was a cold, smart, *cheap* bitch, as far as Alf Byron was concerned. When it came to negotiating for manuscripts, she acted as if the money came from her own pocket. Alf knew he never would have gotten Susann's contract out of Pam Mantiss. It was a funny thing: In his experience, men in publishing showed their power by spending huge amounts on acquisitions—the more they spent on an author, the more important they were. Women, on the other hand, tried to get things as cheaply as possible. Oh, well. Alf hunkered down, relishing the fight.

"I know he's going to go with us, Alf. He'll take the one-fifty," Pam said flatly. "And if he doesn't, take him elsewhere."

Alf considered. "There was another option. You're only talking hardcover. Look, why don't you go to paperbacks and put together a hard/soft deal."

"Fuck that." There was a lot of bad blood between Steve Weiss, head of Paperbacks, and Pam. While most of the risk was in hardcover, most of the profit came from paperback. Pam sold off paperback rights to the highest bidder, even if it was to a competitive house. "I tell you what I *will* do," Pam said after a moment's silence. "I'll make it one seventy-five, but I own sixty percent of whatever we get for paperback rights."

"Oh, come on!" Alf whined. "If the book goes big, we could get an extra million for paperback. And if it sells to the movies, we could get more."

"And if my grandma had balls, she'd be my grandfather," Pam told him.

"It's a rotten deal for the professor."

"Look, Jude wants the money now, not at an auction a year from now. *Tempis fuckit,* as they say in Latin. Make up your mind. And who knows. If the book flops, no one will want paperback rights. So I'll give him this money now. If he makes money later, I get to keep some of it. It intensifies my commitment to making the hardcover a success."

"It intensifies your profits when the hardcover becomes a bestseller. It's highway robbery, Pam."

She shrugged. There was another pause. "Tell you what, Alf," Pam said, "I can't go any higher on the advance, but I can sweeten the deal for you a little bit. I'll add television advertising to Susann's marketing campaign."

"Network or cable?" Alf asked. Needless to say, advertising for Susann wouldn't do a goddamned thing for Daniel Gross, but then again, Daniel Gross wasn't Alf's major client. And Susann needed all the help she could get. This would give her a boost.

"Forget network!" Pam snapped. "We can't afford it. We go Lifetime. It's a good women's channel. We've been having luck with it."

"You should do the ads anyway," Alf said. "It has nothing to do with Jude Daniel's book. No deal."

"Okay," Pam said, but she sounded sly. "One last thing." He knew it. She had something up her sleeve. "I've spoken to Jim Meyer about this problem with Kim Baker. It could be a costly legal battle, Alf. Put another nail in Susann's coffin and drain you dry. Legal fees. Money right out of your pocket. But I'd be willing to commit Davis & Dash to handle the legal costs. We can push them to the limit, stop Kim's book," she paused again. "Meanwhile, a hundred and seventy-five thousand dollars is not a bad advance for a first novel," she reminded Alf. She waited. "Deal?" she asked.

"Deal," he told her.

# 35

It is more blessed to give than to receive.
—*Acts 20:35*

Emma was jubilant over the editorial-meeting results. *The Duplicity of Men* would be published! Emma had stood up for what she believed in, and it had paid off.

Standing up to Pam had been the second brave act of her life; the first had been to come to New York after Wellesley and go from publishing house to publishing house, looking for work in a market where jobs just weren't available. Both acts had made her more happy than anything ever had. Perhaps, Emma thought, she should be brave more often.

Emma did admit that bravery had a price: She was tired from the meeting, the fight, and the long week. She'd have the weekend to recover, and—for a change—no work to take home. She'd sleep for two days! Light-headed, she walked down the messy hallway to her office and, heard her phone begin to ring. She hurried to reach it. "Emma Ashton," she said.

"Hi, Emma, it's Alex."

Immediately her heart begin to thump almost painfully in her chest. She clutched the side of the desk. Alex was calling back! It was so rare, so very rare for Emma to like someone, in *this* way. She'd given up hope that Alex had felt the same. And now, after weeks of silence, Alex had called.

"How are you?" Emma tried to sound friendly but cool. After all, Alex *hadn't* called immediately. Emma told herself not to act berserk with joy, but somehow, inappropriate as it was, she did feel joyful.

"I just got back from Los Angeles. I'm exhausted, that's how I am. I know everyone puts down L.A. to be cool, but I'm different: I *sincerely* hate it."

Emma laughed. "What were you out there for?" So, Alex had been away. Was it true? Maybe there was a reason for the weeks of silence.

"I had to meet with power agents out there. Book-to-movie guys. Todd Harris and Michael Siegel. You know. Anyway, I have a book that's just been optioned by Warner Brothers. My first movie deal."

"Congratulations," Emma said, and then she couldn't resist bragging herself. "And I've just managed to get a really brilliant first novelist signed."

"Wow. Lots of firsts here. Congratulations. Does he have representation?"

"The novelist?" Emma had to smile. "First of all, *he's* a she."

"Oops." Alex giggled. "My first mistake. Caught out in really inappropriate political incorrectness. Me, of all people. Well, can I represent her?"

"Not unless you're into seances," Emma continued, trying to sound stern, though she was actually smiling. "She's dead."

"*A first novelist who's dead*?" Alex asked. "Doesn't look good for the backlist. What's up? Death before publication is not a good career move."

Emma explained the situation and told about meeting the mother in the reception area. "I know what a long shot it was, but the book is brilliant. Absolutely brilliant. And I made them see it. The editorial board has agreed to publish it."

Alex paused only a moment. "Well, just because she's dead doesn't mean she doesn't need representation," Alex laughed. "Maybe I could help the mother."

Emma laughed, too. And then, as natural as breathing, she said, "Why don't we get together and celebrate? Have a drink. Talk it over." God, she'd been brave again! And she was rewarded.

"You took the words right out of my mouth," Alex told her. "I've been thinking about you since we met."

Emma could hardly believe it. Could Alex really be as interested in her as that? When Alex suggested that they meet right after work that night at the Royalton, Emma agreed immediately. For a minute or two she felt almost too happy, but the feeling faded quickly. Within fifteen minutes Emma was second-guessing herself. Fear set in. Perhaps she should have played harder to get. Perhaps Alex's story about being out of town was bullshit, and worst of all, perhaps Alex was more interested in cadging a new client than in Emma herself. Oh God, she thought, Frederick was right. He'd always warned her not to be so prone to second thoughts, self-doubt, and caution. Stop it! she told herself. Emma decided she would throw caution to the wind. She'd just go for what she wanted. She'd let herself be happy. What the hell.

Emma smiled to herself. Life was holding new promise: an important novel *and* the chance at romance. She'd go for it. In fact, she wondered how she would be able to hold her impatience and manage to get through the rest of the day.

Reluctantly, she sat down at her desk. She looked at the stack of new work in front of her and groaned inwardly. Even the pile of unopened mail was inches deep. No wonder all the Davis & Dash offices were always so jammed with paper. Emma began to sort. There were a few memos: one about filling in expenses more accurately and another about medical benefits. She threw both into the trash. There was the weekly printout of book sales and orders. Quickly Emma skimmed the list to see how some of her books were doing. Not particularly well. The phone rang, and she decided to let the automated system answer it. But what if it was Alex, calling again to change the time—or to cancel? Emma's stomach lurched. Ridiculous, and if it was, she'd take the call later and call back.

She ignored the phone and opened a small package:

There was a handwritten note from Susann Baker Edmonds, and it included a gift—a really beautiful leather wallet. "I'm so delighted to finally get the chance to be working with you." Yeah, right! Emma knew that Susann didn't want to be edited by anyone. Susann and her agent had already made that very clear. Still, it was a nice gesture, if insincere. Well, actually the *gesture* was pretty lame, but the *wallet* was nice. She'd have to write a thank-you to Susann. Emma added that to her "to do" list.

She opened a few more letters, filed a couple of memos from the sales department, and dealt with a set of galleys that had just come in and needed to be sent on to the author. Heather should have done this but seemed always to be busy on one of the other editors' work. There was another package, and when Emma saw that it was from Italy, she smiled. Frederick. A gift! He was so good and generous about gifts. Even while he was having a romance—if that's what he was having and if it was still on—he'd thought of her. Unless, of course, it *wasn't* still on. Maybe he'd shopped for consolation.

It wasn't his handwriting on the brown paper. Well, he probably wouldn't write it himself. But she bet it was a nice gift—Frederick had more money than she, along with a generous streak and good taste. Maybe the handwriting was his girlfriend's. What could be nicer than a surprise gift from an indulgent brother? She felt terrific. She would have drinks and possibly dinner tonight with Alex, and the prospect of a weekend loomed before her now as an invitation to fun, not work. Emma snipped the string and tore off the paper. There was a white, tissue-wrapped something that looked suspiciously like a manuscript within. Oh, no! Surely Frederick had not secretly been writing a book! Emma lifted the folded cover note.

It was difficult to read, as it was in Frederick's ever-more-illegible handwriting, and she felt her good mood begin to ebb. It *was* a manuscript, though not by him. It was written by "a good friend" of his, and he had underlined *good*. He was asking her to read it, and begging her—only if she thought it was good, of course—to do what she could for it. Emma threw the letter down. God! How could she handle this? Weren't manuscripts from dead authors represented by their aging mothers enough to deal with? The chances of this thing being any good were minimal. And disappointing Frederick and his new friend would be such a drag.

Lately, thinking about Frederick always made Emma feel guilty and anxious. The phone rang. Great! More trouble to finish off her anticipatory mood! She decided she would not answer the phone; she wouldn't even take the messages until Monday. The hell with it. With a sigh Emma began to load up her backpack.

Had she really wanted to be an editor? Emma asked herself. Had she really thought that it was the best of jobs, a tremendous privilege to get to spend her life reading? What drug had she been on? Tired, her good mood ebbing, she put the manuscript in her backpack. She hoped that Frederick, somewhere in Italy, was going to have a good weekend, even if she did not.

# 36

> One of the oldest human needs is having someone wonder where you are when you don't come home at night.
>
> —*Margaret Mead*

Frederick took Camilla's hand as they left the Helvetia & Bristol Hotel. The weekend crowd was noisy and pleasant. They'd been a part of it, talking about her book, a possible title, the tour group, and the two new shirts he'd bought. He told her about his job and his flat—which he called an apartment—in New York. Then he'd offered to walk her home. Camilla had been relieved that he had not invited her up to his room, though she was sure it was elegant and seductive. She just didn't want to be put in that position.

But she realized as they walked through the Firenze evening that she would like to sleep with him. Somehow, his lack of expectation, the very lack of pressure from him, had made the difference. Unlike Gianfranco, who had wooed her with passionate words and romantic little gifts, Frederick's calmness had reassured and attracted her. Unlike Gianfranco, Frederick really listened to her, and helped her in ways that mattered. Camilla made up her mind. She would sleep with him tonight, back at her own tiny room. Assuming, of course, that he wanted to.

She thought he did. His hand—all long, slim fingers—was wrapped around hers in a gentle but possessive way. His whole arm pressed against hers, as if he were taking her lead on every step. It was surprisingly sexy. He was not a dominant-male type, that was certain, but he was far from weak. He was her height and didn't weigh much more than she did. But despite his unprepossessing physique and looks, his deep enthusiasm for her, for her writing and her knowledge of art, moved her. After all, what had good looks in men brought her before? Yes she was definitely attracted to Frederick on some deeper level. Though she could ill afford another disappointment, Camilla felt that Frederick could be something more in her life than an ill-fated affair. And she needed something more.

Being alone so much had taught Camilla to be brutally honest with herself. She was attracted to Frederick's intelligence, his wit, and his kindness. More than anything else, she was attracted to his stability. She'd liked his solid, protective, upmarket mother, and she liked the description of his life in New York. She admitted to herself that there was none of the breathtaking excitement here that there had been with Gianfranco and others, but Camilla knew just where *that* kind of excitement would lead her—to obsession, unrealistic expectations, and disappointment.

They rounded a corner onto the Via Cistone. Her *pensione* was just a few steps up the street. As they approached the door, Frederick stumbled over a cobblestone and she had to spin and shore him up with her free hand. He shook his head and apologized. "I'm worse and worse," he said. But she patted his arm. He was nervous, and so clearly awkward and vulnerable. It was a nice change that, for once, it was the man, not she, who was at a disadvantage.

There, in the dim light from the street lamp, she turned to him. "This is where I live," she said. "It's not much. Would you like to come upstairs?"

He lifted his hand up to her face, gently touching her cheek and then her forehead. He moved his hand under her chin and brought her mouth to his for a kiss. It was a promising kiss. Not shy at *all.*

"I'd like that very much."

Camilla opened the enormous door and brought him over to the steps. They were shallow and marble and curved in a gentle ellipse up to the floors above. Hesitant at first, once Frederick grasped the rail, he moved smoothly beside her. At the top of the second staircase Camilla gave Frederick her arm and led him down the long, dark hallway. He held her arm firmly with one hand, dragging his other hand along the wall. Her room was at the very end of the second floor and had two windows, one facing east and one facing south. There was no real view to speak of, just some red-tiled roofs, stucco walls, and a bit of the church of San Giovanni. As quietly as she could, Camilla opened the door and let Frederick in. Although her landlady seemed to like her, Camilla felt that discretion was more than desirable, especially as Signora Belleccio had turned a blind eye to Gianfranco's first visit.

Frederick stood very still while Camilla closed the door behind them. She was about to turn on the light when Frederick, his voice thick, said, "Let's leave it dark." He was very close to her; she could feel his breath against her cheek. He stood there, deeply still, but now she didn't feel any nervousness or tentativeness from him. Slowly, he put one arm behind her, his hand low on her back. With his other hand he cupped her head and brought her face to his for another kiss. Camilla relaxed, her body drawn to him as much by her loneliness and attraction as by his hand pressing her against his chest. The kiss was luxurious, long, and searching. He tasted sweet, as if he had somehow turned the wine they'd drunk to sugar. Camilla sighed. Then he took her hands and held them together, gently, at the wrists. "Take me to your bed," he said, and she did.

Camilla lay on her side, cuddled against Frederick. Because he wasn't much taller than she, he fit her nicely in several senses of the word. In the darkness, her back to him, she smiled. She felt rapturous. Frederick's passionate, gentle, insistent lovemaking had come as more than a surprise. His hunger, and his skill, had almost been a shock. Had she imagined him awkward, inexperienced? There was nothing rushed or fumbling about him in bed. As awkward as he might be when vertical on his two feet, he was masterful when he was horizontal in bed. Camilla nearly giggled with the sheer joy of it.

Perhaps she *had* felt some doubt about his performance, sensed something amiss, what with his hesitancy, and his mother and all. Perhaps she *had* taken him to bed partially as a sort of recovery, or through lack of other options. But he was a wonder, far better as a lover than Gianfranco had ever been. He had made her shiver, and he had made her laugh, and then he had made her come. Afterward, without discussion, he had taken out a condom—something Gianfranco had fought every single time. Frederick was sure of himself but so very considerate. He'd entered her, and after he'd had his own release, he had actually brought her to orgasm again. She'd laughed then. "Where have you been hiding all of my life?" she'd cried. Now they were crowded on the narrow bed, but tired as she was, Camilla felt neither uncomfortable nor sleepy. She felt as if it were Christmas or some other usually disappointing holiday, and she had opened an unpromising package to find a splendid treasure that was all hers. She couldn't help it—she *did* giggle aloud.

Frederick moved against her and gently blew in her ear. "Are you laughing at me?" he asked, but his voice was indulgent. "Ready for more?"

"How old are you?" she asked. "I thought all this was supposed to peak years ago."

Frederick laughed. "I'm a late bloomer," he said. "I'm thirty-six. I think I can hold it together for another eighteen months or so."

Camilla did a quick mental calculation. He was almost seven years older than she, though somehow he seemed older. She'd been too shy to ask until now. Camilla raised herself on one elbow and kissed her surprise package on the mouth, then on each of his eyes. "Are you sleepy?" she asked. He shook his head. "Then what should we do?"

"Why don't I tell you how much I like your book?"

"Been there. Done that," she said, but she blushed with pleasure.

"Then why don't you describe your room to me," he suggested.

"What? This room?"

"Well, this room to start."

"I'm afraid it's not much. A bit of a tip, really."

"A tip?"

"Oh. A mess in your language." She kissed his nose and snuggled nearer to him.

"Then describe this room as you would like it to be," he told her. "It's too dark for me to tell the difference."

Camilla lay back down beside him. He tucked the sheet over her shoulder and put an arm under her head. She liked his quirkiness. She thought of a favorite room of hers, one in a private villa just outside Ravenna, to which she had taken several special tour groups. It was a salon overlooking the river, and it had enchanted her. So, lying in the dark in her small narrow room, Camilla described the lofty frescoed ceiling, the Palladian windows, and the magnificent mosaic floor of the Villa d'Amica. She described the open loggia, covered with wistaria vines, that ran beside it. Frederick listened so quietly, his breathing so deep that after a little while she was afraid he might have fallen asleep. But when she dared to look over at him in the darkness his eyes were open, though unfocused. He must have sensed her looking at him and turned his head.

"Nice place you got here," he said, and she laughed. He paused, then lowered his voice. "I love to hear your descriptions, Camilla. They make me see things as if I'd never seen them before. Or as if I were seeing them now, here in the dark. You bring everything you describe to life. That was the wonder of your book. Right now I would swear that if I put my foot over the side of the bed, my feet would touch mosaic."

"No. You'd only step on my knickers, I'm afraid." She

smiled at him. It was the last smile she would give him for a long time.

"I have something to tell you," Frederick said, and his tone of voice told her everything she needed to know. She felt the ocean of loneliness outside the room, just waiting to rush in and engulf her. God, she should have known! What was it going to be? That he was married? That he was leaving for five years of missionary work in China? That there was some woman back in New York? That he didn't really want to be involved with anyone? Whatever it was, Camilla knew she didn't want to hear it. Not now, not ever. She turned her back to him, huddling away from his body, toward the cold stucco wall.

"I don't want to know," she said.

He put his hand on her shoulder. She didn't want him to touch her, but all at once she felt so tired that she didn't have the strength to shrug it away. "Perhaps I should have told you before," he said, using that old line that they all did. Only he had used it a little sooner, after a particularly good bonk. That was all it was. A bonk.

"Perhaps you should have," she said coldly, without even bothering to turn around.

"Well, I thought you suspected. You've been so understanding. That's the only reason I put it off."

What in the world was he talking about? He'd paused. "I really thought you suspected, so I didn't come right out and say anything. I mean, it's not an easy thing to hide. I didn't make any moves on you. I left that up to you. And when you invited me up . . . well, I couldn't resist. Anyway, I didn't say anything. Because of that, and . . ." he paused. "Because of that, and because I didn't want a pity fuck. I thought you really liked me."

Camilla couldn't help herself. "Like you? Of course I like you. Are you mad, or just insulting? What would I go to bed with you for if I didn't? Why in the world would *I* pity *you*?"

"Because I'm going blind," Frederick told her.

# 37

> My definition of a good editor is a man I think charming, who sends me large checks, praises my work, my physical beauty, and my sexual prowess, and who has a stranglehold on the publisher and the bank.
>
> —*John Cheever*

It was a wet and windy day, and though it wasn't yet noon, all the lights were on in the bookstore. Opal squatted before a low shelf and heard both of her knees creak. New York dampness was hard on the joints. She put two paperback copies of Styron's *Lie Down in Darkness* onto the fiction shelf and had to steady herself against it to help her rise. She looked around the bookstore. There was a student type in an oversized army jacket looking at hardcovers. Well, *he'd* never buy a twenty-five-dollar book. A well-dressed older woman was paging through cookbooks at the back. Although Opal had spent close to twenty years in a library, it was interesting to see how a short time in a bookstore had completely changed her relationship to books. She didn't enjoy seeing people reading anymore. Now Opal wanted them to *buy*. Since she'd started working here, Opal had learned that Roberta had problems. Business was slow and the rent still had to be paid. Opal was concerned, and not for Roberta's sake alone. After all, Roberta was not only her one friend in New York—she was also the only person Opal knew who had been kind to Terry. So it was the least that Opal could do, helping out at the store.

Across the floor, Opal saw the young man look around, as if to see whether he was being observed. There was more pilferage than Roberta could afford, and Opal disapproved of all those jacket pockets. She put on her can-I-help-you smile and walked up behind the young man. "Anything I can do for you?" she asked. He started a bit, then spun around.

"No. No, thanks," he said, then walked away from her up the aisle and made a beeline for the exit. Well, either she'd insulted him and queered a sale, or she'd just prevented a theft. She was about to turn away when she saw Roberta across the street, making her way against the rain and wind to the shop. Roberta had had an early-morning dental appointment. Painful and expensive gum work. Opal had always prided herself on taking very good care of her gums.

Roberta came through the door, her discomfort making her long face appear even longer. "How was it?" Opal asked.

"About as bad as it gets." Roberta tried to smile, but it ended up a grimace. "When this work is done, I'll be even longer in tooth than I am now."

"Could you drink some tea?" Opal asked as she followed Roberta back to the small stockroom where they also kept their coats, the book-keeping, mugs and spoons, uncrated books, and other bookstore detritus.

"I don't know. I know I'll never eat again."

Roberta might not be able to eat food, but she had devoured Terry's manuscript. And she had loved it. She'd called Opal in the middle of the night the moment she'd finished it, and the two of them had gone over it in loving, delighted detail. It was a two-and-a-half-hour phone call, and the only time since Terry's death that Opal had felt happy.

"Try some tea," Opal now urged Roberta.

"I could drink it if it isn't too hot," Roberta agreed, putting her coat on a hook and brushing her damp hair back with her hand. "Thanks so much for covering for me. You really have to let me start paying you."

Opal shook her head, then started heating up the water.

"We'll talk about it later," Roberta warned her. "I'd better get out front. How was the morning?"

"Not too bad," Opal reported proudly. "One of your regulars, that designer with the adorable Chinese baby, came in. She bought one hundred and forty-six dollars' worth of children's books."

Roberta tried to smile. "What would I do without Mrs. Kahn and Lily?" she asked.

"That was about it. UPS was late. I haven't opened the boxes." Opal paused. "And something else." Roberta raised her brows. "Mrs. Kahn had a woman with her. French, I think. But black. Madame someone. Do you know her?"

Roberta shook her head.

"Well, she was introduced, she looked at me, and said, 'I'm so sorry for your loss.'" Opal paused. It had been very strange. She couldn't really explain the feeling of shared sorrow and warmth that seemed to flow from the woman. "Then she told me, 'Your daughter's words will live.'"

"What?"

"Well, I wondered if you'd talked to Mrs. Kahn about—"

"Certainly not! Who was this woman?"

Opal shrugged. Then the front door chimed. "We better get out front," Roberta repeated. She was almost to the cash desk when the phone rang, so Opal left the call to her. But after a moment, Roberta put her head around the door to the back room again. All the pain was erased from her face, replaced with a look of—what? Expectancy? Excitement? "It's for you," Roberta said to Opal. "Emma Ashton, from Davis & Dash," she whispered. "Wasn't she the one who took the manuscript?"

Opal felt herself freeze, as if she had turned suddenly to ice. And then she felt as if she were melting, going to water. She had told Roberta about the young kid with the backpack who had agreed to take the manuscript home.

But Opal had not dared to hope to hear from Emma Ashton. She figured she would give it another few weeks and then call her. But it had been only ten days. Opal blinked, then swallowed. She couldn't just stand there doing nothing in the middle of the stockroom. She made herself take the two steps over to the extension and lifted the phone. Her hand was trembling.

"Hello," she said. "This is Opal O'Neal."

"Mrs. O'Neal? This is Emma Ashton from Davis & Dash. I called your number but there was no answer. I got this number off the manuscript. I took *The Duplicity of Men* with me. Remember?"

Remember? Opal had had to use every bit of willpower not to allow herself to think about it for the last 240 hours. But, she told herself sternly, you knew this would be a long haul. So what if this girl, this child, doesn't like it? Opal was prepared for that. She would not allow herself to be disappointed. Whatever it took, however long it took, she was prepared. If this girl couldn't understand the manuscript, there would be somebody who did. Eventually, if she kept at it, somebody would.

"I can come pick the manuscript up this afternoon," Opal said into the phone.

"What?" the girl asked. She probably was busy today. Opal had to remind herself not to be pushy or resentful.

"Or I could come first thing tomorrow," Opal told her.

"I'm sorry. I'm in an editorial meeting all morning tomorrow."

"Well, you can just leave it with the receptionist," Opal said, exasperated. "I could pick it up from her. Sandy is her name. She's very nice."

There was a pause, increasing Opal's exasperation. "I don't think you understand, or else I don't understand you," Emma Ashton said. "I don't want to give you back the manuscript. I want to publish it."

Opal stood there for a moment and actually stared at

the receiver in her hand. "You want the book?" Opal asked, afraid to hear the answer.

"It's a wonderful book, Mrs. O'Neal. You were right. Your daughter is—was—very, very talented. I can't say what we can pay for it yet. I'm not authorized to do that. It is an unusual book, and its length is a problem, but Davis & Dash would like to talk with you about publishing it."

Opal stood there, and once again she felt frozen. Instead of joy she was flooded with a terrible anger. These were the words that would have kept Terry alive. Why couldn't they have come sooner? Why couldn't Terry have lasted just a little longer? Once again, Opal's hand began to shake, but she managed to keep her voice calm. "When should I come in to talk to you?"

"Would Friday for lunch be all right for you?"

Friday lunch, Saturday morning, Sunday at midnight, Opal thought. Any time from now until my natural death. But all she said was, "What time?"

"Would one o'clock be all right?" the girl asked. "We can meet at the Four Seasons."

"Yes." She hadn't a clue where the restaurant was, but Roberta would know. "I'll be there at one o'clock on Friday," Opal told the girl, then remembered herself. "And thank you. Thank you for reading it," she said, then hung up the phone.

She stood there for another few moments, still shaking. She would never thank them for publishing the book, she promised herself. That is just what it deserved. But the girl *had* been good to take it home and look at it, and hadn't it been lucky that she was good enough to recognize its worth? Too late, though. Too late for Terry. But at least Terry's words would live beyond her. It might bring Terry no joy, and it might bring little joy to Opal. Still, it was something. It was more than something. It was what Terry had always wanted and what Opal had always wanted for her.

She walked out of the stockroom, through the center

aisle of the shop, past mysteries, science fiction, and literature, and got almost to the cash desk before Roberta, ringing up the cookbook purchase, looked up and saw her. She raised her eyebrows. "Bad news?" Roberta asked, and Opal managed to shake her head before she loudly and wetly burst into tears.

# 38

> Publishers are all cohorts of the devil; there must be a special hell for them somewhere.
>
> —*Goethe*

Gerald looked up from the manuscript in front of him. Pam Mantiss, for all of her faults, had managed to do it again. It had been quite some time since she had brought an important book into the house, but her timing couldn't be better. *The Duplicity of Men* was a real work of art, something Gerald could be proud to publish. Something Gerald's *father* would be proud to publish, he thought. If there was some pain he felt as he placed the last page neatly on the high stack of typed sheets, it was only that his writing would never achieve this. He was no genius.

Well, you couldn't have everything, he told himself, though he knew he tried. You have intelligence and taste, you have a social position, you have a fascinating job, and wives and children. Not to mention a name known to every media savant in the country and a string of books that all sold a lot more copies than this book ever would. Still, a lasting work of such intelligence and insight did cause Gerald a momentary stab of regret. Would I give up everything I have to have written this book, he asked himself? He thought of his perfectly austere study at home, the twilight view of the Central Park reservoir, and the dinner party he was about to host. The wall-mounted antique chenets would glow and the company would as well. Could he give all that up? No, he couldn't, he wouldn't give any of that up, but it would have been nice to have written *The Duplicity of Men* as well.

Still, he'd have the honor of publishing it, and it couldn't have come at a better time. After the Weston fiasco, Gerald had been putting off sending a copy of his own book to Senior for fear of his father's overreaction. It seemed to Gerald that after all these years, Senior should be able to make the distinction between fiction and biography, even if the fiction *was* loosely based on events of the past. Anyway, who cared about forty-year-old scandals? They simply made for a good read. And wasn't that what it was all about, if you couldn't write with genius? Sometimes Gerald thought that Senior only bothered with his endless moral scruples to annoy Gerald and make him look bad.

Senior had lived in a world where gentlemen put up capital to publish books because they chose to, because it interested and amused them, and the 10 percent return on investment at the end of each year was all that was expected. In that long-ago world a commitment to an author lasted a lifetime, and editors served as bankers, marriage counselors, and muses to their writers. But those days were gone. And it was time that Senior woke up and smelled the Jamaican Blue Mountain. At that moment, Mrs. Perkins buzzed the intercom. "What is it?" Gerald asked huffily.

"It's your father on line one."

"I'll take it." As if Gerald had the choice. What would Senior blame on Gerald now? If Senior had wanted everything to remain the same, he shouldn't have sold the firm when he retired. Now he had no responsibility except as a board member. Gerald sighed, and with great confidence he picked up the phone. "Hello, Father."

"Gerald, I have seen the proposed fall list, and I think we need to go over it along with some other things. Come over to the house."

Gerald didn't get annoyed at his father's demand this time. He decided how he would handle his father. He'd send him a group of manuscripts, including his own and *The Duplicity of Men*.

*Duplicity* would certainly make Senior sit up and take

notice. This was the kind of work that won prizes for publishers. And perhaps—just perhaps—it would soften the flak Gerald would have to take on his own book. His own book had certainly been improved by the suggestions Emma Ashton had provided him with. Clever girl, and not altogether unattractive. Too bad she was a lesbian. According to Pam Mantiss, anyway. Sometimes Gerald wondered if Pam might not be feeding him disinformation.

He looked at the next memo in his stack. It appeared as if intelligent and massive revisions had been outlined for the dreadful Susann Baker Edmonds book and were under way. Perhaps they would be able to salvage some of his investment there. He was admitting—but only to himself—that he had bet on the wrong horse. The $20 million contract that stole her from Imogen Clark had become publishing legend. Now it would turn to egg on his face if something wasn't done to improve the manuscript. He thought of Freud's overquoted question: What did women want? Gerald certainly didn't know, and his list reflected that. He'd *thought* they wanted Susann Baker Edmonds, but his timing or her plotting may have been off. Well, he'd see what came out of this revision cycle.

Meanwhile, the fall list was slowly beginning to shape up. The list meeting he had been dreading, the one that would make or break their profit picture for next year, looked as if it might produce quite a few viable titles. There were some nonfiction gems, and he was determined to get his own book on the bestseller list by any means necessary. With this heavy editing, the Edmonds book just might fly—especially if they got this problem of her daughter's book straightened out. The Jude Daniel manuscript had three advantages: Pam had bought it cheaply, there already seemed to be a lot of industry buzz about it, and the currency of its subject could be exploited. Like that Joyce Maynard novel a few years back. Perhaps he'd send it over to his father as well. Yes, he decided, he would. Anything to deflect Senior's contempt.

Then there were the long-shot fillers, but certainly possibilities. The Hollywood tell-all by Brando's housekeeper, the story of the cult members who believed they'd been impregnated by Elvis after his death, and the new novel by Annie Paradise. All they needed were a few more titles, and they'd manage to stave off a head-rolling coup for another fiscal year. Then he picked up *The Bookseller*, a U.K. trade magazine.

There, in one of the savant's columns, was a wrap-up of events at Frankfurt:

## BENT'S NOTES

Oh, what bliss it was to be alive! Well, not quite bliss, perhaps. One can imagine prettier places than Frankfurt in which to spend a few days in autumn.

But this year's book fair was not without its moments of light relief. Like the sight of uniformed book fair officials bearing down on Archibald Roget to announce, "Your erection is too high"—the dimensions of the Peterson booth were, they alleged, in contravention of the fair regulations.

A taxi driver shared an interesting fact with me. Prostitutes in Frankfurt dread Fair Week. "Trade slows down to barely a trickle," they complain.

---

*It was, as has become the custom, a "quiet but workmanlike fair"—God forbid anyone should be caught having fun. It was, however, good to see Eddie Bell, back on form selling the latest volume of Margaret Thatcher's memoirs. You'd've thought that THE EARLY MIDDLE YEARS might be a greater challenge to Eddie's salesmanship than THE DOWNING STREET YEARS and THE EARLY YEARS, but Eddie was showing not a hint of strain, claiming a print run of "in excess of 14 million copies, including 50,000 to Uzbekistan, wherever the fuck that is."*

---

**A brief encounter with the ever quietly self-satisfied Ed Victor, who was even more quietly satisfied than usual after his "multi-million dollar worldwide sale" of a book by publishing supremo Dick Snyder entitled *Healthy Wealth,* a management guide with the subtitle *Sustainable Wealth Creation Through Emotional Reengineering*—"an unexpected book from Dick," said Ed, "but I've never seen such interest from so many publishers."**

*But, hard as it is to admit, there was rather more life in the American aisles. On the Friday morning, I ran into Morgan Entrekin, who invited me to a party later that night.*

*"But it's the Bertelsmann party tonight," I pointed out perspicaciously.*

*"It's after the Bertelsmann party," Morgan explained patiently. Turned out he and Cario Feltrinelli were co-hosting, and Ken Follett would play with his rock 'n roll band. I declined the invitation gracefully, since even the Bertelsmann party is past my bedtime. But I gather a wild time was had by all, which is hardly surprising.*

*Indeed, publishing folk seem as keen nowadays on playing guitar for the masses as they are on providing fodder for the web offset machines. In addition to Ken Follett's Hard Covers (also starring Douglas Adams), you have Stephen King, Dave Barry, Amy Tan, and other bestselling authors making music in Kathi Goldmark's Rock Bottom Remainders, and Robert Waller insisting on recording country and western ballads. Olivia Goldsmith recently wrote (and sang, if you use the term loosely) a ditty called "Book Tour Blues." And a host of authors appeared at a North Carolina Book Fair in a group called The Grateful Deadlines. Mort Janklow may have put his finger on it when he advised Ken Follett to hold on to his day job.*

*It was certainly in the American aisles where the big rumour of the fair emerged—on the Davis & Dash stand, to be precise. Gerald Davis ("There is no such thing as a Davis & Dash book") and his boss, the redoubtable David Morton, were, so the rumour goes, having a quiet natter about the merits or otherwise of one of Davis's forthcoming titles, SCHIZOBOY by Chad Weston, when the natter got progressively less quiet and developed rather rapidly into a cadenza followed by a crescendo, all of which has reportedly left relations between the two somewhat strained.*

*SCHIZOBOY, so I'm told, is a no-holds-barred novel so graphic that it has even prompted the usually broad-minded literary editor of the SUN (who reportedly read an early leaked copy of the manuscript in the expectation that the SUN might wish to serialise it) to describe it as "giving pornography a bad name."*

*SCHIZOBOY, I understand, was Davis's discovery, but so disgusted by the book was Morton (chairman, president, born-again chief executive and chief operations officer) that Davis's future at the firm his forebears created is said to be distinctly unclear. All of this is rumour, of course, and I'm sure they'll sort things out.*

*Back in the British aisles, at the Citron Press stand, Craig Stevens was selling what he claimed was "the most unlikely book of the fair since Mohammed Ali"—a "heavily illustrated" biography entitled THE PRIVATE LIVES OF GERALD FORD, which purports to prove that, somewhat contrary to popular belief, Ford was "the most complex and interesting American president this century."*

*"I know it sounds unlikely," Craig tells me, "but that's precisely why it's such a brilliant book. People from every major market have been queuing up to see it. The photographs are just amazing."*

---

**Yes, it was that sort of fair. Even submissions for the Diagram Group Prize for the Oddest Title of the Year were thin on the ground: the best I saw was a new edition of a very old title: *Sex Instruction for Irish Farmers*, and the rather too specialist *History of Dentistry in Oregon*. Way off the quality of past runners like *Big and Very Big Hole Drilling*, I'm afraid.**

---

*I was, therefore, reduced to looking instead for oxymorons. You know the sort of thing; Royal Family, Friendly Fire, Military Intelligence, Happy Birthday (at least when you get to my age).*

*I was, needless to say, on the lookout*

*for bookish oxymorons, and I'm happy to say that I found a few, and some not half bad.*

*"Exciting new English writer" was Gary Fisketjon's suggestion; "Exclusive offer" Liz Calder's. And, from some wag whose name I forgot to write down, the best of the bunch—"Literary agent."*

**Horace Bent**

Gerald, who usually enjoyed the wit and inside jokes of Horace Bent's column, felt the blood drain from his face. He'd been able to convince himself that his humiliation had been, well, semi-private. He'd been wrong.

He thought of the dinner party tonight and nearly squirmed. Despite the soft light from the antique chenets, the guests took on a new complexion. They'd be secretly sneering. And, if that wasn't enough, he had to see his father.

He could only hope that Senior wouldn't criticize him too harshly.

# 39

> Once a book has been written, I could never explain how I managed it.
>
> —*Selma Lagerlöf*

Judith had managed to take Flaubert for a long walk on the campus. She had even stopped at the small boutique near the humanities building and bought herself a new long skirt. But it wasn't an act of true optimism. She had to do it: Daniel was taking her out to dinner tonight, and she couldn't fit into any of her other clothes. Now, getting ready for their date, she stood up in the bathtub, her long dripping hair clinging all the way to her waist. She looked down at herself, pink and wet from the heat of the bath. Her belly pouched out so that she couldn't see her pubic hair unless she sucked in her gut. How much weight *had* she gained? She had been so depressed. Eating had been her only comfort and distraction. But this afternoon, at last, she felt a little better. Today had been a good day. Daniel had been attentive last night. She'd managed to get up early this morning and straighten the place up a little. And the anticipation of dinner with Daniel was almost exciting.

It was also unusual. They never went out to eat. For one thing, they couldn't afford to. And though he had never said so, Judith knew Daniel didn't like running into students or faculty members at the local restaurants. Was that just his nature? Sometimes Judith was afraid that Daniel was ashamed of her, or of himself for getting involved with her. She'd tell herself that was foolish—that he was just a private person, bad with small talk and too busy with his work and their book for shallow socializing.

But—whether out of shame or awkwardness—she did know that he refused any invitations they got. After all, he had said, they couldn't afford to take anyone out, and they couldn't entertain in what he called "our rat-trap apartment." Judith had only thought of being with Daniel when she had married him. The pleasure of that had seemed enough—more than enough: It was overwhelming. But in the last year she actually saw very little of him. And she saw virtually no one else. She'd certainly never imagined when she married him that she wouldn't be a part of his life on the campus or off.

She shook her wet hair and picked up a towel to wrap it in. Well, she wouldn't think about all that now. She wouldn't spoil the first pleasant day she'd had since she finished the book. Because Daniel said he had a surprise for her tonight. Her birthday had come and gone almost three weeks ago, and Daniel had only remembered with a card—a bland one. She suspected he'd gotten it at the last minute. Well, his monthly paycheck came yesterday. Maybe he had a gift for her now. She smiled. That would be nice. Or it could be that he'd finished editing their book. Maybe Daniel had even managed to get the manuscript retyped. Maybe he was ready to submit it. Judith actually smiled with anticipation. She'd be fascinated to see what changes he had made. Odd how it would be a comfort to have the manuscript back again.

Judith wrapped herself up in her robe, pulled the old rubber plug from the bathtub drain, and walked into the bedroom. Her new skirt lay on the bed. Tomato red, it glowed and warmed the room. She sat down on the bed, which she had stripped and made up neatly, and began to brush out her hair. She wondered where they would go tonight. She preferred the Italian place to the diner or the only Chinese restaurant in town, but she knew the Villa JoJo was more expensive than either of the others. Well, she'd be happy with whichever one Daniel picked. It would still be a treat. She glanced at the bedside clock. She was supposed to meet him in front of the student union at six. She only had half an hour. Smiling, she began to dress.

"How can I help you?" the woman in the salmon-colored suit asked. Daniel had been careful to approach one of the woman bank officers. He was nervous, and the fat older man in rumpled brown plaid was more than he could handle right now. Daniel had always been better with women. He looked over at the rectangular name plate on the woman's desk. Patti Josephson. She was slightly overweight, and the gray roots were showing in her brown hair. He smiled at her but not too widely.

"My name is Daniel Gross. Dr. Daniel Gross. Just an academic doctor, I'm afraid." He laughed self-deprecatingly. No dice. She didn't even acknowledge the mild joke. "I want to open an account," he said. "Could you help me do that, Ms. Josephson?"

"That's my job," she told him flatly. She reached her hand out and paused over several piles of forms. "What kind of account? Checking? Money market?"

"Checking, I think." She wasn't looking at him. He wanted her to. He needed to make a friend of her. He paused, waiting until she did look up. "Look," he said with a bit of a frown, "I'm not very good at business. I need some expert advice." He paused again, and she waited, raising one brow. But at least she kept looking at him. "Let me explain my situation. You see, I'm a professor here. And I'm also a writer."

Ms. Josephson nodded and looked at him expectantly. Did her eyes flick to his ring finger? He'd taken off the band before he came in. He'd have to bring up the subject now, but he was so goddamned nervous. Why? There was nothing wrong with this, he told himself. Absolutely nothing. But Ms. Josephson wasn't very responsive. She didn't seem to like him. Well, what did he expect from an overweight *über*-teller woman in a cheap poly-blend suit?

"Here's the thing," he explained. "I have a pen name. I mean, I've written this book and I've just sold it to Davis & Dash, the publishers."

"Oh. Congratulations. What kind of book? A textbook?"

It was only feigned interest, but at least he'd gotten a rise out of her. Still, he felt insulted. Did he look like the kind of guy who could only write a textbook? "Not at all," he said. "That's the problem. It's a novel, and they think—well, they *hope*—that it's going to be a big hit. My agent is sending it out to Hollywood. There might even be a movie." Byron had told him it was a long shot, but it wasn't a complete lie. "April Irons, the producer, is looking at it." Lie or not, it worked. The woman's eyes seemed to come alive. Sure, everyone loved show biz.

"Really?" she asked. Now the interest wasn't feigned. "What's it about?"

"It's a story of a woman pushed beyond her limits."

Ms. Josephson actually laughed. "Aren't we all?" She looked at him straight in the face for the first time and smiled.

He'd better play to his strength, Daniel thought. "Tell you what," he said, "I'll give you a copy as soon as it rolls off the press."

"Oh. That would be lovely."

"Well, wait until you read it before you decide that," he told her. "The problem is it has a lot of—well . . ." he paused for effect. "It's not an academic book at all." He raised his brows.

She laughed. "Hot stuff, huh? Well, that's what sells."

"I certainly hope so. Anyway, it's sold for quite a bit of money. And I'll be getting a first check soon. So what kind of account do I need?"

She launched into a long, boring harangue about the benefit of money markets versus some other bullshit. Was it his imagination, or was she actually getting flirtatious? "This is great of you, to help," he said. "Maybe I could thank you by taking you out for a drink sometime."

Ms. Josephson smiled but shook her head. "I don't think my husband would like that," she giggled.

Thank God. Off the hook. But contact had been established. "Maybe you could just sign the book for me?" she suggested.

The perfect opening. "Well, if I did sign it with my legal name, I think it would ruin it. See, I have a pen name." He felt like rushing through this, but he forced himself not to. "My contract and all the rest acknowledges that I am writing under another name. It's perfectly legal," he assured her.

"Of course," she said, "it's a pka."

"What?"

"A pka." She wrote it on a form. "Professionally known as. We have a few actors and voice-over people with pkas. It's no problem." She pointed out the place on the form. "You're Daniel Gross, pka what?" She had started to write. Daniel took a calming breath. Mrs. Josephson continued briskly. "I'll have to ask for your Social Security number and some other form of identification. Can I see your driver's license or your passport?"

He handed her both, because he had brought them, just in case, along with the Davis & Dash contract. He spread the contract in front of her and saw her eyes flicker over the amount. "I don't have the check yet," he told her, "but you can see it's going to be a nice one, and I want to be ready for it."

She looked at the contract again, then smiled at him. "Congratulations," she said. She filled in more information boxes. "Anybody else on the account?" Ms. Josephson asked. "Is it in trust for anyone, or a joint account?"

"No," he said. Was this where the trouble started? His heart sped up again.

But it was over. And it was all just that simple. She merely filled out a few more forms, then asked him for an initial deposit to open the account. He checked his wallet. He only had three twenties and two fives, and he needed to hold on to most of it to take Judith out to dinner tonight and break the news. His MasterCard and Visa were maxed out. Could he get away with Chinese? No. He was determined to do this in a very public place, where there couldn't be a major scene. That meant Villa JoJo's, though he hated the idea of running into anyone from the faculty there. He'd have to keep at least fifty bucks for dinner. Could he open an account with only twenty dollars? Would Ms. Josephson laugh at him, after his big talk of movies and foreign rights? Daniel tried not to show his embarrassment. How could a grown man be living so hand-to-mouth?

His stomach tightened at the thought of his upcoming dinner with Judith. Even at a public place, could he count on her not making a fuss? Lately, she seemed to be unraveling. No wonder he had been so easily comforted by Cheryl. Judith looked like hell, and so did their place. Why was everything so messy? It wasn't as if she had anything else to do all day. Daniel thought back to Cheryl's neat apartment and fragrant bed with regret and longing. He shouldn't have done it. He knew that. And maybe he shouldn't be doing this. But he had to. He had to survive and move on and make some sense out of his life. He'd make Judith understand. And, before he made any permanent arrangement, he'd move the two of them into an apartment in the townhouse complex Cheryl lived in. They'd spend a little—a very little—of the book money on that. Maybe Judith could keep a new apartment clean.

Daniel fished a twenty-dollar bill out of his wallet and handed it to the banker without comment. It was all he could spare. She made no comment, and Daniel felt great relief. He *was* getting organized. He was doing everything he had to, step by step. He'd opened the account, and now he would have to tell Judith. He had put it off too long already. But he looked down at the fifty bucks left. What a waste. The thought of his wife, stringy-haired, puffy, and depressed, filled him with a lethal combination of distaste and guilt.

Ms. Josephson bustled back from a teller with a deposit slip and smiled at him one last time. "Okay, we're almost all set," she said. "You merely have to sign these and we'll be ready for your ill-gotten gains." Alarmed, he glanced up from the signature card at her face, then realized it was just a mild joke.

"No problem," he told her, and neatly signed "Jude Daniel" at the bottom of the two cards.

Daniel had been late to meet Judith at the student union and greeted her without an apology or a kiss. But as he walked her in the direction of Villa JoJo, things had improved. Judith looked around at the noise and bustle of the restaurant. Daniel had gotten them a booth at the side, which always made Judith feel protected, yet also part of the scene. Across the room she could see Don, the head of Daniel's department, who was just finishing dinner with his family. A student of Daniel's, here with his parents, had stopped by the table to say hello. Daniel had even introduced her. Then Daniel had ordered wine, and now Judith was on her second glass. She felt better than she had for weeks; this special treat pleased her so much. She thought the new skirt looked good on her, and her hair felt light and soft on her shoulders. Daniel had even insisted that she order the antipasto appetizer, though he usually dispensed with a first course to save money. Now she was finishing the last olive—her favorite part. She always saved her favorite part for last.

It was all so nice. Daniel was really attentive. Whenever she said anything—anything at all—he'd look at her in a searching way. She should make more of an effort for him. For a moment, Judith felt a stab of guilt. Perhaps it was because she looked good, and he had seen her looking that way so rarely lately. Daniel lifted the Chianti bottle and refilled her glass. Then he took her hand. "I have some good news for you," he said.

Judith looked up from the empty antipasto plate and smiled. Was it the wine, or the food, or the setting that made her feel so happy? Or was it Daniel's hand on hers? She looked at him expectantly.

"The book's been accepted," he said.

For a moment, his words didn't register. What book? Her head felt muddled by the wine. *Their* book? Did he mean their book? *Accepted*? "Accepted by whom?" was all she could manage to say.

"By Davis & Dash," Daniel said, and he held her hand tighter.

She felt a flush begin to rise from her belly to her chest and on to her throat. She opened her mouth, but for a moment the flood of feeling left her speechless. "You mean for publication?" she asked, her voice coming out as nothing more than a whisper. "It's accepted for publication?" She asked again, and Daniel nodded.

"Oh, my God! You're kidding! I can't believe it!" She paused for a moment, trying to collect her thoughts. "I didn't even know you'd *retyped* it. Or finished editing." Her head felt as if it was spinning. How much wine had she had? "God! I can't believe it." She began to laugh with pleasure and relief. It was all going to be all right! He was so wonderful. No wonder he'd been ignoring her, busy with his own work. He'd done this, just as he said he would. And she'd done nothing but sleep and mope. She had to stop being so paranoid, so depressed. "How did you do it, Daniel?"

Daniel explained about Alfred Byron and the submission to Gerald Ochs Davis. Judith listened, enraptured. It was the best story she had ever heard. Like a child, she wanted him to tell it all over again. She still couldn't believe it. She laughed again, her delight making her feel light-headed.

"But it's been so fast. It's all so fast." How could she ever have doubted him? She'd been afraid that she'd wasted her time, that he might not be able to deliver, and in reality he'd sold the book already! "Oh, Daniel! I've been miserable and depressed and thinking I'd failed, while you've been doing this! I love you!" She leaned across the table to kiss him, but he didn't lean in to meet her. Well, he wasn't affectionate in public. "They liked it? Tell me what they said again. They weren't just being polite?"

"I don't think they bother to pay money to be polite," Daniel said dryly. Money! Of course. Now there would be money. Before Judith even had a chance to ask about the money, Daniel said, "There are a couple of problems, though."

That was him all over! Always worrying. Judith laughed. "Daniel, what problems can there be? I can't believe it. They're going to publish *In Full Knowledge*. Elthea will be read by thousands of people. And we'll be famous! Oh, Daniel, this is such an outrageous surprise! Thank you!" She leaned across the table again, this time all the way, and kissed him wetly on the mouth.

Daniel looked around the room. "Shh," he cautioned. "Let's not spread it around. Not till it's signed, sealed, and delivered." He smiled at her.

When was the last time she'd felt this good? Maybe when he'd said that he'd marry her. All of those long, dark winter days alone in her makeshift office working on the manuscript seemed to take on a clear golden light. It *hadn't* been wasted effort. She *wasn't* talentless or deluded. Other people, professionals—Gerald Ochs Davis, for God's sake—liked her work. She could write. She should never, ever doubt herself again. Remember that, she thought, and she felt flooded with energy. She would clean up the apartment, lose weight, and get back to writing her real one. She looked over at Daniel, and tears of gratitude and joy rose along the bottom of her eyelids. "You said I could do it. You said I could do it, and you were right."

The waiter came and put their plates on the table. Judith felt as if she would never have to eat again. The wine, the soft lighting, the good news all converged and, for a moment, Judith felt as if her life was perfect, specially blessed. Everyone in the room must envy her, with her handsome husband and her writing talent.

But Daniel had stopped smiling and patted her hand. "Judith. Listen. There are a couple of changes they want made to the manuscript. Big changes. It will be a lot of work. But we have to do it. And the money isn't as much as we'd hoped. Getting it sold wasn't as easy as I thought. It takes a lot to make a new novel into a bestseller. A lot of money and a lot of time. We're not going to get much now, and you'll have to do a lot of rewrites."

"Oh, Daniel. It doesn't matter. It's a start. It *proves* we can do anything. We can do anything together." She looked at his worried face. Misery in victory. That was Daniel all over. She almost laughed again. He worried when things went badly, *and* he worried when things went well. She, on the other hand, knew how to celebrate. She picked up her glass of wine, but he reached over to stop her.

"Eat something," he said. "Before it gets cold."

She looked across at him as he picked up his knife and sliced into the veal. She hadn't really focused on how very subdued he was. It wasn't just victory worry. Why, he hadn't even made a toast. What was wrong? Something *was* definitely wrong. Despite the haze from the wine, Judith suddenly went into sharp focus. The lipstick smudge on her wineglass, the sweat on Daniel's forehead across the room, the burned-out lightbulb in the wall sconce. It was all clearly visible. "What is it?" she asked.

Daniel had his head bent over his order. He'd cut several pieces of meat, but he'd only moved them around on his plate. Judith noticed a speck of tomato sauce where his mustache joined his beard. He looked up at her. "They think I wrote it, Judith. It was an accident. They just assumed Jude Daniel was a man. That it was me. And they loved the idea of a book so clearly from a woman's perspective that was written by a man. That's what sold it, more than anything. I was afraid to tell them. I was afraid to lose our chance." He looked directly into her eyes. "It's harder than I thought, to get published. Alf Byron owed me favors, but he didn't even want to *read* it. And if *he* hadn't, no one would." Daniel looked away, across the room, but his eyes were unseeing. "And it's not just about getting published, but then, afterward, its about getting advertising and exposure, enthusiasm and support from the publishers. I was afraid, Judith. I was afraid that we'd wind up rejected, or that they'd print five thousand copies and we'd go nowhere." He stopped to wipe his already clean mouth with the napkin. "These guys wanted me and the book. They've promised to push it. I was afraid to queer the deal. These people are savvy. They can make it happen for us." He paused. "Did I do the wrong thing?"

She wasn't sure that she had gotten it. "You mean they don't know about me at all?" Judith asked. "Not at all?"

Daniel shook his head.

"But I wrote the book," Judith cried, and this time tears actually rolled over her lids and began to run down her face. "Daniel, I *wrote the book.*"

Daniel stiffened. "It was *my* idea, Judith. We did it together," he said, his voice lowered.

"But my name. Jude. It's my name, too."

"They thought it was me. That's all. They just assumed it would be me." He didn't look at her. He looked from his plate to his glass and back, then all around the room. "Please lower your voice," he told her. The restaurant was beginning to clear out, but Judith didn't care who heard or saw her. How could this be happening?

"It was my work. I worked so hard." Her voice was a childish wail.

"Judith. Please. You have to be quiet."

"I won't," Judith said. "I *won't* be quiet."

Daniel looked around the restaurant, then reached across the table and put a hand on each of her shoulders. "Listen," he said, "we did this for the money. And eventually there *will* be money. Alf Byron talked about a TV movie or maybe a miniseries. He's talking to April Irons out in Hollywood. A really big producer. There might be foreign-rights sales. Let's get the money, Judith. We can tell them all later, once we're in. You'll do the book tours, you'll be recognized then, once it's safe. And, in the meantime, we'll have enough to get a nicer place. To live better. We can go on a vacation. Maybe go to Cape Cod." He was talking fast now, so fast that his tongue left little bits of saliva at the sides of his mouth. Where was his napkin when he needed it? "Cape Cod. You like that. Who knows, maybe we can even rent a house there for the summer. And we could both write. You could write what you want." He smiled at her, an attentive, apologetic small smile. But the saliva was still there. He placed the palm of his hand against her face, brushing her cheek and her temple. "We'll have some money, we'll be together, and we can write seriously. What's so terrible about that?"

Judith looked across the table at her husband. "I don't know," she said.

# 40

I am true love, I fill
the hearts of boy and girl with mutual flame.
Have the will
I am the Love that dare not speak its name.
*—Lord Alfred Douglas*

Emma opened her eyes. The light that filtered through the backyard tree branches was playing on the ceiling of her sleeping alcove. The light was beautiful, and she watched the dancing movement lazily until she realized both that it was Saturday morning and that she had spent the night with Alex. Carefully, superstitiously, she turned her head to the left. It hadn't been a dream. Alex's short blond curls lay on the pillow next to hers. Sleeping, Alex was even more attractive than Emma had remembered. When she was awake there was something tense, almost nervous, about Alex's flashing, always moving, eyes and tight jaw. Now Alex in profile was a Burne-Jones painting, all translucent skin, long eyelashes, and glorious ringlets.

Emma looked away, as if her enjoyment was an invasion of Alex's privacy. She would have to watch herself. She couldn't visibly dote on Alex. She shouldn't move too fast. This was only a beginning and maybe just a one-night stand. Emma should take nothing for granted, expect nothing. It was the only way she'd have a chance with someone as mercurial, as attractive and entertaining as Alex. Emma lay quietly in her bed, Alex stretched beside her, and tried to simply live in this glorious moment.

Emma knew she had always been too serious. It wasn't that she was humorless; at least she hoped not. It was just that she took everything so much to heart. She had never been able to take an affair lightly. She'd had two in college, and both had ended badly, with Emma accused of jealousy, of suffocating her lovers. She'd sworn she'd never let that happen again.

Instead, nothing had happened. Emma hadn't had a date, much less an affair, since she'd come to New York. Work had kept her busy, but it hadn't stopped her from aching with loneliness. Still, she wouldn't jump into bed with just anyone. She'd waited a long time to find someone as interesting and as passionate as Alex.

When Alex took her hand, Emma almost jumped. She turned her head and tried to keep a really loopy smile from washing over her face. Instead she forced herself to be light, and gave Alex a quick peck on the nose.

"Is that the best you can do for a good-morning kiss?" Alex asked. Then Alex rose on one elbow, bent her face over Emma's, and kissed her deeply. Emma put her hand up to Alex's taut cheek and ran her fingers through her curls.

"That's more like it," Alex said approvingly, and lay back down on the pillow. They lay in comfortable silence for a few minutes. Emma found it hard to catch her breath. "What are we going to do today?" Alex asked.

Emma felt her heart jump in her chest. Alex had said "we." Did she mean them to spend the whole day together? It was too good to be true. Better not assume anything, Emma thought. "I have a manuscript to read," she said tentatively.

"Oh, yes. Maybe a new client for me." Alex smiled. She stretched, pushing her long, shapely arms high up over her head and arching her toes till they almost reached over the end of the bed. I need a bigger bed, Emma thought, then told herself sternly that she was being premature. "I'm starving," Alex said. "Are you? Do you have anything to eat? Or should we go out?"

Alex stood up, long and lean and beautiful in the early light. Though thin, she had surprisingly full breasts. Emma hadn't seen her naked yet, not standing from a distance, and now she forced herself to tear her admiring eyes away, though she felt like devouring every bit of Alex. Nude, Alex walked to the window and looked out over the back gardens. Emma was free to look at her perfect back, the curve of her buttocks, and her long, long legs. "It looks like it's going to be a nice day," Alex said and turned from the window, catching Emma in the middle of her worshipful stare. Alex smiled and lifted one eyebrow. "Of course, if you're hungry for other things . . ." She made it back to the bed in three long strides and jumped under the blanket. "I got cold," she complained, pushing her now cool body up against Emma's warm one. But Emma didn't complain. She just clasped Alex to her and felt grateful.

Alex lay on the sofa. From time to time Emma surreptitiously looked up. She loved seeing Alex's long form stretched comfortably on the yielding cushions. Alex was reading the book review section from the Sunday *Times*—even though it was Saturday night. In New York it was a dating tradition to pick up the *Times* and bagels for the next morning on Saturday night. They had spent the entire day together. After a walk along Hudson Street and the piers, lunch at Elephant & Castle, and a long afternoon in bed, they were sitting here now, just hanging around. Emma was trying to keep herself from hoping that Alex would stay the night. She didn't want to press her luck. Last night had been so magical, and today had been perfect. It's enough, she told herself.

It was just that this was so very, very nice. And that was the problem. Emma was already dreading their separation. When Emma felt the relief of companionship, when she felt the warm, wet surrounding of love and friendship, the coldness of her everyday life alone seemed far worse. She would have to guard against any appearance, any hint of desperation. She had lived alone, and she knew how to do it, she reminded herself firmly. But it was so nice to have somebody here. Someone as funny, as beautiful, as sexy and smart as Alex.

"Work to do?" Alex asked, and Emma nodded.

"Flap copy," she said.

"New, improved novels," Alex suggested.

"Now with plotting, the advanced secret ingredient." Emma laughed.

"Reduced adjectives!"

"Less description—fat free!"

"And more powerful verbs!"

Alex had insisted that Emma take out her work. "I don't want to ruin your weekend," Alex said, and then laughed as if she knew how ridiculous that idea was. She had settled herself on the sofa at her right, and Emma had taken the much less comfortable sling chair for herself. Then, more out of habit than desire, she pulled out the manuscript that Frederick had sent. She needed to look normal, to keep from staring at Alex. At first Emma had had trouble concentrating: As she began the novel she looked up at Alex over and over again. But she didn't want to embarrass herself by getting caught, so she had allowed herself only one look at the end of each page. She had done that throughout the first chapter, as she was introduced to the American ladies on tour, their British guide, and the handsome young Italian who drove their bus. But after a while the story had picked her up and swept her along. Now she was so engrossed she forgot about her end-of-page peeks. She even forgot about Alex. Emma felt she was in Italy, on the bus with the widows and Catherine, their diffident guide. There was a clarity to this writing, descriptions so perfectly honed that Emma *saw* the sights, observations so economical yet so deft that Emma quickly understood the various half-dozen older women and their yearning young guide. When the luggage got confused and Mrs. Florence Mallabar lost her temper, Emma actually laughed out loud.

"Is it good?" With an unsettling tumble, Emma was back

in her living room, Alex stretched out before her. "Is it good?" Alex repeated. "It seems as if it must be."

"It is good, so far."

"Can I read it?" Alex asked. She threw the *Times* onto the coffee table.

Emma thought for a moment. She didn't want to seem hesitant. After all, this was just an informal submission from her brother. Surely the writer didn't have representation. Still, Emma felt a little uncomfortable. But how could she say no? She looked across at Alex's expectant face. Emma's interest in the book was impossible to hide. This was something they shared. They both loved books. Emma nodded.

"Great!" Alex said. "Let's call out for Chinese, eat it in bed, and read the manuscript together."

Emma had to laugh. Hardly anyone's idea of a wild Saturday night, she thought. But she knew it would suit her right down to the ground.

Later, much later, Emma could never figure out if it was the manuscript, the excitement of being with Alex for the first time, or a combination of the two that made reading the book so wonderful. Reading was almost always such a solitary activity that it was truly peculiar fun to finish a page and pass it directly to Alex. They both loved the book: the quirky, dry humor; the insights into women, both young and aging; the temptations and disappointments of romance; and the terrific, gentle ending.

"It's a wonderful book," Emma said. It was close to two in the morning. They were up, out of bed, and sitting at the kitchen counter, drinking tea and eating the leftover Chinese food. Emma's microwave was on the fritz, so they were eating moo shu pork pancakes cold.

"It's terrific," Alex nodded. "You're going to publish, it, aren't you?"

For the first time in twenty-four hours, Emma felt her heart sink. She had just cashed in all her chips with Pam. The fight for *The Duplicity of Men* had been tricky, and

Pam was still touchy about Emma's ultimatum. How in the world could she get Pam to agree to publish this one? It certainly wasn't a typical bestseller: not what Pam would call a Spook or an Uh-oh, or even a Pink. Emma sighed.

*The Duplicity of Men* was a great book, and she was glad and proud that she had been instrumental in getting it on the list. This untitled manuscript wasn't in that category, but it was a tremendously compassionate, readable book with a lot of wisdom and charm. Maybe it was a bit too literate for a mass audience, maybe it was missing a "hook," but surely there was some place for it. Oh God! Emma hated to even think of Pam's face if Emma pitched this book. How in the world could she get Pam to agree to do it? She looked across at Alex and shrugged.

"It won't be so easy," she said truthfully, and then she told her all about Opal O'Neal and the strong-arm tactics she had had to use with Pam. Alex listened. She seemed to be a good listener, nodding knowingly at parts, shaking her head over the insanity of some of it.

"Very ballsy," she said approvingly. "You did the exact right thing." She paused. "You said this Opal O'Neal had no representation?"

"No," Emma told her. "If she did, she wouldn't have had to sit in the lobby for weeks."

"Will you recommend me to her?" Alex asked. Though she was again uncomfortable, Emma nodded.

Alex lifted the new manuscript. "So, because of the other book you don't think you can get them interested in this?"

Emma shrugged. "It's good. I know it's got something. I even think with the right handling it could sell. Look at Barbara Kingsolver. Or Anne Tyler. Or Alice Hoffman. There's a real market for quality women's fiction. Pam calls it artsy-fartsy, and it makes the middlebrows feel good. I think it could sell. But I'm not sure Pam will think so."

"I could sell it," Alex said boldly. "I could sell it to Pantheon."

Emma felt another stab of discomfort. Was that disloyalty on Alex's part? Did she feel abandoned because Alex seemed so quick to take the booty and run? Was she jealous already? Ridiculous, she told herself. Alex was helping her solve a problem.

Alex smiled at her. Had she seen the look of dismay cross Emma's face? "*You* can get it published," Alex assured her. "It's a terrific little book. And Davis & Dash is really weak on women's books. Tell Pam Mantiss it will help balance the list. Tell her it's a long shot that she can buy cheap. Tell her I'm optioning it to Fox. And tell her she can negotiate with me for the rights." Alex flashed her devastating smile at Emma. "You *will* let me write to the author, won't you?"

Emma nodded. "But I don't think that will do it," she said. "Pam is really smart. She'll know the book is good but risky. And I think if the recommendation comes from me again, she'll resent it."

"Go over her head. Give it to Gerald Ochs Davis himself."

Emma looked at Alex with surprise. Would Alex do something like that? Looking at her, Emma thought she would. But Emma herself wouldn't. She shook her head. They both sat, still and silent, until Alex reached for the last of the moo shu and popped it in her mouth.

"I know," Alex said.

Emma looked at her expectantly. "Bring it to Pam with a strong letter from me," Alex said. "But recommend passing."

"Pass on it? Tell her I *don't* like it?"

"Tell her you do, but it's not for Davis & Dash. That it's not a Davis & Dash book. That they can't do women's fiction well. And be sure to put a cc to GOD."

Emma laughed. "He'll hate that." She considered it for a while. "It might actually work," she agreed. "Especially if I give a copy to Jim Meyer. *He* sends everything to Gerald's father. And this is just the type of thing that Mr. Davis Senior might really like."

"And if he doesn't, I'll sell it to Pantheon," Alex added. "Or if not I can submit it to Bill Henderson at Pushcart Press. He does worthy books no one else will." She took Emma's hand. "But enough about all this. Now, my little moo shu, it's time for bed."

# 41

> There are days when the result is so bad that no fewer than five revisions are required. In contrast, when I'm greatly inspired, only four revisions are needed.
>
> —*John Kenneth Galbraith*

Susann sat at the desk by her window, the one overlooking Central Park. The day was cold and the park looked deserted. She had not put on any makeup, and the reflection off the window glass was merciless. Despite the heat in the room, she shivered. She picked up the cashmere afghan that Edith had knitted for her. Edith's knitting had so irritated Susann. Visions of Madame Defarge and retirement homes. After all, she wasn't an old woman, nor was Edith. Edith should have found better things to do than knit. Now, however, Susann was grateful. Somehow she couldn't get warm. She held the soft blanket around her and looked across the room at the logs flaming in the fireplace. Despite the thermostat set on high and the burning wood, the heat didn't seem to reach her.

She knew why. She looked at the massacred manuscript in front of her. Blue lines of editorial comment were everywhere, and color-coded strips of paper were glued to virtually every page. It was the manuscript that was freezing Susann's blood. She couldn't fix it, and if she *didn't* fix it, she was doomed. She picked up the long, demanding editorial letter that was signed by Pam Mantiss but that Susann knew Emma Ashton had prepared. Phrases jumped out at her. "Ridiculous supposition," "unmotivated action," "unlikely coincidence." Tears rose in Susann's eyes. She had never been treated this way by Imogen

Clark. To be virtually dismissed, insulted, and ridiculed by a girl younger than her own daughter!

Of course, *that* thought brought up the problem with Kim, and Susann actually shuddered. Alf had somehow sicced the entire Davis & Dash legal team on Kim, and Susann had not had the courage to stop them. She knew that Kim's slender resources and the limited resources of her little publishing house would probably not be able to stand up to the onslaught. There would be no novel by Kim Baker Edmonds this fall. But that didn't end the problem. It would be just one more area in which Kim would fail—because of her mother. But what else could Susann do? Like most of her problems, Kim had brought this on herself. Why did she have to compete with me and my very survival? Susann asked herself. The thought of her own new book failing frightened her so deeply that she shuddered once again.

"Here, drink this." Edith had appeared and put a steaming cup before Susann. "It's tea, but it's got some rum in it. That will help."

Susann looked down at the manuscript, a bleeding blue abortion. "I doubt it," she said. But she took the cup by its dainty gilded handle and sipped from it. After a few minutes, she felt the warmth move from her throat to her stomach and then further down. She looked up piteously at Edith. "I can't do this," she said. "I just can't."

"Oh, yes you can. And you will." Edith said in that no-nonsense Cincinnati accent. "I know you're tired. You shouldn't have agreed to do this new book in the first place—it's too much extra work. But you *can* do it."

"I don't know where to start. There's just so much they want changed."

"Well, I have a novel idea," Edith paused. "Get it? That was a pun."

Susann eyed her without even the ghost of a smile.

"Anyway, we start at chapter one, fix it, and move on to chapter two. I admit it's original, but it just might work."

"I wish Alf would help," Susann said.

"Well, he won't. So I'm going to heat up a can of consommé, and we're going to sip soup and rewrite until ten o'clock. Then I'm going to make a good old Cincinnati four-way, with onions. You'll feel better once we get started. And then you can sleep."

"I haven't been able to sleep in weeks," Susann moaned.

"You'll sleep after this work. And tomorrow, after breakfast, we'll work on chapters two and three."

Susann began to shake her head wildly. "It's too much," she said. "It's too hard. I'm too tired and we don't have enough time. What if I do all this and the book is *still* no good?"

"This is a lot easier than editing that first one we did. Do you remember?" Susann shook her head. "You were working all day at the law firm and we were trying to get it into shape at night. Harlequin was going to take it only if you cut it by seventy pages. Remember? Remember how confused and tired you were? We didn't have a clue, and we only had three nights to do it and get it back."

And then Susann did remember. She remembered exactly what it was like—the two of them working in the kitchen of her awful trailer, Kim asleep, the endless cups of coffee. It had been hard, but they had done it. She wasn't sure if it was harder than this, but it had been hard enough. "I was younger then, Edith. There was less at stake."

"You *looked* older," Edith told her, "and there was a hell of a lot *more* at stake. If they hadn't accepted that one, you would never have written anything again. There are eight thousand members of Romance Writers of America, and each one would like to be in your shoes." Susann looked at Edith and slowly nodded. She was right, for a change.

"But this one is so complicated," Susann almost cried. "And I don't have much time. And Edith, they really don't like me. It's not like with Imogen. You know they really don't. I'm afraid of them, and afraid I'll miss the deadline."

"Sue Ann Kowlofsky, you have never missed a deadline in your life," Edith said. "You won't miss this one either. Now let's go through it page by page until we get it right."

"But I'm so tired. I've already finished this book. I can't go back to it again."

"Well, you have to." Edith paused and looked again at the editorial letter. "You know," Edith said, "these suggestions are pretty good. I think they might make all the difference. This girl's no fool." Edith looked at Susann. "You might just manage to pull off a bestseller."

Susann drained the cup of cooled tea, then picked up her pen. "All right," she said.

# 42

> Publishing is not exactly a business; it's more an activity.
>
> —*Ruth Nathan*

Opal was to meet the miraculous Emma Ashton and her boss for lunch, but since she had nothing else to do and she was far too nervous to stay home and scrub or read, she showed up at The Bookstall as usual. Well, not exactly as usual, she admitted to herself: She was wearing a new navy blue rayon dress that belted at the waist. She had even put her gold Cupid pin on the collar. It was the first time she'd had a skirt on since she'd arrived in New York, and when she walked into The Bookstall Roberta looked up and smiled. "Perfect," Roberta said approvingly, and Opal wondered if, perhaps, Roberta had worried that Opal might not have or even *know* the appropriate thing to wear. "You look dignified and businesslike. Very nice."

Roberta and Opal had spent the last two days talking about nothing but the upcoming lunch at the Four Seasons. Roberta had dined there several times, back when the book business was better. She talked about the New York landmark restaurant in the Seagram's Building and described its two vast, austere rooms. "If you're meeting with someone senior," Roberta said, "you'll probably eat in the Grill Room. It doesn't look as fancy as the Pool Room does—it's just a series of levels off the bar—but those are the most fought-over lunch tables in Manhattan."

Opal had shrugged. She just wanted to talk about whether these people would really publish Terry's book. Since the phone call she had told herself a hundred times not to get her hopes up, but, of course, she couldn't help it.

Roberta had told Opal that she needed a literary agent or lawyer. Opal had merely shook her head. "Who?" she asked. "How? I couldn't get any of those agent jaspers to talk to me up till now. I don't want to get this any more complicated than it has to be."

"But you'll have to have someone read the contract."

"Well, I'll take care of that when we come to a deal," Opal had said.

"I don't think that's the way it's done," Roberta had told her. "Your agent is the one who makes the deal and gets the money for you."

Opal had looked at Roberta with big eyes. "Money?" she had said. "That's the least of it. Why, at one time I thought I'd have to pay to publish this myself!"

Now Roberta came from around the counter and handed Opal a thin flat box. "It isn't new, I'm afraid," Roberta said. "But it's a good one and I've never worn it, and I'd like you to wear it today." Opal blushed with pleasure. She couldn't remember the last time she'd had a gift. She opened the box and found a tissue-wrapped scarf; a scarf so beautiful and of so many colors that it silenced her.

"You don't like it," Roberta said. "Well, don't feel you have to wear it."

Opal shook her head, then took out the heavy silk square. She knew it must be French and tremendously expensive, even before she saw the Hermès signature at one corner. She'd already admired Roberta's beautiful scarves. She knew they cost a fortune. Now, recovering from her surprise and pleasure, she remembered her manners. "Oh, it's too nice. It's absolutely exquisite. I can't let you give me this."

Roberta smiled with relief. "You like it? Listen, you can't stop me from giving it to you: I've already done that. And you can't stop me from tying it on you, either." Roberta wrapped the scarf into a precise knot around Opal's neck. "Come on, take a look," she said, and walked the reluctant Opal back to the mirror.

The scarf was breathtaking, and it transformed Opal. She didn't look like an Indiana librarian. Instead she had become, well, if not fashionable, at least in the running. "Let's move the pin," Roberta suggested kindly. They did, and with the Cupid readjusted, Opal felt as if she could stand up to the Four Seasons or any other restaurant.

But Roberta wasn't yet satisfied. She was looking at Opal critically, her eyes half closed. "Almost," she said. "Almost." Then she pulled her own earrings off. "Lose those little pearls temporarily, and put these on," she insisted. "Just a loan," Roberta assured her. Opal didn't even argue. Roberta's earrings were big, each one a kind of modern wing shape, and they framed either side of Opal's face. They weren't anything Opal would have chosen or worn, but she had to admit they were impressive. "There you go," Roberta said. "The woman with the biggest earrings runs the meeting." Opal laughed.

And it was a good thing that Opal was armed with Roberta's earrings and scarf, because *everything* about the restaurant was intimidating. She walked into a large, bare marble room that seemed to have nothing in it. Well, nothing but a window in one marble wall where people handed over their coats; that and a huge suspended staircase. No signs, no other doors. There *was* a sofa, so Opal sat down on it, but after a few minutes she realized that everyone else who entered had made their way upstairs. That must be where the restaurant was. Roberta hadn't told her that crucial bit of information! Now she'd be late.

When Opal did make it to the top, an enormous room opened up in front of her. There was a four-sided bar on the right of the staircase and a large lectern on the left of it where three or four restaurant staffers stood. She looked past them to the banquettes behind the lectern and tried to recognize the face or form of Emma Ashton. But no one looked familiar. After all, Opal reminded herself, she'd seen the girl only for a few moments. And since then she'd heard her voice just once on the phone. Opal looked around again, telling herself not to panic. From Roberta's description, she knew this was the Grill Room. Perhaps they had been seated in the other area of the restaurant. What was that place called? Opal thought it had something to do with billiards, but that couldn't be right. She looked at the group at the lectern and steeled herself to approach them. After all, here she *was* expected and *did* have an appointment. What did she have to be frightened of?

The answer to that question was, of course, a rejection. Emma had said they liked the book but they had some things to discuss. What things? Opal forced herself to push her fears out, into the corner of her mind, and went up to the desk. "I'm here to meet Miss Ashton?" she said.

The woman at the desk looked down a list. "Ashton?" she asked. Then she shook her head. She was polite, and looked concerned. "No Ashton, I'm afraid."

Opal's stomach lurched. Had she gotten it wrong? Was there some mistake? Certainly, it couldn't have been a joke. And certainly she had not gotten the day, the place, or the time wrong. Just then Opal felt a hand on her shoulder and turned to see that she did, indeed, recognize Emma Ashton, though the girl was dressed more like a grown-up today, wearing a severe gray knit.

"Um, Mrs. O'Neal," Emma said. She sounded a bit unsure herself. Opal nodded. "It's so good to see you. Please come over to our table. Pam Mantiss is dying to meet you. She's our editor in chief."

Well, that was something. The editor in chief. Opal was led back to a corner table against a kind of niche. She was introduced to Emma's boss, Pam. Opal tried not to take an immediate dislike to the woman—after all, she reminded herself, she may want to publish Terry's book. But there was something in the woman's glittery eyes, in her too-tight sweater and her immediate barrage of questions that was unnerving and off-putting.

"So, did your daughter really write this book?" Pam Mantiss asked before Opal even sat down. "It's remarkable really. What was her background? Where did she go to school? Has she written anything else? Was she published before?"

Opal, startled as much by the nonstop delivery as by the questions themselves, took a deep breath. Only Emma's calm face made it viable to stay. Emma seemed to wince a bit and nodded at Opal. "Yes, of course Terry wrote the book," Opal said, trying not to show her exasperation. "She'd been working on it for almost a decade when . . . she died."

"One of *my* authors just died," Pam exclaimed, as if that was a bond between them. "Peet Trawley. Terrible. We have a contract and no book." Pam smiled. "While *you* have a book and no contract. Right?" Opal couldn't even nod; she felt too paralyzed. "You haven't been talking with any other publisher?" Pam Mantiss continued.

Opal thought back to all those useless hours and hopeless conversations in reception rooms. It seemed, though, that this bizarre woman was afraid of competition. Opal wasn't cagey by nature, but she could commit a sin of omission on Terry's behalf. "Well, I *have* spoken with a couple of other houses, but not in a serious way," she said. It wasn't exactly a lie.

Pam Mantiss shot a look at Emma. What, Opal wondered, did *that* mean? Did they mean to publish the book or not?

Just then the waiter arrived and asked for their drink orders. "Pellegrino," Emma said, whatever that was. Pam ordered wine.

"Coffee, please," Opal told the boy. Then they consulted the menu. Opal couldn't believe the prices. She ordered the salmon and was surprised when it came—it was the best thing she'd ever eaten. Well, of course Opal knew there was such a thing as fresh salmon, but there wasn't much of it in Indiana. While they ate, Opal answered questions and told them a little about Terry's background—valedictorian, her undergrad and grad school scholarships, her Yale and Columbia degrees. The entire time she felt as if she were being tested. Would they publish *Duplicity* or not? She didn't know what to omit, what to add. She didn't mention the rejection letters, but she did tell them Terry took her own life.

"So did my father," Pam said, between bites of steak tartare. "It really fucked me up."

Emma and Opal looked at each other, then sat in silence. Pam didn't seem to notice. Opal couldn't tell if Pam liked her or not—or if Pam liked the book. She watched as Pam cleared her plate, ordered an extra side of creamed spinach, ate that, and, Opal noticed, finished the rolls. "Do you want that?" Pam asked, pointing at Opal's own dish. Opal shook her head and Pam took the plate, cleaning it. She ate with a peculiar intensity, as if nothing stopped her hunger. Opal couldn't help but stare. The waiter broke the silence when he asked for their dessert order.

"Nothing for me," Pam told him. "I'm on a diet. But I *will* have another glass of wine." Opal wasn't sure if it was Pam's third or fourth. At lunch! Then Pam turned to her. "The thing is," Pam said, in a serious voice, "we would love to publish this book. It's a brilliant, brilliant work."

Finally! Opal took a deep breath. "Well. It certainly took you long enough to say so," Opal said tartly. But she guessed that was just the way these people did business. Four glasses of wine, enough food for a week, rude questions, and then the praise. They wouldn't talk to you if they didn't think the book was worthwhile. Weak with relief, Opal leaned back in her seat. She was in one of the fancier restaurants in the city talking to one of the best publishing houses. She had done it. She had found a home for Terry's work, and soon *The Duplicity of Men* would be in bookstores and libraries all over the country. Thank

God. Thank God for that last manuscript, and for Emma Ashton, and for Roberta Fine, and even for this crazy woman Pam. "Thank you," was all she managed to say, but it was all she really needed to. She lifted her coffee cup to her lips. Ah.

"Have you an agent?" Pam asked. As usual, before she got an answer, Pam went on to another point. "Listen, there's no way that we can pay you much. This is actually the kind of book that university presses put out. *Confederate Widow,* that kind of thing. And they pay squat. But we believe we can create a wider audience for this book. Still, it's a gamble. In terms of the actual advance . . ."

"It doesn't matter," Opal said, shaking her head slightly. "By 'advance' you mean money? Well, the money isn't the point."

Pam Mantiss's eyes narrowed. They were almost the same yellow as a cat's eyes. She smiled, but only with her teeth. "Good. Now, the other thing is, it's going to need a lot of pruning. Hopefully the manuscript will be significantly shorter. It's got to be cut down by at least twenty percent, and I'd like to see it cut even further."

Opal looked up from her coffee. The others had been served coffee too, along with a plate of tiny, tempting cookies. But she ignored the treats. Opal could barely believe what she had heard. First of all, there was that dreadful use of *hopefully*—and by a New York editor in chief! *This* editor was not going to work on Terry's book. Hopefully not, anyway. And how could the woman think the book could be cut? Opal put down her cup. "Not one word," she said.

Pam Mantiss, who was finishing the last of the little cookies, smiled—or at least she showed her teeth. "What?" she asked.

"No cuts," Opal said. She felt on firm ground at last. "Absolutely no cuts, no editing, no 'pruning'—as you called it. This isn't a tree, it's a book. And it's complete. No changes. There are a very few typos that I *have* noticed, but other than that, none of Terry's words are to be deleted or changed."

"What?" Pam asked again, her voice rising harshly.

Opal's stomach tightened, but so did her resolve. Publishing a bowdlerized book would not be publishing Terry's book. "No cuts," she repeated calmly, and finished her coffee.

Emma Ashton broke the silence. "Mrs. O'Neal, you don't understand. I love the book just as it is. But the economic reality of publishing a book of this magnitude is a frightening one. Especially with the cost of paper and the limited sales prospects for *Duplicity of Men*. It's a brilliant book, perhaps even a great one, but we can't—"

"How many libraries? How many real bookstores?" Opal interrupted her with the questions. "This is not a book to be read only today. It is for generations to come. Every college, every university will need copies."

Pam Mantiss smiled. This time it was more than showing her teeth: It showed her contempt. "Mrs. O'Neal, I think you have to reconsider—"

There was no point in listening to her. Opal had pegged that one right from the beginning. Her way or no way. "I'm sorry," she interrupted. "There's nothing to consider or reconsider." Opal paused. Emma Ashton's face was a study of concern. Well, Opal couldn't back down. "My daughter spent her entire adult life making that manuscript as perfect as she knew how. That is the way the work must be published. Nothing deleted, nothing changed, nothing edited. Anything else would show a lack of respect for her." Opal paused and gained control of her voice, which had risen. "She's not here to approve any suggestions, and you weren't there to give her any before she died." Opal said quietly. "So it's published as it stands or not at all."

Emma looked across the table. For a moment, Opal glanced into her eyes and felt that the girl knew what this was costing her. But even if it cost her publication of the book, she would not waver. Terry's work must stay intact.

"Well, I guess that's it," Pam said flatly. To her credit, Emma looked stricken. Pam Mantiss searched through her bag, pulled out a credit card, and handed it to the hovering waiter. Then she handed a business card to Opal. "Looks like it's a university press for you," she said. The bill came, and Pam scribbled her signature. Then she struggled into her leather jacket. She stood up.

"It's been nice to meet you," she said. She motioned for Emma to follow her. "We're outta here," she announced. "Give me a call if you change your mind."

# 43

It's necessary to publish trash in order to publish poetry.

—*Herbert Mitgang*

Gerald stepped out of the company limo and was greeted by the new doorman at his father's Fifth Avenue apartment building. It was one of the smaller but more exclusive structures on what was called "Museum Mile"—the Guggenheim, the Met, the Frick, and the Cooper-Hewitt were all in the neighborhood. Senior lived on the floor *below* the penthouse—penthouses, he felt, were ostentatious. Gerald glanced at himself in the gilt-framed mirror in the elevator vestibule. His hair was on straight, his tie was tight, and his jacket was admirably cut. Too bad he felt *he* was about to be cut as well.

The walnut doors of the elevator drew back, and William, eyes downcast and white-gloved as always, greeted him. "Hello, Mr. Gerald," he said. One of the smaller riddles of Gerald's life was how William identified everyone by their feet. Gerald stepped into the elevator and looked down at the gleaming parquet floor and the tiny upholstered divan across the back wall. In all the years he had lived in the building—as a boy, as an adolescent, and on all his visits as an adult—he had never seen anyone sitting on that seat. William, wordless, carried him up to the penultimate floor of the building and rolled back the door.

Senior's apartment was the only one on the floor. Gerald stepped out of the elevator directly into the gallery, a thirty-foot-long space hung with a few old portraits and carpeted with an ancient and somewhat tatty Kirman rug.

There were five imposing doors off the gallery—one huge one to the salon, another, its twin, opposite the dining room, and three smaller ones that led to the library, his father's study, and the bedroom wing. Gerald shot his cuffs and then, annoyed with himself, promised that he would not allow himself that habitual tic until he was safely out on the avenue again. He looked around for Matilda, the housekeeper, but it was Senior himself who appeared, standing in the doorway to the library. Trouble. Gerald nodded and walked across the long and empty space to where his father stood.

Formal as ever, Senior held out his arm, his elbow bent at a ninety-degree angle, and gave Gerald two quick handshakes. There were no hugs or even eighties air kisses in the Davis family. As always, Senior was immaculately groomed, his full head of white hair brushed back, his cheeks clean-shaved and pink, his mustache perfectly trimmed. He was attired in what Gerald thought of as his retirement afternoon uniform: gray flannels, a white Brooks Brothers shirt, and a cashmere cardigan the watery blue color of his eyes. His only acknowledgment of age and infirmity were the soft black kid slippers he wore instead of his usual lace-up shoes.

Gerald followed his father into the library, one of the four rooms that overlooked the Central Park reservoir. Oddly, at least to Gerald, his father had situated the desk at the window, with his chair behind it so that he sat with his back to the splendid view. For a moment, Gerald thought of T. S. Eliot and *his* desk—resolutely facing the blank wall. But Senior was no poet. Ever the devoted reader, Senior *had* once explained that the western light over his shoulder best helped him peruse a manuscript. Gerald took the seat opposite him and decided to lead with his strongest punch.

"So, do you think as highly of *The Duplicity of Men* as I do?" Gerald asked, stopping himself from grabbing at his cuffs. He forced his hands to lay in his lap and looked across the desk at his father, backlit by the glare of the setting sun.

"Of course I do. It's a wonderful book. A truly wonderful book. You should be proud of it. I only wish your mother could—"

Somewhere, at the other end of the apartment in a room that faced east, Gerald knew his mother continued to deteriorate. Alzheimer's had stricken early and hard, and she hadn't recognized any of them for more than a decade. The joy that his parents had shared in reading and talking and long consultations over the *Times* crossword puzzle had long ago dissolved, along with her frontal lobe. Senior must have cared very deeply for the book for him to even mention her.

"It's a shame the author is dead. It could still be nominated for the Tagiter, but winning would be a long shot. I think it could be a National Book Award winner, but I believe to be nominated it has to be a living author."

Gerald had forgotten that, then wondered briefly about whether the rule actually meant only contemporary authors were eligible. The O'Neal woman was so recently dead as to make a posthumous award possible, wasn't it? Gerald couldn't help but smile. The National Book Award. Senior thought it was worthy indeed, and Senior was no fool. Plus, he still had connections. Just getting a *nomination* would help with sales, not to mention selling the paperback rights, along with increasing Gerald's status and credibility this difficult year.

"Couldn't we see if that stipulation could be waived in this case? She isn't, after all, *long* dead."

Senior's face tightened. "Dead is dead, Gerald," Senior said. "It's binary. Length of time dead is no factor at all." Gerald felt as if he had been set up to be chastised. He'd acquire the book. He had to, or face his father's contempt. He'd tell Pam she had to buy it, though she'd had difficulties of some type with the author's mother. Senior turned to the other corner of his desk and slid over what

Gerald recognized, with a sinking feeling, as his own manuscript. He wasn't surprised; he didn't expect his father to like it. He'd listen to the lecture, try not to look like a whipped schoolboy, and then life would go on.

Senior leaned forward, his shoulders hunched against the light, his white hair haloed by it. "Gerald, we *must* talk about your book. There is no way I can allow you to publish this. It's a monstrosity. Whatever possessed you? It was one thing to allow that disgusting, tasteless, psychotic book by Chad Weston into the house. But he was your author. His first book had shown some promise. There was a contract. A moral dilemma. I think you should have turned it down, Gerald, but I understand why you didn't." Gerald tried not to flush, wondered if his father had read the Horace Bent column, and if he'd secretly enjoyed the David Morton fiasco. "But *this* book, Gerald. A family tragedy recycled and transposed into tabloid trash? It will shame you, the family, and the house. Publishing doesn't need any more irrelevant tell-alls. You cannot publish it. If a Davis has to do that sort of thing, leave it to Patti." He shrugged in distaste. "Next you'll be doing sequels!" Senior shook his head. "Sequels, prequels! Disgusting! The shameless Larry Ashmead came out with *Cosette*. Can you imagine? A sequel to *Les Miserables*? What's next? *The Penultimate Mohican*? Would Salinger's estate sell *Catcher in the Pumpernickel*?"

Gerald tried not to visibly squirm. He was actually considering a sequel right now. Not that he was alone. Partly inspired by the huge success of *Scarlett*, the Alexandra Ripley follow-up to *Gone with the Wind*, publishers and agents had signed up authors to write continuations of everything from *Star Trek* to the novels of Jane Austen. Recently, Vagrius, one of Russia's most respectable publishing houses, had signed an author to write a sequel to Tolstoy's *War and Peace*. Would it be called *Truce*? Gerald wondered.

Despite his resolution, Gerald shot his cuffs and blinked.

He had been prepared for disapproval but not for this blanket contempt, nor the restrictive command. Senior had overstepped himself. Was he prohibiting publication as Gerald's father or as the past chairman of the firm? Did he refer to the *SchizoBoy* scandal because he would talk with David Morton or simply to humiliate his son and heir? In either case, Senior had no real power to stop the presses. Still, despite his anger, Gerald felt his stomach drop and the empty place fill with a frightening hollowness. "I think you might be overreacting," he said. "First of all, this is fiction. Secondly, any events that might have inspired me happened nearly fifty years ago." Gerald thought of his mother. "Those who might care won't remember, and those who might remember won't care."

"I beg to differ with you," Senior said coldly. "Your uncle is still alive, and so, I believe, is Mrs. Halliday. Not to mention those left in *my* circle of friends." Senior shook his head, sending rays of fading light into Gerald's eyes. "What in the world would possess you to rattle this skeleton? It reflects badly on everyone. The only possible advantage is that it might make you a few ducats. But surely, Gerald, you can't possibly be thinking the book has any merit or that any merit would be reflected on you. What *could* you have been thinking? It's never going to make Harold Bloom's *Canon*."

Gerald squinted and turned away. The sunset was hurting his eyes, and he couldn't see his father's face. In the room around him, beautifully bound books and first editions stood on mahogany shelves next to his father's Chinese porcelains. The carpet was a precious silk Tabriz, a campestral pattern that, though worn, was still magnificent. The furniture was American Hepplewhite, all museum-quality. His father had bought this sumptuous twelve-room apartment—complete with three working fireplaces and three maid's rooms—for ninety thousand dollars almost forty years ago. Today Gerald was barely managing the mortgage on his apartment—half the size—

at twenty times the price, and there was no Tabriz on *his* floor. His first wife had their rug collection, his second wife most of the paintings, and both had better addresses than he did. How dare his father sound so contemptuous about "making a few ducats." All of Senior's needs had been taken care of perfectly for decades. No, Gerald corrected himself, for Senior's whole life.

For a moment, Gerald felt tremendous self-pity. It had been so hard to find a legitimate place for himself in the world his father had created, a world his father had both inherited and expanded during a time when there were no inheritance taxes, when income tax was nominal, when a million dollars was a lot of money. In those days you could buy an original Philadelphia highboy for a few thousand dollars. Now a few hundred thousand wouldn't guarantee it at a Christie's auction.

Gerald looked around at the immaculately beautiful room. It had been his privilege to grow up here, disciplined by his father and ignored by his mother, but it wasn't his fate to get a room like this of his own. Or the respect his father had gotten. Or the autonomy. His father had sold out his birthright and now despised him, Gerald, for surviving as best he could.

There was no way he could *not* publish the book. Senior was mad. It was on the list, about to be featured with a two-page spread in the catalog, and Gerald would receive the acceptance check in a matter of days. For a moment Gerald thought about changes that could be made to the galleys; but that, too, was madness. He looked across the desk, directly into the sunset, and squinted again. Just as well. There was no need for Senior to see what was in his son's eyes.

"Well," Gerald said. "I hear your point of view. Stephanie and I have a dinner this evening." He rose, though he hadn't yet been dismissed, and walked to the door. Let his father think what he wanted; that his word was still law, that the publishing world as a whole—and his son in particular—trembled when he spoke. The fact was, Gerald *was* trembling, but more from rage than from fear.

Senior was up and across the room with him. The old man was surprisingly spry. He'd live forever, and if he didn't, his wife would. With his sisters still alive, Gerald knew he'd inherit nothing but the valuable first editions anyway. He glanced once more at the perfect room and turned to leave it. His father followed him into the gallery. Never a bright space, it was dim now, lit only by the smear of bright sunlight that poured from the library's open door. Gerald stepped out of the light and strode the long, dark walk to the elevator. He was determined to say nothing, nothing at all. But his father broke the silence.

"By the way, Gerald, I really like that little Italian book. It has a *je ne sais quoi*, a certain charm."

My God, Gerald thought. Now he's reading manuscripts I haven't even gotten to! It was ridiculously insulting. His father was muttering on. "I know the business has changed, that there's no visible market for a book like this, but I think that its optimism, humor, and wisdom might have a broad comfort and appeal. Anyway, at least it's literate. You could do a whole lot worse."

"Yes. I understand. You've already told me I have," Gerald said icily. He pressed the button for the elevator while he and his father stood together in the wide and empty entrance gallery.

# 44

Everyone needs an editor.
—*Tim Foote*

Camilla lay on the bed that Frederick had deserted. She hadn't moved since he'd told her that he couldn't undertake a relationship right now and it was wrong of him to try. Though it was a warm afternoon, Camilla felt so cold that her body trembled and her teeth chattered. Every part of her seemed to hurt, except her eyes. They roved, taking comfort in the view out the window, in the Canaletto reproduction over her desk, and in the still life that her vase full of pinks and oranges made. But her brain wasn't really making sense of what her eyes took in. She was shattered. To have been held so closely, loved so deeply, and then discarded was more than she could bear.

After their coupling, Frederick had told her all about macular degeneration. She'd never heard of it, but he had haltingly explained that it was a leading cause of central-vision loss. He still had some peripheral sight, but he was rapidly going blind. Most people who developed the illness didn't begin to lose vision until their late fifties or sixties, but for some reason Frederick's eye problems had begun early. He'd made this trip to Italy as a kind of visual good-bye—the rate of degeneration had been increasing lately—and he'd needed his mother to assist him.

Going blind! It was such a tragedy. Yet it didn't give Frederick the right to sleep with her and discard her! She felt sorry for herself, but that didn't mean that she didn't also feel pity for Frederick Ashton. How wretched he must feel. But that was no excuse for his behaviour. He had used her, deceived her, and then rejected her. It was the last straw—her back was broken and she could no longer bear her burden of loneliness and self-care. She'd lie in bed for a long time. Then she'd return to Birmingham. She'd been a fool to think she could ever escape.

For what else could she do? This guide job would take her nowhere. She had no life, no community of friends here. She'd seen that before Frederick's arrival, and only more clearly since. The affair with Gianfranco had been hurtful and ill-advised; now this misadventure with Frederick had ended everything. Even this room in this beautiful city had become dangerous. The only thing left was to go back to the drabness she had come from. The thought was unbearable, and, worse, Camilla could barely imagine a step beyond her defeated return to her mother's flat. She could go to ground there for a while, live on high tea of beans or canned spaghetti on toast and an egg, return to her childhood survival ploys of visits to the library and the Birmingham Museum, but then what? Beg Sister Agnus for a teaching job? Visit her "patroness," Lady Ann, and be patronized? Never. Camilla's tears turned bitter.

Perhaps the worst part of it all had been how very good it had felt to be in Frederick's arms. Ah, the comfort of touch, of skin on skin, and the human need for congress. He'd been a wonderful lover, far better than anyone she'd ever slept with. Bastard! He had opened up that need, that female side that now, once again, would have to go begging.

In bed with him, after she had recovered from her mute surprise at his disclosure, she managed to ask him to leave. He'd seemed shocked by that. Whatever had he expected? He had apologized over and over again, but that was hardly the point. Only several hours after he had left did it occur to Camilla that he may have needed help getting back to his hotel in the dark. He'd been horrid, but she supposed she had, too.

Why had Frederick assumed she was so negligible? Was being a guide the same as wearing a signpost: "I'm here to help"? Was it because he was from a patrician class, used to being serviced? Camilla's eyes teared up. How could she have let herself believe that a normal, able-bodied, well-off, healthy man from a good family would pursue her in a serious way? How had she let herself think that? "Her kind," as her mother had put it, was sought after merely as a mistress, a nurse, a paid—or in this case unpaid—companion, a guide, a governess. Weren't these the only roles suitable for nineteenth-century women who had been educated beyond their station? Things hadn't changed for women like her in a hundred years.

Finally she was cried out. Camilla could almost imagine herself lying under the high flaking ceiling until she ceased to exist. But life, more's the pity, didn't work that way. She was not Lily Bart, and this was not *The House of Mirth*. Unfortunately, those women with the taste and desire to live amidst beauty who didn't have the wherewithal to do so didn't just tragically expire nowadays, as they did in Edith Wharton's time. They soldiered on, usually at some nasty job of work. Camilla admitted defeat. She couldn't look forward to the future—a job in a High Street bookshop, or whatever was next on the agenda—but she would move on to it because she had no choice. Slowly, and only because she had to, she rose.

She looked around the room and sighed. What she needed was a removal man. How had she collected so much flotsam? Packing up would be a trial. She would have to either get more cartons or buy another suitcase. She could go to the straw market tomorrow and see if there was something decent Emilio would give her at a knocked-down price, since she'd sent so many visitors to him. She'd never taken a kick-back or a percentage, just as she had refused to drag trusting tourists through a "tour" of cameo factories or other rubbish, even though owners had offered her significant bribes to do it. So she could only afford a cheap case. That was her in a nutshell—a cheap case. She was, as usual, short of cash, but if she left in two weeks, she needn't pay any more on her room, and she could sell the little clock

Gianfranco had given her. It was the only valuable thing she had. She stood up and took the clock off her table, wrapped it in newspaper, and put it in her purse.

It was then she saw the envelope, lying on the floor half under her door. Frederick had already sent one note—almost illegibly written—full of apology and pain. He had asked to see her again—just as a friend—and she had not responded. She couldn't. She was far too shy to tell him how she felt, and far too honest to lie. She kicked this new note across the floor—she didn't need to decipher another one. Apparently, in the five days since their night together, he had neither left Florence nor quite given up. For a moment, Camilla was tempted to kick the note back under the door, or to pick it up, and, unopened, tear it into a thousand tiny pieces that she could sprinkle out the window as her confetti *arrividerci* to Firenze. But she couldn't quite manage to do it. Ah, that was her problem. She was weak. What can I possibly be hoping for, she asked herself? She took the envelope over to her desk.

It was, as she knew it must be, from the Helvetia & Bristol. But once she opened that envelope, there was another enclosed. Confused for a moment, Camilla looked at the printed return address and the postmark. Davis & Dash, New York, New York. Had Frederick returned to New York and written her already? But the envelope was addressed to him in Florence and the seal already torn. She pulled out the one-page letter inside.

Dear Frederick,
Mother told me you had remained behind in Italy, and I hope you're doing well. Can you manage? How are you reading this? Anyway, in hopes that you have some help, I'm writing to tell you that while architecture is out of the question for you now, you seem to have a pretty good nose for literature. An alternate career, perhaps? I truly enjoyed the Camilla Clapfish manuscript. I think a lot of other readers will as well. I won't go into

all the gory (and they are) details, but I'm almost certain we will make your writer an offer. I suspect it won't be much—twenty thousand dollars or so, but a first novel is not usually a good bet and this is probably the best we can do. Needless to say, Ms. Clapfish is free to go elsewhere, but we would like to hear from her as soon as possible should she be willing to accept our terms.

*Entre nous,* I should say that an agent has read the manuscript and is willing to represent her with us or elsewhere. The agent is certain of a sale. If Ms. Clapfish can possibly come to NYC, it would also aid in the process. Needless to say, it's a bit of a conflict of interest for me to recommend this, but Alex Simmons is an aggressive young literary rep and truly enthusiastic about the book. If Ms. Clapfish does decide to contact her, just have her promise that she will never mention at D & D that the recommendation came from me. I do this only because Mother led me to believe you had a personal interest in the author. Way to go, bro.

I'm writing to you at the Helvetia with a request for them to forward it to you, if you've moved on. Mother said something about Assisi. Generally, I would be a little more impressed with your literary management skills if the two of you amateurs hadn't forgotten to enclose an address for the author. Definitely not good form, old boy. SASE, please. Even for submissions from brothers.

Anyway, give me a call to let me know when (and if) you're coming back. Meanwhile, I'm thinking of you. And I'm grateful to report that my own private life is looking up. Which is to say, I almost have one.

I would write more, but I don't know who will be reading this to you. The telephone works.

Love, Emma

Camilla, utterly amazed, scanned the letter again, and then a third time. It was like a beam of light, not just cutting through her darkness but illuminating a future—a real, potential future. Frederick truly had liked the book, and his blessed sister did, too.

Then for one horrible moment, Camilla wondered if this wasn't some hoax, a misguided attempt by Frederick to "make it up" to her or recapture her attention. But a scrawl across the bottom of the paper reassured her. "I am leaving for New York tomorrow. Please come to the hotel this evening. Business only. And congratulations." Underneath that, in even more uneven handwriting, he'd written, "*You owe me nothing.*"

Camilla stared at the single page before her. She could hardly believe the power it had. Twenty thousand dollars! She'd never had more than five hundred pounds at any time in her life. She got up and, without even realizing it, virtually waltzed across the room and threw herself back down on the bed. Her book was good enough to be published, and by a New York publisher! She was so shocked, so delighted, that she threw herself onto her stomach and began to giggle. How strange: She had been lying here less than fifteen minutes ago in despair, and now she was enraptured. Everything had changed. Somewhere in New York a woman liked her story of middle-aged American ladies and was willing to give her a pot of money. Should she stay on here in the city that she loved and begin a second book? Should she go on to London? Or should she return to New York, the city she had been defeated by? One thing she did *not* consider was a ticket to Birmingham. Again, Camilla giggled. It was just far too outrageous. She'd been rescued. Was she dreaming?

The only thing she knew was that she *would* go to the hotel. Whatever damage Frederick had inflicted, he had more than made up for it with this wonderful boon. She would see Frederick tonight, and she would thank him. But she would never talk about her feelings for him again. It would be all business and platonic friendship. Camilla would not let herself be hurt anymore.

# 45

> There are men that will make you books and turn
> 'em loose into the world with as much dispatch
> as they would do a dish of fritters.
>
> —*Miguel de Cervantes*

The list meetings were always a double ordeal for Gerald: It wasn't just that they were long and rancorous; or that future sales depended on them; or that everybody had a pet peeve or a personal agenda; or that people took each decision personally. Because, as if all that was not enough, Gerald *also* felt as if his father attended every meeting with him, second-guessing him and (too often) silently criticizing his decisions. After all his years of therapy, Gerald might have shaken the ghostly feeling if he wasn't totally aware that Jim Meyer, corporate counsel and mole, would give his father a full report of everything. Gerald nervously looked down at his almost-invisible monogrammed initials. Before a list meeting he certainly wished sometimes that he were *more* godlike, at least in his omniscience.

The list meeting was where he and Pam Mantiss finalized the editorial acquisitions for the season and presented them to the key marketing and sales staff. Then the team, under Gerald's despotic guidance, began to structure publication dates, print runs, quotas, sales strategies, advertising budgets, publicity campaigns, author tours, and all the other necessities that would support the list. Dickie Pointer, VP of sales, was tough and battle-scarred: There wasn't a bookseller he didn't know or a quota he couldn't argue. Other attendees were Amy Rosenfeld, head of marketing, and, unfortunately, Chuck Rector. Wendy Brennon, vice president of publicity, was the only new player. The meeting would position books relative to one another and whatever else they guessed or knew would be out there in the marketplace. Books were ranked not necessarily by quality, though Gerald did like to consider that. Personal enthusiasm in a book among staff counted, but with something like Susann Baker Edmonds's new novel there was the overwhelming consideration of how much Davis & Dash had paid for the book—and how much, therefore, had to be further invested to recoup. Well, Gerald thought, he wouldn't open the meeting with *that* hot potato. Nor would he mention the Chad Weston fiasco. And, if they knew what was good for them, none of the others would mention it either.

His buzzer rang. "They're all waiting," Mrs. Perkins said.

Gerald already knew that. The woman annoyed him, so he played a childish—but to him amusing—game of annoying her back. "I'd like a cup of coffee," he told her. "No, make it espresso." That took longer. "I'll have it in here." This was his company, his offices, his conference room, despite what David Morton might think. It was his meeting and his goddamned list. The publishing house still had his name on the door, the letterhead, and the Quotron stock data. He'd take his time.

He looked down at the memo for the list meeting. They would never get through all of this today, he thought, and lifted his thumb and index finger to the arching bridge of his nose, pinching the place that got tight from tension. Well, he would do his magic, work his way through and see if, yet again, he could come up with a list of books that would manage to make money, give some status to the house, *and* get them on the bestseller list. It wouldn't be easy.

Worse than the lack of confidence in the Edmonds book, worse than the gap that *SchizoBoy* had left, would be facing down Dickie Pointer and Chuck Rector as he insisted on a huge printing for his own book. Well, Gerald wouldn't start with that, either. *He'd* make the agenda and see when the time was right for that particular skirmish.

Mrs. Perkins knocked and entered. The tiny demitasse cup rattled in her hand. She put it down on his desk, and he could see how difficult it was for her not to prod him to get up. Spitefully, he picked up the spoon and slowly stirred the deep brown liquid, though, as he didn't take sugar, there was no need to. Then he put the spoon down on the thin saucer. "Any biscotti?" he asked. He watched as her thin lips tightened. She nodded her head. He didn't really want one, so as she was returning with a plate, he passed her in the doorway, shrugged, and crossed the wide reception area to the conference room.

Everyone was already assembled, waiting, and Chuck Rector, at the far end of the table, was pontificating. "All that I'm saying is that if each editor simply cut ten pages—only ten pages—from each of his or her books, I estimate that we could save close to eight hundred and seventy-five thousand dollars per year."

Gerald saw Pam Mantiss roll her eyes, but Lou Crinelli's pockmarked and irregular face was turning deep red. If anyone could take Pam's place it might someday be Lou. It was his first list meeting, and it looked as if he, like the tape on *Mission Impossible*, might self-destruct. "That's the stupidest thing I ever heard," he said. Crinelli was pretty rough around the edges, but he was a truly good and aggressive acquisitions editor, and in this case, he was absolutely right. Gerald cleared his throat and took his place at the Chippendale chair at the head of the table. Lou continued, "I suggest revisions that *have* to be made. Sometimes they're cuts, sometimes not. How the hell can you cut ten pages from *everything*? Try cutting ten pages from *The Sun Also Rises*."

"I was merely pointing out the relationship between paper costs and the bottom line," Chuck said, bristling. "You know, paper and binding costs have been spiraling, while we—"

Gerald leaned forward. They all looked at him expectantly. When he had their full attention, he began, "It's always amused me to notice how few people really see themselves as others see them. For example, just in this room Chuck probably thinks he's intelligent. And Lou may think he's attractive. And I, I think I'm a nice guy. But all three of us are deluded. So let's drop opinions and get down to work."

And so the list meeting began.

They had already waded through a few midlist titles and were on to the books that mattered. "Are we going to have the Peet Trawley book in time?" Gerald asked. The Trawley book was more important than ever.

"Dead men tell no tales," Dickie Pointer cracked, sotto voce.

Pam shot him a poisonous look. "Yes, we'll have it on time," she told Gerald. He wondered at her new confidence. She'd been having a hard time of it, and—to tell the truth—it had made him more gleeful than it should have. For years Pam had edited and critiqued the work of others, always ending with: "I could write twice as good as that." It had been nasty good fun to see her leveled. But Gerald needed this book, and she seemed calmer. Perhaps she could draft the Trawley trash.

"We've got to have it," Dickie growled. "As long as it says 'Peet Trawley' and has an omega on the cover, it'll sell. But we've *got* to deliver on time. I don't want to be pissing off my booksellers."

"You'll have it," Pam assured him.

"Well, at least the rollout on it is automatic," Amy said. "We have a good marketing plan. We'll just trumpet this as Peet Trawley's last book."

"The fuck you will," Pam Mantiss said.

Amy looked at her. "But I—"

"Peet left several manuscripts," Pam announced. "They might take a little more editing, but this *isn't* his last book."

"Ha!" crowed Dickie. "It's like V. C. Andrews. The longer she's dead, the more she's written."

Interesting, Gerald thought. Pam, it seemed, has found a sideline. Well, it would be good for the house. "Am I the only one who needs a coffee?" Gerald asked calmly. He hit the silent buzzer under the table with his foot, and Mrs. Perkins opened the door. After everybody's complicated coffee orders were given, but before Mrs. Perkins and Andrea returned, the plans and positioning for Peet's book were completed. No blood had been spilled. Well, Gerald thought, only twenty-seven more to go. Would that they were *all* dead authors. There was a lot of it going around. Hadn't the late Lucille Ball just penned an autobiography? Actually, he noticed from the agenda, the next one was dead too.

"This next one is a truly magnificent book. I hope you all read it," he said, looking around the table. Dickie read very little, Chuck less. "But there is no way we can do this book without significant cuts," Gerald declared, his hand on the outrageously high pile of the *Duplicity* manuscript.

"Mrs. O'Neal still says it's out of the question," Pam admitted. She was bitter that he'd forced her to make the acquisition.

"Did you tell her it's out of the question for us to publish it at this length?" Gerald barked. Pam didn't even blink, merely nodded and shrugged. He turned to Chuck Rector. "What would this cost?"

Rector shrugged. "Minimum, thirty dollars," he said.

Gerald felt as if his head might explode. The trend was clearly toward shorter, cheaper novels. He turned to Pam. He hated vulgarities, but he had to exclaim. "Mind and mustache of Muhammad! We can't put a thirty-dollar price tag on a first novel. It absolutely can't be sold that way, if it can be sold at all. Are you certain you can't get her to revise it?" He *had* to have this book on this list. He'd authorized Pam to pay anything reasonable, though Senior would despise him if he didn't.

Wendy Brennon cleared her throat. "You know, I think there is a tremendous angle on this book. First of all, it will appeal to women as well as men. The title alone is going to do that," she said. "We also have this wonderful human-interest story: The Book That Refused to Die, Even Though the Author Did. I think I can get *People* to do a 'Pages' story on it. And if the mother will go on Oprah and Sally and Ricki Lake and, you know, cry a little bit, well, I think we really have something here."

Gerald didn't let anything register on his face, but he was pleased. That was what he had hired Wendy for. She'd better find some equally good angles for *his* book. Then Dickie Pointer spoke up. "Yeah, yeah. Publicity is swell, but the book's too big. People want little reads. Even twenty-five dollars is too much, especially for a first novel. The thing is too literary, and even if it hits, it's a oner: There's no follow-up. After all, she's dead." Then Dickie grinned and shot a glance at Pam. "Unless you find a sequel in her attic, too, Pam."

Pam ignored his gibe and looked sour. "All right. We know the chains aren't going to take this book. That's clear from the beginning. So it's got to be the independents. I say we pass. She won't let us cut it. Fuck her."

"Fuck the poor bereaved mother?" Crinelli asked with wide eyes.

"Fuck yourself," Pam said.

"Children, children," Gerald warned. "Look, I want this book. And it can be sold. We make it an event, send out advance reader copies to the literary bookstores. They'll hand-sell it. And we can get some blurbs. Who among the literati owe us a favor?"

"Who cares? I don't care if you get a blurb from the Holy Father himself," Dickie said. Since the pope had written a book, there had been a lot of pope jokes. The nine-million-dollar advance Random House had paid spurred some to call the book "Poprah." Dickie turned and looked directly at Gerald. "How many copies are you going to ask my reps to sell? If you do a first printing of more than two thousand, you're crazy. And trust me, there'll be a second coming before we do a second printing."

Wendy spoke again. She was the only one who seemed to Gerald to be calm, but then, she hadn't worked with any of these people long enough to hate them. "I think we can get some really good reviews on this," she said. "All it takes is the front page of the *New York Times Book Review* for this novel to really—"

"Now *there's* a revelation," Dickie said nastily. "You put my *address* book in a review on the front page of the book review and we'll get three hundred thousand hardcover sales."

Pam leaned across the table toward Dickie. "If you could read instead of just talk, you'd know this book is that fucking good," she said. "It *could* get a *Times* cover. But the mother's a pain in the ass."

Gerald cleared his throat. He didn't want things to deteriorate with Dickie before they got to Gerald's own book. He was going to have to hit him with an undeliverable quota on that one. "Okay," he said, "regrettably we take the book at its current length. We print five thousand copies. Dick, I'm asking you to get four thousand out there. That means you'll probably come in with thirty-four hundred. Wendy, let's test your enthusiasm to see what you can do on the 'mothers-whose-daughters-write-books-and-commit-suicide' talk circuit." He raised his brows. "Pam, see who you can blow to get respected writers to give us a blurb."

Pam made a moue. "Dickie, can I borrow your knee pads?" she asked dryly. She looked around the table. "Does anyone have Saul Bellow's private phone number?" Nobody laughed.

Gerald looked at his agenda. "Okay, so now let's talk about something that could make us money," he said, moving the meeting on. "We've got this first Jude Daniel novel."

The atmosphere around the table immediately perked up; Dickie actually smiled. "What we need for this," Dickie said, "is a fabulous cover. Can we show the three kids' graves, with the bitch crying over them?"

The man was a ghoul. And an obvious thinker, which to Gerald was a bigger sin. "Perhaps we don't have to be quite so literal," Gerald suggested. "But a cover *is* going to be very important. Do we already have Eddie working on something?"

Pam nodded. "This has got to be a really classy preprint, sent out to our hot list. There's already a lot of industry buzz on it. Some people are pissed off that they didn't get a chance to bid on it. It's a page-turner. It's got sex, murder, and yet it's a great women's read. This could be a lot bigger than Miller's *The Good Mother*."

"Maybe we could retitle it *The Bad Mother*," Dickie joked.

"What's Jude Daniel like?" Wendy asked.

"The guy is a publicist's wet dream," Pam assured her. "Here's the pitch: a handsome, sexy, sensitive man who truly understands what it's like to live in a woman's skin."

"Women writers used to rule soft fiction, but in the last five years, that's changed," Gerald said. "Grisham and Waller are writing the kind of books that women used to write, and now men as well as women are reading them. Jude Daniel is a part of that sea change: I think this could be our *Horse Whisperer*."

"As my grandmother used to say, 'From your lips to God's ears,'" Lou joked. "But I'm not so sure. I don't know if women want to read about a kid killer, and I don't know if men want to read about a woman."

"Yeah?" Pam asked. "Grisham didn't seem to have too much trouble getting them to read *The Client*: That was a woman protecting a boy from kid killers."

"A fluke."

"It's a great read, Lou," Pam said, her voice rising. "Your grandmother would love it."

Gerald turned to Dickie. "We're going for a super release here," he said. "Thanks to Pam we got the book at a good price and we can afford to push the hell out of it. This one's got to go out of the ballpark. What are you thinking of lining up?" he asked Amy.

"Well, we can do a twelve-book in-store display and dump, and maybe a contest."

"Yeah," Dickie said. "Kill your kid and win a free plea bargain."

Amy laughed.

"We'll try to tie it into a sweepstake or something. And if the guy can schmooze, if he can talk, we can do a ten-city tour," Wendy added.

"He can schmooze," Pam guaranteed. "How about fifteen cities?"

"He'll be dragging his ass by the time that's over," Wendy said. "You ought to know how hard it is to get much interest in a first novelist."

Pam shook her head, exasperated. "Forget about that. This isn't *about* a first novelist. It's the nonfiction angle. Women who kill their own children. C'mon, use your head: He's a college professor. He can be positioned as an expert."

Dickie nodded. For once he and Pam were in agreement.

"Okay," Gerald said, "I want to see a really great marketing plan *and* a terrific publicity package. I think we're in good shape on this one. Let's plan a tentative print run of a hundred and fifty thousand copies, and if orders look strong, let's kick it up to two hundred."

Chuck Rector rolled his eyes and mumbled something about remainders. Gerald would have liked to slap him down, but with the memory of handling his own remainders so fresh, he abstained. Well, the meeting was at the highest point it would reach. He'd best get on to his new manuscript. "Now, about my oeuvre" he said. There was silence. "I know I can say we were all disappointed by the performance of *Lila*. But I don't have competition from

Laura Richie on this new one. I have the inside story, and I know I can deliver."

Gerald looked around the table. No one but Wendy was meeting his eyes. "I've rewritten the opening. It's much stronger now." He kept his voice low; he refused to feel embarrassed. He couldn't prevent himself from tugging at his cuffs, though. "Listen: I'm going to send the preprints out to all my old friends. Liz Smith will write something positive. So will Helen Gurley Brown, if she's not out of there. But I don't want the book circulated too widely. Blurbs are better anyway."

He couldn't admit that he was afraid of negative reviews, but they knew—all but Wendy—that that's what he was saying. "There are a lot of people close to me who owe me one. We won't have trouble getting quotes." Certainly not, Gerald thought, since every author he published would be obligated to say something nice about the book. That is, if they wanted another contract. He cleared his throat. "Dickie, I need you to sell three hundred thousand copies."

Dickie pushed back his chair, partially rose, then fell back. "Gerald, please . . . you have to listen to reason on this. The bookstores know exactly how many copies of *Lila* were shipped. And how few sold. Everything is computerized. They know their returns. You *can't* expect—"

"*You* can't expect me to listen to this," Gerald said coldly. "*I'll* be at the sales meeting. *I'll* present this book. And I'm going to ask for a personal commitment from each of our sales reps, promising to place their quotas. Anyone who can't make that promise can rep someplace else. Have I made myself perfectly clear?" He paused, his eyes narrowing. "We aren't talking about *options* here, Dickie." Gerald turned his cold eyes on Wendy. "See what *you* can come up with as a publicity plan. But no tours. Let's just talk to a few of my journalist friends. I think we might be able to get a *New York* magazine story, or maybe something in the magazine section of the *Times*. We'll certainly get coverage in the *Observer*—maybe an interview. There's this whole New York socialite/crime-story angle. Dominick Dunne has done so well with it. I want to see that kind of coverage. Go to *Vanity Fair* and *The New Yorker*. They're into recycling old scandal. Wendy, you're in with the Condé Nast people. With all that, a big advertising budget along with the quota, we ought to do it." Case closed. It was, after all, his company. He paused. "Now, on to Madame Edmonds?"

Shell-shocked, the staff turned to Pam. "What about that prima donna?" Dickie asked. Gerald knew they were all afraid to say what they were thinking: that he'd bought a dated novelist at an inflated price as she began her decline.

"I like it," said Wendy. "It's better than Jackie Collins.

"Hardly a recommendation," Gerald said.

Dickie spoke up. "I think her problem was that she'd lost touch with her typical readers. And the average age of her core audience is 'deceased.' This book is more realistic. It deals with today's women's problems and yet fulfills more wishes than her last one."

Gerald smiled grimly. "She will," he said. "So what can we do to turn her around and get her back on the very top of the bestseller list?"

"Well," Pam suggested, "there's already a lot that we're contractually obligated to do: Alf Byron has us tied up. We *have* to do the national advertising—"

"Shit, that doesn't sell *anything,*" Dickie said. "She just wants to see her airbrushed picture in the papers." He shook his head. "We've committed a quarter of a million dollars to the campaign."

Chuck whistled and smacked his head with his hands. "Good money after bad," he muttered. Gerald ignored him.

"Look," Lou said, "I'm not on the sales end, and I don't pretend to be an expert there. But it seems to me the only way to get this writer back on the rails is to get her back on the rails. Know what I mean?" Everyone stared at him. No one did know. Sometimes Lou made no sense at all. But this, as it happened, was not one of those times. "Maybe they didn't buy her last book, but they all know her name," Lou said. "She's still a celebrity. She's got some glamour. Not in New York or L.A. or even Chicago, but she does in the whistlestops. Get her out there to every little bookstore. Spend the money on that. People won't show up for a Jude Daniel. Who the hell ever heard of him? But for twenty years Susann Baker Edmonds has been a name on every bookrack in every airport and every drugstore and every supermarket in the country. And am I the only one who's noticed that she's used the same photograph for twenty years? Anyway, she's an institution. Put the broad on a forty-city tour. She'll get coverage in every small newspaper in the country."

"It's a *great* idea," Dickie said. "My reps will love it. We have her visit the Heartland. No Dallas-Fort Worth bullshit. Let's see her in Cincinnati and Rutland, Missoula and Sacramento. Omaha. Kansas City. *Definitely* Kansas City. Ken Collins can sell the hell out of her in Kansas City. None of the garden spots."

"She's gonna *love* this," Pam intoned, then couldn't stop a wicked giggle. Even Gerald grinned. Oh, it was evil. He imagined Susann and Alf stuffed on a four-seater commuter plane over the Puget Sound. For the millions they'd paid her, Susann Baker Edmonds would take their marching orders. She'd weep and wail, but she'd do it. And he'd bet that people in the boonies would come out and buy.

"Will that consume the whole budget?" Chuck asked. "We're contractually obligated to spend it all." He stopped to calculate. "Between the tour, the advertising, some posters for the bookstores, and the usual promotional stuff, what else is there?"

"How about bumper stickers?" Wendy asked.

"Yeah. 'Honk if you remember Susann Baker Edmonds,'" Dickie said, and they all laughed.

Gerald grimaced at a vision: Susann Baker Edmonds as the Anna Morrison of the future. Christ, he hoped he was wrong. "All right, we're in agreement that we have to bring Susann back to the top and we have the means and money to do it. Let's move on." Everyone grumbled in low tones, as if they had just been punished by their school principal. "Now, the last beauty on the agenda is this untitled bit by one Camilla Clapfish."

Since his visit to Senior, he'd read the manuscript and agreed with Senior's view. "We haven't quite acquired it yet, but I like it, Pam, despite Emma's pass." Pam smiled at Gerald. "It will cost us a nickel, and it might go places." Frankly, he was surprised that Emma Ashton, who had seemed so savvy about his own book and the O'Neal, didn't see the possibilities. Well, maybe she wasn't as bright as he'd thought. "Anyway, the angles for it are the fact that its author is a Brit and she writes charmingly. You know what Priestley said: 'An Englishman is never so happy as when he's explaining an American.'"

"It sucks," said Dickie. Gerald ignored him.

"What the hell are we going to call it?" Pam asked. "Does she have an idea?"

"How about *Florence in Florence*?" Wendy offered. "Isn't one of the main characters Mrs. Florence Mallabar?"

"Oh, come *on*," Pam groaned.

"How about *Boring*?" Dickie asked.

That remark made Gerald think of the Charles Willeford book with the best title in the world: *New Hope for the Dead*. But he didn't want to encourage Dickie. "Let's get serious," he said. "Pam, have you got a contract with her?"

"No problem. She's coming in next week to sign."

"So? A title?" Gerald asked the group.

"How about *A Week in Florence*," Wendy suggested. "Undertones of *A Year in Provence*, but shorter."

"It should only sell like Peter Mayle," Dickie said.

"Let's say *A Week in Firenze*," Gerald suggested. "It adds that little something, the spice of the foreign." He nodded.

"I really like this little book. It seems to me it's really got something. I don't think we should expect much of it, but we throw it in as a long shot. Let's use the word *charm* a lot in the marketing copy."

"So, what do we give it in support?" Amy asked. "Advertising? A poster? A book tour?"

"You've got to be joking," Pam said. "This one makes it on its own or not at all. Maybe those characters up at Misty Valley Books will give her a reading in their 'New Voices for a New Year' program. We're not investing enough for it to matter either way. We'll just throw it out there and hope it gets some good reviews."

"But without any publicity or advertising the chances of a first novel going anywhere are just about zero," Wendy protested. Pam looked at her as if she were a fool.

"Ain't life a bitch?" Pam asked.

# PART THREE

# *In Chains*

Publishing is no longer simply a matter of picking worthy manuscripts and putting them on offer. It is now as important to market books properly, to work with the bookstore chains to get terms, co-op advertising, and the like. The difficulty is that the publishers who can market are most often not the publishers with worthy lists.

Gerald Ochs Davis, Sr.
*Fifty Years in Publishing*

# 46

> The Author lacking superb sage advice
> Is grist for editorial malice;
> Or onward, where the rude Publisher's haste
> Drives the Author to new heights of angst.
>
> —*Paul Mahon*

Camilla had forgotten how deeply nasty American immigration was, involving standing in long, crowded queues after hours of sitting in a cramped, crowded plane. She got through it as painlessly as possible, but she'd had quite enough of people in close quarters, thank you, by the time she got to the rude bureaucrat who wanted to know the purpose of her visit and to see her return ticket, which she didn't have. "I'm here from Italy for business, and I'll be getting a ticket to London after the business is completed," she said coolly, though she had no idea if that was true.

"And what kind of business are you in?" the immigration officer asked.

Only then, with a certain amount of pride, did she hand over the Davis & Dash letter. "I'm here to talk to my publisher," she said, and the sentence rolled off her tongue delightfully. *My publisher.* She had a publisher.

A tiny voice inside her, like a flicker of cold flame, said, "Not yet, you don't." The letter was not a contract after all. But she shook off the negative thought.

If the clerk didn't seem impressed with the letter, at least he let her pass. Next she battled a gaggle of Italians to get to the Alitalia carousel, where she picked up her bags. Exhausted, she got through customs in only a moment and moved, out past the stanchions that blocked luggage carts, into the chaotic milling crowd of Kennedy Airport's international-arrivals terminal. She knew there was a coach to Manhattan, and she would have to find the place to purchase tickets. But there, before her, in very large black letters on a cardboard sign, was her name: CLAPFISH, it said, unmistakably. She walked over to the man who was holding the sign. He was dressed in a black suit and white shirt. She was almost afraid to address him—after all, this was New York—but her name was unusual enough for this to be more than coincidence. "Who are you looking for?" she asked, playing it cagey.

"Camilla Clapfish. That you? We're here to pick ya up. Mr. Ashton is in the car waiting."

The man picked up her two bags and, without another word, began shouldering his way through the crowd. Was it some sort of luggage-stealing dodge? Camilla didn't know what to do, so she simply followed. Frederick hadn't said that he was picking her up, but it was very kind of him—if a little bit stifling. They had agreed to stay friends. Frederick had begged her to forgive him and to promise to forget that their one night together had ever happened. She had agreed, but she broke the promise often. She dreamed about his hands on her, his mouth over her own. Still, she would never let that show. Never. So, why had he come to the airport for her?

Camilla followed the driver's broad back as he pushed his way out to the electric exit doors. But she didn't expect the sleek black limo that awaited her outside. The driver opened a back door and held it for her while she hesitated. Camilla had never been in a limo. For a moment—only a moment—she wondered again if it might not be dangerous—a whiteslaver plot or something—but she figured she really wasn't worth much on that market, if there was one. She did peep inside, though. Frederick was sitting there in the dimness. Was his smile nervous? It was hard to tell.

"You made it," he said and reached out for her hand. He missed and grabbed her at the elbow, but she made up for it by leaning forward and timidly pecking him on the cheek.

"Well, this is an elegant surprise," she said. "Do you always travel by limo?" She meant it as a joke, but she really didn't know the answer: After all, there was so very little she actually did know about him.

"Oh, yes," he said matter-of-factly. "We keep a fleet." Then he laughed, and she knew he was joking. "This is one of the strange and few bargains in New York," Frederick explained as the driver got in front and smoothly moved them out into the mayhem of airport traffic. "It costs almost as much to take a dirty cab out and back to the airport as to hire a limo. I figured the splurge was worth it."

"It's certainly nice to arrive as an aristocrat. I just hope I don't pique their expectations at the Lesley." From another tour guide Camilla had found out about a very modestly priced hotel on Riverside Drive, at the western edge of Manhattan.

"Well, as Mark Spitz used to say, it's nice to begin with a splash."

"Who's Mark Spitz?" Camilla asked.

Frederick shook his head. "My goodness. It's good I picked you up. You're *not* prepared to live in New York without some help. You don't even know who Mark Spitz is. That alone could affect your success here." He leaned forward and addressed the driver: "Bobby, tell her who Mark Spitz is."

"I know the name. Is he that serial killer they caught out on Long Island? No. No. He was that guy before Greg Louganis."

Frederick rolled his eyes and shook his head. "The dumbing of America." He raised his voice. "An Olympic swimmer. Won six gold medals. How soon we forget." He turned to her. "So, Camilla, what are your plans?"

"Well, I've written to Alex Simmons for an appointment. Then I thought I might start to look for a flat." She paused, waiting to tell him the best news. "And I'm already on the third chapter of my new book." She was quite chuffed about it, actually.

"Wonderful! It sounds like you'll be busy." Frederick turned to look out the tinted window, though Camilla doubted he could see anything. "I've decided to register for some classes myself."

"Are you going back to university, Frederick?" What would he study instead of architecture?

Frederick barked a laugh. "Not exactly. Lighthouse for the Blind offers a program in Braille for the NSI: the newly sight-impaired. I've decided to take it. I just wonder if I'll still move my lips when I read, or only my fingers." He turned back to her. "Mother has invited you for dinner in Larchmont tomorrow," he said. "I don't know if you have other plans, but I designed the place and I'd like you to see it, though I can't speak for the meal itself."

"Oh, I'd love to," Camilla said. "It's very kind of her. Did she really want to go to all that trouble?"

Frederick shrugged. "It was her choice. Dinner for you or a beating from me with a tire iron. I think she showed good judgment."

Camilla laughed, then wondered just how much of that was true, and whether Mrs. Ashton would be happy to never set eyes on her again. But Camilla decided not to inquire too deeply.

They crossed over the Triborough Bridge, and Camilla remembered to look to her left to watch the amazing Manhattan skyline come into view. The afternoon was hazy, but despite that the thrilling agglomerate looked as magical as ever. She turned to Frederick and felt a pang for him as he stared blankly ahead. But she reined in her pity: They were not to have a relationship based on that.

As they crossed Manhattan, Camilla had become more and more excited to recognize personal landmarks, but she tried not to be too effusive. After all, Frederick was oblivious. It was still hard for her to realize that she had returned to this city—the one that had defeated her—as a success, as a novelist about to be published.

It was only at the Hotel Lesley that reality began to set in.

The building was nicely situated on an Upper West Side street at the corner of Riverside Drive. It was what was inside the building that got frightening. First, there was the smell. As Bobby carried the bags and held the door, Camilla and Frederick navigated the three steps up to the lobby and were hit with a scent that seemed a combination of unclean clothes and something nastier. Ammonia? Urine? Frederick actually wrinkled his long nose. Before them was a torn linoleum floor and a battered counter, behind which the palest man Camilla had ever seen, wearing the most obvious black toupee, stood listening to the complaints of an old woman. She was supported by a walker and dressed half in nightclothes and half in combat wear. "It should have come already," she whined. "Didn't it come? Or did one of you sonsabitches steal it?"

"It hasn't come," said the man behind the desk. "It never comes until five. Why don't you go to your room until then?"

"One of you sonsabitches stole my Meals-on-Wheels. I'm stayin' right here. I'm gonna watch you to see if you eat it. I'm gonna watch you."

To Camilla's left was a sofa that looked like nothing so much as a backseat from a 1940s DeSoto. Perhaps it *was*. On it, a cadaverous young man lay sleeping, his legs stretched across the floor, his head hanging at an ominous angle. Camilla tried to ignore them all and simply announced her name. After some brief paperwork, she was awarded a key for her courage and directed to a room on the third floor. She asked if there was nothing available higher in the building, and the toupeed clerk didn't even bother to look up. "Forget about it," he said. She was too addled to ask about a view.

They waited a long time for the lift, and when it arrived,

a demented-looking old man, his greasy, shoulder-length hair plastered to his head, stepped out. He was shirtless and wore stained electric blue trousers. He was already talking at the top of his lungs, though the lift was empty. He continued talking as he walked by them. Camilla took Frederick's arm, and with Bobby behind them, they got into the elevator. Bobby pressed 3.

The third floor was incredibly dim. Frederick's hand tightened against her arm. She was sure he could see nothing at all—she barely could—and for that she was grateful. The hall was incredibly narrow and meandered in a strange way, with random room numbers and cul-de-sacs. There were holes in the middle of the tatty carpet. The three of them negotiated the best they could. But the strangest thing was that the rooms, many of them, were locked only with padlocks, as if people had been thrown into them for storage and then locked up. Or locked out, Camilla supposed. They found her room, 334, and the moment she fit the key in the lock and pulled open the door, her modest fantasy of the table by the window, the new manuscript, and the view of the river was shattered.

The room was perhaps five feet by nine feet, with a bed pressed against one wall, a broken bentwood chair, and an overhead light. There was no night table, much less a desk, and the window was partially paned with painted plywood, the rest of the window so filthy and facing such a dark airshaft that no light came in at all.

The three of them couldn't fit in the room. Bobby, in the doorway, was the first to break the silence: "Oh, man."

"Camilla, you can't stay here," Frederick told her. "You really can't."

"He's right," Bobby agreed. "Forget about it."

"But I have to," Camilla said, though her voice was very small. The whimpering from down the hall was really the worst of it. Was it an animal or a person in pain? Camilla had converted all of her money into dollars, but despite the good exchange rate, she had less than a thousand of them. She didn't know how long it would take to get her book money, but she knew she wouldn't find a place less costly than this one. "I have to stay here," she said, "I can't afford—"

"She's on drugs," Frederick explained to Bobby. "Pay no attention to her. Use force if necessary." He turned to Camilla. "Come on, let's go."

For a moment Camilla thought they meant they were leaving her, just like that. Panic set in. But then she felt Frederick's hand propelling her from behind. He pushed her as far as the lift, though she began protesting mildly. But when the door opened and she saw another guest, this one worse than the first two, she closed her lips and stepped into the car with relief.

They were out on the street and into the limo in minutes. Frederick gave Bobby an East Eighty-sixth Street address.

"You can stay at my apartment," Frederick said. "Don't worry. It's empty. I've been staying with my mother. This will just be temporary, until you figure out what you're doing."

And since she didn't have a better choice, Camilla merely nodded in mute gratitude, not remembering that Frederick couldn't see her.

# 47

> It's not the most intellectual job in the world, but
> I do have to know the letters.
>
> —*Vanna White*

It was done at last! And not just done, but done pretty well. Susann handed the last edited page of her book to Edith and stood up. Oh, Lord, she was stiff! The small of her back still ached, despite the pillow that Edith had stuffed against the chair back. Susann had been sitting at that desk for days. But Edith, bless her heart, had kept her going with dozens of cucumber sandwiches and endless cups of black coffee. That and bouillon were all Susann could keep down: Her anxiety had kept her queasy throughout the whole editing process. It had been torture, but now it was over.

There were only three good things about the experience, Susann reflected, other than the fact the book was done. One was that her hands, for some mysterious reason, had stopped aching. The second was that she had probably lost weight from the anxiety and all the caffeine. Last but most important was that through every minute Edith had been so supportive, so nurturing and enthusiastic that Susann found herself not just grateful but actually loving. Susann looked over at her, still bent over the word processor, and felt such a rush of feeling for her old friend that when Edith turned around, Susann had to blink to see her clearly.

"Oh. This is good. This is *really* good," said Edith, looking at the last page. And Edith wasn't one to throw praise around loosely.

"Do you really think so?" Susann asked anyway.

"Oh, yeah. This is wonderful. This is vintage Susann Baker Edmonds. I mean, it's like your old books. Ruby is a great character. She's not so perfect; she's more real. And then this ending . . ." Edith looked back down at the page. "It's *really* good," she repeated, and sighed gustily.

"How would you grade it?" Susann asked, then held her breath.

Edith turned to look at her, her pudgy, aging face taking on that serious expression it always did when considering the Edmonds oeuvre. Susann knew that Edith took their work very seriously, and that she respected it, admired it, a lot more than Susann did herself. A long time ago Susann had run out of inspiration and operated simply on discipline and craft. But Edith expected—and sometimes saw—art. Usually Edith's naive attitude irritated Susann, but during this editing trial-by-fire she found it surprisingly comforting and endearing.

"So?" she prompted. "What do you say?"

Edith looked back at the manuscript as if she would find the answer written there, but Susann restrained her irritation. Edith was slow, meticulous, sincere, and loyal. Susann would do well, she told herself, to remember that all the time. While Alf had been busy traveling, negotiating, and being generally consumed with his new Boy Wonder, Edith had been here, working out each sentence, patiently listening as Susann unknotted the plot and tightened the characters. Amazing, Susann reflected, that for all this Edith received only fifty thousand dollars and a tiny room in the attic, while Alf would get two and a half million, his 10 percent of her newest contract.

Edith now looked at Susann. She pursed her lips, which deepened all those lines that radiated from her mouth. Edith really *should* have derm-abrasion, Susann thought, then chided herself. She was shallow. Here, when everyone else had abandoned her—her editor, her agent and lover, her daughter—Edith had not just done her job but had comforted and encouraged Susann. And Susann was petty enough to be turned off by the poor woman's lip wrinkles.

The lips opened, and "A minus" came out. She paused and considered for another minute. "It would have been an A, but the coincidence of the miscarriage was always a little hard for me to believe. You know, it was so convenient."

Susann's eyes opened wide. She hadn't received an A from Edith since *A Woman and a Lady*. Susann distinctly remembered that Edith had given *The Lady of the House* a B minus, and Susann had been deeply offended (though she had secretly agreed, or thought even less of it). When it hit number one, Susann had been particularly pleased to point it out to Edith, and gave her a bonus to rub it in.

Now the hairs on Susann's arms rose as she went goose-fleshed. Edith, her personal weather vane, felt that this one was that good. Perhaps all the work had been worth it. Susann put her hands on her lower back and arched it against the pain. She'd take a long hot bath and call her masseuse. But first Susann and Edith would drink a bottle of champagne to celebrate. Because Susann suddenly felt that Edith was right: This book would fly up the list. She wouldn't have to settle for, be humiliated by, two weeks at number twelve. She'd regain her glory and see this one at the very top, kicking the hell out of Waller and Grisham and that dog Crichton. With this one she'd do something not just for herself but for women, and then she'd be up there again with reigning queens Danielle Steel and Barbara Taylor Bradford. Everyone at Davis & Dash would treat her with respect. She'd insist that she get a new editor and that they fire that annoying girl. Then she'd have a long, stern talk with Alf about *his* role. Perhaps it was time to renegotiate his percentage. Or even to drop hints about a new agent! Yes, that might get Alf's attention.

"Edith, break out the Moët. Then I'm taking you out for the best dinner in the city. To hell with cholesterol. We're going French. We deserve it."

"*You* deserve it," Edith said fervently. "Though that editor's comments were really helpful."

Susann watched Edith as she rose from the word processor and went to fetch the champagne. Well, Susann decided, she wouldn't insist on the firing of Emma Ashton, then. But once she had her power back, Susann thought, she *would* do the rest.

The phone rang. Great! Maybe it was Alf and she could coolly share her good news with him. It wasn't too soon to begin to get the upper hand again. Perhaps she'd invite him over to share the champagne. Or out to dinner. She'd have to cancel dinner with Edith, who'd be disappointed. Still, she could always reschedule *that*. It wasn't as if Edith's dance card was filled.

But it wasn't Alf. "Call off your dogs." It was Kim's voice, and she didn't sound clean *or* sober. Susann hadn't spoken to her daughter since Kim had revealed her publishing plans over tea. God knows what Alf had instigated since then with the help of Davis & Dash. Susann's stomach fluttered, and at the same time a pain in her right hand stabbed viciously. Oh God, the arthritis was back!

"Kim, where are you?"

"Why the fuck should *you* care? Want to send a subpoena?" Then the bitterness in her voice seemed to seep away, leaving only despair. "Listen, when Craig Stevens, my publisher, got those letters, he caved. He can't afford any legal battles right now. He won't do the book if you threaten."

Susann sighed in relief, but she was careful not to let Kim hear it. Ah, she must be so disappointed! Though Susann had never connected with Kim's hunger for drugs and booze, she could identify with the hunger to be published. And she could always deal with Kim when she was depressed—it was her daughter's anger that frightened Susann. "Listen, he can do the book, Kim. Just not with my name."

"Oh, come off it," Kim snapped. "It's my foot in the door. Citron is a new small house. What the fuck is going to sell my book *except* the name? What sells yours now, for God sake? The deathless prose? The originality?"

"All that we were asking—"

"I want to do this," Kim interrupted urgently. "The book might not be much, but it's mine, and no worse than a lot of others. If the name is the only wedge I've got, then let me use it. It beats working as a waitress, or that probation job in the auto-supply store." She paused, but not before Susann thought she heard her daughter sob. "Stop this blackmail. I'm asking you to call off all of those fuckers, to send Citron Press a letter granting permission, and to let me be."

"Kim, I have a lot riding on my new book, and I just don't want your release to muddy the—"

"Fuck you, you selfish old bitch! It's *always* you." Kim's voice deepened into the voice that terrified Susann with its rage. Susann clutched the phone, though her knuckles ached. Then Kim's voice continued, but the anger was gone: Her voice was slower, more powerful somehow, and infinitely sadder. "Can't you see you had your turn? You made your choices. You went as far as you could. Isn't three husbands, ten bestsellers, and a lot of money enough? It's ending now for you. Now the ride is ending. But please, please give me a shot at a turn."

Susann put down her champagne flute. How dare Kim do this? Ruin everything, make her feel old and wasted and finished! Kim had always been jealous, dangerously jealous.

"Kim, you're being unfair. Unfair and—"

"Oh, don't bother," Kim snapped. "You're so very fair yourself, right? Listen: I'm making a simple deal with you. You understand deals. You try blackmail, I try blackmail. Drop the legal thing. Let me alone, and I'll let you alone."

"And if I don't?"

"Then I'll kill myself. I'll do it publicly, off a very high roof, and I'll leave a note. I'll sign your last name to it. And that, I guarantee, *will* get published, Mother."

Then the phone clicked.

# 48

The cat does not negotiate with the mouse.
—*Robert K. Massie, The Artistic Cat*

Emma turned over the last page of the new Peet Trawley manuscript. If the Trawley books had been bad before, they certainly weren't going to be improved by being written by Pam Mantiss. In fact, Emma was shocked at just how bad, how bankrupt, this one was.

Of course, that didn't mean it wouldn't climb to the top of the list, as his books always did. There was a certain golden circle of authors who had previous sales and positioning so high that a new book of theirs automatically generated enough advance orders to guarantee bestseller status, even before the book was written. They were the "brand name" writers, and in America brand names sold. There was a whole new breed of readers, readers created by the superstores, who actually only read a single brand name: "I'll have the new Steel," or "I want another Clancy," they'd say. Since they'd never read novels before, Emma had thought it was a good development—at least new readers were being created. But when the brand names started pushing dozens of other authors off the shelves, Emma began to worry. Peet was Davis & Dash's brand name, along with Susann Baker Edmonds, but after reading Peet's manuscript, Emma couldn't help but wonder if, dead or alive, his luck would continue.

Emma was about to lift the phone to call Lucille Bing, who managed production and copyediting, but the instrument of torture beat her to it and rang first. For a moment her heart thumped. She was hoping to hear from Alex. Instead she lifted it up and heard Pam, already uttering a stream of profanity before Emma had even gotten the phone up to her ear. "Have you seen the fucking cover art for Gerald's goddamned reader's copies?" Pam was asking.

"No," Emma admitted.

"Well, it sucks. He fucking hates it. You know how anal he is about covers, and he *really* hates this one. When are the cocksucking reader's copies scheduled to go out?"

Emma didn't know why *she* felt guilty: Thank God, art was one thing she *wasn't* responsible for. She also didn't know why Pam had to call her to tell her this, or to ask her about the production schedule—Pam had her own copy of it but was apparently not comfortable lifting it off her windowsill. Easier to call me, I guess, Emma thought as she pulled the printout toward her and reviewed the timetable. "We have two weeks," she said.

"Oh, shit. He's in the Hamptons till Thursday. He'll just have to see what that prick Jack pulls together then. I swear to God, Jack is shitting bricks over this."

Emma was sure, without the overly scatological description, that art director Jack Weinstock was indeed uncomfortable. He was a sensitive man, and though he had managed to survive for years through the frequent personnel urges and purges that GOD provoked, he seemed to live each day in fear that his head was on the block.

"Listen, I have an important meeting," Pam snapped. "But while I'm gone come up with a plan for controlling the distribution of those motherfucking reader's copies. You remember what happened with the reviewers last time? Gerald doesn't need any third-rate stringer for some pathetic, bullshit book section in Albuquerque taking potshots at him. *No* review copies to critics."

Emma didn't bother to repress her smile. Paperbound preprints of all major books were manufactured and distributed specifically so critics *could* see them early. In fact, they used to be called "review copies." But times had changed, and some publishers felt more comfortable quoting friendly celebrities rather than hostile critics on the back of book jackets. The two appeared to carry equal weight with book buyers, and the former were much easier to control. Since Gerald knew *everyone*, he would manage to get celebrities or authors who owed him a favor to say something about *Twice in the Papers*. Emma was always amazed to see legitimate writers—or prominent people with taste—stoop to recommending a patently bad book, but it was done all the time. "A landmark." "Delicious." "A spellbinder." The public didn't seem to get it, and if the blurb was later paid back with a blurb for their book, a new contract, or even just a slightly larger advance, no readers were the wiser.

"Listen, I've got to go. I have to convince a first author that he's got some revisions to do. It'll take hours," Pam moaned. "By the way, have you heard about the nominations yet?"

Emma rolled her eyes. Pam was absolutely obsessed—well, Pam was obsessed with *everything*—but her latest obsession was this year's Editor of the Year Award. "I don't think the nominations are announced until the end of the month," Emma told her, as if Pam wasn't completely aware of that fact.

"I know, but I just thought you might have heard something. Like, through one of your many friends." Emma didn't like Pam's tone, but then there were so many things about Pam that she didn't like. "Anyway," Pam continued, "call production about Gerald's cover art, and make sure they don't go ahead with Jack's piece of shit."

Emma hung up, then sighed when the phone rang again. It might be Alex, but it also might be Jack Weinstock, ready to argue or to weep.

The bar at the St. Regis was deliciously cool. Pam Mantiss sat in the midst of true luxury actually enjoying herself. Jude Daniel was really a very attractive man, in a professorial way, and he knew how to fence.

"I understand your point," he was saying. "But I'm not

sure that I can completely agree. It's a given that Elthea won't be sympathetic to all readers. There's no way. So why try and water down the character in the small hope of gaining a few more readers? Think of those we might lose. After all, she *is* a murderess. And not just a murderess, but a child-killer. And not just a child-killer—she's killed her *own* children." He paused. "Strange as it may sound, some people just won't warm to a woman like that."

Pam laughed. "Yes, I know. But I have a child. And sometimes I feel I *could* kill him," she admitted. "We all have that unspoken guilt we have to work against. Know what I mean?" Jude nodded. "You know, I actually think you do. That's the insight that's going to sell this book."

Jude smiled. "Well, I do have a daughter. But she doesn't live with me."

"Oh, divorced, huh?" Pam paused. "Me, too." This was getting interesting. She simply *had* to find a way to make him see her point of view, do the editorial changes, and then . . . well, she'd see. He was really rather attractive. Now, what could she use as an incentive? She crossed her legs, and in the coolness, her thighs slid one over the other. Her left leg touched his. Suddenly Pam got an enormous craving for a drink, though she'd absolutely forbidden herself booze at lunch. "Have you got a cigarette?" she asked.

"I don't smoke anymore," he told her.

"Not even after sex?" she asked. It was an obvious line, but she pulled it off.

He smiled. "I never looked," he told her, turning her come-on into that old joke. His smile warmed. "But I think I produce a sufficient amount of heat."

"I bet you do." Pam lowered her voice to a husky whisper. "You know, I really loved the sex scenes you wrote, especially Elthea's last fuck with the boyfriend. When she's reduced to begging him for it."

"I worked a long time on that," Jude said. "I wanted to be graphic but not pornographic. It was very hard."

"I'm sure it was," Pam said with a leer. She knew what

game they were playing now. God, she'd have to lose some weight! No way she could get on top of him—everything would jiggle.

The waiter came over and asked if they wanted another round. Jude was having white wine, while she was only drinking Pellegrino, but the hell with that—she asked for a dry white. "*And a cigarette,*" she told the waiter, "if you can get me one."

"My pleasure," he told her. Thank God they still allowed smoking in New York bars.

The waiter left, and Pam realized there was still someone standing beside her. She looked up into the young but wasted face of Chad Weston. "Remember me?" he said.

Oh, Christ. She didn't need this now, not when she was wooing a new novelist. The Weston imbroglio was becoming a real liability. She glanced quickly at Jude Daniel, hoping he didn't recognize the little yuppie prick. Thank God, Jude was out of the loop. He probably wouldn't know anyone or anything. Still, she'd have to shut Chad up any way she could. "Did you get my message?" she asked.

"What message? Don't bullshit me, Pam. You haven't called."

She widened her eyes as best she could. "Chad, I *did* call. *And* I put my career on the line for you."

"Yeah, and I'm Marie of Romania," Chad said bitterly. "Will it be published?"

"I give you my word," Pam said.

"If it isn't, I walk." Weston stood silent for a moment, then turned and walked away. It was as if he was too tired or beaten to fight.

Well, it could have been worse. Pam looked at Jude and shrugged. "Another novelist," she said. "I pushed the hell out of his first book, but his second book sucked. I bought it anyway, out of loyalty, but it went nowhere. Now he's angry because there's some concern about his third." She shrugged again. "Nobody else liked the book but me," she said honestly. "What can I do? I told him how to fix it, but he wouldn't listen. Still, I'm fighting for him." She sighed deeply as if with regret. Jude, she noticed, looked down at her chest when she heaved it. Oh, he was interested and scared.

Pam loved mixing business with pleasure. It made both of them so much easier. She reached out and took Jude's hand. "Listen," she said, "I really love the book, and I want the best for it and you. It's *your* book, and I'm not telling you what to do. I don't work like that. It's just that I want to see the widest acceptance, the widest possible readership. This book could be really big, but only if we get it right. And if we get it wrong, well . . ." She paused and gave the silence enough beats. Enough beats for the fear to set in. She shrugged, and as she did, her left breast brushed his right hand, just for the slightest moment. She let his other hand go. "Well," she said, "I don't have to tell you how tough the competition is or how many first novels fail."

Had his eyes widened? She couldn't tell, but she did see his Adam's apple move. He was really kind of sexy in a geeky Jewish way. And his hand had been sinewy, with long fingers. Pam narrowed her eyes and looked meaningfully at Jude Daniel. She was sure now that he'd make her revisions. She wondered about the size of his dick.

Pam walked down the long hallway and stuck her head into Emma's cubicle. She was feeling that feeling—tingling with energy—and she wished she was back with Jude Daniel instead of here. "Move it," she said, though Emma had her head down and was clearly busy with some paperwork. "Come on." Pam turned before Emma could answer and continued to her office, sailed past her secretary, and threw down her coat. She went to the refrigerator and pulled out a Snapple bottle just as Emma walked through the door. She didn't offer her any.

Pam sat down at her desk, swiveled the chair so she

could get her feet up, and swigged at the iced tea. "Listen," she said, "we have to sign that old bitch to a contract. We have to do it right away."

"Which old bitch is that?" Emma asked.

"The O'Neal woman, for chrissake. The O'Neal woman. GOD has taken a shine to her daughter's fucking doorstop, and we've got to publish it. But I'll be dipped in shit before *I* call her."

"You mean we can publish it as it stands? The whole thing?"

"The whole fucking thing. If it doesn't sell one fucking copy, I don't want to hear about it." Pam was afraid that Emma might be enjoying her discomfiture. That was all right; Pam had a perfect punishment for Emma. "And I really have to question your judgment about that little Italian book. You shouldn't have passed on it. Somehow it got passed up to Gerald. Not only do I really like it, so does Gerald. Anyway, we're going to stick it on the fall list, to fill in some of the holes. That means that you've got to edit it quickly."

"All right." Emma, who usually had her feelings written all over her face, seemed surprisingly calm. Pam just shrugged and took a long sip of her iced tea. "Well, get to it."

Emma turned to leave. "Oh, and by the way," Pam told her, "I'll handle all the Jude Daniel stuff myself. I'll leave the girls to you."

# 49

> Writers and readers are expected to kneel before the latest hardware gods.
>
> —*Herbert Mitgang*

Judith looked down at the wrinkled, stained manuscript. It had a thick brown rubber band cinching its middle and what looked like hundreds of yellow Post-it notes blooming around its margins. The look of it offended and upset her, as if somebody had drawn a mustache on or otherwise defaced a child. She leaned both elbows against the card table and put her head in her hands.

"Oh come on, Judith," Daniel said. "It's not a tragedy; it's only an editing job. You just need to go through the manuscript and fix it."

*She* had to fix it? Judith sat open-mouthed, struck dumb. That had never occurred to her. Wasn't it enough that she had written it? Wasn't it *more* than enough, now that Daniel had taken *In Full Knowledge* as his own? The lumpy typing chair was pushing into her back and thighs as if she weighed a thousand pounds. And the dust in the turret room seemed to be choking her. She couldn't breathe, she couldn't move, she couldn't speak. What was happening to her? She tried to get a few breaths down into her empty lungs and realized Daniel was staring at her. She must be gaping like a fish, but she didn't care.

When she managed to breathe again, she spoke for the first time. "You've stolen the book," she said. "You've stolen the book from me. And now you want me to *fix* it for you? It's not enough that you're taking all the credit? You also don't want to do *any* of the work?" That had taken all of her air. She gasped. She couldn't believe that she'd said her thoughts aloud. But all of this was making her feel crazy, absolutely crazy. Was she being unreasonable and oversensitive, or was *he* out of his mind? And if it was him, if it was *Daniel* who was crazy, how had she made the horrendous mistake of letting him become the only person in her life? *She* must be crazy. Though she had just turned twenty-two and knew she should feel very grown-up, she suddenly felt as lost as a child.

"Come on, Judith. Don't go crazy on me," Daniel said, and she froze again. Could he read her thoughts? Was he controlling them? He certainly had been controlling her actions. What in the world had she been thinking? Had she been thinking at all this last year? Or had she been in some kind of sex dream, some spell from which she was, at last, awakening? But unlike waking up to reality, she was waking up to a nightmare. For a moment, everything seemed perfectly clear, and then, like the heat mirages that wavered over the highway but disappeared when you got there, reality shimmered and was gone. Or came back. Judith simply couldn't tell. She tried to take another deep breath. She trusted Daniel. She *had* to trust Daniel. But she looked back at the manuscript, and her lip trembled.

"Look, honey, you're making this all too personal. This isn't about you or me. It's about *us*. And the first thing we're going to do to make this easier is we're going to move. This place is a rat hole. I know you hate it. There's a really nice garden apartment available outside town. Fox Run. We're going to get you out of this dump and into a place where it will be really comfortable to work. A real office. And I'll help you." He paused and patted her shoulder. "I mean, I still have to teach—can't give up the day job yet," he laughed, though it sounded forced. "And I'll probably have to meet with Gerald Ochs Davis and other publishing people." He paused. "Listen," he continued, "we'll get a nice place, and then you'll meet with them too. I'll tell them you're helping on the editing. If we can just get these changes made, they'll really get behind this book. That's the critical thing now: for them to get behind the book. Because if they don't, we might as well have not bothered to write it, Judith." He sighed and leaned onto the dusty windowsill.

"You can't imagine how competitive it is. Once you get these edits done, it's all going to be about marketing and how much money and effort they're willing to put into this. I saw something really scary in New York. This author came up to the editor I was with. Davis & Dash had done two of his books, and now they've dumped him. The guy looked like a zombie. He wouldn't make the changes that they wanted. We can't afford to take that risk." He smiled, came slowly toward her, and gently rubbed her cheek. "You remember the plan: First we get rich, *then* we get famous."

Judith took a few more deep breaths. She flipped through the yellow-stickered mess on the table before her. He was probably right. But look at all the changes they demanded! How much work? Judith felt tears coming. Better to be angry. Daniel had just assumed that she'd agree. She gestured at the pile of yellow-stickered papers. "It's not a manuscript, Daniel. It's a goddamned forsythia bush. You're taking the credit, *you* do the edit." She stood up, disturbing Flaubert, who slept at her feet, and walked to the other turret window. "Anyway, it's not just the manuscript. It's the concept. They just don't get it. I should have known a male publisher would never allow it to be printed as is. These changes aren't right. I mean, I understand wanting to soften Elthea a little, not that I agree. But most of it doesn't make sense. She wouldn't behave the way she did if she was softer, if she was stronger. And the ending! I just can't see—"

Daniel came to her at the window. He lifted her chin with his hand and made her look at him. "Listen. I know it's hard for you. Editing is hard for *anybody,* and when it's a work about to be published, there's this extra feeling, pressure, because of the irrevocability of it."

For a moment, the thought that he knew nothing about what he was telling her flashed through Judith's mind. Daniel had never had a book published, so he'd never edited one. This "pressure of irrevocability" or whatever he was talking about was something he'd made up or read. She looked up at him for the first time, eye to eye, and she saw that he didn't know Elthea. Or, if he did, he didn't really care. The knowledge shocked her, and as if embarrassed, she slid her eyes to the right—but she said nothing.

"Look, I know it's daunting," Daniel said. "I know it's a lot of work, but it's for our future. We get through this last part and we're home free." He put his arms around her and hugged her to him, his chin resting on the top of her head. Before, always before, Judith had liked when they stood this way. But today, her face pressed against his chest, his head holding hers down, she felt smothered.

Yet he was right. This book wasn't the best she could do. It was only meant to be commercial, so why was she so conflicted? Was it because she was still so angry over the way he was taking the credit? Maybe she shouldn't make such a fuss. They'd written a book to *be* commercial. And weren't these people the experts? They published dozens of bestsellers each year. What did she know? Maybe she was being too sensitive. And maybe she was expecting too much of the reading public. All of those things were possible. But what she *did* know, down to the very last molecule in her body, was that these editorial changes—which very well might sell books—made no sense as far as the character went and would spoil whatever had been good and authentic in Elthea. Judith sighed and pushed herself off Daniel's chest.

"I brought you something," Daniel said, and despite herself, Judith felt a small thrill of pleasure. Daniel so rarely bought anything and then only when he had to. He didn't believe in birthday gifts or Christmas. Now his excitement showed. He was proud of himself, like a little boy.

She couldn't help it. "What is it?" she asked.

He took her hand and led her down the three little steps into the kitchen and through to the living room. A wrapped flat carton sat on the wooden crate that they used as a coffee table. The wrapping was blue, and there was both a stick-on bow and a card attached. Silly as it seemed, Judith felt as if it were Christmas. Daniel *was* thinking of her, and though he had gotten all the attention so far, he had not forgotten her. Here was her reward. Relieved as well as curious and grateful, she approached the carton. A winter coat? She needed one. It was too big to be jewelry—her first choice—but as soon as she touched the box and felt its heaviness she knew it wasn't clothing. No sexy nightgown or silky underwear. It weighed at least ten pounds. Books, she thought, and tried to keep the disappointment out of her face. She did not want a new thesaurus or the American Heritage dictionary. She wanted something deeply personal, something luxurious and special. Well, it *might* be. Making the moment last, she picked up the little card and opened it. There was a drawing of flowers and a mortarboard. Across the front, in purple lettering, it said, "For Your Graduation." It was the kind of card that every shop in this university town carried at all times. Nothing special or appropriate about it. In fact, it seemed as if Daniel had just grabbed the first thing he saw. She blinked and opened it. Inside, Daniel had handwritten the message: "Now that you're a real writer, I thought it was time for you to graduate to real writer's tools. Love, Daniel." She put down the card and began to remove the paper carefully. "Oh, come on," he said. "Have fun with it. Tear the goddamned paper."

Surprised at his language—Daniel rarely swore—she did as she was told, and the picture on the laptop-computer carton became visible. It was one of the newest models, the really portable ones.

"You'll need it now," he said, handing her a diskette that Cheryl had given him. "You'll need it to make the corrections. You can get the editing done much faster this way. I've gotten you two programs: one for word processing and a dictionary. It's supposed to be really great." He paused, proud. "Do you like it?" he asked.

"It's just peachy," Judith said.

# 50

> To me and my kind, life itself is a story, and we have to tell in stories—that is the way it falls.
>
> —*Rumer Godden*

Emma never looked forward to Sunday dinners at her mother's, but her curiosity about Camilla Clapfish, both as an author and as a companion to her brother, made this Sunday evening different. She had actually put on a dress—not to please her mother, but because for her this was almost a business meeting.

She stood before the full-length mirror and surveyed herself. "Will you zip me up?" Emma asked Alex, who was stretched across the sofa watching Emma's preparations. Emma had told Alex about the evening on Friday night, but now, two days later, Alex seemed in no hurry to leave, instead watching Emma dress. It felt both cozy and a little stifling to Emma. "Come on," Emma said, "help with the zipper." Languidly, Alex pulled herself up from the sofa, came up behind Emma, and put her hands on Emma's shoulders. But instead of going for the zipper she bent her head and nibbled at Emma's neck.

"Should I give you a hickey to take home to Mama in Larchmont?" Alex asked. Emma laughed but pulled her head away. "Or should you be bringing *me* home to Mama?"

Surprised, caught off guard, Emma stared into the mirror and caught Alex's eye, but before she could respond Alex bent her head over the zipper. Was that why Alex was hanging around? Had she expected an invitation? Emma was out; her mother knew her sexual preference, but Emma had never brought a girlfriend home. Why was it that parents and children don't want to hear about one another's sexuality? It seemed that would rub her mother's long nose in it. And surely she and Alex weren't intimate enough yet for the come-home-and-meet-the-parents trauma. But perhaps Alex felt they were. Alex had felt her jerk away and had stiffened. She reached down for the zipper, all business. Oh God, Emma thought. This was the price you paid for being a lesbian. If men were always rushing *away* from commitment, feeling smothered and "needing more space," women were overeager. The old lesbian joke was that the first thing a couple did on a blind date was move in with each other. Emma really liked Alex, more than she had liked anyone before, but with their busy schedules they had barely spent three weekends together. Emma needed to take things one step at a time. She valued Alex already, and one reason she wasn't ready to introduce her was that Mrs. Ashton, when she met either of her children's potential mates, was not the type to improve the chances of a successful relationship. But now Emma had to worry about whether she was hurting Alex's feelings, creating resentment that, in the end, would exact a price.

"It's stuck," Alex said, referring to the zipper. "I think you have to take it off and then maybe I can wiggle it."

"Oh God, I don't have time for that! The train leaves in twenty-five minutes. Mother hates it when I'm late." Emma tore the dress off over her head and threw it onto the closet floor. Fuck dresses anyway. She pulled out a pair of black slacks, thrust her legs into them, and grabbed a white, man-tailored shirt from the hanger. Perfect. She looked exactly like a dyke, one of her mother's favorite looks. Emma sighed. Maybe if she tied a scarf around her neck? She wasn't the scarf type. She did have an Indian silk one stashed someplace, but she couldn't remember where. Well, she'd just have to settle for a sweater. After all, this wasn't formal.

"So Camilla Clapfish is going to be there," Alex said. If

she was angry, her voice didn't show it. "She's just gotten to New York, I think." Emma nodded. "I'm seeing her this week, you know," Alex reminded her.

"Great," Emma said. "Just keep me out of it." God, that sounded abrupt. But now that she was editing Camilla, this triangle could get intense. Stop being so self-conscious, Emma told herself, but that never worked. Now that it seemed as if Alex really liked her, now that Emma knew that she was crazy about Alex, all of the madness would begin: the I-didn't-mean-to-sound-so-harsh-but-you-didn't-have-to-push-me-like-that stuff. Relationships were *so* hard, and the Ashton household had by no means been a proving ground for relationship-training. Our motto must have been "Knock politely if the door is closed, and keep your feelings to yourself," Emma thought. What did that translate into in Latin, she wondered, and was it too long for the family crest? (There *was* an Ashton family crest, but her mother was far too appropriate to use it.) "I've got to go," she said to Alex, who didn't make a move. "Just pull the door shut when you leave."

They were at the awkward phase where they hadn't yet exchanged keys, but they did leave each other at their apartments "alone." Emma kissed Alex on the cheek, but Alex didn't respond. She must be hurt, Emma realized. But it was too late to do anything about it now. "See ya," Emma said and rushed out to the subway.

Emma made the train and was met at the station by her mother, who brought her home to meet "Miss Clapfish." But Emma couldn't quite figure it out: Camilla was a cool customer. It was clear that she and Frederick liked each other, and apparently she had moved into his apartment. But it also seemed that Frederick was still living here with their mother. Were they together or not?

It was none of her business, of course. But Emma hoped Frederick had found someone, and their mother *had* implied that he had. He certainly deserved to, and now that her own happiness with Alex was blooming she especially wanted her brother to be loved. But it didn't seem to Emma as if the connection had held, if it was ever there at all. She reached over to the wine bottle and refilled her glass, noticing that Frederick's was almost empty. "Shall I give you more Bordeaux?" she asked, and he nodded.

They had spent most of dinner discussing Frederick's trip to Italy, Mrs. Ashton's recent trouble in the Larchmont ladies' bridge tournament, and, briefly, Camilla's life in Florence. Somehow, Emma felt it premature to jump into the business conversation. Yet she had to let Camilla in on the politics at Davis & Dash. How could she start? She didn't think it was necessary to tell her about the Chad Weston fiasco or the way it had affected Camilla's luck. But some preparation was clearly necessary. There was a lull in conversation as the salads were removed by Rosa, the housekeeper. Now was as good a time as any, Emma thought. "You know, Camilla, I'm not really here, and we haven't really met," she said. "Not yet."

"What?" Camilla asked.

"I have to explain that you are Pam's purchase, not mine. In fact, Pam Mantiss thinks I disapprove of your book. It was the easiest way I could get it accepted. Not that it wasn't worthy, but if I like something, Pam has a corporate policy not to. So I resorted to child psychology. Please don't blow my cover when you meet her."

"What is all this about?" Mrs. Ashton asked, her arched eyebrows arching even higher. "Do you have to dissemble to get your job done?"

"Dissemble?" Frederick asked. "Mother, you've been reading Henry James again. And after you promised."

Mrs. Ashton pursed her mouth in an attempt at disapproval, but the right side flicked upward in what Emma always thought of as a charmed and charming half smile. Frederick had a way with their mother, a way of teasing her while keeping his boundary firm and doing so with grace and good humor. Emma envied him that. She had never had the skill, but perhaps that was because of the mother-daughter thing. Or the lesbian thing. Emma knew that she simply didn't please her mother the way Frederick did. Yet her mother did love her. She knew that too. Mrs. Ashton may not approve of the actions of either of her offspring, but in her restrained yet powerful way, she loved them. Well, it wasn't her mother Emma had to worry about, she reminded herself. It was Davis & Dash's fledgling author.

Sure enough, Camilla Clapfish was leaning forward over the table with a look of concern. "I don't understand," Camilla said. "Aren't *you* my editor?"

"I guess I ought to explain," Emma said. "Pam Mantiss, *my* editor in chief, is a brilliant but admittedly rather—um, eccentric—character. She doesn't see it as *my* job to acquire manuscripts, at least not any that are guaranteed to sell fewer than fifty thousand hardcover copies. I had just presented another noncommercial book to her when your manuscript came in." Emma paused and smiled. "It's a lovely book. I knew it was something we ought to publish, but I had to"—Emma looked over at her mother—"*dissemble.*"

Frederick was smiling. Camilla seemed to lean back in her chair. Emma went on to explain the ruse, and how—by seeming to reject the book for the wrong reasons—she'd gotten contrary Pam and desperate Gerald interested. "Right now he's so worried about the list that he would publish the phone book if it had *commercial* written across it," Emma finished with a laugh.

Mrs. Ashton asked. "You would think a man of his stature, from his family—"

Emma laughed again. "Oh, Mother, what *does* family have to do with anything?" Before Mrs. Ashton could respond, Camilla, looking rather pale, spoke up.

"So you mean I've gotten in on a fluke?" she asked. "You *tricked* them into wanting my book?"

Oh God! Emma had forgotten, for just a moment, about

author handling, especially first-time novelists. All writers were insecure, but new authors were the especially so. She had left out the worst of it—*SchizoBoy* and all that—but she could have been more diplomatic. That last remark about publishing the phone book was dumb. What had she been thinking of? Being with her mother always made Emma awkward. "Not at all," she said, as warmly as she could. "You would have been *rejected* by a fluke. Because, by coincidence, I had just fought a battle for another first novel. So I didn't want *that* to happen. The fluke was that I hadn't ever fought for a book before, and right then I'd have had to fight for a second one. So I went another way. And it worked." Emma took a deep breath. "Pam sincerely likes the book. It's her baby. Really, it's best for you. She's far more important than I am. I'll just edit you." Emma looked at the woman across the table, at her level eyes, her scrubbed appearance. It was actually hard to imagine Camilla Clapfish and the overblown Pam Mantiss in the same room. They looked like comics drawn by very different cartoonists: Pam was "The Far Side," and Camilla was an English Jules Feiffer. "Anyway," Emma said, trying to summarize, "what this means is that you and I haven't met. Your manuscript came in through an agent, and I may not even see you this week over at Davis & Dash." Was Camilla mollified? Emma tried one more attempt. "Since I didn't, and since Gerald Ochs Davis showed enthusiasm for your book, Pam is *very* interested. Don't let her scare you, though, if you can help it. She's pretty intimidating, but she's smart, and she can make your book. Just remember that her bark isn't as bad as her bite."

"Well, *that's* a relief," Camilla said. "I shall just try not to get bitten. I suppose the bad news that you had to use guile is offset by the good news that important people like the manuscript. There's the fluke." She allowed herself a very small smile. She was really a cool one, Emma thought. But nice, definitely nice.

"No, the fluke was that you met me and I submitted

the book to Emma," Frederick said. "If you had gone through any normal channels, the book would have been accepted anyway."

"In my opinion, the fluke is just being served," Mrs. Ashton said as the platter of flounder filet was brought around by Rosa. Mrs. Ashton looked over at Camilla. "I would love to read the manuscript. I'm sure that neither Gerald Ochs Davis nor his editor in chief could be tricked by anyone." She glanced over at Emma as if to reprove her for her bad manners and to remind her to toe the line. "I hope you haven't done anything wrong, Emma."

Emma tried to smile. "The only thing I did that was remotely suspect was to give your manuscript to Alex Simmons, the agent. That's against Davis & Dash's best interest, I suppose. But you ought to have some representation. Still, that advice shouldn't come from me. So I think it would be a good idea if you went to more than one agent, just so I don't feel responsible."

"I will," Camilla said. "Do you have a list of them?"

"I'll get you a list," Emma said, "or you could call the Writers' Guild." They all looked down at their flounder then, and in the ensuing silence Emma wondered again what was going on between her brother and this woman. She was afraid she'd handled it all pretty awkwardly. She looked up and tried to seem upbeat while she managed to ask Camilla whether or not she was excited about the prospect of being published.

"I'm thrilled, actually," Camilla said. "It's a new start for me. And I'm very grateful to all of you." And Emma wasn't certain, but she thought she saw tears in Camilla's dark brown eyes before she returned them to her plate of fish.

# 51

Let every eye negotiate for itself, and trust no agent.
*—William Shakespeare*

"I'm here for some advice," Opal admitted and looked across the desk at the white-haired older man across from her. His office was as impressive as he was—it looked a little like the Rare Book Room back at the Bloomington Library except that, with the practiced eye of a librarian, Opal could see that none of the books were actually valuable. In fact, most of them were barely what Opal would call books: those fine leather-bound, gold-embossed volumes on her right were all Susann Baker Edmonds! Who would have bothered to bind *that* pulp in pigskin? Opal suppressed a shrug. Emma Ashton had advised her that she needed an agent or a literary attorney and that Pam Mantiss had suggested Mr. Byron. So, here she was, but she certainly didn't know what should happen next. Did she write him a check and hire him, or was this more like an audition? Well, first things first. "You've read my daughter's book?"

Mr. Byron's big head nodded. "Most of it," he then said, "and I—"

"Most of it?" Opal asked. She knew it was a lengthy manuscript, but how could this man nod and tell her that he'd read it if he hadn't come to the magnificent ending? "I don't think we can talk about her book until you've read it *all*," Opal said, and picked up her purse, preparing to leave.

Alfred Byron made a gesture to restrain her. "Now, now, Mrs. O'Neal. You'll have to excuse me. It wasn't that I haven't been completely drawn in by the power and the magic of your daughter's work. It's merely been the press of my own schedule. I can't tell you how busy I am. I'm representing a *very* important new author, and his launching is taking a tremendous toll. Plus Susann Baker Edmonds has just finished a novel, and it's also taking a lot of my attention."

Well, that explained the bound books. Opal wondered if Pam Mantiss really considered that the agent for that sort of foolishness would be right for Terry's work. "You know," Mr. Byron continued, "I am a very hands-on kind of agent. It's important for me, and for my clients, that I guide not only their careers but often their actual writing. I can't tell you how much editing and rewriting I do myself."

"You *rewrite* manuscripts?" Opal asked.

"All the time," Mr. Byron told her proudly. "My clients are very grateful. I can't tell you how many have dedicated their books to me." There seemed to be a lot of things this man couldn't tell her. He walked to the shelf on the right, browsing along and pulling down three different volumes. Though he meant it to look casual, Opal had the distinct feeling that the books were not randomly selected, though he tried to make it look as if they were. "Ah. Here's one." He flipped it open to the dedication page. "'To Alfred Byron. Without whom this book would never have been *written*.'"

He handed it to Opal, and she looked at the spine. She'd never heard of the author. It appeared to be some kind of science fiction. Mr. Byron flipped open another book and smiled, looking down at the page before him. He sighed. "Here," he said, "I'll let you read this yourself."

He handed her the book, opened to the dedication page. Opal, ever the librarian, couldn't help but notice that the rest of the book seemed in pristine condition. It was obvious that the book was only opened to this page. "To Alfred Theodore Byron, my agent, my muse, my editor, and my friend." It was signed Susann Baker Edmonds. Opal closed the cover primly and returned it to Alf's wide desk.

"Well," Opal said crisply, "I won't need the muse or the editor part. The book is written by my daughter, as I'm sure Pam Mantiss told you. She edited it herself before she died," Opal explained. "It's to be published as is."

Mr. Byron smiled, perhaps a bit condescendingly. "You have to please yourself," he said. "But it reminds me of the old saw about lawyers who represent themselves: They find they have a fool for a client."

"I don't think I take your point," said Opal, although she certainly did.

"Well, it's just that your daughter, like every other writer, may have needed the clear, cool eye of an outsider to do a decent edit. I wrote a whole chapter about that in my book. The need for an outside eye."

"Oh, now I understand," Opal told him. "If you're implying that my daughter was a fool, or that I am, I think I disagree."

"Not at all. Not at all," said Mr. Byron, and he stood up, walked around the desk, and patted her on the shoulder. She had virtually decided by now: He was a pompous reptile, and she didn't like him one little bit. "I think you misunderstood," he was saying. "I didn't mean to offend. The book is a masterpiece; no doubt about it. And I promise you I wouldn't have taken time from my heavy schedule to see you if I didn't think so. I can't tell you how many people want to see me. So, I'm not talking about changing your daughter's work. But sometimes some tightening, some judicious pruning, some cutting back—always so painful to the author—can make all the difference."

"All the difference to whom?" Opal asked.

"To sales," Byron told her. "Regretfully, a book this length is not an easy sale. It can be intimidating, not to mention expensive."

"Mr. Byron, I know this book won't have commercial success on the scale of Susann Baker Edmonds or Stephen King." Opal paused. "But real readers, deep readers, will appreciate it. They'll know its worth."

"Not if they never see it on a shelf of a library or bookstore, Mrs. O'Neal," he said. "If a book isn't promoted, it simply sits in a warehouse. And this book—a first novel, an unwieldy length, a challenging style, and a high price, looks like one of those books that never leave the warehouse."

The thought of all those unread books, like an unlived life, made Opal unutterably sad. She saw there was more to this puzzle than simply getting published. "But don't the publishers take care of publicity and all that? After all, they're the ones who lose money if a book sits in storage."

He laughed unctiously. "In theory they take care—but Davis & Dash has almost fifty titles on the fall list alone. I assure you that all books will not be treated equally. My job is to fight to get Terry's book reviewed in the right places, to use my contacts to have it written about, to push them at D&D to do what they should."

"Well, what are your terms? I don't need any editing, but I need someone to review the contract and handle the rest of the business."

Mr. Byron sat down in one of the burgundy leather chairs opposite her. "To tell you the truth, we have a bit of a problem. You see, normally I work on a fifteen percent commission. But as there won't be another book from your daughter, or a career to build, in this case I would be putting in a huge amount of work for a very small financial reward."

Opal didn't think 15 percent of the advance was a small reward, nor that Mr. Byron had to do all that much work. "Don't you merely have to review the contract and oversee?" she asked. "Call your contacts? Could that take very long?"

"Oh, it's much more complicated than that. Though I don't expect this book to have very many sales, there may indeed be some foreign rights sold—Scandinavians like this kind of thing, and there's a considerable market there. Plus, I have some very good contacts in the U.K. I think I could manage a London sale, and maybe even a South African. All of the contacting of foreign publishers and the contracts entailed involves a lot of effort on my part."

Opal thought not of the money but of the chance to have Terry's book translated into Swedish, Norwegian, and half a dozen other languages. She'd never thought of that. The idea thrilled her, but this man did not. She hated beating around the bush, and he was doing so much of it that the bushes were dead. He obviously had something in mind. Why didn't he just come out and say it? "Well, Mr. Byron, why don't you tell me what you suggest?"

He smiled. "One obvious approach would be for me to take a higher commission. But I'm sure you can use all the money you can get right now."

Opal was offended by that. Did she look indigent? Why did he assume that? Opal was quite competent financially, and if she returned to Bloomington relatively soon, she could live comfortably for the rest of her life. But she felt it was irrelevant to point any of this out to the arrogant Mr. Byron. "So?" was all she said.

"So I have another idea." The man interlaced his fingers and placed his palms behind his head, his elbows winging out on either side. "I think there's a better way to go," he said. "I think *your* story would make an excellent movie. Not a feature perhaps, but a television movie-of-the-week. It has all the elements: your daughter's tragic death, your brave struggle to get her recognition. We could even gloss it up a bit and have the thing become an enormous bestseller, vindicating your belief. It certainly could affect sales very positively." He paused, but Opal was speechless. "I had a very preliminary discussion with a contact of mine at ABC. He's bought two of Susann Baker Edmonds's books and has done them as miniseries. We might be able to attach Tyne Daly. She would play your role, of course. Anyway, I think we could interest him, and we're talking mid six figures."

Mr. Byron looked over at Opal, and he must have misinterpreted her expression. Opal realized that her mouth was probably hanging open. She snapped it shut. But before she had a chance to say anything, Byron continued. "I know. It's a lot of money. Now, I would insist on twenty percent of this *and* executive-producer status for myself. But you could look at it as an unexpected windfall."

"I most certainly could not. Mr. Byron, you are either the most insensitive man I have ever run into—and that's saying quite a lot—or you're certifiable. Why would I want to exploit my daughter's tragedy? It's painful enough that it's happened. I don't need to relive it, share it, or make a financial killing on it. And I must say it was totally out of line for you to discuss this with anyone at a television network or anywhere else without my permission. I did *not* retain you, and it is clear that I am not going to." Opal lifted her purse and stood up. She was out the door and down the hall to the elevator before she saw even the slightest humor in the ridiculousness of it. As she stepped onto the elevator, she imagined telling the whole story to Roberta. Tyne Daly indeed.

"A made-for-TV movie?"

"I told Roberta you wouldn't believe it," Opal said to Emma Ashton over the phone that afternoon. "But then, who would?"

"What did you say?"

"I told him what I thought of him and walked right out. I may not live in the country anymore, but I still know a weasel when I see one." Opal thought perhaps she'd gone too far, but when she heard Emma's laugh she felt relieved and vindicated.

"Well, Alf Byron does have something of a spotty reputation," Emma admitted. "More like a cheetah than a weasel, I think. I was sorry that Pam had even suggested him, and I'm glad that you've decided not to work with him."

"The only thing I regret," Opal said, "is that he tempted me with foreign sales. I *would* like to see Terry's work in other languages, but I don't have a clue as to how to pursue that. Heavens, it was hard enough to get you to look at it in English!"

"Well," Emma said, "there *are* other agents."

"Oh, I just don't think I'm the agent type," Opal said. "There's something unhealthy about the setup. I mean, why don't they charge an honest fee for their time, the way other professionals do? Just because a book sells a million copies doesn't mean they should make more. At least it doesn't to me. But then, I'm from Indiana."

"So, what are you going to do?"

Opal thought of the nightmarish image of books stashed unread in the warehouse. But she pushed the thought from her mind. "I just want you to draw up the contract, Emma. I trust your house. Davis & Dash has a good reputation. I'll have my lawyer back in Bloomington look it over."

"Oh, Mrs. O'Neal, I'm not sure *that's* the best thing. Publishing contracts are very complicated documents, and even though a lot of it is boilerplate, it ought to be looked at by a professional. At the very least, go to an attorney who specializes in entertainment law."

"Entertainment? Are we talking about television movies again?"

Emma laughed. "No, it's just what the field calls itself." She paused. "You know, Mrs. O'Neal, I *do* have a solution to the foreign-rights issue. You could call Alex Simmons. She's a reputable agent, a friend of mine, and she could represent your foreign sales."

"Well, there's an idea."

"Do you want her number?"

"No. It isn't necessary. You call her and send the contract over. If you trust her, I will, too."

"I'm sure she'll be able to review the contract for you, too. And I doubt she'll charge for it."

"It's a deal."

"It's a deal," Emma agreed. "Oh, one more thing: If you *do* ever consider a television movie, if I were you, I'd hold out for Olympia Dukakis."

For a moment, Opal thought the woman was serious. Then she realized the joke. "I'll keep it in mind," she told Emma.

# 52

> No passion in the world is equal to the passion to alter someone else's draft.
>
> —*H. G. Wells*

Pam threw the ghosted Peet Trawley manuscript across the long, narrow table and hissed at Stewart. "You call this a first draft? I told you I wanted it fast and good. You seem to have forgotten the *second* part of that directive." She crossed the room to the half-opened casement window, coated with dust, pigeon droppings, and who knows what else. The place was nasty and depressing. It wasn't dirty, exactly. It just had that air that apartments lived in by single loser men in their forties always acquired. Maybe it was the piles of old newspaper and the lingering odor of cheap take-out food. Pam shuddered.

They had decided to meet at Stewart's apartment in Stuyvesant Town, a sprawling ten-block mass of middle-income housing, and from Stewart's dirty window all Pam could see were other boring brick buildings exactly like this one. It was unseasonably hot, and Pam was sweating, but the gritty breeze that blew in did no good. They shouldn't have met here, but Pam didn't want to be seen with Stewart while he was finishing this book—if he *could* finish it. "Don't you have any fucking air conditioning in this place?" she asked. "I can't work in this heat."

"The buildings were built back in the thirties," Stewart told her calmly, as if she wanted an architectural history lesson. "They didn't have air conditioning back then, so of course, they didn't wire for it. Rents are cheap here, and you put up with it. Air conditioners aren't legal, though some people cheat. Still, they get fined or even thrown out of the development if they're caught."

"Christ! Air-conditioning condo commandos?" Pam grumbled. "Don't people have better things to do than police their neighbors?" She looked back at Stewart. No, people like him probably didn't. God, she'd have to lick him into shape fast. She sighed. "Look, I'll make this easy for you. There's only one thing wrong with this draft: It sucks. Now, let me break that down for you. It sucks because of three things: The characters are either dull or unbelievable, the plot is obvious, and the pacing is uneven."

The manuscript *was* bad, but Pam had to admit—at least to herself—that Stewart had at least managed to get the damn thing written. Which was more than she had done. But she now realized she hadn't done it precisely because she'd feared that her version would be almost as bad as Stewart's was. Pam thought of handing this mess in to Gerald and shuddered. After looking down on his work all these years, he'd now be able to look down on hers or what he thought was hers. It made Pam feel a little sick to imagine Gerald's sly smile and raised false brow.

She looked across the room at her writer-for-hire. The difference between her and Stewart was that while she would be deeply shamed by writing crap as obvious and bad as this, *he* was stupid enough to defend it. Well, she supposed that was good, in a way. Peet's books had been badly written, too, but they had energy and belief. She had to get Stewart to put more energy into this draft.

Stewart looked up at her. The guy wasn't even smart enough to stand and meet her on eye level. He was pussy-whipped before they even started! Pam sighed again. "But Peet's characters were always unbelievable," Stewart was saying. "Ice cream men who are actual demons, a nursery school staff that's a coven of baby-eating witches. You know."

Pam narrowed her eyes. "Well, they might have been

a trifle larger than life, but that's a lot different from dull. People don't have to read to be bored. They can be that all by themselves." Pam wiped her upper lip. The sweat had collected along her spine and was making a damp patch on her lower back. Her crotch was wet, too.

Stewart licked his lips. Despite the heat, Pam noticed he wasn't sweating. There was something wrong with a man who didn't sweat. She liked sex sweaty, wet, and slippery. But why was she thinking of *that* now? Stewart repulsed her. The little worm. And it was a good thing, too. They had too much work to do to get involved with *that*. Anyway, she had promised her shrink she wouldn't sleep with anyone for six months. Her shrink had suggested that there was a compulsive element to her sexuality. She'd denied it and agreed to the celibacy, though she didn't like it. It made her antsy. And why should she deny herself something she liked? For a moment she thought of Jude Daniel's long, sinewy hand. Pam shrugged. None of that. It had been almost two months, and she could do another four easy, just to prove to her shrink she could do it. It was the heat that was making her horny, not Stewart, who was mounting another defense.

"Look, I used *your* plot," he said. "Remember?"

Pam was away from the window and jammed into the chair next to Stewart in less than three seconds. She could see by the way he froze that it frightened him. Good. Did he think she'd stab him like the student had? "If you had used *my* plot, the plot would work," she said. "What happened to the double cross? And why wasn't Samantha a twin?"

"Pam, those elements just didn't work. When I got there it was so unbelievable that—"

*"I'll* tell you what's unbelievable. What's unbelievable is that you're getting six figures for this work and you can't even follow directions." She pulled out the editorial letter she'd prepared. "I don't have time to go through this thing with you page by fucking page." She had to get out of this

suffocating place. Pam threw a folder at Stewart. "I've put together these notes, and I expect a new draft by the end of next week. A *usable* draft."

"Next week?" Stewart looked at the sheaf of notes with an expression on his face more pained than dismayed. He leafed through the lengthy letter. "Pam, nobody could get these revisions done by next week and—"

"Peet Trawley could," Pam lied. "And don't tell me Peet's dead. I know that, or else I wouldn't be wasting my time talking to a limp dick like you."

"Pam, I haven't brought this up, but my mother's dying. I can't possibly make this deadline."

Pam paused. "Were you close?"

"Pam!"

"It was just a question." She stood up, deeply regretting every fucking penny of the money she had paid this idiot. "This book is not just on the fall list," she said coldly. "It's the *lead* title, okay? So if you want the rest of your money, if you want me to publish your next piece of shit, or if you even ever want to work in publishing again, you'll get these rewrites done by next week. I'm busy as a cat covering shit, but I made the time to edit it, so get it *done*." She felt another drop of perspiration trickling down from under her arm. It felt as if an insect were crawling on her. Well, Stewart and this place gave her the creepy-crawlies. And no wonder. It looked like the public housing she'd grown up in on the West Coast. Pam never wanted to be reminded of those days! "I'll be here next Thursday," she told Stewart. "I'll need the revisions to read over the weekend." She turned and let herself out.

"I *really* love your book," Pam said to Camilla Clapfish. The girl smiled. They always glowed when they heard those words. Pam launched into the obligatory three-minute praise: the lyrical descriptions, the acutely drawn characters, the blah, blah, blah. Camilla actually blushed with pleasure. She wasn't pretty exactly, but she had that peachy English skin and her hair glinted with reddish high-lights. She must have been about ten years younger than Pam, but Pam knew that a decade ago—or even two—Pam hadn't had that air of vulnerability and freshness. The comparison didn't make Pam warm to Camilla.

"Would you like a coffee? Or are you a tea drinker?"

"Coffee would be lovely, thanks."

Lovely. Yes, Pam was sure that coffee would be lovely for Camilla Clapfish. And so would everything else. She was clearly one of those little English girls who had always been taken care of, who spent their spare time writing little literary novels to amuse their friends. A regular Jane fucking Austen.

Pam wondered who Camilla Clapfish's friends were and whether she was connected in any high places. Did she hang out with Di or Fergie? And did she know the editorial world? More importantly, Pam wondered who *else* was about to see the manuscript.

The good news was that Pam had gotten in at the ground floor, had already made her offer and could probably buy it cheap. If it moved, it moved. If it didn't, she could play up its literary side and use it to enhance her editorial reputation. It paid to be careful. Since the *SchizoBoy* débâcle, she felt the ground had moved under them. Without Gerald at the helm, she knew her job would be jeopardized. The show-down with David Morton did not enhance either of their career paths. But this book was a pretty one, to make up for *SchizoBoy*. Not that it would appeal to the same market. Yet it could possibly take off. The problem was she had lied to Gerald and told him she'd already acquired it when she hadn't—not quite. If she could only manage to snag this book and parlay the rest of the list so she was voted Editor of the Year, Pam would feel more secure.

She looked over at the demure Camilla Clapfish. When did this girl have to worry about job security? She was wearing a pathetic skirt and blouse with a little schoolgirl jacket. But English women rarely knew how to dress. This was a woman who didn't know shit about business either, and if Pam played her cards right, she could buy this manuscript for a nickel, have it in galleys in two weeks, and shoot it out there with the rest of the fall list. Now Pam's job was to make sure that their offer was accepted. The coffee arrived, and Pam began the little dance. "Is this your first visit to New York?"

"Oh, no. I was here for school. I went to Marymount and Columbia."

Marymount, of course—little-rich-girl school. "Oh, really. What did you study?"

"Art history."

Pam nearly smiled. Of course. And then she probably worked for two weeks at Sotheby's before she met Chauncy or Percy or Charles. Well, it was time to get down to business. "We're prepared to publish your book. Have you thought about a title?"

"Actually, I think about it quite a bit. But I don't seem to come up with anything appropriate."

"Yes," Pam nodded. "Titling is an art in itself, and very important. A good title sells books. We're thinking of *A Week in Firenze.*"

The girl paused. "Isn't that just a bit . . . prosaic?"

"Well, we'll work on it. So, I have the contract drawn up. Do you have any questions?"

"Well, you will have to be just a bit patient with me," Camilla said. "I'm very greatful for your interest, but I'm in the process of retaining an agent and I don't quite know what ought to go into the contract."

Shit. "Who's your agent?" Pam asked.

"I haven't committed yet, but I think it will be Alex Simmons."

Alex Simmons. Who the fuck was Alex Simmons? On the one hand, dealing with an unknown agent was good news, because at least it wasn't Lynn Nesbit or one of the piranhas who would insist on Pam's tonsils plus rewards for sales. On the other hand, an unknown could be a real pain in the ass. "He knows about our offer?"

"Yes, and we're meeting over it this week. May I take it with me? I want you to know that I'm here because I have every intention of doing my book with you, if you'll have me. It's just that I've been advised that it's best to have an agent."

"Sure." Pam paused. She thought fast. She had a good way to kill two birds with this stone. "You know," she said, "if you're selecting an agent, this might be a good time to meet with Alfred Byron. He's one of New York's best, and I'm sure he'd be delighted to represent you." Yeah, delighted to take his cut and leave well enough alone. Alf owed her, and there'd be no bullshit about book-club bonuses or extra payouts for each week the book made the list. If this little book *did* succeed, it could be a bonanza for both of them and very little risk or trouble for either. After he'd blown it with Opal O'Neal, Byron better snag this one. Pam smiled at Camilla. "Why don't I give Alf Byron a call? He's very busy, and he represents some of our finest authors, but if I ask him to see you, I'm sure he'd make time."

"That would be very kind of you," Camilla Clapfish said.

# 53

> There's only one thing more frightening than being asked to do a book tour, and that's not being asked to do a book tour.
>
> —*Gerald Petievich*

"Forty-two cities! Are you crazy?" Susann stood up and walked across the old Persian carpet on Alf's office floor. She felt like walking right out but stood in the farthest corner instead. "You're joking, right? They don't really expect me to do forty-two cities?"

"Expect you to? Susann, I *begged* them for this. This is exactly the strategy you need."

"I need forty-two cities like I need a coronary thrombosis! How many bookstores is that? Eighty-four? Or is it three in each city? One hundred and twenty-six stores to sit behind a table and sign stock in? I don't know which is worse—when I have three hundred women who each want a personalized note, or when they throw me a party and nobody comes because the rinky-dink bookstore forgot to advertise or was too cheap." Susann heard her voice rise. She wouldn't cry or lose control, but she was upset and frightened. Since Kim's call she hadn't slept through a single night without a horrible dream of Kim's threatened suicide.

"Alf, it will take months. *Months* out of my life. And I have the next book to get on with."

"It won't take months. It's six weeks. That's all."

Susann walked back across the room and gripped the corners of his fancy antique partner's desk. Her money had bought it for him, along with the rug and the leather chairs and the ornate bookcases. She felt as if she could rip it all apart bare-handed. She lowered her voice. "Forty-two cities in six weeks. That's one city a day! Not including traveling time. Did they get me confused with Naomi Judd? I'm not a goddamned bus tour, Alf, I'm a writer. Don't get the Airstream customized for me."

"Calm down, Susann. I have their absolute guarantee that everything will be top-drawer. First-class flights, first-class escorts, first-class hotels."

"Oh, I know about first-class escorts: middle-aged women who work part-time and pick me up in Cleveland in their Honda Accords. Then they're late to get me to the radio station because they can't find the address, even though they had to bring Clive Cussler there last week and they've lived around the corner their whole lives. And what's the name of the four-star hotel in Akron, Alf?" All at once her anger deserted her and all she felt was tired. She slumped into the chair across from his desk and looked at him. "I am fifty-eight years old, in case you've forgotten. It takes me over an hour to put on my face. That's not counting getting dressed. How much luggage will I have to drag, how many outfits for forty-two days when I'm not staying over two nights anywhere and I can't get anything dry-cleaned?"

She looked at him, but she didn't see his face. Instead she saw those unwelcoming hotel rooms, the blank television screen, the lamp beside the bed with a bulb invariably too bright or too dim to read by, a telephone with a blinking message light. She imagined forty meals with third-string journalists whom she would have to charm, twenty local interviews by radio deejays who had never read her books, a hundred bookstore managers whose names she would have to remember. "I can't do it, Alf," she whispered.

"Of course you can. You *have* to. You have more than two million readers out there, and we have to remind them to get out to the bookstore and buy this book. They don't just like your writing, they like your lifestyle. They like *you*. And if they come in to see you and hope that a little of your glamour rubs off when you sign a book to them, then you're going to accommodate. Gladly." He looked into her eyes. He *was* a compelling presence. "It will put you on the top again, Susann. You *need* this. It hasn't been cheap and it hasn't been easy to arrange, but it's going to be great. And you won't be alone."

Susann looked up. "Will you come with me?" *That,* she realized, would change the picture entirely. It would still be hard, arduous work and tiring travel, but with Alf along it might actually be fun. It would be like the old days, when he'd arranged every book signing, gone with her, and opened each and every book she signed. They hadn't spent time like that together in the last few years. "Oh, Alf, are you coming with me?"

He looked away. "Well, I'll go to Boston and Chicago. And then you can go on from there. I'll meet you in San Francisco, and then again in Los Angeles."

"While in between I do Bakersfield, Sacramento, and Oakland," Susann said, trying to keep the bitterness out of her voice. And Omaha, Milwaukee, Detroit, *and* Akron. She should have known better! She stood up, crossed her arms, and paced back to the corner again. Why did she always wind up in a corner? Why did it always seem to get more difficult, rather than easier? As she overcame each obstacle, another molehill turned into a mountain, right before her eyes. She'd left her beloved editor, negotiated this new deal against her will, was dealing with a hostile editor, and had rewritten the book according to direction. But this, this was so unspeakable, so tedious, so exhausting, depressing, and lonely that she wondered if even the number-one spot on the bestseller list was worth it. Susann stood absolutely still, her arms now hanging at her sides. She looked at Alf and wondered, not for the first time, whether her career was his attempt to take care of her, an outgrowth of his own ego, or—at this point—merely a paycheck.

"This is important, Susann," Alf told her.

"What are *you* going to be so busy doing? If this is so important, this tour, why can't you come?"

Alf looked down at his huge desk blotter. Who used blotters anymore? Susann wondered irrelevantly. God, that was Alf. All for show. No real staying power.

"I have to manage the business. Plus Jonathan is getting married. I have to be around for that."

"And I don't?" Susann asked. She knew that Alf's son had become serious about the woman he was dating, but she didn't know anything about a wedding; obviously, she was not invited. Clearly, she was not supposed to know. She bit her lip.

As if to distract her, Alf stood up and began to talk quickly, his voice raised. "It's going to be small. I can't tell you how small it's going to be. Just immediate family. Nothing at all. And remember: You're not my only client." He came around the desk, drew her out of her corner, and continued holding her hand. "Of course, I love you and you're my most important client, but Jude Daniel's book comes out simultaneously and I have his first tour happening at the same exact time. Someone's got to watch the store, Susann. You know I have business to attend to."

"How many cities is *he* touring?" she asked. "Where is *he* going?" Her voice had a nasty screech to it. She was shocked by the surge of jealousy she felt.

"Uh, only four or five. Nothing like yours. You know, the usual: New York, Boston, Chicago—"

"San Francisco and Los Angeles," Susann finished. "Which are the cities you'll bother to see me in. Two birds with one stone, Alf?"

Susann knew what she had to do—both to survive this and to punish Alf. "There's only one way I'll do it, Alf," she told him. "I have to have two things."

He looked up at her, and this time his face had the attentive look, the look he took on when he knew she meant business. The bristly eyebrows had lowered, and he had his good ear cocked toward her.

"I'll do it if you make Davis & Dash drop the case against Kim."

"What? Now, Susann, you know—"

"That's the deal, Alf. I do the tour, you drop the case. Make it all right with her publisher, make it all right with Davis & Dash. Send them a letter, have the lawyers make phone calls. Let her use the name. Do whatever you have to do. Leave her alone and let her book come out. Stop torturing the girl."

"Susann, I don't think—"

"I know what *you* think. Now I'm telling you what *I* think. It's the only way I'll do the tour. Also, I'm taking Edith with me. That's the other thing. And she has to have first-class accommodations, too. I'm not going to be sitting up in first-class eating a filet while she's stuck behind the curtain with a stale ham sandwich."

"That'll cost a lot of money, and Davis & Dash has already appropriated the budget. I can't tell you how hard it's been to negotiate it. We don't want them to cut back on the ads or television commercials."

"Try to get them to pay for it, and if they won't, then *you* pay for it. You should be with me anyway. And you can afford it: You'll be getting a hefty percentage from this acceptance check." She saw him wince. Alf was so predictable: Hit him in his wallet and he hurt. Susann almost smiled, but she was too sad and tired.

Still, there was an appropriateness to having Alf pay for Edith's first-class travel. It was Edith who had gotten her through, while it was Alf who collected the big checks. This might even things out, at least a little. "That's the deal," Susann told him. "Kim gets her book, and I don't have to drag myself alone through America."

She didn't wait for him to answer. She just turned and left the office.

Susann would calm down. She always did. Alf buzzed his secretary. "Please send Susann some flowers. Seventy bucks' worth." Well, maybe he should do better than that. "Seventy-five," he amended. "But don't use that Park Avenue goniff. Call the guy on Thirty-fourth Street. You know what she likes. Have we heard from the West Coast?"

"Not yet," Natalie told him. "And you have a three o'clock."

"Right," he snapped. Alf Byron hadn't been this excited in years. At last he was in the action again. He'd actually hired another assistant because with Susann's book tour and the buzz about Jude Daniel, Alf knew it was going to be a good year. He tried to imagine what it would feel like having two books on the top-ten list. He knew that some people in New York thought he was finished, that he was a *putz* from Cincinnati, but if *In Full Knowledge* hit big, and he was sure it would, who would be the *putz*?

He lifted the phone and dialed the William Morris Agency in Beverly Hills. *In Full Knowledge* was definitely movie material—and not some stodgy TV miniseries either. This was feature stuff, dark but gripping. He knew there was a bias against women's stories for the big screen, but there was sincere interest from the biggest female producer in Hollywood.

His call was answered by electronic voices. Alf hung up. He wasn't leaving any message. They could call him. And they would. He didn't want to look too hungry. So he called his pal over at *BookNews* and fed him the latest: that Davis & Dash was planning a print run of 150,000 copies on *In Full Knowledge* and that two producers were already fighting for the screen rights. Meanwhile, he'd worked through his foreign agencies. If enough people believed it, it would become true. And the foreign sales *would* roll in, though not at record-breaking levels. At least not yet. The movie option would change that.

He looked down at his list and realized he had to call Jim Meyer to pull them off the Kim Baker thing. He also had to see this girl that Pam Mantiss was sending over.

He'd read her manuscript the previous evening. It was nothing with nothing. Pretty writing, no plot, and he certainly didn't care very much about those annoying older women. In fact, they reminded him of his mother.

But as a favor to Pam he would represent the old girl, this Camilla Clapfish. And who knows, there could be a few bucks in it—though Pam had let him know that this was not a deal for him to renegotiate. She scratched his back, he'd scratch hers. He'd caught hell from Pam for losing that stubborn Mrs. O'Neal. He'd just tell this English lady to take the offer, get the contract signed, and see if he could collect a percentage. Why not?

"She's here."

Alf grunted, reached into his briefcase, and pulled out the manuscript Pam had messengered over to him. Miss Clapfish turned out to be one-third the age that Alf had expected. She wasn't some wizened old English spinster—she was a peachy young girl.

"Well, well, well," Alf said. "Miss Camilla Clapfish. Notable new author."

She held out her hand in response to his. He took it. It was cool and amazingly soft. Alf had the strangest impulse. He wanted to take this kidsoft palm and rub it all over his own leathery face. For a moment he thought of Susann's hands—despite her care and surgery, they showed her age. And the arthritis hadn't improved them. They were swollen at the finger joints and as spotted as his own. He looked down at Camilla Clapfish's smooth, white skin. How long had it been since he had held young flesh? There was something about it that was more than seductive: It was invigorating, as if the life in her cells could rub off on his own. He looked up, into her fresh face. She looked a bit alarmed, and he dropped her hand. "So. Come. Sit down." He forced himself to go back to his seat on the other side of the desk. No point in frightening the girl. It was back to business.

"I read your book."

"And what did you think?" Her voice was fresh and youthful. Alf was a pushover for an English accent.

"Very nice. Very nice. Not commercial, but nice. You can certainly write."

"Thank you," she said. Those English always sounded so classy. He wanted to hear more.

"Why don't you tell me a little about yourself?" he prompted.

He let her talk for a few minutes while he listened more to the rhythm than to the content. This one would be easy. "So, what can I do for you?"

"Well, as I say, it's very good of you to see me at all. What I have to do is retain an agent and get this business at Davis & Dash taken care of." The girl paused and actually seemed to blush. "But do you think there's a chance that they might raise their offer a little bit? I'm very grateful for their interest, and I mean to sign with them, but money is an issue."

"So, what else is new?" Alf asked, smiling. Now was his chance to make peace with Pam Mantiss. "Listen, can I give you some advice? This is not a very commercial book. I don't think I could raise interest in it anywhere else. Pam Mantiss is um . . . unpredictable. She likes it. All well and good. But she has the luxury of a couple of giants like Peet Trawley and Susann Baker Edmonds to support an artsy-fartsy book like this. No offense intended."

The girl blinked but nodded. Her hair was smooth and shiny. Alf thought that every strand must be a slightly different tone of chestnut, red, and ash. It looked so alive and healthy. Unconsciously he ran his fingers through his own mop of frizzled white hair. He got an idea. Pam Mantiss would kill him, but he'd cope with that later.

"I think you have two choices," he told the girl. "And whether you sign with me or not, I believe this is excellent advice. I can't tell you how many people pay me money to advise them like this. I think you either leave the book as it is and take this offer quickly, before it melts away, or you make some significant changes and we rethink it." As far as he was concerned, the book was a lot like Listerine: 98 percent of the text was inert, though there were a few good scenes.

Camilla Clapfish leaned forward. "What changes do you suggest?"

"Well, first, we need more sex. Second, we need more plot. Third, we need these characters to be a *lot* younger. Think about it: Who's going to care about a bus full of old broads—you should excuse the expression—that nothing really happens to? It's not a story. It's a sketch. Artistic, I grant you, but not engaging. You get my meaning?"

"Yes," she said. "Absolutely. But I think you're talking about a different book."

"Exactly. A different book. A book that will sell. If they were college students, a bus full of girls from college. *That* could be a movie. Well, maybe a television movie."

"But I—"

The phone rang, and Alf put up his hand. "I'm expecting an important call," he said.

He snatched up the receiver. "Is it William Morris?" he asked his secretary, and when she told him it was, he took a deep breath. Don't be too eager, he told himself. He counted to twenty. "Put them through."

"Scott, how ya doing? What news?"

"Good news, Alf. April Irons is interested. She sees it as a vehicle for Jodie."

Feature! Feature! At last he'd get something onto the big screen.

"Uh-huh." He tried to keep the excitement out of his voice.

"Now, she's not attached to the project yet, but April worked with her on *Suddenly Sane*. And she wants to have her husband, Sam Shields, direct."

"How much?"

"Not much. A hundred thousand, against six hundred when it goes into principal photography."

"You've got to be kidding? That's peanuts."

"Look Alf, April figures she could do this film without the book. The story is out there. But she likes the title, and if she attaches Jodie, you've got a real shot at this thing happening. Any money she doesn't spend on the option she'll pour into the script. I'm telling you to take the deal. If I shop it around, we'll lose April, guaranteed. I need your decision by five o'clock my time."

"What's the rush?"

"She's leaving for location. At least that's what she says. So talk to Jude Daniel and get back to me."

Alf put down the phone, his heart beating loud in his chest. He wondered if he should take a pill but decided not to. This was good excitement. He'd make the deal. The professor would be thrilled. So would Pam Mantiss. He looked up, into the dark brown eyes of Camilla Clapfish. He'd forgotten all about her. But she'd witnessed his triumph.

"I've just sold an author's book to the movies," he said. "I rewrote most of it. He listened to me, and now it's going to star one of the biggest actresses in Hollywood. So, what do you think?" He had to wrap this up. He had more important things to do and wondered where he could reach the professor.

"Well, thank you for taking this time to see me," she said. "I'm committed to meeting one other agent before I make my decision."

What the hell was this? "You're seeing another agent?" Alf asked. Pam Mantiss hadn't told him that. What had this been? An audition? As if Alf Byron had time to waste! He stood up. "Well, if you think that someone else can give you better advice than I just did, I suggest you take it."

Camilla Clapfish paled a bit. "Oh, I didn't mean that—"

"Look, I'm a busy man and I'm not looking for new clients. You talk to your other agent, and you work with him. And good luck to you," he said. Camilla stood up, and he moved her to the door.

"Natalie," he shouted, "can you see Miss Clapfish out?" His secretary appeared, and Alf didn't bother to take Camilla's pretty hand again. "Best of luck," he repeated and turned his back. If Pam was pissed that he had not nailed the girl down, he'd more than make up for it with the good news about the option on *In Full Knowledge*.

And who knows, maybe this little English chit would be back, begging him to take her on. At 20 percent.

# 54

> Unhappy endings in books are better than happy ones because readers believe life is sad and feel less manipulated.
>
> —*Maureen Egen*

Judith sat at the new word processor, carefully typing in her handwritten revisions to *In Full Knowledge*, hitting the "save" key at almost every line. She was paranoid, but it was justifiable. She had worked all day yesterday, forgotten to save her edits, and lost it all when she'd reached across the keyboard for her coffee and hit some unknown combination of buttons. She'd been highlighting something to put into italics, and she still wasn't sure if she hit the trackball or accidently touched the mouse or both. The whole thing made her sick.

Judith burped, patted her chest, and took a few more gulps of ginger ale, though Daniel had forbidden her to eat or drink around the computer. She hated everything about the stupid machine, even the words; *trackball, mouse.* It sounded like some demented game that Tom and Jerry would play. And how user-friendly was the thing if she couldn't even drink her coffee near it? A whole tedious day's work wasted!

She hated the laptop almost as much as she hated the dead space that was their new apartment. It was five rooms on the first floor of the Fox Run Green Garden Apartments, but there were no gardens, no foxes, and not even much green. The place was perched on three levels up a hillside. Their own apartment was dark because it faced north, and there were balconies on the two floors overhead, blocking the light as effectively as awnings.

Judith admitted that the walls—all beige—were straight and clean, and the wall-to-wall carpet—a light blue—was brand-new. But the cleanliness seemed sterile to her, and their mishmash of old furniture looked even more pathetic in the setting of these middle-class walls. She missed her turret room and the lively view of the campus. The extra space only made her feel lonely. In fact, she felt buried alive.

Even Flaubert was uncomfortable—he followed her from room to room and lay his head on her foot the moment she sat anywhere long enough. Now she looked down at him and scratched behind his crooked left ear. His tail thumped twice in gratitude, two halfhearted thwacks against the floor, and then he sighed. Hadn't someone written that there was nothing more heartbreaking than the unconscious sigh of a dog? "You're right," she told Flaubert. "This place sucks."

There was also something about the new-carpet smell that made her constantly sick to her stomach. She left the windows open almost every day, but the nausea kept coming back. Daniel said it was all in her head, but she knew for sure it was in her nose and belly. What did they make this glistening, springy rug out of, anyway? Nothing that had ever grown on a sheep's back, that was for sure. Probably from by-products of a nuclear reaction or a *Valdez* spill. *Synthetic* was such a cold, scary word. God knows what these fumes could do to her liver. Judith was even worried about Flaubert lying on the stuff all day, so she'd put down blankets for him.

Judith thought back with some embarrassment to all the complaining she had done about their old apartment. Now, in comparison, the place seemed heavenly. It had windows long enough for Flaubert to look out of. Here the windows began at chest height, narrow slits along the top of the rooms. She guessed that it was considered "modern," not to mention cheaper to build. There were other modern conveniences. The dishwasher and the trash compactor and the microwave, all in almond, were lovely, if you cared about microwaves and dishwashers and trash compactors. To her surprise, Judith found that she didn't, not at all. She'd complained about the nasty kitchen and the splintered floors at their old place, but she preferred them to this nylon hell that needed constant vacuuming. Somehow, when she let the dust and clothes and books and papers collect around their old apartment, it looked bohemian. Here it merely looked tacky.

Meanwhile, Daniel had introduced her to Cheryl, who lived upstairs. She was the only possible fox at Fox Run. Her one-bedroom apartment looked like a picture from one of those second-rate women's magazines you could only buy at supermarket checkout counters. The place was stuffed with dried-flower arrangements and flounced lace curtains and gingham throw pillows, all color-coordinated in salmon and mint green. The girl even had one of those repulsive new brass beds that were reproductions of the originals, which hadn't been hip for a decade. Judith might be a slob, but she was also a snob—and proud of it. Cheryl's little nest of horrors with the flowered Melmac dishes was nothing Judith wanted to emulate. What was the point of Daniel introducing them, and later asking how she liked Cheryl and her place? Was Daniel trying to help her find friends or give her homemaking tips? The girl was sweet, and she obviously adored Daniel, but then, they all did. Anyway, Cheryl *was* not a potential friend, and it didn't look like there were any other potentials at Fox Run. It was a long walk from town, and without a car Judith felt more isolated than ever.

But perhaps that was her sickness: Maybe she was a chronic complainer, which Daniel had just accused her of. He said that each time she got something new, she regretted what she had lost, though she had been unhappy with whatever *that* had been. Judith had to admit there was some truth to his accusation.

Depressed and confused, Judith patted Flaubert, typed

a few more lines, and hit Command S to save. She looked down at the next yellow tag on the manuscript page. It was one she hadn't noticed before, but then there were so many. It was a key scene, right after Elthea realizes her boyfriend has been cheating and is going to leave her. Over the course of a night, Elthea, in despair, calls his answering machine and leaves a dozen begging messages, each one more desperate, more pathetic, and more angry than the last. Then, in horror and disgust, she decides to drive to his house, get in, and erase the messages. Though it's past three in the morning, she packs her sleeping boys into the back of the car and takes off on her doomed mission. That's when she sees him with the other woman. Judith was proud of the chapter. It stretched out the horror to the breaking point.

The yellow slip merely said, "Cut scene. Too long. Pick up the pace. Anyway, impossible for so many messages to fit on a tape."

Judith looked at the comment in disbelief. This was the turning point of the book. Elthea's obsession, her need to connect and the impossibility of doing so had to be shown. And it would take a dozen messages to do it. Judith lifted her hand to the note, tore it off the manuscript, and crumpled it up. Her hands were shaking. She thought of Elthea, disintegrating this way before the reader's eyes. One could understand what propelled her, with her children, into that suicidal, homicidal dive. To cut the scene would destroy the only possibility that a reader would have to truly understand Elthea, her utter humiliation and her outrageous act.

Judith stood up, and Flaubert's head fell off her foot onto the synthetic carpet. *Synthetic.* That was the word, all right. They wanted to make the book synthetic, faster-paced, stupid. Who *was* this editor? Certainly Gerald Ochs Davis couldn't be this thick. As Judith lifted the page, her nausea increased. If she drank any more ginger ale, she'd burst, but the queasiness wouldn't go away. She leafed through the next few pages to see if the comments got worse. And they did, in a way. There, written not on a yellow note but right on the manuscript, in the margin next to the flashback sex scene, was another comment she hadn't noticed. Part of the paragraph had been circled, and in the same handwriting as that on the little yellow Post-its the editor had written, "I wish you'd do this to me." Judith felt her stomach heave and took two deep, fast breaths. What in the world was *this*? Surely Gerald Ochs Davis wasn't a homosexual, or was he? Judith stared at the words. *I wish you'd do this to me.* For a moment, Judith was tempted to laugh. Someone, a man or a woman, had written that to Daniel, but the irony was that it was she, Judith, who had created the sex on the page. If Mr. Davis was gay, wouldn't he be disappointed to find that out? And if a woman had written those words, wouldn't she be confused? *I wish you'd do this to me.* Judith did begin to laugh, and as she did Flaubert jumped up, unaccustomed to that noise. But after a couple of moments, the laughter became a spasm in her stomach and her gorge rose. Before she had time to get to the bathroom, Judith vomited, splattering the pristine blue carpet, Flaubert, and the edge of the laptop's screen.

She threw up again, this time only on the carpet, then dry-heaved until even the last bit of ginger ale was emptied from her. Shaking, she sat back down. What had just happened?

She looked down at the mess she had made. Her resentment, her jealousy, her suspicions, fear, and anger had all overcome her. She had been holding it down for days, weeks, and it had to come up. She was furious with Daniel, her only friend, for his betrayal. She was furious with herself for being used, for being stuck here and taking on this editing job. And she was frightened—truly and deeply frightened—that Daniel was cheating on her in more than one way: that he wasn't just taking credit for the book but that perhaps he had taken Cheryl or some editor woman who had been near this manuscript as his new mistress, while she was becoming his discarded wife.

The stench of her vomit rose from the floor. Of course, Judith told herself, she could just be overreacting. Maybe she was coming down with a stomach flu. It was going around. And the toxic smell of the carpet was enough to make anyone sick. So was this editing job. But, as nausea rose again, Judith thought for the first time about whether there might not be another reason for her sickness. Judith wondered whether she might be pregnant.

# 55

We must cultivate our garden.
—*Voltaire*

Opal needed more bags. That was the problem. Maybe some cartons, too, for the heavier stuff, but definitely more bags. And not these thin, white kitchen ones. She needed the heavy lawn-and-garden bags. How, she wondered, could an enclosed, fenced space collect so much trash? How did these cans and plastic forks, sodden newspaper pages and broken bottles find their way back here? Did people throw them out their windows? Opal sat back on her heels and surveyed what she had done. A small corner, about five feet square, was cleared, but she had filled four large bags to do it. She'd have to quit now and go and get more bags.

Actually, she hadn't even been thinking about clearing this backyard wasteland, but with the book actually sold, Opal found herself with time on her hands. She'd done as much cleaning as she could bear to do in Terry's apartment—at this point she felt as if she could map every permanent stain on the blue-painted walls. So, this morning, after a bracing cup of tea and with nothing else to do until she went to The Bookstall at one, Opal had donned the thick yellow rubber gloves she used for housecleaning and had gone out into the small yard.

There was, she found, some order to the chaos out there. Despite the weeds, broken branches, and dead leaves, she found evidence that someone had once at least tried to garden there. Under the trash she had unearthed a flagstone walkway. At the far end of the yard, where she was working right now, there was a brick wall and, before it, a kind of raised bed had been built, though it had been completely obscured by the weeds and garbage. At one time it must have been a bed of roses, because Opal could recognize the two thorny stumps she had already uncovered and pulled from the unpromising soil.

She didn't have any tools, so she made do with the house broom, which she used to awkwardly sweep up the piles of dead leaves and pulled weeds. She also improvised with the metal dustpan, and had even employed its edge to scrape away at the dirt, once the leaves and weeds were cleared. But what she needed to do the job efficiently was a rake and a small shovel, not to mention a weed whacker. Opal thought longingly of her garden shed back in Bloomington. She didn't suppose they had weed whackers in New York City. She wouldn't make the investment, anyway. After all, she was in no rush. This was merely something to do while she waited for the contract from Alex Simmons and made sure the book was really on its way to publication.

The cleared earth gave off a rank odor—it smelled more than a little of cat. But the old leaves and the dead tall grasses smelled just like her garden back in Indiana. Suddenly, Opal experienced a wave of homesickness. She had only two more months before her library job was lost. She wondered how the tenants were treating her house. She turned back to one of the bags she had filled and tried to stuff a few more handfuls of twigs into it. Funny how heavy all that light grass got when it was shoved into a plastic bag. She could barely move this one, and as she tried to, she saw a branch press out through the plastic, three quarters of the way toward the bottom. It tore a hole the size of a half-dollar. Opal sighed. It would all tear now if she moved it. She'd have to double the bag.

"What are you doing?"

Opal jumped at the sound and turned to see Aiello. How had he gotten in? It was only then that she noticed the recessed door at the side of the building, set back from

Terry's apartment and obscured by a scratchy holly bush.

"What are you doing?" Aiello asked again, always the master of the obvious.

"It's Sunday," Opal told him. "I'm going to church."

"Man is closer to God in a garden than anywhere else on earth," Aiello quoted, and Opal nearly fell over sideways. "It's a poem," Aiello told her, though he pronounced it *pome*. "My mother had it on a plaque in her yard."

Opal had actually known the poem for years. It wasn't much, as poems went, but the only poetry she'd figured Aiello knew would be a limerick about a boy from Nantucket. Opal was surprised, to put it mildly.

"You need more bags," Aiello commented. Well, for once his base-level perceptions could be useful.

"Have you got any?" Opal asked.

"Sure," Aiello said, and without any further nagging or requests he disappeared from whence he came and returned with a whole roll of sturdy black plastic trash bags.

"These here ones won't hold," he told her, pointing to her own with his chin, and Opal tried to avoid being exasperated. Effortlessly, he picked up the first two white sacks and placed them in one of the larger, heavier-gauge black ones. In two minutes he had consolidated all of her work into a single, twist-tied mound. "You need a hoe," he said, "and a scythe to cut this down." Opal just shrugged and turned back to pulling weeds from the long bed. "I got a scythe," Aiello added. "You want me to cut all this down for you?"

"You have a *scythe*?" Opal asked in disbelief. Aiello as the grim reaper was a disconcerting image. What was the man doing in the midst of this urban blight with a tool as Bruegelesque as a scythe?

"My grandfather had a big garden out in Corona," Aiello volunteered. Opal didn't know where Corona was, but she supposed it was somewhere in the country. "Grew vegetables, had fruit trees. Even grew his own grapes. I used to help him. When he died, I kept the scythe."

Opal wasn't sure if she was comfortable with the combination of Aiello and a large curved blade, but the temptation to get the worst part of the mess cut down was more than she could resist. Not that she was planning to stay, or that she might even get around to planting this place. It was merely the librarian in her, the part of her that liked things to be tidy. "Certainly," she said. "That would be very kind of you."

He turned to go, but as he did, he stopped at the gate. "Oh, here," he said, handing her an envelope bearing the small green sticker that meant it was registered. "You got this, and I thought you might want me to sign for it. Save you a trip to the post office." That was Aiello! Just when she thought he might actually be reasonable and pleasant he'd do something nosy or rude or out of line. Receiving other people's mail was a federal offense! And surely it hadn't come on Sunday. How long had he been holding it?

"When did it come?" she asked.

"Yesterday," he said. "Or the day before." She very nearly snatched it from him, but before she could express her annoyance, he was gone. He had no right to sign for her mail. What if it was something important? He'd held it all day yesterday and made two trips out here before he'd even remembered to give it to her. The man was impossible!

Opal pulled off her thick rubber gloves while she held the envelope between her teeth. Then she took it in her hands and looked at the return address. Davis & Dash. She trembled as she turned the envelope over. Although she was usually extremely careful, she tore at the back of the flap, and, hands shaking, she scrabbled to open the folded sheets inside. She nearly ripped the cover letter, which was a handwritten note from Alex Simmons.

Well, here's the contract. You'll receive a check on signing, which is standard.

I'll begin negotiating foreign rights once we have review copies. Such a long and complex novel presents special problems for both translation and printing. Still, I believe it will sell well abroad, though not fetch high advance money.

I am really thrilled and deeply grateful for the opportunity to be involved in this book. Let's hope that Davis & Dash can give *The Duplicity of Men* the worldwide audience it deserves. Call me if you have any questions.

All the best,
Alex Simmons

Opal took a moment to look at the enclosed cover letter from Pam Mantiss to Alex Simmons, then she checked to see that the attached pages were indeed what looked like a legal contract between Davis & Dash as publishers and Opal O'Neal as proprietor. Her hands began to shake harder. She glanced at the advance amount and realized that she would be receiving two payments—one of fifteen thousand dollars when this very contract was fully signed and another for the same amount when the book was published.

When the book was published! Opal clutched the papers against her chest. A breeze riffled them. She would never forget this moment, standing here amidst the trash and the garbage bags, the buildings looming around her, the empty pewter sky overhead. When she lay dying, it would be this moment that she would recall, the feel of the paper in her hands, dead grass against her leg, the faint smell of cat that the earth gave out. She felt such a deep gratitude, a bittersweet joy. Now Terry would become not dead but immortal.

Opal looked around her, as if she were seeing the space for the first time. She would plant a tree here, a weeping, flowering tree. And under it she would put a little plaque, or maybe a stone, to commemorate the moment. There were trees in other yards—she had been gathering their leaves, and she could see some big ones over the back fences—so if she planted one here, it might remain for a hundred years.

When Aiello returned with the scythe he was astounded to find Opal standing where he left her, silent tears coursing down her cheeks.

# 56

> The publisher is a middleman, he calls the tune to which the whole rest of the trade dances; and he does so because he pays the piper.
>
> —*Geoffrey Faber*

Sales conference was a hallowed tradition at Davis & Dash, despite the terrors and boredom involved. It was the chance for the house's two enemy camps—the editorial and the sales staffs—to meet, catfight, lay blame, and then be united in the huge joint effort to push and sell the ever-growing number of books on the fall list.

For his own comfort, Gerald made sure that the sales conference was held at a decent resort hotel, and that he, of course, was housed in the very best suite. But to contain costs, he made sure that it was off-season, at greatly reduced rates. Another cost-saver was forcing all junior staff to double up with roommates. This season's sales conference was being held in Palm Springs, and though he himself blanched at the thought of the climate there in mid-April, he was smart enough to know that those who had never been to Palm Springs would be all a-twitter. It had cachet, and Davis & Dash was known for that. Because the sales conference was not just for getting business done, but a motivation and a reward. It was also an opportunity for staff to make their mark; to be singled out as a presenter of books was to be awarded the *cordon bleu*; some salespeople received accolades and a special emolument for best sales performance. They knew, most of them, that this was one of only three shots a year at exposure to him, Gerald Ochs Davis, and a chance to clamber up a few rungs of the ladder. A lot of effort went into making the sales conference as slick, as professional, and as motivational as it could possibly be.

That didn't mean that it didn't bore the shit out of Gerald, and gearing up for it was even worse.

Apparently, it bored the shit out of Pam Mantiss as well. She had asked Emma Ashton to take her place today and run down the books each editor would present to sales staff. The young editor was stiff and cool, but Gerald sensed her underlying nervousness and smiled. It annoyed him that Pam had ducked this meeting, but alternatively he'd enjoy teasing Emma Ashton. There was something removed about her that ignited the impulse in him to bully—if she were a fly, he'd be forced to pick off her wings.

"So, how is our video star?" Gerald inquired.

This season, because she was a new acquisition and because her book was so important to the fiscal health and well-being of Davis & Dash, Susann Baker Edmonds was going to be presented via a videotape. In it she explained her past work and would tell the salespeople about her new book. It was costing a packet, and Gerald had heard it had caused all kinds of problems. "It's finished?" he asked Emma.

"Not quite," Emma admitted. "But it will be done in time," she assured him.

"What's the problem?" Gerald had received word that Susann was miserable about how she looked on tape, insisting the whole thing be shot again. "Will it run over budget?"

"I wouldn't know," Emma said coolly. "You'd have to ask Dickie Pointer or someone in charge of it. I only have the lineup of the program and editorial presenters."

Disappointed that she hadn't risen to his bait, Gerald looked at the schedule Emma had handed him. Of course senior editors would present their books, and the publicity and marketing people would give the sales reps the usual follow-up rap about the support each book would get, though the reality was that only the big books, the Trawleys and Edmondses and the like, got much beyond a wave good-bye. Like nineteenth-century orphans, once they were released they were on their own. And usually as lost.

"How about the Daniel book? Pam presenting it?" She was their best presenter, and even after all these years, when she was hot on a book she could ignite the crowd. In this case, from long experience, Gerald suspected Pam was hot on the author as well—perhaps literally and at this very moment. Maybe that was why she'd canceled their meeting.

"Yes," Emma said, either ignoring his jibe or running with it. "Jude Daniel is also going to make an appearance. As our new rising hope, we're pretty pleased and excited about the presentation."

"So I would wager." His own book would be presented, not by him alone but also by Pam. And she'd better be at her most perfervid. For *Twice in the Papers* they had made an extrazealous effort, Emma assured him, as if he didn't know. A multimedia presentation—which showed the newspaper clippings from the original scandal, family photographs of Gerald's aunt and uncle, and even a picture of the murder scene complete with the victims—had been pulled together, along with old newsreels that described what was at the time called "the High-Society Crime of the Century." Gerald hoped that the fact that the event happened fifty years ago wouldn't be a noticeable marketing problem. Of course, Jim Meyer's department *did* have something of a legal problem, since Gerald was using all this as a promotion while simultaneously insisting the book was fiction (and he had indeed added quite a few flourishes of his own). But, as he had explained to Jim, the presentation was only in-house, to set the tone, and it included a full disclaimer at the end. That, of course, didn't mean that anyone would believe it. Gerald was going to try to play this game from both ends, rather as Joe McGinniss had played the Kennedy book—but reversed.

McGinniss had insisted that his creation of the private thoughts and conversations of Ted Kennedy and his family was *non*fiction, while Gerald was insisting that these actual historical events were all invention.

Gerald smiled. It was one of the developments in publishing over the last decade that made purists like his father weep and cynics like Gerald laugh. A book like *Mutant Message Down Under* was self-published first as nonfiction. After questions were raised about whether the author had actually been abducted for a month-long walkabout with Aborigines, the book was simply reissued as fiction and became a bestseller.

"So, the presentation has been vetted with Meyer, and Pam has it all prepared?" Gerald asked Emma. He knew Pam was always working until the last minute, courting disaster in her quest for excitement or self-destruction, Gerald was never sure which.

"I haven't seen it," Emma said blandly. "But Pam says she's prepared. And I believe that Jim has a memo on the presentation for you." Emma handed him a copy. Gerald smiled at her. She was a cool one—no doubt about it.

The memo was a typical Meyer legal CYA maneuver. Everyone loved gossip, and Gerald was desperately counting on the fact that old gossip retold would sell as well as new gossip. Adultery, high society, a guilty man going free, and the piquancy of lesbian love should make a potent combination. Lesbians were hot right now, Gerald reflected. Except perhaps for this one. Gerald smiled again at Emma. Idly, he wondered if she swung both ways. Or if she'd consider a *ménage*. He glanced at the memo. Jim Meyer didn't trouble him; it was only the fear of word getting back to his father that held any terror. But he could not allow this book to fail. Not after the Chad Weston fiasco, the death of Peet Trawley, and Susann Baker Edmonds's recent poor showing. If it did, there would definitely be trouble with David Morton over another big contract and questions might even be asked about past contracts that Gerald would not like to have to answer to David Morton or anyone else.

Mrs. Perkins rang to tell him that Carl Pollenski was waiting. Gerald sighed and dismissed the little dyke, telling Mrs. Perkins to send Pollenski in. Carl was the manager of MIS—Management Information Systems—the computers that they all depended on but nobody really understood, except perhaps for Carl. And Carl was now probably the highest paid MIS man in publishing. But then, Gerald reflected, people who kept secrets should always expect to be well paid. Keeping secrets and publishing them were two ways to get rich.

Carl was tall and broad. He wore his hair in a buzz cut that might be fashionable except that he had worn it that way since the last time it was stylish. He was rarely invited up to Gerald's lair, and, unlike the unflappable Emma Ashton, he looked uncomfortable. His suit was light green—why couldn't these nerds who were queer for their gear learn how to dress? When Gerald got up from behind his desk and moved to the sofa, Carl awkwardly sat on the sofa too, which meant they were at oblique angles to each another, their knees virtually touching. It was too much for Gerald, who got up and sat in the chair opposite. More proof that it was best to keep Carl busy with machines. "Do we have all of the backup information for sales conference?" Gerald asked.

Carl nodded. The whole industry based its print runs, shipping, and sales projections on the computerized results of the author's last book's performance, and the ones before that. Because the booksellers, especially the chain stores, had also automated, there was now very little left to opinion, luck, or chance: Advance orders were based on the number of books the author had previously sold, and all the hype in the world, all the advertising and all the buzz, did very little to change that. Gerald thought back to the old days, when a brilliant PR guy had once sent an advance copy of a novel to people in the phone book—people with the same names as important reviewers and authors. Then he'd put their positive opinions in huge ads, with their names—Tom Wolfe, Norman Mailer, et cetera—printed boldly across the two-page spread. A ploy like that wouldn't work today. Past performance was all that mattered. It was only with a new author, one without a database, that there was not just leeway but an opportunity to make a killing.

For Gerald, the dismal sales of his last book had been so disastrous that there was no way, despite his special presentation, despite the pushing from Pam, despite the big catalog spread, that *Twice in the Papers* was going to initially be ordered in any kind of numbers that pleased him. Unless, of course, he had a special strategy.

"Well, I wondered if you've come up with a strategy yet, Carl."

"You mean for your book?" Carl asked. No, Gerald was tempted to snap, for world peace. But he kept his temper in check. Regretfully. Because when it came to perceptions of performance, that was where Carl came in. Because while Carl couldn't control what the bookstores *actually* ordered, he could change what Davis & Dash's sales sheets *indicated* were ordered. And what Gerald had found was that to top management, printouts reflected reality more than reality itself. A few keystrokes from Carl and an extra ten or twenty thousand copies of Gerald's book were reported as ordered, or even shipped. Take that, David Morton.

On the last book débâcle, Carl had developed a complicated system where book orders and shipments were "borrowed" from other authors, adding to Gerald's bottom line. Though Gerald had never admitted it, it had saved his ass. Carl had explained it to him. A bookstore in Kansas City might reorder fifty copies of Trawley's latest. The bookstore received the fifty Trawley copies, but the order was credited as an order of Gerald's books. Trawley never knew the difference, though what made Gerald nervous was that an author at Trawley's level could afford to actually pursue an audit and compare a printout to warehouse shipments. That's why ever-cautious Carl had refined the system and decided this time it was best to spread appropriated sales over several midlist books. The trick was to be sure the selected authors would sell enough so that five or ten thousand copies could be purloined and to be sure that the book price was exactly the same as Gerald's. Carl had now developed a way to set it all up in advance. The purpose of this meeting was to decide which books were likely candidates for poaching.

Because of his help, Carl was receiving not only forty thousand dollars more a year in his annual salary, but he also had a generous expense account that Gerald himself signed off on. And he had been given the use of a corporate car and driver whenever he requested it. A small price to pay to help ensure Gerald's next million-dollar contract, especially as it didn't come out of Gerald's pocket.

"So, Carl, have you some suggestions?"

"Sure do, Mr. Davis. Sure do." But despite his words he just sat there. Perhaps he mistakenly supposed Gerald actually enjoyed his company or gazing at his noxious verdant suit. Carl was originally from Brooklyn, and if his suit didn't give that away, his voice did. He'd been working on Wall Street for Drexel Burnham when it closed its doors, and he had been grateful for the job at Davis & Dash. Gerald needed to keep him grateful.

The oaf just sat there sweating. Gerald allowed himself a tiny bit of sarcasm. "Well, Carl, I thought we might take a look at the list before sales conference, just so we could be sure everything was set up." Carl nodded his bristly head, which the remark had flown right over, and took out a list, which he handed to Gerald.

"These are my candidates," he said. "The price is right, and the ISBN numbers are similar." Carl always hoped that—if unearthed in any way—their joint fraud could look like miskeyed entries. Gerald doubted that, but *he* was determined that there would be no discovery in the first place.

He looked over the sheet that Carl had handed him. There were only four titles on it, but none of them would be able to "lend" more than five or six thousand copies to *Twice in the Papers*. Gerald looked up at Carl. "This won't be enough," he said flatly.

"Well, with your legitimate sales, and a boost of twenty or twenty-five thousand copies—"

Gerald shook his head. "I have to be guaranteed a minimum of seventy thousand hardcover copies," Gerald told Carl.

Pollenski shook his head. "*Seventy* thousand?" he asked. "That's including your actual sales?"

"Sales or no sales," Gerald told him. "I want to touch a hundred thousand. I don't want there to be *any* doubt about the success of this book. I'll make sure that it will appear in the media as a success. You'll make sure it appears that way on our bottom line. If it doesn't make the *New York Times* bestseller list, well, that's the luck of the draw and their Byzantine weighting system." Gerald shrugged. No one knew for sure how the *Times* compiled its list. He remembered the article in *Business Week* exposing the fact that large numbers of books were bought from specific bookstores that were involved in calculating the placement of bestsellers on the list. In the old days, fifty thousand copies would guarantee you a place on the list. Now the framework had changed. A Crichton or a Waller could sell a million hardcover copies and throw the rest of the list off. "So, Carl. That's our target."

Carl swallowed. "Look. I would like to. But I can't get seventy thousand copies onto your account sheet," Carl said. "Not without taking bigger risks than I'm prepared to take."

Gerald smiled, but it was the smile he used to freeze men's blood. "Carl, I know you can if you simply think about it a little longer. Let's choose another dozen books we could borrow from."

"A dozen! You don't understand. Every new book we bring into this represents a significant risk. It has got to be keystroked. The chances of misposting a credit are good—it happens all the time—but the chances of misposting sales of a dozen books, and all to one account, are virtually nil. If anyone examined—"

"No one is examining anything," Gerald snapped, "and I need another seventy thousand hardcover sales."

He was implacable, and he knew it, and he didn't care. This book would not be a failure, not in anyone's eyes. He needed the next contract forlornly. And this book would sell. And if it sold a hundred thousand copies on its own, he would *still* add to the figure. He merely had to make sure that his figures did not contradict those in *USA Today,* which had started a revolutionary bestseller list based on actual point of sale.

"Too bad about *SchizoBoy*. It would be a pleasure to have credited some of Weston's sales against mine." Gerald went over the list again, picking out a few backlist titles he expected would continue to sell modestly. Then he added three new titles. At last he circled half a dozen more. He handed the list to Carl, who looked it over glumly.

"This is only eleven. You got another one in mind?" Carl asked. Gerald thought of his father and his prediction about "the little Italian novel." "We could add the Clapfish book to the list," Gerald said. "No one will notice if some of her sales disappear."

# 57

> Editors seek out the first novels with the seductiveness of Don Juans; the pleasure of discovery is one of the obvious reasons.
>
> —*William Targ*

Camilla showed up at the Chelsea address of Alex Simmons fifteen minutes early, bringing a copy of her manuscript and the precious letter from Davis & Dash along with her. It wasn't as if she thought that Alex Simmons might doubt her word—she knew Alex had been put in the picture by Emma Ashton, but carrying the little portfolio made her feel more secure, more like a real writer, whatever that was. And after the meeting with Mr. Byron, Camilla needed all the support she could muster.

Alex Simmons's office was not what she expected, nor was the neighborhood. Chelsea, nothing like London's Chelsea, was a collection of residential brownstone streets mixed with wide commercial avenues. It was on Manhattan's West Side, just above Greenwich Village. Several of the streets she'd walked from the tube stop had been very attractive, but this one looked a bit down-at-the-heel, and the several steps she had to negotiate to descend to the ground level at Ms. Simmons's address were cracked, while the foyer was littered and bare of plants or ornamentation. In London there would be a neat garden, or at least box hedge and a few evergreens. In Italy there would be a profusion of flowers to dispel the prison-yard atmosphere. The windows were also barred, not to mention dusty. Camilla shrugged. Although she had expected something more upmarket, or even more uptown, she was still grateful for this woman's interest.

That she would be one of Ms. Simmons's first clients would bring certain advantages, Camilla thought, but that must be weighed against the disadvantage that Alex Simmons surely was not yet a well-established agent: hardly an Andrew Wylie, whom tabloids in London had labeled "The Jackal" for the killer deal he made for Martin Amis.

Well, I suppose I'm not in the killer-deal category, nor will I ever be, Camilla thought. She would never own a Canaletto, drive a Roller, or even own her own flat. It was enough that she was here, in New York, with a book about to be published and at least two agents apparently eager to represent her. Camilla smiled and buzzed the intercom.

The office was a single room that held file cabinets along one wall, a colorful framed Jasper Johns over a desk, and a small sitting area. It wasn't much, but it was orderly, and the woman who turned to greet her was tall, well groomed, and very well dressed. Could she be the P.A.? Camilla wondered. As usual she felt awkward and shy with any new person, and this woman made her feel a bit dowdy in her plain skirt and sweater. But no. It was surely Alex Simmons herself. This was a start-up—she didn't seem to have a secretary.

"You must be Camilla," the tall woman said and extended her arm. Her handshake was very firm, and she kept hold of Camilla's own hand a bit longer than Camilla thought was quite necessary. But Americans were like that. "Come sit down." There was a small loveseat, a low table in front of it, and a straight-backed chair. Camilla took the chair, though she wasn't sure she was expected to. Still, she was so eager for this meeting that her physical comfort hardly mattered.

"I loved your book," Ms. Simmons said. "But somehow I expected you would be older."

"I expected you would be, too." Camilla smiled. Ms. Simmons laughed.

"I would say that we are both protégées, but neither of us is *that* young. Still, pretty accomplished for a first novel."

Alex Simmons paused. "It *is* your first novel?" she asked. Camilla nodded. "You haven't published under any other name? Or published in London?" Camilla shook her head. Why was the woman looking at her so intently? Alex smiled. "Well, jolly well done, then, as you might say."

"I doubt I'd say anything like that," Camilla told her coolly. Somehow this meeting wasn't going quite as she expected it to. They weren't clicking. In fact, she wasn't sure she liked this woman at all. Was it something about agents? Why the suspicion? Was it complimentary, indicating that Camilla's work seemed very professional, or was it denigrating, because she was under suspicion? "Do you doubt my word? Or my ability?" Camilla asked her.

Ms. Simmons laughed. "Oh, God! Neither one. Just getting things clear. You know, it's just that there's always a certain advantage to working with a first novel. Critics are eager to discover a new voice. For some reason they're just as eager to be disappointed by a second novel." She shrugged. "Human nature? Envy of their own creation? Who knows? Anyway, I wanted to be sure what I was working with here."

Camilla hardly knew what to do. This woman seemed very savvy but also more than a little off-putting. Perhaps it was best to get up and walk out of the office. But where would she go, except back to Mr. Byron, who was unthinkable. If Ms. Simmons felt Camilla's discomfort, she didn't show it. Instead, she gave her a sunny smile—all those white American teeth—and said, "I think we really have something here, Camilla. Middle-age romance is in. Just now the market is hot, especially for short books. Readers don't want the old Michener and Sheldon behemoths." She lifted a couple of smallish books from the neat stack on her desk. "They want a quick, light read for less than twenty bucks, and they want a little sentiment. They also want to feel smart, if it's at all possible. Your book will do it all. It has wit, but it also has the sentiment. I think we might get the literary market *and* the commercial one if we play our cards right."

"But I really didn't see this as a particularly sentimental book," Camilla protested, surprised. In fact, she was offended. She had tried to imbue her woman characters with dignity, despite their fussy ways and little foibles. And the actual romance was very minor, just a subplot and not the point of the book at all. She looked again at Alex. "Of course, I'd be grateful if it was a commercial success, but do you really think it's likely?"

"Not likely, but possible." Ms. Simmons leaned forward. "I know you're going to talk to some other agents. Fine. And maybe you're not sold on me yet. Perhaps you don't think highly of me. But let me tell you what your agent is supposed to do for you." She paused. "Your agent is *not* your editor, nor your business manager, nor your mother. What we should do for you is see your greatest market potential and help you achieve it. We do it by placing you with the right publisher, selling your foreign rights, overseeing your publicity, and positioning you in the publishing world." Ms. Simmons flashed her another winning smile. "I'm prepared to do all of that. It's going to take some work. And you won't have this chance—to be making your debut—ever again. If you miss it, the boat is gone. I'm willing to get on your team. And I think that together we might have quite a potential."

Camilla nodded. This woman was not stupid, and at the very least Camilla was getting an education. But she was also getting rather frightened. Was that part of a ploy? Well, she'd question her based on what Alfred Byron had said. Despite her shyness, Camilla asked, "Do you think the characters need to be younger?"

"Younger? No."

"Do you think there should be more sex?"

"Certainly not! Did Pam Mantiss suggest that?"

"No. Someone else did."

"Well, forget about it. Everyone is a writer manqué."

Alex Simmons stopped smiling then. She looked hard at Camilla. "Let me ask *you* a question: Have you started another book?"

Camilla nodded.

"Great. Then let me ask you *another* question: How are you going to live while you finish it? Do you have money of your own?"

"Not really. I thought I'd live on the advance."

Ms. Simmons actually snorted. "You *do* think highly of me," she laughed. "I know I can do better than the twenty thousand that Davis & Dash offered, but not much. How long can you live on that in New York? And anyway, you'll only get half of it. You won't get the other half until publication, and I wouldn't expect the book to come out until next spring, at the earliest." She was talking quickly, turning over papers on her desk. "How in the world are you planning to live for more than a year in New York City on twelve or fifteen thousand dollars, less my fee—which is ten percent—less taxes, which I suggest you pay right up front."

"I only get half the money?" Camilla asked, stunned and dismayed. She didn't know that most crucial fact, and of course she hadn't thought to inquire of Emma over dinner, or of Mr. Byron. It wasn't just her shyness. She'd been taught never to talk of money. It was rude, even shocking. Yet one had to, to live. Camilla felt a knot of panic tighten in her chest.

"You only get half the money," Ms. Simmons told her, nodding knowingly. "*And* you'll have to go through a pretty onerous editing cycle, then probably be involved in some publicity for the book. At least we hope so. Publicity is very important. Meanwhile, you'll also have to be working on your new manuscript. With all that, do you think you could still have it done in a year?"

Camilla shrugged. She had never tried to do a book by schedule, and she'd never been through an "onerous editing cycle."

"Look, here's one way we could approach this," Ms. Simmons said. "I *could* go to Davis & Dash for a two-book deal. I know that Pam Mantiss will fight like hell against it, because she doesn't want to buy a pig in a poke and—if she does—she certainly will want to buy it very cheaply. But the advantage of a two-book deal, *if* I could get it, is it would give you more money up front—maybe thirty thousand dollars." The knot in Camilla's chest loosened for a moment. "The disadvantage is that if your first book does well, you've sold your second one for peanuts," Alex Simmons continued. "Of course, you'll make it up eventually in royalties, but you'll be waiting two years before you'll see your first check."

"Two *years*?" Camilla asked. The knot came back. Her voice sounded faint in her own ears. "Why so long?"

"Publishers do their accounting and issue royalties only twice a year, and then they are always reflecting with the period that *ended* six months before. Plus, they'll deduct your advance from the first royalties. That's why smart agents try to get the biggest advance they can—otherwise the publisher is holding your earned money for over a year. Think of the interest they earn on the float! And Davis & Dash, because they're so big and they can get away with it, is one of the worst. I hear they've just redone their reporting system and now they're four months behind what they usually are."

"What's the alternative?" Camilla asked, more frightened than before. She'd come to New York with the expectation of a check, a career, and a new way of life. Instead, it seemed, everything had become more costly, the money wasn't there at all, and she had nothing to fall back on. Oh, she couldn't bear to go back to waiting tables or those other jobs from her student days!

"Well, we *could* try to auction the book. It's not what's usually done with a book like this, but all I need for an auction is get two publishers interested. And then get them bidding against each other. Still, I'd have to submit it to a lot of publishers."

Camilla paused. "You mean take it back from Emma Ashton?" she asked.

"Not take it back, exactly. They don't own it. They've got no contract with you."

"No, but she was the one who helped me."

"Yeah. And I'm trying to help you now. We're talking business. We try to get a few editors, the more literary types who are looking for the next Amy Tan, and we tell them you're it. I probably couldn't get more than fifty thousand for the book, maybe less, but half of that ought to hold you for a while, at least until you get the draft of your next book finished."

Camilla sat there stunned. She couldn't possibly withdraw her book from Davis & Dash. The Ashtons had been kinder to her than her own family. They were the only people she knew in New York. Emma had even been so kind as to send her to Alex Simmons, who in return was suggesting she betray Emma! Camilla shook her head. "I'd prefer to stay with Davis & Dash," she said coldly.

The agent shrugged. "Well, they're a good house. And Pam Mantiss is smart, no doubt about it. Let's just hope she really likes the book and wants to get behind it. Because what they propose to do to promote it is as important as what they pay for it. But what will *you* do? Financially, I mean?"

"I guess I'll have to get a job," Camilla said, and the whole bubble that she had built for her future seemed to burst right there in that small dim office. There would be no charming flat, there would be no mornings of contemplation over her tea. There would be no relaxed but agonizingly pleasant choice between this word and that, no long lunches with her editor, afternoons in the library reading room, meetings with other writers.

Though she hadn't had it long, the thought of giving up the writing life gave her a physical stabbing pain. She couldn't bear to. She couldn't say writing made her happy, but it wasn't about happiness, in the long view, was it? It certainly didn't satisfy her—her work wasn't nearly good enough, would probably never be good enough. But it was the striving, the movement from nothing to something and then on to something better, that mattered. Editing, though onerous, was necessary in writing just as mistakes were necessary in life. It was the hope for perfectibility and the hopelessness of it that kept Camilla at her desk. What in the world was she going to do? What had she been thinking? She'd returned to New York, the toughest city in the world, without a means of earning a decent living. And Camilla simply couldn't face going back to the dreadful, pinched life of a student again. She felt far too old and tired for it.

Alex Simmons was looking at her closely. Camilla hoped her agony didn't show. "It's imperative you finish your new book within the year. Otherwise you'll lose momentum. The market forgets quickly nowadays." The two of them sat there silently for a few moments. "Maybe I could get you a part-time job," Alex offered. "Something in publishing. It wouldn't hurt you to get to know a few people. What do you think?"

"I don't have a clue," Camilla told her.

"Hello, Emma. It's Camilla Clapfish."

"What's up, Camilla?" Emma asked. She was up to her neck in a dozen things, but she focused on Camilla. She liked the woman.

"Well, actually, I just thought I'd report in after my meeting with Alex Simmons."

Emma felt herself blush at the sound of Alex's name. Luckily, she was just on the phone. "Oh, great. How did it go?" she managed to ask.

"A bit of an eye-opener, really. I guess it was a necessary step. There's so much I don't know about the business of publishing. It's all really very complicated, isn't it?

Contracts, advances, foreign rights, commissions." She paused. "I'm actually rather more confused than I was before," Camilla admitted.

Even over the phone Emma could hear her discomfort. She needed new-author pep talk number eleven. "Well, it seems that there are two kinds of authors," Emma told her. "The ones who really like and understand business. They stay involved with it. But the majority are the ones that don't. They just let their agents handle it. I imagine you'd be one of the latter type."

"Well, actually I'd like to be. And I think Alex Simmons is quite good. At least she seems so. But her advice has really presented me with a problem."

"What's that?" Emma asked brightly.

"Well, it's really rather awkward. It seems that she's recommending that she do something she calls 'shop the manuscript around' or even auction it, to get me the greatest advance. Though I admit I need the money, I feel I'm committed to you. What do you think? I won't go with Alex Simmons, though I think she's most competent, if you tell me not to. And I certainly won't withdraw the manuscript without your permission."

Emma's eyes had already opened wide, and her mouth was hanging open as well. Alex had suggested shopping the manuscript around? To take it away from Davis & Dash? Emma couldn't believe it. Aside from the trouble it would make for Emma with Pam and Gerald, how could Alex betray her like this? After all, *she* was the one who sent Camilla to Alex in the first place. What was going on? Surely Camilla had gotten something wrong, but the terms she was using—"shopping around," "auction"—were agent's terms. Emma tried to take a deep breath, to not make a judgment, and to be sure not to show her surprise and concern to Camilla, who had continued talking without realizing Emma's attention had wandered.

"The point is," she was saying, "I feel very grateful to you and Frederick. I know that, as Alex Simmons put it, business is business, but I certainly would prefer to work with you than anyone, and I don't want to do anything that might be disloyal. What is the protocol? I'm all new at this, you see. So I'm calling you to help me decide what to do."

Emma very nearly groaned aloud. This was getting worse and worse. She knew she never should have suggested an agent to Camilla, and now the conflict of interest had deepened in four different directions at once! First, Emma was paid to serve Davis & Dash's interest, and she took her responsibility seriously. She shouldn't be looking after Camilla's interests. But she already felt that Camilla was a friend, new to publishing and New York City, and she ought to be given some good business advice. As if that wasn't enough, Emma certainly didn't want to turn Camilla off about Alex and lose a client for Alex, especially since Alex had been so enthusiastic about the book and seemed dedicated to it. Finally, Emma's feelings kept asking over and over how Alex could possibly betray her in this way. *Why* would she? What had Camilla quoted? "*Business is business.*" Was that how Alex felt? Emma sat, miserable and confused.

Camilla must have sensed her discomfort. "Perhaps I shouldn't be bothering you with this," she continued. "I know I'm expected to take care of myself, and you've been ever so generous already. I do like Alex Simmons. She seems much more on-target than Mr. Byron."

"Byron?" Emma said and rolled her eyes. Alf Byron, the hyena of agents. "What did you see *him* for?"

"Pam Mantiss suggested it."

Of course. One hand washing the other. But Emma was in no position to criticize Pam, since she wasn't clean on this. Still, Alf Byron. An illiterate so crass that he thought *Howards End* was a gay novel. "What did Alf Byron say?" she asked.

"That I should rewrite the book and make them college girls on a summer holiday."

Emma hooted with laughter. "Perfect! Well, why don't we meet for a drink and talk?"

"I'd be very grateful," Camilla said, sounding sincere.

"Why don't I come over tomorrow evening?" Emma proposed, looking at her appointment book. "Shall I just drop by Frederick's?"

"Oh, could you manage it?" Camilla asked. Her relief was obvious. They agreed on a time, though Emma *wasn't* so sure she could manage it. Not without being deeply upset by whatever was going on with Alex.

# 58

> I see my [editorial] role as helping the writer to realize his or her intention. I never want to impose any other goal on the writer, and I never want the book to be mine.
>
> —*Faith Sale*

Opal sat at Terry's desk, the enormous pile of galleys on her left. On her right was the tower of Terry's manuscript, and Opal was attempting, line by line, to compare each and every word to make sure that *The Duplicity of Men* would be produced exactly the way Terry wrote it. She agonized over every correction. What had Terry meant? Opal pushed her reading glasses up to the top of her head and pinched the part of her nose, just above the bulbous end, where her glasses always left a mark.

She looked out the window at the cleared yard and the beginnings of the garden she had started there. Will the flowers have bloomed and faded and lost their petals before she was done with this job? Opal looked down at the two pages before her. She'd never had any idea before of how much tedious work it took to actually make a book happen, beyond just the writing of it. This was making her hand cramp and bringing on a headache. Of course, most manuscripts were not 1,114 pages long, and most authors were working from their originals, not this blurry, third-generation photocopy of Terry's manuscript. But surely all authors had to work with typesetters, and though the manuscript may not have been easy to read, Opal was appalled and frightened by the mistakes she had already found. One chapter had the last three pages lopped off, and it had taken Opal almost three hours to find that the missing text had been inserted ninety-one pages later. Characters' names were misspelled in such original ways that Opal herself got confused. And the spelling in general! The spelling and the punctuation errors were beyond conception: colons interspersed almost anywhere, word breaks hyphenated willy-nilly, a peculiar bracket that did not seem to be part of the English language popped up again and again, while quotes opened but never closed. As for paragraphs! Well, Terry might almost have not bothered with them, since these on the galleys so often bore no relation to her own indents. There were sentences duplicated from the bottom of one page to the top of the next. How, Opal wondered, did authors have the strength to go through galleys again and again, when she herself knew that even a missing italic could have such an impact on the way a sentence read? Opal sighed and promised herself that, despite the tedium, despite the dreadfulness of the work, she would make sure that every page was carefully checked as many times as necessary.

But there was the rub—when, by accident, she had reread a page that she had previously corrected, Opal had found not one but *two* inconsistencies she had failed to notice. Disgusted, she got up from the desk, walked to the stove, and put some water on for tea. Not that she wanted any, but perhaps the caffeine would freshen her. And maybe the job wouldn't look so impossible when she returned to it.

As she poured the boiling water into her mug to steep, she made a quick mental calculation. She had been able to do about thirty pages a day during this first week. If she could keep up at that pace, or do a little better—why, it would still take her over a month to get the corrections made! And she didn't have a month. Emma Ashton had explained that to get on the fall list they had to have the galleys back by the end of next week. Then they would be sent to these same pathetic typesetters and—Emma had explained to Opal's despair—the process would be gone through again to be sure the corrections had, in fact, been made. Opal figured that the whole thing might take her another three or four months.

That brought up the question of whether or not she was to give up her job in Bloomington, because before then the library would insist they had to know. With a sigh, Opal picked up her tea and went to stand by the window. Though it was already dark in the apartment, sunlight fell on the raised brick bed against the far wall. To her surprise, Opal saw that Aiello was out there, stirring up some of the earth, several plastic bags arranged around him. She rapped on the window with her knuckles.

Aiello heard the noise, turned, and approached her. She pushed open the window so she could talk to him, but he spoke first. "Just thought I'd help you with the weeding," he said, though it was clear there were no weeds at all. "And I thought I'd put in a few marigolds for you, while I was at it." That explained the bags, she realized.

"Thank you, Mr. Aiello. That's very kind, but I don't care much for marigolds."

"Everybody likes marigolds," Aiello told her. "Hey, you plant them now, they'll bloom all summer."

"I know," she said. "They'll bloom and bloom in orange and yellow. They'll smell very strong. This garden will have very few flowers, and all of them will be lightly scented and white."

"Listen," Aiello told her, "you can't beat marigolds. You know, they keep away bugs."

"I did know that," she told him. "It's because of that objectionable scent. You see, both the bugs and I don't care for them, and I told you that I'm only planting white flowers. Sort of a memorial to my daughter, you know." She was embarrassed to resort to it, but she had to stop him.

"Right." Aiello nodded, then paused. "I could just put them in along one side," he offered. "Pity to waste them."

"No, thank you," Opal managed to say without snapping. Then, mercifully, she was saved by the bell.

"Who could that be?" Aiello asked, and though it was true she had virtually no visitors, Opal didn't appreciate the comment.

Of course, it was Roberta. "I left Margaret to close up—most probably a mistake," Roberta admitted. "But I thought you might come over to my apartment this evening. I miss you at the shop. I want to know how the galleys are coming along. Anyway, I made too much dinner last night for one, and it seemed a pity to waste it today in unappreciated leftovers."

Opal smiled at her friend's tact. "I would *love* to get out of here," she said. "You couldn't have come at a better time. Just let me get my sweater."

Roberta stepped in while Opal went to the closet.

"So what do *you* think of marigolds?" Aiello asked her from the window. Roberta jumped.

"Oh, it's you," she said when she recovered herself.

"He's helped with the garden," Opal explained, lifting her eyebrows to express exactly how helpful he was.

"Marigolds," Aiello repeated. "She should plant them, right?"

"But I thought this was going to be a white garden," Roberta said. "All white."

"Yeah, yeah," Aiello agreed dismissively. "It can all be white, except for the marigolds. What do ya think of them? I mean, in general."

"As Miss Jean Brodie put it, in regards to chrysanthemums, 'A very serviceable flower,'" Roberta quoted.

"See!" Aiello told Opal triumphantly.

"Mr. Aiello, it wasn't meant as praise," Opal explained and flung on her sweater. "Now, *no* marigolds. But thank you for the thought." She closed the window firmly, and she and Roberta went out to the street.

"I think you've made a conquest," Roberta said. For a moment Opal hadn't a clue as to what her friend was talking about, and then, with horror, it came to her.

"Oh, you don't think Aiello could . . . no! Oh, absolutely not! I'm older than he is, and . . . and he's an idiot."

"A cat may look at a queen," Roberta said mildly, grinning a rather feline smile. "I stand on my position. He fancies you."

"Well, I assure you that his love is unrequited—unless, perhaps, he has a hidden proofreading talent. Then I might consider a liaison worthwhile."

Opal had never been to Roberta's home. She stepped out of the elevator in the doorman building and was momentarily confused to find herself in a tiny vestibule that seemed to open right into someone's home. Then she realized that Roberta's apartment was the only one on the floor, and it was the penthouse. She followed Roberta into the small but very attractive living room. Three walls were covered with floor-to-ceiling bookshelves, except for the alcove where the fireplace was located. The fourth wall opened to a terrace. In the dying light Opal couldn't help but be drawn to the doorway and the view of bedded plants, birch trees, and the sparkling city lights arrayed behind the parapet wall. "Oh, my," she said. "This is really impressive." Roberta, already on her way into the kitchen, turned for a moment and smiled.

"Yes, the garden with the city view behind it is fun, isn't it? I'm lucky. I rented this place right after I opened the store. Back in the days of rent control. Since then it went co-op, but I never bought it. I've lived here for twenty-two years, and my rent now is only up to eight hundred and seventy dollars. Other people in the building pay three times that in maintenance alone! It hasn't made me popular, but I didn't do it as an investment strategy. I simply didn't have the money, or whatever I *did* have I always put into stock for the shop. The store is my only equity." She shrugged. "Probably not a wise financial move."

Opal followed Roberta into the spacious kitchen and helped her set the table. In just a few moments Roberta pulled together a salad, heated the French casserole, and sliced the seven-grain bread. She took out a demi-bottle of wine and, over Opal's protests, poured a little into her glass. Then they sat down in companionable silence and ate.

It wasn't long before Opal began to talk about the task in front of her. Roberta was all sympathy. "Oh, typesetters and proofreaders are all getting more and more careless. Books now are just unbelievable! I catch typos in almost every one." She shook her head. "It's an enormous job for you," Roberta said sympathetically. "Perhaps you could hire somebody to help you."

"I haven't the money, and I wouldn't trust just anyone, anyway," Opal told her. "But now I know where the term 'galley slave' came from!"

Roberta laughed, then paused. "Perhaps you would let me help. After all, you've been helping me and you haven't taken a dime. Turnabout is fair play, Opal."

"Oh, I couldn't let you. It's just too much work and too tedious."

"Unlike bookstore work," Roberta said dryly. She paused. "You know, Opal, you are a lot better at giving than you are at taking. That is not a particularly healthy way to be. Trust me, I speak from experience on this."

Roberta softened her voice. "Your daughter, I think, shared the trait. She couldn't ask for help when she needed it. But it's not too late for you to change."

Opal blinked and thought of the endless galleys awaiting her. She thought of Terry, toiling alone at a task much more difficult, more isolating, and with less companionship than she had. If only Terry had asked for help. If only . . . Opal shook her head, picked up her glass of wine, and drank it down. It was nasty stuff—not the least bit sweet. She ran her tongue against the roof of her mouth. What Roberta had said hurt, but it wasn't said to be hurtful. "Yes," Opal agreed. "I do need help. Thank you for offering."

# 59

> An editor's job is to push you, teach you, and to wear miniskirts with black mesh stockings.
>
> —*Howard Stern*

Daniel lay flat on his back, panting. Beside him, Pam lay naked, her eyes closed, wild blond hair hiding the rest of her face, one of her heavy breasts resting against the crook of his arm. He dared to glance at her again. She was as ferocious in bed as she was in business, and Daniel couldn't remember ever having fucked like this before. Even now, his penis hardened as he remembered her on her knees, then straddling him, and that last position! She had moved on him and under him with more urgency, more crazed energy, and more noise than he had ever experienced. She was frightening, but undeniably erotic. Her huge breasts alone were fascinating, almost freakish. He thought about his first wife, and Cheryl, and Judith, all small-breasted dark women. Daniel could have been smothered by Pam's enormity. Even now, the weight of her breast on his arm was arousing and alarming at the same time.

He was satisfied, and not just sexually. He had long suspected, he had hoped, that he was special, that he deserved something more than just an untenured teaching position in an obscure school. He wanted fame, and money, and recognition. He wanted access to the likes of Gerald Ochs Davis, coverage from magazines like *Vanity Fair*, and sexual gratification from women like Pam Mantiss. He turned his head toward the bedside table and the two bottles of Moët they had drunk. Vintage. What did a bottle of *that* cost here? Two hundred dollars? Three hundred? What was this room costing for the few hours they'd use it? Davis & Dash was willing to pay for it, to pay for him. And if he hadn't actually written every word of the book, well, the *idea* had been his, the nerve to do it had been *his* nerve, the strategy, the entrée through Alf Byron, all of it had taken courage, determination, and skill. He had pulled it off, and this was his reward: knowing he had "graduated," that he had made it into a new world, one he had longed to enter.

He had delivered the revised manuscript a week ago. Pam had read it and suggested they meet to "discuss" it: This tryst had resulted. Daniel smiled to himself. Apparently he had been accepted in both senses of the word. He looked over at Pam again, and her eyelids fluttered. When she opened her eyes, he looked away, then nearly jumped to find her hand wrapping itself around him.

"Mmm. Nice. Is this for me?" Even when she was being seductive, Pam managed to sound a little bit threatening. "I'd hate to waste a hard-on," she told him.

Before he could say anything, her mouth was on him. Daniel looked down at her bobbing head, and though the delicious warmth and the feel of her magic tongue made him long to close his eyes, he fought the temptation, exchanging that pleasure for the one of watching the editor in chief of Davis & Dash gobbling him. It made him harder, and it made him smile, until Pam looked up and pulled her mouth from him with a wet, sucking sound. Oh, he could hardly bear to have her stop.

"Now my turn," she said. "Since I started the Prozac it's been a bitch to come. Here, let's try this." She got up on her knees and moved them to either side of his face. Before he could react, she had settled herself on his mouth. "Now, work me, baby," she told him, her voice a growl. And, pinioned between her legs, how could he refuse?

Judith sat primly on the sofa, her hands folded on her lap. "Is it all right?" she asked. "Did they accept it?"

Daniel nodded his head, drained in every sense of the

word. All he wanted was a long hot shower and unconsciousness. But Judith, he realized with a sinking feeling, was ready for a blow-by-blow. "Everything went fine," he told her, trying to circumvent the inevitable.

"Oh, great!" She ran to him, threw her arms around him, pressing her lips to his mouth. Daniel recoiled, thinking of Pam's other lips, but then he remembered himself. He kissed Judith on the top of her head. This was unlike her. Judith wasn't demonstrative. "I'm so relieved," she was saying. "I don't think I could touch the manuscript again for any amount of money." Her eyes opened wider, reminding him of Little Orphan Annie's circles. Daniel couldn't help but compare them to the elongated slits of Pam's yellow eyes. "So, we got the money?" Judith asked. "We got the acceptance money?"

Exhausted and—for some reason—depressed, Daniel slumped into the only comfortable chair in the living room. Why was everything his responsibility, he wondered? Why was all the pressure on him? He looked at Judith again, and if his resentment was colored by guilt, he chose not to feel it. He would make *her* feel guilty.

"Yes, I got us the money. I mean, it'll be sent. But it wasn't so easy."

"I thought you said everything went fine."

"Only because I made it happen," Daniel said. "He went through every damn page. We fought chapter by chapter. It was a wrestling match." The image of Pam's legs coiled over his torso intruded, and he put his hand up to his eyes, rubbing them wearily. He'd been careful not to mention Pam's name to Judith; he's only referred to Gerald Ochs Davis.

"What about the answering-machine chapter? Is it all right? I softened it a little, but Elthea's obsession just has to be—"

Christ, he couldn't take this now. "He said he's going to think about it. He still wants it cut, but he said he'd think about it."

"And what about the ending? He can't want that happy ending. Will he take my new version?"

"I'm not sure, Judith. He said it was better, but he still thinks we have to go for something more upbeat."

"It's not better. It's much worse," Judith said angrily. "But it's not as dark as it was. He can't really expect—"

"Judith, I don't want to talk about it! I spent the whole day fighting for us. Now I don't want to spend the whole night fighting with you. I've had it." Judith looked away for a moment and bit her lip. Then she walked out of the room. Oh, Christ! Now there'd be another whole scene. Just what he needed. Daniel sighed, feeling the martyr. But instead of pouting, Judith surprised him by returning with a smile on her face and two glasses in her hands.

"Here," she said. "Drink this up and you'll feel much better." Daniel looked at the dubious contents of the ugly tumbler. The liquid was pink, and it bubbled.

"What's this?" Daniel asked suspiciously.

"Asti Spumanti," Judith said proudly. "And I made dinner to celebrate. Pot roast!" She took his hand and led him into the kitchen. The table was set with candles and a bunch of unnaturally blue carnations. Judith lifted her glass and clinked the one that Daniel was holding gingerly in his own hand. "To the acceptance check," she said. And he was forced to raise his glass as she took a tiny sip from hers.

The sweet taste of the cheap wine was disgusting. He had had vintage Moët only hours before, and he had no intention of going from that to Asti Spumanti, not now or ever. He looked at Judith and the pathetic little suburban kitchen. The smell of cooking mingled with floor wax hung in the air. He was nauseated, his jaws were tired, and he knew that he couldn't possibly manage the pot roast. Well, for appearance's sake he would have to sit down. He walked to the table and sank into one of their new kitchen chairs. He'd let her have all this when he left, he decided. He could be generous. Judith went to the refrigerator, brought out two salads, and placed one before him. Iceberg lettuce and unripe tomatoes. He thought of the subtleties of the grilled portobello mushrooms he'd had with Pam. That was the problem with Judith; she had no subtleties. It made her easy to deceive but damn difficult to live with. He sighed.

"So what did he think of chapter eleven?" Judith asked.

Daniel couldn't even remember chapter eleven. Was that Elthea's back story or the one where her husband leaves her? "Judith, I managed to get him to accept it. It was very hard work, but I managed to do it. You have no idea what it's like. I had to negotiate on every point. I did what I could, okay? And now I'm very tired and I don't really want to talk about it." Judith looked at him, her doe eyes big and round as quarters. He couldn't bear to sit there, opposite her, as she pulled her babybird-with-a-broken-wing routine. All at once he was incensed. He shouldn't have to put up with this. It was sad, and it was unfair, but the reality was he was out of her league. He'd help her to understand that, when the time was right, and then he'd leave her. She was young. Everyone's first marriage was a fiasco. She'd get over it, as he had. He laid his fork down, his salad untouched. "I'm tired and I'm going to bed," he said.

Daniel didn't bother to put on the light in the bedroom. He walked to the bed, shedding his jacket and shirt and dropping them to the floor. He sat down on his side of the mattress and pulled off his good shoes, for once not bothering with the shoe trees. He slipped out of his trousers and let them fall to the rug. Flaubert had followed him and now jumped onto the bedspread, putting his cold nose up against Daniel's naked back. "Off," Daniel told him and gave the dog's rump a push. Then, naked but for his shorts and too tired to slip into his pajamas, he lifted the blanket and inserted himself under it. He stared up at the ceiling, one of those blown-on, irregular-textured affairs. He took a deep breath. Exhausted as he was, he knew he wouldn't be able to sleep because his mind was racing.

He had been right. That's what he had to remember. He was one of the elite, one of those people who, despite obstacles, can grab at the brass ring. Well, in this case it was a gold one, and he would keep a hold of it. He was not going to fall back, be dragged back, into the old life: begging for tenure, boring sex, drinking Asti Spumanti, saving up for a winter coat. He had known he was special, and Pam Mantiss confirmed that. He might not like her, but she was smart and tough and she recognized talent when she saw it. The fact that she wanted to sleep with him was the equivalent of winning a writing prize. He was hot, and she wanted to keep him, and they both knew his book would succeed. So would he.

On the next contract there would be a lot of money. Alf Byron said that Hollywood was interested in the book. They'd meet with producers. Maybe Daniel would write the screenplay. And without the teaching job, he'd have all the time in the world to turn out the next book himself. The trouble, of course, was Judith, still sulking in the kitchen. He could see now that he had never loved her; that he had merely felt sorry for her. That was his problem: He was always adopting birds with broken wings. Cripples. That wasn't the basis for a relationship. He would have to escape, but this time it would be easier because he wouldn't stay here and have to face Don and the rest of the faculty. It would be hard on Judith for a while, sure, but then she'd go back to her daddy, finish school, and her real life would begin. In a way, she'd been lucky to have the experience.

He sighed. He knew there'd be some ugly times ahead, with lots of crying and possibly even hysteria, but unlike before, he had a cushion of money deposited in his name and the promise of this large acceptance check as well. He'd survive.

From the floor he heard Flaubert's tail thwack the carpet,

and he looked to the doorway to see Judith's dark form against the dim light from the hall. She walked across the room. Now there'd be accusations and recriminations. He sighed.

But Judith merely took off her shoes and slipped into bed, fully clothed, beside him. Gently, wordlessly, she put her arm around his torso, and Daniel had to will himself not to recoil. They would have to separate, he told himself yet again. He had another life waiting for him, and she would have to make her own. But he couldn't discuss that yet. Not tonight, when his legs were tight with exhaustion, his back hurt, and his jaw felt as if it were being pinched in a vise. He lay as stiffly as possible, but Judith managed to insinuate her arm under his neck and roll her head against his unresponsive shoulder.

"Daniel?" she asked, and he was flushed with irritation. Who else would he be? Mahatma Gandhi? She moved her warm body against his. Irrelevantly, Daniel remembered that Gandhi used to like to sleep with two young girls, one on either side, to test him and keep him warm. Judith's warmth seeped through the thin cloth of her dress. "Daniel," she said, "I wasn't just celebrating the acceptance check. I have some news, too."

Oh, Jesus! Just what he needed. Show-and-tell at this time of night! What was she going to share with him? The results of Flaubert's visit to the vet? How she'd conquered page styles on Microsoft Word? "Yes?" he asked, and tried not to let his boredom and irritation express itself in that single word.

He felt her hand searching for his, and by an act of will he didn't pull his back when she wrapped both of her small ones around it. She leaned her head against his and then, in a whisper—a whisper of doom—he heard her.

"I'm going to have a baby," she told him.

# 60

> The job of an editor in a publishing house is the dullest, hardest, most exciting, exasperating and rewarding of perhaps any job in the world.
>
> —*John Hall Wheelock*

Emma winced as she picked up the receiver. Thank God, the voice at the other end of the phone was the pleasant, down-to-earth alto of Opal O'Neal. "Emma, I have good news," she said.

"Great. I could use some."

"Why? Is anything wrong?"

How do you explain the overload and chain reactions, the constant deadlines and endless work that was Emma's daily lot? And why complain? She had chosen it. But sometimes the pressure of the workload and the corporate games in a firm as big as Davis & Dash got to her. The real botheration was that she had a growing and most unpleasant suspicion, just a small one, that if she hadn't been in publishing she might not have sparked Alex's interest. She'd written it off as unworthy of her and of Alex. But now she was afraid that it wasn't just a paranoid fantasy. Why hadn't Alex called her? Emma hadn't heard from Alex since her meeting with Camilla Clapfish. Even if Alex didn't call to make a date, why hadn't she at least called to explain about Camilla so Emma knew what was going on? Whatever the reason for Alex's silence, it plunged Emma into suspicion and misery. Don't overreact, she'd told herself. Wait and find out what's going on.

"I'm fine," Emma lied now to Mrs. O'Neal. "It's just good to hear your voice. What's your news?"

"I'll have the galleys finished right on schedule," Opal

said. "But my goodness! I hope you don't pay those people who do the typesetting very much. There were mistakes on every page. They certainly aren't good at their jobs."

Emma laughed. "Who is?" she asked.

"You are," Opal told her. "You're *very* good at your job. Why, I don't know where I'd be if not for you."

For a moment, despite the mail piled on her desk, Heather walking in with a distracted look on her face, and the list of calls she still had to make, Emma felt a calmness and pleasure. Yes, some of what she did was worthwhile. "I've asked the marketing department to get together a really good program for *Duplicity,*" Emma told Opal, while Heather mimed "emergency" and tried to point to the phone as she ran her index finger across her throat. Emma nodded at Heather and raised her index finger to indicate she needed just one minute more.

"Should I bring the galleys down to you when I'm done?" Opal was asking.

"Oh no, don't bother," Emma told her. "We'll send up a messenger."

"Oh, I wouldn't want to do that," Opal said. "What if he lost them?"

Emma smiled. "They never do. But I'll tell you what. I'll come up when they're ready and get them myself."

"Oh, that would be terrific." Opal sounded sincerely pleased. Meanwhile, Heather was waving her arms in some kind of we're-going-to-be-chopped-meat semaphore. Emma quickly said her good-byes to Mrs. O'Neal and hung up.

"What *is* it?"

"Do you have the edited manuscript from Jude Daniel?" Heather asked. Emma shook her head. It was more work she wasn't looking forward to; another book about to go into galleys for their fall list. So far, Pam had been handling it herself, a sure indicator that she expected a runaway with this one, but at this mechanical phase she'd dumped it on Emma, as she did so many thankless tasks.

"I haven't seen it," Emma told her secretary.

"Well, Pam says she got it from Jude and left it here, on *your* desk."

"When?" Emma asked. Ridiculous. After just telling Opal O'Neal how careful they were, was there a manuscript missing? An edited manuscript. My God! "When did she leave it here?"

"She didn't say. Last night or the day before." Emma's stomach dropped. She'd been through everything on her desk since this morning. There was no edited Daniel manuscript.

"Okay, let's not panic," Emma said in a voice calmer than she felt. Heather's eyes were already big with panic. "She said she left it on my desk?"

"Yes, or on mine," Heather whispered. "But I swear there hasn't been anything new on my desk in the last two days except for the Trawley thing and the mail."

"Listen, I'm sure it's here somewhere, probably on *Pam's* desk. That is, if she didn't leave it in a taxi." Heather's eyes grew even bigger. A mistake to mention *that* possibility, Emma realized. If Pam *had* done that, they knew they'd take the fall.

They spent the next forty-five minutes—time Emma couldn't spare—searching her office, Heather's cubicle, both desks, Pam's secretary's desk, and the hallways in between. The manuscript had disappeared, but Emma kept calm. She'd been through enough of these false alarms with Pam to take it one step at a time, the way you had to with alcoholics. She wondered if there was a twelve-step program for codependent editors, then wondered if that wasn't a redundant phrase. After all, weren't *all* editors codependent?

When the phone rang again Emma considered not answering it, but it might just be Alex. She had left only one message for Alex; she didn't want to seem too needy. Emma picked up the phone. "Emma Ashton?" a voice inquired. Not Alex's.

"Yes," she said, disappointed and a little—just a little—more concerned.

"Please hold for Susann Baker Edmonds."

God, Emma hated to be called by a secretary! She thought it was the height of rudeness and, on impulse, hung up. She knew it was wrong, but sometimes she just couldn't help it. When the phone rang again she sighed and decided to take her medicine now instead of on her voice mail. "Emma Ashton?" the voice asked again, and again Emma indicated it was she. "We got cut off."

"Oh, it's been happening here all day," Emma lied.

"Well, let's hope it doesn't happen *now*," the voice said. "I'll put Miss Baker Edmonds on." There was an irritatingly long pause.

"Emma, dear." Susann's voice purred in Emma's ear. "I have some sketches here that I'd like picked up."

"Sketches?" Emma asked. Was the woman now illustrating her books as well as writing them? Emma couldn't help but wonder which she'd do worse. "Sketches of what?"

"They're sketches of the clothes I'm going to be wearing for my book tour. I'm sure the publicity department would like to distribute them. I thought they might be sent to the newspaper's fashion pages. It's such a big tour, and I'm sure people in those smaller cities will be interested in my choice of designers."

Emma almost laughed aloud. As if anyone cared what a *writer* wears, Emma thought. It was hard enough to get the public to care about what writers wrote! "Well, send them over," she said. "I'll bring them to the publicity department." And *they'll* laugh for twenty minutes and then toss the sketches into the circular file. Let *them* deal with it.

"Would you mind sending over a messenger?" Susann asked sweetly.

"Certainly," Emma agreed, and jotted a note to herself. She would have to call the mailroom, fill out a form, have

Heather bring it down, and have the cost deducted from her budget. Meanwhile, Susann Baker Edmonds had a car, a driver, *and* a full-time secretary, not to mention the millions of dollars in advance money. Oh well. Emma merely shrugged.

"Thank you," Susann said, and mercifully, she hung up.

Heather walked in, her face pale. "I just can't find it," she said. It looked to Emma as if tears were rising in her eyes.

"Don't worry," Emma assured her, though she too was becoming distinctly nervous. "It's going to show up. And anyway, in case of emergency Jude Daniel probably has another copy. Why don't I just call and check on it before we do anything else?"

"But if he finds out that we've lost it—"

"I'm not going to tell him *that*. I'm merely going to ask if he has another copy. Meanwhile, we'll keep looking. One step at a time. But it will give us another option." Heather took a deep breath and nodded. Emma smiled at her. "Keep looking. By the way, while I was on the phone, did I get a call from Alex Simmons?"

"No," Heather said, and left Emma alone to contact Jude Daniel.

Emma looked through her card file and found the upstate number. She picked up the phone, but instead of a dial tone there was a caller already on the line. "Emma?" a crackly voice asked. "Hello. Are you there?"

Not now, Emma thought with a sinking feeling. Not Anna Morrison. Emma just didn't have time to be kind to her today. "Hello, Anna," Emma said as if her last breath of air was being used to get the words out. "What can I do for you?"

"Have you found out if there have been any more sales on my book?"

What was this? Anna hadn't even had a book in print for over a decade. Had the woman finally moved over the line from loneliness to delusion? Emma had no time to find out. "As a matter of fact, Anna, I was just going to call a marketing meeting. It might come up. I'll call you as soon as I can."

"You're such a darling, Emma. Thank you." Mercifully, Anna too hung up.

Emma couldn't get on top of this day. She dialed Daniel's number and waited while the phone rang. She knew the chances of getting anything but an answering machine nowadays were slim: Emma spent the largest portion of her time talking to machines and listening to her own recorded missed calls. Was all of this technological advance really so efficient?

But by the fifth ring she realized that Jude Daniel was one of the last dozen Americans left who did not have a machine. Emma was about to hang up when the call was actually answered, and by a live voice. "Hello?" a woman asked. Was this his secretary or his wife? Emma wondered. What could she say; what message could she possibly leave, that wouldn't make their new about-to-be-a-star author feel they treated his work cavalierly?

"Is Jude Daniel there?" Emma asked.

She heard a sharp intake of breath, and then the woman said, "My husband isn't home."

Well, there was a place to start. May as well be cordial and social. "Oh. Hello, Mrs. Daniel. This is Emma Ashton. I work at Davis & Dash. We're publishing your husband's book."

"Yes, I know," Mrs. Daniel said, her voice almost inaudible. "What do *you* have to do with it?" Emma wondered if there was something wrong with the connection. Had she really heard that? "What do you have to do with it?" Mrs. Daniel repeated.

As little as possible, Emma thought, but she tried to sound enthusiastic. "Well, I'm one of the editors here."

"Are you my husband's editor?" the woman asked, and now her voice was much stronger, but also tight and hard. "I thought Mr. Davis was his editor."

Emma couldn't help but smile. GOD didn't even edit his *own* books, let alone other people's. Still, she couldn't afford to offend. Perhaps they'd been told the editing was Gerald's. But she doubted it. "No. Mr. Davis has been involved, but he's not actually editing the book. Pam Mantiss is. She's our editor in chief and *very* important." Emma wanted to be sure that the wife wouldn't be put off.

"Is she pretty?" Mrs. Daniel asked. Or at least that was what Emma thought she heard. What the hell was going on? Could the woman be drunk? Or perhaps crazy?

"*Is* this Mrs. Daniel?" Emma asked again.

"My name is Judith Gross. My husband is Jude Daniel," the woman said, then laughed bitterly.

Oh Lord, Emma thought. Why was every single thing so damn complicated? All she wanted was to find a copy of a manuscript, which wasn't even her responsibility in the first place. Well, she'd just push on. "We know that Mr. Daniel has finished his revisions to *In Full Knowledge*," Emma said tentatively, and she could almost swear she heard a snort on the other end of the phone. Maybe the woman *was* drunk. "Anyway, I was wondering if there was a copy of the manuscript up there with you?"

"Yes," Ms. Gross said flatly. "I have a copy."

Thank God! "Well, we just might want to see it," Emma said, relieved. Worst case, they could get this copy FedExed down to them. At least there *was* a copy. "We've had a few problems reading this one," she lied. "I don't *think* we'll need to see it, but it's good to keep it available. May I call you for clarification, or if another copy of the manuscript is necessary?"

"Sure," Ms. Gross said. Then she paused for a moment. "Did Pam Mantiss like the changes?"

This was one of the stranger conversations Emma had had, and she'd had plenty of strange conversations with authors, their family, and friends. "Well, I wasn't directly involved, but we're going into galleys soon, so I think that she did." Emma tried to be placating. "You must be very proud of your husband. There's a lot of excitement about this book here. That's why Pam Mantiss herself is involved." There was a pause at the other end of the line, and after a moment or two of silence, Emma thought the woman had hung up. But she hadn't. Instead, Emma distinctly heard her clear her throat.

"So, is she pretty?" Judith Gross asked again.

Emma didn't know what to say. As far as she was concerned, Pam was a gorgon, and why would this woman care, anyway? "Well, she's . . . attractive."

"How old is she?"

"I'm not sure. Um. About forty, I guess."

"And is she married?" Ms. Gross asked.

"No, she's divorced." This woman *was* crazy, and Emma only needed to get off the phone. "Well, it was nice to talk to you, Ms. Gross. I'll ring back if we have any more trouble reading our copy." The hell she would. If they couldn't find the manuscript, Heather could make the next call. "Anyway, if we need it, you can send one down to us at our expense," Emma said cheerily and hung up, shaking her head.

"Heather!" she yelled. "Jude Daniel has a copy of the manuscript if we need it."

But Heather came in doing some kind of break dance and waving an interoffice envelope. She pointed to it and sang, "*In Full Knowledge*. Pam put it in the interoffice mail. It was in the mailroom all the time." Emma nodded and shrugged. Typical Pam Mantiss move. "Can you believe it?" Heather asked. "All that pain for nothing! She never gave me the manuscript. She *didn't* drop it off on my desk. *She* sent it in the interoffice. Look, the envelope is in her writing! Instead of walking twenty feet down the hall to my desk, she sends it twenty stories down to the basement for one of those idiots to lose it on a back shelf until now." Emma didn't have the energy to do more than nod, clearly disappointing Heather, who was obviously looking for a common outrage.

"Well, at least we have it and I don't have to call that madwoman upstate again," Emma sighed.

"Who's that?" Heather asked, and Emma told her about the odd conversation with Jude Daniel's wife. "Pretty?" Heather echoed. "The woman is Medusa. But Pam turns men *and* women to stone. Everyone knows the 'Preying Mantiss' hunts down and sleeps with all the men authors. Ecc-ch! Who in the world cares what she looks like?"

"Obviously, Mr. Daniel's wife does." And it occurred to Emma, for the first time, that the woman's paranoia was not that different from her own. Emma thought of Alex. Of course, Pam's always been a star-fucker. And Jude Daniel is the next rising star. His wife *isn't* crazy. She's probably on to something.

Heather shrugged and went back to her desk, leaving Emma alone with a room full of unpleasant thoughts. God, what was Alex doing now? Why hadn't she called? Was there someone else? Had Emma let herself be used? She never should have introduced Camilla and Alex. She never had and never will again mix business with pleasure. She sighed. Was it a Chinese proverb that promised that no good deed would go unpunished?

She lifted the phone and dialed the number she already knew by heart. And after all that, Emma was greeted only by Alex's voice on a machine. For a moment Emma considered hanging up—she certainly wasn't prepared to face this in a cold recorded message. But it had to be faced. So when the beep came she simply announced her name and asked that Alex call her at home in the evening. After all her anticipation, she knew she wouldn't look forward to this call when it came.

# 61

> In America there seems to be an idea that writing is one big cat-and-dog fight between the various practitioners of the craft.
>
> —*William Styron*

The woman with the bad perm and the lipstick painted too far outside her lip line looked up from her reception console. "Yes?" she asked.

Susann gave the woman her best smile and, reading the woman's name off the Davis & Dash ID card hanging around her neck, said, "Miriam, please call Mr. Davis's office for me."

"Does he expect you?" the woman asked.

"Of course," Susann told her briskly. Miriam would, no doubt, be embarrassed in a moment when she realized to whom she was talking, but Susann could be gracious.

"Your name?" the woman asked.

"Susann Baker Edmonds," the author told her, and gave her an understanding look.

But without even a glimmer of recognition the receptionist flicked her eyes away and punched in an extension number. She looked up without a smile on her clownish lips. "The line is busy," she reported flatly. "Take a seat."

Susann blinked. It was outrageous behavior. This would never have happened to her at Peterson. Imogen used to wait for her in reception! There she had been treated with respect, her name and her face recognized. But Susann managed, once again, to give her best smile. "Why don't you try calling Mrs. Perkins's line?" she said. "I've come to discuss my book tour. I know Mr. Davis wouldn't want to be kept waiting, Miriam."

"It's *Marion*," the receptionist said. Then she shrugged, consulted her screen, and punched in another extension. She looked up at Susann. "What's *your* name again?"

Susann's smile dropped. She repeated her name, enunciating clearly. But the woman was already saying to Mrs. Perkins or whoever had picked up, "I got a Susan Almond down here." There was a brief pause during which Susann clenched her painful hands into fists. "Susan Almond," the receptionist repeated. "She *says* she's got an appointment."

Susann reached forward and snatched the receiver out of the idiot woman's hands. "This is Susann Baker Edmonds," she said. "I have an appointment with Mr. Davis."

Mrs. Perkins's voice over the phone was very soothing and apologetic. "Yes, of course you do. I'll come right down myself to bring you up. It won't be a moment."

Susann thanked her and handed the receiver back to Marion. "She's coming down to get me," Susann said, and turned her back on her. She was so annoyed and flustered she'd forgotten to ask if Alf had arrived yet. Well, he must have and gone upstairs.

The reception area at Davis & Dash was a large windowed showroom that had space for not only the idiot receptionist and security desk, several sofas and chairs, but also book displays and a changing special exhibition. Today the exhibition was of children's book illustrations, and Susann ignored it. But she made a beeline for the shelves of recent releases. Most prominently displayed was a life-size cardboard cutout of a moronic Hollywood has-been clutching her ghostwritten autobiography. There also were a dozen hardcover and softcover copies of the Trawley garbage, along with an "as told to" book by a fashion model (whose claim to fame was how badly she'd been slashed by her boyfriend, ruining her not particularly successful career). There were also three books—*three*—by television sitcom actors who seemed to think they had something to say. Susann restrained herself from shaking her head. Why was it that everybody wanted to horn in on the book business? Writers didn't take side jobs as models or deejays. If you *were* an obscene radio deejay, couldn't you be satisfied with that? Why did you also have to write a *book* about being an obscene radio deejay?

Well, this was obviously the dross. She walked to the other shelf but was equally disappointed there; seven paperback romances by no-name authors, Gerald Ochs Davis's last release (now more than a year old), a book by a woman who claimed to have been raped by aliens (complete with pictures of her baby), and high on the shelves and almost out of view, three legitimate novels.

"Mrs. Edmonds." Susann turned to be greeted by Gerald's secretary, who welcomed her and ushered her into a waiting elevator. Feeling the chill, the woman tried to warm the atmosphere. "Mr. Davis is *really* looking forward to seeing you," Mrs. Perkins said.

"Has Mr. Byron arrived yet?" Susann asked.

"No," Mrs. Perkins told her, making her stomach lurch nervously. "But Mr. Davis has been waiting." Yet when Susann arrived at his office, she was surprised to find that Gerald Davis was not alone. Alf wasn't there yet, but Gerald Davis's henchman was on time. The publisher stood, extended his hand, and then introduced the young woman beside him.

"Susann, this is Wendy Brennon, our new head of publicity. I wanted her to personally supervise every moment of your tour, and I thought this was a good time for you to meet."

Susann gave Wendy her best smile and held out her hand, though her knuckles were swollen today with arthritic pain. The girl's overly firm handshake was excruciating, but Susann managed to keep the smile splashed on her face. This insignificant-looking young woman was important; she was the key to it all. But she seemed *so* young. They got younger and younger, these publicity people.

The three of them sat down in a corner of Gerald's vast

office. "We're so delighted that you're doing this tour," Gerald said. "It's going to be great for you, and great for business. Look what touring did for Newt Gingrich."

"Well, he was thinking of running for president, wasn't he?" Susann asked. "Now, after he toured, he's not." They laughed, but Susann merely waited. Where was Alf? She didn't want to have to do this meeting alone, especially not with two of them facing her. Oh, how could she bear to drag herself all around this vast country alone? "Newt must have gotten tired," she said.

"Perhaps. But I hear he sold a hell of a lot of books."

Susann smiled and nodded. "Yes. I'm looking forward to that." Should she engage in small talk and stall or face it alone? She'd kill Alf for this. She smiled again. "So, do you have the schedule?" she asked Wendy.

"Well, I have part of it," Wendy answered, handing her a three-page printed sheet. On the left margin it listed the date and the city. In the center was a listing of the scheduled interviews, radio, local TV, et cetera. On the right margin were the travel arrangements and local contacts. Susann quickly scanned the densely covered sheets. Aside from Chicago, Cincinnati, Seattle, and Los Angeles, there didn't seem to be *any* firm appointments—just "interview with press as scheduled" and "radio interview tk." Susann put the papers down in her lap and held her hands together so they wouldn't be so obvious. Is this all that had been booked so far? This was nothing. It was a nontour, a nonevent. Did they think they could get her to give up two months of her life to sign stock in the backroom of a B. Dalton in a suburban mall?

At that moment the door was flung open and Alf Byron appeared. Susann was so relieved to see him that she didn't bother to give him the look of pure annoyance she'd been preparing.

"Hello, hello." Alf slipped into a chair and turned to the disappearing Mrs. Perkins. "Coffee, please," he said. "Black with sugar." She could hear his heavy breathing.

Susann knew he shouldn't have caffeine with his heart medication, but she said nothing.

"Hi, Wendy. Hello, Gerald. Sorry. I was negotiating with April Irons. We've sold Jude Daniel's book to Hollywood! International has bought the option. They want to attach Drew Barrymore to the project."

"Congratulations," Wendy said.

Susann noticed he didn't apologize to *her*, and that he already knew this incompetent little publicity girl. And why did Jude Daniel interfere with *my* business life? He had yet to sell one damn copy of any book. Of course, she thought bitterly, she had yet to option a book to Hollywood. Men had all the luck. Women got TV miniseries.

"Hello, Alf," Gerald Davis said coolly. "We're just going over Susann's tour schedule." Wendy passed a copy to Alf, who looked it over quickly.

"Mm. Thirty-six cities already. It's starting to shape up nicely."

"Nicely?" Susann asked. "The list is very neat and very organized, but I don't quite agree. I don't see anything major and virtually nothing firm."

"Oh, I should have mentioned that we have book signings in every city," Wendy said. "I just haven't listed them here."

Book signings! As if *that* took any clout or did any good! My God, Susann could walk into any bookstore in the city, or the country for that matter, and sign copies of stock. It was media exposure that sold books—and created crowds at book signings. Howard Stern had a line of ten thousand people at one of his signings—but only after shamelessly promoting himself on radio for hours before. Without television, radio, and heavy newspaper-feature coverage there was no point to this tour. Susann looked over at Alf, waiting for him to explode. For years they'd played the good cop/bad cop game. He knew what was necessary.

But there was no explosion. Alf merely nodded mildly.

"Things will firm up as we get closer to the dates," Wendy Brennon assured them.

Susann couldn't believe it. Alf just nodded again. "That isn't good enough," Susann said.

The girl glanced at her and then back at Gerald, who had sat quietly throughout. "It's a little difficult right now to set up things so far in advance."

But Susann was having none of that. If *she* had to drag herself to Fort Worth and to Portland and to Detroit, *they* had better be certain that at the very least she was on local radio and TV, the all-important local morning show. Otherwise, what was the point? She didn't need to hide in a hotel room for hours only to duck out once or twice to bend her arthritic fingers around a pen and sign a few hundred books. "Well, this won't do. How long will it take you to get a *real* schedule?" she asked. "Because I don't leave for a tour unless a real tour is scheduled."

"It'll come, Susann," Alf said. "It will come."

Susann looked at him. Since when wasn't he pushing for commitments? Since when was he so patient? Since he'd gone Hollywood? Since he was late for her meetings because he was busy with Jude Daniel talking to some famous woman studio head? She turned back to the pages. "I don't see *any* national television here," she said. "Nothing. How do we stand on that?"

"I'm working on it," Wendy assured her. "It's just that with the sweeps at that time, and the way the talk-show lineups are going lately, there really isn't a venue for you."

"Are you *serious*? I'm not booked for *any* national shows? I've done Donahue. I've done Sally Jessy. I've been on the *Today* show twice."

Wendy hunched over. "I haven't been able to get much interest from producers for any of our writers, except for Jude Daniel."

That name again! Susann felt her mouth go bitter with bile. Jude Daniel. She hated him.

"All the shows are piling on guests—ten or a dozen per

show." Wendy was gabbling. "They want screamers or celebrities. They don't want novelists. They want cross-dressing fathers who sleep with their daughter's guinea pigs. We don't even know that the talk shows sell books anymore."

Susann stood up. "You better find an angle," she spit. "And if you don't get me on television, you can forget the tour." She looked over at the publisher. "There goes all that advance money you paid out down the drain, Gerald. I don't think Mr. Morton will like that. So I'll wait until you *find* an angle." She walked to the door. She would not be treated like some paperback original, some drugstore romance writer. "Meanwhile, we have a meeting with the marketing department," Susann reminded Alf. "That is, if you don't have any Jude Daniel Hollywood business to attend to."

Leaving his coffee unfinished, Alf followed her out of the room.

"That is the worst cover I've *ever* seen," Susann said to Jack Weinstock, who winced. "I don't mean it's the worst cover I've seen for one of *my* books. I mean it's the worst cover ever. On any book."

She surveyed the sick green-and-beige mottled jacket with the black type. Jesus! Did they think she was writing textbooks? And why was her name so small? And her photo! She was used to a huge airbrushed glossy portrait on the back cover. Instead she had been reduced to a postage stamp on the top of the back flap!

"We were trying for a *Bridges of Madison County* kind of look," Jack stuttered. "You know. Subdued. Classy."

"My jackets have always been classy. But not boring. This is boring. And ugly. This is *not* a bestselling cover."

"A bestselling cover is the cover on a bestselling book," Alf quipped. "I don't think it's bad. It's a departure, sure, but maybe you need something new."

Susann narrowed her eyes and turned on him. "Maybe I do," she said.

# 62

> When I sit at my table to write, I never know what it's going to be till I'm under way. I trust in inspiration, which sometimes comes and sometimes doesn't. But I don't sit back waiting for it. I work every day.
>
> —*Alberto Moravia*

There was no doubt in Camilla's mind that Frederick Ashton's flat was the nicest place she had ever lived. It was four enormous rooms; a drawing room that faced south and had three ten-foot French doors that opened to a Juliet balcony, a book-lined dining room, a corner master bedroom with huge south and east windows, and a combination guest room-study. There was also a tiny but efficient galley kitchen. Throughout the flat the floors were magnificent—parquet with the most beautiful, subtle woodworked designs around the borders of the rooms. The floors shone in a way that Camilla hadn't seen since she'd left the convent school.

The furniture was sparse, simple, and almost nondescript. It was the space and its light that made the flat so exquisite. Camilla also thought that perhaps Frederick avoided clutter and excess since he couldn't see it now, and from a practical point of view, all of it could prove an obstacle to knock down or trip over. In the bedroom, for instance, there was only the high four-poster bed, two nightstands, and a low tufted bench at one window. There wasn't even a bureau. Clothes were all stored in closets and cabinets that were hidden from view. Surprisingly, the simplicity and emptiness didn't seem stark to Camilla—at least not after she got used to it. In fact, the flat seemed a restful oasis in a visually overloaded, merciless city.

In the short time she'd spent in these rooms, Camilla had come to love them deeply. This was a New York she had never known before or even dared dream of. She watched the light play on the walls and floor of the flat as the sun moved through the day. Even the shadows at twilight were exquisite, and she almost hated to turn on the lamps at night. Camilla felt very secure in the apartment. But she had not unpacked—her clothes were neatly stored in her suitcase in a wardrobe—and she had, after her talk with Emma, determined that she would have to leave it, and soon. She had decided to take on Alex Simmons as her agent, to stay with Davis & Dash, and get a job. She would live within her means. There was a limit to how much debt one could be in, even to a friend. And she needed to be sure that Frederick understood that her tenure here was not a prelude to anything more in their relationship.

Frederick was not indicating otherwise. Camilla tried not to think of their night in Firenze. He was a friend, not a lover. He must want it that way. He was the opposite of pushy—he called only once or twice a week, inquiring about her writing, and at her invitation, he sometimes dropped by.

He came to his flat as if he were a visitor, and half a dozen times he had taken her out to dinner. He brought her to a different restaurant each time, and he seemed to be known at each one. Talking and dining with him was the bright spot in her days—but that didn't mean that they should be anything more than friends. After dinner she'd sometimes read to him, and she found it helpful reading her words aloud. It was a great editing tool. Frederick commented very little, though she knew he liked what she'd done so far. She'd seen it in his acute reaction to her words.

Frederick was also advising her on business. They had discussed Alfred Byron and Alex Simmons. Both had agreed that Alex was the only choice, and yesterday Camilla had signed on with her. In fact, Camilla had never felt so well taken care of, so buffered. It was lovely, but it also made her both sad and anxious. This must be what it was like to be born into a family with retainers, solicitors, trust funds, and contacts in all the right places. That the Ashtons were so willing to share all of this with her, a virtual stranger, was both touching and rather eerie. She wondered when it would all be withdrawn.

Since her arrival in New York, Camilla had spent her days divided between her work on the new book and long walks through Manhattan. While she had not unpacked her clothes, she had made the study her own and sat each morning before the window at Frederick's desk, which she had littered with new pads of lined paper, a framed Canaletto print, and a Venetian blue glass vase in which she kept some tulips.

She worked for three or four hours in the morning, walked from eleven to almost three, and then worked in the afternoon for two hours more. In the evenings, when she didn't see Frederick, she watched American television—all those channels with nothing on any of them!—or went out to the cinema. She had spent one glorious afternoon at the Metropolitan Museum of Art, but oddly, she didn't feel up to returning. Right now she was focused on words—the words that were growing in a magical, organic way on her pages. She was writing about a student's adventures in New York and revisiting some of the places she had lived during her student years. Her story was developing nicely.

But this suspension could not go on indefinitely. She couldn't accept much more of Frederick's hospitality. She would have to leave fairyland. Like all the other struggling people outside this perfect flat, she would have to get a day job and find digs. Manhattan seemed financially out of the question, but Brooklyn or The Bronx seemed within reach. Today she was going to meet Craig Stevens about a job with his small firm and then take the subway to The Bronx—where she had seen a bed-sitter advertised in the paper for just five hundred a month.

Camilla dressed carefully for her interview. Alex had called her with the address and an appointment, telling Camilla that she had already spoken to Craig Stevens on her behalf. Camilla walked out of the apartment, and Curtis, the elevator operator, greeted her. So did the doorman, George. She would miss being pampered with their daily salutes. She walked to Lexington Avenue, checked to make sure she had the requisite tube token, and disappeared into the underground entrance.

Craig Stevens was a handsome man, but a good part of his charm resided in the fact that he seemed unaware of it. His hair was very dark and thick, and he wore it without a part. His face was strong, with a square chin and intense eyes. Most attractive was his ruddiness, a healthy glow to his skin that seemed either about to bloom or darken into whisker shadows along his jawline. Camilla couldn't help thinking of Stendhal's title *The Red and the Black* because Craig Stevens's hair was so jet, his color so high, his jaw so dark. There was a vitality about him that created a feeling of excitement and confidence.

She was drawn to him. He was physically impressive. He wasn't tall, but his shoulders were broad. There was something solid about him, both in his build and his attitude. He was young to be a publisher, at least she thought so. He couldn't be more than thirty-five, forty at the outside, but his energy and enthusiasm made him seem even younger.

Citron Press was his own creation, and it was small but sturdy. Right now it consisted of four offices in this loft building on Twenty-second Street, but he confidently assured her they'd be moving in just a matter of months to larger quarters. Alex had told Camilla that the young publisher had had a modest upbringing and that he'd made a fortune in book packaging, whatever that was. He also had the courage, skill, and charisma that attracted a following of investors willing to bankroll Citron Press.

"We thought of a lot of names before we came up with Citron Press," he told her. "Stevens Publishing sounded a little grandiose. I wanted Miracle Books—you know the old gag: If it's a good book it's a miracle." Camilla laughed. "Anyway," Craig continued, "some of the investors were afraid Miracle might sound like a Christian press, so we're Citron. Give us lemons, and we'll make lemonade."

Camilla smiled. She liked his energy and silly jokes. Then she looked at the wall to her left. She stood up, galvanized. "It's genuine, isn't it?" she asked. She moved toward the small painting. It was a Canaletto, a small study of the Grand Canal, right after the Rialto.

"Yes. It was my grandfather's. He left it to me. He bought it in London in a sale room at the turn of the century." Camilla stared at the tiny, beautiful scene. The sun always shone from a perfect Adriatic blue sky, it would seem at high noon. It was what she loved about Canaletto—the control, the microscopic detail, and the way he encapsulated the atmosphere of the whole city of Venice in a five-by-twelve-inch piece of canvas.

"It's beautiful," she whispered.

Craig nodded. "My favorite possession," he said.

Camilla sat opposite him again, listening while he leaned forward and placed his hands on his knees. "Here's what we've got going," he explained. "Publishing has become such a big business that authors aren't treated like authors anymore. Publishers look at them as manufacturers of their 'product,' and their books are treated that way. Like products. What we're managing to do is attract a select group of writers who want to be treated as *writers,* who want their work respected and understood by their publisher. We think we can do that *and* make money, though neither one is easy. We've got almost fifty titles, and we're out of the red." Camilla nodded. Though she knew so little about the business, she could recognize this as an achievement. She was definitely attracted to this vibrant, intelligent, enthusiastic man. Her eyes moved back over to the Canaletto. Amazing. He stood up and moved to the shelf behind him. "We publish Walter McKay," Craig Stevens said proudly. "He left Random House for us. And we've just signed Veda Barlow. She's been bouncing from house to house, with one horror story after another. They've totally mishandled her, but I think she can be really important, and a lot more than a regional writer. Do you know her work?" Camilla admitted she didn't. Craig smiled and shrugged. "That's the problem," he said, "but you will."

Camilla believed him. If anyone could succeed in this difficult, challenging city, it would be a man like Craig Stevens.

"We're also trying a few first novels. Ron Fried. I'm trying to sign Susan Jedren. And Kim Baker Edmonds. A mix of literature and popular stuff. Small presses are really important to America. We're the ones that will keep new blood flowing to the readers and other publishers out there. The problem is, only small bookstores buy from small presses. And once an author hits it big, they often move away to a giant house. Oh, well." He paused. "So, Alex told me a little about you. Davis & Dash is doing *your* first novel. I'd like to read it."

Camilla smiled. "I'd be happy to show it to you," she said.

"And you're working on a new one?" he asked.

"Oh, yes. But I can't afford to do it without working at a paying job as well, it seems."

Craig was nodding. "Well, I have a part-time opening. Reading manuscripts, some books from the U.K. we might want to publish over here, answering phones." He shrugged, almost apologetically. "Nothing too literary. A little of this and a little of that. No title, no health insurance, and a lot of flexibility required. But if you're interested and we work well together, we can try it out for six months. Then either put you on full-time or give you benefits."

"You'll hire me?" Camilla asked. She hadn't even been paying attention. He hadn't gone over her résumé, had he? Or even questioned her about her schooling? She tore her eyes away from the painting.

"Sure," Craig said. "You're obviously smart, educated, and you'll work cheap. Alex even tells me you're talented." He grinned. "And maybe we'll do your next book."

Once again, Camilla marveled at how easy things became when you had the proper introduction. "I've never worked in publishing before," she felt obligated to tell him.

He laughed. "Great! No bad habits." Then he got serious. "Hey, listen, you *write* books. You know what a lonely, insecure life it is. You'll know how to care for authors. That's what we're about." He stood up and pulled on his jacket. "You want to go out and get a bite?" Craig asked. For a moment Camilla wasn't sure what he was talking about. Then it dawned on her that he'd just invited her to dinner.

"Oh, I can't. I have another engagement." Was the job dependent upon *that*? Did this mean he was interested in her in *that* way? It was so hard to tell with Americans. Craig shrugged. Just then, Susan walked in.

"Where are we eating tonight?" Craig asked Susan.

"At Tutta Pasta," Susan said. Craig made a face.

"Well, you're not missing much," he told Camilla. "Can you start next week?" Camilla nodded, and Craig turned to Susan. "Meet the sixth employee at Citron Press," he said, and put his hand on Camilla's shoulder. "About to be underpaid and overworked."

"Any other abuse we can offer you?" Susan asked with a wry smile.

"Find me a cheap flat," Camilla joked. "I was going up to The Bronx this afternoon to look at one."

"The Bronx?" they both asked, looking at each other with alarm.

"How cheap?" Susan asked.

"Five hundred dollars a month?"

Craig shook his head as if that was impossible, but Susan nodded. "Park Slope," she said.

When Frederick arrived that evening, Camilla greeted him with a smile and a statement: "I'm taking *you* to dinner tonight." She still had $140 in her purse and meant to return to the nicest restaurant Frederick had taken her to—a tiny French place off Madison Avenue called Table D'Hote. But as they began walking down the street, Frederick grasping her right arm gently for stability and guidance, he demurred.

"I don't really want French," he said, "if you don't mind." He paused, as if considering. "Could we have Chinese? I've got a yen for it, you should pardon the pun." Camilla groaned. She hadn't yet been to a Chinese restaurant in New York.

"Certainly, if you know of one."

Frederick laughed. "They're on every corner. But I know the good ones." It was only once they were seated at First Wok that Camilla realized she'd been outsmarted. Dinner for two would hardly cost more than twenty dollars. She looked up from the menu and smiled at Frederick.

"You've been very naughty," she told him.

He raised his brows, his face innocent of guile. "What?" he asked, but then he broke into a guilty grin. "So what are we celebrating?" he continued, changing the subject. "I know there must be a celebration here. Have you already finished the new book?"

Camilla laughed. "I've barely finished the new chapter," she said, though she was pleased with her progress. "No. What I've done is gotten a job."

"A job?" Frederick asked, his smile fading. "What do you need a job for?"

"For the money, Frederick. Obviously, for the money. I can't depend on your hospitality forever."

"Why not?"

"Why not? Because it's . . . preposterous. I can't live on charity. Now that I've realized how little I'll actually get for the book, even with Alex's help, I shall have to cut my cloth by my pocketbook."

"What the hell does *that* mean? Is that some limey expression about fashion?"

"No, Frederick. It means that I will have to work, and find an inexpensive place to live, and get on with the book more slowly. So I've found a part-time job with a small publisher, and I'm looking for a place to live in Park Slope."

"Brooklyn? You want to live in Brooklyn?"

"Want has nothing to do with it. It's just what I have to do right now."

"No, Camilla. What you *have* to do right now is get your next book written before the first one comes out. That's so that no matter what happens—if the book is well reviewed or if it bombs, you already have your vision established."

"Well, I shall endeavor to do that," Camilla said stiffly.

"But why do it so slowly? Why be distracted by a job? What kind of job is it, anyway?"

So Camilla told him about Craig Stevens, Citron Press, and her new, minuscule salary. "But that and the advance ought to keep me, if I can find a place for five hundred a month. And they know of a few buildings in Brooklyn, one of them where another Citron Press writer lives. Park Slope seems to be a great enclave of writers."

"I don't know. It seems to me Manhattan is the center of everything." He paused. "Isn't my apartment comfortable?"

Camilla could hear the hurt in his voice. It was the very last thing she had meant to do, and yet she had done it. Oh, she was so awkward and hopeless with this sort of thing! She reached her hand across the table, past the moo shu pork, and took Frederick's long hand in her own. "Your apartment is absolutely splendid, and so are you.

It's just that I can't live on your charity. It isn't right for me."

"It isn't charity!" Frederick said loudly. Heads turned. "It *isn't* charity," he repeated in a much quieter voice. "It's friendship. And it also allows me to support the arts. All right—I admit I'm not Lorenzo il Magnifico, but there's no reason why I can't be your patron."

Camilla thought of Gianfranco, ready to keep her as his mistress. She couldn't repress a small shudder. That wasn't what Frederick was proposing, but it still would not do. "This isn't Firenze, and it's not the fourteenth century, Frederick," Camilla said gently. "You've already done so much for me. You've done *everything* for me. You've started me on a whole new life. But now I have to take care of myself."

Frederick withdrew his hand. "Yes. It isn't easy being taken care of, is it?" Camilla heard the pain in his voice and realized anew what he was going through. "I wish I didn't have to depend on anyone either."

She bit her lip. He hadn't talked much about his program at Lighthouse for the Blind, but she knew he was having difficulties. Who wouldn't? "We all depend on people, Frederick. I *have* depended on you. I still will. It's just a matter of degree. You've been really marvelous. I don't know what I would have done without you. Truly. I want to keep you as a friend, always, keep reading to you, and I want to keep seeing you."

"I won't keep seeing you," Frederick said. "My sight is going very fast now."

"Oh, Frederick. I am sorry." She paused. "I'll help any way I can."

"In Brooklyn?" Frederick asked.

"Here, there, or wherever it suits you," Camilla told him.

# 63

> Things in the publishing world are seldom what they seem.
>
> —*Anthea Disney*

The moment she walked into the hip Chelsea restaurant, Judith knew she was dressed all wrong. The restaurant was called Bistro du Sud. It looked like somewhere in France—not that Judith had ever been to France. It was a narrow, long room with a pressed-tin ceiling, signs advertising French beers, and a dark wood bar at the entrance. Around it several dozen people clustered, and all of them, even the men, were dressed better than Judith was. She looked down at her navy blue dress with the white collar and cuffs and wondered what she had been thinking. Compared with all of her cheap, flowered clothes, this had looked sophisticated upstate. Now she realized, too late, that she was wearing a truly suburban dress. She had costumed herself perfectly for the part of the dull wife.

The party was to celebrate the movie option that had been sold to Hollywood. April Irons, the producer of *Jack and Jill* and *The Extinction*, was going to make it. Daniel had been so excited by the news that he hadn't slept for two nights. But he looked good—full of energy and excitement. He'd told Judith that there was another important reason for the party: One of the book clubs was interested in *In Full Knowledge* but wouldn't make it a main selection. Apparently, Davis & Dash wouldn't sell it to them as an alternate. So, to break the deadlock they were having this party and the book-club people would get to look the author over before a final decision was made.

Funny that they wouldn't look at the real author. Judith

felt invisible from the moment they entered the bistro. She couldn't stop herself—as they approached the bar she took Daniel's arm, just above the elbow, though she knew it was another one of those giveaway gestures that made her look like the suburban wife. Still, she couldn't face walking unattached into this crowd, most of them dressed in black, all of them thinner and hipper-looking than she was. Daniel moved forward and was greeted by a tall, broad-shouldered woman who looked about Judith's age. Judith tried to smile. Had she left that note for him in the manuscript? Was this Pam Mantiss? But even Judith, for all her suspicions, could see that there was no attraction or connection between this woman and Daniel—unless they were the greatest acting team since Olivier and Leigh.

"The author of the year," the woman was saying pleasantly but without much real warmth. "How about that movie sale?"

Daniel smiled modestly. "Yeah. Pretty good," he said. "They're a hot team."

"*You're* the hot one," another woman said with her own heat. She was older, and her face had a lot of mileage on it. But despite her thin lips and the lines that ran from her nose to her mouth, her wild blond hair and her voluptuousness were appealing. Judith could sense she had a kind of sexual attraction.

"And you must be Mrs. Daniel," the older woman said. Her eyes, which were long and narrow, seemed to sweep over Judith, focusing particularly on Judith's bad haircut, her stupid dress, and wide hips. She felt appraised in a millisecond. The thin lips smiled, but it wasn't a smile of approval. The woman extended her hand. "I'm Pam Mantiss," she said. "I'm your husband's . . ." There was a pause—wasn't there an inappropriate pause?—"editor. *And* greatest fan." Judith wondered if the woman had considered saying something else, but she didn't have time to. She was distracted by the first woman, who had extended her hand. "I'm Emma Ashton," she said. "We spoke on the phone a while back." Judith took her hand and nodded, distractedly. She remembered that morning. She couldn't think of anything to say.

"I was in my bathrobe," she said. Emma blinked. Judith realized she didn't sound coherent, but the moment of that call came back to her and the words popped out. She'd been vomiting all that morning. "I was in my bathrobe when you called," Judith repeated, trying to explain. But what else could she say?

"Come on, Jude. I want you to meet Jim Reiner from the book club," Pam Mantiss said and took him by the arm. "I'll get you a drink, introduce you around. The book-club people are dying to meet you since they heard about the option. I smell a main selection," she sang throatily and led him away.

"Well, what do you do?" Emma Ashton asked Judith.

"Uh, I . . ." She stopped. What could she say? She was a college dropout? A ghostwriter? A housewife? Judith simply stood there, in her stupid dress, pretending not to be the author, pretending not to be distraught, pretending not to be so angry at Daniel that she wished that drink he was raising to his lips at the bar was battery acid instead of Beaujolais. She looked around the room. People were clustering around Daniel and Pam Mantiss, who held the central position at the corner of the long bar. A young man with a ponytail said something, and Daniel's laugh rang out. Judith counted the people who were grouped there, waiting to talk to Daniel. She stood rooted to her spot, invisible and alone. Daniel, as always, was the center of a crowd, but this time—unlike those times in the past when the students and faculty gathered around Daniel and she felt his importance reflected onto her—Judith only felt her insignificance. And her resentment. The glory he was basking in was *hers*, and she had allowed it all to be stolen from her. She realized that Emma Ashton was still beside her, now looking at her with some alarm.

"Are you all right?" Emma asked. Judith could only nod

her head. "It is a *very* good sign, this option," Emma said as if she were trying to be reassuring. "You must be very proud of your husband."

Judith's head snapped up, and for a moment she was about to blurt out the truth. She wondered what this woman's reaction would be. She looked across at Daniel. What would his reaction be? She would *have* to talk with him. There was no way she could continue with this. He would have to tell them all, whatever it cost them in money and whatever it cost him in ego. Because, Judith realized, if this goes on much longer, it will kill me.

A force she didn't know she had moved her through the crowd to Daniel's side. Pam Mantiss was holding his arm, and they were talking to an older man, small and very well dressed. Judith took Daniel's other elbow and gave it a tug. He was impervious and continued to stare at the small man. Judith tugged again, this time almost viciously. She wasn't just invisible. Perhaps she was dead—a real ghost. What was the name of the woman in *Topper*? Marian Kirby. No one could see *her* but Topper himself.

At last Daniel looked down at her mildly. "Oh, excuse me," he said—not to Judith but to the little man. "Gerald, this is my wife, Judith. Judith, meet Gerald Ochs Davis."

Judith barely managed a nod and said, "I have to talk to you." Daniel smiled blandly and ignored her completely. Had Topper ignored Marian? Judith thought so, but when he did Marian had acted up.

"Gerald was just saying how we would both be fighting each other for a place on the *Times* list," Daniel told her. "But I—"

"I have to talk to you *now*," Judith said, and her voice was so loud that all the conversation at the bar stopped. Daniel looked at her and then back at his coterie. He raised his eyebrows.

"Excuse me," he said with a shrug and a smile. "My wife seems to need me."

Still holding his elbow, Judith pulled him from the

group. But where to go? Not outside on the street. They needed some privacy. She moved toward the back of the long restaurant, past the empty banquet tables readied for the dinner, and into a hallway that led to the toilets.

"What are you doing?" Daniel whispered with a snarl. "Are you drunk?" His voice was angry, but for once she wasn't intimidated.

"I can't do this, Daniel," she told him. "It isn't fair. It isn't right. No more secrets. We have to tell them."

"We have to tell them what?" Daniel asked, and she looked at him. He stared back angrily. Was he crazy? Could there be any question of what secret had to be revealed?

"We have to tell them about me. That I wrote the book."

"Are you insane?" Daniel hissed, his eyes opening. "Are you completely insane?"

Just then someone scurried past them, someone who apparently had been using the bathroom. "Judith, you're drunk again," Daniel said in a voice so loud that Judith jumped.

"I'm *not* drunk," Judith protested. "I haven't had time to even have a drink. Anyway, I can't drink. Not with the baby." Judith began to cry.

Daniel paused. Was it her imagination, or did he at last look guilty? Maybe he'd see what had happened, how this had gone too far. Maybe it would be all right. "Judith, there isn't time for this now. There's been so much on my mind. There was so much I've been coping with."

"So much *you've* been coping with?" Judith asked, her voice finally rising. "Daniel, this isn't going to work. We've *got* to tell them. And if you won't, I will. Right now." Daniel looked at her, and even in the dim hallway she could see his face pale. Topper turned into a ghost.

"Are you nuts or stupid?" He grabbed her arm. He held her so tight that she winced. "We're not telling anybody anything. Anyway, there's nothing to tell." Then he put both of his hands on her shoulders and lowered his voice. "Judith, we made an agreement. We are playing this a certain way. Don't you see what's happening? Don't you see the opportunity for us? Do you think Gerald Davis shows up at every first novelist's little party? Does every book get optioned by April Irons? It's all very complicated. The guy from the book club wants to play golf with me this weekend. This book could *really* take off. He has connections everywhere. It would be reviewed by the *Times*, the *Washington Post*. It would appear in the columns. And if any of them think there's a problem with it, if anything looks odd to them, they'll just let it die. We won't make any more money. Everything will have been for nothing."

"I don't care. I don't care if we never make another dime. I am not going to stand here and be ignored and left out." Her voice had risen, and he tried to shush her. She felt his fingers digging into her shoulders, but she didn't stop, though she did lower her voice.

"Daniel, you tell them tonight, or else I will. It's not complicated. It's as simple as that."

The Davis & Dash people were seated at several large tables at the back of the restaurant. Judith was separated from Daniel, who had Gerald Ochs Davis on one side of him and Pam Mantiss on the other. Judith sat between the ponytailed guy—an art director named Jack—and Emma Ashton. It was hard to hear what was being said around the big table. She couldn't hear her dinner companions because she was so busy trying to listen to what was being said across the table. She watched Daniel. Was he telling Pam Mantiss now? But the woman laughed. Surely she wouldn't do that if Daniel had told her the news. Maybe she was laughing in disbelief.

Every now and then Mr. Davis would begin to make some pronouncement and everybody would fall silent and then everyone would respond, but a lot of the time Pam Mantiss seemed to monopolize Daniel's attention. She had draped her arm across the back of his chair in the masculine gesture boys use with their dates in movie theaters. She kept leaning into him and whispering. The rest of the time she chatted with the book-club man on her other side. But with Daniel she whispered. Well, if it wasn't quite whispering, it was murmuring, and Daniel kept drinking and laughing. In all the time she'd known him, he hadn't drunk this much or laughed this much. Well, if that's what it takes for him to get up his courage, it's all right with me, Judith thought. So long as he talks.

Gerald Ochs Davis had made a toast, and that had been followed by Pam Mantiss's, during which she and Daniel made a lot of eye contact. Judith didn't care anymore. She'd stand up in the middle of all this hero worship and make herself the heroine. She would. Just then, to her astonishment, Daniel stood up. Well, he was going to do it in front of them all. Perhaps that was the best way.

"I want to thank you for the tremendous help you've given me," he said, looking around the table. "I don't think any new novelist has been welcomed into a house as I have at Davis & Dash. But there's something I have to tell you." Judith felt her heart beat harder and tried to compose herself. Whatever their reaction, she would be prepared for it. This was important. Her stomach lurched, and all at once she began to tremble. Despite her threat, she couldn't believe Daniel was making the announcement this way. She smoothed down her skirt, adjusted her collar. "Writing is a lonely business. But, in a way, I've been lucky. I haven't been alone the whole long, painful way. This book wouldn't have been what it is, it would not have achieved its potential, without the help of one woman. A woman of true literary genius, to whom I am very grateful."

Judith lifted her head up and stared across the table at Daniel. She was almost faint, but her cheek flushed. He lifted his glass. "To Pam Mantiss. My editor."

There was an echoing murmur, and everybody else lifted their glasses and drank. But Judith was so stunned that she actually let go of her glass. It dropped to the table but didn't break, though the wine splattered halfway across the white tablecloth. There was a minor scramble to get out of the way of the moving stain. Then, as smoothly as she could, Emma Ashton righted the glass and the ponytail filled it for Judith, but of course, she didn't drink. She stared across the table at her husband. He looked back at her, and then his eyes flicked away. What had she read in his eyes? "There's someone else who needs to be thanked," he said. "No novelist who's married ever underestimates the contribution of their spouse. I'd like to thank Judith for all of the time she put in, and all that she had to put up with. And if your typing wasn't great, honey, at least your attitude was."

People laughed and raised their glasses, and Judith sat there paralyzed. Was that it, then? Was *that* his acknowledgment? His confession? He'd made her sound like an idiot. She was about to say something, anything, and then Gerald spoke up and the table hushed again.

"Well, Jude, now that the book has been optioned for the movies, what are you going to do with the money?" he asked.

"Get some shirts like yours," Daniel said. And everyone at the table roared with laughter—everyone but Judith.

# 64

> Not all writers can work with all editors. A project that is taken on with great enthusiasm by an editor may bog down because the chemistry isn't right.
>
> —*Betty A. Prashker*

"Mrs. Trawley's on the phone."

Pam tried to decide which would be worse: speaking with the Widow Trawley or having periodontal surgery. Not that it was a choice—she would have to speak to the Widow Trawley, *and* her dentist had told her her gums were shot. Pam picked up the phone. "Hello, Edina," Pam said in her toughest voice. "What can I do for you?"

"What you can do for me is fix this manuscript," Edina Trawley snapped. "I don't know how you could have edited my husband's works for as long as you did and be able to miss the point altogether." Pam was always amazed to hear a honey-dipped Southern girl spit her words out, as Edina did now. "Peet's work had a spiritual undercurrent, a subtext that is completely missing in this draft. I am *very* disappointed."

Spiritual undercurrent? Subtext? Edina had been at the literary bottle again. She was drunk with editorial power. What the fuck was she talking about? Peet Trawley's books were Gothic trash with a lot of satanism and sex thrown in. Subtext? The only subtext Peet could have ever written would have been a submarine manual.

"Edina, I'm not sure I'm following you." Pam knew she was merely vamping for time and knew also that Edina didn't have a clue as to what she was talking about. There *was* a problem, but it didn't involve spiritual currents or lyricism. The problem was that the book sucked.

Unbelievable and badly plotted as Peet's books had always been, this new one, somehow, managed to be worse. She had already edited it twice and squeezed two total rewrites out of the suffering Stewart, to no avail. Pam had come to believe that Peet had passionately believed in the idiocy he wrote, and that gave it an energy totally lacking in her own work, and now Stewart's pathetic draft. A reader could always smell an author's bad faith. Danielle Steel's stupidities were readable because of Steel's own sincere belief in her female fairy tales.

"What I'm *trying* to say is that the book lacks Peet's essence. His authenticity. You have to make it an authentic Peet Trawley."

"Edina, it can't be authentic. Peet's dead," Pam said flatly. And this is the first time you ever bothered to read one of these manuscripts, much less critique one, you bitch, she wanted to add silently. Before he died Peet always complained about how uninterested Edina was in his work. Now, all of a sudden, she'd known about his fiction's spirituality and subtext? Get the fuck out of here!

But Pam had already spent her share of the ghosting money and couldn't afford to say what she wanted to. She didn't like the feeling at all. As editor in chief, she'd been telling authors about their inadequacies for years. She didn't need this turnabout. She could hardly believe she had to listen to some poor white-trash moron talk about literary imperfection. Next Daisy Mae would be explaining to her the difference between a metaphor and a simile. "Well, what do *you* suggest, Edina?"

"I think you should fix it. I think you should make it better."

Pam almost laughed out loud. Now, *there* was an example of editorial direction. From now on she'd just tell all her authors to "make it better."

"Listen, Edina. I do think I have to tighten up the ending a little bit. And I can try and make Marie more sympathetic.

I think those things would help, don't you?" Pam promised herself she would kick the shit out of Stewart the next time she saw him. She would never work with the motherfucker again! Not only would she withhold the rest of the money she owed him for *this* book, but she'd never publish another one of his own stupid novels again. "Do you think that would help, Edina?"

"Well, I think it should be more like *The Celestine Prophecy*. I read that it sold a lot of copies and it's very spiritual."

Yeah, if you consider seventy-nine weeks on the *New York Times* list and over two million hardcover copies sold spiritual, then it was a spiritual book. Pam considered it a fucking miracle. But it had nothing to do with Peet Trawley's oeuvre.

"Anyway," Edina continued, "I'd like you to fix it up, and then I wondered if we could talk about doing three more."

"What?" Holy shit! First the bitch complains, and then she expands the contract? Pam smiled for the first time that morning. This wasn't about lyricism. This was all about money. *That* was the subtext for Edina Trawley. Pam quickly tried to figure how much she could ask for, and how much of that she'd have to pay off to Stewart. She'd work with him if she had to. "Well, we could certainly talk about it. I'm sure Mr. Davis would be interested."

"Well, fine then," Edina drawled. "Fix this one up, and why don't you talk with our lawyers?"

Pam sat down, took a swig of her Snapple, then picked up the phone and dialed Stewart Campbell's number.

Pam's apartment was a pigsty. She couldn't blame it on Christophe—he was as messy as any nine-year-old, but he pretty much contained it in his bat cave of a room. No, the mess was mostly hers. Take-out containers littered the counter from two nights of quick dinners; glasses and bottles—empty and half-filled—were scattered on most horizontal surfaces; shoes were flung into corners; and layers of clothes she'd peeled off hung over the side of the sofa, except for those that lay in wrinkled piles on the floor. Unopened mail and unpaid bills, along with manuscript pages, were everywhere. What she needed was a full-time housekeeper, Pam thought. And the money from the Trawley contract—the new three-book contract—would get it for her, along with a nice car, some new furniture, and a down payment on a country house. All she had to do was bully Stewart through the final rewrites, get him on board for the next ones, and cash the check.

Stewart would be there any minute. Pam got two black plastic garbage sacks from the kitchen, closed the door on the chaos in there, and then went through the living room and dining room throwing everything—clothes, papers, glassware, and cutlery—into the bags, which she then stowed in the hall closet. She had barely finished by the time Stewart rang up.

Pam was prepared for warfare. And the struggle between editors and writers was like a war. She wondered briefly if all editors both admired and hated writers as she did—and envied them. It was odd how learning that she couldn't write a book hadn't diminished her hate but had intensified it. The last time she had seen Stewart he was less than a whipped dog. She had thrown the manuscript at him and demanded the second rewrite. He'd whined, and she had resorted to insult and threat. The problem was that she resented like hell the fact that Stewart, hack though he was, could sit down and write, while she—who had always told herself she would someday—could not. The only way she could cope with the knowledge was by torturing him.

Her doorbell buzzed, and she walked down the long hallway and opened the door, but it wasn't a whipped Stewart who greeted her. Pam had the survival instinct of a feral wolf, and she could smell any change in the wind. Something had changed, and Stewart, messy and disheveled as ever, looked different. She thought it was something about his shoulders—up to now she'd never even noticed Stewart *had* shoulders. He seemed thinner, too. God, she wondered, is he sick? Does he have AIDS? He's just the type to be bisexual. And I probably slept with him. She told herself to keep cool, and led Stewart down the darkness of the hall into the open space of the combined living room/dining room. She sat down on her leather sofa, crossed her legs, and then decided perhaps it was best to be a little more accommodating. "Are you losing weight on purpose?" she asked.

It was as if he didn't hear her. Stewart threw the bulky envelope containing the latest revisions onto the coffee table. "This is it, Pam. I've done the best I could. I don't know if you'll be happy with it. I don't know what would make you happy. But I'm finished."

Pam felt her stomach tighten. He didn't just mean finished with the draft. She could tell. "You're sick?" she asked.

"Sick of you," he said, and she realized it wasn't AIDS that had caused the weight loss; it was aggravation. Her relief was tinged with concern. The idea of finding a new author, of getting him or her to agree to total secrecy, of the possibility that Stewart would now start to talk, all terrified her almost as much as the idea of a fatal disease. The industry would not look kindly on an editor who fraudulently presented a ghostwritten book as a posthumous one. And, almost worse, if word got out that she had written it, she'd be embarrassed by its poor quality and the critical jibes she would have to take. Worst of all would be to have it known that she had subcontracted the book out while she retained most of the money—a clear conflict of interest and violation of her fiduciary responsibility to her authors. But she told herself to keep her cool, and she managed to do it, at least outwardly. She recrossed her legs and managed, "Do you want a drink?"

Stewart shook his head and refused even to sit down. It was obvious to Pam that it was taking all of his will to stand up to her both literally and figuratively. That was a good sign.

"I think you're finished, too, Stewart." She looked at him, hoping for a wince. But his face showed no reaction, except perhaps a softening of the mouth—was that relief? "And you know what? I think I owe you an apology." Still no reaction, not even surprise, but she wasn't sure how much Stewart was actually hearing, he was so intent on speaking his piece. "I know I was hard on you, Stewart. But I had a lot of reason to be. You're good, you know. You're really good. But you lack discipline and structure. I've told you that before. I thought if I could push you with this one, if I could get the best possible work out of you, that it would help you with your own writing. I thought you could take it. That was my mistake. I had your best interests at heart, but if I rode you too hard, I apologize."

Stewart remained standing, but he took a deep breath. He was such a decent guy Pam almost laughed. "Okay," he said. "There's the final. Pay me if you want to and don't if you don't. But I am not touching it again."

Then, unbelievably, Stewart turned and started to walk down the hallway. Pam almost panicked, but then, using all of her self-control, she burst out laughing. Stewart stopped in his tracks.

"Stewie. Stewie." She drew out the syllables the way a kid would. "Hey, Stewie, don't take it so personally. Sure, I screamed and threatened. Like I said, it was a test, and you passed. You passed with flying colors, Stewie. But you don't get a grade. What you get is a nice fat book contract. Actually, two of them." Stewart turned and looked at her. "Come sit down for a minute." She held her breath while he hesitated. But finally he took the four crucial steps back into the center of the living room and lowered himself into the chair farthest from her. Pam was sweating, but she hoped it didn't show. Her fish had seen the spangle of the lure. But would he take the bait?

She made her face as serious as she could. She couldn't use the fish analogy on him. Go for the veldt, she thought. "Listen, Stewart, this was a trial by fire and I know you feel burned, but you came through it like a lion jumping through a flaming hoop." She put her hand on the manuscript on the table. "Without even reading it I know it's good. It was good in your last draft. But now it's *really* going to be right. A job well done, and you get your reward." She paused, picked up the manuscript, and put it on her lap. "Stewart, I'm ready to offer you a three-book contract for your own work. And I'll double the advance to fifty thousand per book."

His mouth opened, then closed, like a little guppy. He'd taken the bait. But was the hook set? He sat quietly for a moment and then said, "Can I do the ecology one?" Pam, confident, began to reel him in. For years Stewart had been talking about a stupid novel with an eco theme. Those books never made any money. But Pam smiled at him beneficently. With the Trawley books millions of dollars were at stake.

'As your third book, Stewie. When you're up to your full powers. But that's not all," she told him. "I want you and I to privately agree to another three-book contract—three more Peet Trawleys. That, my dear, will bring you three hundred thousand dollars," she paused for full effect. It would bring her over a million. "You could move into an apartment with air conditioning," she said, smiling.

Stewart paled, and even across the room she could see the sweat glistening on his forehead and upper lip. Did fish sweat? Pam wondered idly.

"I can't ghost another Trawley book," Stewart said, his voice so low it was almost a whisper.

"Of course you can. Now that you've gotten his style down, it'll go much more smoothly."

Stewart shook his head. "I can't."

They sat there in silence. Pam knew the next person who spoke would be the loser in this battle of wills. She kept her eyes focused on Stewart. She had to land him. She wanted to mention the money again, but she kept her thin lips shut. What was the first line of *The Old Man and the Sea*? The silence stretched out between them. "I don't get my contract if I don't do the Trawley, do I?" Stewart asked.

Pam silently shook her head and waited for Stewart to jump into the boat, as she knew he would.

Pam couldn't get a goddamned taxi, and she had to get back to the office for a meeting with Gerald by three. It was so fucking inconvenient that she couldn't meet Stewart in public. At last, desperate, she hailed a gypsy cab and agreed to pay ten bucks to be brought back to the Davis & Dash building. The cab was hot and smelled of body odor. Pam probably did too. She threw the ten dollars at the driver and jumped out of the car the moment it pulled to a stop. She had four minutes to make it through reception, up the elevator, and down the hallway to Gerald's office. He hated people to be late for his meetings, though he invariably made them wait for him. She dashed through the lobby and to the elevator as the doors slid open. Chris from marketing and an older woman Pam didn't know stepped out. "Congratulations," Chris said as Pam pushed by them. She paid no attention.

She punched a button to get her upstairs. Just before the elevator doors closed three secretaries stepped into the car, and of course, they all punched different floors. Pam tapped her foot with impatience. The secretaries were eating frozen yogurts and talking a mile a minute. When the the first one got out, she actually held the door open to finish her stupid comment. "Give it up," Pam barked and pushed the "door close" button. The two others fell silent and looked at each other, but Pam didn't give a shit. Finally, she got to her floor, and as she was stepping out of the elevator, Dickie Pointer stepped in. "Congratulations," he said, and the doors slid closed. Pam began to walk as fast as she could past the receptionist desk.

"Congratulations, Miss Mantiss," the black woman said, but Pam kept walking. It wasn't until she rounded the corner by Heather's desk that Heather stood up and said the same thing. Pam, already late for Gerald, stopped. Then Emma Ashton came out of her office, holding her hand out as if to shake Pam's.

"Congratulations," Emma said.

"What? What?" was all she snapped.

"You've been nominated for Editor of the Year," Emma told her.

# 65

It's those damn critics again.
—*Irwin Shaw*

Emma looked around at the empty tables surrounding them at Zöe, the huge SoHo restaurant. Eight o'clock was early for dinner in SoHo. Emma knew that within an hour or so every table would be filled, and the noise in the high-ceilinged, tile-floored restaurant would be overwhelming. In SoHo people seemed to like noisy spots. Perhaps it made them feel like they were in the middle of something happening. And they were. Dan Hedaya, the dark, intense actor from *Nixon* and *First Wives Club*, was at a table to her right. Elise Atchinson and her young director husband were just behind them. The place was hip, but Emma knew that the din would tire her brother, and she hoped that they could finish the awkward celebratory dinner quickly and be out before the worst of the crowd kicked in.

"Editor of the Year!" Alex picked up her glass of wine by its long stem and laughed.

"That takes the biscuit," Camilla agreed.

"She means the cake," Frederick said.

"No, wouldn't I say 'cookie'? That takes the cookie?"

Frederick shook his head. "Biscuits are cookies, but the expression here is 'That takes the cake.'"

"Excuse me for interrupting this transatlantic summit, but for what, exactly, did Pam Mantiss receive this nomination?" Alex asked.

Emma shrugged. "Oh, you know how political the association is. Pam's been on their steering committee for years. She's been pushing for it like crazy—you know, campaigning without campaigning, like a cardinal for the papacy."

"Will they send up a puff of white smoke if she's elected?" Frederick asked.

"Black, I'm sure," Emma joked. "She's not well liked. She's expected to be nominated almost as often as Susan Lucci for an Emmy; she finally campaigned for the thing and this time she may finally manage to bag it."

Alex laughed and raised her glass. "To Pam Mantiss, the Susan Lucci of publishing," she said, and Frederick and Emma laughed.

Camilla wrinkled her brow. "I'm afraid I don't quite see it," she said. So Emma explained about *All My Children* and the Emmy Awards. Camilla nodded. "Rather like Tony Warren's brilliant creation *Coronation Street,*" she said, "although I don't think anyone in the U.K. ever tried to give any of *them* awards. But the queen watches regularly." Camilla paused. "I felt she was quite mad actually. Not the queen," she hastened to explain. "Pam seemed mad."

"Oh, she's always mad about something," Emma agreed.

"Let me translate again," Frederick said indulgently. "Camilla was just speaking English. She didn't mean angry. She meant crazy. You know, like the Mad Hatter."

"Oh, she's that, too," Emma agreed.

"It's Emma who ought to be mad—I mean angry," Alex said. She looked at Emma directly for the first time that evening. "You've done all of her editorial work for years. And what's she getting the most buzz on now? *The Duplicity of Men,* which *you* found."

Emma shrugged. There was a silence. Just as it became awkward, Alex turned to Camilla and asked how her apartment hunting was going. Emma was surprised: She'd thought that Camilla was comfortably ensconced in Frederick's place. Had Camilla and Frederick had a fight, just as she and Alex had?

Well, it hadn't been a fight, exactly. Emma had finally heard from Alex after days of silence and had told her how disturbed she was by the way Alex had handled Camilla. She accused Alex of disloyalty, if not directly, then by implication. And Alex had become very defensive. "Look, business is business," she'd said. "It's a question of ethics. I have to tell my clients all their options. There are enough sleazebags in the business who don't."

Emma had been hurt by Alex's attitude—as if she were accusing Emma of unethical behavior. Alex's ethics hadn't seemed so visible when she'd benefited from Emma's contacts. Emma had been so pained by Alex's attack that she didn't raise any of her other doubts—why she hadn't heard from Alex in two weeks and the feeling she had that once she had been useful in sending over Opal O'Neal and Camilla, she might be dispensable. Alex should have called her, should have apologized, should have pursued her and would have, if she cared. Emma didn't argue when hurt. Certainly now Alex had cooled, and this "celebratory" dinner they were having was not going as well as it should. Her brother also seemed distant, and he and Camilla seemed estranged. The conversation seemed to flow smoothly only between Camilla and Alex.

Alex was praising and complimenting Camilla on everything from her haircut to the first chapter of her new book. Was she sincere, or was she doing it to antagonize Emma? The thought occurred to her that Alex might be interested in Camilla as more than a client. Emma pushed the thought out of her mind as unworthy, even paranoid, and tried to think of something to interject. "Well, the good news is we really need your book, and they're actually talking about moving you up to the fall list. Quite unusual since we don't even have a signed contract! Pam thinks your book doesn't need any line editing—she's putting it right into copyediting."

"Well, that sounds promising," Frederick said.

Alex put down her wineglass and sat up straight. "Wait a minute," she interjected. "Why is that? Is Pam too damn lazy to do a careful edit?" Alex turned to Camilla. "The book is good, but it could be tightened just a little bit. I'm thinking particularly of chapter three and maybe the last chapter."

Camilla nodded, then shrugged. "I don't know. What do you think, Emma?"

"Why is she coming out on the fall list?" Alex demanded of Emma. "I thought it wasn't scheduled until spring of next year? What's the rush? She'll be buried." Alex turned to Frederick and Camilla. "All the big books come out in the fall—it's the busiest time of the year. It'll be much harder to get you reviewed or to get publicity, or even shelf space in the bookstores." She turned back to Emma. "Why the hurry?"

Now it was Emma's turn to shrug. "Pam likes the book. And maybe it's filling a gap. You know, we did expect to do the Chad Weston book."

"Oh, great," Alex said. "Replace some sleazy, male, misogynistic porn with a sensitive, literary first novel. Someone's got their brains where they sit."

Camilla's face clouded. "Is this bad?" she asked. Emma noticed she asked Alex, not her.

"Well, if they put you in the Weston spot and spend the money advertising you that they were going to spend on Weston, then it's fine. But somehow I don't think that's the plan. Is it, Emma?"

Emma looked up from her drink. Alex knew very well that it wasn't. She felt attacked, and this time she was sure it wasn't oversensitivity. Why was Alex being so hostile? Why was she making Emma look bad to her author?

"I thought it was good news!" Emma said. She looked at Camilla. "You'll get your second check this September instead of having to wait until April. I don't think it's bad to have the book come out in the fall. It means it's important. There *are* a lot of big books that come out then, but you're not competing with them anyway. With first novels it's always a crapshoot."

There was a silence. The next course was served. The

dinner was far from the cheerful event that Emma had hoped for. There seemed to be as much tension between Frederick and Camilla as there was between her and Alex. No one ordered either dessert or coffee. It was not a table anyone wanted to linger over. At last they were through, and Alex insisted on picking up the tab.

"Anybody for a drink?" Alex asked as they were leaving. It was raining, and they stood for a time under the canopy of the restaurant, hoping that an available taxi would whirl by.

It was a vain hope, and in the end Emma had to run to the corner and flag down two cabs—first one for her brother and Camilla and the second one for Alex and herself. When she got into it, wet and breathless, she saw Alex hesitate. Then she got in. Relieved, Emma directed the taxi uptown, to her apartment. "Come with me. We have to talk. Unless you want to be dropped at your place."

Alex shrugged. Emma cleared her throat. "I don't think it was very helpful, you being so negative about early publication."

"Why? It *is* a negative. You know she'll get buried. They're probably just doing it to fill a hole. They're not making it a major offering, are they? Have they even sent it out to the book clubs?"

"No. But it's not a book-club kind of book. You still didn't have to bring it up that way over dinner. It upset Camilla and embarrassed me."

"So what? That's my job, Emma. It's my job to protect Camilla and her book. Don't make it personal. I know the publication date wasn't your decision."

"Wait a minute. Don't talk to me about your professional duties. Tell me instead why you tried to lure Camilla away from our house."

Alex opened her eyes very wide. "Emma, I wasn't 'luring' her. I was trying to do the best I could for her. It's just business." Alex paused and looked out at the rain. "Anyway, isn't this Pam's project?"

Emma snorted. God, it was so unfair! "I *sent* her to you, Alex. How would it look if we lost her because of you?"

"Nobody knew you sent her to me. It wouldn't have damaged *your* reputation."

"*I* knew. You seem terribly worried about what's best for Camilla Clapfish. How about what's best for *me*?"

"I think it's best for you to calm down," Alex said coldly.

But Emma, for once, wouldn't calm down. For once, she wouldn't be a turtle. "I meet you and we see each other for weeks in a row. I send you clients. And then, once you sign them, you become so busy I don't even hear from you. You try to steal an author, and when you don't succeed you embarrass me in front of her. And you tell me not to take it personally? As Camilla might say, you're mad."

"Well, if that's the way you see things, maybe I'd better get out of this cab."

"Maybe you had better," Emma snapped back, though it took all her pride to clip the words out.

Alex rapped against the Plexiglas that separated them from the driver. "I'll be getting off at this corner," she told him. They were on the Bowery, somewhere below St. Mark's Place. It was a dicey neighborhood, especially at night. The driver pulled over, and Alex, without a look or a word, stepped out into the rain, slammed the door hard, and began walking across the wide avenue. Emma's last view of Alex was of the tall woman illuminated by headlights, flagging down a taxi of her own.

# 66

> An absolutely necessary part of a writer's equipment, almost as necessary as talent, is the ability to stand up under punishment, both the punishment the world hands out and the punishment he inflicts upon himself.
>
> —*Irwin Shaw*

Daniel couldn't believe his luck. Just when everything was going perfectly, this trouble with Judith had to hit. He wondered for a moment if she might not be lying. How could she possibly have gotten herself pregnant? He'd always insisted they use a diaphragm. Had Judith purposely forgotten? He put his elbows up on his desk, placing his head heavily in his hands. On the desk lay the check for the movie option, made out to Jude Daniel and perforated along the bottom with its explanatory memo, "film option." The number—so many dollars all at once—was exhilarating.

There was a knock on the door. He sat in his hot, tiny office and spun the chair around. "Yes?" he called out. His voice sounded anything but welcoming. When Cheryl's blond head intruded he couldn't withhold a sigh of irritation. Just what he needed! Another dumb, dependent woman.

"Daniel, I—"

He rose and started walking toward her. "I'm late," he said by way of explanation. "Walk with me to the car."

"But I wanted to—" They were in the hallway, and she was interrupted by a greeting from Dr. Esther Ruden. Since the news of Daniel's book had traveled, he had more than regained his old popularity in the department. It appeared that divorce was permissible in an about-to-be published commercial author. In fact, when news of the movie option had leaked, Don and his wife had actually offered to throw a little party in his honor. And all of the faculty was planning to drop by—invited or not. No business like show business, Daniel thought ruefully.

"Hello, Esther," he said. Although he hated the witch—a women's studies professor—he was tempted to stop and talk with her, just to deflect Cheryl. But he knew Cheryl would cling to him like a limpet. Moving into Fox Run had been, in the end, a bad idea. Cheryl had too much access. Esther nodded at him, but her slightly raised brow as she took in Cheryl at his side dissuaded Daniel from inviting conversation.

He quickened his steps, and Cheryl had to almost skip to keep up with him. "Will I see you tonight?" she asked.

Daniel shrugged. "I have a lot of work to do," he said, and saw Cheryl's lip tremble. God! These women would drive him insane.

Daniel had been thinking hard. A time came when each man had to act—to take action and change the course of his life. And you couldn't do it halfway—you had to go the distance or lose out altogether. Most people didn't get even one chance to change their lives. He was one of the lucky ones who had. If one missed that opportunity, lacked the courage to take all the actions, one could be lost forever. He would not wind up one of the lost, one of the losers.

"Daniel, I really need to—" They were in the parking lot, and Daniel was already unlocking the door to the brown Subaru.

"Cheryl," he said, "you know how much I value your friendship. But I'm very late and I just can't talk now. I'll try to come up to your apartment tonight. We can talk then." He got into the car and put the key in the ignition. But when he looked up, Cheryl was standing right at the door, her hand on the rearview mirror, tears flowing down her perfect, unlined face.

"I just wanted to—"

Daniel extended his hand and pushed her gently away from the side of the car. "Tonight," he told her and drove out of the campus parking lot.

It was very clear to him what he had to do. He would resign, pack up, and move to Manhattan. He had close to a hundred thousand dollars in his bank account. He'd get a deal to write the screenplay for *In Full Knowledge*. He would leave the school, the town, his ex-wife, his baby daughter, and leave Judith. She could have the apartment, their furniture, and the dog. She could get a job or finish school. He'd even offer to pay her tuition.

Of course, with a baby . . . well, that was insanity. This pregnancy was the worst possible luck. But then, Judith's timing had always been bad. The pregnancy, plus her threat to insist on credit for the book, had been enough to finally move him in the direction he should have taken before. Damn it. Now he couldn't leave her. Not until the pregnancy was taken care of. Daniel thought of the ABA convention and the party for him there. He wouldn't even tell Judith about it. He'd just go. But before he could leave Judith permanently, he would have to convince her that a baby was just not on. She wouldn't like it, because of her past, but he could tell her that there was plenty of time, that they had other priorities, and promise her a baby later. He sighed. There would be a scene, and tears. He'd have to hold her and comfort her. His skin crawled. He thought of Dreiser's *American Tragedy*, which now seemed more poignant than he had ever realized.

Daniel found himself gripping the wheel and grinding his teeth at the thought of the scene that awaited him. He hated to lie, but it was Judith who had put him in this position. All of this was Judith's fault.

"Cheryl's called three times," Judith told her husband. She had promised herself she wouldn't greet him that way, but the third call was more than she could take. If the girl was this nervous about a term paper, she was a psycho. But Judith suspected that term papers had nothing to do with it. She remembered how she had felt, a student of Daniel's, when they were having their affair. Was it her imagination, or did Cheryl have the same sound of urgency and fear? But Judith, unlike Cheryl, had never called Daniel's wife. Of course, Daniel hadn't moved her into the same building with his wife. Judith looked across the room at her husband. Was he sleeping with Cheryl? Or was Judith's pregnancy making her oversensitive, dependent, and suspicious? "She says she has to see you," Judith told him. Daniel threw his briefcase, not quite so new anymore, onto the chair beside the door.

The phone rang, and he snatched it up. "Hello? Yes." He listened for a moment. "I understand. She told me. I'll try to drop by later." Wearily, he hung up the phone.

It must have been Cheryl.

"Aren't office hours good enough?" Judith asked. "You don't have to go up there every time she buzzes for you."

Daniel walked past her to the kitchen and opened the refrigerator door. "Oh, come on, Judith," he said. "Let it alone." He looked into the fridge. "Don't we have anything cold to drink?"

Judith had herself finished the last bottle of soda water—it was the only thing that kept her from constant nausea. She'd been too tired and dispirited to trudge the four long blocks to the nearest 7-Eleven. Now that Daniel was back with the car, he could get himself something to drink or they could both go to the supermarket. But the idea of walking up and down the aisles of food made Judith dizzy and sick to her stomach again. She put her hands across the little bulge of her belly and sat down in the only comfortable chair.

Daniel came in from the kitchen, making do with a glass of tap water. It wasn't hot in the apartment—Judith had left the fan running on low all day—but Daniel was sweating. He sat down on the folding chair across from her. "We have to talk," he said. For a moment, a terrible moment, Judith thought Daniel might admit to an affair with Cheryl. What would she do then? But he merely looked at her, paused for a moment, and asked, "What are we doing?"

Judith looked back at him. "About what?" she asked and then followed his eyes as he looked down to her belly. "You mean about the baby?" And this time the wave of nausea that hit her was different; she broke out in a cold sweat and felt her mouth fill with bile.

Daniel sat there saying nothing. Judith looked at him, frightened that she might have understood his meaning. For once, just for once, she outwaited him. "This isn't a good time for us to have a child," Daniel began. "It was never in my plans, but now, of all times, it's a real problem."

"Why?" Judith asked. "Now that we'll have some money coming in, and you'll probably get tenure—"

"Having a baby is tremendously expensive."

"The school's insurance covers it," Judith said. "And we'll have more money now than we've ever had."

"You don't understand," Daniel interrupted. "This isn't about money. I don't plan to stay at school. We won't have insurance. And there will be traveling for the book, and for the movie."

"What do you mean?" Judith asked, her voice a whisper. "Do you mean that you don't want this baby?"

For a moment Daniel refused to meet her eyes. Judith couldn't believe it. She'd told him about her date rape in high school, about her father's reaction to that pregnancy, and the forced abortion. He couldn't . . . Daniel stood up. "It's bad timing," he said, turning away and walking back toward the kitchen.

Judith stood as well. "You don't want our baby?" she asked. It felt like the last straw.

"It's not that I don't want our baby, I just don't want it *now.*"

Judith's hands clutched her stomach, and then she

dropped them to her sides as she followed him. "What do you mean?" she asked in a voice so quiet that she saw Daniel stop to hear her.

"I just don't think we should have this baby now. I have the book tour, and I am thinking of leaving the school, and I have to get started on the next book. We'll have to go out to California when they start filming the movie. I want to write the screenplay. It's just not a good—"

"You son of a bitch," Judith whispered. She couldn't believe it, but it was time. "Why don't you come out and say it? Be honest for the first time in your life. You want me to have an abortion? That's what you want?" She picked up the lamp and, whipping the cord out of the wall, threw it directly at Daniel's head. He ducked, but the plug at the end of the cord caught his neck and the lamp fell to the floor. The damned toxic carpet muffled the crash, but Judith picked up the next handy object—a copy of Melville's *Typee*, and hurled it at Daniel. "You're crazy," she said. "You're sick." The book hit him in the chest, and he jumped up, knocking over the chair.

"You're the crazy one," he said, but Judith merely hefted a flowerpot from the windowsill and sent it flying toward him. It hit the wall with a satisfying smash, pottery shards and soil flying everywhere. "Judith, stop. You have to . . ." he took two steps toward her, his arms out as if to restrain her.

The phone rang, and Judith snatched it up and threw it at Daniel, the receiver hitting his forehead with a satisfying chunk. "It's for you," she said. "It's always for you." He moved toward her. "Don't come near me. I hate you. And I am not going to have an abortion. I won't." She knew she was screaming, that her spittle was flying, but she didn't care. "You're disgusting. You're a liar and you're disgusting." Judith started to sob, but she didn't want to cry. She wanted to kill him. She ran to the kitchenette and picked up the saucepan beside the sink.

"Judith, don't," Daniel began, but when he saw the

heavy pot in her hand he turned and ran for the door.

"You're disgusting!" she screamed and threw the pot, but he was already out of the apartment. She knew where he was going, but suddenly she didn't care. She looked around at the havoc and realized it wasn't enough. This apartment, this stupid life they had made together, should be torn apart, just as he wanted to tear apart the life that was inside her. She ran to the bookshelf and began pushing his precious volumes off the shelves, onto the floor, almost taking the fax machine with them. In moments, the carpet was littered with books. She threw over the table and then went to his desk and dumped each drawer into the middle of the room. Still, it wasn't enough. Then she saw his briefcase.

She got the vegetable peeler from the kitchen and sat down with the case. The leather was very fine. She slid the vegetable peeler across the smooth surface. A satisfying curl of brown leather lifted itself, leaving an ugly scar. She worked at the case for a few minutes, then opened it and dumped the contents onto the floor, along with everything else. She picked up a notebook and tore it in half. Childishly, she crumpled all the papers into small spheres and threw them in different directions across the room. Let Daniel try and grade those papers! Then she noticed a perforated bit of paper that looked, almost, like a check. She lifted it up. It had clearly been torn off a check, but it seemed to be the long stub or memorandum. "To Jude Daniel, option payment for *In Full Knowledge,* first installment $50,000 less agent commission of 20%." Judith stared, blinking at the amount. Daniel had received forty thousand dollars and hadn't told her about it. He had said that it would take months, or maybe more, before any money came in from the movie option! She had believed him. She was stupid. She scrabbled through the rest of the papers from the briefcase, but there was nothing else there. Then she went through everything that she had dumped out of the desk. Nothing. Then she noticed his sports jacket. She got up from the floor and went through his pockets. There, in the inside breast pocket, was a checkbook. She pulled it out.

The checks were printed with the name Jude Daniel. They used Daniel's school address. Judith wondered how long he had had this account. She flipped to the check register. There was an initial deposit of twenty dollars, followed by a deposit of twenty-five thousand, then another twenty-five thousand dollars deposited more than a month ago, followed by the forty thousand that was dated today. Despite a few small withdrawals, there was close to ninety thousand dollars in the account! Judith stared at the register. Why hadn't Daniel told her about this? Was he a thief as well as a liar?

It was then that she heard the whimpering. She stopped for a moment and, confused, wondered if it was the baby. That was crazy. On her hands and knees she followed the noise to the corner, behind the TV. Flaubert was lying there, whimpering, his long nose buried in the deadly carpet, his paws on top of his nose. She had never heard this noise from him. In fact, she realized that he had never been frightened or abused since they'd adopted him. Now the noise that came from his throat was a frightened, heartbreaking sound, and it seemed to express perfectly her own emotions. Gently she reached out to him and put her hand on his head. On her hands and knees, she put her face up against his. The dog was trembling all over, and she tried to hold him.

"It's all right," she said. "It's all right. You're okay. No one's going to hurt you." But the dog continued to shake, and Judith knew that he doubted the words as much as she did.

# 67

> For booksellers and publishers, [the ABA] puts us into a loop. It reminds us that we all love the business and that we're all part of the intellectual society of books.
>
> —*Bruno A. Quinson*

The ABA, the American Booksellers Association, holds a mammoth convention each year in late May or early June. Aside from the booksellers—from tiny independents with a gross of less than twenty thousand a year to the buyers for Borders, Barnes & Noble, and the other massive chains, every agent, every publisher, most important editors, and all the authors of the moment attend the grand institution.

In the taxi on the way to the Chicago convention center, Gerald felt a headache coming on. In a way, the ABA was an anachronism. Despite the presence of national buyers whose pencils could write orders in the millions, nobody wrote orders at the ABA anymore. Now sales were all made long in advance through reps, computers, and catalogs. Gone were the days when booksellers gathered to actually press the flesh, judge the wares, and make their selections. But the ABA remained a kind of annual circus—in Gerald's opinion—where publishers with much fanfare presented their fall list.

It was a time for beating the drum and garnering publicity. In the last few years, particularly in light of some of the political books, it had also been more widely covered in the general press. Gerald supposed that the publicity had to be good for the book business, but the thought of personally marching down all those aisles filled with books, giveaways, agents, authors, would-be authors, bookstore owners, and all the related hangers-on and sycophants of the publishing trade made Gerald wince.

But worst of all was the fuss that Archibald Roget of Peterson had created over that little pissant, Chad Weston. He was the *cause célèbre*, and Davis & Dash had been made to look like a repressor of the arts. Not that the ordure Weston had poured into his work could count as art with anyone but the American Civil Liberties crowd. So now a bad book that no doubt would have simply disappeared into the muck from which it came was being touted by liberals as a political rallying point. No wonder the Republicans had come down so hard on the National Endowment for the Arts!

He'd avoid all the hypocritical hoopla that Archie had concocted. It would be easy—he had a killing calendar already—meetings, parties, the lot. And there were the speaker breakfasts each morning—another event Gerald abhorred and that this year he would certainly manage to miss. Life was far too short to spend time listening to Ivana Trump prattle on about the hardships of life as a single woman. When he had been forced to attend *her* speech he hadn't listened to a word but had become fascinated with the woman's hairdo. What a load! There was something there that defied gravity, mused Gerald, always conscious of his own hairpiece. It had turned out to be the most diverting breakfast lecture he had ever attended.

Jude Daniel's book had all the early indicators of a runaway hit, and Gerald simultaneously felt grateful for a shot at a megaseller and a stab of personal envy. Davis & Dash was throwing a big party for that. Booksellers—many of whom collected preprints—had been flooding the switchboard with calls for *In Full Knowledge* bound galleys. In comparison, despite the items that had been planted in columns and magazines, there was little early spontaneous interest in *Twice in the Papers*.

Each year the temptation to simply hide in his hotel suite became stronger and stronger. In his father's time, the ABA had been dignified, a gathering of book people. Now, like all other American businesses, it had devolved into nothing but a huckster's heaven. Gerald, always despising the mob, prepared to join it.

Pam turned over and lifted one eyelid. Jesus Christ! It was already nine-fifteen. Fuck! She'd missed the breakfast lecture that the vice president was giving. Not that she gave a shit about his book, his views, or anything else about him, but she *had* hoped to meet his wife, whom she was working on for a tell-all after the administration folded. Pam scrambled out of the bed and began pulling on her underpants. Shit! She had left her bags in her own room, and she didn't have time to go up there now. She slipped off the old underpants and turned them inside out so that the stiff side was away from her body. She and Jude had been playing footsy for over an hour in the bar last night before they ditched the rest of the crowd and came up to his room. Her panties still showed effects.

Pam walked around the bed, past Jude's sleeping form, and went into the bathroom. She washed her face and ran his comb through her hair. It was a nightmare, but she didn't have time for a blow job now. Not in either sense of the word. She used Jude's toothbrush, deodorant, and styling gel, then left the bathroom in disarray.

She had a meeting with Joy Dellanagra-Sanger, the fiction buyer for Waldenbooks and still the world's most enthusiastic fiction reader. Christ, how could she face that double-barreled Italian-Norwegian energy first thing in the morning?

She kept on the lookout for the most important book buyers. The fiction buying at Borders was shared between the soft-spoken, very literary Robert Teicher and the much younger, hip Matthew Gildea: Teicher handled the front half, and Gildea covered the back. Pam found it amusing that they split the responsibility alphabetically. She wondered where they divided authors; somewhere in the

*LMNO*'s? No one had split them since kindergarten.

She struggled into her dress, stuffed her panty hose into her bag, and slipped her bare feet directly into her heels. She went to the mirror over the bureau and did a quick makeup job. If she hurried, she could get a cab to the convention center and might just manage to catch the second lady before the breakfast meeting broke up. As Pam strode toward the door, Jude sat up, bleary-eyed from the wine, the blow, and the sex of the night before. "Where are you going?" he asked.

"I have appointments," she snapped. "So do you. You must have hung up on the wake-up call. Get yourself cleaned up and get over to the Davis & Dash booth."

"What am I supposed to do there?" he asked, his voice perilously close to a whine.

"Try selling a book," she told him. "And don't forget the party tonight. Get yourself a haircut and make sure you have a good shirt." Men! They never grew up, never took care of themselves. "I'm your editor, not your mother," she pointed out and marched out of the room.

Daniel walked up the entire first aisle of the convention center before he began to shake. In his dreams, in his nightmares, he had never imagined so many books. And this was only the first aisle! There must be thirty aisles, and every one was crammed with books, posters for books, light boxes displaying books, and walls of shelves of featured books. Somehow he had never imagined this. This river, this mountain, this avalanche of volumes in which his one small offering could so easily be buried.

He wasn't well. The night of drinking, sex, and cocaine was not what he was used to. He felt drained. The trembling in his hands moved up his arms. He had to sit down, get a breath, hold on to something, and get it all under control. Up to this very minute, Daniel had thought the success of *In Full Knowledge* was a fait accompli. Alf Byron's support, Pam's enthusiasm, their intimacy, and the sale to

Hollywood had all made it clear that Daniel had a hit on his hands. Up to now, the only problem he'd foreseen was Judith—a thorny complication but not truly catastrophic.

Now, confronted by all the competition at the convention center, Daniel felt both humbled and deeply frightened. Oh, he could charm Gerald Ochs Davis. He could even bullshit Alf Byron. He could screw Pam Mantiss, and—as long as he had to—he could manipulate Judith. But how in the world, Daniel thought, could he cajole store and chain buyers into picking out his book amid this juggernaut? How could he be certain they'd make his novel a bestseller?

It was Emma's first time at the ABA, and she was thrilled. Each year there were internal squabbles and jostling among the junior editors for the dubious honor of attending, while the senior editors tried like hell to avoid it. The Davis & Dash booth was one of the largest, with eleven enormous light boxes featuring the best—or at least the most commercial—of the fall offerings. Emma was impressed by the professional look of the booth, which actually included tables for meetings, shelf displays, and even half a dozen easy chairs, which weary booksellers seemed grateful to sink into. But it was the energy of the place that excited Emma more than anything else. It was a hive, a huge colony of booksellers and buyers who, if not all equally dedicated to the written word, at least made their living by it.

Her only disappointment was that neither of the books she cared about had been chosen for a light box or a special display. *A Week in Firenze* had been quickly run into very inelegant advance copies—no special cover and no typesetting. A mock-up of the proposed cover was on a shelf toward the back of the booth. Other than that, not a lot was being done for it. Emma wasn't really surprised. But it was the handling of *The Duplicity of Men* that truly upset Emma. A book as important, as beautiful as this one deserved more than the bit of shelf space and the page in the catalog that it had received. This was the reality of books as commerce, but seeing *Duplicity* here, treated so cavalierly by its own publishers, and knowing that of all the hundreds of thousands of volumes here that this was one of the handful of worthies was truly dispiriting.

What Emma thought of as the "Creepy Crawly Trawley" was featured in the light box right beside her. Its lurid cover featured a three-dimensional element that made the sea of blood and the severed finger seem to flow off the cover. Emma noticed that in the ebb and flow of the crowd, one man stood staring at the display. Dark-haired, gaunt, and hollow-eyed, he remained like flotsam on the beach while waves of people came and receded. As if mesmerized by the blood, the finger, or something. Emma was just beginning to get nervous. It wasn't just *The Catcher in the Rye* that attracted a following of disenfranchised kooks. Trawley's work definitely had a fringe cult of admirers. She looked more closely at the man's name tag: Stewart Campbell. He was a Davis & Dash author; he'd done a few mediocre mysteries for Pam. While his books were no worse than Trawley's, Trawley's sold in the millions and his sold remarkably little, and Emma wondered if this was at the root of his fixation. He seemed to be in so much pain that, for a moment, she considered telling him he shouldn't take it personally.

Pam had already made it clear among the cognoscenti that she had been the author. And it wasn't worth her job to divulge the secret to Stewart.

"Well, hello," an unmistakably deep voice said.

Emma looked up to see Alex surveying her with a cool grin. Emma couldn't help it; she blushed and hated the feeling of her face going hot. She hadn't seen Alex since they parted that night in the rain, though they had spoken once, briefly, on the phone. Neither had apologized, and now, standing opposite each other across the Davis & Dash table, Emma wondered how they'd bridge the impasse.

And then Alex did it, as simply and completely as it needed to be done, with nothing more than a wicked smile.

"You're looking good," Alex said, and Emma blushed again, but this time with pleasure.

"You too. The Armani was worth it," Emma told Alex, who looked down at herself and then grinned again.

"Where are you staying?"

"At the Hilton. But Davis & Dash assigned roommates."

"You're kidding! Who did *you* get?"

"Nancy Lee."

"Ooh, I'm jealous," Alex laughed. "How about dinner? I'm at the Sheraton, and *I* don't have a roommate—yet."

"I've got to go to the dinner for Jude Daniel," Emma said. "Come to that?"

"Sure. He's supposed to be the Next Big Thing. Who's *his* agent?"

"Alfred Byron."

"God! I thought he was dead."

"Wishful thinking. No, he's still torturing me on Susann Baker Edmonds's behalf."

"How'd he snag Daniel?"

They talked industry gossip for a while, and then Emma gave Alex a tour of the Davis & Dash booth. They giggled over the flap copy for GOD's new novel and sniped at the sell-out authors whose overblown accolades were on the back cover. Then they came to the shelves in the back. Alex lost her smile. "What the hell is this?" she asked, gesturing with a sharp jab at the shelf holding *A Week in Firenze*.

"Not much, is it?" Emma admitted.

"Jesus Christ, Emma. Is that all you have to say? Couldn't you *do* something about it?"

"I have nothing to do with the displays, Alex. That's all the marketing department. It's not even *my* book. Pam's the editor."

"Oh, for fuck's sake," Alex snapped. She grabbed the mock-up of the book and walked to one of the front shelves, clearing an armful of Gerald's *Twice in the Papers.* "Here, even *I* can do this." She walked to the back of the booth, setting Gerald's books down on the floor. Then she proceeded to the display of *A Week in Firenze* and brought them all up to the prime location of the featured book display. "There. That's better," she said, surveying her work.

"Alex, you can't do that. They'll only move them back."

"Well, in the meantime, someone might actually get a chance to see Camilla's book. Maybe one will even buy it. And then I'll get ten percent of the money—not enough to pay for my room at the Sheraton, but at least it's a start." She turned and started to walk away.

"Will I see you at the party?" Emma couldn't stop herself from asking.

"Sure," Alex said, but her smile was gone.

Roberta Fine was tired of schlepping. In her left hand she carried a tote bag from Houghton Mifflin, stuffed with a Random House poster, a Morrow calendar, and a plethora of advance copies. In her other hand she gripped a shopping bag provided by HarperCollins, almost as full.

Roberta had made it a point to see some of the publishing movers and shakers. Linda Braun of Doubleday and Scribner's, feisty, slimmed down, and coppery-haired, was terrific to deal with. She and Roberta shared diet secrets. At the Barnes & Noble booth Roberta had spotted the blond hair of brilliant Sesselee Hensley, buyer for the dreaded superstores. Roberta enjoyed listening to her Texas twang. Her last chat was with Karen Paterson of B. Dalton. Karen was not as commercial as Linda and Sesselee, which was a nice change. Roberta enjoyed her sense of humor.

Roberta had already had her picture taken with the vice president and had waited in line for Anne Tyler to autograph her latest offering. She'd also had a cup of coffee with Neil Baldwin, the mustached, tweedy director of the National Book Foundation. He'd charmed her. Such a lovely young man. A full morning, indeed. Now, all Roberta wanted to do was find someplace to sit down. When she saw the Davis & Dash booth ahead, complete with inviting upholstered chairs—rare as a literate best-seller at the ABA—Roberta made a beeline for one of the vacant ones. It was good to feel the cushion at her back, which had begun to ache in that nagging way that only a visit to her chiropractor would fix.

Roberta arranged her bags and packages around her feet and then had a chance to look around. From where she sat she could see the lurid cover for *Twice in the Papers* and the latest Susann Baker Edmonds. Roberta wouldn't bother to stock either one—they were the kind of books that her regular customers didn't buy and that the super-store down Broadway would sell at 30 percent off. She craned her neck to see if she could find the light box that featured *The Duplicity of Men*. But it must have been in one of the few beyond her view. Of course, she must take a photo of it and any other special part of the display so that she could give it to Opal when she returned to New York. If only she could sit here comfortably for just a few more minutes without feeling guilty. After all, she could sit when she got back home, but she'd spent more money than she really could afford to be here right now. She should maximize every minute. Roberta thought of the T-shirt that was popular at last year's ABA—"So many books—so little time." Well, it was true. And after all these years despite all the difficulties and the obvious financial problems she was facing now, Roberta still loved books passionately. At least some of them, anyway. And so she pushed herself out of the chair, fished her flash camera from her bag, and went looking for *The Duplicity of Men* display.

But there wasn't one. She checked every light box and the front of the booth. There was nothing. It was only when she got to the back that she found the small display and the inelegantly bound advance copies. Nobody would notice the book back here. Was this all that Davis & Dash was planning to do for the most literary book on their fall list? Roberta spotted a young woman standing idly beside the shelf of catalogs. Her name tag identified her as Nancy Lee of Davis & Dash. Roberta approached her. "You're publishing *The Duplicity of Men*?" she asked.

"*Publicity for Men*?"

"*Du*plicity," Roberta corrected.

"I don't think so, but let me check the catalog," the young woman said agreeably.

"Never mind," Roberta told her, and picked up her bags and strode away.

It was really quite unbelievable! After all the work Terry had put in, all of the heartbreak and rejection Opal had had to face. And now, at last, the book was being published and even the publishers didn't know it. *Publicity for Men*, indeed! There was no chance Terry's book would be noticed and bought by bookstores, which meant that there was no chance it would be read.

Roberta felt, for a moment, every year of her age. She couldn't troll the aisles any more today. For a moment she thought that she hadn't the strength to get on the shuttle and back to her hotel. She looked around at the faces of the other booksellers; then she got her idea. A letter cost only thirty-two cents to mail, and Roberta knew scores, maybe hundreds, of booksellers. She couldn't talk to them here, but she would write to them. She would write to them all and tell them just how good this book was. How it deserved to live.

Susann knew what to expect, but it seemed to her that every year it got worse. As she arrived a man had actually recognized her, but when he asked for her autograph and she agreed, he handed her a copy of *Border Music*. "But I didn't write it," she told him. "It's by Robert Waller."

"Yeah," he had said, "but *his* line was way too long."

Waller! Waller! Always Waller! Or Grisham. Last year the very average-looking John Grisham had been listed by

*People* magazine as one of the fifty most beautiful people in the world. Susann still seethed over that. Why have plastic surgery when book sales made you beautiful? And without book sales, was she then . . . There was no way to deny that her line was not nearly as long or robust as Anne River Siddons's, James Finn Garner's, and Chad Weston's. Janet Dailey seemed to have a pushing, endless stream of readers begging for her inscription. Peterson had—due to her leaving—dumped her book on the market with virtually no publicity. It was out, but Peterson was having no signing of it. But that only emphasized the spindliness of Susann's own line, where there used to be an endless and sometimes even violently enthusiastic crowd, complete with an occasional fracas. Susann knew what it meant when she was visibly reduced to a very thin trickle of supplicants. Perhaps they all were right, Susann thought. Perhaps she did need to tour the country and get closer, reconnect to her readers.

She looked at Pam Mantiss, who was obviously bored and distracted, waiting for the next bookseller to come by. The woman looked as if she had thrown her clothes on. Why couldn't she, Susann, work with a stylish, enthusiastic editor like Susan Sandler?

An older woman approached Susann and from out of a shopping bag pulled a battered copy of *A Woman and a Lady* and laid it on the desk. "I can't tell you how much this book meant to me," she said. "Could you sign it for me?"

Susann knew she shouldn't, it was a Peterson backlist title, but then again this was someone who had probably been reading her books from the start. "Certainly. And thank you, my dear," Susann told her, signing it gratefully.

"I'm your greatest fan," the woman said and pulled out a copy of another of her early novels. "Would you sign this, too?"

"Of course," Susann told her. Readers still did care. This woman had carted these books all the way to the ABA because they meant something to her. Susann's fingers were cramping, but she was touched, and signed her name with a flourish.

The woman now pulled out of her bag a paperback copy of *The Lady of the House,* truly dogeared and missing its cover. "Would it be asking too much?"

Before Susann could take the book, Pam Mantiss came from behind her, putting her face almost offensively close to the fan. "I'm afraid it would," she said. "You see, Miss Edmonds is very busy right now."

Susann looked at her editor, shocked. "Surely I can—"

"We didn't publish *any* of those fucking books," Pam hissed at Susann. She turned back to the tiny woman. "Ms. Edmonds only signs hardcover. You can get her to sign a copy of her new book when it comes out."

The woman turned to Susann and looked embarrassed. "I won't be able to afford to buy it until it comes out in paperback. But I'm sure I will like it," she assured Susann. Humbly, she put the unsigned book back in her bag and walked away.

Just then a bookseller came up and started talking with Pam. Pam approached Susann and slapped a copy of her last book in front of her. "Sign this. Write 'to my niece Rachel, with love from her Aunt Sissy.'"

Susann looked at Pam in dismay and blinked. "I can't write that," she explained. "After all, Rachel isn't *my* niece. And besides, you just said that I—"

"If you want these guys to order your *new* book, you'd better start writing," Pam snorted, handing Susann a pen.

Alf Byron was just hitting his stride. He had walked up and down the ABA aisles as if he owned them. He was back in the action, respected by all. The buzz about Jude Daniel's book was getting louder and louder. And when he walked into the party for Jude, Alf felt as if the party was in fact for him and his return as a player in the New York publishing scene.

It had been a long time between rains, but Alf had weathered the drought. For too long he had been thought of as an agent with one client, a kind of joke, a literary gigolo. And with Susann fading, whatever positioning he'd managed had been fading too. But now Susann was reborn. And the icing on the cake was the heat being generated by Jude Daniel, his new boy wonder. Had he been an Italian *gavone,* Alf would have clutched his crotch and readjusted his testicles; the fact was, he had a pair of balls now.

The moment he walked into the crowded room, Pam Mantiss spotted him and made her way over. After the bitter negotiations over Susann's contract and the possibility of a bad performance of her first book for Pam, this was a nice change. For a moment Alf felt guilty, because he knew he'd given Jude's book away. But he'd make it up on the next contract. Once this one hit the bestseller list any publisher would be happy to pay six figures to get a hold of the professor. Pam knew that as well as Alf did, and her smile and extended drink were only a premium on the insurance policy she was trying to establish.

Alf accepted the glass and took a sip. "Not bad," he said. The white wine was crisp and chilled, not the usual lukewarm Gallo chardonnay.

"I'm drinking it," Pam said, emptying her glass. She looked around the room. "Don't you hate this shit? People who hate you pretending they don't, and people who are envious pretending they aren't."

Alf nodded, but he actually loved it. "Well," he said, "a lot of people are envying both of us tonight. Editor of the Year, huh?"

Pam nodded. "Big fucking deal," she said.

"Well, you got a hell of a list," he said. "I don't know how you manage to pull it out time after time."

"Neither do I, Alf, neither do I." Pam grabbed two more glasses off the tray of a passing waiter and offered one to him. Alf shook his head, his glass still half filled. Pam shrugged, drained the first glass, and placed it on the floor, where it was sure to be stepped on. Then she gulped half of the wine from her second glass. Alf decided she would not be good company by the time the glass was empty.

"Where is the professor?" he asked.

"Look for the knot of women. He'll be in the center."

The room was jammed with the usual crowd. Binky Urban was talking with someone Alf didn't recognize. A new writer? If Binky was interested, so was Alf. Fredi Friedman, blond and elegant, was coolly listening to some minor agent. Alf walked by and heard the guy saying, "I have the hottest book in town, and we want two point five for it." Alf nodded to Michael Korda and was gratified to receive a nod in return. Finally, he made his way to the tight group near the bar. It was all women—editors, bookstore owners, and two of the buyers from the chains. The professor was in the middle of them, and as Alf shouldered his way into the crowd, they all laughed at some remark he had made.

"Well, you know it's true," Daniel continued. "Most men think there are only four things a woman should know."

"What are they?"

"How to look like a girl, how to act like a lady, how to think like a man, and how to work like a dog."

Again, the crowd broke into convivial laughter. "Of course, you're married," one of the women said flirtatiously. "None of us would be lucky enough to find out you're not."

Jude's face got serious. "Actually, I'm not. I was, but we're in the process of divorce." He sighed. "It isn't easy to live with a writer."

Alf looked around at the faces of the women. They looked as if they'd like the opportunity to see how hard it might be. The professor played them like a violin. The kid had a big future. Across the room, standing with Wendy Brennon, was Susann. Her eyes were on him, but when he looked at her she didn't change her expression or acknowledge him. Alf felt a momentary stab of guilt. For years, at parties like these, Susann had been the center of the group of women. He ought to go to her. He ought to find out how the book signing had gone. But here, in the center of the action, it was as warm as a Caribbean beach. Alf couldn't face the trip across the room to the frigid look, the tundra, that was Susann's corner of the room.

Alf elbowed a short woman aside and put his hand on Jude Daniel's shoulder. "Well, Professor, you don't seem to need my help now," he said heartily. "Not like when you first brought that manuscript to me."

The women turned their heads to look at him. Jude made some introductions, but Alf waved his hand. "I know most of you," he said. "Some talent we got here, huh? And I was the one who found him." Then he launched into the story of the letter he got from an obscure college professor to sit on a panel and how he, Alf Byron, had encouraged and created this new literary star.

# Part Four

## *The Bestseller*

The release of a book is rather like Jesus' presentation to the Temple: Anything might happen, from worship of the rabbis to attack by the Philistines. But whatever the initial reaction, over time very few books are remembered. Of the fifty thousand published each year in America perhaps three dozen become true national bestsellers. As the Bible puts it in Matthew 22:14, "Many are called, but few are chosen."

—Gerald Ochs Davis, Sr.
*Fifty Years in Publishing*

# 68

> When writers die they become books, which is,
> after all, not too bad an incarnation.
> —*Jorge Luis Borges*

Opal pulled hard, feeling as if her knees were about to give way. She was in an undignified and uncomfortable squat, clutching the narrow trunk of the weeping cherry tree that had been delivered just the day before. Aiello had worked most of the previous afternoon digging the hole, and now he, Roberta, and Opal had managed to drag the surprisingly heavy sapling to the center of the little lawn and sink the root ball into the waiting site. As Opal and Aiello strained, Roberta stood at the other side of the little garden and directed them to be sure that the trunk was perpendicular to the handkerchief square of lawn. Opal, usually appreciative of Roberta's perfectionism, snorted. It was almost as frustrating as having a sidewalk bystander help with parallel parking.

"Still more to the right," Roberta said, motioning with her long hands. Opal pulled in that direction as hard as she could. Sweat had broken out on her forehead. The sun was surprisingly hot. Who would have thought such a slender tree would have such heavy roots?

"Is this all right?" she managed to shout, despite her breathlessness, and Roberta paused before she nodded, as if she wasn't quite certain.

"Quick, Aiello," Opal gasped. "Get the dirt in. Pack it around to hold the tree at this angle." To her it seemed the tree was lopsided, as if she were pulling it over herself in an almost recumbent position. But she knew she was probably too close to it to tell and—as with a few other things she was too close to judge objectively—she would have to trust Roberta.

She was trusting Roberta more and more, anyway. They worked together now at the store every day and usually lunched or dined together several times a week. Roberta had introduced Opal to off-Broadway theater, and in return Opal had bought them a subscription to the symphony. Roberta had helped Opal with the garden and had brought her to the banker she herself had used for more than twenty-five years. Now Opal's out-of-state checks were credited as cash when she requested it, instead of after nine seemingly endless business days. It certainly made New York City a friendlier place when you knew people who knew people.

And Roberta knew people. She had told Opal all about the disappointing placement that Terry's book had gotten at the ABA. Then Roberta had handed Opal a letter, a letter that beautifully described *Duplicity* and urged booksellers to stock it. Roberta had asked permission to send it out to the list of independent bookstore owners, many of whom she knew. Needless to say, Opal had agreed. Yes, she was trusting her friend. Roberta had even found the Westchester nursery from which Opal had ordered this beautiful tree, this memorial to Terry.

Opal kept pulling at the trunk, though her arms felt as if they were being pulled from their socket. "Hurry up, Aiello," she said. "I can't hold it much longer."

"I know what you mean. I'm literally sweating bullets."

"You are not speaking literally," Opal had to say. She couldn't bear it when people used *literally* as an emphasis. "You might say *virtually*."

"I might say 'shut up and hold the tree.'" Aiello shoveled in two or three more spadefuls of earth and then stood on the spot, stamping the soil down around the tree. "Anyway, what's the diff?"

He was hopeless in a lot of ways, but he did know how to plant a tree. For the first time, Opal felt the pull the tree had been exerting start to lessen. She dared to loosen her grip and turned her head to Roberta, across the way. "Is it okay?" she asked, and Roberta nodded, coming to hold on to the trunk herself. Aiello went back to shoveling, and Opal slowly managed to come out of her undignified squat, listening to her knees crack, stretching her legs, and moving her arms in circles in their joints. She'd be sore tonight.

"Take a look," Roberta said, and gesturing with her chin. Opal walked back to the farthest corner, near the door to the apartment. She turned around, and the tree was perfectly centered in the middle of the perfect new green lawn. Behind it the white flowers, mostly impatiens and stock already in bloom, and the dark green of the two budding rosebushes made a perfect counterpoint to the brick wall behind them and the graceful tree in front.

Her two helpers, one on each side of the tree, looked at her expectantly. Opal nodded to show her approval, but she couldn't say anything more because her throat was choked with tears.

"Looking good?" Aiello asked, and Opal nodded again. Even Aiello was looking good to her. I must be on sentimental overload, she told herself. But he *had* been more than kind. In his own berserk New York way, he was a friend, too.

"So. We got something else for you," Aiello called and looked over at Roberta. "Just stay where you are." The two of them left the garden through the back doorway and reappeared a moment later, struggling with a bulky, heavy burden. It was a white wrought-iron bench, which they moved with difficulty into position under the tree.

"Is this about right?" Roberta asked.

"Do you like it?" Aiello called.

Opal nodded and came across the grass to the two of them. She was deeply touched. How had Aiello gotten the bench? As if he knew what she was thinking, he shrugged and said, "I had a friend in Queens. He gets this stuff sometimes."

Roberta looked at Opal and then put her finger on the plaque at the center of the bench back. Opal didn't have her reading glasses, but from where she stood she could make out the inscription.

In memory of Terry O'Neal,
beloved daughter of Opal O'Neal
and author of *The Duplicity of Men*

Opal could barely read the dates under that because of her tears. They rolled down her face and mixed with the sweat and the dirt she had unknowingly smeared across one cheek and the bridge of her nose. "Oh, it's really beautiful," she told them. "And a beautiful gesture," she added. Roberta nodded, silent.

"We got a great price on it," Aiello said. "My friend gave me a real break." Opal couldn't help but wonder whether the bench might have fallen off a truck or, worse, whether it might have been "liberated" from someone else's garden. One never knew with Aiello. But her thoughts didn't stop her tears or her gratitude. He took out a surprisingly clean handkerchief from his back pocket, blew his nose, and then offered it to Opal. She smiled and shook her head, preferring to wipe her cheeks with the back of her hands. "You got dirt all over yourself," Aiello informed her.

Opal looked down at her grimy hands. "I think I better wash up," she agreed, needing time to gather herself, so all three of them walked across the little lawn and into the apartment. When Opal looked into the mirror in the bathroom she very nearly burst out laughing. Her face was a mess of gritty black dirt and tear tracks, complicated by what looked like a sunburned nose and the mottled perspiration rash she sometimes got at her hairline. "You're no beauty, Opal O'Neal," she told her reflection, shrugged, and washed her hands and face. As she came out of the bathroom, Roberta was taking a bottle out of the refrigerator.

"I don't know if we should drink this or break it over the bow of the bench," Roberta said, indicating the champagne bottle.

Another lovely gesture! Roberta was so thoughtful. "Oh, I don't think the bench needs a christening," Opal exclaimed.

"Thank God," Aiello answered, "'cause I need a drink. But do you got any beer?" Sadly enough, Opal didn't. But she looked up at her two friends.

"Why don't I get some for you, and make a pitcher of iced tea? It's a bit early for drinking. We can have some lunch and save the champagne for after." She looked at Roberta, careful not to hurt her feelings. "Would that be all right?"

"Of course," Roberta told her. And then the doorbell sounded. Aside from Margaret, at the bookstore, Opal couldn't think of anyone else she knew who might drop by. She went to the virtually useless intercom and inquired who was there. Through the static it was hard to hear, but it was certainly a woman's voice, so Opal pushed the buzzer. They had a female mail carrier, but she did not usually buzz. Perhaps there was a registered letter?

Opal opened the door to find Emma Ashton standing there, beaming at her. "I took a chance you might be in," Emma said. "I wanted to surprise you." Then she saw the other guests and paused. "Oh. Perhaps this is a bad time," she said. "It's just that—"

"These are my friends, Emma." Opal made the introductions. "How very nice of you to come by. And it couldn't be a better time." She was about to take Emma's arm and show her the tree and bench, just visible from this angle, but Emma interrupted.

"Yes, it *is* a perfect time," she said. "Look what I have for you."

"Another gift?" Opal asked. "I've certainly been treated well today." And then she saw what Emma was extending toward her and stopped talking. It was a book—a really thick book bound in maroon buckram and covered in a midnight blue dust jacket. Emma held the book up, and Opal could see the title—*The Duplicity of Men*—in dull gold across the top. And there, in smaller letters across the bottom, "A novel by Terry O'Neal."

"Isn't it beautiful?" Emma asked. Opal nodded. "I hope you're as pleased with it as we are." Pride showed in her young face.

Opal reached out and took the satisfying heft of the book in her hands. There it was, as perfect as it could have been in any dream.

"It's the very first copy we received," Emma continued. "I . . ." She paused. "I brought something else as well," she said, and pulled a bottle of champagne from her tote bag. "There won't be much for all of us," she said. "I wasn't expecting a crowd."

"Oh, there will be plenty," Roberta laughed and retrieved her bottle of bubbly from the refrigerator. "Opal always keeps champagne on ice, just for occasions like this. Emma, why don't you help me with this?"

The two women got out glasses while Aiello struggled with the cork. Meanwhile, transfixed, Opal sank onto the daybed and began to reverently thumb through the book. If only Terry . . . She began to think, then shut that part of her mind firmly. I have done this for her, Opal told herself. It's not enough, but she would have been glad. And there was something wonderful, truly magical, about the word becoming flesh—well, at least ink and paper—something great about the bulk and smell and corporal reality of the book sitting there in her lap.

Emma handed her a glass of champagne, and Opal looked up. Her friends already held glasses. "To *The Duplicity of Men* and to Terry O'Neal," Emma said. They all drank, though Aiello didn't seem to relish his.

"Thank you," Opal said.

"Let's hope it gets the success it deserves," Emma said.

"Hardly likely with its placement at the ABA," Roberta sniffed. "You couldn't find it, much less buy it."

Emma's smile faded. "Were you there?" she asked. Roberta nodded. "It was too bad. The book deserves more," Emma agreed.

"It's going to get more," Roberta said and explained her letter-writing plan.

"That's great!" Emma said. "It's just what *Duplicity* needs. Word of mouth! Terrific." She paused. "How can I help?"

"Who do you know who'll send out letters?" Roberta asked.

Opal spoke up. "Surely you've done enough, Emma," Opal said. "The book would never have been published if not for you. Isn't that enough?"

"No," Roberta and Emma said together, and they smiled.

# 69

> There's an enormous difference between being a critic and a reviewer. The reviewer reacts to the experience of that book.
>
> —*Christopher Lehmann-Haupt*

Judith picked up the extension and listened to Pam Mantiss's voice. Daniel was in the kitchen, and Judith had been careful not to let the bedroom extension click as she lifted the receiver. Flaubert came to her side and looked up trustfully at her. Judith felt awful—she knew it was wrong to do this, but she simply *had* to get more information. Now she stood in the bedroom, dripping from the bath and listening in on a conversation *she* should be having with *her* editor. So why did she feel so guilty? Flaubert licked at the water on her legs. Daniel had reduced her to this, to sneaking information about her own book.

"A star," Pam Mantiss was saying. Was she talking about Daniel? Was he a star already? "You know how many first novels get a star in *PW*? And have you seen *Kirkus*?"

Daniel said he hadn't. Judith wondered who Kirkus was and looked around the bedroom—as if he might be there. But Pam screeched. "You didn't *see* it?" Kirkus was clearly an it, not a who. "I didn't think so," she continued. Judith wondered how Pam could be both shocked that Daniel hadn't seen Kirkus and at the same time expecting that he hadn't. "It comes out tomorrow," Pam explained, "but *I* have an advance sheet. I'm faxing it to you now."

Judith could hear the beep of their new fax machine. It was in the hallway, and she desperately wanted to see the review. But she had to hear this conversation. "Read it and weep—for joy," Pam Mantiss was saying. "And the pricks at *Kirkus* try so hard to disagree with *PW*, but they *still* had to give you a bullet. I'm telling you, advance sales are going to skyrocket. You've got to get in to New York," Pam said, her voice lowering to an even sexier tone. "I'm really hungry. Want to eat?"

Daniel cleared his throat. "I'll try," he said. Judith hung up.

When she walked into the kitchen followed by the dog, Daniel was greedily devouring the review on the faxed page in front of him. "What's that?" Judith asked as innocently as she could. Daniel was too busy reading to answer. Judith tightened her hold on her elbows in order not to snatch the paper out of his hands. Kirkus must be some kind of magazine or something. What had it said? What was *PW*, and what had *it* said? Judith could barely contain herself.

She looked at the back of the paper in Daniel's hand. She'd been reviewed! She almost danced in place, she felt so impatient. Flaubert felt her excitement and began waving his plumed tail. Hadn't Daniel finished reading it yet? Judith moved beside her husband and took his arm, trying to look over his shoulder, but he didn't even shift the page to accommodate her. She couldn't act as if she knew what it was.

Judith let go of Daniel's arm and, in return, was handed her review. The page contained short reviews of a few different novels. It wasn't like the long *New York Times* reviews she was used to. Her eyes scanned the titles until she found *In Full Knowledge*.

> Rarely does a first novel open with such power and authority. Twenty-two-year-old Elthea Harris is trying to cope with a boring job, financial problems, and single-motherhood, when she is abandoned by her lover, the third of three men to betray her. This final blow pushes Elthea over the edge, and she murders her three boys.

Because the grim story is so beautifully drawn, the unimaginable violence appears nearly an understandable response to the patriarchy that has murdered Elthea's spirit. The author movingly conveys flashbacks to Elthea's childhood, her father's suicide, and incidents of molestation by a stepfather.

But then some of the power of the book fades. Jude Daniel has done an admirable job of shedding light on the darkest parts of a woman's psyche, but in the last third of the book the plot becomes predictable and the ending trite. Still, the amazing power and clarity of the writing, the illumination of a woman in this much pain, is more than worth the price of admission. Jude Daniel is no Chekhov, but this is an unusually strong, highly commercial first novel.

Judith looked up to find Daniel staring at her. "But this isn't good," Judith said. "This isn't a good review." Flaubert, looking up at the two of them, stilled his tail.

Daniel smiled at her in an infuriating way. "It is, actually. It's got what we call 'money quotes' in it." Judith noted the *we*.

Gently Daniel took the page from Judith and began to read aloud. " 'Daniel has done an admirable job of shedding light on the darkest parts of a woman's psyche,' " He looked up and smiled at Judith. " 'Rarely does a first novel open with such power and authority,' " he continued. "We could put both of those excerpts on the back of the jacket. Or in ads. That, along with the *PW* review—"

"There was *another* review?" she asked, as if she didn't know. "But the book hasn't even come *out*."

Daniel smiled, his smile so damn condescending. "There are a couple of publications for booksellers," he explained. "They have to review books before they come out so that bookstores know how to order. *Publishers Weekly* is the big one."

"So they review all books, not just the good ones?" she asked.

"They review about eighty-five percent of all novels," Daniel said. Judith wondered where he'd learned this. "For a first novel, an author with no track record, the *PW* review is critical. My review is a good one." Daniel went to the hallway and got out his briefcase. He didn't seem even to notice the scars that the vegetable peeler had made on it. It was as if she couldn't cause him any pain. "I've got to get to the train," he said, looking at the schedule. "I have a dinner to go to."

"Since when?"

"Since my review. We're celebrating because the *PW* review was so very good. It was given a star, which means it was a notable, maybe an important, book. That star will be worth hundreds, maybe thousands, of advance orders from bookstores. It's really very important for my career."

His career. His review. And he didn't even show me, Judith thought. He didn't let me know at all. What else don't I know? She thought of the checkbook, and the sound of Pam Mantiss's voice over the phone. She remembered all the phone calls from Cheryl. "May I see the *PW* review?" she asked, and was embarrassed that her voice came out in a shaky whisper.

"Sure," Daniel said casually. "It's here someplace." He continued to search through his briefcase. Finally he pulled out a crumpled page.

Judith had to restrain herself from snatching the review out of his hands. Her eyes ran over it, and phrases—what Daniel would call "money quotes"—jumped out at her.

> First novels don't often achieve the authority of voice that this one has." "The compassion created for a woman who has committed this heinous act is a masterful achievement. Daniel shows how an action so wrong can, at the worst of times, feel so right." "More than a crime saga, more than a page-turner, the novel,

> like Flaubert's *Madame Bovary*, gives us a heroine whose actions are morally indefensible and self-destructive yet human and understandable to the core.

Judith held the page tightly, but her hands began to shake and the tears in her eyes stopped her from what she really wanted to do—go right back to the beginning and read the review over and over again. It was a miracle to her that this person—someone with the power to write a review read by thousands of book buyers—understood. All of those months alone in her little turret room had added up to this, this moment when someone else had read what she had written and had known what she had tried to do with every word; more than that, they had felt what she wanted them to feel. The power of that made it hard for her to breathe, and she felt the tears at the corner of her eyes begin to slide down her cheeks.

"Daniel, why didn't you tell me about this? How come I didn't know?"

"Oh," he said. "I meant to. It's just that I've been so busy. There was the ABA, and then planning my book tour—"

"Daniel, it's our book. And I didn't even know that it had been reviewed. What else don't I know, Daniel?" She stared at him for a few moments, and as he looked back at her she thought that just possibly he might actually tell her the truth, come clean, and be the Daniel of old. But she was wrong, or the moment passed.

"Judith, you're blowing this completely out of proportion," he said. And she realized that she'd lost him.

# 70

> The *New York Times* list is a bunch of crap. They ought to call it the editor's choice. It sure isn't based on sales—
>
> —*Howard Stern*

"What do you mean, we're lost?"

The limo driver didn't answer. His name was Biff. Susann should have known not to trust a man over fifty named Biff—or under fifty, for that matter. He didn't respond. Certainly Biff had heard her. She raised her voice. "What do you mean?" she repeated. "You said you knew the way between Albuquerque and Santa Fe. You said this was your country. How can you be lost?"

"It's not so much that I'm lost as much as I don't know where we are."

"Well, *there's* a comforting distinction," Susann snapped.

"You were the one who wanted to get off Twenty-five," the driver said accusingly. "Twenty-five would have taken us right into Santa Fe."

"Edith wanted to see a pueblo," Susann explained, not for the first time, and then was irritated with herself for even bothering. As if a Biff deserved a word of explanation. What had the Duchess of Windsor said? "Never complain, never explain." Well, Susann agreed with the second part, but certainly not the first.

She leaned forward, sliding open the panel beside the seat. Nothing. No ice chest, no drinks, no television. None of the pleasures or comforts she'd been promised. Perfect. "This thing isn't a limo," she muttered. "It's a hearse."

"It could be worse," Edith said.

"How?" Susann snapped.

"Well, you could be traveling in a coffin instead of the backseat."

Susann laughed. Anne Rice had made a spectacle of herself, starting her last book tour riding in a coffin through downtown New Orleans. Since when were writers side-shows? In Susann's opinion the only thing bigger than Rice's royalties was her hunger for publicity. And her bad taste.

"I haven't gotten to see a single thing on this trip," Susann complained.

"What a lie," Edith said serenely, knitting away. Damn her nimble fingers! "There have been countless hotel lobbies, bookstores, and radio studios. Not to mention airports. *Lots* of airports."

"I mean a sight. A cultural landmark." Susann sighed. These first two weeks had been grueling, but Edith had been a gem. Unperturbable, always prepared, she returned phone calls, packed and unpacked, ironed Susann's clothes when necessary, kept her supplied with bottled water, opened the books for Susann's signatures, and kept her eye on the huge pile of luggage.

Susann looked out the tinted window. The light was beginning to fade. The road, a single-lane highway through the desert, was paved, but that didn't stop the limo from throwing up clouds of dust into the twilight. If Biff didn't know where they were, why didn't he stop? She'd have to tell him what to do.

She was so tired. She'd started the morning at five, done a radio call-in show where they had given away a dozen copies of her book while she answered questions from the locals, including what she thought of the new Albuquerque city manager. As if she knew. Then she'd done two bookstore signings, had lunch with the manager of the New Mexico Borders stores, and as if that weren't enough, finished up with another signing. It had all been as dreary and tiresome as the previous sixteen stops. The only relief and comfort Susann had was Edith. That was why, when

Edith asked to see a pueblo, Susann—who had no interest herself—had asked Biff to oblige.

Alf had abandoned her almost completely. He hadn't even called for four days. He was all caught up in the Jude Daniel nonsense. When he did call last night, it was only to tell her that the *New York Times* had phoned Davis & Dash to verify the title and their summary of her book's plot, a sign that it was being considered for the list. It wouldn't be reviewed, of course. Her books never were. But even the *Times* had to admit that they sold.

How the *Times* weighed and balanced its very subjective list was a mystery. Commercial books always got a bad deal. Why, one week, when Howard Stern's book had sold fourteen thousand copies, it had dropped to second place behind Colin Powell's, which had only sold three thousand! Alf had managed to worm out the fact that Susann's book was number seventeen on the hardcover fiction list. That was not as good as she'd hoped, nor as good as it had once been. Until the last two, her books had always zoomed up to number one during their first week in the stores. But she was struggling back from the failure and couldn't expect to be launched at the number-one spot—although she had secretly hoped for it.

Number seventeen was a start, but achingly hard to accept, because the *Times* only published the top fifteen bestsellers. Seventeen was as useless as twenty or fifty or seventy-three. Still, there was plenty of time to hope. Tomorrow they would get the early results from the *USA Today* list, which reported the top fifty. She'd surely be on *that* list.

"It's getting dark," Edith said, peering out the window. "I don't think we'll be able to see a pueblo anyway."

They were driving through a canyon, and though the sun might not have set up above, the floor of the canyon was already dark. "Turn around," Susann told Biff.

"Turn around?" the idiot at the wheel repeated.

"Let's get back to Twenty-five," Susann told him. From

the rear seat she could see the driver shrug. If his neck wasn't so thick, she would have liked to put her knobby fingers around it and do some of her arthritis exercises.

Then, as if he had read her thoughts, the driver swerved in a diabolical U-turn, throwing Edith up against Susann and the two of them to the side of the limo. Edith nearly skewered her with a number four needle. Biff had done a wide turn, fishtailed off the road, and now the heavy limo seemed to sink in the soft sand. Biff gained control of the wheel but then gunned the motor. With a sinking heart, Susann heard the whine of a wheel spinning and going nowhere.

"Oh, shit!" Biff said, and gunned the useless motor once more. Susann looked at Edith, who leaned forward and lifted her knitting bag, which had been thrown to the floor.

"Don't worry, I have sandwiches," Edith told her and patted Susann on the knee.

# 71

> I think a book should have a very good chance of earning out or you shouldn't buy the f—cking book.
>
> —*Roger Straus*

Gerald had just finished going over the advance orders with Pam when she paused. There was nothing for her to be so cheerful about—David Morton had announced his disapproval of last quarter's results, not only to Gerald but to the press. Still, Pam had been smirking for most of their meeting, and Gerald suspected it was because the Trawley book was already number four on the *Times* list. An author's death usually precluded further financial success, except in Peet's case. In its first week of release, despite his threats and an ultimatum to the the sales force, actual initial orders for *Twice in the Papers* had barely reached thirty thousand hardcover copies.

Of course, Carl's computer wizardry would begin to change all that. With Morton on the warpath, Gerald couldn't afford any vulnerability. His book, at least on paper, would look as if it were doing respectably well. But meanwhile, Gerald knew that Pam, with her nose for an advantage, would be weighing his monies against hers. He'd received a $1.1 million advance on sales of thirty thousand copies while she'd gotten a paltry $250,000 payment on hardcover sales that were already approaching 750,000 copies. She felt she'd succeeded where he'd failed again. Next she'd be hitting him up for a book contract of her own.

Gerald sighed. "The Annie Paradise book looks pretty good. Maybe we should goose it with radio ads. We need something to show Morton."

Dickie Pointer shook his head. "It's topped out. It won't sell any more than that."

Gerald looked at the initial orders for Susann Baker Edmonds's book. They had been light, but there had already been some feedback from the field based on her tour. Slowly but surely the old bag was really charming the orders out of the sticks, and Gerald's hope that this book would not be a fiasco rose. He'd shelled out such a monstrously big advance that Morton would surely use it against him if this book didn't move. They had barely spoken since Frankfurt, and then only at board meetings. Gerald winced at the idea of another dressing-down.

"What is Edmonds at now?" he asked.

"Number seventeen on the *Times* list. It might move up."

More worrisome was *In Full Knowledge*, which, for a first novel, had received healthy orders after the ABA but hadn't any apparent sell-through. Gerald *knew* the book would be a hit but was surprised at how slowly it was taking off. He didn't even want to *think* about what he would do if the quarter of a million books he'd printed began to flow back to their warehouse.

"I want the two of you totally prepared for the meeting with Morton. Pam, you better know your numbers inside and out." Pam nodded. Dickie shrugged. Dickie never knew anything *but* numbers.

"Anything else?" Gerald asked, facing Pam's smirk for the final time before he dismissed them.

Pam asked, in her very least inflected voice, "Did you see that ridiculous review?"

Gerald looked up at her. He knew her well enough to recognize her lack of affect for a setup. "What review?" he asked.

"The *Times* review of *Twice in the Papers*. You mean you *haven't* seen it?"

For a moment Gerald actually thought she was joking—a bad joke—and one he would have punished her for, but the smirk and her narrowed eyes told him she was serious.

"The *Times* reviewed me?" he asked. It was impossible that it would happen without him knowing it. He was friends—or at least socially familiar—with Christopher Lehmann-Haupt. But since his first book, the *Times* had politely not condescended to even mention his work—it was too commercial. Still, Gerald knew if they did review it, they would be savage, and he had been grateful. No mention was an accommodation rather than an embarrassment. "What *are* you talking about?" Gerald snapped, trying to sound bored rather than frightened.

Pam was po-faced. "You haven't seen it? Well, it's running tomorrow. A friend faxed it to me." She innocently looked through her messy pile of papers. "Wait, I'll see if I can find a copy. I just *assumed* you had already read it."

Gerald shot his cuffs as an alternative to strangling Pam. He didn't know who she blew to get *any* advance word from the *Times*, but she must have known he hadn't seen a review from there: They were demons about leaks. She shrugged, shifting her large breasts.

"I must have left it in my office," she said. He watched her as she sashayed out of the room, and he and Dickie sat there silently, waiting for her return. It didn't take long for Pam to reappear. Gerald tried to be prepared.

Pam glided across the vast, carpeted space of his office and handed him the faxed page. Gerald scanned it. "This roman à clef pretends to be literature when it's in fact a badly reported, fictionalized account of a long-dead scandal." Gerald ran his eyes further down the page. "If this account of these tragic events was compassionately rendered or offered the reader some insight into why things happened as they did, the book might have a vaguely redemptive quality. Instead . . ." Gerald kept his eye moving, allowing himself to feel nothing, to show nothing. "Hackneyed . . . presumptuous . . . turgid . . . ultimately boring." Gerald forced himself to smile. "Ah," he crooned dismissively. "The *Times*. The bastion of middle-class morality."

Pam raised her eyebrows and ventured another small smile. "You know how I feel about being the bearer of bad news," Pam said with exaggerated concern. Gerald knew *exactly* how she felt and would never give her the satisfaction of showing even a flicker of his feelings.

"Well, this can only help," Gerald said. "Exposure is the name of the game. Thank God."

Pam raised her brows, as if questioning his view. Ah, well, Gerald comforted himself, all the more mysterious to her, then, when—with the help of Carl Pollenski—Pam would see sales for *Twice in the Papers* escalate.

"I think this may work in the book's favor," he repeated as cavalierly as he could manage. "After all, they spelled my name right."

Dickie reached for the review, but Gerald shook his head. "I'd like to go over it again later," he said. He could not bear to have Dickie read it in front of him. Even less did he want to imagine David Morton gloatingly reading it tomorrow over breakfast. And Senior! His father would choke on his toast.

Gerald managed a smile, though it felt to him more like a death's-head grin. "Well," he said, "with the full-page ad we're running, that puts me twice in the papers. Which, as my book points out, is all that anybody needs in their lifetime."

# 72

> For several days after my first book was published,
> I carried it about in my pocket and took surreptitious
> peeps at it to make sure the ink had not faded.
>
> —*Sir James M. Barrie*

Camilla looked up, responding to the knock at the door. It was probably Will Bracken, the writer from across the hall. Camilla didn't want to leave her desk or her manuscript, but she rose and crossed the little room.

The flat that she'd rented in Park Slope could be a lot worse. It was the front half of a floor in a brownstone, what was called a dumbbell apartment because of the two largish rooms with a tiny bath and kitchen in between. It reminded her a bit of the North London digs that students used to cluster in near Camden Lock. The floors here were just as splintery, the walls just as cracked and desperately in need of a paint job, and the light fixtures and appliances were truly ancient. It would not have been too grim if Camilla had had the time and money to fix the place up.

But she had neither, nor the interest. Somehow, after living in Frederick's pristine and truly beautiful apartment, Camilla didn't feel there was much point in trying to make a silk purse out of this place. It would never be all right. For one thing, the light was all wrong, and so was the view—the back gardens reminded her of Birmingham. She missed Manhattan, the haven of Frederick's apartment, the doormen, and Frederick himself.

Seeing him in the evenings had punctuated her day. She wrote better, knowing that she would be reading her words to him later. And, while she had been alone at Frederick's flat, she had never felt lonely. Why had she traded all that away? In retrospect, her prickly pride seemed stupid. In return, all she had gained was what she could laughingly refer to as her "independence": her menial job with Craig at Citron Press, her lonely flat, and her distressing neighbor, Will, now knocking again at the door.

"Who is it?" Camilla asked. There was no security in the building other than a front-door buzzer system that was broken as often as it worked.

"It's Will. You working?"

Camilla opened the door. "I was," she said pointedly, but Will merely shrugged an apology. He was tall, thin, and balding, with small blue eyes and a beaky narrow nose. William Bracken was a serious writer, and a good one, but life usually didn't reward either trait.

"I could come back later," Will said, but Camilla shook her head and held the door open. Will had helped her move in, given her a few bits of furniture, and shown her around the neighborhood. He was a nice man, and she actually liked him and respected his work. It was just that he was so depressing, and that she had so little time for her own writing.

Will sat down in her one chair and crossed his long legs. "So, how's it going?"

"Slowly," she said, and he nodded understandingly.

"The second one comes slow," he said. He'd already written eight books, all of which had been published, most to glowing praise. But each dense and beautifully written novel had sold fewer copies than the one before. Will had explained that in the last decade of persistent writing he had seen his advances drop from their initial modest amounts to a pittance. "When Elmore Leonard was asked what was the best thing to write to make money, he said 'Ransom notes!'" Somehow Will managed to exist without taking a teaching job or any other work. Despite sales of less than three thousand copies of his last book, despite the refusal of his publishers to put out another, Will had written on his beautiful text enough to keep him satisfied, his frugal way of life enriched only by his manuscripts.

"Let me take you for a walk," Will said. "You could use a little stretch, and I want to show you something."

Camilla looked at the manuscript but only for a moment. She respected Will's advice. "All right," she agreed and grabbed a jumper. They walked out the narrow hall and down the two flights of stairs to the street. Prospect Park was to her left, so Camilla was surprised when Will turned to the right and began walking in the direction of the little street of shops and services that catered to many of the Park Slope residences.

"How's Craig?" Will asked.

"Hyper and enthusiastic as usual," Camilla told him. Will worshipped Craig, who had found him in his obscurity. Will's long-suffering wife had finally tired of him and left. Shortly after that Will's publisher had refused his seventh novel—which Will felt was his best. Will had contemplated suicide, but soldiered on for the sake of the books still unwritten. Then, after a really rough year, Craig had found him in Brooklyn and not only offered him a three-book contract but told him how much he'd always admired Will's work and how proud he would be if Will would sign with the newly formed Citron Press. It had been like a rebirth for Will, and he wanted to sing Craig's praises at every opportunity.

Craig and Camilla had given him renewed hope. In return, Camilla had learned from Will's example just how easy it was for a novel and for a writer to be lost. Alex had promised her that she would fight for additional advertising dollars, book signings, and publicity, but Camilla had been more frightened by Will's life than she liked to admit, even to herself. This was *not* the life she had envisioned. Will had admitted that he couldn't even pay for the dental work he desperately needed and had been suffering a toothache for weeks.

Now Will seemed to be over the pain—his jaw was no longer swollen—and was leading her past a few cafés and the greengrocers. He turned and opened the door to the bookstore. "Here," he said, "I've got something to show you." She followed him into the cool darkness of the shop, and he led her to a shelf beside the window. "Look," he commanded. He pointed to the bookshelf. There was Pat Conroy's latest, along with books by Tom Clancy and . . . she blinked at what she saw: the cover of *A Week in Firenze*, and under the title her own name.

"But, but . . ." Camilla knew she was gasping like a fish. Although she had received her first copies of the book, it was not due out yet. "I thought its publishing date was next month," she said. "How could it—"

"Oh, no one pays attention to pub dates in this country," Will said, "except maybe reviewers. They have such a backlog of advance copies that they publish their critiques by pub date. But bookstores receive copies in advance."

Camilla stared at the book, taking its place there in the orderly rows among the others. Her book. "How extraordinary," she said.

Will nodded. "Quite a feeling, huh? Now I'll tell you something. You don't get tired of it." He grinned. "I've never passed a bookstore anywhere where I didn't go in and check. And I feel a thrill every single time I find my books." He paused. "I check libraries, too," he admitted.

Camilla could only stand in the little Brooklyn bookstore, far from Birmingham and Firenze, and experience the greatest thrill of her life.

"Congratulations," Will said and stuck out his hand.

"Thank you," Camilla responded, taking Will's hand and suddenly, desperately, wishing Frederick were there.

# 73

> The family only represents one aspect of a human being's function and activities . . .
>
> —*Havelock Ellis*

"You know what Mother would say," Frederick told Emma.

Emma nodded, though she wasn't sure Frederick could see her nod. "You can't be nice to some people," she said, in a perfect imitation of her mother's intonation.

Frederick laughed. "I was thinking she might say we've been dissed by love."

Emma laughed. "There are a lot of things that Mother says, but *dissed* is not one of them." Talking about loneliness and failure wasn't something Emma did easily, but she knew it wasn't easy for Frederick, either. "I think we try too hard," Emma ventured.

Frederick nodded. "Our generation of Ashtons seems to have lost all feeling of entitlement," he said. "Along with some of their eyesight. Why do we give people things? Why did you give clients to Alex? Why did I give the apartment to Camilla?"

Emma shrugged, then realized that Frederick couldn't see her response. "I don't know. What's your theory?" She took his arm. They were walking through the Conservatory Garden, a fenced-in section of Central Park that was beautifully planted and maintained. Frederick liked it because the ground was even, and there was a statue in the south garden that he could run his hands over. There were also the scents from the herbs, roses, and what was left of the perennials. It was a small oasis in the city, a beautiful place, and Emma was glad that her brother could enjoy it, even with his dimming vision.

"It's a very bad thing to have someone feel indebted to you," Emma opined. "I think it makes us paranoid—we feel we're in danger of being used—and it makes them resentful."

Frederick laughed. "So, why do we seem always to put people in our debt?" he asked. "Well, no good deed goes unpunished." He looked at his sister, tilting his head, birdlike. "You know," he said, "I really love her."

"I know," Emma said softly. "But I think you scared her off. I'm sure she felt odd being kept by you."

"Emma, that wasn't my intention! Kept? You don't keep people. Not in the nineties. I was only lending her my empty apartment."

"Oh. So you never slept with her?"

Frederick paused. "Well, not in New York."

"What did you do? Go to Jersey?"

Frederick didn't even laugh at her joke. "No," he said. "What I mean is, that part was over *before* we came to New York."

"Say what?"

"We slept together in Florence," he explained. "I hadn't really meant to, but then we did. Afterward I told her about my sight, and that I wouldn't bother her in that way."

"Let me get this straight: You slept with her and *then* you told her?"

Embarrassed, Frederick merely nodded. "And then you told her you wouldn't have sex with her again?" Frederick winced.

Emma kept quiet and waited. Frederick broke first. "I hadn't told her *yet,*" he said. "I meant to. Then she invited me up to her room, and I—"

"*She* invited *you* up, you slept with her, and you told her about your eyes. Then you never slept with her again?"

Frederick nodded.

"Was the sex awful?"

"No! It was wonderful. But she wouldn't want to be put in the position of having to reject me—"

"You're an asshole, Frederick," Emma said, shaking her head. "I'm surprised she didn't kick you in the nuts. You know, you were my only proof that all hetero men aren't jerk-offs, and here you go, blowing my theory."

"What did I do? I mean, I know I should have told her first. But then I made up for it. I let her off the hook."

"Did you give *her* the choice? Did *she* want to be 'let off the hook' as you so quaintly and I hope only figuratively put it? Maybe it feels like *you* rejected *her*. It would to me."

"Are you speaking from experience?" Frederick wanted to know.

Emma looked at him. "No. It was different for me. Alex acted as if she liked me, then I gave her Camilla and Opal O'Neal as clients, and then she ignored me. I didn't ignore *her, she* ignored *me*. She was using me."

"Maybe she was just busy."

"No, Frederick. I didn't hear from her for a week at a time. Then she would call me and yell at me about how Camilla's book wasn't being handled properly."

"That doesn't sound like ignoring."

"Once she got so mad she got out of the taxi we were in and left me on the Bowery."

"That doesn't sound like being ignored either. It sounds like you were mixing work and your personal life, but it also sounds like she's passionate about both." He paused. "She yelled. Then I bet you got too proud to call her."

Emma looked at him. "Are you speaking from experience?" she asked.

Frederick laughed. "How about a new book? I could write it. *The Ashton Siblings: Love Fuck-ups.*"

"Is it fiction or nonfiction?" Emma asked, grinning.

"It's self-help."

# 74

> Being a woman is a terribly difficult trade, since it consists principally of dealing with men.
>
> —*Joseph Conrad*

Judith didn't know where to turn. Because she knew now that she *had* to turn somewhere, take some action to try and protect herself, to take back what was hers. But how hard would it be? Humiliated and enraged, she still couldn't face calling her father, the only person she knew who dealt with lawyers and courts and suits. Admitting to her dad that his low opinion of Daniel was right was beyond her.

She was also afraid she'd weaken and wind up installed back in her old bedroom in Elmira. She was equally afraid to go to the three or four small law firms in this town, for fear that word would get back to Daniel and the faculty, though why she cared was beyond her. Somehow, it just seemed best to keep this secret. Perhaps, if she could threaten Daniel, he could see what he'd done wrong and they could patch things up, before it was all too late. Stealth, it seemed, was the only tactic she could use.

Judith decided that Albany might be her best shot—there were nothing but lawyers in the state capital. But which one? She had no one to ask, so in desperation she let her fingers do the walking. From a phone booth near the student union she began to make her calls. She opened the list at an *S* page, and Mr. Slater was the first lawyer who answered his own phone and took her call. "I have a legal problem, and I need help," Judith managed to blurt out. Just saying it out loud made it more real, and her hand began to sweat against the plastic of the telephone receiver.

"Is this a marital case? I don't do marital law, though I could—"

"No. Not really. It's about theft, uh, plagiarism." Judith realized she really didn't know a word to describe Daniel's betrayal. "You see, I've written something and someone else has published it."

"And you haven't gotten paid?" Mr. Slater asked. "That would be a contract dispute. Do you have a written contract?"

"Yes. Yes, well, a contract without my name on it."

"I don't understand," he said. "You had a contract to write something, but you didn't put your name on it? Whose name *did* you put?"

"A made-up name, a pen name. And now my husband is saying that it's *his* pen name." Oh, God, it was so confusing. It was so hard to explain. "Could I come in and see you?" Judith asked, her voice shaking. And when Mr. Slater said yes, she quickly accepted the first appointment he offered. She hung up the phone, her hands drenched in sweat.

"So, what you're saying is that you wrote this book of your husband's," Mr. Slater summarized. He was a big man with freckly skin and thinning reddish gray hair. He folded his hands and set them comfortably under his paunch while he leaned his chair back and surveyed Judith.

"The book is *not* my husband's," Judith corrected. "It's mine."

"So you say. Well, I'm no expert in copyright law, but this would seem to be a copyright case. That's a federal issue. Expensive to pursue. Anyway, if it *is* a copyright issue, then what proof do you have?" He paused. "You say you wrote these drafts in your own handwriting. We have those, to start with." He lifted up a pencil to take notes.

Judith felt her stomach drop. She shook her head. "No," she said.

"No, what? You didn't write them by hand?"

"I did, but I don't have them. I've given them to Daniel."

"Then what did he do with them?"

"Correct them and give them back to me. But I'd type them, and when I was done he took the typed manuscript and the drafts."

"And what did he do with those?"

"He corrected the manuscript from them. You know, to make sure I got all the typos and changes. I don't know what he did with the first draft."

"So you have in your possession nothing, not one page, of your original handwritten work?"

"No," Judith admitted, her voice very small.

He sighed. "What did you type on?"

"A regular typewriter. Mine from college."

"You *do* have the manuscript you typed?" Mr. Slater asked. "That might be a start."

"No, I don't," Judith admitted. "Daniel had it retyped. I don't know what he did with my typed version."

"You don't seem to know a lot," Mr. Slater said.

"I didn't know any of this would happen," Judith protested.

"How long was this book, Mrs. Gross?"

"Seven hundred and twelve pages in manuscript," she admitted. At least she knew something.

"And you don't have *one* page, either in your handwriting or from your typewriter?"

Judith's lips trembled. She shook her head.

"And you have no contract or written agreement with your husband?"

Judith shook her head again.

"And he is a professor? He teaches creative writing?"

She nodded her head.

"And did *you* graduate college, Mrs. Gross?"

Judith shook her head. "I quit when I married Daniel.

Instead of going to school, I started on this book. We were doing it together."

"Well, you just said you wrote it alone."

"I did," Judith assured him, but she felt flustered. "I wrote it while he was busy teaching classes. It was a project we came up with together."

Mr. Slater stared up at the high ceiling, tapping his pencil against his legal pad. Then he shook his head, sighed, and looked back at Judith with that narrowed look of dismissal and contempt she'd seen often enough on her father's face. "Mrs. Gross, let me put it to you this way: Your husband, a recognized professional in the arts, has presented a manuscript to an agent, found a publisher, and gotten a contract on it. You say *you* wrote it, but you have no written agreement with him, no handwritten draft, no typewritten manuscript, no witnesses. In fact, you have no proof at all to substantiate your claim." Mr. Slater paused and tapped his pencil again. The sound click, click, clicked. He cleared his throat. "Sometimes, women—wives—of prominent men get confused. They help with a project, or hear a lot about it, and start to think it's their own. It's not a lie on their part, it's more like an exaggeration—"

"I'm not lying or exaggerating." Judith snapped. "I wrote that book."

Mr. Slater sighed. "Even if it *is* true, I don't believe you could get a court to listen to you. And as I told you, federal-court copyright cases are an expensive endeavor. Do you have the resources to undertake one? I'd require at least a five-thousand-dollar retainer."

Judith shook her head. "I thought perhaps you'd just take your fee after we won."

"I'm sorry, Mrs. Gross. I don't work on a contingency fee. And I don't think there's a judge or jury who would believe you. For what it's worth, I can tell you that I don't either."

*

Judith managed to get down the hall of the office building, find the ladies' room, and lock herself in a booth before she began to sob. She had at least that much dignity. For a moment she stood leaning her head against the back of the stall door, but the purse hook got in the way. She moved to the toilet seat—it had no lid—and sat weeping.

How could everything be so wrong? The affair with Daniel, quitting school, losing her friends, the marriage, the lonely months of writing; all of it added up to this humiliation. She'd been a fool, and she'd been used. Remembering how disappointed Daniel had seemed when her father had disowned her, she wondered whether she would rather have had him steal her money or her words. Well, actually, he had managed to do both. He'd take not only the credit but probably the money, too. Judith pulled some of the toilet paper off the huge roll and wiped her runny nose, but it was hopeless to try and stem the flow. She had turned to liquid, and it was running out of her eyes and nose and mouth. She leaned her head against the side wall and continued to weep, for how long she didn't know.

She was surprised when, sometime later, she heard a noise in the stall beside her. Someone must have come in. She'd been making so much noise she hadn't heard the door open or any footsteps. Judith tried, for a moment, to calm herself and stop her gurgling and sobs, but she couldn't do it. After a few moments the sound of her weeping was accompanied by the noise of a tinkle in the next booth, then the flush of the toilet.

Judith tried again to take a few breaths and get control of herself. But then the memory of Mr. Slater's face and his tone of voice as he told her that no one would believe her came back. She couldn't help but moan and continue crying. Her eyes were badly swollen by now, and she could barely see, but when there was a knock on the booth she managed to look down and observe the chubby legs of a woman in scuffed suede flats. Oh God. This was so mortifying. Judith couldn't stand it.

"Excuse me. Are you all right?" the woman asked. Judith tried to clear her throat but didn't manage to. The voice continued. "I mean, obviously, you're not all right, but can I help?"

No one could help, and that realization sent more tears, this time silent ones, dripping out of the corner of Judith's eyes. "I'm fine," she choked out.

"That's ridiculous," the woman's voice said. "You're not crying for goddamned joy in there." She had a thick city accent—Judith couldn't tell if it was Brooklyn or some other part of New York City, but it was definitely not local. "Come on," the woman coaxed. "Open the door."

"You can't help me."

"How do you know? And I won't hurt you. Hey, trust me. I've done my share of crying in toilets. Come on, open the door."

Sitting there, alone in the stall, Judith felt more lonely than she could bear. Whoever the woman was, she was trying to be nice, and no one had been nice to Judith in a long time. So without thinking, she leaned forward and threw the bolt. The door to the stall swung open, and a heavy, dark-haired woman stood there. She looked Judith over. "It's your husband, right?" she asked, and once again Judith burst into tears. The woman put an arm around her, and Judith leaned against her shoulder, sobbing for what seemed like a long, long time. The woman didn't try to stop her or pat her or question her. But her bulk was comfort enough. Finally, Judith was empty of tears, and when at last she finished, the woman silently walked her over to a basin, ran some cold water, took down a few paper towels, and gave them to Judith so she could wipe her face.

"My name is Brenda Cushman," the woman said. "You don't have to tell me your name, not if you don't want to." Judith pressed the cold towels against her eyes.

"I'm Judith," she managed to say.

"Well, Judith, if you're trying to get a divorce from the bastard, my friend Diana has an office down the hall. She's a good attorney. She's not looking for work, but—"

"It's not that simple," Judith gasped.

"It never is," Brenda told her. "But if he's hitting you, we can find a place for you to stay. And if he's withholding money, we can probably get you some interim financial help. And if it's about custody, well, Diana is the best when it—"

"He's cheating me," Judith said, her voice still thick.

"They *always* cheat on you," Brenda told her.

"No, not cheating *on* me. I mean, he's stealing from me."

"Stealing your money?"

Judith shook her head.

"He's stealing the kids?"

"We don't have children," Judith told the woman. "Not yet, anyway. It's worse."

Brenda lowered her heavy eyebrows. "You're upset. I'm confused. What the fuck *is* this guy doing to you?"

"He's stealing my book," Judith wailed, and began to cry again.

After humiliating herself with the first lawyer, Judith was more hesitant, as well as more organized, in telling her story to the second one. Brenda Cushman had brought her down the hallway to the office of Diana La Gravenesse. Diana was a tall, cool blond in an elegant suit who sat and listened quietly without asking any questions until Judith was through. "I know it sounds impossible," Judith said. "I know I sound really stupid and like it didn't happen this way, but it really did. It's unbelievable, but it really did."

"And it's happened before," the lawyer said. Judith looked up at her. "Have you ever heard of Colette?"

"She's a French writer, isn't she?"

"Well, she was. She's been dead for quite some time.

But her husband used to lock her in their room until she passed manuscript pages under the door. For every page she wrote, he'd pass in a slice of buttered bread. Then he took them and had them published under *his* byline."

"Did he kill her?" Judith asked.

Diana La Gravenesse smiled. "Well, I'm sure she felt as if he did. No, she eventually left him and began writing on her own. In the end she wrote a lot of wonderful books, all with *her* name on them."

Judith blinked and took the first deep breath she'd been able to inhale all day. "You believe me?" she asked.

"Yes, of course, I believe you," Diana La Gravenesse told her. "Unfortunately, I'm not a judge. And I don't specialize in entertainment or copyright law, so I don't know if I ought to handle this case for you. Probably not. But I *do* know it would be helpful if you could get your hands on your original manuscript *and* typed draft. Do you think you could do that?"

"I don't know," Judith said. "We packed everything up when we moved. But I can try."

"What I suggest," Diana explained, "is that you say nothing to your husband yet. Try to gather these documents, and then we will assess the situation: whether to go to the publisher, to confront your husband directly, or to simply begin court proceedings. But generally going for a settlement first is your best, least painful option. If you go to federal court, we'll certainly have to get you another lawyer."

"I have no money," Judith whispered.

"I understand, but after you sue or settle, there will be money. And I think I can convince an attorney I know to work based on a percentage of that expectation."

Judith leaned toward the woman. "Thank you," she sighed. "You've been so kind." Diana La Gravenesse simply patted her hand and gave her a card.

"I hope you can find the manuscript," she said. "Or even the typewritten draft. Call me one way or the other."

Judith stood and picked up her bag, stuffing the card into the side pocket. She walked to the door. The lawyer had already put her head down, writing notes and looking at her calendar.

"One more thing," Judith told her.

"Yes?" Diana responded, looking up.

"If I have to have one, will you also handle my divorce?"

# 75

> Some writers thrive on the contact with the commerce of success; others are corrupted by it. Perhaps, like losing one's virginity, it is not as bad (or as good) as one feared it was going to be.
>
> —*V.S. Pritchett*

Opal looked up from the counter and turned toward Roberta, who was busy boxing returns. "Do you have any more stamps?" she asked.

"They're in the left-hand drawer," Roberta told her, and Opal pulled it open and found the neatly stacked books of postage.

"I'm paying you back for all of this," Opal said. Roberta shrugged.

"Believe me," she said, "it won't make much of a difference." Opal watched her friend as she addressed the carton being returned to Random House. Sales were not good, and there had been a lot of returns lately. With all of the daily worries of running the bookstore, Opal was deeply touched that Roberta had found time to put together a mailing campaign to most of the independent bookstores across the country. Each day, the two women tailored several dozen letters about *The Duplicity of Men*, hand-addressed them, and sent them out. Opal had no idea if it was doing any good, but she supposed it couldn't hurt. And Emma Ashton had helped. Two evenings a week she stopped by with lists of important people in the book trade.

Book sales on *Duplicity* in the shop were certainly good, but that was due mainly to the big window display Roberta had created, as well as her insistence that every regular customer buy the book. They had already sold close to sixty copies, but Opal knew there was no other bookstore in the country that was going to do that.

"Is Vivien Jennings at Rainy Day Books a Miss, Mrs., or a Ms.?" Opal asked as she began to address an envelope.

"Definitely a Ms.," Roberta said, straightening up from her last carton. No one had been in the shop all morning, and Opal wondered if it was the gloomy weather or the superstore that was keeping them away.

When the doorbell sounded, Opal looked up to see a young man in a good black jacket over an undershirt swagger into the store. He looked around for a moment and, once oriented, moved toward the fiction section. Roberta dusted off her hands, pushed the carton to the side of the counter with her foot, and prepared to assist the young man, if he needed it. He was already running his finger back and forth across a shelf and turned to Roberta as she approached him.

"Have you got *SchizoBoy*?" he asked.

"The Chad Weston book? No, I'm afraid we don't," Roberta informed him. He looked back at the shelf.

"You don't have any of my books," he said. "This is unbelievable. Man, I'm not prepared for this shit. I was told that you ran a literary bookstore. That's why I came up here."

Roberta blinked. "Are you Chad Weston?" she asked. From behind the desk Opal watched her friend. "I don't like to discourage any writer, Mr. Weston, but we don't carry every book, and personally, I was—"

"Every book? I'm not talking about *every* fucking book. I'm talking about *my* book. Don't you read *Time*? How about *Vanity Fair*? Or the *New York Review of Books*?" Weston had raised his voice and now was shouting. "Do people like you understand the important issues of the day? The ACLU is going to handle my suit against Davis & Dash. It's not just my book, it's a blow for literary freedom everywhere. It's a First Amendment issue. Not that I expect *you* know what free speech means."

"Mr. Weston, I'm very well aware of the controversy around your book, and I received an advance copy long before Davis & Dash decided not to publish. I read it. I didn't like it then, and I don't like it now. I know you say it's satire, but I believe good satire has to come from anger, not a prurient delight in the subject." Roberta paused. "Frankly I don't think the book has any literary merit."

For a moment Opal thought he might strike Roberta. He pulled back his hand and in a fury pulled a book off the shelf, throwing it across the bookstore. "Censorship!" he yelled. "How would a dried-up old bitch like you know literature anyway?" he sneered. "You wouldn't feel it if it was shoved up your tight, pathetic ass."

Roberta walked across the room calmly and picked up the book Chad Weston had flung. It was a novel by Susan Jedren. "Mr. Weston, this writer—whose book you've just damaged—is a hundred times the artist you'll ever be. You, young man, have made the terrible mistake of believing your own PR. Political issues aside, your books are simply bad and heartless. Apparently, so are you." Roberta was pale. "Not only that, but in the interest of frankness I also have to tell you that your sales technique leaves something to be desired."

"Like you know about sales techniques, or anything else," Weston spat.

"Mr. Weston, I wouldn't stock your book on principle, but if a decent author came in and asked me to carry their *first* novel, and did so in a pleasant way, I assure you I'd be willing to accommodate." The young man looked at her with obvious contempt and disbelief.

"What the fuck is with you?" he asked. "You talk like a character out of Dickens or something." He shook his head, but Opal had had enough. In a moment she was standing beside him. She took him by the arm. Before he seemed to know what was happening he was propelled down the aisle to the door. He tried to pull his arm away, but Opal was strong—stronger than some skinny little city-boy drip.

"What?" he cried. "What are you doing?"

"You're leaving. Good-bye."

"No, I—"

Opal pushed him out the door and closed it in his face before she could even hear what he was attempting to say. "Good-bye," she repeated through the glass, and locked the door behind him.

"You fat old fuck," the young man screamed. He screamed other things, but Opal ignored his ravings.

"Thank you," said Roberta, clearly shaken. "When you think about it, it's surprising that authors don't start behaving like postal workers. You know, spraying bookstores with machine-gun fire."

"Perhaps," Opal said to Roberta, "we could learn something from this little experience." She pointed to her stack of letters to bookstores. "We might be going about this *Duplicity* marketing thing the whole wrong way."

The afternoon was long and silent, with only a few lookers and no buyers to break up their mailing. When the phone rang at four o'clock, both of them jumped—it had become that quiet. Roberta lifted the phone and spoke briefly. Then she handed it to Opal, covering the receiver with her hand and mouthing, "It's Pam Mantiss."

Opal shrugged. She hadn't heard from Pam, nor had Pam returned her calls in more than three weeks. It was, Opal knew, one of the early indicators that *The Duplicity of Men* was not selling even as well as the modest expectations Davis & Dash had had. "Opal O'Neal," she said, as if the bookstore were manned by two dozen people and someone else might have inadvertently picked up the extension.

"Opal? I have great news. It's finally happened."

Opal blinked. "Yes?" she asked. Had Lehmann-Haupt reviewed the book? Had it been nominated for a prize? Had one of the chains finally decided to stock it?

"You're on *Oprah,*" Pam said. For a moment, Opal was

left silent. What was the woman talking about? Opal had never been on television in her life.

"I'm *what*?"

"You're going on *Oprah*. They want to do a show for sweeps week about devoted mothers of suicides. We've got you on the first segment. You talk about Terry, her book, and how difficult it was to get it published until you met me. They've promised to use at least one still shot of the book. We're negotiating to have Oprah hold it up herself, but they aren't promising that yet. Still, I think she'll like you. Now that she's cleaned up her act, this is her kind of story."

"It's not my kind of story," Opal said coldly.

There was silence for a moment. "What are you talking about?"

"It's not the kind of thing I'll do."

There was a longer silence at the other end of the phone. Then, "Are you out of your fucking mind?" Pam asked.

"I don't think so," Opal told her.

"Writers, publicists, *anybody* would give their left tit to get a chance to push their book on *Oprah*. It guarantees success. Well, at least a couple of hundred thousand books. She *made* Marianne Williamson. You remember her first book? *Return to Love*. It went into so many editions that they started calling it *Return to Printer*, and she followed it up with *A Woman's Worth*. It should have been *A Woman's Net Worth*. You are *not* going to turn this down."

"You are not going to turn my daughter's life into some kind of spectacle," Opal responded. "I wasn't doing this so people could mock Terry or judge her."

"Oh, for Christ's sake!" Pam Mantiss said. "Nobody is going to judge her. What they're going to do is buy the fucking book."

"Well, then they're buying it for the wrong reason." Opal heard Pam gasp at the heresy. It seemed she'd finally managed to shock the woman. Opal supposed everybody had a religion of sorts, and apparently one of Pam's commandments was that there was no wrong reason to buy a book.

"Jesus Christ! Have you any idea of how goddamned hard we worked to get this opportunity? Are you crazy or stupid?"

"Neither one," Opal said. "Just bored with this conversation." Then she hung up the phone.

The fact was, *The Duplicity of Men* wasn't selling, not even modestly, according to the informal reports Opal got from Emma. "It'll take a while for the independents to kick in," Roberta reassured her. "It's not over till it's over." She calmly dished out some rice and beans. They were having dinner at Flor De Mayo on upper Broadway, where you could eat rice and beans and barbecued pork and fried plantains and still leave with change from a ten-dollar bill. The afternoon had been filled with calls from Wendy Brennon, Emma Ashton, an Oprah Winfrey producer, and even Gerald Ochs Davis himself, all trying to change Opal's position. They hadn't.

"More plantains?" Roberta asked.

"Yes, please." They ate for a while in silence. "Do *you* think I should do it?" Opal asked.

"It's a lot to give up," Roberta said, honest as she always seemed to be. "The sales would be very nice. But, no, I don't think you should do it, and I don't think you should let it worry you."

"I don't think Terry would want me to, do you?"

Roberta shook her head. "Terry had a lot of dignity," Roberta said, and Opal felt reassured and much better than she had since the disturbing calls had begun.

"It's too bad there isn't a dignified television show that wants me," Opal said with a sigh. "I suppose dignified television is an oxymoron."

Roberta paused. "But there is," she said. "God, why didn't we think of it before? Why don't you do the Elle Halle show? If Oprah wants you, Elle probably would. And she could do the show with sympathy and some class. She only does one guest per episode. No mothers-of-suicides garbage."

"Would she have me on?" Opal asked. "She's really fancy."

"Well, instead of calling you, all of those fools over at Davis & Dash could be calling her and finding out."

"But doesn't Elle Halle always try to make people cry? Isn't that her trademark?"

"It might be her trademark, but it doesn't have to be *yours*." Roberta paused. "It's an evening show. Prime time. It's an audience that *can* read. If you do anything, it should be Elle Halle."

Opal nodded. "Roberta, you're brilliant," she said and reached for another fried plantain.

# 76

> In today's media culture, the actual book is becoming an incidental by-product of a writer's career—something to keep his or her name in circulation.
>
> —*James Wolcott*

"What do you mean, you're not going to make it?"

Susann turned from the window and the splendid view of the San Francisco harbor to gesture to Edith, who had just entered the suite. Edith looked at Susann on the telephone and raised her eyebrows before she made herself scarce.

"I have dragged myself through twenty-two cities," Susann said to Alf, her voice low. "You promised me you'd meet me here in San Francisco and go on to Los Angeles with me. Two cities out of more than forty. It wasn't a lot, Alf, but it was something."

At the other end of the line Alf began his litany of excuses—the problem he had back at the office, the difficulty with his son, and the slightly disappointing performance to date of Jude Daniel's book. But Susann didn't need to hear any of it again. She hadn't needed to hear any of it the first time. The only thing she needed was for Alf to be here, in San Francisco now, glad to see her, comforting, strong, and capable—as he used to be. Susann was tired of excuses, tired of lies, and, she realized all at once, tired of Alf. Alf began with his new promises—how he'd meet her in Los Angeles, how he'd take her to Morton's for dinner, but Susann wasn't interested.

Instead she simply hung up. She turned to the stunning view. She could see both bridges from here, her favorite suite at the Mark Hopkins. There was no fog, and blessedly, her hands were not hurting. She told herself that there was no reason for her to be unhappy. Nothing had really changed. Alf would not be here, but he had not been there for a long time. She had gotten through a rough landing in Houston; a night in a limo in the desert; a signing in Austin, where only a dozen readers showed up; and close to fifty interviews where everyone asked the same questions and she gave the same answers. Despite all these efforts the book, for the third week, still languished at seventeen, just below the cut-off point of the published *New York Times* list, and had only moved up to twenty-seven on the *USA Today* list. It hadn't made *Publishers Weekly*'s list at all! And Susann knew she was running out of time. Well, the national television satellite campaign would begin this week, and she would do that, too, alone. The radio and television advertising would also begin this week, and that would be the final push. It had to do the trick. It just had to. The book hadn't failed, she told herself. It simply hadn't succeeded yet. She looked out at the breathtaking view and told herself again that there was no reason not to be happy.

The telephone rang, and Susann let Edith pick it up. She wouldn't speak to Alf. Edith poked her head into the room. "The escort is waiting downstairs," she said. "Are you ready?"

Susann picked up her purse and nodded. Silently they left the suite, took the elevator downstairs, and met Kathi Goldmark, the queen of the author-escort business. Always carrying books, press kits, schedules, and the like, Kathi was famous for both her organization and the canvas bags she had made up. She carried one now that said, "Cheerfully schlepping authors since 1983."

Kathi took them out to the car and got them settled, or as settled as Susann was going to be. She consulted her schedule, informing Susann of a slight reshuffling. Susann merely nodded, and Kathi pulled the car into the traffic going down Nob Hill. Susann tried to relax. Kathi was a real professional—Susann had worked with her many times before. She would get them to the signings and the radio stations on time. But although she hadn't seen Kathi since her last book tour, Susann was too tired and disappointed to try to make small talk.

"I met your daughter last week," Kathi volunteered. "I took her to a Marin bookstore."

Susann sat up. "You saw Kim?" she asked. She hoped there would not be a horror story—syringes left in Kathi's car, or worse.

"Oh, yeah. I guess talent runs in the family," Kathi said warmly. "She was very nice too, unlike *some* of the first novelists I've trekked around."

That was good to hear. "I would think that first novelists would be grateful," Susann said.

"Well, some are. But more than a few are worse than divas. You know, they're novices. They just can't put things in perspective. It's taken them their whole lives to get that first book out, and they think everybody else's life should stop to appreciate it. What did Dickens call it? *Great Expectations*?"

Susann laughed. "They'll get over it," she said grimly.

"Which authors are easy?" Edith asked, knitting away in the seat beside Susann.

"Norman Mailer. He's a real pro. He's always on time, and he knows exactly what's expected of him. E. L. Doctorow is great; so is Amy Tan. They know how to give to their fans without draining themselves dry. Anna Murdoch was a real lady. Some old woman asked what her husband did, and she smiled and told her he sold newspapers. The old woman said she had a brother-in-law with a newsstand and it was a tough business. Anna agreed." Everybody laughed, thinking of Rupert Murdoch's immense wealth and influence. "Charlton Heston toured with his book. Apart from the movie buffs, he had two kinds of fans: old women who told him that they loved him in *Ben Hur* and kids who loved him in *Wayne's World*. He was a trooper though. He knew the business. I guess that's why Kim was so good—she already had learned the ropes from you. Anyway, she left me something to give to you." Kathi began shuffling through papers and bags on the front seat beside her. Susann squirmed. Oh God, what next? A writ? A severed ear? A letter bomb?

"I guess you've carried all kinds of packages," Edith said, as if she too was imagining the possibilities.

"Sure," Kathi agreed cheerfully. "I've transported just about everything but hazardous waste. Unless you consider Peet Trawley in that last category."

Susann laughed but waited nervously. What was it that Kim had left for her?

By then they had arrived at the radio station, and Susann had to prepare for Alex Bennett—the deejay who did clever interviews with a live audience and a sidekick—a different comic every week. Each hungry comedian was trying for the most airtime possible, and in the past Susann had sometimes found it difficult to get a word in edgewise. She also occasionally found herself the butt of their youth jokes, but she got through this morning unscathed. Then there was an interview with the *San Francisco Chronicle* and after that the book signings.

At last it was over. Kathi took them back to the hotel. She still hadn't presented Kim's package, and Susann decided to let the matter drop. Gratefully, she got out of the car and turned to go into the hotel. "Wait. You forgot this," Kathi said and gave her a package: Susann took it gingerly.

"Thanks," she said.

Susann and Edith went up the elevator, the parcel almost ticking between them. "Well, open it, for heaven's sake," Edith said at last.

Susann handed the package to Edith. "You do it," she coaxed.

Edith rolled her eyes, and once they were safely in the

suite, she tore off the wrappings and opened the box. "It's her book," Edith said, and handed the volume to Susann.

Taking it seemed to use up her very last bit of energy. "I'm going to have dinner in bed," Susann told Edith. "But don't let me stop you. Go out if you would like."

"I would like to see Ghirardelli Square," Edith admitted. "And take a cable car."

"Knock yourself out."

Edith left her, and Susann soaked her weary bones in the huge bath-tub, using almost half of her Chanel bath salts. Then she crawled into bed, but she didn't sleep. She picked up Kim's book and began to read. She didn't put it down until she had read it from cover to cover. It was a tidy piece of work, and there was even some really good writing in it. The plot could have been tighter, but as Susann got to the end and was surprised by its little twist, she realized that she was proud of Kim. She *did* have talent.

On the last page was a message handwritten by Kim herself. It made Susann stop and hold her breath.

Dear Mother,

I don't know if you'll think this is any good or not. I don't even know if you will read it and see this note, but I hope you've done both. I want to thank you for your generosity in letting me use the name. I know the book wouldn't have been published without it, but I think it's no worse than lots of other books.

It's also taught me how hard you have had to work all these years. I'll try to forgive you if you can try to forgive me.

Love,
Kim

# 77

> The successful editor is one who is constantly finding new writers, nurturing their talents, and publishing them with critical and financial success.
>
> —*A. Scott Berg*

Pam sat in her office, like a she-spider in the very center of her web. She was waiting for the last little fly to buzz in—a fly it would be a pleasure to wrap in silk and hang up as a trophy. Today was the day that they announced the Editor of the Year, and Pam couldn't leave her desk. She was afraid to show her anticipation to anyone, just in case the award didn't come through. She wanted to be at her phone to hear that bitch who chaired the committee give her the news.

She got up from her desk and walked over to the refrigerator. It was only ten after ten, but there was no way she'd get through this morning without help from Dr. Snapple. She took out a bottle, walked back to her desk, and was just popping it open when Emma's voice startled her. "Have you heard anything yet?" She was standing in the doorway in one of her typically disheveled arrangements—Pam couldn't call them "outfits," they were too nonfashion. She seemed to select her clothes by throwing them against the wall; anything that slipped to the floor in a wrinkled mess was wearable.

Pam looked at her with a narrowed eye. Did Emma resent her? Correct that; she knew Emma *must* resent her, but she wondered how much. After all, it was Emma who had found *Duplicity*, which was beginning to get a lot of critical praise. And the Clapfish book, overseen by Emma, was giving Pam a touch of class and showing that she could still do literary fiction. And Emma had practically rewritten the Susann Baker Edmonds abortion, as well as the first chapter of Gerald's pathetic book. In fact, if Pam won Editor of the Year—and she absolutely *had* to—it would be in large part due to Emma's work this year and last. Amazing how much *she* resented Emma.

"Have I heard about what?" Pam snapped, taking a swig from her Snapple bottle. She wasn't going to admit to a moment of concern.

"From publicity about the Elle Halle show for Mrs. O'Neal."

"No, I haven't heard a word. If that old bitch won't go on *Oprah*, I don't give a shit if she gets on anything else."

"Well, let me know if you hear anything," Emma said and turned to leave. "Oh," she said casually, "and good luck with the award."

Fuck! The girl pissed her off, and Pam thought of the old Chinese question: "Why does he hate me so? I never did anything for him." She shrugged. Human nature was a bitch.

So much for philosophy. She had to win this year. She quickly went over in her mind her strengths and weaknesses for the award. The big question was the Chad Weston thing. The little prick was making the Davis & Dash rejection into a *cause célèbre*. Pam didn't think it could work against her—it might actually work in her favor, as long as the spin was right. After all, it had been her book and it was common knowledge that it wasn't she who had rejected it. In fact, the whole business could ace it for her. If she had come out with *SchizoBoy*, the feminists and puritans who were shocked by it would be attacking *her* now, instead of Peterson. She got to look like a civil libertarian without taking the heat. And though Weston was busy dissing everyone in public, he had not yet attacked her—at least not in print.

The phone rang and Pam jumped, but she wouldn't let

herself answer it. She waited, pretending to be a lady, until her secretary took the call and then buzzed her. Her stomach knotted up—she hadn't eaten, and the Absolut iced tea was churning. "Jude Daniel on line one," her secretary told her, and, exasperated, Pam snatched up the phone.

"What?" she demanded.

"I'm leaving for Boston," Jude said. "What are the chances of you meeting me there tonight?"

Pam covered the phone with her hand, closed her eyes, and sighed gustily. Sex with Jude was certainly not good enough to travel for. "Maybe," she said. "Can I call you back?"

"I'm at the airport," he told her.

"Right. Well, I'll call you at the hotel." Just hang up, she thought, her eye on the light of the other line.

"I'm having a lot of trouble with my wife," Jude said.

What else was new? Pam didn't give a flying fuck. Just get off the phone so she could get her call. "I'm sorry to hear that," she said.

"Are you?" Jude asked, his voice intimate. "I'm going to leave her."

"Great," Pam said. "I'll call you at the hotel."

"But Pam, she's getting very odd. I'm worried. She may give me trouble. She thinks she contributed more to the book than she did."

"They always do," Pam said, thinking of Edina.

"No. I mean she's really acting unbalanced. She says the book is half hers."

"Only in divorce court. New York's law is equitable distribution. But she'll have to prove it first. Anyway, we have a whole legal department to deal with infringement and this kind of stuff." Christ. Get off the phone. "Don't worry. Just knock 'em dead at the bookstores."

"I—"

"I'll call you at the hotel," Pam interrupted and finally

hung up. It was a good thing she did, too. Because just then the phone rang with the call she had been awaiting so many years.

"To Editor of the Year," David Morton said, and everyone lifted their glass to her. Pam smiled demurely. She couldn't believe her luck—that David Morton had been in New York, in Gerald's office, when the announcement was made. In publishing in the nineties there was no such thing as job security, but this was as good as it got. Pam looked around the table. They were lunching at Palio, and the expansive room with its enormous high ceilings and marble floor fit her mood.

David Morton was sitting beside her, and Gerald was opposite them. Pam, with her radar for trouble, could feel the tension between the two men. She hadn't been invited to their meetings, but she had heard from Jim Meyer that all was still far from well.

Pam wondered if the long-awaited restructuring was in the making. How would she fare? It would be almost impossible to match this job. She had little work and a lot of salary, a nearly impossible combination in publishing. The only better job was Gerald's.

"I'm so glad to get a chance to know you better," Pam purred to Morton. For a born-again Christian, he wasn't a bad-looking man.

"Did you read this totally disgusting garbage that Davis planned to publish?"

"You must be talking about the Weston book," Pam said, all innocence.

"It was horrific. Only a madman would write it, and someone worse would publish it."

"Well, I know a lot of women here, aside from myself, who were deeply upset about it," Pam said calmly.

"You've read it then? I'm ashamed to think a woman had to read this as a part of her job."

"Oh, Gerald gives me a lot of unpleasant things to do,"

Pam said smoothly. "All in a day's work. I was just afraid we were publishing it."

"Listen, there was no way that Davis & Dash would have published the book. This is a Christian country. Who the hell wants to read about a man who kills and rapes and eats women?"

Perhaps Jeffrey Dahmer would, Pam thought, but knew that discretion was the better part of valor. Somehow she didn't think Morton had a sense of humor. Anyway, Dahmer would only like the book if it were *men* being raped and eaten. And wasn't Dahmer dead? Not much of a market there. Pam tried to refocus her mind on the business at hand. There was an opportunity *here*.

"I couldn't agree with you more," she said. "What did you do?"

"I told Gerald to track down that crazy son of a bitch and tell him we're not publishing that crazy goddamned book." He paused. "Pardon my French," he apologized. "I don't usually use raw language, but I was appalled."

"As was I," Pam told him.

"I said 'Stop the presses,' or whatever you people say to make a book not happen."

"Really?" Men loved to show their power. Even born-again Christian men. "And you weren't worried that his lawyers would sue?" Pam asked in an awed voice.

"Let 'em sue. I said, 'We are not publishing this book.' You can ask Gerald yourself."

"Wow!" Pam purred. "That was heroic." She paused. "And I do want to tell you, Mr. Morton, that I'm not only speaking for myself but for a lot of the staff here when I tell you how relieved I am by your decision."

"Well, well. Nice of you to say so. I thought all of you publishing types might get on your high horses with me."

"Not at all, not at all," Pam said. "I think it is a deeply wise decision and one that neither of us will ever regret." She stared into his eyes.

"Well, good then." He paused, but he didn't look away.

"It's really very nice getting to talk with you. I look forward to working with you more closely in the future."

"I couldn't agree with you more."

"You're really great at what you do," David murmured to her. She raised an eyebrow and looked back at him.

"And you don't even know *all* that I do," she said in a husky whisper.

He looked at her, and for a moment she feared that his shock would turn to distaste. But her mojo was so powerful tonight that she carried it off, even with a born-again southerner like David Morton. Was he physically attractive, or was it his aura of power that enticed her? After all, Graydon Carter of *Vanity Fair* had named Morton number two in his list of the most powerful men in America. Looking at him, Pam realized she could have him. And that she would.

She looked across the table to find Gerald's eyes on her. His face had a glazed look. Pam smiled at him. He didn't smile back.

# 78

> Writing is not a profession but a vocation of unhappiness.
>
> —*Georges Simenon*

Daniel walked down the long hallway to the very end of the hotel corridor. Behind him a bellman far older than he carried his bag, and in front of him an obsequious concierge far younger than he carried the keys to the suite.

Daniel hadn't been in Boston since his student days, and he'd never stayed at a Swissôtel. It was a lot more luxurious and elegant than he had expected—he'd imagined some kind of corny motel with a Heidi motif. When they got to the room, he was surprised to see on the door a brass plaque that said AUTHOR'S SUITE. The concierge threw open the door with a flourish, and Daniel entered. There was a fabulous marble bathroom to his right off the hall and then two fairly small but exquisitely plush rooms. The bedroom was visible through an archway—all soft pastels and beautiful woodwork. The living room was even more welcoming, furnished with a sofa, a silk-covered easy chair, and two vases of colorful flowers. There was also a tray wrapped in cellophane—it seemed to be filled with fruits, candies, and other goodies.

"Sir?" the concierge asked from behind him. Daniel turned to see an antique desk with a bookshelf, and the concierge was holding out a copy of *In Full Knowledge*. "Would it be too much trouble for you to sign this for our collection?"

Daniel blinked. At first he thought the kid was pulling his leg, but he appeared absolutely serious—in fact deferential. Daniel shrugged. "Sure," he said. He was actually thrilled, but he didn't want to look like an amateur. He opened the book to the title page, picked up the pen, and began to scrawl, then realized he'd begun to sign his own first name. He paused for a moment and glanced to see if the kid noticed. He hadn't, so Daniel simply wrote "Jude" above his first name. Jesus, he'd have to remember to keep his wits about him. After all, this was a book-signing tour.

"Thank you, sir," the concierge said and added the book to the shelf. Daniel was too flustered to do anything but nod—he forgot to tip either the concierge or the bellman.

Once he was alone in the room he had a chance to catch his breath and orient himself. The view was lovely, but then Daniel had always liked Boston. Maybe he'd live here. He flicked on a few of the lamps. He was drawn to the desk and the shelves above it. There, beside his book, were two dozen or more. Daniel pulled out a William Styron. He opened it up, and inside Styron had written, "Thanks for the hospitality." I should have written something like that, Daniel thought, and sat down at the chair in front of the desk. A beautifully bound, gold-trimmed volume lay flat on the leather surface of the dropleaf. It was a guest book, and Daniel paged through it. He saw famous name after famous name—all writers—and their comments. I'm sitting in a chair Saul Bellow sat in, Daniel thought. He looked down and saw an inscription from Pulitzer Prize-winner E. Annie Proulx. A few pages later James Finn Garner wrote, "When I read the sign on the door that said 'Author's Room,' I pictured cigarette burns on the table and unfinished cups of coffee around the room, plus a feeling of general ennui. Thanks for dispelling those images. Unfortunately, now I have to go back to the 'Author's House,' which is much less orderly and quiet." Phyllis Naylor had written, "Last night it was Motel 6 in Danvers, tonight the author's suite in the Swissôtel. Yesterday I thought this gig would never end, now I'm sorry that it will. What a wonderful respite!"

Daniel knew what she meant. He had no idea where he

would go after this tour was over. He couldn't go back to Judith. Perhaps Pam would invite him to move in. A writer and an editor living together seemed an ideal situation. But was he a writer? Could he write another book? He looked down at the real writers on the pages before him. Jane Smiley, another Pulitzer Prize-winner, had been at the hotel May 6, 1995. She'd written: "Good colors, nice light, well-shaped rooms. I had *great* dreams here. Thank you for thinking of us. May I see the movie-star room?"

When he walked into the bedroom, Daniel noticed an envelope beside the phone. He opened it up to find a welcome note from the media escort, his guide for tomorrow's book signings. There was also a schedule outlining all of his activities. He'd be on radio during drive time, then sign some books at Barnes & Noble and meet with a *Boston Globe* reporter in the afternoon.

On the other side of the bed was a standing ice bucket. In it was a bottle of wine—good wine, Daniel noticed—sent by David Gibbons, the executive director of the hotel. Daniel smiled. He could get used to this.

Daniel opened the Chablis, stretched out on the living room sofa, and poured himself a glass. The phone rang. There were five extensions; one beside the sofa; one on each side of the bed; one at the desk; and another on the wall in the bathroom! Each had two lines. "Hello?" he said. Alf Byron's gruff voice greeted him.

"Hello, Professor. You got there safely?"

"No problem." Daniel took an appreciative sip of the wine.

"Great. Listen, I'm going to fly up tomorrow morning. I'll be with you every step of the way. And I have some good news about your visit to L.A. I set up a little meeting with April Irons and her staff. What do you think about writing a screenplay?"

"A screenplay? You mean for *In Full Knowledge*?" Daniel felt his stomach tighten. "I've never written a screenplay before."

"You never wrote a bestseller before either. Nothing to it. Let's pitch her. She's willing to listen."

"Sure," Daniel said, and took another swig of his wine. "I can do it. I can do anything."

# 79

> My family used to tell everybody that the first word I said was "book." I tell everybody that my second word was "terms." And by the time I was three, I could spell "co-op advertising."
>
> —*Len Riggio, CEO of B. Dalton Booksellers*

The book wasn't selling. It was as simple as that. Camilla had called Pam Mantiss's office regularly. At first she had been put through to Pam herself. Then, as it became clear that the book wasn't moving, a secretary had taken the messages and Pam had been slow to ring back. Now her calls were simply transferred to Emma. Alex was upset. She was trying to work with people at Davis & Dash to get some publicity and reviews, but they didn't seem to be co-operative.

"Don't worry," Alex tried to reassure Camilla late one rainy autumn day when she stopped by after work. "We can still make this happen. I'm arranging for some local book signings and really pushing for more reviews." Camilla nodded, but she didn't feel very hopeful. The actual publication date of her book had been an anticlimax, the calm after the calm. Nothing had happened. But something had to happen, for financial reasons as well as career ones. "The problem is," Alex continued, "that there's no co-op advertising, no shelf space bought for you. There won't be a paperback sale if the hardcover doesn't sell better." She looked at Camilla. "It's a good book. It *will* find an audience." Alex patted Camilla's hand. "How's the job?"

"Great," Camilla said, and that, at least, was true. She enjoyed her work at Citron. She loved gazing at the Canaletto, living with it, as it were. She liked the people she was surrounded by—Susan and Jimmy O'Brien and Emily, who did the photocopying and helped cover the phones. And Craig of course. Working with Craig was exciting and sometimes difficult: His extraordinary energy made him volatile—sometimes he yelled and even threw things—but so vibrant and interesting. He had also started romancing Camilla, though she didn't tell Alex about this. Camilla didn't know if she'd accept Craig's overtures or not. She was tempted, but there was something about his nervous energy, his aura, that warned her of potential disaster.

"How's the apartment?"

"Rather dreadful, really. I feel buried alive there."

"That isn't good."

"No. I can't seem to sleep there."

Almost as bad as that was the fact that Camilla simply couldn't write there. Perhaps it was the rejection, the disappointment of her book sales—or lack of them. Perhaps it was the overwhelming silence and bleakness in her Park Slope apartment. Or perhaps it was the money worries, which never seemed to cease. Whatever it was, Camilla was having trouble turning out even a page or two a day.

"Camilla, you have to be able to write. It's a necessity."

"Yes, I know." But the next morning, and the next, and for all of the next week she couldn't. She sat at her desk, stared at her pad, and nothing came at all.

Camilla sat with her notebook in front of her on the café table. It had taken her almost a month—a month of sleepless nights and nightmares—but she had found, at last, a place where she could work. She had gone to the superstore around the corner from Citron Press and spent four hours at one of the tables in the coffee bar. Somehow, the noise and bustle around her became a comfortable, comforting hum, and Camilla found that she could move forward easily. When she got stuck she simply got up, walked down the few steps that led to the rest of the bookstore, and wandered through its enormous space, picking books off the shelf and reading a few bits; then refreshed, she would return to the café and sit down for another stint of writing. If she walked to the superstore right after she left Citron Press, she could work from two until six or even seven.

The only bad thing about the superstore was that they didn't seem to carry her book. She'd told Craig about it, and he had laughed. "Of course they don't carry your book," he'd said. "Your last one didn't sell more than ten thousand copies."

"But there *wasn't* a book before this," Camilla said.

"Catch-22," said Craig. "You can't get a job without experience, and you can't get experience without . . . A store like that doesn't bother to take chances. They're looking for volume sales, authors with a proven track record. They'd rather carry two titles that each sell a million books than two million titles that sell one each."

Despite her book not being there, Camilla loved the superstore. She liked to watch the young mothers pushing toddlers in foldable prams making their way to the children's books. She liked the teenagers, who came in and skivved about. She watched the older women who made their way over to such a wide variety of sections—poetry or anthropology or the most bloodthirsty crime novels. And she watched the young singles who seemed to cruise the aisles, picking up volumes and one another virtually simultaneously.

She had a routine now: She left Brooklyn by eight, worked until one o'clock at Citron, then spent four hours at the superstore in Chelsea. She had a rule: She had to finish three pages each day. It was tiring, and it was hard to focus on the manuscript after a morning of dealing with Citron Press emergencies, but slowly, very slowly, Camilla was beginning to build the vision of her new book. She often ate at the little bistro on Ninth Avenue, sometimes meeting Citron Press people there. Then, alone, she'd head for the tube and Park Slope.

But just this week three things interfered with her comfortable routine. Alex called her about a book-signing tour, Frederick showed up at the superstore, and Craig Stevens asked her out.

The first one wasn't a surprise—Alex had been working at getting the Manhattan bookstores to invite her. At last, she'd lined up Bookberries, Books & Co., The Corner Bookstore, and Shakespeare & Company. Camilla had had to ask for a day off, and Alex had taken her around to introduce her to the bookstore managers, and Camilla had signed a few copies at each store. It had not been dramatic or thrilling, but Camilla deeply enjoyed it.

Frederick had not been dramatic or thrilling either. He'd merely been a surprise. He showed up at her elbow at the superstore without any warning, sat down across from her, and took her hand. It surprised Camilla in two ways. She certainly hadn't expected him, and she didn't know how he had found where she came to write, but it also surprised her to find how much she had missed him. Not just his kindness, but his physical presence, a certain electricity.

"I have been trying to reach you," Frederick said.

"Yes, I know. I've been calling you back, but I only get your machine. We've been playing Cox and Box, haven't we?"

"Not that I know of," Frederick said. "What the hell is cocks and box, and is it as dirty as it sounds?"

Camilla laughed. "I suppose it does sound rather sexual," she admitted. "I was just speaking what you call 'English' again. I think you call it telephone tag. You know, we keep missing each other."

"Well, I know I keep missing you," Frederick said tenderly.

Camilla looked down. "What I meant was about Cox and Box. It was a play in the West End, I think. They shared a flat. One worked the night shift and the other the day shift. They slept in the same bed, but not at the same time."

"No, that would be kinky."

"Oh, Frederick, you know what I mean."

"To tell you the truth, I don't care what you mean. I just like the sound of your voice. Camilla, let's see each other." He paused. "Well, of course I can't see you very well, but you know what I mean."

"I don't think I do," Camilla said.

"What I mean is, could we start over? I was very stupid in Florence. I should have told you about my vision. And then I shouldn't have said 'no more.' I was afraid that you pitied me—"

"I do pity you," Camilla said. "I also like you. And respect you."

"Camilla, could we go out on a blind date? Of course, that's the only kind of date I can have."

His jokes were so painful. "I don't know, Frederick . . ."

"I think I hurt your feelings, Camilla. I think I've been very stupid. But I'm not *always* stupid. Will you at least consider it?"

"Yes, Frederick. I'll consider it."

Camilla had a lot to think about. After Frederick left she sat alone, staring at her manuscript but seeing nothing. Frederick wanted a fresh start. Will was definitely getting ideas. And then there was tonight.

Camilla had to admit that she felt a great attraction to Craig. He was lively, aggressive, and very persistent—all the things that Frederick was not. She felt not just complimented but threatened by his interest in her. He did not seem like a man who believed in settled, monogamous relationships. Thinking back to her romance with Gianfranco, she reminded herself that it was dangerous to swim out beyond your depth.

Still, she had to admit that life was getting interesting.

# 80

Few men make themselves masters of the things they write or speak.

—*Tirso de Molina*

Opal pulled the rake toward her one more time. The letter campaign was going nowhere, it seemed. Only in physical activity did she find comfort. Her left arm was hurting, and her right hand had already developed a nasty little blister on the web of skin between her thumb and forefinger. "It's amazing how the city softens you up," Opal said aloud.

Aiello, who was on his knees stuffing the raked leaves into the bag, paused and looked up at her. "I don't think so," he said. "The city toughens you up. It don't get tougher than the Big Apple."

Opal shook her head. The man was always misinformed. "Before I moved here," she told him, "I could rake all of my property in one afternoon."

"How many acres?" Aiello asked.

Obviously, the man was thinking of *The Big Country* or some other movie. Why did easterners think everyone west of New Jersey lived on a ranch? "A quarter," she told him.

"Big deal," Aiello said. Then, as if to prove her right, "You have any cows out there?"

"No. No buffalo either. And no Indians. It wasn't the Wild West."

"No Indians? Then why do they call it Indiana?"

Opal rolled her eyes and put down the rake. She looked at the blister. She ought to go put on a Band-Aid before she tore the skin any further.

"You hurt yourself," Aiello said, taking her hand in his.

"A blister." Opal shrugged and tried to take her hand back. But Aiello didn't let go. He was still on his knees, the big plastic garbage bag twist-tied beside him.

"Would you do me the honor?" he asked. Opal furrowed her brows and tried to take her hand away again. But Aiello clung on. "Would you do me the honor to take my hand in holy matrimony?"

Opal stared. "Are you joking?" she said. Aiello, his face serious, shook his head. "Then you're out of your mind," Opal told him, and immediately saw the damage her thoughtless response had done.

Aiello narrowed his eyes, as if to close her out, and then lowered his head so that she couldn't see his face. All that showed was the circular bald spot at the top of his head. He had dropped her hand and slowly stood up.

"Mr. Aiello, I—"

"I didn't think you would. I knew you were too educated and too classy. I was just asking."

Opal was almost speechless. She bit her lip. She hadn't meant to belittle the man. "Well, it was a very nice thing for you to do."

"Hey, I'm a nice guy." Aiello looked at her. He seemed to have recovered already. "Is this a definite no or a maybe?" he inquired.

"It's a definite no," Opal told him. "But I hope we can still be friends." The phrase came up automatically from some barely remembered period of her life, centuries ago. The formula still seemed to work.

"No sweat," Aiello said and hefted the bag of leaves to his shoulder. Perhaps, she thought, he was a bit relieved. But what does one say next? Just then the door chime sounded. Saved by the bell, Opal thought.

"Have you seen it?" Roberta asked. She was standing in the doorway, her coat open, the scarf halfway down her back. "Have you seen it?" she repeated.

"Seen what?" Opal asked.

"The *Times* book review."

Opal had seen last week's, but she remembered that today was Monday, the day that bookstores and publishers received advance copies of the next week's book review. "Look at this," Roberta said and pushed the book review at her. Her hand was trembling.

Opal took the paper in one hand and her friend's elbow in the other. "Come in," she said. "I have to find my glasses."

"Here, use mine," Roberta said, lifting the glasses that she wore on a chain around her neck. "Hurry up."

"You act as if it's printed in disappearing ink," Opal said, but she felt her heart beginning to flutter. Nothing was more important than a review in the *New York Times*. The paper rarely disclosed who it was reviewing or when. Sometimes a book waited months for a review that came out too late to help it. Opal moved to the window and put Roberta's glasses on. The review was on the bottom half of page eleven. "Posthumous Greatness," read the headline, and underneath it, in smaller letters: "First and only novel by deceased author is a work of brilliance." Opal blinked. There was a large picture of Terry—the one taken in Roberta's shop. The caption underneath it read: "The author, before her suicide early last year." Opal began to read the review. "It's a man's world," it began. "But never has it been so clearly, so lyrically, so completely pointed out to us as in 'The Duplicity of Men,' a first novel by the late Terry O'Neal. As if the book was not in itself a brilliant argument, as well as a totally engrossing story, the author's own tragic experience echoes her beautifully imagined tale."

Opal couldn't read any more because of the tears gathering in her eyes. For heaven's sake! All she did was cry! Tears blotted the page, and she held the paper away from her to be certain that, once she was in control of herself, she could read it. In the meantime, Roberta took her hand. "It gets better," she said. "It's a rave."

Aiello came in and looked at the two of them. "Bad news?" he asked, as on-target as ever.

Roberta shook her head. "Terry's book just got a rave review," she explained.

"It's gonna make money?" Aiello asked.

Roberta shrugged. So far their letter campaign didn't seem to be affecting sales. They'd only heard from Mitchell Kaplan at Books & Books in Coral Gables and Cari Ulm at Bearly Used Books. "It's going to be *read,*" she said. She looked back at Opal. "Are you okay?" she asked.

"Yes," Opal told her and turned toward the garden.

"Aren't you going to read the rest of it?"

"Yes," Opal told her, "but I'm going to go out in the garden and read it to Terry."

# 81

> A novel should be an experience and convey an emotional truth rather than arguments.
>
> —*Joyce Cary*

Something had changed in the atmosphere at Davis & Dash, and Emma was sure it wasn't just her imagination. Business news was not good: Although Peet Trawley's book was climbing the list, Davis & Dash didn't seem to have another big commercial success this season. There was a celebrity bio that was disappointing, and a hostage book that seemed to prove that America had at last tired of endurance sagas. Susann Baker Edmonds, despite the work Emma had put into the editing, had not yet scored, and Gerald's novel, though doing better than his last, was certainly no bestseller. No one had expected anything but modest sales from *Duplicity* or the Clapfish novel, but the big surprise was how badly Jude Daniel's book was selling. It looked like they were going to have enormous returns. Emma shrugged. She had never really believed that the book would attract a mass audience—it was like expecting a book set on death row to become a big summer read. It was too grim. Emma was grateful that she had had nothing at all to do with *In Full Knowledge*. She knew that Pam would probably be feeling the lash for it, and that meant the search for a fall guy was on. Perhaps that was what gave all the editors the look and posture of scurrying mice.

And if GOD lashed out at Pam, the rumor was that David Morton had begun lashing out at Gerald Ochs Davis himself. Last week Mr. Morton had arrived unannounced and several meetings had been interrupted so that GOD and Pam and Dickie Pointer could all be pulled into emergency sessions. Since then everyone seemed to be keeping to their burrows, like small mammals who knew a predator was about. Emma was no exception.

The phone rang and Emma picked it up.

"Unbelievable!" Without an introduction, without a hello, Emma recognized Alex's voice. Since her talk with her brother, Emma had been thinking of calling Alex, but she hadn't done it. Now Alex sounded happy rather than angry. "Isn't it unbelievable?"

"What, Alex?"

"Haven't you heard? Terry O'Neal has been nominated for the Tagiter. It's the most prestigious annual literary prize. Well, I guess *she* won't get it, except posthumously."

"*The Duplicity of Men* has been nominated?"

"Yep. I made sure Pam did, and my little elves tell me it's a strong contender. Isn't it unbelievable? If it wins, foreign sales will go ga-ga."

Emma didn't care about foreign sales. Or even the prestige this would bring to Davis & Dash. This was *her* book, despite the credit Pam had been taking for it. Emma had found it, believed in it, and gotten it published. She'd been right. Her flesh raised in goose pimples. "Does Mrs. O'Neal know?" Emma asked. Oh, God, Opal would be so thrilled.

"Well, I haven't told her. No one answers her phone. Can you believe she doesn't have an answering machine?"

"She's on her way to Pennsylvania. She's doing National Public Radio to promote the book." Emma paused, savoring this reward. "You really think she might actually win?"

"I don't know. It's a long shot," Alex admitted. "Stranger things have happened. If it wins, it's good news for Davis & Dash."

"Yeah." Emma smiled. Boosted by the confirmation that her instincts had been right about *Duplicity*, Emma realized that with Alex it was now or never. "So, do you want to get together and have a drink to celebrate?"

"Sure."

They made plans to meet, and Emma hung up, feeling better than she had in weeks. She tried unsuccessfully to reach Opal, leaving a message with Wendy's office and the Philadelphia contact at NPR. She wanted to give Opal the news herself.

Rumors about the fate of Davis & Dash abounded: heads would roll; cutbacks would ensue; the company might be sold off or closed down—but Emma felt good. With all of the gigantic restructurings, acquisitions, reorganizations, and downsizing that had gone on in publishing over the last decade, Emma would be surprised by nothing. She'd been lucky so far. As a little fish in the Davis & Dash ocean she merely hoped she could hold on to her job and keep paying her rent. And she was thrilled that she had helped get a Tagiter-nominated book published, even if she wouldn't get much credit. If the killer sharks really were circling Gerald, Emma wondered if the nomination would help him, and if the coming shake-up would affect the minnows like her.

In fact, the atmosphere was so tense lately that Emma had started lunching out. She couldn't really afford the time or the cost, but at least it gave her a break from the terrified looks of the others. Today, in celebration of the good news and the rapprochement with Alex, she decided to go to the sushi bar a few blocks away. Emma had found it only a week ago, and though it was small and dark, the sushi was both fresh and comparatively cheap. It was late when she walked in—almost two-thirty—and she took her seat at the bar with a nod to the chef behind the counter. After placing her order—two California rolls and an order of agae tofu—she sat there leafing through a new manuscript.

Just behind her a waitress slid back a shoji screen and emerged from one of the three private dining rooms. The only other customer at the sushi bar called for his check, and Emma was served. She put down the manuscript, wiped her hands on the hot washcloth she was given, and sank her teeth into the avocado and crab. It was bliss, her own private celebration. She even ordered a saki. It was then she heard the voices behind her.

"I tell you I'm not going to do it. I *can't* do it," a man's voice said.

Emma shook her head. People were so rude, so unaware of others. They talked in movies, they shouted in restaurants. There was no place you were left peaceful.

There was a murmuring response, but the man's voice broke into it and continued even louder. "Not for another fifty thousand, not for a hundred thousand. Davis & Dash is making a fortune on my work. I wrote a book that's number three on the list, and I can't even get my manuscripts read." Again there was the murmuring voice. And, though now she was fascinated, Emma couldn't hear any more of the conversation. Who was number three on what list? she thought. The only Davis & Dash success right now was Peet Trawley, and he was dead. But his book was number three on the *Times* list.

Emma took a few more bites of her California roll. Then the man's voice roared, *"No, you didn't. You tortured me, but you didn't write it. I wrote every goddamned word!"*

Now, after a loud "Shhhh!" Emma could hear his companion's spoken response. "You'd better calm down." Emma felt gooseflesh rise on her arms. Surely that was Pam's voice. "This is a good gig for you, and you'd better not blow it," Pam's tough voice barked. "You're so self-destructive."

"Fuck you! Self-destruct this. Get yourself another ghost. If it's such a great gig, *you* take it." There was a pause and some murmuring. "More money or you can tell Edina Trawley she can get herself another boy. Or I'll tell her myself."

"Don't you *dare* speak to Edina Trawley," Pam snapped.

Emma didn't know exactly what she was hearing, but she knew she shouldn't be hearing it. As quietly as she could, she asked for her check. She looked regretfully at the tofu, the remaining sushi. But she knew she had to get out.

"What's the matter, you no like California roll?" the chef asked, gesturing to her almost untouched plate.

Mute, Emma just shrugged and smiled, then began searching in her purse for her wallet. She'd better just leave a twenty and get out.

"You take them with you?"

"No," she whispered. "I have to go."

The argument was getting louder. "Yeah?" she heard. "Well, Daisy Maryles might be interested in seeing my work-for-hire contract. And so would the Writers' Guild."

Emma knew that Daisy Maryles was the executive editor of *PW*—she also wrote its "Behind the Bestsellers" column. Emma threw the money on the counter, stood up, and hurriedly reached down to pick up her bag. As she turned to go, the screen to the dining room was pushed open and a thin dark man stepped off of the platform. Emma recognized him but couldn't quite place the face. He grabbed his shoes but didn't stop to put them on. He was out of the restaurant before Emma could move, and then it was too late.

There, on her hands and knees on the small tatami mat in front of her, was Pam, who looked up into Emma's face.

"Pam!" Emma said, feigning surprise. "What luck."

"Yeah," Pam said. "All of it bad."

# 82

> Every novelist has a different purpose—and often several purposes which might even be contradictory.
>
> —*Irwin Shaw*

San Diego was in reality a beautiful city, but that hardly mattered to Susann, who knew that there was no reality but the reality of her book sales. The view from her hotel window—sun splashed off the harbor and marina—could have been a dirty brick wall for the amount of pleasure it gave her. She was dressed and ready to begin her last day of book signing—all that was left was the New York satellite session that would include another dozen radio stations and television shows but would all be done from the comfort of a lower Park Avenue studio.

"Are you ready, Susann?" Edith asked. Susann nodded, though she'd never felt more exhausted in her life. She didn't dare to glance in the mirror—she'd probably get so demoralized that she wouldn't be able to show up at the superstore downtown.

She had worked very hard. No one could deny her that. On their last stop, in L.A., Alf had met them and cheered her with the news that sales were climbing and there was some interest from the network for a miniseries. But the meeting with NBC had gone badly. It seemed Alf had exaggerated their enthusiasm and had embarrassed both of them. She had failed. Despite the days, the weeks of touring, despite all of her smiles, her nights alone, and the discomfort of travel, she still had not made the *Times* bestseller list. The book had hovered in the high teens and then dropped down into the twenties, only to rebound to number seventeen.

"Let's go," Edith said, and puppetlike, Susann obeyed, following Edith down yet another hotel corridor into another elevator, through another lobby, and out into another waiting car.

The two of them were silent. They had spent so many hours together there was nothing left to talk about. But Susann found comfort in Edith's presence. And it wasn't absolutely hopeless. Tonight, Wednesday, the *New York Times* would fax the new list to subscribers of the early information. Maybe, just maybe . . . Susann thought of Robert James Waller and Alexandra Ripley signing thousands of copies of their books in advance. She sighed heavily.

"It isn't the end of the world," Edith said, patting Susann's arm.

"No," Susann agreed. "It's just the end of my career."

"Oh, aren't we feeling a little sorry for ourselves?"

Susann looked down at her gnarled hands. "Aren't we entitled to?" she asked.

"Entitled? Certainly not. We can pity ourselves if we choose to, but we are definitely not *entitled* to. Haven't you wound up with more than you ever expected? Haven't you had a good run up to now?"

"Yes," Susann agreed, "but I don't want it to stop." She felt that with the late start she'd gotten she was owed more. "I don't want it to change. Why should it have to?"

"Because everything changes," Edith said. "It's just the nature of things."

"Well," Susann said, setting her mouth. "I don't want it to change *yet*."

"Then you're greedy," Edith told her, but she softened her words by patting Susann's arm again.

They arrived at the bookstore early, as they always did. It was one of the largest of the chain, and Susann had signed books here two years before. "Who's the manager?" she asked Edith.

Edith consulted the card in her purse. "Stacy Malone," she said. "But Stacy is out on maternity leave. The assistant manager, John Brooks, is going to be here. Ask about Stacy's baby." Edith kept complete notes on every bookstore they'd ever visited and corresponded (in Susann's name) with many of the store managers.

"Did we send Stacy anything for the baby?" Susann asked.

"You knit her a sweater," Edith said with a smile.

Susann looked down at her hands. "I think we're going to have to stop using that one," she murmured. They got out of the car to be met by John Brooks.

The cheerful bustle inside the store perked Susann up. She really did love bookstores; all the fuss that was made over her, and the opportunity to meet her readers. John Brooks had a very nice table set up, complete with a cloth and a vase of flowers, though they were only chrysanthemums.

"We have more than a hundred people waiting," John said. "It looks like it's going to be a really big signing. Stacy wishes she could be here."

"Well, the baby's much more important than I am," Susann said with a smile.

"Would you like to put your things in the back?" John asked, smiling at her modestly. "A few of our own girls wanted to meet you, and they have books they'd like you to sign."

"Of course," Susann said. How could there be all this interest, all these people, and yet no place for her on the list? She knew her touring would have a cumulative effect—that lists were based on sales of two weeks prior. She just felt that there was a build to this tour—that finally her perseverance would pay off and she would be rewarded. This would be the week.

She met the staff in the storage room at the back of the

store. "What a beautiful sweater you knitted," one of them said.

"Stacy loved it so much," another one told her. "She sends her love."

A third clerk took out a picture of a young blond woman with a surprisingly dark baby. "Here's Thomas," one of them said.

"Isn't he beautiful?" Susann cooed. "And Stacy looks great. She didn't gain any weight from her pregnancy."

There was a moment of silence, and Susann looked around the room while the clerks looked at one another and avoided her eye. What had she done? John Brooks cleared his throat. "Your public is waiting," he said, and he opened the door to lead Susann out to the table. Edith followed her.

"That wasn't Stacy," Edith whispered. "Stacy is black." Susann shook her head. This was the sixtieth bookstore on her tour. There was no way to keep up with this sort of thing. How was she to know? Susann sat down behind the table, flustered after her gaffe but smiling brightly. There was a long line of readers, as well as a tall pile of books stacked behind her, ready to be signed. John Brooks patted her on the shoulder. "We're going to work you really hard," he said. "It's such a relief to have a pro like you come in. We had an author scheduled last month who never even showed up. Didn't even call." He shook his head; then smiled at Susann and eyed the big crowd. "This is great," he said. "It's so nice to have a fill-in until Waller's book comes out next week."

Susann froze. Her hand painfully clenched the arm of the chair. "Fill-in?" she said. She turned to Edith. "Robert Waller has a book coming out next week?"

The assistant manager nodded his head. "We received them today."

Susann looked from Edith to the bookstore manager and then back at the crowd. Waller would blow her off the list! There'd be no space, no hole for her to fill. Susann stopped and swallowed. Fill. That's what she was now. What had this boy just called her? A fill-in. Susann turned to the crowd and then burst into uncontrollable sobs.

# 83

> I am forced to say that I have many fiercer critics than myself.
>
> —*Irwin Shaw*

Gerald sat drumming his fingers on the side of his chair while Dickie Pointer droned on. He glanced down at the printout. After all these years, he still couldn't read the goddamned things. They were confusing and badly organized, but he supposed he should be grateful for that. After all, if they weren't so obfuscating, it would be far more difficult, or even impossible, to "borrow" sales credits the way he had. Yet even with the extra "sales," *Twice in the Papers* wasn't performing well enough. Still, it was early. The official pub date was a week away. There was time, and Gerald was about to redouble his campaign for column mentions and advertising. He'd see Wendy Brennon about publicity this afternoon, and if she couldn't deliver more, she'd better be prepared to start looking for another job.

Mrs. Perkins, wearing a dress with a campestral print strewn across it, entered the room and made her way around the conference table to Gerald. She handed him a pink message slip. There was nobody that Gerald would interrupt the sales meeting for, with the exception of David Morton. He frowned at Mrs. Perkins for her bad judgment and then looked down at the slip. It said, "Your father on the line. Bad news." Gerald shrugged. He hadn't heard from his father since the reader's copies of his novel had been sent out. It was the big chill. This could only mean that his mother had—at long last—taken a turn for the worse or even died. Well, she'd been as good as dead for more than a decade.

For a moment Gerald played with the idea of snubbing his dad, letting Senior hold on, only to be told by Mrs. Perkins that his son was in a meeting and unavailable. But that was childish. Best to make up and help with whatever preparations were necessary. It would heal their little breach. Gerald hated funerals. He wondered if his black Armani double-breasted suit would still fit; he'd put on some weight.

He nodded and walked from the room without excusing himself. Dickie stopped momentarily, but Gerald heard his drone resume as soon as he stepped beyond the door. Mrs. Perkins, always one to appreciate a possible drama, looked whey-faced. "He said it was urgent to reach you," she whispered, as if there was anyone in the empty hall to disturb. Gerald just nodded calmly and walked to his office. He thought, for a moment, of the length of time Senior had been on hold.

Mrs. Perkins followed him into his office, as if she could give him some kind of moral support. The woman was presumptuous. He looked at her, arching a brow. "Please close the door as you leave," he said coldly, and lifted the phone. She went.

"Hello, Gerald. Is that you?"

"Hello, Father. Is Mother—"

"Your mother is fine, Gerald." He hesitated, always a stickler for accuracy. "Well, she's as fine as she usually is. Thank God she's in her condition. I don't think she could bear this."

Was it Senior himself who was ill? Cancer? Gerald stood at the desk, his imaginary world expanding. What had prompted this call? "What is it, Father? Are you all right?"

"I certainly am not, nor should you be. But I'm calling about your Uncle Bob."

"Uncle Bob Ochs?" Gerald asked.

"Yes, your Uncle Bob Ochs," Senior snapped. "The man whose privacy you invaded for profit. Your mother's brother. The man who lived down a terrible scandal and had some peace in these last years. Your uncle, who blew his brains out this morning."

"What?" Gerald fell into his chair. "He couldn't have! He was so old."

"Not so old that he couldn't pull the trigger on a forty-five," Senior said coldly. "Not so old that he could ignore all the new talk and innuendo that you started up again."

"When did this happen?" Gerald managed to ask.

"Last night, or early this morning. His housekeeper found him. Unfortunately, she didn't call me. She called the police. I'm afraid the story will definitely make the papers."

Gerald was silent. His uncle was nothing to him—a distant figure. He'd been there at family occasions, and he'd always sent the obligatory gift at Christmas and birthdays. But he had been ghostlike for years. Still, the knowledge that he had caused the man's death frightened Gerald for a moment. He'd never been responsible for a death before, even if it was only the death of an eighty-two-year-old living ghost.

"I'm very sorry," Gerald said. "Are you sure this had anything to do with the book?"

"Don't be an ass," Senior snapped. "Of course it was the book. Charles at the club told me that Bob had stopped coming in. He lunched there every weekday for the last eighteen years, and right after your book came out he stopped. When I called him he was deeply shaken, but I didn't realize it was this bad. Of course I didn't, or I would have done something. Apparently, he stopped going out altogether. The housekeeper said that he mumbled about how everybody knew. That everyone on the street stared and pointed."

"Oh, that's ridiculous," Gerald said. "The book isn't even selling that well, and how would people know it was him?"

"It was his delusion, Gerald," Senior explained, using the tone of voice he'd used when Gerald had failed a subject in school. "But *you* sparked the delusion." The old man paused, and Gerald tried to brace himself for what he knew was coming. "I asked you not to do this book, Gerald. You told me that you wouldn't, or you led me to believe that you wouldn't. And then, without as much as a rewrite, you published it. You killed your uncle, and if your mother knew, I'm sure it would kill her. It was an utterly craven, selfish act, and I am deeply ashamed of you. I want you to know that you no longer have my support. There is no forgiveness for this. Your Uncle Bob was not an easy man to know. He was distant, and he had his own demons to fight. But he didn't deserve a death like this. They're still cleaning his brains off the walls." He paused, and Gerald wondered, for the briefest moment, if his father was crying. But Senior merely took a breath and continued relentlessly. "You are an unnaturally ambitious, avaricious man. You were born with more advantages and gifts than most, and they still weren't enough for you. You've managed to choose the low road over the high one at every juncture. And I am deeply, deeply ashamed of you."

Gerald opened his mouth, about to protest or apologize, he wasn't sure which. But the phone clicked, and in a moment a dial tone buzzed. Slowly, he put the phone down.

He sat for a few moments. Well, it was unfortunate that his uncle had taken his own life, but the man *was* eighty-two. He was probably senile. His sister was—had been for years. And really, how tragic was it? What did he have to look forward to at that age? Not that it was his fault, no matter what his father implied. Gerald hadn't used his uncle's name, and he had changed plenty of the details. Nobody was pointing the finger at Robert Ochs. The only finger that killed him was his own finger on the trigger. I actually depicted him sympathetically, Gerald thought. For all I know, he never even *read* the book.

And then the thought occurred to him, small and flickering, at first like the tongue of a snake: How much coverage would this get? And if it *did* get a lot, what would it do for the sales of *Twice in the Papers*? After all, he thought, Bob is already dead. He has no survivors. It can't hurt him, and it could significantly help me. The spin on this matters. Coverage could bring the scandal right into the present again. And I could issue a statement, be bereaved and saddened by this tragedy. Perhaps *People* could do a coping piece on me, the tragedy and my remorse. Remorse sells.

Gerald leaned forward and buzzed Mrs. Perkins.

"Are you all right?" she asked, and he was repulsed by her morbid curiosity.

"Get Wendy Brennon up here right away," he snapped.

# 84

> At some point those of us who are about what is called "truth" have to be as willing to fight for our reality as those who are fighting against us.
>
> —*Nikki Giovanni*

"And you had never even read the book during your daughter's lifetime?"

Opal blinked at the question. It didn't really matter: This was National Public Radio, and listeners couldn't see her face. All she had to do was answer Terry Gross's questions and not shuffle the papers in front of the microphone.

"I read bits over the years, Terry," Opal said. But so little. So very little. Her daughter had been so secretive, so alone, so bitter. Opal blinked back tears.

Saying her daughter's name aloud to this woman was very painful. As if she understood, Terry Gross reached out and touched her hand.

"The important thing is that it's a wonderful book, a brilliant book, that traces the emotional failure of American men. Their inability to love, their irresponsibility to themselves and to their families," Terry Gross said while Opal recovered herself and nodded.

"We have a nation full of single mothers and motherless children. Deadbeat dads. My daughter's father was one," Opal admitted. "And we have a corporate structure in the United States as irresponsible as the fathers running it. Terry's book illuminates the tragedy."

"I understand the manuscript was very nearly lost."

"It wasn't lost. It was destroyed. My daughter burned it and all of her notes before she died. It was only by luck that a publisher had retained a rejected copy and forwarded it to me."

"Amazing!"

These questions were irritating her. "What was amazing? That my daughter was rejected twenty-seven times? Personally, I only find the twenty-seven rejections amazing."

"So how did you go about getting it published?" Ms. Gross asked. "Did you have any connections? Did you know any agents or members of the literary world?"

Opal snorted. "We don't have a lot of them in Bloomington, Indiana." Then she launched into the story of how she'd gone from publishing house to publishing house.

Pam Mantiss and Wendy Brennon had been nervous about this. They had even insisted that Opal be sent to a course in communication strategies, where a woman with too much makeup had set her in front of a video camera and pretended to interview her. Then Opal had to watch the tape while the woman critiqued her. It was all pretty foolish: The only thing it had changed was Opal's hairstyle—when she'd seen herself on the TV she realized she needed a new perm. Pam had told her to give short answers and to mention both the title and Davis & Dash whenever she could. Instead, Opal just answered Ms. Gross's questions. That was enough.

Wendy and Pam had started her with a radio program, and a good one at that, to see how she did. Since the *Times* review a lot had changed. They were going to send the tape to Elle Halle, who was considering a show about Terry. Opal was still turning down the tabloid shows, though Pam had begged, threatened, bribed, and even wept a few crocodile tears trying to get Opal to change her mind. But Opal had been firm: She'd do only the shows where the host had actually read the book and where the program was focused not on personalities, gossip, Terry's suicide, or Opal's supposed bravery but on *The Duplicity of Men* itself. Terry Gross's "Fresh Air" on NPR was an intelligent program, and Opal would do Connie Martinson's cable TV show, and Elle Halle, and that was it.

Now Ms. Gross turned to her copy of the book and began to read. Usually she asked the author to, but Opal had known she wouldn't be up to it. Ms. Gross did it well. Opal listened to her daughter's words spreading out over the airwaves, being communicated to tens of thousands, maybe even hundreds of thousands of people. It was hard to believe that this day had finally come. Opal was satisfied; she had done her job, and now Terry's book belonged to the ages. It would find its own readership. It was no longer up to Opal. She could go home now.

"Opal O'Neal, it was a real honor to have you on," Ms. Gross said.

"Thank you. Good-bye, Terry." Speaking the name out loud to Terry Gross startled Opal again. She'd just said "Good-bye, Terry" over the air to thousands of people. Yes. Maybe it was time to say good-bye.

Terry Gross was saying a few more things into the microphone, and then, just before the ending of the show, there was some sort of commotion in the control booth, where engineers with headsets and Wendy Brennon were sitting. They couldn't hear anything in the studio, but Wendy began to jump up and down, as if she had a trampoline instead of the silencing carpet under her feet. One of the engineers gave a thumbs-up sign through the glass, while the other scrawled a note across an unlined pad. Wendy held the pad up, and Opal looked across the microphone, the tangled cables, and the control console in front of her. "*Duplicity* a top contender for the Tagiter," the sign said, and for perhaps the first time on National Public Radio, both the guest and the host were speechless.

# 85

> I've always believed in writing without a collaborator, because where two people are writing the same book, each believes he gets all the worries and only half the royalties.
>
> —*Agatha Christie*

Judith had searched the entire apartment, looked through Daniel's desk and briefcase, gotten into his office on campus, and even snuck into Cheryl's apartment, but she hadn't found a single page or note on *In Full Knowledge*. She couldn't believe it. How could all those drafts, all her notes, all the manuscript copy be gone? She thought back to the move. Had she packed up all her office papers, or had Daniel? Had they even brought them here at all? Had they thrown them out?

She felt sick, but it wasn't morning sickness. That had stopped. She was sick from betrayal, loneliness, and abandonment. Daniel had been touring, calling her from Chicago, Los Angeles, and Dallas, and each time, all he had asked was whether she was still "being stubborn." She was.

Judith protectively laid her hand over her stomach. Daniel was coming home tonight, and she would confront him. It had taken her all day to get her courage up. She had already called Diana La Gravenesse four times and gone over it with her each time. Even now, as Judith sat waiting for Daniel to walk in the door, she could barely believe that she was going to threaten him. But she agreed with Diana that this was the only way. Surely, in the end, Daniel would care about this child and his wife. A part of Judith hoped—no, believed—that Daniel would come to his senses. That he was only upset and confused by all of this new attention, and that in a little while, once he had adjusted, he would come around.

But Judith had to admit that Daniel hadn't been himself for a long time. Once Daniel had been open, affectionate, responsible, and antisocial. The "new" Daniel was none of those things. He was secretive, cold, and undependable, and he seemed to love his new social life.

Judith sighed. Her palms and her armpits were damp. She didn't want to have to do this, but what other option did she have? She couldn't find the documents that Diana had asked her for. Judith thought of the checkbook in Daniel's name. Even that had disappeared. Before he had left, Daniel had given her five hundred dollars and told her he'd see her in two weeks. He'd also reminded her there was another five hundred in their joint account, in case she decided to "go for the procedure." Judith shivered. He hadn't mentioned the Jude Daniel bank account. She supposed that she had nothing to lose in confronting Daniel and demanding her rights. But then why did it all feel so dangerous? And why, despite Daniel's treatment of her, did she still balk at the idea of threatening him with legal action?

Judith wanted two things, and Diana La Gravenesse had pointed out that she might have to settle for only one of them: She might get to disclose her authorship, or she might get to stay married. Diana didn't believe she could get both. She had left it up to Judith to make up her mind which one she wanted.

Judith would confront Daniel. She didn't have a choice about that; she had to somehow. But she hoped that she could make him see reason. She wanted fairness, and credit for her work, but she also wanted Daniel and she was hoping that she could manage to do what Diana said was impossible—to have it both ways.

When she heard Daniel's key in the lock, Judith moved a hand toward her hair—as if straight bangs would help her. One thing she knew: No matter what, she wouldn't have an abortion. She wouldn't kill their baby. And, crazy as it seemed, it was the baby that Judith felt she had to stand up for tonight. Somehow she could do what had to be done for the baby even if she couldn't do it for herself. As the door opened, she told herself to be calm, to be firm but controlled. She told herself all those things, but she knew she wouldn't succeed with any of them. All she could hope for was that Daniel's feelings for her and his sense of fair play were still strong enough to make a difference.

"You waited up?" Daniel asked, casting a glance at her but walking right past her on his way to the kitchen. He dropped his bag on the carpet. Judith followed him. He looked exhausted, and for a moment Judith felt sorry for him. But that would only weaken her resolve, so she looked away while he took off his jacket, took out a glass, and poured himself some wine. He'd told her over the phone that he'd been drinking wine almost every night—once he'd even called her when he was drunk—and that was another one of the things about the "new" Daniel that worried her. Jewish men didn't drink—it was one of the reasons she had married him: She'd known she'd never have to face one of those screaming scenes her father used to perpetrate on her family when he was intoxicated.

"Daniel," she said, and even to her her voice sounded small and inconsequential. "We have to talk."

"Wrong," Daniel said, and sailed by her on his way to the bedroom. "I have to sleep. I've never been so tired."

"Stop," she told him. "We *do* have to talk."

He turned and looked at her. "Judith, I explained to you once, but I will explain to you again, I have nothing to say to you until after your abortion."

Judith felt the tears rising along her lower lids. "I'm not talking about *that*," she said.

"Then I'm not talking at all," he told her, then turned to walk into the bedroom.

"Daniel! I'm going to sue you if you don't give me credit for the book."

He spun around, his mouth open, his eyes big. Surely now he would see how insane this had all become. Judith braced herself, prepared for him to either yell or break down in tears. But Daniel did neither.

Instead, he began to laugh.

Judith watched him, thinking at first that he might be so overtired that he was hysterical, and he was, but not in the way she first thought. Daniel laughed and then kept on laughing, his face crinkled up. The lines she'd always considered so handsome showed beside his eyes. He was laughing so hard that his wine almost spilled on the wall-to-wall carpeting. "You're going to what?" he finally asked.

"I'm going to sue you if you don't immediately contact Davis & Dash, in writing, and acknowledge my coauthorship." There, she'd said it and she'd said it right. She took out the document that Diana La Gravenesse had supplied. "Here," she said, "you have to sign this."

Daniel reached out and snatched the paper from her, spilling more wine and making bloody blots on the carpet as he did so. He looked at the paper in disbelief and then back at her. "Well," he said, "haven't you been a busy girl." He shook his head. "Busy, but stupid." He paused as if considering. "Yes, we could describe you that way."

Judith's lip trembled, but she didn't move. Diana had warned her he might get nasty. "My lawyer is pretty smart," she said.

"Oh, yeah. Brilliant. Sniffing out a bestseller and working on the come. Lots of brilliant lawyers work for free," he sneered. He threw the wineglass across the room, where it fell against the couch and rolled off, spreading its bloody stain in a wide arc. Judith winced.

"Daniel, can't you be nice? You know that I wrote the book. Can't you just do the right thing? Can't we be the way we used to? Please, Daniel."

"Please, Daniel," he imitated and added a sneer. "What exactly do you want to be like it used to? You want to be broke? You want to go back and live in that dump? You want me to be wasting myself teaching morons all day long?" He turned his back on her and walked to the bedroom.

"I want you to love me. And I want you to be fair. Just tell the truth. That I wrote the book." Daniel turned to her, and his expression, almost a snarl, frightened Judith. Involuntarily, she took a step backward, almost stepping on Flaubert, who was crouched at her feet.

"The book was *my* idea," Daniel growled. "*I* thought of it. *I* picked the subject. And *I* told you what to write. You never would have done it except for me. And you didn't even do it well. I had to edit every word. And even then, Davis & Dash rewrote it again. It's *my* book, and I won't be publicly humiliated or called a liar."

"Then I will sue you."

Daniel looked at her—simply looked, but his eyes grew small with anger, or contempt, or something even more unpleasant. Then he laughed. For a moment, only a moment, Judith thought that they might end this fight—this most horrific argument—the way they used to end all their tiffs: with a joke, a laugh, and forgiveness. But, as usual, she was wrong. "Don't you have a clue?" Daniel asked. "Don't you have the slightest fucking clue? Do you think that I'm as stupid as you are?" He picked up the wine bottle and held the long neck up to his mouth and drank. Then he put down the bottle and stared at her. "You're talking like a child," he said. "Just *try* to sue. I have the entire book written in my own handwriting, complete with cross outs and corrections."

"In *your* handwriting?" Judith echoed.

"In *my* handwriting. In a dated journal. Which I read aloud in some of my writing groups. To which I added notes with their comments. All would testify on my behalf. I have Cheryl, who typed the manuscript for me, with my handwritten corrections because you did such a bad job. She'd testify to that. I have everyone from Don Kingsbury to Pam Mantiss who can testify, and *will* testify, that they saw me writing. What have you got? Who have you got? People here already think you're crazy. They've seen your scenes in restaurants and at parties. I've told them how jealous you've been. They're convinced that you're neurotic, envious, and agoraphobic—and that you live in a fantasy world.

"And the other people at Davis & Dash think you're nuts, too. Remember the spectacle you made of yourself at the Chelsea party? You think they won't testify on my behalf? They have lawyers who do nothing but this kind of work, coping with nut cases and scam artists all day long. So sue. It will make us even. 'Cause I'm suing, too. I'm suing for divorce." He turned and headed for the door. "By the way," he said, "don't try to get any of the money. I'm going to make sure the court knows how you stood in my way at every point on this book. How you drained me. You never worked. You just sat on your ass while I sweated blood. So that you deserve none of the income. They might not agree completely, but in the meantime, I'd suggest you get a job at the 7-Eleven and try to work for a living." He paused. "Oh. And about the divorce. Forget it. I want an annulment. And I'll contest that the baby is even mine."

Judith started to weep, and Flaubert began to growl again.

"Shut up," Daniel said, but Judith didn't know which of them he was talking to. He just turned and slammed the door.

# 86

> I have never begun a novel without hoping that it would be the one that would make it unnecessary for me to write another.
>
> —*François Mauriac*

"It's unbelievable!" Alex Simmons said. "I had to pull an awful lot of strings."

Camilla didn't know what the proper response was, so she said, "Thank you." But she had quite a few doubts. She certainly didn't want to discourage her agent, but she had given up. She'd had to. Looking ahead and working on her next book was the only way to be sure that her heart didn't break. Will had told her that, and it was good advice.

"Camilla, I've been working so hard to keep *A Week in Firenze* on the bookshelves."

Camilla sighed. "When and where is the interview?" she asked.

"They want to come to your studio."

"You mean, they're coming to Park Slope? But the flat is a tip."

"A tip?"

"You know, a garbage dump," Camilla said, remembering to translate into American.

"That's the *point*," Alex said. "They *want* a dump. The whole angle here is 'little penniless English girl makes good.'"

"Don't be mad. How have I made good?" Camilla asked. "The book has failed. I've failed."

"If you ever say that out loud again, I'll come there and rip your heart out," Alex said, and the tone of her voice was convincing. "None of my clients fail. It's too early in my career to have any failures," Alex barked. "You are a critical success. Americans root for the underdog. It's a standard *People* story. They just plugged you in because somebody over there owes me a favor."

"But isn't that the magazine that always has a scandal or a tragedy on the cover? Do people who read it buy books? Do they read?"

"They move their lips when they do, but they all have credit cards and a Barnes & Noble located conveniently nearby."

Camilla shrugged. "It sounds rather undignified and futile," she said, "but of course I'll do it. And thank you, Alex. You're a wonderful agent."

"I want that in writing," Alex said. "Anyway, I'll get back to you with the day and date. They're talking next week."

"You're going to be in *People*? You're kidding? That's fabulous."

"Is it?" Camilla asked Craig Stevens. He had taken her out to dinner at Rain, a restaurant that made her think of the South Seas and sweating planters back in the days of the British empire. Not that they were sweating. Though the restaurant was done up in rattan and mosquito netting, the ceiling fans were pushing only cool air that had clearly been conditioned. It was all rather posh and funny, Camilla thought, but the menu looked interesting and the bar scene more so.

"*People* magazine is big," Craig said. "Giant. Jesus, I wish I could get Will into *People* magazine."

"Well, maybe he could knock on my door and they'd put him in the picture."

"Oh, great," Craig said. "A literary Kramer."

"Kramer?" she asked. "What did *he* write?"

"A coffee-table book," Craig told her. "Anyway, Camilla, this might make a big difference to your book sales."

Camilla shrugged. "I think it's a lot like our *Hello* magazine. Rock stars and their wives at home, a duchess who's done a cookery book, and endless stories on Paula Yates and Princess Caroline of Monaco. I don't see how it will sell a single copy."

The waitress appeared and they ordered. Craig reached across the table and took her hand.

"Camilla, I don't know how to do this without seeming to harass you."

"Do what?" Camilla asked. Craig, who was always so smooth and funny, seemed speechless and ill at ease. Her hand felt good in his. For a moment, Camilla wondered what it would be like to kiss him. She knew he was a big flirt and had a string of girlfriends. She could understand why.

"Listen," Craig said. "I don't want you to feel that I'm asking this because you work for me or that you have any obligation or that I expect anything of you. I just really, really like you."

"I like you, too, Craig." Camilla knew what was coming and didn't know what to do.

"Yes, but do you like me in *that* way?"

"Which way?"

Craig groaned. "You're not making this easy for me," he said. "I'm asking your permission to make a pass at you. I'm not harassing you, and I don't expect it or demand it or anything like that, but I certainly would like it if you like me, you know, feel attracted to me sexually and would sleep with me. Is that clear enough?"

"Oh, I see," Camilla said and blushed. "You're being politically correct."

"Yes, and to put it in your terms, it's a damn bloody nuisance."

"Those aren't *my* terms at all," Camilla said. She looked at him and began to giggle. "Actually, I think it's very funny."

The waitress placed their first course before them. She

looked at Craig. "Is there anything else you want?" she asked.

"I've already made what I want abundantly clear," Craig told her. Camilla giggled again. The waitress stood there confused until he dismissed her.

"I'm very complimented," she said, "but I'm a little bit fragile right now. I don't think a casual affair would work for me."

"I'm not talking casual affair, Camilla." He looked at her across the table, and, silly as it might be, she believed him. "I know you must think I'm a bit of a tart," Craig said.

"A bit," Camilla agreed.

"You know I was married, right?"

Camilla nodded.

"Well, one of the reasons we broke up was because we couldn't have children. It was a great disappointment to me and to my wife. It was also a humiliation."

"Why should that humiliate you?" Camilla asked. "Your wife couldn't help it."

Craig smiled but shook his head. "The problem wasn't with my wife. I think low sperm count is always the husband's fault, isn't it?" He looked away, over to the bar.

"Still," Camilla said. "It isn't as if it's your fault." But even as she said it, Camilla wondered why wounded men were the ones attracted to her. Was it some message she gave off? Some attitude? But perhaps she shouldn't take it so personally. Perhaps *all* men were wounded in one way or another.

"Is this a ploy?" she asked. "I mean, I've been told by Emily and Susan that there are a lot of lines men use in this city." Craig's face hardened, and Camilla realized she'd made a mistake.

"I'm very sorry," she said. "I'm sorry for what I just said, and I'm sorry about your marriage." She paused. "But it isn't totally tragic, Craig. There are a lot of babies in the world who need parents."

Craig shrugged. "I think it was the blow to my ego. The fact that I'd been blaming my wife, that we'd just assumed it was her. I did a lot of damage. I've had time to get over it. Time to change. But I want a wife, and I want a family. And I really care about you. Let's get to know each other better. What do you think?"

"Craig, is this a proposal?"

He grinned. "It's more like a proposition," he said. "I felt full disclosure was the way to go with you. Now that you know: If you're interested, well"—he paused—"we could rent with the option to buy."

"It would be a tempting way to get my hands on a Canaletto," Camilla joked.

"It wasn't the first thing I was thinking of you getting your hands on."

Camilla smiled at his wickedness. She liked Craig. Was it something more? She thought of Frederick but put him out of her mind. Maybe this was a way to get over him. "My place or yours?" she asked.

"Most definitely mine," Craig told her. "It's just around the corner."

Camilla was late getting back to Park Slope, and the people from *People*—a funny phrase—were already there. There were three of them: a male journalist, a woman photographer, and a dogsbody who seemed to help with the lighting and carrying the bags. Alex was there too, and rolled her eyes as she saw Camilla walking down the block.

"I'm so sorry to be late," Camilla said.

"At least it isn't snowing," Alex remarked caustically.

"Picture of the struggling writer coming back from work?" the photographer said, aiming an absolutely enormous lens at her.

"You have a daytime job?" the journalist asked.

"Yes," Camilla told them. "At Citron Press." But that was not where she'd been. She'd been lying in bed at Craig Stevens's flat. They had spent the night together. He was a tender and energetic lover. Funny how that hadn't moved her. It had been pleasant to be with him, but something was missing, and it certainly wasn't sperm. She'd been trying to forget Frederick, but it had reminded her vividly of her night with him.

Camilla had fallen asleep disappointed. She and Craig had made love again in the morning, and she had felt very little toward him. Camilla didn't understand it, accepted it as one of the odd tricks of life. But she certainly couldn't discuss it with this magazine interviewer. "Please come up to my flat," she said. "I'll make you a proper cup of tea to warm you up."

"Could you put some Jack Daniel's in it?" the dogsbody suggested, stamping his feet. Alex gave him a look, then gave Camilla another look as they all trooped into the tatty foyer and up the stairs.

"We could shoot on the staircase," the photographer suggested. "I like these broken banisters, they look like missing teeth."

"Whatever," the journalist said in a bored voice, and Camilla wished she'd been there a little bit earlier.

# 87

> One should fight like the devil the temptation to think well of editors. They are all, without exception—at least some of the time—incompetent or crazy.
>
> —*John Gardner*

Pam had already put her sunglasses on and crossed the dim lobby of the Waldorf-Astoria without looking in either direction. David Morton wasn't a particularly good lay, but you didn't have to be when you owned as many companies as he did. Pam didn't even think of it as sex; it was more like insurance payments—a necessary precaution.

Still, it wasn't necessary for anyone to see her slipping out of the Waldorf. She wished that David had picked a more discreet hotel, but it was clear that he didn't often carry on with women. He'd spent half the evening talking to her about his troubled marriage and then had been as tentative and polite as an Eagle Scout. David Morton had probably *been* an Eagle Scout, Pam thought. She ran her fingers through her blond, curly hair and descended the steps. Shit! There was a line of people waiting for taxis; she'd have to hoof it crosstown over to Davis & Dash for the big meeting with Edina Trawley and her gang of lawyers.

The sun was shining, and the morning was fresh and pleasant. Pam smiled. David Morton was very impressed with his Editor of the Year. He wasn't from the book world, and like many of the moguls new to publishing, he still believed its PR. Funny how men who knew how to manipulate the buzz on Wall Street to float a stock offering believed the buzz in the book world. Pam thought of all the trouble, all the sucking up she'd had to do, to get the fucking award. It had been worth every minute of it. She was David Morton's little Editor of the Year. David Morton was proud of her and, after talking, had confided in her. He thought Gerald would have to go. Pam had faked a torn loyalty but at last had let him coax out her views. She'd given him all the support she could after decimating Gerald. David hadn't promised her Gerald's job as publisher—not yet—but given time, he would. Perhaps a walk over to the office was just what she needed—it gave her time to think of how she'd decorate GOD's Little Acre.

Then she felt a tap on her shoulder. She turned around, surprised.

"When are you going to meet with me?" Stewart Campbell asked. "When are you going to take my calls? You promised me a new arrangement. You promised, and now you don't even take my calls."

Pam gave him a withering look. "And what are you doing now, stalking me? Have you gone completely crazy?"

"I'm not stalking you. I'm following you because it's the only way I get to see you. That's your choice. You made some promises to me, Pam, and you better live up to them."

Pam's stomach clenched. How long had he been following her?

"Since last night," Stewart said, as if her question had been voiced.

"I will not be blackmailed," Pam said in a voice as strong as she could manage. "I told you: I'm meeting with Edina Trawley and her legal corps today. I'll get it all straightened out."

"Good," Stewart said. "Or I talk to my own legal corps."

"Stewart, I told you: Contractually you deserve nothing more. You signed on as a writer-for-hire. I'm doing the rest simply because I like working with you."

Stewart laughed. "Yeah, and I'm Elvis. I'll talk to *PW* this afternoon, Pam, if you don't take my call."

"I am not having a fucking business meeting at the corner of Fiftieth and Park," Pam yelled. The light changed, and she walked toward Davis & Dash. Her stride was steady, but her hands were shaking.

"You better take my call!" Stewart shouted above the noise of the traffic.

# 88

Good swiping is an art in itself.
—*Jules Feiffer*

"I can't do it, Mr. Davis."

Gerald froze, and then, after a pause long enough to intimidate anyone, he moved his hand up to his cheek and lay two fingers along his temple. "What?" was all he said.

"I can't do it," Carl Pollenski repeated.

"You can't? Or you *won't*?" Gerald asked in his most withering tone.

The MIS drone had had the nerve to call him and insist—insist—on a meeting. "We're in trouble here," he had said, and although Gerald had told him he was simply too busy to fit him in, Carl had demanded a half hour of his time. In principle, Gerald felt that allowing Carl to dictate to him set a bad precedent. But the man's nervousness had begun to infect Gerald, not unlike a nasty contagion.

Carl told him that he felt frightened by the questions of his chief analyst, and he wanted to abort all future transfers of sales. Gerald told him not to be an ass, advising him simply to fire the analyst. The Polack looked at him as if he were crazy, but Gerald knew that he was the only one who saw things clearly and had the power to achieve his goals. To hear any protest from this computer dweeb, who had accepted Gerald's generous salary and very special benefits, enraged him. Gerald told him to forget about the analyst, fire or reassign him, and double the orders for *Twice in the Papers*, taking most of them from *A Week in Firenze*, which was doing surprisingly well. Gerald had consulted the order sheets. Too bad *The Duplicity of Men* was priced so high—it had a lot more sales than Gerald had expected, and he could have stolen at least a thousand orders from there.

But when he poo-poohed Carl and gave him new instructions, Carl balked. "Look, things aren't like they were," Carl said. "I can't do it."

Gerald, when he was most angry and most dangerous, grew icy cold. He looked at the big idiot with the crew cut through teeth clenched so hard they were almost chattering. "You can and you will," Gerald told him.

"But someone's going to find out," Carl said, almost whining.

"Don't be ridiculous. Nobody expected any sales from the Clapfish book. We could take twice as many and no one would be the wiser, least of all the author. Edina Trawley isn't going to miss nine thousand copies when it's selling double that in a week. And I'm taking full responsibility. As they say at Nike, just do it."

"Look, it's my career that would be at stake."

Gerald never ceased to be amazed at the worry and grandiosity of all the little people with little lives that they never failed to think actually mattered.

"I'm not putting my career on the line," Carl said more harshly.

"I'm afraid you already have," Gerald told him smoothly. "I'll report that you did this without my permission as a way to curry favor, and I'll also discover your abuse of company privileges—the car, the catering, the theater tickets."

# 89

I think it's unfortunate to have critics for friends.
—*William Styron*

Susann lay on the sofa, a cold compress on her forehead, her hands wrapped in a moist hot towel. She'd finished the tour almost a week ago and returned to New York with unbearable pain in her hands. The New York dampness didn't help, but Susann didn't have the energy to travel. Her house in France during this wet season was certainly no better, and expensive as they were, she didn't really feel good in either of her homes.

She'd already been to Columbia Presbyterian twice for hot-wax treatments. They had done little to relieve her, but immersing her hands in the warm gluey wax had at least been a momentary respite. The moment she pulled out her hands, the aching intensified. Her only distraction from the pain was to think about her failure. She hadn't made the list, and she knew she wouldn't. Other books had moved in, and hers was finished, topping out at an invisible number, part of the unpublished list, the list that didn't matter, the list that did not include bestsellers.

She had called Pam Mantiss and Gerald Ochs Davis twice a day for the last four days and had not even received a call back. She knew she wouldn't. She was nothing but a burden on their list, an author who would never earn out her advance, and one they might decide was not worth publishing. The thought of turning out three more books very nearly made her weep.

She would become a nobody, a nothing, for what was she if not a bestselling author? For almost fifteen years, her name and that phrase had been married in a joining far more meaningful to her than any of her actual marriages. *Susann Baker Edmonds number one bestselling author . . . bestselling author Susann Baker Edmonds is arriving in . . . and now let me introduce bestselling author Susann Baker Edmonds . . .*

She wasn't a wife. She wasn't even a mistress—when was the last time she had seen Alf, much less slept with him? She wasn't a successful mother—despite Kim's book, her trouble with drugs and Susann's guilt at not protecting her from her stepfather certainly proved that. So what was she? Despite the face-lifts, despite the money she had earned, Susann returned to her apartment and lay on the sofa, facing the fact that her time both as a publishing star and as a sexual woman had come to an end. She was a middle-aged woman alone, about to sink into the oblivion into which all middle-aged American women without the buffer of fame, family, and status disappear. She would become invisible, no longer in magazines, no longer quoted in *Publishers Weekly*, no longer sought after as a speaker or television guest. She would become a nobody, and the thought was unbearable.

Edith, another middle-aged nobody, walked into the room. "How are your hands?" Edith asked.

Susann just shook her head. What was the point in describing her pain?

Edith brought the heated mitts and gently, carefully, inched them over Susann's curled claws. Then she sat down in the small chair opposite Susann. "I think there's been about enough of this."

"Enough of what?" Susann asked.

"Enough mourning. Okay. The book hasn't succeeded. So what? You've had eleven that have. You have money in the bank, a house in France, this apartment, and enough clothes to fill ten boutiques on Madison Avenue. It's time to get over it and move on."

Susann looked at Edith resentfully. "Move on to what?" she asked.

Edith shrugged. "Who knows? That's the fun part. Figuring it out."

"There's nothing to figure out. It'll be more of the same. I have a contract to do three more books. I'll hate them. Pam Mantiss will hate them. The public will hate them. And then I'll be seventy."

"Who says so? You might finally fire me for saying this. That's okay. I've put plenty by for my retirement, and it's got to be said. Susann, I've never known a woman who was so smart and so dumb at the same time. Screw the contract. Screw Gerald Ochs Davis. Screw the public. You don't have to write another word, not if you don't feel like it. And you certainly don't have to try to do some silly knockoff of *The Bridges of Madison County*."

"But I have to. My contract . . . Alf—"

"SCREW ALF!" Edith crossed her chunky legs. "Alf is a lying, manipulative, greedy, ungrateful, disloyal agent. I know that's redundant. Let's face it, he's always been a power-crazed prick. He rode you until he found another horse. Well, throw the jockey and let him get trampled. If it's any satisfaction to you, Jude Daniel's book tanked. Word over at Davis & Dash is that it's the big disappointment of the season." Edith tsked sarcastically. "Such a disappointment for Alf Byron. I guess his mummy never taught him not to count his chickens before they were published."

"Oh, Edith, I can't face knowing that I'll be alone for the rest of my life."

"Alone? What am I? Chopped liver? And I think that you should see Kim again." Edith leaned forward gently and put her hand on Susann's shoulder. "Sue, dear, it's time to put down the reins. You've worked long and hard. No wonder your hands hurt. They're tired. It's time to move on."

"Move on to what?" Susann asked. "A crippled old age?"

"Well, old age certainly, but how about moving on to

some fun and selflessness? They're not mutually exclusive."

Susann sat up. "What are you talking about?"

"It's time to stop worrying about the career. It's time to stop being a hostage to it. You don't have to worry about chapter eleven ever again. It stopped being fun a long time ago. You don't have to worry about your place on the list, the number of advance orders, or your meeting with the Literary Guild. Think about what you would really enjoy doing. You have the means and the time."

"What about my contract? What about—"

"Let the lawyers handle it. That's what they're paid for."

Susann thought for a moment of what it might feel like to lay the burden down. It had been so much work, so much unrelenting pressure for so long, Susann could barely imagine her life without it. "I don't know what I'd do," she whispered.

"I know. Isn't it exciting?" Edith asked. And for a moment Susann felt the thrill of possibilities.

"Hawaii," Edith whispered. "The South Pacific. Pueblos. Rafting down the Colorado. An apartment in Paris. Arranging your own flowers. Giving money to Chinese orphans. Shopping on the rue de Rivoli. Breakfast in bed. Scholarships for creative writing. The emptiness could be filled."

"But what about Alf?" Susann asked.

"I say fire the bastard. But then, what do I know?"

The telephone rang. Susann knew better than to expect it might be anyone from Davis & Dash, but she still hoped. She managed to sit up and hold out her twisted fist. "Who is it?" she asked Edith.

"It's your daughter," Edith told her innocently.

# 90

> Opinions cannot survive if one has no chance to fight for them.
>
> —*Thomas Mann*

Opal's life had changed more than she would have liked in the last few weeks. The letter campaign to the independent bookstores had finally worked, spawning not only more book orders but also dozens of phone calls from the bookstores asking for Opal to appear. It was the Tagiter nomination, of course, that had done it. That and the *New York Times* rave. But Opal wanted to deal with the stores that had shown an interest before all of this happened. So she wrote back to Liberties in Boca Raton, Vivien Jennings at Rainy Day, and Dwight Currie and Michael Kohlman at Misty Valley Books. She thought that they would do best by Terry's book.

"It's the most ridiculous thing in the world," Opal said to Roberta as she tried to do something with her hair. "I'm not a sideshow. Why would anyone want me to sign my daughter's book?"

"Oh, Opal, it's just the way people are. Look at Pat Conroy. He tours with his father—the one he wrote *The Great Santini* about. And the *father* signs the books."

"Totally shameless," Opal snapped. "Have they no dignity?" She shook her head. "I'm not making a spectacle of myself."

"Look, the Elle Halle show is certainly not a sideshow. People are begging to be on it."

"People! People? People are having unsafe sex. People are destroying the ozone layer. People are using *unique* with a modifier. That doesn't mean it's all right."

Roberta laughed. "Opal, *you're* unique with a modifier."

They were waiting for Wendy Brennon and Emma Ashton, who would be conveying them by limo over to the Elle Halle studio. Pam Mantiss, of course, had tried to horn in, but Opal had refused to even consider an appearance with Pam Mantiss there. "I won't cry," Opal said now to Roberta. "I don't care if the woman brings out Terry's baby pictures. I am not going to weep on television."

"Oh, Opal, it's not the worst thing in the world," Roberta said. "Elle Halle just wants to make good television."

"Good television! An oxymoron. Isn't Elle Halle the one who asked Michael Jackson and his wife if they have sexual intercourse?"

"I think that was Diane Sawyer."

"Well, shame on her, then. Good television indeed! This is about books, not gossip or show business."

"I'm afraid you're wrong, Opal. The book business has become mostly gossip and show business, at least for the successful." The buzzer rang, and the two women left the mirror. Roberta spoke over the intercom. "The limousine is here," she said. "Come along, my reluctant media star."

The time on camera went very quickly. Elle Halle, perfectly dressed, perfectly coiffed, and perfectly cool, had asked the usual questions. Terry's suicide, how Opal felt about getting the call from the police ("How would *you* feel?"), how Opal had found the manuscript ("I didn't find it. It was sent to me."), how did Davis & Dash get it ("From the wonderful Emma Ashton."). At first Ms. Halle seemed taken aback by Opal's abrupt, no-nonsense answers, but after a little while Opal could see that the woman, intelligent as she was, figured a way to use Opal's style as a kind of humorous understatement.

Elle Halle told the story of the rejections, showed some of the rejection letters on the monitor, and then asked Opal what she thought of the distinguished list of editors who had turned down Terry's book. "A confederacy of dunces," Opal had said.

"Well, either they are or the Tagiter committee is," Elle laughed.

Opal shrugged. "One thing I've learned about New York publishing," Opal told her, "is that it's a lot like what my husband used to say about the used-car business: 'There is a seat for every ass and an ass for every seat.'"

Elle had asked about Terry's father's desertion, about Terry's childhood, and about the book itself. "Have you read it?" Opal asked.

Elle Halle smiled. "From cover to cover," she said. "Will there be a test?"

When Opal returned to the green room, Emma, Wendy, and Roberta gave her a round of applause, and that was after the standing ovation from the technical crew. Opal guessed she'd done well. She was pretty tired. It wasn't every day she was on national TV; she was grateful for that. Elle Halle came back and asked her to sign a copy of Terry's book, giving Opal an autographed picture of herself in return—"Not that I'd asked for it," Opal said in the limo on the way home.

The limousine phone rang. Wendy Brennon took the call, then covered the mouthpiece. "Katie Couric wants you on the Today show," she said. "What do I tell them?"

Opal, exhausted, leaned back in her seat. "Can we discuss this tomorrow?" she asked.

# 91

> Cool and calm are important, but, paradoxically, so is warmth and energy.
>
> —*Betty A. Prashker*

"Those orders have got to be wrong," Alex was saying. "Check with your computer department. I see *A Week in Firenze* everywhere." Emma shrugged and had to think of what to say.

"It's a small book, Alex. It's a small book, maybe achieving cult status, but just because you see it in bookstores doesn't mean people are buying it. I guess there's no sell-through."

"Well, call MIS anyway. I'm calling Ingram myself. I'm telling you, the book is being reviewed in a lot of literary journals, and it's moving. I know it's moving." Emma looked at the printout and shrugged again. She was trying to tell herself that Alex's anger was not directed at her. Alex's voice softened. "So, how are you?"

For a moment Emma thought she might keep up a good front. Then, thinking of her conversation with Frederick, she decided to be truthful. "I'm upset here at work," she said. "I think there are going to be a lot of changes. There are all kinds of rumors."

"Hey, it wouldn't be publishing if there weren't a dozen rumors a day."

"Yeah, but it's never seemed like this before. The corporate people have come in, and they seem to be combing the place. I don't know what they're looking for, but GOD is frayed around the edges."

"You would be too if your novel was taking a dump, your highly touted new writer's book has gone south, you were forced to dump Chad Weston and his book zoomed, while the only thing you got that's selling was written by a newly dead author."

"I don't think it *was* written by a newly dead author," Emma murmured.

"Yeah, yeah. Pam Mantiss probably rewrote most of it."

"I don't think so," Emma said. And, despite her better judgment she told Alex about the conversation she had overheard.

Alex listened breathlessly. "So you're telling me that not only does Peet's ghost have a ghost, but that Pam, who is a ghost, has a ghost too?" Alex hummed a fragment of a spooky-sounding tune. Then she began to intone, "The literary dead are restless in their tombs. Skeletal fingers click upon an insubstantial word processor. What haunts these haunts, keeping them from their eternal rest?"

"They haven't earned out their advance," Emma said, finishing the gag.

"So who is this guy?"

"He's a midlist author. Stewart something. Stewart Campbell. You know, I remember seeing him mesmerized by the Peet Trawley display at the ABA. I thought the guy was some kind of weirdo fan."

"Sounds like a weirdo hack to me. I wonder what he got paid to write the country's number-one bestselling book?"

"There was a rumor that Pam was getting a quarter of a million."

"Hmm," Alex said. And for a moment the conversation seemed over. But Emma desperately wanted to continue the contact.

"Isn't it great about *Duplicity*?" she asked Alex.

"I'll say. I've already received fourteen inquiries about foreign rights. Would you believe one is from Croatia? You'd think they'd have more important things to do."

"That will make Opal happy." She told Alex about the taping of the Elle Halle show and how touched she'd been by Opal's compliment.

"Jesus, I hope it doesn't air. They better cut that out."

Emma scowled. Was Alex jealous? It was such an unkind thing to say. "Why?" she asked. "Don't you think it's true?"

"Of course, but that has nothing to do with it. Don't you ever think politically, Emma? How is Pam going to feel if she hears Mrs. O'Neal say that after *she's* taking all the credit."

"Oh, yeah. Right," she said. "That's why I need you. I forget things like that. Listen, Alex, do you think we could—"

"Yeah, seven-thirty at Le Petit Café. Be there or be square."

Emma smiled.

But Emma wasn't smiling an hour later when Mrs. Daniel appeared at her desk. She looked even worse than the last time Emma had seen her; in fact, she hadn't recognized her. She had called, earlier in the week, and begged for an appointment. She said that neither Pam Mantiss nor Gerald Ochs Davis would take her calls (which certainly didn't surprise Emma, based on the performance of Jude Daniel's book and the corporate trouble that Davis & Dash was facing).

Emma had felt sorry for the woman, and her punishment now would be the endless list of complaints that wives often made to publishers. How their husband's book hadn't been advertised enough, how the publicity should have been reorganized, how . . . But looking at Judith, her long disheveled hair, her weight, her Indian-print skirt and big cardigan top, Emma realized this woman was not going to try to tell her how to do anything. "Sit down," she said as kindly as she could. "Would you like a danish and coffee?"

"No," answered Mrs. Daniel, who remained standing. She wet her already chapped lips with her tongue. "I've given it up," she said. "I'm . . ." she looked down at the bulge beneath her breasts.

Emma raised her eyebrows. Mrs. Daniel *was* fat, and sloppy. "Are you dieting?"

The woman began to sob. Startled, immobilized, Emma just sat there. "What's wrong?" she finally asked.

"Daniel and I are divorcing," Judith said. "I'm having a baby. I don't have a job, and I don't have any money."

"Oh, surely Jude won't leave you right now—"

"*I'm* Jude," the woman said. "And Daniel will leave me. He has left me. And if he hadn't I would have left him."

Emma didn't have the slightest idea why this stranger had decided to come to her and discuss her marital problems. She liked the young woman, despite the fact that she was clearly unstable. She had a kind of directness that made it appear she was painfully honest. If it was an act, she was a fine actress.

"How can I help you?" Emma asked gently. "I don't really know Jude, but if you think it might help—"

"*I'm* Jude," the woman said again. "That's what I came to tell you. *He's* Daniel Gross, and I'm married to him. And we're getting divorced. I'm Jude Daniel. I wrote *In Full Knowledge.* I did it myself, chapter by chapter, and it took eighteen months. Daniel said we would share the money and then I could go out and write what I wanted to. He was going to get the book published, but I wrote it."

Emma looked at her. The black makeup around her eyes had softened and smeared. The pink lipstick she had applied too quickly had been eaten off most of her lips, but some remained on her teeth. She looked mad—in both senses of the word.

"Sit down," Emma offered. "Sit down and we'll talk."

There were dozens of deluded people, pathetic souls who truly believed that they had written *War and Peace,* or *Valley of the Dolls,* or the latest Anne Tyler. And there were nuisance suits, a fairly large industry in California, of people claiming to have contributed a movie idea, a character for a book, or the idea for a title. Changes in copyright law had cleared most of that up. Emma looked at the unraveling woman who now sat in front of her. There was also the issue of marital property. If this was a marital problem, things became fuzzy—as they did over custody. Emma reminded herself that in speaking to this woman she was putting Davis & Dash in jeopardy. She should immediately call Jim Meyer in legal. But thinking about Meyer's fish-eyed stare made Emma feel greater compassion for this truly disturbed woman. What should she do?

"Would you like a glass of water? Something else to drink?"

Mrs. Daniel nodded, and Emma buzzed for Heather. As usual, there was no response. Could Emma leave her alone? She decided to take a chance. After all, what could the woman do in her office except tear up a few books? "I'll be right back," Emma said, then left in search of a soft drink.

The little kitchenette, as so often happened, had already been ransacked, and Emma couldn't even find clean paper cups. She thought of the little refrigerator in Pam's office—Pam was away—and though it was strictly forbidden, Emma dashed down the hall and into Pam's office, threw open the refrigerator door, and removed two Snapples, being sure to rearrange them so that the missing soldiers were less obvious.

When she got back to her office, her guest had found some paper napkins, had taken a mirror from her purse, and was mopping her face. "I'm sorry," she said in a calmer voice. "I know you must think I'm crazy."

"Not at all," Emma lied. She handed Mrs. Daniel the Snapple bottle. "Not very civilized, I'm afraid. We don't have any cups right now." The woman shrugged as if that were the least of her problems, and Emma figured it was. She had just managed to seat herself when Mrs. Daniel, after taking a swig from the Snapple bottle, spat across Emma's desk, her bookshelf, the carpet, and Emma herself with her mouthful of iced tea.

"What are you doing?" she coughed. "I don't think it's funny at all. Do you know I'm pregnant? Is this the kind of thing you sophisticated editors do as a little practical joke? Spike the tea?"

"What are you talking about?" Pregnant, poison? Was the woman delusional as well as paranoid? "It's just iced tea," Emma said.

"The fuck it is."

She sounded violent, and Emma was frightened. She had better call security. She handed another napkin to Mrs. Daniel. "I'm so sorry," she said as calmly as she could, but it came out as a croak. Emma felt her palms go wet as her mouth went dry. She picked up her telephone and tried to smile. "Just one minute," she said. And again her voice was a dry croak. She dialed the number for security and picked up her own Snapple, popped off the lid, and took a sip.

God! Emma nearly spit the liquid into the receiver. How much vodka was in there? And how had it gotten there?

This explained Pam's obsession with her sacrosanct Snapple. She was drinking. All day. No wonder she guarded the refrigerator. No wonder she could come in sober and be bombed before lunch. What else was Pam doing? What was she doing with Stewart Campbell? What was she up to with Jude Daniel? Emma turned to Mrs. Daniel. "You're right." she said. "It *is* spiked."

Emma continued to stare at the woman. As Mrs. Daniel tried to wipe up her skirt, she pressed it against herself and Emma could see the contour of her belly. She *was* pregnant. And the Snapple had been spiked. Emma continued to stare at her. What else was true? "You're telling me the truth, aren't you?" she asked.

"You believe me?" Mrs. Daniel asked, her voice soft with surprise.

"I think I do," Emma said.

# 92

> . . . when the author goes a-roving on that thing known as "the book tour." These are the dangerous times, and they are part of what is so blithely referred to as "the writing life."
>
> —*E. Annie Proulx*

Daniel shifted from his right leg to his left and then back again. In front of him, on the long narrow table, there must have been fifty copies of his novel. The Corner Book Store manager had also thoughtfully provided a chair, a pitcher of water, a drinking glass, and a pen. But Daniel didn't need any of them. Despite the sign in the window and the one beside the table, it appeared that absolutely no one in the city of New York was interested in having him sign a copy of *In Full Knowledge*. Worse, they weren't interested in buying it either.

Daniel couldn't believe it. Despite the advertising, despite his book tour, despite the interviews and his charm and the push the book had received at the ABA, despite all of that and in the face of Alf Byron's certainty and Pam Mantiss's hunch, *In Full Knowledge* was failing, and Daniel Gross knew that he was failing along with it.

He shifted to his other leg. "Sign the books," Alf muttered and elbowed him. "Each one they sign they can't send back. It counts as a sold book."

Mechanically, Daniel picked up the pen and began to sign. But what good would a few dozen book sales make in the sea of volumes that would be returned to Davis & Dash from bookstores all over the country?

"Sign the books," Alf Byron hissed again, but at that moment a man approached the table with a copy of *In Full*

*Knowledge* already in his hand. Thank God. At least there was one reader who wanted a signature, and despite his mortification, Daniel was relieved to oblige.

"Hi," the man said. "I'm Lenny Golay."

"I'm Jude Daniel," Daniel told him with what he hoped was a modest smile. "Shall I sign the book 'To Lenny'?"

The man laughed. "No, thank you. I'm the owner. Actually, I'd prefer that you didn't sign any more copies." He smiled again. "Chris," he called to another guy. "Could you bring some stickers and help me box this stock?"

Chris joined them, a roll of "Signed by the Author" medallions in his hand. "Why don't you let me put them on the books Mr. Daniel has already signed, and then you can bring the rest of these back to the stockroom."

Daniel felt his face darken with a blush.

"Wait a minute," Alf said. "We have plenty of time to sign the rest." Daniel watched with deepening embarrassment as Alf laid his age-freckled hand on Chris's arm. "We're happy to sign them."

"No, we're not," Daniel told them all, and laid down his pen.

# 93

Never look on the bright side; the glare is blinding.
—*Florence King*

There was a knock at her door, and Camilla looked up from her manuscript. She hoped it wasn't Will. Since she had been interviewed by *People*, he had been peevish—almost as if he was hurt. Camilla could only suppose that Will was either jealous of that silly article or felt that she was about to abandon him along with her status as a non-commercial penniless author. Not that it was likely—Davis & Dash still wasn't returning her calls. The knock came again. This silliness was beneath Will. Camilla went to the door. To be careful she looked through the peephole and was surprised to see a uniformed face topped by a cap. "Who is it?" she asked.

"It's Bobby. Frederick Ashton's driver."

Camilla opened the door. She said hello before she saw the roses—dozens and dozens, maybe *hundreds* of roses—some bunched under Bobby's long arms, others piled in cellophane at his feet, and the rest stacked along the staircase. "Oh, my goodness," she said. "What—"

"Where shall I put them?" Bobby asked with a grin.

"I have no idea," Camilla told him. She walked into her tiny kitchenette looking for a vase. It was ridiculous, absolutely ridiculous. If she put them in her garbage pail, her mop bucket, every one of her drinking glasses, as well as filling the sink, she still couldn't possibly get them all into water. Bobby kept returning with yet more roses, rather like the sorcerer's apprentice. They seemed to be every color, from white to the lightest pink blush to a darker pink to an almost magenta. They were magnificent.

"He's quite mad," she said. "Your boss is quite mad."

"Mad about you," Bobby said with a nod, and Camilla blushed almost as deeply as the roses.

"Oh, I think not."

"Ha! The two of you ought to have your heads examined." Bobby brought in yet more flowers.

"Whatever shall I do with them?" Camilla asked.

"Beats me." Bobby shrugged.

"The bath!" Camilla rushed to fill the tub with lukewarm water. When she came out of the bathroom, Will was standing in the doorway.

"Chelsea flower show?" he asked.

"A bloody funeral, more like," Camilla said. "They're all going to die if I don't put them in water." She began to transfer the roses to the bath. "How did you know I was here?" she asked Bobby.

"You weren't," he said. "Not when we came earlier." Camilla had gone out early for a quick breakfast and the Sunday paper. "We came back."

"We?" Camilla asked.

"Yeah. Frederick's downstairs, sitting in the car. He—"

Camilla didn't wait. She ran down the stairs without a coat, without a thought, to see Frederick. Will yelled something, but she didn't hear it. The car was parked across the street. Despite the cold, Camilla stepped between a parked van and the truck at the curb and crossed over. Frederick, sitting in the backseat surrounded by still more roses, didn't see her, but when she knocked on the window he immediately lowered it. "You are totally bonkers," she said.

"Hello. So nice to see you, too. You're very welcome for the flowers."

"Yes. Of course. Thank you, you madman. They're brilliant. Absolutely brilliant. But you *are* mad. They must have cost a fortune."

Frederick nodded somberly. "Yes. Now I'm poor and I'll have to move to Park Slope. Will you like me better then?"

"Oh, Frederick, I've always liked you." Camilla pushed her face through the opening to kiss him on the cheek. He didn't see it coming, moved his head, and her lips touched his. His hand rose and held her cheek, and the kiss became serious. Her hands were braced against the side of the car, her back bent at an awkward angle, but the kiss went on and on and she loved it.

At last she pulled back.

"You like me," Frederick said. "You really like me." His hand moved down her neck to her shoulder. "God, how can a woman so cold be so hot? You don't even have a coat on! Get in here before you get sick. I have something to show you." She opened the door and he moved over, crushing some of the roses beneath him.

"Be careful of the flowers," she cried.

"I'm only worried about the thorns," he said as he pulled one stem. He leaned across and closed both the door and the window. Then he put his arm around her. "For medicinal purposes only. You've got to be warmed up or you'll die of pneumonia." Bobby got into the front seat, increased the heat, and without a word, pulled out onto the street.

"Where are we going?" she asked. She felt better than she had in months. "Am I being kidnapped?"

"Don't kid me, honey," Frederick said. "You haven't been a kid in years. I don't care what *People* magazine wrote. 'The Little Author That Could,'" he mimicked.

Camilla shrugged. "I didn't write it," she said apologetically. "Anyroad, I must lock my door and get a coat."

"All taken care of," Bobby said, handing her her keys and thrusting her blue jacket over the divider.

"But what's the rush?" Camilla asked. "Where are we going? And what about these roses? They need to be put in water."

"You're a woman with a lot of worries," Frederick commented.

"I'm a woman with a lot of roses," Camilla retorted. "Where are we going?"

"Patience, patience," he counseled. "You are on a need-to-know basis."

"What?"

"Military term. For security reasons you only need to know what you need to know. No more."

"What is this, the army?"

Frederick ignored her. "There are a few things you *do* need to know," he said. "The first is that I'm going blind."

"I know *that,* Frederick," Camilla said, her voice serious.

Frederick continued to ignore her. "The second is that I love you."

"I didn't know that," she said, and she felt her heart quicken.

"That's because of the third thing. I'm very proud. And independent."

"Is that the fourth thing?" Camilla asked in a small voice. "That you're independent?" She was still thrilled over the second thing—Frederick loved her.

"No," Frederick told her, "that's part of the third thing. Those two things go together. The fourth thing is that I've never made love to a woman and had it feel the way it did with you."

"I think I'll close the privacy panel now, if it's all right with you," Bobby interjected from the front seat.

Frederick shrugged. "Have it your way. The man is a nut about his privacy." He turned to Camilla. "The fifth thing is that even though I'm visually challenged, as we now say, I think I'm worthy of you. It took me a long time to decide that, but you'll have to decide for yourself whether I'm right or not."

Camilla sat back. She thought of Craig and how . . . how she didn't love him. She looked at Frederick. They had crossed the Williamsburg Bridge and were driving up the FDR, heading to Midtown. The East River was silver outside the limo window. "I don't know what to say," she began.

"Wait," Frederick interrupted. "There's one more thing

you need to know. There's no question of financial dependency. There's absolutely no question."

Camilla felt the color drain out of her face. Was he talking about some kind of salary for her? Or even a contract, that she would not expect any of his money? A prenuptial? Or was he *offering* her money? Ready to be insulted, Camilla told herself to calm down and not be so quick to rush to judgment. "I don't know . . ."

The car turned off at an exit and pulled over to a corner. It was Sunday morning in New York, and all was deserted. "Get out," Frederick said. Bobby was already circling to open the door, and Camilla was completely confused. Was he throwing her out? Had she offended him already?

"What is going on?" she asked aloud.

"Be patient, Little Author That Could." Frederick stepped out of the car with her and made his way from the curb to the window of the shop. "Take a look," he told her. She did.

The window of Bookberries was completely filled with copies of *A Week in Firenze*. "Oh my God!" she said.

Bobby took a pile of cellophane-wrapped roses and put them in front of the bookstore. Camilla stared and stared. "Have you taken it in?" Frederick asked. "Bobby already took photos. Want to get back in the car? We have a few more deliveries to make." Frederick ushered a reluctant Camilla back into the limo. Their next stop was the Madison Avenue Bookstore. Again they got out of the car and again the window was filled with copies of *A Week in Firenze*. Camilla was speechless.

"We took the liberty of signing your name to the cards," Frederick told her. They left another bouquet and drove on to Books & Co., then Burlington Books, and finally made their way across Central Park to the West Side. There they stopped at The Bookstall, which had one window filled with *The Duplicity of Men* and the other stuffed with *A Week in Firenze*. At Shakespeare & Company there were only a few window copies. "That's probably because they're sold out," Frederick said cheerfully. "Yesterday it was full."

"Frederick, is this some kind of a joke? Did you arrange this?"

Frederick laughed. "Drive down Fifth Avenue," he told Bobby. And in Doubleday, Barnes & Noble, and all the other Fifth Avenue shops Camilla saw her book in huge displays. They left flowers everywhere, and then Frederick opened a bottle of champagne. They drove down to the Village to visit the bookstores there.

"Is it all because of the *People* article?" Camilla asked in a daze.

"You mean you haven't seen it?" Frederick asked.

"Seen *what*? There's something else?" Camilla asked.

Frederick shook his head. "You are on a need-to-know basis only, but this you do *need* to know. Didn't you get the paper this morning? Didn't Davis & Dash call you?"

"Know *what*?" Camilla asked again. "I will throttle you in another moment."

Frederick knocked on the privacy panel. "Bobby, could you please give me the copy of the book review?" He turned to her. "The *New York Times* put you on the cover," Frederick explained. "You didn't know that either? Because that's the last thing I had to tell you. Number six: You're rich. You're a bestselling author. *A Week in Firenze* is reviewed on the front page of the book review. And it is number three."

"*What*? How?"

"*People* magazine? Word of mouth? The booksellers getting the *Times* on Thursday? Listen, Camilla; here's the point. You're going to be very, very rich. You don't need me at all. Not that you ever did. But I hope that you *want* me. I want you. I know that, and I'm not afraid to tell you. I'm just afraid to hear your response."

"I think I'll close this privacy panel again now," Bobby told them.

"Camilla, are you in love with this guy you work with?

If you are, I want you to know that *I* blew it. If you did care about me, I know that I blew it. But it wasn't a lack of feeling for you. It was stupidity, pride, and fear. Are you in love?"

Camilla felt as if she couldn't breathe, but oddly, it was a wonderful feeling. "I *am* in love, Frederick." But she couldn't bear, even for a moment, to see the disappointment that crossed his face. "With *you*, Frederick. Since Italy. Since before I knew about your vision, and after. And not because I'm a martyr. Or because you're rich." She paused. "I think it's because you're very, very good in bed."

Frederick laughed and extended his hand toward hers. She took it and put it against her mouth. "You ain't seen nothing yet, honey," he told her.

# 94

> As repressed sadists are supposed to become policemen or butchers, so those with irrational fear of life become publishers.
>
> —*Cyril Connolly*

"It seems that there are significant discrepancies in the orders and the actual shipping," said the tall fool from Price Waterhouse. He was black, and he looked a lot like a Dobermann pinscher.

"I'm shocked to hear that," Gerald told him. "Is it more than the typical irregularities of inventory control?" He was perfectly calm. CPA's were like dogs—they could smell fear on you, but Gerald had none. Whatever Carl had done could be written off to human error or, at the very worst, some misguided loyalty nonsense on the part of one of Carl's subordinates. He looked at these two pencil counters, careful not to show his scorn. If the tall black one looked like a Dobermann, the short, thin, white one looked like a terrier. He would just pat them on their heads and send them on their way. With the Trawley/Mantiss scandal breaking, the poor showing of Susann Baker Edmonds, the incredible returns expected on *In Full Knowledge*, and the earlier flap over the Chad Weston book, the last thing he needed was deeper inquiries into their record keeping. He was already on thin ice. As long as Carl kept his cool there was absolutely no problem.

"Have you discussed your concerns with Carl Pollenski? I'm really not as computer-literate as I should be. He's in charge of all that."

"I'm afraid that Mr. Pollenski is part of the problem, Mr. Davis."

"Well," Gerald said smoothly, "I had hoped he was a competent man. He's only been here for a year or two, but he came with the best recommendations."

The little terrier spoke for the first time. "Mr. Davis, do you know that *A Week in Firenze* is about to make the *New York Times* bestseller list?"

"What?" Gerald felt himself grow pale and lightheaded as the blood drained from his face. Was the stupid little book selling that well? How many sales had he and Carl reassigned to *Twice in the Papers*? How in the world could it get on the list? Gerald attempted a smile. "What good news. We've been praying for another bestseller. I guess our prayers have been answered."

The Dobermann shook his head. "Something is wrong, Mr. Davis. By your records you've only sold and printed thirty thousand copies. But it must be at least three times that."

Gerald shrugged. "Nobody understands the weighting of the *Times* list," he said. "It's a science, an art form, or something. If it's a literary book, it has to sell far fewer copies to make the list than a commercial book does." He was talking too much. He stopped and shrugged. "Well, I'm sure you'll get to the bottom of it."

"I think we have," the terrier told him. "But we're reporting our findings to Mr. Morton. Carl Pollenski has made a statement."

# 95

> And we meet, with champagne and a chicken, at last.
>
> —*Lady Mary Wortley Montagu*

"Oh, Mother, I'd love to."

Susann looked across the table at Kim's face. Her daughter had changed. Susann wasn't sure if it was the modest success of Kim's book or the process of writing it. But somehow her daughter seemed calmer, more accepting, yet optimistic. "I'm returning the Davis & Dash advance, and I have the co-op up for sale. And I've already had a few nibbles. Should we plan for a May embarkation?"

"Now, there's a good word," Kim said with a smile. "And one you don't get to use much in conversation, unless of course you're discussing an around-the-world cruise with your author mother."

"I do think it will be the perfect way to write: spend the morning with our manuscripts and then in the afternoon we come to a port and sightsee."

"And shop," Kim said, laughing. "Oh, Mother, it really sounds wonderful. It's an absolutely great idea. Just the two of us."

Susann paused. "Well, not exactly. I did want to invite someone else."

Kim's face darkened and for a moment she looked like the old Kim—resentful, angry, and jealous. Not that Kim didn't have every right to feel those things, Susann reminded herself. I squandered too much of the time that belonged to my daughter on my writing and undeserving men.

"It's not Alf," Susann assured her daughter. "I want to take Edith."

"Edith! Oh, how wonderful."

"I thought so, too," Susann said.

# 96

Nothing beats a good book.
—*Nunzio Nappi*

Opal was dreaming of fish. One of them was also Terry. Opal watched the fan of a speckled fish tail. She herself was a fish, but once she realized that she became confused. Was she, or was she drowning? Then the telephone rang and Opal was pulled from the dream.

She must have dozed off. She reached for the phone beside her elbow. The chair was not a good one for sleeping, and her neck hurt. She put the phone to her ear and winced as it compressed her stiff neck.

"Hello."

"Mrs. O'Neal?" It was Emma Ashton.

"Yes, Emma," Opal confirmed."What is it?"

"Mrs. O'Neal, your daughter has just been awarded the Tagiter."

# 97

> Editing can, and should be, not only a life-enhancing profession but also a liberal education in itself . . .
>
> —*M. Lincoln Schuster*

Emma was sorting through her piles of reading. She had them laid out on the floor of her apartment, and the place was an absolute mess. Emma got through the long weekends by doing her reading—she was actually almost all caught up. She smiled to herself grimly. What time is it when an editor is all caught up with her reading? Time for an editor to get a life.

There were a few memos and trade magazines left to go through. Emma didn't mind—it was actually a pleasure to read *Publishers Weekly* with enough leisure to enjoy it. This was actually the current issue—sometimes she didn't get to look at them until they were two or three weeks old. Emma went to her couch and settled down among the sofa pillows. She read Judy Quinn's "Hot Deals" column and Paul Nathan's "Rights" column. Alex was mentioned there—she had sold foreign rights for *The Duplicity of Men* to thirteen countries already. Emma had to smile. Alex was a hustler, no doubt about it.

Then she turned to her favorite column—"Behind the Bestsellers" by Daisy Maryles.

*The talk at Davis & Dash has moved from a whisper to a rumble—and much of the noise is about who is behind which bestseller. Apparently, the latest Peet Trawley hit was not written by the late author before his death. Neither, we learn, was it written by his editor, Pam Mantiss. Facts seemed to indicate that Mantiss—who accepted a hefty payment from the estate to write the book—actually jobbed it out to Stewart Campbell, one of her midlist authors, who now threatens to sue. As if that wasn't enough of an ethics problem, in the deceased-author category there is also talk about* The Duplicity of Men, *a novel that has been bumping the bottom of the* PW *list, hovering just below number 15, since its high acclaim. Apparently, Mantiss, sometimes known as Preying Mantiss for her tough deals, didn't attempt to write this one—she merely takes the credit for finding it. Meanwhile, the deceased author's mother tells us a very different story: that Mantiss was actually "rude and very negative about the book. She wanted it drastically cut." (This, remember, from the editor who deemed Chad Weston's book worth publishing.) Last but not least, there's an unsubstantiated rumor that the big bomb of the Davis & Dash list—the highly touted but largely unsold* In Full Knowledge*—also has authorship in question. Jude Daniel, recently separated from his wife, is accused by her of purloining much of her work on that book, yet another Pam Mantiss volume. As a final note, we point out for those of you with short memories that Ms. Mantiss was recently dubbed Editor of the Year.*

*The editorial torch does burn at Davis & Dash, although somewhat lower. Apparently, it was editor Emma Ashton who discovered* The Duplicity of Men. *"She took it from me when no one else would read it," Mrs O'Neal reported. "She recognized its worth and then fought to get it published." This unsung heroine was also responsible for finding another of this year's sleeper hits—*A Week in Firenze, *moving up our list to number three. The author, Camilla Clapfish, says, "Emma Ashton read my book in manuscript, and it was she who got it into print."*

Holy shit! Emma bolted upright. This was unbelievable. Actually it was believable and the truth, so far as Emma knew, but how did Daisy Maryles know it? And what would Pam Mantiss say when *she* read it? Emma read the column all over again. It was a thrill to read her name, and to imagine everyone else reading it. Even Pam Mantiss. But tomorrow, Monday, was not going to be pleasant.

"You little bitch, traitor! You fucking bitch!"

Emma winced but didn't recoil. "Stop it," she said. "I told you I didn't speak with *PW*."

"Right! And I'm the Virgin Mary! Nobody else knew all of this, nobody else! What did you think? This would get you *my* job? Is that it?"

"Pam, I had nothing to do—"

"Shut the fuck up! First of all, that's not true; secondly, you went over my head to Gerald; and C, you're fired! You were never very good, and now it's clear that you were never even loyal." Pam took a swig out of her ever-present Snapple and almost choked on it. Emma couldn't help wishing she would. "What the fuck do I need you for?" Pam continued. "Just one thing—don't expect a fucking reference, okay? Don't expect a reference, because you're not going to fucking get one! *Or* a going-away party. Or a chance to get sympathy from your fucking coven, you little witch. And forget about one of those sweet little corporate memos that explains how you are leaving us 'to pursue other interests.' You're leaving us to get on the unemployment line, and that's where you're staying as far as I'm concerned."

Emma stood up. "Pam, I didn't report any of the column to *PW*. It doesn't matter if you believe me or not. I'm leaving. But the really interesting part is that it's all true, the *PW* stuff. I wasn't a hundred percent sure, but your anger validates it." Emma took a deep breath. "In five years you've never thanked me or praised me. You're smart, Pam. You're very, very smart, and talented, but nobody is so smart that they don't need a friend. I don't think you have a single one." Emma started walking to the door, her hands shaking, but she carried herself with dignity.

"You cunt!" Pam screamed. Emma just managed to see the Snapple bottle fly past her right ear and shatter in an explosion of iced tea and broken glass on the doorjamb. She was sprayed with the brown liquid and a few bits of the glass, but she didn't stop. She wiped her face off with her hand and didn't even bother turning down the hallway toward her tiny, precious windowed office. Emma just walked past Heather and the crowd that had assembled, past GOD's Little Acre and the receptionist, into the elevator, and out of the building forever.

# 98

> I write for the same reason I breathe—because if I didn't, I would die.
>
> —*Isaac Asimov*

Judith sat in the dusty little turret room, the card table in front of her, Flaubert sleeping at her feet. She squinted at the laptop screen. She was on page seventy-two of her other book, and either she was insane or it was truly good.

Each morning she seemed to go into a kind of writing trance. Time passed, but she wasn't conscious of it. She only knew the flow of words that sometimes gushed, sometimes trickled, from her pen. It was a lyrical wave, like a tide that washed up, crested, and then ebbed, leaving her empty as a wave-washed beach.

She patted her stomach. Of course, the possibility that she was insane was very real. Here she was, pregnant, broke, and about to be divorced, back in the dump she had lived in with her soon-to-be-former husband. And the odd thing was, she was happier than she'd been in a very long time.

Well, not happy actually. Just more at peace. She had begun her new book because it was simply that or go crazy; that was the same reason she'd moved out of the other apartment. What she felt was probably a lot like the old joke about banging your head against the wall. It really did feel good when you stopped.

Judith didn't know how she would feel if *In Full Knowledge* had been a huge success. All the criticism of the book had been aimed at the parts she felt were weakened or compromised by Daniel's rewrites. But the fact that it had failed made it somehow easier for her to move on. Daniel would eventually have to give her some of the money—Diana La Gravenesse had assured her of that. That was assuming that there was any money left. Apparently, Daniel had quit the department, and she had heard from Emma Ashton that he had not been given a contract for a second book.

Flaubert woke up and stretched. He seemed happy to be back at their old haunt, and oddly enough, so was she. Without Daniel the place seemed larger. And she *had* to live here—it was the only place she could write. The landlord had actually welcomed her back, and Judith had enough money in their joint checking account to pay rent in advance. She'd also registered for the next semester at school and qualified for a student loan. She wasn't sure if she would take a full course load, but she had enough money to go on until the end of the year and the birth of her baby.

She didn't know if it was a daughter or a son. And she didn't care which it was, but her new book was titled *To My Daughter*. It was the book Judith had always wanted to write.

Judith looked down at the screen of her laptop. She nodded. She was probably insane, she decided, but she thought her new book was truly good.

# 99

> By and large, the critics and readers gave me an affirmed sense of my identity as a writer. You might know this within yourself, but to have it affirmed by others is of utmost importance. Writing is, after all, a form of communication.
>
> —*Ralph Ellison*

Perhaps it was a failure of imagination, but Camilla had simply never imagined success on this level. Had someone once said it about Elvis Presley? That he had redefined how big "big" could be?

She was temporarily living at the Gramercy Hotel after journalists had begun to ambush her in Park Slope. The guests at the hotel must think she was a nutter, the way she flinched in the lift. But it was all a bit too much. She needed the security of the front desk, as well as the operators at the switchboard to take her messages. These seemed to flow in a never-ending stream of pink message slips. People she hadn't heard from in years, those she had known briefly, and some she'd never known, had never even heard of, were all calling for her time, asking for interviews, for her to speak at luncheons, at fund-raisers, to give signed copies of her books to charity auctions. *Publishers Weekly* had profiled her, *Entertainment Weekly* had run a full-page picture along with an article, and *In Style* was hoping to follow up the *People* coverage with a look at her home. Too bad she didn't have one.

What she did have, though, was an incredible amount of money about to be paid for the paperback rights to *A Week in Firenze*. Alex had made a brilliant deal: D & D got only 30 percent of the paperback money. In addition, there were a dozen publishing houses begging her, absolutely on their knees, hoping for a deal on her next book. Alex had taken care of everything beautifully—she'd even arranged a short-term loan until the money started to flow in, though Davis & Dash was quite willing to advance her money against royalties. It was funny, Camilla thought, that people were so reluctant to lend one money when it was needed and so eager to when it was not.

She was over the moon, not just about the money or the reviews or the attention—which was actually rather difficult and embarrassing—but because she knew now that she had succeeded. Despite all odds, she would be allowed to live a writing life, and as Alex told her, her next book could be anything she wanted it to be. Happily, it was coming along nicely, though all of this commotion had certainly slowed her down.

The phone rang and Camilla winced. It was only Alex. Alex was her lifeline, her banker, her investment counselor, and her organizer. "We're riding the serpent, Cam."

Camilla never had a nickname and wasn't quite sure if she liked having one now, but Alex was so protective and good-hearted, had done such a brilliant job, that certainly Camilla wasn't going to object. "I just heard the news from the horse's mouth: You've moved up to number one on the *Times* list. That means, by the way, another five thousand dollars this week." Alex had structured Camilla's contract with a lot of bonuses. Davis & Dash had not objected at the time, feeling that it was unlikely she would ever get them. But she was getting them all. She received twenty-five hundred per week for every week her book was on the lower part of the *Times* list and five thousand a week for every week it was number five or above.

"You're going to be a main selection."

"A main selection of what?"

"That I can't tell you yet. Both the Literary Guild and Book-of-the-Month are bidding for you. By the way, you get to keep half of the money. It ought to be another seventy-five thousand, at least. But that's not why I'm calling."

Camilla giggled. Alex took such a delight in business that it was infectious. "So why did you call?" Camilla asked, just as she knew she was supposed to.

*"I called because Paramount, Warner, and Fox all want to turn your book into a movie!"*

"You can't be serious? A movie about a busload of old ladies?"

"Cam, they're saying that you're going to do for old women what *Bridges of Madison County* did for middle-aged ones. Olympia Dukakis, Shirley MacLaine, Anne Bancroft, and Joanne Woodward are panting for parts." To the tune of "God Save the Queen," Alex sang, "One million bucks for sure. One million bucks or more, less ten percent."

Camilla laughed. "They *really* want to make my book into a film? I can't visualize it."

"Cam, you don't know what the thing will look like when they're done with it. It's like putting your baby up for adoption: You can't insist on the wardrobe and the schools—it's not your baby anymore. If I make this deal, I suggest you hand the baby over and focus on your next one. Hollywood does what it has to do. For all we know, instead of a busload of old ladies, they'll become a space capsule filled with orangutans."

Camilla giggled again. "I should like to see that, actually."

"So, we're agreed? You sell the book to Hollywood."

"Absolutely," Camilla said, hardly daring to believe it. Orangutans aside, it was almost a biblical thrill to imagine her characters being made flesh by actresses who would enact her story for people all around the world. Tears came to her eyes.

"And Camilla?"

"Yes?" Camilla asked.

"Next week I think you'll make number one again."

# 100

Everybody doesn't have to be in the movies!
—*Samuel Goldwyn*

He'd been kept waiting in the fussy reception room for more than half an hour, and he was about to consider it an insult when Byron's secretary appeared and hustled him into the inner sanctum. Alf looked, somehow, much smaller than the man Daniel had met in this office just over a year ago. "Well, Professor?" Alf said in a voice that sounded tired.

Daniel needed some preliminaries. After all, it wasn't easy to ask for a loan. "Well, Alf, I just wanted to know what you've heard from Hollywood. Have they got a script yet?"

Alf looked at him. His eyes looked bloodshot, and the lids hung slackly, showing a watery, light pink flesh. "There's no script, Professor."

"He couldn't do it, could he?" Daniel felt his hope leaping. Despite the withering meeting with April Irons, Daniel felt there might be an opportunity here. He *knew* he could write a good screenplay. "Do you think there's another chance?"

"No."

The minimum price for a screenplay was $250,000. "But I know I can write a good script."

"Write a script? I was talking about another chance at a book! Forget the movie, Professor. There isn't going to be a movie. Nobody makes a movie of a book that bombs."

Daniel paled. "But my option money."

"The option runs out in another few months, and I'm sure they won't pick it up."

"But they were so interested," Daniel sputtered.

"Hollywood interest is like interest on a loan from your father—it's completely waivable."

Daniel sat there trying to recover. It didn't seem like a good time to ask for a loan, but since Byron had brought it up . . . "Do you think I might get a loan—you know, just an advance against royalties to help me out? Until I finish the next book."

"What royalties?" Byron asked. "There won't be any royalties. I don't think the book will ever earn out. And as far as the next book goes, I don't think we could sell it unless you changed your name. But that's a possibility." He leaned back in his chair. He sighed deeply. "What's the next book?" he asked.

Daniel didn't have a clue.

# 101

> In this world, politics is like navigation in a sea without charts and wise men live the lives of pilgrims.
>
> —*Joyce Cary*

"You're fired."

"No, I'm not," Pam said to Gerald.

"Excuse me? I don't think you heard me, and I'm certainly sure that I didn't hear you correctly." Gerald looked at Pam and for the first time allowed himself the luxury of showing his true feelings. "You're fired," he said. "I'm not firing you because you're a slut, or because you slept with David Morton, or because you took credit where none was due. I'm not firing you because you gave away seventy percent of the paperback rights on the biggest hit of the season or because you bet on a losing horse. All of that is par for the course, Pam. I'm firing you because you tried to fuck me over, and that, Miss Mantiss, is simply not allowed at Davis & Dash."

"I'm not leaving." Pam smiled.

"Don't be insubordinate. You've had a long run. You've gotten away with murder. Now take it like a man."

Pam's smile became even more insolent. "I think that you're the one who's being fired," Pam said. "I'll only accept a dismissal from David Morton."

"You got it," Gerald told her, and threw the letter signed by the chairman onto her desk.

Pam looked at it in disbelief. "Surprised?" Gerald asked. "He didn't like the Trawley stuff. Edina nearly drove him mad. And he certainly didn't like the *PW* article." Gerald smiled grimly. "I also made sure he knew you'd slept with me as well as Jude Daniel. I think it hurt his pride." Gerald laughed. "He thought you were his one true love. It's sad to have to spoil a man's illusions."

"You prick!" Pam yelled. "I'm not leaving."

Gerald walked to the door. "You shouldn't have fired Emma Ashton," Gerald confided. "Morton doubted my word until you did that. Too bad, Pam. Clear out by noon. Security will be up to be sure that you do."

Gerald strode down the hall. He had a lot of problems, but he would solve each one. He always did. He'd neutralized Pam: The *PW* article had given him the ammunition he needed to do that. He had gathered all the information on Carl—the limo use, the high expense-account spending. He'd be ready to present it when the time came. David Morton was beginning to doubt his own judgment, and Gerald knew he'd be able to keep his job as long as Morton realized there was nobody else who could fill it. Pam would never get it now, and Gerald had not groomed any other successor.

He walked almost jauntily past Mrs. Perkins's desk. "I'll have a cup of Jamaican Blue Mountain," he told her. But she looked up and shook her head.

"Mr. Morton is in there waiting for you."

"In my office?"

Mrs. Perkins nodded. "Mr. Morton and—"

But Gerald turned and almost ran to his sanctum. He opened the door and was shocked to see David Morton sitting in his chair at his desk, with another man beside him. A third man, his back turned toward Gerald, was in one of the low chairs in front of his desk. How dare they! Gerald was in a rage but tried to keep calm. In the corporate wars he had learned that anger was best kept under control. Cunning, patience, and ruthlessness were required, not explosions of childish temper.

"Gerald, this isn't going to be pleasant, so I'd like to make it brief," David Morton said. "I have your resignation here. I'd like you to sign it."

"Are you insane?" Gerald asked.

"Sign it, son," his father's voice said. Gerald walked to his desk and faced Senior, sitting in the low armchair.

"I'm not signing anything," Gerald said. What the hell was his father doing here? What did Senior have to do with any of this?

"We'll press charges if you don't," David Morton said. "We'll call the SEC. We don't know how long you've been pulling the switcheroo on your book sales, or how much you knew about the Trawley business, or a lot of other things, but we certainly have enough to get you jailed."

"Jailed?"

"This is a publicly held company, Gerald," Morton said.

"Sign the paper, son."

It was unbelievable. Gerald tried to take it all in. "But you can't want me to resign," Gerald said nervously to his father. "You may not have agreed with all of my decisions, but this is Davis & Dash. I'm the one with all the contacts in the business. I'm the one who brings in the big authors."

"Like Susann Baker Edmonds?" Morton asked with a sneer.

Gerald saw his father sigh and shift in the chair as if he were in physical pain. "I didn't want to have to say this in front of a stranger, Gerald, but I'm deeply disappointed in you. I don't understand why you've done what you've done, and I don't excuse it. I hold you responsible for your uncle's death and the shameful publicity blitz that surrounded it, and now I'm shocked to find that you've been dishonest as well. This gentleman from Price Waterhouse has explained the whole ugly scenario."

"Carl Pollenski is singing like a diva," David Morton drawled. Gerald's desperation became panic.

"Give me a little time," he said. "There's no one else to run the company. Let me do it until you find someone else. I'll help with the transition."

"I'll do that, son," Senior said. "It's the least we can do for the shareholders."

"But what am *I* supposed to do?" Gerald asked.

"Sign the paper and then walk away," David Morton told him.

# 102

> It is important for an editor in chief to remain calm in what can be difficult circumstances . . .
>
> —*Betty A. Prashker*

The Editor of the Year sat in the tiny space between the bottom of her office bookshelves and the small refrigerator. Despite her ballooning weight, Pam had managed to insert herself into this corner because it seemed to her that only here could she feel even a modicum of safety. The floor was littered with empty Snapple bottles. They had sustained her through the siege outside her office. She didn't want to think about what would happen when she ran out of Snapple, but that wouldn't happen for a long time—there was at least a case of doctored iced tea in the fridge.

Because Pam was not leaving her office, not even to pee. She knew that if she did, her nightmare would come true—she'd be locked out of the corner office it had taken her twenty years to achieve, and she'd have no place, no place at all, to go.

Littering her office floor were red-circled printouts, copies of torn-up trade magazines, and shredded newspapers. Pam didn't like the news in any of them. The Chad Weston book was number two on the *New York Times* list, the only bestseller—aside from Trawley—she'd selected that season. And it was earning money hand over fist for the fucks at Peterson.

Worse was the absolute collapse of Susann Baker Edmonds's book. Pam had warned Gerald that the woman was on the decline, but Pam was the one who was living day-to-day with the results of *that* corporate acquisition. Despite an initial sales surge from the advertising and tour, the book had risen only to the high teens and then, in a week or two, disappeared off sales radar completely. Gone with the wind.

*Gone with the Wind*. Now *there* was a book, thought Pam as she picked up another Snapple bottle. She once read that there were more than fifty fully developed characters in Margaret Mitchell's pulp masterpiece. As a girl, she had read—no, devoured—it and had identified with Scarlett so completely that she'd asked to use it as her confirmation name, much to the priest's dismay. She only remembered now that Scarlett had wound up loveless and defeated. When she was a girl, Pam had *always* believed that Scarlett would regroup, would find Rhett and convince him that tomorrow was another day.

It was only now, crouched in the corner beside the refrigerator, that it occurred to Pam that Scarlett had made too many fatal mistakes—she would not rise from the ashes but decline into lonely middle age. Tears for Scarlett, and herself, flooded Pam's eyes.

The phone rang, but Pam didn't move. It could only be more bad news. She had already been summoned to a meeting in Gerald's office, a meeting she did not choose to attend. She wasn't going to let that bastard fire her again. Not after all these years. Her secretary had been banging on the door at regular intervals, but Pam wasn't moving. The phone stopped, and she smiled, taking another swig from her bottle. Enjoy those calls now, she told herself bitterly. Your phone isn't going to ring for a long time, girlfriend.

Pam's legs were cramping, and she shifted her weight. She could understand the Susann débâcle, and the Chad Weston backlash. She had even expected the failure of Gerald's book. What she couldn't understand was *In Full Knowledge*. All the signs of success had been there—the early buzz, the movie sale, the current-events tie-in. The book was even well written, not that that accounted for much in today's market. *In Full Knowledge* hadn't just failed, it had bombed, and she was left holding the bag. She appeared to have wasted hundreds of thousands in promotion—promotion of a book she'd bought cheaply and whose author she was known to be sleeping with. Though her excuse was she had saved all of the money up front, because of the deal she had worked out with Alf Byron, it looked to David Morton and his minions like she had simply pushed her lover's book. Unprofessional *and* immoral. How could she tell David that the book would have cost them a million dollars if it had gone up for auction? That she had worked a covert deal with Alf? Preying Mantiss had struck again. But this time she'd fucked herself. Even if she got David to believe her, which she doubted, she'd look like a whore. And Alf Byron would never back her up. So she was left with no defense for the expensive Edmonds book campaign, either.

Now, as she rocked back and forth on the floor, she had two very serious problems—well, three. First was that Gerald knew she had betrayed him to David and she'd lost Gerald as a protector. The second was that David Morton was no doubt personally hurt, and she didn't look as pristine as she had. Third, she simply had to pee, and she couldn't leave her office to do it.

There was more pounding on her door. Not all the office doors at Davis & Dash locked, but when Gerald had given her a budget to redecorate, that was one of the first things she'd installed. "Pam, you have to unlock this." It was Dickie Pointer's voice.

"Fuck you, Dickie!" she yelled. He'd be happy to see her go down in flames. She took another swig from her Snapple bottle. Going down in flames reminded her of a filthy Sophie Tucker joke about Cointreau and cunnilingus. Pam laughed out loud. She actually felt very comfortable, except for the terrible pressure her bladder was exerting.

Everything would have held together if it wasn't for that little fuck, Stewart. If he hadn't called Edina Trawley herself, Pam could have managed everything. But, like living dominoes, Stewart had called Edina, Edina had called David Morton, David Morton had called Gerald (and probably the newspapers as well). Pam remembered the *Times* publishing column by Doreen Carvajal.

Davis & Dash Editor in Flap

*Insiders at Davis & Dash say that Pam Mantiss, editor in chief well known for her commercial-fiction instinct, has lost a writer. While house jumping isn't new, house jumping by dead authors is a twist. But the estate of Peet Trawley, the late bestselling author of . . .*

Pam hated their hypocritical, holier-than-thou attitude. Like everybody didn't ghostwrite *everybody's* books. So she was an editor and a ghostwriter who employed a ghostwriter. Big fucking deal! Margaret Truman didn't even *read* the books she turned out, and Ivana Trump probably couldn't read her own.

Pam realized she was very, very drunk, but she didn't care. The phone began ringing again, but Editor of the Year wasn't going to answer. She wasn't going to answer the door either, no matter how hard they banged on it. What she *was* going to do was take a piss—she had to piss like a racehorse. Pam reached over for one of her empty Snapple bottles, and without leaving her tight corner, she pulled up her skirt, pulled off her panties, and crouched over the bottle.

The release felt wonderful, and for a moment Pam felt nothing but good as she voided her bladder. But after only a few seconds she realized that the bottle was almost filled and she couldn't stop. It overflowed, and hot urine ran down the side of it and over her hands onto the carpet. Shit! Or, she wondered drunkenly, should she more accurately say piss? She laughed, spilling some more urine. Goddamn it! Now she'd have to sit in the wet spot. Well, she'd been doing that with men all her life!

Crouching on her toes, her skirt around her waist, the Snapple bottle under her, Pam reached for the *New York Times* column. She'd wipe herself with it. That was what you did with that kind of journalism. Yellow journalism, she thought, and laughed again as the urine turned the page sallow. What's black and white and yellow all over? She was very drunk, she realized again. It was only when the door flew open, and Dickie, followed by two security guards, Pam's secretary, and a host of others, pushed into the room that Pam, in her half-naked crouch, realized she was not nearly drunk enough.

# 103

Failure feels bad.
—*Nan Robinson*

Alf simply couldn't believe it: *In Full Knowledge* had not just disappointed, it had bombed. He stared at the current issue of *Publishers Weekly*. In the featured article, "Unhappy Returns of the Season," *In Full Knowledge* was listed at the top. He knew he'd be seeing it on remainder tables for years to come. He wasn't sure what exactly had gone wrong, but it had gone wrong drastically.

> Among this year's major disappointments was the much touted but little-bought *In Full Knowledge*. This first novel was optioned by International Studios while still in manuscript, and the ABA buzz was that it would be *the* Big Fall Book. Believing it a new *Horse Whisperer*, Davis & Dash ordered a mammoth first printing of 250,000 copies. But it fizzled . . .

Shit! Alf threw down the magazine and got up from his desk. Pam Mantiss wouldn't return his calls, much less discuss a second book contract for the professor, and he knew that there would be no interest from any other publisher after the widely publicized failure. What did Michael Cimino do after *Heaven's Gate*? No. More importantly, what did his agent do?

Thinking of Hollywood, Alf shuddered at the memory of the enraged call he'd gotten from April Irons, who'd told him he was "a stupid old *putz*," among other unkind things. There would be no movie, that was for sure. Now

Alf wished he hadn't negotiated quite so hard with her, but it was too late. Another burned bridge.

It was too late for almost everything. He looked ridiculous to the industry and even to himself. Worst of all, Irons's comment stuck in his mind. He *was* a stupid old *putz*. He'd been fooling himself. He had only one client—he'd always had only one client who was worth anything—and that was Susann. Her latest book hadn't done well, but it hadn't been the utter débâcle Jude Daniel's had been. Susann still had her contract, and Alf felt sure he could help her to come back. Maybe she wouldn't be as big as she had been, but if once again he focused his attention only on her, he could make sure they both had plenty of money for years to come.

He'd been a fool. It had been just a silly mistake after all these years. Susann would understand. In fact, there was probably no need for apology.

Alf buzzed his secretary. "Call the florist," he told her. "I want a box of roses to bring with me tonight."

"How many?" his secretary asked. "What color?"

"Red, and make it two dozen." Alf stopped and considered. Roses were expensive. "No," he said, "make it a dozen and a half."

"Alf is downstairs," Edith said and raised her eyebrows. "I didn't know he was coming over."

Susann looked up from her sorting. They were going through the bookshelves, getting ready to pack. The apartment had sold quickly—it did have a stupendous view—and they needed to be out by the end of the month. Susann knew she was disheveled, and she hadn't checked her makeup since this morning. "I need lipstick," she said and stood up.

Edith smiled from across the room. "I'll entertain him until you're ready," she said in a girlish voice, then laughed. She sat down in the large winged chair and picked up her knitting. "Can I watch?" she said. "I'll feel like Madame Defarge."

Susann walked through her bedroom to the bath. She switched on the light and looked at herself in a mirror. She was pale, and the puffiness under her eyes was more visible than ever. But it wasn't a bad face, not a bad face at all.

She looked into her own eyes, ignoring the lines and the hooded lids. "You're fifty-eight years old," she said aloud. "You've got a twenty-nine-year-old daughter. You've been married three times, and you've been Alf's mistress for almost fifteen years. Can you face this? There won't be any more men. Anyway, it's not likely." She watched as the eyes in the mirror filled with tears. Something hurt her, in her chest and throat. She stood there, watching her reflection and feeling the pain.

"Silly bitch," she said. "It's not like they were anything but trouble." Quickly—well, as quickly as she could with her hands—she put on some lipstick and dusted her cheeks with blush.

When she joined Edith in the living room, Alf was ensconced in his chair, and a bunch of red roses was placed in one of her Lalique vases. "Flowers," Susann said. "How nice."

"A dozen and a *half,*" Edith said with wicked emphasis.

Susann almost smiled. Alf would never change. It had been so long, and he still didn't remember that she hated red roses. Well, perhaps she had never told him. She took a seat on the sofa, almost across from him. "This is a surprise. To what do I owe the honor?"

Alf glanced over at Edith, then shot a meaningful glance at Susann. She ignored it. Whatever he was going to say he was going to say in front of both of them. "Susann, I . . ." he paused. "What are you doing with the books?" he asked.

"Packing them up," Susann said calmly.

"How come?"

"Because we don't think the new owners of the apartment want a library exclusively made up of various editions of *my* novels."

"The new owners?" Alf paused. "Are you putting the apartment up for sale?"

"No," Susann said, "I've already sold it."

Alf jumped up from his chair. "Sold it?" he said. "Are you going to live in France?"

Susann shook her head. "Selling that too," she said. "Though it may take a little longer."

"I don't understand," Alf said.

"I'm sure you don't," Susann agreed calmly.

He ran his fingers through his white mane—he still had lovely hair. But Susann watched as his face got red. She almost told him to be careful, to remember his blood pressure, and to take another pill, but that wasn't her job anymore. Alf looked at Edith, who was calmly watching while she clicked away at her needles. "Susann, can we talk alone?" he asked.

"Oh, I don't think so," Susann said sweetly. "I've been doing so much alone already. I only had Edith to help me." Susann smiled at Edith, who didn't even look up. "I had to deal with my editor all alone, I even had to do my book signings all alone, I had to break down in the desert all alone." She looked at Alf. "Not actually alone, though," she said. "I was with Edith, and I'm with Edith now. So I wasn't alone, Alf. I was without you, though. And at first I didn't like it. Then I got used to it. And now, Alf, I really enjoy it. I really enjoy being without you."

Alf stood up and ran his fingers through his hair once again, looking down past his belly to his Belgian loafers, then at her. Too bad he'd never practiced a best smile, Susann thought. He could have used it now instead of the ghastly grin he'd plastered on his face.

"Susann, I know you might be a little angry with me," he said. There was a noise that sounded like a snort from Edith's direction. Alf paused, looked at her blackly, and then went on. "I know how you feel."

"I doubt it, Alf," Susann told him. "I don't think you've thought about how I feel in a very long time." She looked over at the flowers. "If you did, you'd know I hate red roses. If you did, you would have insisted that I be invited to your son's wedding. If you did, you never would have made me leave Imogen and put me in the hands of that maniac, that insect, Pam Mantiss." She paused, letting it sink in. "If you knew how I felt, Alf, you wouldn't have sent me around the country, dragging myself from place to place, without coming with me. And if you knew how I felt, Alf, you *certainly* wouldn't have broken your promise to show up in San Francisco and finish the tour with me. Alf, we're finished. It's all over."

Alf sat down heavily, not in his chair, but on the sofa. He let his hands fall between his knees. "I've been very blind," he said. And for a moment, just out of habit, Susann felt sorry for him. He wasn't a young man. He wasn't even middle-aged. Alf Byron had gotten truly old, and in a way, she felt compassion for him. Then he lifted his still magnificent head and looked at her. "This doesn't mean I won't be your agent anymore, does it?"

Susann felt her face flush, almost as if she'd been slapped. This was it then. The bottom line to Alf had always been the bottom line. "I'm afraid it does, Alf."

He stood up. "Wait a minute," he said. "I'd like to think we can work out the personal side, over time, but in terms of business you have a contractual obligation . . ."

Susann tried to hide her hurt. She would keep this on a professional level, because it was clear to her that she meant more to Alf as a paycheck than as a person. "No, thank you," she said crisply.

Alf's face once again got very red—whether from embarrassment or anger Susann could not tell. But his next words made it clear. "I'll have to take legal action, Susann. We have a contract. Davis & Dash is instructed to send your checks to me. After I deduct my percentage, I'll send them on to you, but I am the agent of record."

Susann shook her head. "I'm afraid the the Davis & Dash deal is going to be terminated. My new attorney is taking care of it."

"What?" he asked.

"Terminated, Alf. I'm returning the advance. It's one of the reasons I'm selling this apartment."

"But . . . but—"

"Yes, Alf, one of us is a butt," Edith said, looking up brightly. "You got that part right."

# 104

The shelf life of the average trade book is
somewhere between milk and yogurt.
—*Calvin Trillin*

Daniel buzzed but got no response. Daniel knocked, and when there was no response he banged on the door with his foot.

He felt desperate, and he had to get in. He couldn't stand the idea of another night in a hotel. He hadn't slept well in weeks. His money was going too fast, and now that his marriage was over he couldn't go back to the apartment in Fox Run. Anyway, he wanted Pam—he wanted her energy and her body to console him. He wanted comfort, and he wanted her to explain what had gone wrong with the book. He also wanted her to fix it, to fix everything. And then he wanted some athletic sex and a good night's sleep. What Daniel Gross wanted as he pounded on Pam's door was for his new life to begin. At last he heard feet padding down the hallway to the door. "Go away."

"It's Daniel!" he shouted before she walked away.

"Daniel who?"

Daniel shook his head. He was very tired, tired and confused. "Jude! Jude Daniel," he remembered to say.

There was the sound of locks sliding open, and in a moment the door opened. Pam's blond curls looked matted and wilder than ever, dark at the roots. She was wearing nothing but a man's stained shirt that barely covered her pendulous breasts.

"What the fuck are *you* doing here?" she asked.

"I've come to be with you," Daniel said plaintively. She looked at him and his two suitcases.

"Be with me or live with me?" Pam barked. "Anyway, are you out of your mind?"

She began to close the door. Daniel couldn't believe it. Was she drunk? High? "Pam, it's me. Don't you want to live with me?" She paused and looked him up and down.

"I don't even want to *know* you," she said. "You're a bad fuck and a big failure—in my experience always a lethal combination. But believe it or not, you are the smallest of my problems right now, you stupid prick." As she started to close the door, Daniel stopped her.

"What's wrong?" he asked.

"What's wrong? What's wrong? That would take too fucking long. Why don't we talk about what's right? Nothing. Absofuckin'lutely nothing. Meanwhile, I've lost my job, my reputation in the industry, and—" she paused, taking in his rumpled clothes, his red eyes, his air of desperation—"you're an asshole."

Daniel felt his entrails turn to water. What was going on? "I thought you loved me," he blurted.

"Yeah, and I thought you wrote that fucking failure of a book. We were both misinformed. So fuck you, Mr. Greenjeans." She slammed the door, and Daniel, paralyzed, heard the locks slide into place. He stood frozen for a moment. He picked up his bags and started to walk away, realizing he had nowhere to go. He couldn't go back to the college after his resignation. He wasn't going back to Judith. He had no friends in New York except Alf Byron, and after their last encounter, he doubted that Alf would even take his calls. He put his bags down. He needed Pam, and she needed him. How had she been fired? And what had people told her about his book? He'd get this business straightened out. He'd explain about Judith, about how the book was really his idea and Judith had merely done the mechanics. He should have told Pam earlier. He'd apologize. He'd apologize and they'd make love and then he'd move in with her and he'd write. He'd write a *real* bestseller.

Daniel took off his overcoat and laid it on the floor. He'd sleep here tonight. Tomorrow he'd talk to Pam, and then everything would be all right.

# 105

Nothing succeeds like success.
*Alexandre Dumas,* père

When Camilla walked into Citron Press, the little hallway that served as a reception area was decorated with balloons and a big banner saying CONGRATULATIONS CAMILLA. "She's here!" Emily yelled down the hall. Susan, Jimmy O'Brien, and the two college interns began pelting Camilla with confetti. She got her hands up to her face but not before she got a mouthful. It didn't get really crazy until Craig came out of his office, popped a champagne cork, and began spraying them all. Behind him, Alex Simmons squealed and jumped away.

"Not on my Armani!" she yelled as she landed a handful of confetti on Camilla's damp hair.

"Who's number one? Who's number one?" Jimmy began to chant.

"Who's number one?" the others joined in and then formed an impromptu conga line that moved down the hall to Craig's office.

Camilla was touched to see a cake decorated with her name and a book on top, along with a big candle shaped as a 1. Craig began to pour champagne into flutes. Everyone was chattering, but Craig's voice rose above the rest. "I don't know what the hell I'm celebrating for! Citron Press didn't publish you," he mumbled as he handed her a glass.

Alex smiled. "No, but for the right price, perhaps you'll publish her *next* one," she said coolly.

Everyone laughed, and Craig rose to the bait. "Hey, I'll even increase her pay." He smiled across the cake at

Camilla. "Three bucks an hour more. Now, you can't say *that's* not fair."

"That's not fair," Jimmy said. "I've been here longer."

"Well, when *you* write a number-one bestseller, I'll pay *you* three dollars an hour more, too," Craig told him in a universal mother voice.

Susan was about to cut into the cake.

"Wait, wait! First she has to blow out the candle and make a wish," Emily said.

"That's only on birthdays," Susan told her.

While they all argued the point, Camilla stood there, the glass in her hand, remembering she'd come in today to quit. Her guilt was now far exceeding her pleasure at all the fuss. How would she tell these nice people that she was leaving? It was the only fly in her ointment. Last night at Frederick's she'd actually had trouble sleeping, thinking about it. Camilla knew that friends were hard to find and that Craig and the others had been there when she truly needed them. She knew how Craig felt about her and remembered how kindly he'd taken her rejection. Perhaps she should stay. "To Camilla," Craig said. "A woman who, incomprehensibly, would rather write a number-one best-seller than bear my children."

"Good judgment there," Susan said. "I'll drink to it." And they all raised their glasses.

"Speech, speech," Emily and Alex demanded. The others chimed in, and Camilla, blushing, drained her glass.

"Thank you," she said. "Really. Thank you very much. When I came to New York and only knew two people, you all became my friends."

"Even then we knew," Craig said.

Camilla couldn't bear it. Tears sprang to her eyes. "I don't mean to be ungrateful," she said. "But . . . I want to spend more time . . . I can't go on . . ."

Craig started to laugh. "Camilla, are you trying to announce your resignation?" he asked.

Camilla nodded and felt a tear run down her cheek past

her nose. "We're very disappointed in you. We thought we'd latched on to one of those annoying people who win the lottery and announce that they're still keeping their job as a legal secretary."

"Stop teasing her, Craig," Susan admonished. "She's really upset." Susan patted Camilla on the shoulder, then gave her a hug. "It's okay, Camilla, we know you're not going to work here part-time anymore."

"No," Jimmy said. "We figured you'd demand full-time status."

"The question is, are we going to publish your next book?" Craig asked.

"Yes, please," Camilla said.

"Whoa! Not so fast," Alex interrupted. "That is *not* a legal commitment," she told Craig. "You can get in line for the auction with everyone else." Camilla looked around. Apparently, no one was angry with her. Nor did they feel she was being disloyal.

"Camilla, we *want* you to leave," Craig explained. "We want you to finish your new book as fast as you can, then bring it over here, and then we'll get any editor you want and we'll turn it right out. In fact," he said, taking the champagne glass out of her hand, "we want you to go home right now. What are you doing here when you could be home writing another bestseller for Citron Press?" He turned to the group. "It looks like everyone will be paying their rent next year," Craig said.

"Let's drink to that," Susan added.

"Hold on a minute," Alex interjected. "There is no legal—"

"Oh, relax, Alex," Camilla said, at last regaining her equilibrium along with her sense of humor.

Sensing the opening, Craig jumped. "We'll do everything for your book. And we'll be so supportive of you. You might have to wait a bit for a large advance, but once the royalties start rolling in—"

"She needs a major advance, Craig," Alex said.

"I'm sure there's some way to work this out," Camilla told them, "although it *might* involve a small Canaletto." Craig groaned and looked serious for the first time that morning.

"Not the Canaletto!" he cried. "No, Camilla, not the Canaletto."

Camilla merely smiled.

# 106

Stay still, be quiet, and listen to your heart. Then, when it speaks, get up and go where it takes you.
—*Susanna Tamaro*

Emma was definitely moping. Not only that, she *wanted* to mope, and she was going to keep on moping for as long as she wanted. She couldn't believe that she'd been fired. After all the work she'd put in, after all she'd done, especially her dedication to, if not affection for, Pam. This had been her reward.

Since her firing she had spent most of her time lying on the sofa. She'd pulled out the phone and only plugged it in when she'd called out for pizza or Chinese food. The floor was littered with empty take-out cartons, but Emma didn't care. She couldn't face anybody's pity. She didn't feel like starting at the bottom of the ladder again, and she wasn't about to report any of this to her mother.

There was a knock on the door. Emma jumped but didn't get up. When the knock became a pounding, she simply yelled, "Go away!" When the pounding actually seemed to threaten the hinges, Emma finally got up.

"Who is it?" she shouted.

"Open the fucking door, you idiot!" Alex yelled. "You haven't answered your phone. I thought you were dead in there."

Oh, God. She didn't need this, but the pounding didn't stop. Cautiously, slowly, Emma opened the door a crack, but Alex pushed right past her.

"Ah, having a pity party? And you didn't even invite me. God, this place looks like an opium den."

Emma looked at Alex resentfully. She had gotten two

important clients from her, and Emma had gotten the ax. It wasn't fair. "What are you doing here, Alex, gloating?"

Alex looked at Emma, and Emma could see that she was hurt by the comment. Too bad, she didn't care. She walked back to the sofa and threw herself on it.

"Gloating? You're the one who should be gloating. I get you recognition for all of your work, and—"

Emma lifted herself up on one elbow. "You got me recognition?" She paused. "You mean to say that you were the one who fed that information to *PW*?"

"Well, I don't think *fed* is exactly the word I'd choose. But I did let some of the facts drop, shall we say."

Emma jumped up. "You got me fired!" she cried.

"Fired? Word on the street is you walked out."

"Pam fired me," Emma told her.

"Was that before or after David Morton fired her?"

"Pam's been fired?"

"Yeah. She was fired by GOD before his father fired him."

"GOD the father fired GOD the son."

"Yep. That just leaves the holy ghost, but like I said, Pam's gone, too. Wake up and smell the printer's ink," Alex told her. "It's been a regular bloodbath."

"You're kidding? I thought there was trouble in the executive suite, but Gerald is actually fired? No more Davis at Davis & Dash?"

"Oh, who cares about them? I care about you."

"No, you don't. You only care about business."

"Is that what you think?" Alex asked. She paused. "Well, I do care about business, and I always will. I wasn't born with a trust fund, and I have to take care of myself. But I don't only care about business." Alex came and sat down on the sofa beside Emma. "Emma," she said, in a voice that was very gentle, "I love you. I'll always fight for my clients and be tough for their sake, but that doesn't mean I don't love you. Were you afraid I was using you?"

A tear slipped down Emma's cheek. She nodded.

"Oh, baby. How could you think that? I'm sorry. I get so intense I forget other people might not be used to me. Maybe we better not work together in the future."

"No fear, I'll probably never work again."

Alex looked at her as if she were crazy. "What are you talking about?" she asked. "Absolutely *everybody* wants to hire you. David Morton wants you back; I also heard that Putnam wants you. But I think you should become editor in chief at Citron Press."

"Editor in chief?"

"Craig Stevens is a friend. There's no guarantee, but he's dying to meet you. It's a small house, but that's its charm. You could build the list with him, exactly as you want to."

"Editor in chief?" Emma repeated. "He'd consider me? For editor in chief?"

"You sound like Rick Kot's demented parrot. 'Editor in chief, editor in chief.' Yes, I'm sure. Why don't you hose yourself off and put on some decent clothes, if you have any. I'm taking you out to lunch with your new boss-to-be."

# 107

> The trouble with publishing today, says this old man, is that as you look around the arena, you will not find heads of houses who really give a shit about literature.
>
> —*Roger Straus*

Gerald stood beside his study window, a copy of *The Duplicity of Men* in his hands. It was a heavy book, in both senses of the word. He had just read it for the second time, and he was even more impressed than on his first reading. He thought of the writer. She had been dead for over a year now, but her work would live on long after her. What had he done that would live beyond him?

Absolutely nothing. The confrontation with David Morton was humiliating enough, but the words that kept ringing in his ears were his father's—"I'm disappointed in you," "You've deeply shamed me," and, worst of all, "I'm backing Mr. Morton and the shareholders on this, Gerald. It's the only honorable thing to do."

Now he knew—perhaps for the first time—what shame felt like. It wasn't a pleasant sensation. He had been called "shameless" by many people in the publishing world, but he hadn't really thought about it until now. He thought of his uncle's suicide and realized how the old man must have felt. Going on was unbearable.

In fact, Gerald couldn't bear to think about it—any of it. He'd squandered his time on earth, so limited and so full of possibilities, writing stupid, foolish books that hadn't even succeeded on the most crass commercial level. He'd left his first family, abandoned his older children, and then abandoned the woman he'd left *them* for. Terry O'Neal could have been writing about him. His latest marriage was loveless. Despite his huge earnings he was penniless. Nothing made sense in his life. His father was right.

He looked at the book in his hands. It was so beautifully written, so deeply felt. Why hadn't he been able to write something equally good? Why hadn't he written something worthy of a Tagiter? The only worthwhile thing he had done was to insist on the publication of this book.

He put the book on the windowsill. He found the small but adequate gun he kept in his study drawer. He looked down, shot his cuffs, and then shot himself.

# 108

In the book business all success is really just back pay.

*—Molly Friedrich*

Opal had been very busy, what with all the interviews and the Tagiter ceremony and the rest of the flapdoodle. Surprisingly, she hadn't minded the flapdoodle. She felt that it was dignified, that it was Terry's, not her own, and she did her best to live up to whatever Terry's expectations might have been. One of the surprises had been the Tagiter prize money—$173,000. The Pulitzer gave only $3,000. The other surprise was the sale of paperback and foreign rights—sixteen more countries were bidding on the book. In addition to her vindication, Opal also found herself modestly rich for the first time in her life. She even flew out to Los Angeles—at the expense of Paramount—and talked with their executives about a film of *Duplicity*. Opal wasn't sure it could happen or would happen or even if she wanted it to happen, but Miss Lansing, the head of the studio, had been beautiful and charming and compassionate and had given her lunch in a lovely white private dining room. It had been very pleasant to see a woman in charge of all those men. Opal even heard from the Bloomington Library, a congratulatory letter from the snippy boy who hadn't permitted her extended leave. He wrote, at the insistence of the board, to apologize and to offer her her job back.

In less than a year so much had changed. A year ago Opal had believed that her own life and her daughter's life were wasted. Now, though the tragedy of Terry's suicide didn't abate, Opal felt vindicated and, more important, at peace. She had spent her own life reading and last year at this time she'd felt that perhaps hers was a pathetic and wasted life. She hadn't "done" enough. But her adventure in New York had renewed her faith in reading. It wasn't an alternative to experience, or an escape from it. Not if you did it right. Reading was the only way we could transcend our own experience and deeply engage in that of another's.

Opal had never written a book, but she knew now that the reader was as important as the writer. In the beautiful relationship of literature, she, Opal O'Neal, was a talented reader and she was proud. If only Terry . . . Opal stopped herself. Suicide cut off the possibility of what tomorrow would bring. Opal continued to be amazed by her own tomorrows.

Now her adventure seemed finished. Despite the cold wetness of the day, Opal went out into the backyard. The weeping cherry tree was bare, and once again all the ground smelled of cat. But when Opal caught one of the stringlike tips of the cherry branch, she saw the beginning of tiny buds and knew that in the spring not only the tree but the whole garden would come into full white bloom. It seemed a pity to leave it—somehow the garden seemed to be Terry's final resting place. But the bench was cold, and Opal shivered. She had her job, her house, and her friends waiting for her back in Bloomington, and to Bloomington she would have to go. Her daughter's ashes remained to be buried, and she would put them in the Bloomington cemetery in the plot next to her own.

She realized she was feeling morbid as well as sad. She let herself out of the garden by the gate and walked over to Broadway and the few blocks to The Bookstall. She hadn't seen Roberta in almost two weeks and hadn't worked at the store in twice as long. Now she could hardly believe her eyes as she saw the big signs in both windows. Opal stood in the wet, staring from one window to the other in stunned immobility. Then she marched through the door and into the warmth of the store.

Margaret was at the counter, ineffectually fluttering over a credit card sale. In all this time, Opal noted with irritation, Margaret still couldn't handle the simple task of drawing the magnetic strip through the reader and punching in the purchase amount. But Opal had no time for that nonsense now. "Where's Roberta?" Opal snapped. Margaret, looking up, made a fluttering gesture toward the back.

Opal didn't bother to knock on the office door—she went in and found Roberta at the table she used as a desk, filling in inventory forms and using her calculator.

"What in the world is going on?" Opal asked.

Roberta spun around in her swivel chair. "Oh, hello, Opal. I thought you were back today. I was going to call, but I got so busy since the sale started. It's been a madhouse here. There's just so much to do."

"Going out of business?" Opal said. "So much work to do to go out of business?"

Roberta shrugged her thin shoulders. "I should have told you. I know that. But there were so many wonderful things happening for you that I thought discretion was the better part of valor. Don't be angry."

"Angry? I'm in a state of shock."

"Come on, Opal. You worked here. You know business hasn't been good. Not for a long time. And the shop next door is empty. The landlord wants to raise my rent at the end of the lease this year, and when I can't manage to do that, he'll knock the stores together. I just can't compete with the big chains," Roberta said apologetically. "You know, they say competition makes better booksellers. I'm not so sure, but it certainly makes me an unhappier bookseller. I should have put my money into real estate instead of books." She sighed. "If I owned my penthouse, I'd be rich right now, instead of broke."

Opal sat down heavily on the molded plastic chair across from Roberta. "So you're just giving up?" she asked.

Roberta took umbrage. "I don't think that founding and running this bookstore for thirty-one years comes under the category of just giving up," she said crossly. "But if you're asking me whether I'm going to retire or not, the answer is I am."

"But why don't you at least sell the business to some other bookstore owner?"

Roberta shook her head. "It would be difficult with the superstore down the block, and without a lease it's impossible. I've been putting it off as long as I could, Opal. Now I have to face reality. The store has got to close." Only then did Opal see Roberta's lower lip tremble, but even then it was only for a moment. "Heaven knows what I'll do with myself," Roberta admitted.

Opal sat there stunned. Of all the ridiculous things she'd ever heard, this was the most ridiculous. Selecting and selling books was a talent, and Roberta was meant to do both. Opal loved the store, just as Terry had.

"There is another alternative," Opal said briskly. "Expand. Put in a café. Add to your titles. Discount some books. Stay open late. Hire more staff. Compete with the big boys, and do better than they do because you can have some major events here. Once we break through the wall to the next space."

"We?" Roberta asked and laughed. "I'm afraid it's just me, and I don't have the money. Banks don't appreciate the book business. I can't get a loan against my inventory the way hardware stores can. I just don't have the money."

"No, but we do." Opal sat up straight in the uncomfortable chair. "I have close to two hundred thousand dollars, and that's not counting the sale of the house in Bloomington. Take me in as a partner. Margaret can handle the baking and the coffee machine. You and I can do the rest, if we can get a good stockboy," she smiled. "Maybe Aiello will help out."

"But I thought you were going back to Indiana?" Roberta said.

"What for? My life is here now." Opal asked, realizing it was true. "I like New York. It's the very best place for an older woman—it's filled with theaters, museums, movies, bookstores, public transportation, and the best doctors in the world. I'd be a fool to leave," Opal said, all at once quite sure that it was true. "What would it cost to buy in?"

"I . . . I don't know. I'm not sure I know." Roberta paused. "Oh, Opal, do you really want to? Please don't get my hopes up. I've only just managed to adjust to losing the store."

"Readjust, Roberta, and give me the good chair," Opal said. "The first thing we do is buy two of these comfortable ones."

"No," Roberta said. "The first thing I do is kiss you right on the cheek. Then I call Paul Mahon and we start having him draw up some papers."

# 109

> I get a fine warm feeling when I'm doing well, but that pleasure is pretty much negated by the pain of getting started each day. Let's face it, writing is hell.
>
> —*William Styron*

Judith was having trouble walking, but that's what happened, she knew, in the eighth month. Her ankles were swollen and her arches ached. She stumbled a lot. It wasn't only that her feet hurt, it was also that her balance had shifted in some funny way so that her hips were no longer her center of gravity. This walk along the cracked New York City sidewalks felt like an adventure. She tripped at the curb, and Alex Simmons grabbed her arm. "Are you okay?" Alex asked.

"Sure," Judith told her, "I do this all the time. It's just that I'm nervous about meeting the publisher."

Alex smiled. "Nothing to be nervous about," she said. "I promise you, Craig and the editor in chief really *loved* your book. Are you okay?"

Judith sighed. The busy street scene kept changing all around her. The homeless woman was gone, but now a young man walking a dozen dogs—all dalmations—walked by. It was surreal. Maybe this was all a dream, but if it was, she didn't want to wake up. She had been having very strange dreams in the last couple of weeks. Finishing the book and being so close to her baby's due date must be the reason. Whatever the reason, she'd woken up more than once in a total sweat, thinking that she had had the baby and it had been stolen from her. And three times now she'd dreamed that the finished manuscript had disappeared.

"I'm fine," she repeated to Alex, and the funny thing was that she *was* fine. Alone she had seen this pregnancy to term, and alone she had finished her novel. It had poured out of her, just the way she wanted to write it. And if it was dark and harsh, that was all right, too. Life was sometimes both. Judith wasn't happy, exactly, but she was content. She'd had time to do a lot of thinking, and she didn't believe anymore that happy was a goal. Good work was a goal. And happy, with luck, might be a by-product. If it wasn't, that was all right, too.

"Should we take a cab?" Alex asked with concern. "It's another five or six blocks to Citron Press."

"No. I'm fine, really."

"How are things with your divorce?" Alex asked. "I know you're in good hands with Diana. She's a great lawyer."

Judith nodded. "She's been great. She even read the manuscript for me, she and her friend Brenda. So has Emma Ashton. What would I have done if she hadn't sent me to you?" Judith sighed. "My future former husband seems to have gotten a lot crazier since *In Full Knowledge* failed. He even asked if we could get back together. But I think that's because he has no one to do his laundry and he wanted to save lawyer's fees."

Alex laughed, then nodded sagely. "Two reasons to stay together," she said. "Or maybe he's heard you're the one who's going to have the bestseller. Craig is very high about your book. He thinks it's going to hit a responsive nerve. He's got a new distribution deal with Macmillan, so the book could really get out there. I could take it to a bigger house and you might get a larger advance, but I honestly think that Craig—"

"No big publishers," Judith said, holding up her hand and almost losing her balance again. "I think I'm finished with big publishers." She laughed. "Not that they ever had the time for me in the first place. What's happened to Pam Mantiss? I know she got fired."

"I heard she went into a rehab somewhere out in the Midwest," Alex said. "But she kept smuggling in drugs and made such a fuss that they threw her out. Now she's resurfaced as a children's book editor." Alex shrugged. "Hey; it's a bunny-eat-bunny world. She'll fit right in. Listen, how are you fixed for money? With the baby coming and everything. Can your family help out?"

Judith laughed. "Not after they read *this* book," she said. "But Diana managed to scare Daniel enough to get a quick settlement. I got fifty thousand dollars, tax-free. And my expenses aren't very high. Flaubert doesn't eat much. And my rent is only four hundred a month." They turned a corner and walked past the Hotel Chelsea. Three really strange-looking people, all painfully thin and of no clear gender, stood at the hotel entrance. New York City was so wild.

"Well, I think I could probably get fifty out of Craig if I push it. Or I could try to auction it. But then you're stuck with whatever house puts up the most money." Judith remembered the party not far from here in Chelsea and how all the people from Davis & Dash surrounded her husband. She shuddered.

"I don't think so," she said. "I don't think money is the answer."

"Depends on what the question is," Alex said dryly. "If the question is what do you pay for your groceries with, you bet the answer is money." Alex took Judith's arm and led her to the entrance of a building. It was Art Deco, with lofty windows and an interesting tile floor in the lobby, but it was a bit rundown. The elevator operator was sleeping on a folding chair. Alex shrugged. "Sixth Avenue it ain't," she said apologetically. The elevator operator awoke with a start and took them up to the fifth floor.

Judith was surprised by Citron Press—it was clean and bright and busy. A young girl with a shock of raspberry-colored hair greeted them pleasantly with a "Yo, Alex. Craig's waiting for you." Alex led Judith down to the end of the hall. They walked into a large room with a table instead of a desk, three or four comfortable chairs, and floor-to-ceiling bookshelves. A very good-looking man raised his head and turned to them.

"Alex!" he said, rising. "And this must be Judith Hunt." Judith smiled at him and nodded. She wasn't using Daniel's name, not ever again.

The woman sitting across from Craig with her back to the door turned around. Judith stared. The woman stared back.

"Judith Hunt?" Emma Ashton said. She stood up. "Oh my God, Judith. Judith Gross. It's you!" Judith just stood there. Why was Emma Ashton here? She put out her hand to say hello. Emma had been kind to her, the only good person at Davis & Dash.

"Hi," she said.

Emma was blinking. "Judith, you're Judith Hunt?" Judith nodded. "I *love* your book," Emma said. Judith smiled proudly, but she wondered how Emma had gotten a chance to read it.

"I'm so glad," Judith told her, and meant it. "I followed your advice."

"I can't believe this," Emma said.

"I'm confused," Craig told them, "but then, what else is new?"

Alex cleared her throat. "I thought a blind submission was best. I wasn't sure how you two felt about each other. But you seem to like each other," she added. She took a seat and crossed her long legs. "That's a relief. I always prefer my authors to like their editors."

"My editor?" Judith asked.

Emma nodded her head. "I'm editor in chief here at Citron Press," she explained. "I got fired from D&D. Then Craig adopted me. I loved your book, Judith. So did Craig. But I just didn't realize you were Judith Gross."

Judith's face broke into an enormous smile. "*You're* the editor in chief here?" she asked. "You'd be my editor? But what happened at Davis & Dash?"

"Too much to tell you now." Emma laughed. "Anyway, I'm here, and I'd love to work with you." Judith felt a strong kick in her belly and put her hand over it. The baby liked this woman. Maybe she'd name the baby Emma, if it was a girl.

"You believed me," she said. "You were the only one who believed me." She turned to Alex. "She was the only one who did. Of course I like her."

Alex grinned and put her hand on Emma's shoulder. "I'm not surprised. The woman has great instincts."

"So, you'd like to work with us at Citron Press?" Craig asked.

"Oh, God, I'd love to," Judith said. "I'd just really love to." She blinked. Somehow that didn't seem enough to say. "My heart is full."

"And your work is great," Craig continued. He was really a very nice-looking man. "You're *really* good. We can market you as a softer Mary Gaitskill. I think we can get you a big audience."

"Honestly?" she asked.

"I think so." He looked down at her stomach, but, unlike other men, he didn't quickly pull his eyes away in a kind of rictus of embarrassment. "Let's go out to lunch," he suggested. "We have to feed that baby, don't we?"

"Sure," Alex agreed, and took Emma's hand. Craig crossed the room and took Judith's, helping her up from her seat. Her hand felt very good in his. "There are a lot of angles we can use to promote this book," Alex was saying to Emma as they walked down the hallway. Craig kept Judith's hand in his.

"Don't start yelling at me about advertising already," Emma warned.

"Don't start taking it personally," Alex told her.

"When is the baby due?" Craig asked quietly.

"Next month," Judith answered. He gave her hand a squeeze.

"Your first?" he asked. Judith nodded. Maybe she was

crazy, but she felt as if the man actually was attracted to her. Probably that was just his way of being nice to authors.

"Your husband must be over the moon," Craig said.

"I'm not married—not anymore," she said blushing. "Didn't Alex tell you the whole story?"

Craig looked at her, obviously confused. "I don't think Alex Simmons is in the habit of talking about her authors' personal lives. She keeps it to business mostly." Judith laughed as they stepped into the elevator. "This *was* about the business," she told him.

"My God, Craig, you're not going to believe this," Emma said as the elevator doors closed.

# 110

> All the world knows me in my book, and my book in me.
>
> *Michel Eyquem de Montaigne*

Camilla tore open the envelope and took out the note paper-clipped to another piece of paper. "I thought you might be pleased with this," Alex had written. "I certainly am." Camilla looked down at the check. It was notated "Davis & Dash: *A Week in Firenze* hardcover royalties." The check was made out to her in the amount of $811,653.97. Camilla stared at the long slice of gray paper. She didn't know exactly how much it was in pounds, but it was quite enough. She rubbed her finger across her name, Camilla Clapfish, and the huge amount. She was worth that much and more. It was quite amazing, really. Ridiculous. Rather like the fairy tale where the farmer's daughter spins straw into gold.

Alex Simmons had been a very busy girl, and—aside from the thirty-seven weeks Camilla's book had been number one on the bestseller list—the movie rights had been optioned by Laura Ziskin and Kevin McCormick at Fox; they actually *liked* literary projects there. Foreign rights had been sold to eighteen different countries—Camilla would see her words in Thai, in Tagalog and Serbian, along with all the Romance languages. She wondered, for a moment, whether Gianfranco would read it in Italian when it came out there.

Camilla looked around. The apartment was still very spare—but she liked it that way. And there was less for Frederick to bump into. It was a discipline, learning to return everything to its place so that he wouldn't trip or bruise himself. But if he could learn Braille, and he had, she could learn to be orderly.

It was odd: Now that she had all the money she would ever require, she seemed to have very few needs indeed. She had sent a whopping big check and thank-you to Sister Agnus Dei and had bought herself some beautiful clothes. Other than that, she didn't seem to have many expenses.

There was the noise of a key in the lock. Frederick and Rosie came in. Rosie was his new love, and very beautiful. She walked sedately alongside him, her dark brown coloring setting off his gingery beard. "Hello, darling," Camilla said, so that Frederick could place her. He turned to face her with a smile. "Hello, Rosie." Rosie wagged her tail. Camilla had been careful not to become too close to the dog, even though she adored the chocolate Lab. But the bond between Frederick and his guide dog mustn't be tampered with. He was dependent on her, and she must be dependent on him for approval as well as necessities. Only he fed Rosie, and she slept on the floor beside him.

"Have a good day?" she asked.

"Not bad," Frederick told her. He put his hand out, and she took it and kissed his cheek. He moved her mouth to his own.

"What did you do this afternoon?"

"Oh, bumped into a few people," Frederick said, smiling ruefully.

Camilla groaned. Frederick still made every possible blind joke and pun. She thought someday that might pass.

"How was *your* day?" he asked.

"You tell me," she said, and he moved to his accustomed chair, put his feet up on the ottoman, and waited for Rosie to lie down beside him.

Camilla took out her new chapter and began to read. It was a part of their tradition, the life they were building together. He came home each afternoon, and she'd read her day's work to him. After she finished, he would open a bottle of wine and they would have a drink, and then both cooked dinner. Tonight Emma was joining them, along with Alex. Craig and his new girlfriend, Judith, were coming too. Mrs. Ashton couldn't make it—she was busy with their wedding preparations and seemed to want to make a much larger production of it than either Camilla or Frederick did. "As it's the only legal wedding we shall have in this generation, I must be humored," she had said. "After all, Emma refused to wear a bridal gown in her commitment ceremony, so you must let me buy one for you."

Camilla began reading, and Frederick listened attentively. He cocked his head to the right in that way that he had, and Camilla smiled when Rosie cocked her head too. Frederick let his long, beautiful hand hang over the arm of the chair and absently scratched Rosie behind one ear. Camilla looked at them, along with the beautiful room Frederick had created, especially the Canaletto on the wall behind him. Frederick had said that this was where his blindness had paid off—he would have fought not to hang the picture on his pristine walls, but as he couldn't see it, he just considered that it just wasn't there. Craig knew it was there, however, and stared at it longingly each time he and Judith came over.

Camilla looked at the painting and then at Frederick's attentive face. She had more than she had ever thought possible, and tears filled her eyes. Moments of joy were rare, so she savored this one. Remember it all, she told herself, so you can write about it. She had been so happy lately that it made her quite nervous. It might pass, but she'd enjoy it while it lasted. And then she'd write about it, because for some reason capturing life on a page was her talent, the thing that gave shape and meaning to her existence, the gift that had brought all the other rich gifts into her life. Tears filled her eyes until she couldn't see the typed page in front of her.

She'd been silent for a long moment. "Is that the end?" Frederick asked.

"No, Frederick darling," she told him. "There's a great deal more."